McTEAGUE

AN AUTHORITATIVE TEXT
BACKGROUNDS AND SOURCES
CRITICISM

W. W. NORTON & COMPANY, INC.
also publishes

THE NORTON ANTHOLOGY OF AMERICAN LITERATURE
edited by Nina Baym et al.

THE NORTON ANTHOLOGY OF CONTEMPORARY FICTION
edited by R. V. Cassill

THE NORTON ANTHOLOGY OF ENGLISH LITERATURE
edited by M. H. Abrams et al.

THE NORTON ANTHOLOGY OF LITERATURE BY WOMEN
edited by Sandra M. Gilbert and Susan Gubar

THE NORTON ANTHOLOGY OF MODERN POETRY
edited by Richard Ellmann and Robert O'Clair

THE NORTON ANTHOLOGY OF POETRY
edited by Alexander W. Allison et al.

THE NORTON ANTHOLOGY OF SHORT FICTION
edited by R. V. Cassill

THE NORTON ANTHOLOGY OF WORLD MASTERPIECES
edited by Maynard Mack et al.

THE NORTON FACSIMILE OF
THE FIRST FOLIO OF SHAKESPEARE
prepared by Charlton Hinman

THE NORTON INTRODUCTION TO LITERATURE
edited by Carl E. Bain, Jerome Beaty, and J. Paul Hunter

THE NORTON INTRODUCTION TO THE SHORT NOVEL
edited by Jerome Beaty

THE NORTON READER
edited by Arthur M. Eastman et al.

THE NORTON SAMPLER
edited by Thomas Cooley

FRANK NORRIS

McTEAGUE
A Story of San Francisco

AN AUTHORITATIVE TEXT
BACKGROUNDS AND SOURCES
CRITICISM

≫≪

Edited by
DONALD PIZER
TULANE UNIVERSITY

W · W · NORTON & COMPANY
New York · London

W. W. Norton & Company, Inc., 500 Fifth Avenue, New York, N.Y. 10110
W. W. Norton & Company Ltd., 10 Coptic Street, London, WC1A 1PU

Library of Congress Cataloging in Publication Data
Norris, Frank, 1870–1902.
McTeague: a story of San Francisco.
(A Norton critical edition)
Bibliography: p.
1. Pizer, Donald. II. Title.
PZ3.N792Ma23   [PS2472]   813'.4   77–479
ISBN 0-393-04460-2
ISBN 0-393-09136-8 pbk.

2 3 4 5 6 7 8 9 0

Contents

Preface

Frank Norris died of peritonitis (following a ruptured appendix) in October 1902, at the age of thirty-two. His death was almost universally lamented as the premature termination of a great career. Today, we are less certain that Norris would have fulfilled the expectations raised by his best work, but we are agreed that this work—in particular *McTeague* and *The Octopus*—has the vitality and depth which make for permanence.

Like Stephen Crane, Norris came to the study of human degradation and violence from a middle-class background. His father was a wealthy Chicago merchant, his mother was vaguely literary. After desultory schooling in Chicago and San Francisco (the Norris family moved from Chicago to the Bay Area in 1884), Frank drifted into an interest in painting and spent two years in Paris as an art student. He returned to America in 1889, and in the fall of 1890 enrolled in the University of California. At Berkeley he devoted himself primarily to fraternity life. In his junior year, however, he also became deeply absorbed in the novels of Émile Zola and in the theories of evolution expressed by his geology teacher, Professor Joseph Le Conte. By this time he was determined to be a writer. After four years at Berkeley, he entered Harvard in the fall of 1894 in order to escape the distractions of San Francisco and to receive guidance while he undertook several writing projects. Out of his Cambridge year and his work in Professor Lewis Gates's writing class came two novels—*Vandover and the Brute* and *McTeague*. Neither work was in publishable form at the end of the year. But even if they had been completed, it is doubtful that two Zolaesque studies of human sexuality by an unknown writer could have been published in America in the mid-1890s. *McTeague* had to wait until Norris issued a successful popular novel and had a base in a publisher's office, while *Vandover* did not see print until 1914. It was clear to Norris that he could not begin his career by writing naturalistic novels. So after a brief misadventure reporting the opening stages of the Boer War in South Africa, he returned to San Francisco and for almost two years, from April 1896 to February 1898, was a reporter and editorial assistant on the San Francisco *Wave*.

Norris often stressed the importance of his literary apprenticeship on the *Wave*. He wrote San Francisco sketches and short stories, interviewed celebrities, contributed editorials, reviewed books, and undertook whatever else was required of the principal writer on a regional weekly. He derived from this experience a firm sense of popular taste and a conviction that he could do better than merely meet its demands. Initially, however, he exploited his awareness of what the public wanted by writing a fast-moving sea romance, *Moran of the Lady Letty*, which appeared serially in the *Wave* and which brought his work to the attention of the publisher S. S. McClure, who invited him to join his firm in New York. But he also revised and completed *McTeague* in the fall of 1897. Once in New York in early 1898, Norris ground out two more popular novels—*Blix*, a San Francisco story of his courtship of Jeannette Black, and *A Man's Woman*, a romance of Arctic exploration. And after considerable difficulty he also persuaded Doubleday & McClure to publish *McTeague* in early 1899.

McTeague was often praised by contemporary reviewers for its "power" but was even more frequently attacked for its "degraded" subject matter. In any case, with four novels published in three years, Norris's career in early 1900 was fully launched. There was still the need to keep the pot boiling, particularly after his marriage, and he continued to produce much literary journalism, including a substantial body of criticism in a semipopular vein. But from mid-1899 to his death most of Norris's energy went into the preparation and writing of an ambitious trilogy of novels in which the growth, marketing, and distribution of wheat would serve to dramatize the relationship between man and nature. The first novel in Norris's Trilogy of the Wheat, *The Octopus*, deals with the raising of a crop of wheat in the San Joaquin Valley of California during the bitter conflict between the farmers and the railroad for control of the valley. The fictional range and thematic depth of *The Octopus*, as well as Norris's skill in weaving together several complex narrative threads, make *The Octopus* a major epic novel. *The Pit* is much less successful, though Norris's rendering of the collapse of a wheat corner in the Chicago grain exchange is still good melodrama. Norris was planning the third volume in the trilogy, *The Wolf*, when he died.

The present edition of *McTeague* seeks to present an authoritative and annotated text and a body of background material and criticism which contributes to an understanding of the novel. The text is that of the first edition, a printing which Norris saw through the press and which contains his later expurgated passages on little Owgooste's incontinence. (See "A Note on the Text," p. xi.) Norris subtitled his work "A Story of San Francisco," and the annotation, in conjunction with Robert Lundy's pioneering study of the Polk Street background of the novel, attempts in particular to reveal the extent and accuracy of Norris's use of his California setting.

Much of the interest in *McTeague* as an early and provocative example of American literary naturalism has centered on the origins of the novel, and, more specifically, on Norris's documentary source in a San Francisco murder, on his borrowings from Zola, on his use of contemporary scientific beliefs, and on his final shaping, through composition and revision, of these and other sources into a compelling narrative which also constitutes a new force in American fiction. In addition, Norris was the foremost theorist of American literary naturalism. His conception of fiction casts light not only upon *McTeague* but upon the nature and direction of naturalism in America. Both the genesis of *McTeague* and Norris's theory of fiction are amply documented in the Backgrounds and Sources section of this edition.

Early criticism of *McTeague* was dominated by the issue of the impropriety of the novel. In recent decades, there has been an increasing effort to come to grips not only with the vexing but still productive question of the distinctive nature of Norris's naturalism in *McTeague* but also with the configuration of his themes and techniques independent of the tendencies of a particular literary movement. As Richard Chase remarks, it is easy to note Norris's obvious lapses in taste and credibility, but nevertheless one does not forget (among other scenes) McTeague in his dental parlors or the murder of Trina. Whether we approach *McTeague* as a historically significant work or (as Norris wished) a "good yarn," the novel continues to hold. Modern criticism has sought to identify both the relationship of the novel to the important literary movement of which it is a part and the nature of its fictional strength.

DONALD PIZER

A Note on the Text

The first edition of *McTeague* was published by Doubleday & McClure in February, 1899. Since Norris's handwritten manuscript served as printer's copy for this edition, and since Norris was also a member of the firm of Doubleday & McClure at the time, it can be assumed that the text of this edition is authoritative. Shortly after publication, several reviewers commented unfavorably on the scene at the Orpheum Theatre in which little "Owgooste" Sieppe wets his pants. Norris thereupon carefully revised several passages in the scene to remove all traces of the incident (see pp. 59–61 of the present edition); this second impression of *McTeague* served as the text of the novel for all later printings until the Colt Press private printing of 1941. Norris died in 1902 without making any further changes in the text of *McTeague*. Later editions of the novel—in particular the edition in the *Complete Edition* of 1928, which contains Anglicized spelling and a revised punctuation—have no textual authority. The present text of *McTeague* is therefore that of the first impression except for the correction of a few obvious typographical errors, listed below. Page and line numbers and words in boldface are from this Norton Critical Edition; the corresponding words in the first impression are in roman type.

> **hers** her's **9:10**
> **waistcoats** waiscoats **29:5**
> **flat."** flat. **79:2**
> **passed** past **82:33**
> **Mechanics'** Mechanic's **112:6**
> **went,** went. **147:18**
> **she** She **158:38**
> **murmured** murmured **183:38**
> **it** if **184:26**
> **McTeagues** McTeague's **189:5**

The Text of
McTeague

Dedicated to

L. E. GATES

OF HARVARD UNIVERSITY

McTeague

It was Sunday, and, according to his custom on that day, McTeague took his dinner at two in the afternoon at the car conductors' coffee-joint on Polk Street.[1] He had a thick gray soup; heavy, underdone meat, very hot, on a cold plate; two kinds of vegetables; and a sort of suet pudding, full of strong butter and sugar. On his way back to his office, one block above, he stopped at Joe Frenna's saloon and bought a pitcher of steam beer.[2] It was his habit to leave the pitcher there on his way to dinner.

Once in his office, or, as he called it on his signboard, "Dental Parlors," he took off his coat and shoes, unbuttoned his vest, and, having crammed his little stove full of coke, lay back in his operating chair at the bay window, reading the paper, drinking his beer, and smoking his huge porcelain pipe while his food digested; crop-full, stupid, and warm. By and by, gorged with steam beer, and overcome by the heat of the room, the cheap tobacco, and the effects of his heavy meal, he dropped off to sleep. Late in the afternoon his canary bird, in its gilt cage just over his head, began to sing. He woke slowly, finished the rest of his beer—very flat and stale by this time—and taking down his concertina from the bookcase, where in week days it kept the company of seven volumes of "Allen's Practical Dentist," played upon it some half-dozen very mournful airs.

McTeague looked forward to these Sunday afternoons as a period of relaxation and enjoyment. He invariably spent them in the same fashion. These were his only pleasures—to eat, to smoke, to sleep, and to play upon his concertina.

The six lugubrious airs that he knew, always carried him back to the time when he was a car-boy at the Big Dipper Mine in Placer County,[3] ten years before. He remembered the years he had spent there trundling the heavy cars of ore in and out of the tunnel under

---

1. For Norris's use of specific Polk Street business establishments, see Robert D. Lundy, "The Polk Street Background of *McTeague*," pp. 263–68 below. Norris places McTeague's "dental parlors" on Polk between Bush and Sutter.
2. A cheap form of beer which was particularly popular in California. It could be fermented quickly at normal temperatures, unlike lager beer which requires slow fermentation at low temperatures. The "steam" refers to the strong carbonation in this form of beer.
3. One of the principal mining areas of California, midway between Sacramento and Reno.

the direction of his father. For thirteen days of each fortnight his father was a steady, hard-working shift-boss of the mine. Every other Sunday he became an irresponsible animal, a beast, a brute, crazy with alcohol.

McTeague remembered his mother, too, who, with the help of the Chinaman, cooked for forty miners. She was an overworked drudge, fiery and energetic for all that, filled with the one idea of having her son rise in life and enter a profession. The chance had come at last when the father died, corroded with alcohol, collapsing in a few hours. Two or three years later a travelling dentist visited the mine and put up his tent near the bunk-house. He was more or less of a charlatan, but he fired Mrs. McTeague's ambition, and young McTeague went away with him to learn his profession. He had learnt it after a fashion, mostly by watching the charlatan operate. He had read many of the necessary books, but he was too hopelessly stupid to get much benefit from them.

Then one day at San Francisco had come the news of his mother's death; she had left him some money—not much, but enough to set him up in business; so he had cut loose from the charlatan and had opened his "Dental Parlors" on Polk Street, an "accommodation street" of small shops in the residence quarter of the town. Here he had slowly collected a clientele of butcher boys, shop girls, drug clerks, and car conductors. He made but few acquaintances. Polk Street called him the "Doctor" and spoke of his enormous strength. For McTeague was a young giant, carrying his huge shock of blond hair six feet three inches from the ground;[4] moving his immense limbs, heavy with ropes of muscle, slowly, ponderously. His hands were enormous, red, and covered with a fell of stiff yellow hair; they were hard as wooden mallets, strong as vises, the hands of the old-time car-boy. Often he dispensed with forceps and extracted a refractory tooth with his thumb and finger. His head was square-cut, angular; the jaw salient, like that of the carnivora.

McTeague's mind was as his body, heavy, slow to act, sluggish. Yet there was nothing vicious about the man. Altogether he suggested the draught horse, immensely strong, stupid, docile, obedient.

When he opened his "Dental Parlors," he felt that his life was a success, that he could hope for nothing better. In spite of the name, there was but one room. It was a corner room on the second floor over the branch post-office, and faced the street. McTeague made it do for a bedroom as well, sleeping on the big bed-lounge against the wall opposite the window. There was a washstand behind the screen in the corner where he manufactured his moulds. In the round bay window were his operating chair, his dental engine, and the mova-

---

4. However, on p. 152 Norris describes McTeague as six feet two inches.

ble rack on which he laid out his instruments. Three chairs, a bargain at the second-hand store, ranged themselves against the wall
with military precision underneath a steel engraving of the court of
Lorenzo de' Medici, which he had bought because there were a
great many figures in it for the money. Over the bed-lounge hung a
rifle manufacturer's advertisement calendar which he never used.
The other ornaments were a small marble-topped centre table covered with back numbers of "The American System of Dentistry," a
stone pug dog sitting before the little stove, and a thermometer. A
stand of shelves occupied one corner, filled with the seven volumes
of "Allen's Practical Dentist." On the top shelf McTeague kept his
concertina and a bag of bird seed for the canary. The whole place
exhaled a mingled odor of bedding, creosote, and ether.

But for one thing, McTeague would have been perfectly contented. Just outside his window was his signboard—a modest affair
—that read: "Doctor McTeague. Dental Parlors. Gas Given"; but
that was all. It was his ambition, his dream, to have projecting from
that corner window a huge gilded tooth, a molar with enormous
prongs, something gorgeous and attractive. He would have it some
day, on that he was resolved; but as yet such a thing was far beyond
his means.

When he had finished the last of his beer, McTeague slowly
wiped his lips and huge yellow mustache with the side of his hand.
Bull-like, he heaved himself laboriously up, and, going to the
window, stood looking down into the street.

The street never failed to interest him. It was one of those cross
streets peculiar to Western cities, situated in the heart of the residence quarter, but occupied by small tradespeople who lived in the
rooms above their shops. There were corner drug stores with huge
jars of red, yellow, and green liquids in their windows, very brave
and gay; stationers' stores, where illustrated weeklies were tacked
upon bulletin boards; barber shops with cigar stands in their vesti-
bules; sad-looking plumbers' offices; cheap restaurants, in whose
windows one saw piles of unopened oysters weighted down by cubes
of ice, and china pigs and cows knee deep in layers of white beans.
At one end of the street McTeague could see the huge power-house
of the cable line.[5] Immediately opposite him was a great market;
while farther on, over the chimney stacks of the intervening houses,
the glass roof of some huge public baths glittered like crystal in the
afternoon sun.[6] Underneath him the branch post-office was open-

5. McTeague can see the power house
of the Sutter Street cable car line. The
cable car was invented and developed in
San Francisco during the 1870s to provide transportation over hilly streets.
Power generated by steam maintained a
cable slotted under the street continually

in motion; a car moved when its driver
attached his car to the moving cable
with a gripping device.
6. The Lurline Baths, at Larkin and
Bush streets. Public baths provided both
swimming and bathing facilities.

ing its doors, as was its custom between two and three o'clock on Sunday afternoons. An acrid odor of ink rose upward to him. Occasionally a cable car passed, trundling heavily, with a strident whirring of jostled glass windows.

On week days the street was very lively. It woke to its work about seven o'clock, at the time when the newsboys made their appearance together with the day laborers. The laborers went trudging past in a straggling file—plumbers' apprentices, their pockets stuffed with sections of lead pipe, tweezers, and pliers; carpenters, carrying nothing but their little pasteboard lunch baskets painted to imitate leather; gangs of street workers, their overalls soiled with yellow clay, their picks and long-handled shovels over their shoulders; plasterers, spotted with lime from head to foot. This little army of workers, tramping steadily in one direction, met and mingled with other toilers of a different description—conductors and "swing men" of the cable company going on duty; heavy-eyed night clerks from the drug stores on their way home to sleep; roundsmen returning to the precinct police station to make their night report, and Chinese market gardeners teetering past under their heavy baskets. The cable cars began to fill up; all along the street could be seen the shop keepers taking down their shutters.

Between seven and eight the street breakfasted. Now and then a waiter from one of the cheap restaurants crossed from one sidewalk to the other, balancing on one palm a tray covered with a napkin. Everywhere was the smell of coffee and of frying steaks. A little later, following in the path of the day laborers, came the clerks and shop girls, dressed with a certain cheap smartness, always in a hurry, glancing apprehensively at the power-house clock. Their employers followed an hour or so later—on the cable cars for the most part— whiskered gentlemen with huge stomachs, reading the morning papers with great gravity; bank cashiers and insurance clerks with flowers in their buttonholes.

At the same time the school children invaded the street, filling the air with a clamor of shrill voices, stopping at the stationers' shops, or idling a moment in the doorways of the candy stores. For over half an hour they held possession of the sidewalks, then suddenly disappeared, leaving behind one or two stragglers who hurried along with great strides of their little thin legs, very anxious and preoccupied.

Towards eleven o'clock the ladies from the great avenue a block above Polk Street made their appearance, promenading the sidewalks leisurely, deliberately.[7] They were at their morning's market-

7. Van Ness Avenue, one of the fashionable residential streets of San Francisco during the 1880s and 1890s. The Norris family lived on Sacramento Street just west of Van Ness and three blocks north of Polk and Bush.

ing. They were handsome women, beautifully dressed. They knew by name their butchers and grocers and vegetable men. From his window McTeague saw them in front of the stalls, gloved and veiled and daintily shod, the subservient provision-men at their elbows, scribbling hastily in the order books. They all seemed to know one another, these grand ladies from the fashionable avenue. Meetings took place here and there; a conversation was begun; others arrived; groups were formed; little impromptu receptions were held before the chopping blocks of butchers' stalls, or on the sidewalk, around boxes of berries and fruit.

From noon to evening the population of the street was of a mixed character. The street was busiest at that time; a vast and prolonged murmur arose—the mingled shuffling of feet, the rattle of wheels, the heavy trundling of cable cars. At four o'clock the school children once more swarmed the sidewalks, again disappearing with surprising suddenness. At six the great homeward march commenced; the cars were crowded, the laborers thronged the sidewalks, the newsboys chanted the evening papers. Then all at once the street fell quiet; hardly a soul was in sight; the sidewalks were deserted. It was supper hour. Evening began; and one by one a multitude of lights, from the demoniac glare of the druggists' windows to the dazzling blue whiteness of the electric globes, grew thick from street corner to street corner. Once more the street was crowded. Now there was no thought but for amusement. The cable cars were loaded with theatre-goers—men in high hats and young girls in furred opera cloaks. On the sidewalks were groups and couples—the plumbers' apprentices, the girls of the ribbon counters, the little families that lived on the second stories over their shops, the dressmakers, the small doctors, the harness makers—all the various inhabitants of the street were abroad, strolling idly from shop window to shop window, taking the air after the day's work. Groups of girls collected on the corners, talking and laughing very loud, making remarks upon the young men that passed them. The *tamale* men appeared. A band of Salvationists began to sing before a saloon.

Then, little by little, Polk Street dropped back to solitude. Eleven o'clock struck from the power-house clock. Lights were extinguished. At one o'clock the cable stopped, leaving an abrupt silence in the air. All at once it seemed very still. The only noises were the occasional footfalls of a policeman and the persistent calling of ducks and geese in the closed market. The street was asleep.

Day after day, McTeague saw the same panorama unroll itself. The bay window of his "Dental Parlors" was for him a point of vantage from which he watched the world go past.

On Sundays, however, all was changed. As he stood in the bay window, after finishing his beer, wiping his lips, and looking out into the street, McTeague was conscious of the difference. Nearly all the stores were closed. No wagons passed. A few people hurried up and down the sidewalks, dressed in cheap Sunday finery. A cable car went by; on the outside seats were a party of returning picnickers. The mother, the father, a young man, and a young girl, and three children. The two older people held empty lunch baskets in their laps, while the bands of the children's hats were stuck full of oak leaves. The girl carried a huge bunch of wilting poppies and wild flowers.

As the car approached McTeague's window the young man got up and swung himself off the platform, waving good-by to the party. Suddenly McTeague recognized him.

"There's Marcus Schouler," he muttered behind his mustache.

Marcus Schouler was the dentist's one intimate friend. The acquaintance had begun at the car conductors' coffee-joint, where the two occupied the same table and met at every meal. Then they made the discovery that they both lived in the same flat, Marcus occupying a room on the floor above McTeague.[8] On different occasions McTeague had treated Marcus for an ulcerated tooth and had refused to accept payment. Soon it came to be an understood thing between them. They were "pals."

McTeague, listening, heard Marcus go up-stairs to his room above. In a few minutes his door opened again. McTeague knew that he had come out into the hall and was leaning over the banisters.

"Oh, Mac!" he called. McTeague came to his door.

"Hullo! 'sthat you, Mark?"

"Sure," answered Marcus. "Come on up."

"You come on down."

"No, come on up."

"Oh, you come on down."

"Oh, you lazy duck!" retorted Marcus, coming down the stairs.

"Been out to the Cliff House on a picnic,"[9] he explained as he sat down on the bed-lounge, "with my uncle and his people—the Sieppes, you know. By damn! it was hot," he suddenly vociferated. "Just look at that! Just look at that!" he cried, dragging at his limp collar. "That's the third one since morning; it is—it is, for a fact—and you got your stove going." He began to tell about the picnic, talking very loud and fast, gesturing furiously, very excited over trivial details. Marcus could not talk without getting excited.

8. Although "flat" more commonly means a large apartment occupying a story of a building, Norris uses the term in its secondary meaning: a building divided into apartments.

9. A famous restaurant facing the Pacific on the western edge of the city. The picnic was no doubt on the beach close to the Cliff House.

"You ought t'have seen, y'ought t'have seen. I tell you, it was outa sight. It was; it was, for a fact."

"Yes, yes," answered McTeague, bewildered, trying to follow. "Yes, that's so."

In recounting a certain dispute with an awkward bicyclist, in which it appeared he had become involved, Marcus quivered with rage. " 'Say that again,' says I to um. 'Just say that once more, and' "—here a rolling explosion of oaths—" 'you'll go back to the city in the Morgue wagon. Ain't I got a right to cross a street even, I'd like to know, without being run down—what?' I say it's outrageous. I'd a knifed him in another minute. It was an outrage. I say it was an *outrage*."

"Sure it was," McTeague hastened to reply. "Sure, sure."

"Oh, and we had an accident," shouted the other, suddenly off on another tack. "It was awful. Trina was in the swing there— that's my cousin Trina, you know who I mean—and she fell out. By damn! I thought she'd killed herself; struck her face on a rock and knocked out a front tooth. It's a wonder she didn't kill herself. It *is* a wonder; it is, for a fact. Ain't it, now? Huh? Ain't it? Y'ought t'have seen."

McTeague had a vague idea that Marcus Schouler was stuck on his cousin Trina. They "kept company" a good deal; Marcus took dinner with the Sieppes every Saturday evening at their home at B Street station, across the bay,[1] and Sunday afternoons he and the family usually made little excursions into the suburbs. McTeague began to wonder dimly how it was that on this occasion Marcus had not gone home with his cousin. As sometimes happens, Marcus furnished the explanation upon the instant.

"I promised a duck up here on the avenue I'd call for his dog at four this afternoon."

Marcus was Old Grannis's assistant in a little dog hospital that the latter had opened in a sort of alley just off Polk Street, some four blocks above. Old Grannis lived in one of the back rooms of McTeague's flat. He was an Englishman and an expert dog surgeon, but Marcus Schouler was a bungler in the profession. His father had been a veterinary surgeon who had kept a livery stable near by, on California Street, and Marcus's knowledge of the diseases of domestic animals had been picked up in a haphazard way, much after the manner of McTeague's education. Somehow he managed to impress Old Grannis, a gentle, simple-minded old man, with a sense of his fitness, bewildering him with a torrent of empty phrases

1. Immediately across the bay in Oakland, at the foot of the present San Francisco-Oakland Bay Bridge, the B Street Station was a stop on both the Southern Pacific Railroad and the East Bay trolley line. In the 1890s there was of course no bridge across the bay and travel to and from Oakland was by ferry and trolley.

that he delivered with fierce gestures and with a manner of the greatest conviction.

"You'd better come along with me, Mac," observed Marcus. "We'll get the duck's dog, and then we'll take a little walk, huh? You got nothun to do. Come along."

McTeague went out with him, and the two friends proceeded up to the avenue to the house where the dog was to be found. It was a huge mansion-like place, set in an enormous garden that occupied a whole third of the block; and while Marcus tramped up the front steps and rang the doorbell boldly, to show his independence, McTeague remained below on the sidewalk, gazing stupidly at the curtained windows, the marble steps, and the bronze griffins, troubled and a little confused by all this massive luxury.

After they had taken the dog to the hospital and had left him to whimper behind the wire netting, they returned to Polk Street and had a glass of beer in the back room of Joe Frenna's corner grocery.

Ever since they had left the huge mansion on the avenue, Marcus had been attacking the capitalists, a class which he pretended to execrate. It was a pose which he often assumed, certain of impressing the dentist. Marcus had picked up a few half-truths of political economy—it was impossible to say where—and as soon as the two had settled themselves to their beer in Frenna's back room he took up the theme of the labor question. He discussed it at the top of his voice, vociferating, shaking his fists, exciting himself with his own noise. He was continually making use of the stock phrases of the professional politician—phrases he had caught at some of the ward "rallies" and "ratification meetings."[2] These rolled off his tongue with incredible emphasis, appearing at every turn of his conversation—"Outraged constituencies," "cause of labor," "wage earners," "opinions biased by personal interests," "eyes blinded by party prejudice." McTeague listened to him, awe-struck.

"There's where the evil lies," Marcus would cry.

"The masses must learn self-control; it stands to reason. Look at the figures, look at the figures. Decrease the number of wage earners and you increase wages, don't you? don't you?"[3]

Absolutely stupid, and understanding never a word, McTeague would answer:

"Yes, yes, that's it—self-control—that's the word."

"It's the capitalists that's ruining the cause of labor," shouted

2. Californians went to the polls in 1880 and ratified a new and liberal state constitution.

3. Norris attributes to Marcus principally working-class and Democratic Party sentiments. Yet Marcus's allusion to "self-control" and his fear of a Catholic takeover of the schools (see p. 40) ally him with Republican antiimmigration policies. And Marcus is later to become a strikebreaker and a minor functionary in Republican ward politics. Marcus's politics, in short, are those of an inconsistent but opportunistic self-interest.

Marcus, banging the table with his fist till the beer glasses danced; "white-livered drones, traitors, with their livers white as snow, eatun the bread of widows and orphuns; there's where the evil lies."

Stupefied with his clamor, McTeague answered, wagging his head:

"Yes, that's it; I think it's their livers."

Suddenly Marcus fell calm again, forgetting his pose all in an instant.

"Say, Mac, I told my cousin Trina to come round and see you about that tooth of hers. She'll be in to-morrow, I guess."

II

After his breakfast the following Monday morning, McTeague looked over the appointments he had written down in the book-slate that hung against the screen. His writing was immense, very clumsy, and very round, with huge, full-bellied l's and h's. He saw that he had made an appointment at one o'clock for Miss Baker, the retired dressmaker, a little old maid who had a tiny room a few doors down the hall. It adjoined that of Old Grannis.

Quite an affair had arisen from this circumstance. Miss Baker and Old Grannis were both over sixty, and yet it was current talk amongst the lodgers of the flat that the two were in love with each other. Singularly enough, they were not even acquaintances; never a word had passed between them. At intervals they met on the stairway; he on his way to his little dog hospital, she returning from a bit of marketing in the street. At such times they passed each other with averted eyes, pretending a certain preoccupation, suddenly seized with a great embarrassment, the timidity of a second childhood. He went on about his business, disturbed and thoughtful. She hurried up to her tiny room, her curious little false curls shaking with her agitation, the faintest suggestion of a flush coming and going in her withered cheeks. The emotion of one of these chance meetings remained with them during all the rest of the day.

Was it the first romance in the lives of each? Did Old Grannis ever remember a certain face amongst those that he had known when he was young Grannis—the face of some pale-haired girl, such as one sees in the old cathedral towns of England? Did Miss Baker still treasure up in a seldom opened drawer or box some faded daguerreotype, some strange old-fashioned likeness, with its curling hair and high stock? It was impossible to say.

Maria Macapa, the Mexican woman who took care of the lodgers' rooms, had been the first to call the flat's attention to the affair, spreading the news of it from room to room, from floor to floor. Of late she had made a great discovery; all the women folk of the flat were yet vibrant with it. Old Grannis came home from his work at four o'clock, and between that time and six Miss Baker would sit in her room, her hands idle in her lap, doing nothing, listening, waiting. Old Grannis did the same, drawing his armchair near to the wall, knowing that Miss Baker was upon the other side, conscious, perhaps, that she was thinking of him; and there the two would sit through the hours of the afternoon, listening and waiting, they did not know exactly for what, but near to each other, separated only by the thin partition of their rooms. They had come to know each other's habits. Old Grannis knew that at quarter of five precisely Miss Baker made a cup of tea over the oil stove on the stand between the bureau and the window. Miss Baker felt instinctively the exact moment when Old Grannis took down his little binding apparatus from the second shelf of his clothes closet and began his favorite occupation of binding pamphlets—pamphlets that he never read, for all that.

In his "Parlors" McTeague began his week's work. He glanced in the glass saucer in which he kept his sponge-gold, and noticing that he had used up all his pellets, set about making some more. In examining Miss Baker's teeth at the preliminary sitting he had found a cavity in one of the incisors. Miss Baker had decided to have it filled with gold. McTeague remembered now that it was what is called a "proximate case," where there is not sufficient room to fill with large pieces of gold.[1] He told himself that he should have to use "mats" in the filling. He made some dozen of these "mats" from his tape of non-cohesive gold, cutting it transversely into small pieces that could be inserted edgewise between the teeth and consolidated by packing. After he had made his "mats" he continued with the other kind of gold fillings, such as he would have occasion to use during the week; "blocks" to be used in large proximal cavities, made by folding the tape on itself a number of times and then shaping it with the soldering pliers; "cylinders" for commencing fillings, which he formed by rolling the tape around a needle called a "broach," cutting it afterwards into different lengths. He worked slowly, mechanically, turning the foil between his fingers with the manual dexterity that one sometimes sees in stupid persons. His head was quite empty of all thought, and he did not whistle over his work as another man might have done. The canary made up for his silence, trilling and chittering continually, splashing about in its morning bath, keeping up an incessant noise and movement that would have been maddening to any one but McTeague, who seemed to have no nerves at all.

1. For Norris's dependence, here and elsewhere, on Thomas Fillebrown's *A Textbook of Operative Dentistry* for his technical dental details, see Charles Kaplan, "Fact into Fiction in *McTeague*," pp. 284–89 below.

After he had finished his fillings, he made a hook broach from a bit of piano wire to replace an old one that he had lost. It was time for his dinner then, and when he returned from the car conductors' coffee-joint, he found Miss Baker waiting for him.

The ancient little dressmaker was at all times willing to talk of Old Grannis to anybody that would listen, quite unconscious of the gossip of the flat. McTeague found her all a-flutter with excitement. Something extraordinary had happened. She had found out that the wall-paper in Old Grannis's room was the same as that in hers.

"It has led me to thinking, Doctor McTeague," she exclaimed, shaking her little false curls at him. "You know my room is so small, anyhow, and the wall-paper being the same—the pattern from my room continues right into his—I declare, I believe at one time that was all one room. Think of it, do you suppose it was? It almost amounts to our occupying the same room. I don't know—why, really—do you think I should speak to the landlady about it? He bound pamphlets last night until half-past nine. They say that he's the younger son of a baronet; that there are reasons for his not coming to the title; his stepfather wronged him cruelly."

No one had ever said such a thing. It was preposterous to imagine any mystery connected with Old Grannis. Miss Baker had chosen to invent the little fiction, had created the title and the unjust stepfather from some dim memories of the novels of her girlhood.

She took her place in the operating chair. McTeague began the filling. There was a long silence. It was impossible for McTeague to work and talk at the same time.

He was just burnishing the last "mat" in Miss Baker's tooth, when the door of the "Parlors" opened, jangling the bell which he had hung over it, and which was absolutely unnecessary. McTeague turned, one foot on the pedal of his dental engine, the corundum disk whirling between his fingers.

It was Marcus Schouler who came in, ushering a young girl of about twenty.

"Hello, Mac," exclaimed Marcus; "busy? Brought my cousin round about that broken tooth."

McTeague nodded his head gravely.

"In a minute," he answered.

Marcus and his cousin Trina sat down in the rigid chairs underneath the steel engraving of the Court of Lorenzo de' Medici. They began talking in low tones. The girl looked about the room, noticing the stone pug dog, the rifle manufacturer's calendar, the canary in its little gilt prison, and the tumbled blankets on the unmade bed-lounge against the wall. Marcus began telling her about

McTeague. "We're pals," he explained, just above a whisper. "Ah, Mac's all right, you bet. Say, Trina, he's the strongest duck you ever saw. What do you suppose? He can pull out your teeth with his fingers; yes, he can. What do you think of that? With his fingers, mind you; he can, for a fact. Get on to the size of him, anyhow. Ah, Mac's all right!"

Maria Macapa had come into the room while he had been speaking. She was making up McTeague's bed. Suddenly Marcus exclaimed under his breath: "Now we'll have some fun. It's the girl that takes care of the rooms. She's a greaser, and she's queer in the head. She ain't regularly crazy, but I don't know, she's queer. Y'ought to hear her go on about a gold dinner service she says her folks used to own. Ask her what her name is and see what she'll say." Trina shrank back, a little frightened.

"No, you ask," she whispered.

"Ah, go on; what you 'fraid of?" urged Marcus. Trina shook her head energetically, shutting her lips together.

"Well, listen here," answered Marcus, nudging her; then raising his voice, he said:

"How do, Maria?" Maria nodded to him over her shoulder as she bent over the lounge.

"Workun hard nowadays, Maria?"

"Pretty hard."

"Didunt always have to work for your living, though, did you, when you ate offa gold dishes?" Maria didn't answer, except by putting her chin in the air and shutting her eyes, as though to say she knew a long story about that if she had a mind to talk. All Marcus's efforts to draw her out on the subject were unavailing. She only responded by movements of her head.

"Can't always start her going," Marcus told his cousin.

"What does she do, though, when you ask her about her name?"

"Oh, sure," said Marcus, who had forgotten. "Say, Maria, what's your name?"

"Huh?" asked Maria, straightening up, her hands on her hips.

"Tell us your name," repeated Marcus.

"Name is Maria—Miranda—Macapa." Then, after a pause, she added, as though she had but that moment thought of it, "Had a flying squirrel an' let him go."

Invariably Maria Macapa made this answer. It was not always she would talk about the famous service of gold plate, but a question as to her name never failed to elicit the same strange answer, delivered in a rapid undertone: "Name is Maria—Miranda—Macapa." Then, as if struck with an after thought, "Had a flying squirrel an' let him go."

Why Maria should associate the release of the mythical squirrel with her name could not be said. About Maria the flat knew absolutely nothing further than that she was Spanish-American. Miss Baker was the oldest lodger in the flat, and Maria was a fixture there as maid of all work when she had come. There was a legend to the effect that Maria's people had been at one time immensely wealthy in Central America.[2]

Maria turned again to her work. Trina and Marcus watched her curiously. There was a silence. The corundum burr in McTeague's engine hummed in a prolonged monotone. The canary bird chittered occasionally. The room was warm, and the breathing of the five people in the narrow space made the air close and thick. At long intervals an acrid odor of ink floated up from the branch post-office immediately below.

Maria Macapa finished her work and started to leave. As she passed near Marcus and his cousin she stopped, and drew a bunch of blue tickets furtively from her pocket. "Buy a ticket in the lottery?" she inquired, looking at the girl. "Just a dollar."

"Go along with you, Maria," said Marcus, who had but thirty cents in his pocket. "Go along; it's against the law."[3]

"Buy a ticket," urged Maria, thrusting the bundle toward Trina. "Try your luck. The butcher on the next block won twenty dollars the last drawing."

Very uneasy, Trina bought a ticket for the sake of being rid of her. Maria disappeared.

"Ain't she a queer bird?" muttered Marcus. He was much embarrassed and disturbed because he had not bought the ticket for Trina.

But there was a sudden movement. McTeague had just finished with Miss Baker.

"You should notice," the dressmaker said to the dentist, in a low voice, "he always leaves the door a little ajar in the afternoon." When she had gone out, Marcus Schouler brought Trina forward.

"Say, Mac, this is my cousin, Trina Sieppe." The two shook hands dumbly, McTeague slowly nodding his huge head with its great shock of yellow hair. Trina was very small and prettily made. Her face was round and rather pale; her eyes long and narrow and blue, like the half-open eyes of a little baby; her lips and the lobes of her tiny ears were pale, a little suggestive of anaemia; while across the bridge of her nose ran an adorable little line of freckles. But it was to her hair that one's attention was most attracted. Heaps and heaps of blue-black coils and braids, a royal crown of

2. Norris varies in his accounts of Maria's background. On pp. 9 and 36 he calls her a "Mexican woman," but on p. 121 she is described as from Central America.
3. After a long history of corruption, lotteries had been declared illegal by the United States Supreme Court in 1878; they continued to flourish, however, despite federal and state laws prohibiting them.

swarthy bands, a veritable sable tiara, heavy, abundant, odorous. All the vitality that should have given color to her face seemed to have been absorbed by this marvellous hair. It was the coiffure of a queen that shadowed the pale temples of this little bourgeoise. So heavy was it that it tipped her head backward, and the position thrust her chin out a little. It was a charming poise, innocent, confiding, almost infantile.

She was dressed all in black, very modest and plain. The effect of her pale face in all this contrasting black was almost monastic.

"Well," exclaimed Marcus suddenly, "I got to go. Must get back to work. Don't hurt her too much, Mac. S'long, Trina."

McTeague and Trina were left alone. He was embarrassed, troubled. These young girls disturbed and perplexed him. He did not like them, obstinately cherishing that intuitive suspicion of all things feminine—the perverse dislike of an overgrown boy. On the other hand, she was perfectly at her ease; doubtless the woman in her was not yet awakened; she was yet, as one might say, without sex. She was almost like a boy, frank, candid, unreserved.

She took her place in the operating chair and told him what was the matter, looking squarely into his face. She had fallen out of a swing the afternoon of the preceding day; one of her teeth had been knocked loose and the other altogether broken out.

McTeague listened to her with apparent stolidity, nodding his head from time to time as she spoke. The keenness of his dislike of her as a woman began to be blunted. He thought she was rather pretty, that he even liked her because she was so small, so prettily made, so good natured and straightforward.

"Let's have a look at your teeth," he said, picking up his mirror. "You better take your hat off." She leaned back in her chair and opened her mouth, showing the rows of little round teeth, as white and even as the kernels on an ear of green corn, except where an ugly gap came at the side.

McTeague put the mirror into her mouth, touching one and another of her teeth with the handle of an excavator. By and by he straightened up, wiping the moisture from the mirror on his coat-sleeve.

"Well, Doctor," said the girl, anxiously, "it's a dreadful disfigurement, isn't it?" adding, "What can you do about it?"

"Well," answered McTeague, slowly, looking vaguely about on the floor of the room, "the roots of the broken tooth are still in the gum; they'll have to come out, and I guess I'll have to pull that other bicuspid. Let me look again. Yes," he went on in a moment, peering into her mouth with the mirror, "I guess that'll have to come out, too." The tooth was loose, discolored, and evidently dead. "It's a curious case," McTeague went on. "I don't know as I ever had a tooth like that before. It's what's called necrosis. It don't often happen. It'll have to come out sure."

Then a discussion was opened on the subject, Trina sitting up in the chair, holding her hat in her lap; McTeague leaning against the window frame, his hands in his pockets, his eyes wandering about on the floor. Trina did not want the other tooth removed; one hole like that was bad enough; but two—ah, no, it was not to be thought of.

But McTeague reasoned with her, tried in vain to make her understand that there was no vascular connection between the root and the gum. Trina was blindly persistent, with the persistency of a girl who has made up her mind.

McTeague began to like her better and better, and after a while commenced himself to feel that it would be a pity to disfigure such a pretty mouth. He became interested; perhaps he could do something, something in the way of a crown or bridge. "Let's look at that again," he said, picking up his mirror. He began to study the situation very carefully, really desiring to remedy the blemish.

It was the first bicuspid that was missing, and though part of the root of the second (the loose one) would remain after its extraction, he was sure it would not be strong enough to sustain a crown. All at once he grew obstinate, resolving, with all the strength of a crude and primitive man, to conquer the difficulty in spite of everything. He turned over in his mind the technicalities of the case. No, evidently the root was not strong enough to sustain a crown; besides that, it was placed a little irregularly in the arch. But, fortunately, there were cavities in the two teeth on either side of the gap—one in the first molar and one in the palatine surface of the cuspid; might he not drill a socket in the remaining root and sockets in the molar and cuspid, and, partly by bridging, partly by crowning, fill in the gap? He made up his mind to do it.

Why he should pledge himself to this hazardous case McTeague was puzzled to know. With most of his clients he would have contented himself with the extraction of the loose tooth and the roots of the broken one. Why should he risk his reputation in this case? He could not say why.

It was the most difficult operation he had ever performed. He bungled it considerably, but in the end he succeeded passably well. He extracted the loose tooth with his bayonet forceps and prepared the roots of the broken one as if for filling, fitting into them a flattened piece of platinum wire to serve as a dowel. But this was only the beginning; altogether it was a fortnight's work. Trina came nearly every other day, and passed two, and even three, hours in the chair.

By degrees McTeague's first awkwardness and suspicion vanished entirely. The two became good friends. McTeague even arrived at that point where he could work and talk to her at the same time—a thing that had never before been possible for him.

Never until then had McTeague become so well acquainted with a girl of Trina's age. The younger women of Polk Street—the shop girls, the young women of the soda fountains, the waitresses in the cheap restaurants—preferred another dentist, a young fellow just graduated from the college, a poser, a rider of bicycles,[4] a man about town, who wore astonishing waistcoats and bet money on greyhound coursing. Trina was McTeague's first experience. With her the feminine element suddenly entered his little world. It was not only her that he saw and felt, it was the woman, the whole sex, an entire new humanity, strange and alluring, that he seemed to have discovered. How had he ignored it so long? It was dazzling, delicious, charming beyond all words. His narrow point of view was at once enlarged and confused, and all at once he saw that there was something else in life besides concertinas and steam beer. Everything had to be made over again. His whole rude idea of life had to be changed. The male virile desire in him tardily awakened, aroused itself, strong and brutal. It was resistless, untrained, a thing not to be held in leash an instant.

Little by little, by gradual, almost imperceptible degrees, the thought of Trina Sieppe occupied his mind from day to day, from hour to hour. He found himself thinking of her constantly; at every instant he saw her round, pale face; her narrow, milk-blue eyes; her little out-thrust chin; her heavy, huge tiara of black hair. At night he lay awake for hours under the thick blankets of the bed-lounge, staring upward into the darkness, tormented with the idea of her, exasperated at the delicate, subtle mesh in which he found himself entangled. During the forenoons, while he went about his work, he thought of her. As he made his plaster-of-paris moulds at the wash-stand in the corner behind the screen he turned over in his mind all that had happened, all that had been said at the previous sitting. Her little tooth that he had extracted he kept wrapped in a bit of newspaper in his vest pocket. Often he took it out and held it in the palm of his immense, horny hand, seized with some strange elephantine sentiment, wagging his head at it, heaving tremendous sights. What a folly!

At two o'clock on Tuesdays, Thursdays, and Saturdays Trina arrived and took her place in the operating chair.[5] While at his work McTeague was every minute obliged to bend closely over her; his hands touched her face, her cheeks, her adorable little chin; her

---

4. A new and fashionable form of transportation in the 1890s.
5. A private joke by Norris. English 22, the Harvard class for which he wrote an early draft of *McTeague*, met at 1:30 on Tuesday, Thursday, and Saturday.

lips pressed against his fingers. She breathed warmly on his forehead and on his eyelids, while the odor of her hair, a charming feminine perfume, sweet, heavy, enervating, came to his nostrils, so penetrating, so delicious, that his flesh pricked and tingled with it; a veritable sensation of faintness passed over this huge, callous fellow, with his enormous bones and corded muscles. He drew a short breath through his nose; his jaws suddenly gripped together vise-like.

But this was only at times—a strange, vexing spasm, that subsided almost immediately. For the most part, McTeague enjoyed the pleasure of these sittings with Trina with a certain strong calmness, blindly happy that she was there. This poor crude dentist of Polk Street, stupid, ignorant, vulgar, with his sham education and plebeian tastes, whose only relaxations were to eat, to drink steam beer, and to play upon his concertina, was living through his first romance, his first idyl. It was delightful. The long hours he passed alone with Trina in the "Dental Parlors," silent, only for the scraping of the instruments and the purring of bud-burrs in the engine, in the foul atmosphere, overheated by the little stove and heavy with the smell of ether, creosote, and stale bedding, had all the charm of secret appointments and stolen meetings under the moon.

By degrees the operation progressed. One day, just after McTeague had put in the temporary gutta-percha fillings and nothing more could be done at that sitting, Trina asked him to examine the rest of her teeth. They were perfect, with one exception—a spot of white caries on the lateral surface of an incisor. McTeague filled it with gold, enlarging the cavity with hard-bits and hoe-excavators, and burring in afterward with half-cone burrs. The cavity was deep, and Trina began to wince and moan. To hurt Trina was a positive anguish for McTeague, yet an anguish which he was obliged to endure at every hour of the sitting. It was harrowing—he sweated under it—to be forced to torture her, of all women in the world; could anything be worse than that?

"Hurt?" he inquired, anxiously.

She answered by frowning, with a sharp intake of breath, putting her fingers over her closed lips and nodding her head. McTeague sprayed the tooth with glycerite of tannin, but without effect. Rather than hurt her he found himself forced to the use of anaesthesia, which he hated. He had a notion that the nitrous oxide gas was dangerous, so on this occasion, as on all others, used ether.

He put the sponge a half dozen times to Trina's face, more nervous than he had ever been before, watching the symptoms closely. Her breathing became short and irregular; there was a slight twitching of the muscles. When her thumbs turned inward toward the palms, he took the sponge away. She passed off very quickly, and, with a long sigh, sank back into the chair.

McTeague straightened up, putting the sponge upon the rack behind him, his eyes fixed upon Trina's face. For some time he stood watching her as she lay there, unconscious and helpless, and very pretty. He was alone with her, and she was absolutely without defense.

Suddenly the animal in the man stirred and woke; the evil instincts that in him were so close to the surface leaped to life, shouting and clamoring.

It was a crisis—a crisis that had arisen all in an instant; a crisis for which he was totally unprepared. Blindly, and without knowing why, McTeague fought against it, moved by an unreasoned instinct of resistance. Within him, a certain second self, another better McTeague rose with the brute; both were strong, with the huge crude strength of the man himself. The two were at grapples. There in that cheap and shabby "Dental Parlor" a dreaded struggle began. It was the old battle, old as the world, wide as the world—the sudden panther leap of the animal, lips drawn, fangs aflash, hideous, monstrous, not to be resisted, and the simultaneous arousing of the other man, the better self that cries, "Down, down," without knowing why; that grips the monster; that fights to strangle it, to thrust it down and back.

Dizzied and bewildered with the shock, the like of which he had never known before, McTeague turned from Trina, gazing bewilderedly about the room. The struggle was bitter; his teeth ground themselves together with a little rasping sound; the blood sang in his ears; his face flushed scarlet; his hands twisted themselves together like the knotting of cables. The fury in him was as the fury of a young bull in the heat of high summer. But for all that he shook his huge head from time to time, muttering:

"No, by God! No, by God!"

Dimly he seemed to realize that should he yield now he would never be able to care for Trina again. She would never be the same to him, never so radiant, so sweet, so adorable; her charm for him would vanish in an instant. Across her forehead, her little pale forehead, under the shadow of her royal hair, he would surely see the smudge of a foul ordure, the footprint of the monster. It would be a sacrilege, an abomination. He recoiled from it, banding all his strength to the issue.

"No, by God! No, by God!"

He turned to his work, as if seeking a refuge in it. But as he drew near to her again, the charm of her innocence and helplessness came over him afresh. It was a final protest against his resolution. Suddenly he leaned over and kissed her, grossly, full on the mouth. The thing was done before he knew it. Terrified at his weakness at the very moment he believed himself strong, he threw himself once more into his work with desperate energy. By the time he was fastening the sheet of rubber upon the tooth, he had himself once more in hand.

He was disturbed, still trembling, still vibrating with the throes of the crisis, but he was the master; the animal was downed, was cowed for this time, at least.

But for all that, the brute was there. Long dormant, it was now at last alive, awake. From now on he would feel its presence continually; would feel it tugging at its chain, watching its opportunity. Ah, the pity of it! Why could he not always love her purely, cleanly? What was this perverse, vicious thing that lived within him, knitted to his flesh?

Below the fine fabric of all that was good in him ran the foul stream of hereditary evil, like a sewer. The vices and sins of his father and of his father's father, to the third and fourth and five hundredth generation, tainted him. The evil of an entire race flowed in his veins. Why should it be? He did not desire it. Was he to blame?

But McTeague could not understand this thing. It had faced him, as sooner or later it faces every child of man; but its significance was not for him. To reason with it was beyond him. He could only oppose to it an instinctive stubborn resistance, blind, inert.

McTeague went on with his work. As he was rapping in the little blocks and cylinders with the mallet, Trina slowly came back to herself with a long sigh. She still felt a little confused, and lay quiet in the chair. There was a long silence, broken only by the uneven tapping of the hardwood mallet. By and by she said, "I never felt a thing," and then she smiled at him very prettily beneath the rubber dam. McTeague turned to her suddenly, his mallet in one hand, his pliers holding a pellet of sponge-gold in the other. All at once he said, with the unreasoned simplicity and directness of a child: "Listen here, Miss Trina, I like you better than any one else; what's the matter with us getting married?"

Trina sat up in the chair quickly, and then drew back from him, frightened and bewildered.

"Will you? Will you?" said McTeague. "Say, Miss Trina, will you?"

"What is it? What do you mean?" she cried, confusedly, her words muffled beneath the rubber.

"Will you?" repeated McTeague.

"No, no," she exclaimed, refusing without knowing why, suddenly seized with a fear of him, the intuitive feminine fear of the male. McTeague could only repeat the same thing over and over again. Trina, more and more frightened at his huge hands—the hands of the old-time car-boy—his immense square-cut head and his enormous brute strength, cried out: "No, no," behind the rubber dam, shaking her head violently, holding out her hands, and shrinking down before him in the operating chair. McTeague came nearer to her, repeating the same question. "No, no," she cried, terrified. Then, as she exclaimed, "Oh, I am sick," was suddenly taken with a fit of vomiting. It was the not unusual after effect of the ether, aided now by her excitement and nervousness. McTeague was checked. He poured some bromide of potassium into a graduated glass and held it to her lips.

"Here, swallow this," he said.

III

Once every two months Maria Macapa set the entire flat in commotion. She roamed the building from garret to cellar, searching each corner, ferreting through every old box and trunk and barrel, groping about on the top shelves of closets, peering into ragbags, exasperating the lodgers with her persistence and importunity. She was collecting junks, bits of iron, stone jugs, glass bottles, old sacks, and cast-off garments. It was one of her perquisites. She sold the junk to Zerkow, the rags-bottles-sacks man, who lived in a filthy den in the alley just back of the flat, and who sometimes paid her as much as three cents a pound. The stone jugs, however, were worth a nickel. The money that Zerkow paid her, Maria spent on shirt waists and dotted blue neckties, trying to dress like the girls who tended the soda-water fountain in the candy store on the corner. She was sick with envy of these young women. They were in the world, they were elegant, they were debonair, they had their "young men."

On this occasion she presented herself at the door of Old Grannis's room late in the afternoon. His door stood a little open. That of Miss Baker was ajar a few inches. The two old people were "keeping company" after their fashion.

"Got any junk, Mister Grannis?" inquired Maria, standing in the door, a very dirty, half-filled pillow-case over one arm.

"No, nothing—nothing that I can think of, Maria," replied Old Grannis, terribly vexed at the interruption, yet not wishing to be unkind. "Nothing I think of. Yet, however—perhaps—if you wish to look."

He sat in the middle of the room before a small pine table. His little binding apparatus was before him. In his fingers was a huge upholsterer's needle threaded with twine, a brad-awl lay at his elbow, on the floor beside him was a great pile of pamphlets, the pages uncut. Old Grannis bought the "Nation" and the "Breeder and Sportsman." In the latter he occasionally found articles on dogs which interested him. The former he seldom read. He could not afford to subscribe regularly to either of the publications, but purchased their back numbers by the score, almost solely for the pleasure he took in binding them.

"What you alus sewing up them books for, Mister Grannis?" asked Maria, as she began rummaging about in Old Grannis's closet shelves. "There's just hundreds of 'em in here on yer shelves; they ain't no good to you."

"Well, well," answered Old Grannis, timidly, rubbing his chin, "I—I'm sure I can't quite say; a little habit, you know; a diverson, a —a—it occupies one, you know. I don't smoke; it takes the place of a pipe, perhaps."

"Here's this old yellow pitcher," said Maria, coming out of the closet with it in her hand. "The handle's cracked; you don't want it; better give me it."

Old Grannis did want the pitcher; true, he never used it now, but he had kept it a long time, and somehow he held to it as old people hold to trivial, worthless things that they have had for many years.

"Oh, that pitcher—well, Maria, I—I don't know. I'm afraid— you see, that pitcher——"

"Ah, go 'long," interrupted Maria Macapa, "what's the good of it?"

"If you insist, Maria, but I would much rather—" he rubbed his chin, perplexed and annoyed, hating to refuse, and wishing that Maria were gone.

"Why, what's the good of it?" persisted Maria. He could give no sufficient answer. "That's all right," she asserted, carrying the pitcher out.

"Ah—Maria—I say, you—you might leave the door—ah, don't quite shut it—it's a bit close in here at times." Maria grinned, and swung the door wide. Old Grannis was horribly embarrassed; positively, Maria was becoming unbearable.

"Got any junk?" cried Maria at Miss Baker's door. The little old lady was sitting close to the wall in her rocking-chair; her hands resting idly in her lap.

"Now, Maria," she said plaintively, "you are always after junk; you know I never have anything laying 'round like that."

It was true. The retired dressmaker's tiny room was a marvel of neatness, from the little red table, with its three Gorham spoons laid in exact parallels, to the decorous geraniums and mignonettes growing in the starch box at the window, underneath the fish globe with its one venerable gold fish. That day Miss Baker had been doing a bit of washing; two pocket handkerchiefs, still moist, adhered to the window panes, drying in the sun.

"Oh, I guess you got something you don't want," Maria went on, peering into the corners of the room. "Look-a-here what Mister

Grannis gi' me," and she held out the yellow pitcher. Instantly Miss Baker was in a quiver of confusion. Every word spoken aloud could be perfectly heard in the next room. What a stupid drab was this Maria! Could anything be more trying than this position?

"Ain't that right, Mister Grannis?" called Maria; "didn't you gi' me this pitcher?" Old Grannis affected not to hear; perspiration stood on his forehead; his timidity overcame him as if he were a ten-year-old schoolboy. He half rose from his chair, his fingers dancing nervously upon his chin.

Maria opened Miss Baker's closet unconcernedly. "What's the matter with these old shoes?" she exclaimed, turning about with a pair of half-worn silk gaiters in her hand. They were by no means old enough to throw away, but Miss Baker was almost beside herself. There was no telling what might happen next. Her only thought was to be rid of Maria.

"Yes, yes, anything. You can have them; but go, go. There's nothing else, not a thing."

Maria went out into the hall, leaving Miss Baker's door wide open, as if maliciously. She had left the dirty pillow-case on the floor in the hall, and she stood outside, between the two open doors, stowing away the old pitcher and the half-worn silk shoes. She made remarks at the top of her voice, calling now to Miss Baker, now to Old Grannis. In a way she brought the two old people face to face. Each time they were forced to answer her questions it was as if they were talking directly to each other.

"These here are first-rate shoes, Miss Baker. Look here, Mister Grannis, get on to the shoes Miss Baker gi' me. You ain't got a pair you don't want, have you? You two people have less junk than any one else in the flat. How do you manage, Mister Grannis? You old bachelors are just like old maids, just as neat as pins. You two are just alike—you and Mister Grannis—ain't you, Miss Baker?"

Nothing could have been more horribly constrained, more awkward. The two old people suffered veritable torture. When Maria had gone, each heaved a sigh of unspeakable relief. Softly they pushed to their doors, leaving open a space of half a dozen inches. Old Grannis went back to his binding. Miss Baker brewed a cup of tea to quiet her nerves. Each tried to regain their composure, but in vain. Old Grannis's fingers trembled so that he pricked them with his needle. Miss Baker dropped her spoon twice. Their nervousness would not wear off. They were perturbed, upset. In a word, the afternoon was spoiled.

Maria went on about the flat from room to room. She had already paid Marcus Schouler a visit early that morning before he had gone out. Marcus had sworn at her, excitedly vociferating; "No, by damn! No, he didn't have a thing for her; he hadn't, for a fact.

It was a positive persecution. Every day his privacy was invaded. He would complain to the landlady, he would. He'd move out of the place." In the end he had given Maria seven empty whiskey flasks, an iron grate, and ten cents—the latter because he said she wore her hair like a girl he used to know.

After coming from Miss Baker's room Maria knocked at McTeague's door. The dentist was lying on the bed-lounge in his stocking feet, doing nothing apparently, gazing up at the ceiling, lost in thought.

Since he had spoken to Trina Sieppe, asking her so abruptly to marry him, McTeague had passed a week of torment. For him there was no going back. It was Trina now, and none other. It was all one with him that his best friend, Marcus, might be in love with the same girl. He must have Trina in spite of everything; he would have her even in spite of herself. He did not stop to reflect about the matter; he followed his desire blindly, recklessly, furious and raging at every obstacle. And she had cried "No, no!" back at him; he could not forget that. She, so small and pale and delicate, had held him at bay, who was so huge, so immensely strong.

Besides that, all the charm of their intimacy was gone. After that unhappy sitting, Trina was no longer frank and straightforward. Now she was circumspect, reserved, distant. He could no longer open his mouth; words failed him. At one sitting in particular they had said but good-day and good-by to each other. He felt that he was clumsy and ungainly. He told himself that she despised him.

But the memory of her was with him constantly. Night after night he lay broad awake thinking of Trina, wondering about her, racked with the infinite desire of her. His head burnt and throbbed. The palms of his hands were dry. He dozed and woke, and walked aimlessly about the dark room, bruising himself against the three chairs drawn up "at attention" under the steel engraving, and stumbling over the stone pug dog that sat in front of the little stove.

Besides this, the jealousy of Marcus Schouler harassed him. Maria Macapa, coming into his "Parlor" to ask for junk, found him flung at length upon the bed-lounge, gnawing at his fingers in an excess of silent fury. At lunch that day Marcus had told him of an excursion that was planned for the next Sunday afternoon. Mr. Sieppe, Trina's father, belonged to a rifle club that was to hold a meet at Schuetzen Park[1] across the bay. All the Sieppes were going; there was to be a basket picnic. Marcus, as usual, was invited to be one of the party. McTeague was in agony. It was his first experience, and he suffered all the worse for it because he was totally

1. Schuetzen Park, which was located in the small East Bay community of Alameda, faced directly on San Francisco Bay. Although Norris placed it within walking distance of the B Street Station (see p. 37), it was in fact almost five miles from the station.

unprepared. What miserable complication was this in which he found himself involved? It seemed so simple to him since he loved Trina to take her straight to himself, stopping at nothing, asking no questions, to have her, and by main strength to carry her far away somewhere, he did not know exactly where, to some vague country, some undiscovered place where every day was Sunday.

"Got any junk?"

"Huh? What? What is it?" exclaimed McTeague, suddenly rousing up from the lounge. Often Maria did very well in the "Dental Parlors." McTeague was continually breaking things which he was too stupid to have mended; for him anything that was broken was lost. Now it was a cuspidor, now a fire-shovel for the little stove, now a China shaving mug.

"Got any junk?"

"I don't know—I don't remember," muttered McTeague. Maria roamed about the room, McTeague following her in his huge stockinged feet. All at once she pounced upon a sheaf of old hand instruments in a coverless cigar-box, pluggers, hard bits, and excavators. Maria had long coveted such a find in McTeague's "Parlor," knowing it should be somewhere about. The instruments were of the finest tempered steel and really valuable.

"Say, Doctor, I can have these, can't I?" exclaimed Maria. "You got no more use for them." McTeague was not at all sure of this. There were many in the sheaf that might be repaired, reshaped.

"No, no," he said, wagging his head. But Maria Macapa, knowing with whom she had to deal, at once let loose a torrent of words. She made the dentist believe that he had no right to withhold them, that he had promised to save them for her. She affected a great indignation, pursing her lips and putting her chin in the air as though wounded in some finer sense, changing so rapidly from one mood to another, filling the room with such shrill clamor, that McTeague was dazed and benumbed.

"Yes, all right, all right," he said, trying to make himself heard. "It *would* be mean. I don't want 'em." As he turned from her to pick up the box, Maria took advantage of the moment to steal three "mats" of sponge-gold out of the glass saucer. Often she stole McTeague's gold, almost under his very eyes; indeed, it was so easy to do so that there was but little pleasure in the theft. Then Maria took herself off. McTeague returned to the sofa and flung himself upon it face downward.

A little before supper time Maria completed her search. The flat was cleaned of its junk from top to bottom. The dirty pillow-case was full to bursting. She took advantage of the supper hour to carry her bundle around the corner and up into the alley where Zerkow lived.

When Maria entered his shop, Zerkow had just come in from his daily rounds. His decrepit wagon stood in front of his door like a stranded wreck; the miserable horse, with its lamentable swollen joints, fed greedily upon an armful of spoiled hay in a shed at the back.

The interior of the junk shop was dark and damp, and foul with all manner of choking odors. On the walls, on the floor, and hanging from the rafters was a world of debris, dust-blackened, rust-corroded. Everything was there, every trade was represented, every class of society; things of iron and cloth and wood; all the detritus that a great city sloughs off in its daily life. Zerkow's junk shop was the last abiding-place, the almshouse, of such articles as had outlived their usefulness.

Maria found Zerkow himself in the back room, cooking some sort of a meal over an alcohol stove. Zerkow was a Polish Jew—curiously enough his hair was fiery red. He was a dry, shrivelled old man of sixty odd. He had the thin, eager, cat-like lips of the covetous; eyes that had grown keen as those of a lynx from long searching amidst muck and debris; and claw-like, prehensile fingers—the fingers of a man who accumulates, but never disburses. It was impossible to look at Zerkow and not know instantly that greed—inordinate, insatiable greed—was the dominant passion of the man. He was the Man with the Rake, groping hourly in the muck-heap of the city for gold, for gold, for gold. It was his dream, his passion; at every instant he seemed to feel the generous solid weight of the crude fat metal in his palms. The glint of it was constantly in his eyes; the jangle of it sang forever in his ears as the jangling of cymbals.

"Who is it? Who is it?" exclaimed Zerkow, as he heard Maria's footsteps in the outer room. His voice was faint, husky, reduced almost to a whisper by his prolonged habit of street crying.

"Oh, it's you again, is it?" he added, peering through the gloom of the shop. "Let's see; you've been here before, ain't you? You're the Mexican woman from Polk Street. Macapa's your name, hey?"

Maria nodded. "Had a flying squirrel an' let him go," she muttered, absently. Zerkow was puzzled; he looked at her sharply for a moment, then dismissed the matter with a movement of his head.

"Well, what you got for me?" he said. He left his supper to grow cold, absorbed at once in the affair.

Then a long wrangle began. Every bit of junk in Maria's pillowcase was discussed and weighed and disputed. They clamored into each other's faces over Old Grannis's cracked pitcher, over Miss Baker's silk gaiters, over Marcus Schouler's whiskey flasks, reaching the climax of disagreement when it came to McTeague's instruments.

"Ah, no, no!" shouted Maria. "Fifteen cents for the lot! I might as well make you a Christmas present! Besides, I got some gold fillings off him; look at um."

Zerkow drew a quick breath as the three pellets suddenly flashed in Maria's palm. There it was, the virgin metal, the pure, unalloyed ore, his dream, his consuming desire. His fingers twitched and hooked themselves into his palms, his thin lips drew tight across his teeth.

"Ah, you got some gold," he muttered, reaching for it. Maria shut her fist over the pellets. "The gold goes with the others," she declared. "You'll gi' me a fair price for the lot, or I'll take um back."

In the end a bargain was struck that satisfied Maria. Zerkow was not one who would let gold go out of his house. He counted out to her the price of all her junk, grudging each piece of money as if it had been the blood of his veins. The affair was concluded.

But Zerkow still had something to say. As Maria folded up the pillow-case and rose to go, the old Jew said:

"Well, see here a minute, we'll—you'll have a drink before you go, won't you? Just to show that it's all right between us." Maria sat down again.

"Yes, I guess I'll have a drink," she answered.

Zerkow took down a whiskey bottle and a red glass tumbler with a broken base from a cupboard on the wall. The two drank together, Zerkow from the bottle, Maria from the broken tumbler. They wiped their lips slowly, drawing breath again. There was a moment's silence.

"Say," said Zerkow at last, "how about those gold dishes you told me about the last time you were here?"

"What gold dishes?" inquired Maria, puzzled.

"Ah, you know," returned the other. "The plate your father owned in Central America a long time ago. Don't you know, it rang like so many bells? Red gold, you know, like oranges?"

"Ah," said Maria, putting her chin in the air as if she knew a long story about that if she had a mind to tell it. "Ah, yes, that gold service."

"Tell us about it again," said Zerkow, his bloodless lower lip moving against the upper, his claw-like fingers feeling about his mouth and chin. "Tell us about it; go on."

He was breathing short, his limbs trembled a little. It was as if some hungry beast of prey had scented a quarry. Maria still refused, putting up her head, insisting that she had to be going.

"Let's have it," insisted the Jew. "Take another drink." Maria took another swallow of the whiskey. "Now, go on," repeated Zerkow; "let's have the story." Maria squared her elbows on the deal table, looking straight in front of her with eyes that saw nothing.

"Well, it was this way," she began. "It was when I was little. My folks must have been rich, oh, rich into the millions—coffee, I guess—and there was a large house, but I can only remember the plate. Oh, that service of plate! It was wonderful. There were more than a hundred pieces, and every one of them gold. You should have seen the sight when the leather trunk was opened. It fair dazzled your eyes. It was a yellow blaze like a fire, like a sunset; such a glory, all piled up together, one piece over the other. Why, if the room was dark you'd think you could see just the same with all that glitter there. There wa'n't a piece that was so much as scratched; every one was like a mirror, smooth and bright, just like a little pool when the sun shines into it. There was dinner dishes and soup tureens and pitchers; and great, big platters as long as that, and wide too; and cream-jugs and bowls with carved handles, all vines and things; and drinking mugs, every one a different shape; and dishes for gravy and sauces; and then a great, big punch-bowl with a ladle, and the bowl was all carved out with figures and bunches of grapes. Why, just only that punch-bowl was worth a fortune, I guess. When all that plate was set out on a table, it was a sight for a king to look at. Such a service as that was! Each piece was heavy, oh, so heavy! and thick, you know; thick, fat gold, nothing but gold—red, shining, pure gold, orange red—and when you struck it with your knuckle, ah, you should have heard! No church bell ever rang sweeter or clearer. It was soft gold, too; you could bite into it, and leave the dent of your teeth. Oh, that gold plate! I can see it just as plain—solid, solid, heavy, rich, pure gold; nothing but gold, gold, heaps and heaps of it. What a service that was!"

Maria paused, shaking her head, thinking over the vanished splendor. Illiterate enough, unimaginative enough on all other subjects, her distorted wits called up this picture with marvellous distinctness. It was plain she saw the plate clearly. Her description was accurate, was almost eloquent.

Did that wonderful service of gold plate ever exist outside of her diseased imagination? Was Maria actually remembering some reality of a childhood of barbaric luxury? Were her parents at one time possessed of an incalculable fortune derived from some Central American coffee plantation, a fortune long since confiscated by armies of insurrectionists, or squandered in the support of revolutionary governments?

It was not impossible. Of Maria Macapa's past prior to the time of her appearance at the "flat" absolutely nothing could be learned. She suddenly appeared from the unknown, a strange woman of a mixed race, sane on all subjects but that of the famous service of gold plate; but unusual, complex, mysterious, even at her best.

But what misery Zerkow endured as he listened to her tale! For he chose to believe it, forced himself to believe it, lashed and harassed by a pitiless greed that checked at no tale of treasure, however preposterous. The story ravished him with delight. He was near someone who had possessed this wealth. He saw someone who had seen this pile of gold. He seemed near it; it was there, somewhere close by, under his eyes, under his fingers; it was red, gleaming, ponderous. He gazed about him wildly; nothing, nothing but the sordid junk shop and the rust-corroded tins. What exasperation, what positive misery, to be so near to it and yet to know that it was irrevocably, irretrievably lost! A spasm of anguish passed though him. He gnawed at his bloodless lips, at the hopelessness of it, the rage, the fury of it.

"Go on, go on," he whispered; "let's have it all over again. Polished like a mirror, hey, and heavy? Yes, I know, I know. A punch-bowl worth a fortune. Ah! and you saw it, you had it all!"

Maria rose to go. Zerkow accompanied her to the door, urging another drink upon her.

"Come again, come again," he croaked. "Don't wait till you've got junk; come any time you feel like it, and tell me more about the plate."

He followed her a step down the alley.

"How much do you think it was worth?" he inquired, anxiously.

"Oh, a million dollars," answered Maria, vaguely.

When Maria had gone, Zerkow returned to the back room of the shop, and stood in front of the alcohol stove, looking down into his cold dinner, preoccupied, thoughtful.

"A million dollars," he muttered in his rasping, guttural whisper, his finger-tips wandering over his thin, cat-like lips. "A golden service worth a million dollars; a punch-bowl worth a fortune; red gold plates, heaps and piles. God!"

IV

The days passed. McTeague had finished the operation on Trina's teeth. She did not come any more to the "Parlors." Matters had readjusted themselves a little between the two during the last sittings. Trina yet stood upon her reserve, and McTeague still felt himself shambling and ungainly in her presence; but that constraint and embarrassment that had followed upon McTeague's blundering declaration broke up little by little. In spite of themselves they were gradually resuming the same relative positions they had occupied when they had first met.

But McTeague suffered miserably for all that. He never would have Trina, he saw that clearly. She was too good for him; too delicate, too refined, too prettily made for him, who was so coarse, so enormous, so stupid. She was for someone else—Marcus, no doubt —or at least for some finer-grained man. She should have gone to some other dentist; the young fellow on the corner, for instance, the poser, the rider of bicycles, the courser of greyhounds. McTeague began to loathe and to envy this fellow. He spied upon him going in and out of his office, and noted his salmon-pink neckties and his astonishing waistcoats.

One Sunday, a few days after Trina's last sitting, McTeague met Marcus Schouler at his table in the car conductors' coffee-joint, next to the harness shop.

"What you got to do this afternoon, Mac?" inquired the other, as they ate their suet pudding.

"Nothing, nothing," replied McTeague, shaking his head. His mouth was full of pudding. It made him warm to eat, and little beads of perspiration stood across the bridge of his nose. He looked forward to an afternoon passed in his operating chair as usual. On leaving his "Parlors" he had put ten cents into his pitcher and had left it at Frenna's to be filled.

"What do you say we take a walk, huh?" said Marcus. "Ah, that's the thing—a walk, a long walk, by damn! It'll be, outa sight. I got to take three or four of the dogs out for exercise, anyhow. Old Grannis thinks they need ut. We'll walk out to the Presidio."

Of late it had become the custom of the two friends to take long walks from time to time. On holidays and on those Sunday afternoons when Marcus was not absent with the Sieppes they went out together, sometimes to the park, sometimes to the Presidio,[1] sometimes even across the bay. They took a great pleasure in each other's company, but silently and with reservation, having the masculine horror of any demonstration of friendship.

They walked for upwards of five hours that afternoon, out the length of California Street, and across the Presidio Reservation to the Golden Gate. Then they turned, and, following the line of the shore, brought up at the Cliff House. Here they halted for beer, Marcus swearing that his mouth was as dry as a hay-bin. Before starting on their walk they had gone around to the little dog hospital, and Marcus had let out four of the convalescents, crazed with joy at the release.

"Look at that dog," he cried to McTeague, showing him a finely-bred Irish setter. "That's the dog that belonged to the duck on the avenue, the dog we called for that day. I've bought 'um. The duck thought he had the distemper, and just threw 'um away. Nothun wrong with 'um but a little catarrh. Ain't he a bird? Say, ain't he a bird? Look at his flag; it's perfect; and see how he carries his tail on a line with his back. See how stiff and white his whiskers are. Oh, by damn! you can't fool me on a dog. That dog's a winner."

At the Cliff House the two sat down to their beer in a quiet

---

1. The old military reservation on the San Francisco side of the Golden Gate   entrance to San Francisco Bay.

corner of the billiard-room. There were but two players. Somewhere in another part of the building a mammoth music-box was jangling out a quickstep. From outside came the long, rhythmical rush of the surf and the sonorous barking of the seals upon the seal rocks. The four dogs curled themselves down upon the sanded floor.

"Here's how," said Marcus, half emptying his glass. "Ah-h!" he added, with a long breath, "that's good; it is, for a fact."

For the last hour of their walk Marcus had done nearly all the talking, McTeague merely answering him by uncertain movements of the head. For that matter, the dentist had been silent and preoccupied throughout the whole afternoon. At length Marcus noticed it. As he set down his glass with a bang he suddenly exclaimed:

"What's the matter with you these days, Mac? You got a bean about somethun, hey? Spit ut out."

"No, no," replied McTeague, looking about on the floor, rolling his eyes; "nothing, no, no."

"Ah, rats!" returned the other. McTeague kept silence. The two billiard players departed. The huge music-box struck into a fresh tune.

"Huh!" exclaimed Marcus, with a short laugh, "guess you're in love."

McTeague gasped, and shuffled his enormous feet under the table.

"Well, somethun's bitun you, anyhow," pursued Marcus. "Maybe I can help you. We're pals, you know. Better tell me what's up; guess we can straighten ut out. Ah, go on; spit ut out."

The situation was abominable. McTeague could not rise to it. Marcus was his best friend, his only friend. They were "pals" and McTeague was very fond of him. Yet they were both in love, presumably, with the same girl, and now Marcus would try and force the secret out of him; would rush blindly at the rock upon which the two must split, stirred by the very best of motives, wishing only to be of service. Besides this, there was nobody to whom McTeague would have better preferred to tell his troubles than to Marcus, and yet about this trouble, the greatest trouble of his life, he must keep silent; must refrain from speaking of it to Marcus above everybody.

McTeague began dimly to feel that life was too much for him. How had it all come about? A month ago he was perfectly content; he was calm and peaceful, taking his little pleasures as he found them. His life had shaped itself; was, no doubt, to continue always along these same lines. A woman had entered his small world and instantly there was discord. The disturbing element had appeared. Wherever the woman had put her foot a score of distressing complications had sprung up, like the sudden growth of strange and puzzling flowers.

"Say, Mac, go on; let's have ut straight," urged Marcus, leaning towards him. "Has any duck been doing you dirt?" he cried, his face crimson on the instant.

"No," said McTeague, helplessly.

"Come along, old man," persisted Marcus; "let's have ut. What is the row? I'll do all I can to help you."

It was more than McTeague could bear. The situation had got beyond him. Stupidly he spoke, his hands deep in his pockets, his head rolled forward.

"It's—it's Miss Sieppe," he said.

"Trina, my cousin? How do you mean?" inquired Marcus sharply.

"I—I—I don' know," stammered McTeague, hopelessly confounded.

"You mean," cried Marcus, suddenly enlightened, "that you are —that you, too."

McTeague stirred in his chair, looking at the walls of the room, avoiding the other's glance. He nodded his head, then suddenly broke out:

"I can't help it. It ain't my fault, is it?"

Marcus was struck dumb; he dropped back in his chair breathless. Suddenly McTeague found his tongue.

"I tell you, Mark, I can't help it. I don't know how it happened. It came on so slow that I was, that—that—that it was done before I knew it, before I could help myself. I know we're pals, us two, and I knew how—how you and Miss Sieppe were. I know now, I knew then; but that wouldn't have made any difference. Before I knew it—it—it—there I was. I can't help it. I wouldn't ,'a' had ut happen for anything, if I could 'a' stopped it, but I don' know, it's something that's just stronger than you are, that's all. She came there—Miss Sieppe came to the parlors there three or four times a week, and she was the first girl I had ever known,—and you don' know! Why, I was so close to her I touched her face every minute, and her mouth, and smelt her hair and her breath—oh, you don't know anything about it. I can't give you any idea. I don' know exactly myself; I only know how I'm fixed. I—I—it's been done; it's too late, there's no going back. Why, I can't think of anything else night and day. It's everything. It's—it's—oh, it's everything! I—I— why, Mark, it's everything—I can't explain." He made a helpless movement with both hands.

Never had McTeague been so excited; never had he made so long a speech. His arms moved in fierce, uncertain gestures, his face flushed, his enormous jaws shut together with a sharp click at every pause. It was like some colossal brute trapped in a delicate, invisible mesh, raging, exasperated, powerless to extricate himself.

Marcus Schouler said nothing. There was a long silence. Marcus got up and walked to the window and stood looking out, but seeing nothing. "Well, who would have thought of this?" he muttered under his breath. Here was a fix. Marcus cared for Trina. There was no doubt in his mind about that. He looked forward eagerly to the Sunday afternoon excursions. He liked to be with Trina. He, too, felt the charm of the little girl—the charm of the small, pale forehead; the little chin thrust out as if in confidence and innocence; the heavy, odorous crown of black hair. He liked her immensely. Some day he would speak; he would ask her to marry him. Marcus put off this matter of marriage to some future period; it would be some time—a year, perhaps, or two. The thing did not take definite shape in his mind. Marcus "kept company" with his cousin Trina, but he knew plenty of other girls. For the matter of that, he liked all girls pretty well. Just now the singleness and strength of McTeague's passion startled him. McTeague would marry Trina that very afternoon if she would have him; but would he—Marcus? No, he would not; if it came to that, no, he would not. Yet he knew he liked Trina. He could say—yes, he could say—he loved her. She was his "girl." The Sieppes acknowledged him as Trina's "young man." Marcus came back to the table and sat down sideways upon it.

"Well, what are we going to do about it, Mac?" he said.

"I don' know," answered McTeague, in great distress. "I don' want anything to—to come between us, Mark."

"Well, nothun will, you bet!" vociferated the other. "No, sir; you bet not, Mac."

Marcus was thinking hard. He could see very clearly that McTeague loved Trina more than he did; that in some strange way this huge, brutal fellow was capable of a greater passion than himself, who was twice as clever. Suddenly Marcus jumped impetuously to a resolution.

"Well, say, Mac," he cried, striking the table with his fist, "go ahead. I guess you—you want her pretty bad. I'll pull out; yes, I will. I'll give her up to you, old man."

The sense of his own magnanimity all at once overcame Marcus. He saw himself as another man, very noble, self-sacrificing; he stood apart and watched this second self with boundless admiration and with infinite pity. He was so good, so magnificent, so heroic, that he almost sobbed. Marcus made a sweeping gesture of resignation, throwing out both his arms, crying;

"Mac, I'll give her up to you. I won't stand between you." There were actually tears in Marcus's eyes as he spoke. There was no doubt he thought himself sincere. At that moment he almost believed he loved Trina conscientiously, that he was sacrificing himself for the sake of his friend. The two stood up and faced each other, gripping hands. It was a great moment; even McTeague felt the drama of it. What a fine thing was this friendship between men! The dentist treats his friend for an ulcerated tooth and refuses payment; the friend reciprocates by giving up his girl. This was nobility. Their mutual affection and esteem suddenly increased enormously. It was Damon and Pythias; it was David and Jonathan;[2] nothing could ever estrange them. Now it was for life or death.

"I'm much obliged," murmured McTeague. He could think of nothing better to say. "I'm much obliged," he repeated; "much obliged, Mark."

"That's all right, that's all right," returned Marcus Schouler, bravely, and it occurred to him to add, "You'll be happy together. Tell her for me—tell her—tell her—" Marcus could not go on. He wrung the dentist's hand silently.

It had not appeared to either of them that Trina might refuse McTeague. McTeague's spirits rose at once. In Marcus's withdrawal he fancied he saw an end to all his difficulties. Everything would come right, after all. The strained, exalted state of Marcus's nerves ended by putting him into fine humor as well. His grief suddenly changed to an excess of gaiety. The afternoon was a success. They slapped each other on the back with great blows of the open palms, and they drank each other's health in a third round of beer.

Ten minutes after his renunciation of Trina Sieppe, Marcus astounded McTeague with a tremendous feat.

"Looka here, Mac. I know somethun you can't do. I'll bet you two bits I'll stump you." They each put a quarter on the table. "Now watch me," cried Marcus. He caught up a billiard ball from the rack, poised it a moment in front of his face, then with a sudden, horrifying distension of his jaws crammed it into his mouth, and shut his lips over it.

For an instant McTeague was stupefied, his eyes bulging. Then an enormous laugh shook him. He roared and shouted, swaying in his chair, slapping his knee. What a josher was this Marcus! Sure, you never could tell what he would do next. Marcus slipped the ball out, wiped it on the tablecloth, and passed it to McTeague.

"Now let's see you do it."

McTeague fell suddenly grave. The matter was serious. He parted his thick mustaches and opened his enormous jaws like an anaconda. The ball disappeared inside his mouth. Marcus applauded vociferously, shouting, "Good work!" McTeague reached for the money and put it in his vest pocket, nodding his head with a knowing air.

Then suddenly his face grew purple, his jaws moved convulsively,

2. Two traditional examples—the first classic, the second Biblical—of undying friendship and loyalty.

he pawed at his cheeks with both hands. The billiard ball had slipped into his mouth easily enough; now, however, he could not get it out again.

It was terrible. The dentist rose to his feet, stumbling about among the dogs, his face working, his eyes starting. Try as he would, he could not stretch his jaws wide enough to slip the ball out. Marcus lost his wits, swearing at the top of his voice. McTeague sweated with terror; inarticulate sounds came from his crammed mouth; he waved his arms wildly; all the four dogs caught the excitement and began to bark. A waiter rushed in, the two billiard players returned, a little crowd formed. There was a veritable scene.

All at once the ball slipped out of McTeague's jaws as easily as it had gone in. What a relief! He dropped into a chair, wiping his forehead, gasping for breath.

On the strength of the occasion Marcus Schouler invited the entire group to drink with him.

By the time the affair was over and the group dispersed it was after five. Marcus and McTeague decided they would ride home on the cars. But they soon found this impossible. The dogs would not follow. Only Alexander, Marcus's new setter, kept his place at the rear of the car. The other three lost their senses immediately, running wildly about the streets with their heads in the air, or suddenly starting off at a furious gallop directly away from the car. Marcus whistled and shouted and lathered with rage in vain. The two friends were obliged to walk. When they finally reached Polk Street, Marcus shut up the three dogs in the hospital. Alexander he brought back to the flat with him.

There was a minute back yard in the rear, where Marcus had made a kennel for Alexander out of an old water barrel. Before he thought of his own supper Marcus put Alexander to bed and fed him a couple of dog biscuits. McTeague had followed him to the yard to keep him company. Alexander settled to his supper at once, chewing vigorously at the biscuit, his head on one side.

"What you going to do about this—about that—about—about my cousin now, Mac?" inquired Marcus.

McTeague shook his head helplessly. It was dark by now and cold. The little back yard was grimy and full of odors. McTeague was tired with their long walk. All his uneasiness about his affair with Trina had returned. No, surely she was not for him. Marcus or some other man would win her in the end. What could she ever see to desire in him—in him, a clumsy giant, with hands like wooden mallets? She had told him once that she would not marry him. Was that not final?

"I don' know what to do, Mark," he said.

"Well, you must make up to her now," answered Marcus. "Go and call on her."

McTeague started. He had not thought of calling on her. The idea frightened him a little.

"Of course," persisted Marcus, "that's the proper caper. What did you expect? Did you think you was never going to see her again?"

"I don' know, I don' know," responded the dentist, looking stupidly at the dog.

"You know where they live," continued Marcus Schouler. "Over at B Street station, across the bay. I'll take you over there whenever you want to go. I tell you what, we'll go over there Washington's Birthday. That's this next Wednesday; sure, they'll be glad to see you." It was good of Marcus. All at once McTeague rose to an appreciation of what his friend was doing for him. He stammered:

"Say, Mark—you're—you're all right, anyhow."

"Why, pshaw!" said Marcus. "That's all right, old man. I'd like to see you two fixed, that's all. We'll go over Wednesday, sure."

They turned back to the house. Alexander left off eating and watched them go away, first with one eye, then with the other. But he was too self-respecting to whimper. However, by the time the two friends had reached the second landing on the back stairs a terrible commotion was under way in the little yard. They rushed to an open window at the end of the hall and looked down.

A thin board fence separated the flat's back yard from that used by the branch post-office. In the latter place lived a collie dog. He and Alexander had smelt each other out, blowing through the cracks of the fence at each other. Suddenly the quarrel had exploded on either side of the fence. The dogs raged at each other, snarling and barking, frantic with hate. Their teeth gleamed. They tore at the fence with their front paws. They filled the whole night with their clamor.

"By damn!" cried Marcus, "they don't love each other. Just listen; wouldn't that make a fight if the two got together? Have to try it some day."

v

Wednesday morning, Washington's Birthday, McTeague rose very early and shaved himself. Besides the six mournful concertina airs, the dentist knew one song. Whenever he shaved, he sung this song; never at any other time. His voice was a bellowing roar, enough to make the window sashes rattle. Just now he woke up all the lodgers in his hall with it. It was a lamentable wail:

> "No one to love, none to caress,
> Left all alone in this world's wilderness."

As he paused to strop his razor, Marcus came into his room, half-dressed, a startling phantom in red flannels.

Marcus often ran back and forth between his room and the dentist's "Parlors" in all sorts of undress. Old Miss Baker had seen him thus several times through her half-open door, as she sat in her room listening and waiting. The old dressmaker was shocked out of all expression. She was outraged, offended, pursing her lips, putting up her head. She talked of complaining to the landlady. "And Mr. Grannis right next door, too. You can understand how trying it is for both of us." She would come out in the hall after one of these apparitions, her little false curls shaking, talking loud and shrill to any one in reach of her voice.

"Well," Marcus would shout, "shut your door, then, if you don't want to see. Look out, now, here I come again. Not even a porous plaster on me this time."

On this Wednesday morning Marcus called McTeague out into the hall, to the head of the stairs that led down to the street door.

"Come and listen to Maria, Mac," said he.

Maria sat on the next to the lowest step, her chin propped by her two fists. The red-headed Polish Jew, the ragman Zerkow, stood in the doorway. He was talking eagerly.

"Now, just once more, Maria," he was saying. "Tell it to us just once more." Maria's voice came up the stairway in a monotone. Marcus and McTeague caught a phrase from time to time.

"There were more than a hundred pieces, and every one of them gold—just that punch-bowl was worth a fortune—thick, fat, red gold."

"Get onto to that, will you?" observed Marcus. "The old skin has got her started on the plate. Ain't they a pair for you?"

"And it rang like bells, didn't it?" prompted Zerkow.

"Sweeter'n church bells, and clearer."

"Ah, sweeter'n bells. Wasn't that punch-bowl awful heavy?"

"All you could do to lift it."

"I know. Oh, I know," answered Zerkow, clawing at his lips. "Where did it all go to? Where did it go?"

Maria shook her head.

"It's gone, anyhow."

"Ah, gone, gone! Think of it! The punch-bowl gone, and the engraved ladle, and the plates and goblets. What a sight it must have been all heaped together!"

"It was a wonderful sight."

"Yes, wonderful; it must have been."

On the lower steps of that cheap flat, the Mexican woman and the red-haired Polish Jew mused long over that vanished, half-mythical gold plate.

Marcus and the dentist spent Washington's Birthday across the bay. The journey over was one long agony to McTeague. He shook with a formless, uncertain dread; a dozen times he would have turned back had not Marcus been with him. The stolid giant was as nervous as a schoolboy. He fancied that his call upon Miss Sieppe was an outrageous affront. She would freeze him with a stare; he would be shown the door, would be ejected, disgraced.

As they got off the local train at B Street station they suddenly collided with the whole tribe of Sieppes—the mother, father, three children, and Trina—equipped for one of their eternal picnics. They were to go to Schuetzen Park, within walking distance of the station. They were grouped about four lunch baskets. One of the children, a little boy, held a black greyhound by a rope around its neck. Trina wore a blue cloth skirt, a striped shirt waist, and a white sailor; about her round waist was a belt of imitation alligator skin.

At once Mrs. Sieppe began to talk to Marcus. He had written of their coming, but the picnic had been decided upon after the arrival of his letter. Mrs. Sieppe explained this to him. She was an immense old lady with a pink face and wonderful hair, absolutely white. The Sieppes were a German-Swiss family.

"We go to der park, Schuetzen Park, mit alle dem childern, a little eggs-kursion, eh not soh? We breathe der freshes air, a celubration, a pignic bei der seashore on. Ach, dot wull be soh gay, ah?"

"You bet it will. It'll be outa sight," cried Marcus, enthusiastic in an instant. "This is m' friend Doctor McTeague I wrote you about, Mrs. Sieppe."

"Ach, der doktor," cried Mrs. Sieppe.

McTeague was presented, shaking hands gravely as Marcus shouldered him from one to the other.

Mr. Sieppe was a little man of a military aspect, full of importance, taking himself very seriously. He was a member of a rifle team. Over his shoulder was slung a Springfield rifle, while his breast was decorated by five bronze medals.

Trina was delighted. McTeague was dumfounded. She appeared positively glad to see him.

"How do you do, Doctor McTeague," she said, smiling at him and shaking his hand. "It's nice to see you again. Look, see how fine my filling is." She lifted a corner of her lip and showed him the clumsy gold bridge.

Meanwhile, Mr. Sieppe toiled and perspired. Upon him devolved the responsibility of the excursion. He seemed to consider it a matter of vast importance, a veritable expedition.

"Owgooste!" he shouted to the little boy with the black greyhound, "you will der hound und basket number three carry. Der tervins," he added, calling to the two smallest boys, who were dressed exactly alike, "will releef one unudder mit der camp-stuhl

und basket number four. Dat is comprehend, hay? When we make
der start, you childern will in der advance march. Dat is your
orders. But we do not start," he exclaimed, excitedly; "we re-main.
Ach Gott, Selina, who does not arrive."

Selina, it appeared, was a niece of Mrs. Sieppe's. They were on
the point of starting without her, when she suddenly arrived, very
much out of breath. She was a slender, unhealthy looking girl, who
overworked herself giving lessons in hand-painting at twenty-five
cents an hour. McTeague was presented. They all began to talk at
once, filling the little station-house with a confusion of tongues.

"Attention!" cried Mr. Sieppe, his gold-headed cane in one hand,
his Springfield in the other. "Attention! We depart." The four
little boys moved off ahead; the greyhound suddenly began to bark,
and tug at his leash. The others picked up their bundles.

"Vorwarts!" shouted Mr. Sieppe, waving his rifle and assuming
the attitude of a lieutenant of infantry leading a charge. The party
set off down the railroad track.

Mrs. Sieppe walked with her husband, who constantly left her
side to shout an order up and down the line. Marcus followed with
Selina. McTeague found himself with Trina at the end of the procession.

"We go off on these picnics almost every week," said Trina, by
way of a beginning, "and almost every holiday, too. It is a custom."

"Yes, yes, a custom," answered McTeague, nodding; "a custom
—that's the word."

"Don't you think picnics are fine fun, Doctor McTeague?" she
continued. "You take your lunch; you leave the dirty city all day;
you race about in the open air, and when lunchtime comes, oh,
aren't you hungry? And the woods and the grass smell so fine!"

"I don' know, Miss Sieppe," he answered, keeping his eyes fixed
on the ground between the rails. "I never went on a picnic."

"Never went on a picnic?" she cried, astonished. "Oh, you'll see
what fun we'll have. In the morning father and the children dig
clams in the mud by the shore, an' we bake them, and—oh, there's
thousands of things to do."

"Once I went sailing on the bay," said McTeague. "It was in a
tugboat; we fished off the heads.[1] I caught three codfishes."

"I'm afraid to go out on the bay," answered Trina, shaking her
head, "sailboats tip over so easy. A cousin of mine, Selina's brother,
was drowned one Decoration Day. They never found his body. Can
you swim, Doctor McTeague?"

"I used to at the mine."

"At the mine? Oh, yes, I remember, Marcus told me you were a
miner once."

1. A group of small islands just outside the Golden Gate.

"I was a car-boy; all the car-boys used to swim in the reservoir by the ditch every Thursday evening. One of them was bit by a rattlesnake once while he was dressing. He was a Frenchman, named Andrew. He swelled up and began to twitch."

"Oh, how I hate snakes! They're so crawly and graceful—but, just the same, I like to watch them. You know that drug store over in town that has a showcase full of live ones?"

"We killed the rattler with a cart whip."

"How far do you think you could swim? Did you ever try? D'you think you could swim a mile?"

"A mile? I don't know. I never tried. I guess I could."

"I can swim a little. Sometimes we all go out to the Crystal Baths."[2]

"The Crystal Baths, huh? Can you swim across the tank?"

"Oh, I can swim all right as long as papa holds my chin up. Soon as he takes his hand away, down I go. Don't you hate to get water in your ears?"

"Bathing's good for you."

"If the water's too warm, it isn't. It weakens you."

Mr. Sieppe came running down the tracks, waving his cane.

"To one side," he shouted, motioning them off the track; "der drain gomes." A local passenger train was just passing B Street station, some quarter of a mile behind them. The party stood to one side to let it pass. Marcus put a nickel and two crossed pins upon the rail, and waved his hat to the passengers as the train roared past. The children shouted shrilly. When the train was gone, they all rushed to see the nickel and the crossed pins. The nickel had been jolted off, but the pins had been flattened out so that they bore a faint resemblance to opened scissors. A great contention arose among the children for the possession of these "scissors." Mr. Sieppe was obliged to intervene. He reflected gravely. It was a matter of tremendous moment. The whole party halted, awaiting his decision.

"Attend now," he suddenly exclaimed. "It will not be soh soon. At der end of der day, ven we shall have home gecommen, den wull it pe adjudge, eh? A reward of merit to him who der bes' pehaves. It is an order. Vorwarts!"

"That was a Sacramento train," said Marcus to Selina as they started off; "it was, for a fact."

"I know a girl in Sacramento," Trina told McTeague. "She's forewoman in a glove store, and she's got consumption."

"I was in Sacramento once," observed McTeague, "nearly eight years ago."

"Is it a nice place—as nice as San Francisco?"

2. The Crystal Salt Water Bathing Company was located on Bay Street.

"It's hot. I practised there for a while."

"I like San Francisco," said Trina, looking across the bay to where the city piled itself upon its hills.

"So do I," answered McTeague. "Do you like it better than living over here?"

"Oh, sure, I wish we lived in the city. If you want to go across for anything it takes up the whole day."

"Yes, yes, the whole day—almost."

"Do you know many people in the city? Do you know anybody named Oelbermann? That's my uncle. He has a wholesale toy store in the Mission.³ They say he's awful rich."

"No, I don' know him."

"His stepdaughter wants to be a nun. Just fancy! And Mr. Oelbermann won't have it. He says it would be just like burying his child. Yes, she wants to enter the convent of the Sacred Heart. Are you a Catholic, Doctor McTeague?"

"No. No, I——"

"Papa is a Catholic. He goes to Mass on the feast days once in a while. But mamma's Lutheran."

"The Catholics are trying to get control of the schools," observed McTeague, suddenly remembering one of Marcus's political tirades.

"That's what cousin Mark says. We are going to send the twins to the kindergarten next month."

"What's the kindergarten?"

"Oh, they teach them to make things out of straw and toothpicks —kind of a play place to keep them off the street."

"There's one up on Sacramento Street, not far from Polk Street. I saw the sign."

"I know where. Why, Selina used to play the piano there."

"Does she play the piano?"

"Oh, you ought to hear her. She plays fine. Selina's very accomplished. She paints, too."

"I can play on the concertina."

"Oh, can you? I wish you'd brought it along. Next time you will. I hope you'll come often on our picnics. You'll see what fun we'll have."

"Fine day for a picnic, ain't it? There ain't a cloud."

"That's so," exclaimed Trina, looking up, "not a single cloud. Oh, yes; there is one, just over Telegraph Hill."

"That's smoke."

"No, it's a cloud. Smoke isn't white that way."

" 'Tis a cloud."

"I knew I was right. I never say a thing unless I'm pretty sure."

3. The Mission District was a business area (named after the old Mission Do-   lores) in the South of Market section of San Francisco.

"It looks like a dog's head."

"Don't it? Isn't Marcus fond of dogs?"

"He got a new dog last week—a setter."

"Did he?"

"Yes. He and I took a lot of dogs from his hospital out for a walk to the Cliff House last Sunday, but we had to walk all the way home, because they wouldn't follow. You've been out to the Cliff House?"

"Not for a long time. We had a picnic there one Fourth of July, but it rained. Don't you love the ocean?"

"Yes—yes, I like it pretty well."

"Oh, I'd like to go off in one of those big sailing ships. Just away, and away, and away, anywhere. They're different from a little yacht. I'd love to travel."

"Sure; so would I."

"Papa and mamma came over in a sailing ship. They were twenty-one days. Mamma's uncle used to be a sailor. He was captain of a steamer on Lake Geneva, in Switzerland."

"Halt!" shouted Mr. Sieppe, brandishing his rifle. They had arrived at the gates of the park. All at once McTeague turned cold. He had only a quarter in his pocket. What was he expected to do —pay for the whole party, or for Trina and himself, or merely buy his own ticket? And even in this latter case would a quarter be enough? He lost his wits, rolling his eyes helplessly. Then it occurred to him to feign a great abstraction, pretending not to know that the time was come to pay. He looked intently up and down the tracks; perhaps a train was coming. "Here we are," cried Trina, as they came up to the rest of the party, crowded about the entrance. "Yes, yes," observed McTeague, his head in the air.

"Gi' me four bits, Mac," said Marcus, coming up. "Here's where we shell out."

"I—I—I only got a quarter," mumbled the dentist, miserably. He felt that he had ruined himself forever with Trina. What was the use of trying to win her? Destiny was against him. "I only got a quarter," he stammered. He was on the point of adding that he would not go in the park. That seemed to be the only alternative.

"Oh, all right!" said Marcus, easily. "I'll pay for you, and you can square with me when we go home."

They filed into the park, Mr. Sieppe counting them off as they entered.

"Ah," said Trina, with a long breath, as she and McTeague pushed through the wicket, "here we are once more, Doctor." She had not appeared to notice McTeague's embarrassment. The difficulty had been tided over somehow. Once more McTeague felt himself saved.

"To der beach!" shouted Mr. Sieppe. They had checked their baskets at the peanut stand. The whole party trooped down to the seashore. The greyhound was turned loose. The children raced on ahead.

From one of the larger parcels Mr. Sieppe had drawn forth a small tin steamboat—August's birthday present—a gaudy little toy which could be steamed up and navigated by means of an alcohol lamp. Her trial trip was to be made this morning.

"Gi' me it, gi' me it," shouted August, dancing around his father.

"Not soh, not soh," cried Mr. Sieppe, bearing it aloft. "I must first der eggsperimunt make."

"No, no!" wailed August. "I want to play with ut."

"Obey!" thundered Mr. Sieppe. August subsided. A little jetty ran part of the way into the water. Here, after a careful study of the directions printed on the cover of the box, Mr. Sieppe began to fire the little boat.

"I want to put ut in the wa-ater," cried August.

"Stand back!" shouted his parent. "You do not know so well as me; dere is dandger. Mitout attention he will eggsplode."

"I want to play with ut," protested August, beginning to cry.

"Ach, soh; you cry, bube!" vociferated Mr. Sieppe. "Mommer," addressing Mrs. Sieppe, "he will soh soon be ge-whipt, eh?"

"I want my boa-wut," screamed August, dancing.

"Silence!" roared Mr. Sieppe. The little boat began to hiss and smoke.

"Soh," observed the father, "he gommence. Attention! I put him in der water." He was very excited. The perspiration dripped from the back of his neck. The little boat was launched. It hissed more furiously than ever. Clouds of steam rolled from it, but it refused to move.

"You don't know how she wo-rks," sobbed August.

"I know more soh mudge as der grossest liddle fool as you," cried Mr. Sieppe, fiercely, his face purple.

"You must give it sh—shove!" exclaimed the boy.

"Den he eggsplode, idiot!" shouted his father. All at once the boiler of the steamer blew up with a sharp crack. The little tin toy turned over and sank out of sight before any one could interfere.

"Ah—h! Yah! Yah!" yelled August. "It's go-one!"

Instantly Mr. Sieppe boxed his ears. There was a lamentable scene. August rent the air with his outcries; his father shook him till his boots danced on the jetty, shouting into his face:

"Ach, idiot! Ach, imbecile! Ach, miserable! I tol' you he eggs-plode. Stop your cry. Stop! It is an order. Do you wish I drow you in der water, eh? Speak. Silence, bube! Mommer, where ist mein stick? He will der grossest whippun ever of his life receive."

Little by little the boy subsided, swallowing his sobs, knuckling his eyes, gazing ruefully at the spot where the boat had sunk. "Dot is better soh," commented Mr. Sieppe, finally releasing him. "Next dime berhaps you will your fat'er better pelief. Now, no more. We will der glams ge-dig. Mommer, a fire. Ach, himmel! we have der pfeffer forgotten."

The work of clam digging began at once, the little boys taking off their shoes and stockings. At first August refused to be comforted, and it was not until his father drove him into the water with his gold-headed cane that he consented to join the others.

What a day that was for McTeague! What a never-to-be-forgotten day! He was with Trina constantly. They laughed together—she demurely, her lips closed tight, her little chin thrust out, her small pale nose, with its adorable little freckles, wrinkling; he roared with all the force of his lungs, his enormous mouth distended, striking sledge-hammer blows upon his knee with his clenched fist.

The lunch was delicious. Trina and her mother made a clam chowder that melted in one's mouth. The lunch baskets were emptied. The party were fully two hours eating. There were huge loaves of rye bread full of grains of chickweed. There were wienerwurst and frankfurter sausages. There was unsalted butter. There were pretzels. There was cold underdone chicken, which one ate in slices, plastered with a wonderful kind of mustard that did not sting. There were dried apples, that gave Mr. Sieppe the hiccoughs. There were a dozen bottles of beer, and, last of all, a crowning achievement, a marvellous Gotha truffle.[4] After lunch came tobacco. Stuffed to the eyes, McTeague drowsed over his pipe, prone on his back in the sun, while Trina, Mrs. Sieppe, and Selina washed the dishes. In the afternoon Mr. Sieppe disappeared. They heard the reports of his rifle on the range. The others swarmed over the park, now around the swings, now in the Casino, now in the museum, now invading the merry-go-round.

At half-past five o'clock Mr. Sieppe marshalled the party together. It was time to return home.

The family insisted that Marcus and McTeague should take supper with them at their home and should stay over night. Mrs. Sieppe argued they could get no decent supper if they went back to the city at that hour; that they could catch an early morning boat and reach their business in good time. The two friends accepted.

The Sieppes lived in a little box of a house at the foot of B Street, the first house to the right as one went up from the station. It was two stories high, with a funny red mansard roof of oval slates. The interior was cut up into innumerable tiny rooms, some of them so small as to be hardly better than sleeping closets. In the back yard was a contrivance for pumping water from the cistern

4. A German pastry dessert.

that interested McTeague at once. It was a dog-wheel, a huge revolving box in which the unhappy black greyhound spent most of his waking hours. It was his kennel; he slept in it. From time to time during the day Mrs. Sieppe appeared on the back doorstep, crying shrilly, "Hoop, hoop!" She threw lumps of coal at him, waking him to his work.

They were all very tired, and went to bed early. After great discussion it was decided that Marcus would sleep upon the lounge in the front parlor. Trina would sleep with August, giving up her room to McTeague. Selina went to her home, a block or so above the Sieppes's. At nine o'clock Mr. Sieppe showed McTeague to his room and left him to himself with a newly lighted candle.

For a long time after Mr. Sieppe had gone McTeague stood motionless in the middle of the room, his elbows pressed close to his sides, looking obliquely from the corners of his eyes. He hardly dared to move. He was in Trina's room.

It was an ordinary little room. A clean white matting was on the floor; gray paper, spotted with pink and green flowers, covered the walls. In one corner, under a white netting, was a little bed, the woodwork gayly painted with knots of bright flowers. Near it, against the wall, was a black walnut bureau. A work-table with spiral legs stood by the window, which was hung with a green and gold window curtain. Opposite the window the closet door stood ajar, while in the corner across from the bed was a tiny washstand with two clean towels.

And that was all. But it was Trina's room. McTeague was in his lady's bower; it seemed to him a little nest, intimate, discreet. He felt hideously out of place. He was an intruder, he, with his enormous feet, his colossal bones, his crude, brutal gestures. The mere weight of his limbs, he was sure, would crush the little bedstead like an egg-shell.

Then, as this first sensation wore off, he began to feel the charm of the little chamber. It was as though Trina were close by, but invisible. McTeague felt all the delight of her presence without the embarrassment that usually accompanied it. He was near to her—nearer than he had ever been before. He saw into her daily life, her little ways and manners, her habits, her very thoughts. And was there not in the air of that room a certain faint perfume that he knew, that recalled her to his mind with marvellous vividness?

As he put the candle down upon the bureau he saw her hairbrush lying there. Instantly he picked it up, and, without knowing why, held it to his face. With what a delicious odor was it redolent! That heavy, enervating odor of her hair—her wonderful, royal hair! The smell of that little hairbrush was talismanic. He had but to close his eyes to see her as distinctly as in a mirror. He saw her tiny, round figure, dressed all in black—for, curiously enough, it was his very first impression of Trina that came back to him now—not the Trina of the later occasions, not the Trina of the blue cloth skirt and white sailor. He saw her as he had seen her the day that Marcus had introduced them: saw her pale, round face; her narrow, half-open eyes, blue like the eyes of a baby; her tiny, pale ears, suggestive of anaemia; the freckles across the bridge of her nose; her pale lips; the tiara of royal black hair; and, above all, the delicious poise of the head, tipped back as though by the weight of all that hair—the poise that thrust out her chin a little, with the movement that was so confiding, so innocent, so nearly infantile.

McTeague went softly about the room from one object to another, beholding Trina in everything he touched or looked at. He came at last to the closet door. It was ajar. He opened it wide, and paused upon the threshold.

Trina's clothes were hanging there—skirts and waists, jackets, and stiff white petticoats. What a vision! For an instant McTeague caught his breath, spellbound. If he had suddenly discovered Trina herself there, smiling at him, holding out her hands, he could hardly have been more overcome. Instantly he recognized the black dress she had worn on that famous first day. There it was, the little jacket she had carried over her arm the day he had terrified her with his blundering declaration, and still others, and others—a whole group of Trinas faced him there. He went farther into the closet, touching the clothes gingerly, stroking them softly with his huge leathern palms. As he stirred them a delicate perfume disengaged itself from the folds. Ah, that exquisite feminine odor! It was not only her hair now, it was Trina herself—her mouth, her hands, her neck; the indescribably sweet, fleshly aroma that was a part of her, pure and clean, and redolent of youth and freshness. All at once, seized with an unreasoned impulse, McTeague opened his huge arms and gathered the little garments close to him, plunging his face deep amongst them, savoring their delicious odor with long breaths of luxury and supreme content.

. . . .

The picnic at Schuetzen Park decided matters. McTeague began to call on Trina regularly Sunday and Wednesday afternoons. He took Marcus Schouler's place. Sometimes Marcus accompanied him, but it was generally to meet Selina by appointment at the Sieppes's house.

But Marcus made the most of his renunciation of his cousin. He remembered his pose from time to time. He made McTeague unhappy and bewildered by wringing his hand, by venting sighs that seemed to tear his heart out, or by giving evidences of an infinite melancholy. "What is my life!" he would exclaim. "What is left for me? Nothing, by damn!" And when McTeague would attempt remonstrance, he would cry; "Never mind, old man. Never mind me. Go, be happy. I forgive you."

Forgive what? McTeague was all at sea, was harassed with the thought of some shadowy, irreparable injury he had done his friend. "Oh, don't think of me!" Marcus would exclaim at other times, even when Trina was by. "Don't think of me; I don't count any more. I ain't in it." Marcus seemed to take great pleasure in contemplating the wreck of his life. There is no doubt he enjoyed himself hugely during these days.

The Sieppes were at first puzzled as well over this change of front.

"Trina has den a new younge man," cried Mr. Sieppe. "First Schouler, now der doktor, eh? What die tevil, I say!"

Weeks passed, February went, March came in very rainy, putting a stop to all their picnics and Sunday excursions.

One Wednesday afternoon in the second week in March McTeague came over to call on Trina, bringing his concertina with him, as was his custom nowadays. As he got off the train at the station he was surprised to find Trina waiting for him.

"This is the first day it hasn't rained in weeks," she explained, "an' I thought it would be nice to walk."

"Sure, sure," assented McTeague.

B Street station was nothing more than a little shed. There was no ticket office, nothing but a couple of whittled and carven benches. It was built close to the railroad tracks, just across which was the dirty, muddy shore of San Francisco Bay. About a quarter of a mile back from the station was the edge of the town of Oakland. Between the station and the first houses of the town lay immense salt flats, here and there broken by winding streams of black water. They were covered with a growth of wiry grass, strangely discolored in places by enormous stains of orange yellow.

Near the station a bit of fence painted with a cigar advertisement reeled over into the mud, while under its lee lay an abandoned gravel wagon with dished wheels. The station was connected with the town by the extension of B Street, which struck across the flats geometrically straight, a file of tall poles with intervening wires marching along with it. At the station these were headed by an iron electric-light pole that, with its supports and outriggers, looked for all the world like an immense grasshopper on its hind legs.

Across the flats, at the fringe of the town, were the dump heaps, the figures of a few Chinese ragpickers moving over them. Far to the left the view was shut off by the immense red-brown drum of the gas-works; to the right it was bounded by the chimneys and workshops of an iron foundry.

Across the railroad tracks, to seaward, one saw the long stretch of black mud bank left bare by the tide, which was far out, nearly half a mile. Clouds of sea-gulls were forever rising and settling upon this mud bank; a wrecked and abandoned wharf crawled over it on tottering legs; close in an old sailboat lay canted on her bilge.

But farther on, across the yellow waters of the bay, beyond Goat Island,[5] lay San Francisco, a blue line of hills, rugged with roofs and spires. Far to the westward opened the Golden Gate, a bleak cutting in the sand-hills, through which one caught a glimpse of the open Pacific.

The station at B Street was solitary; no trains passed at this hour; except the distant rag-pickers, not a soul was in sight. The wind blew strong, carrying with it the mingled smell of salt, of tar, of dead seaweed, and of bilge. The sky hung low and brown; at long intervals a few drops of rain fell.

Near the station Trina and McTeague sat on the roadbed of the tracks, at the edge of the mud bank, making the most out of the landscape, enjoying the open air, the salt marshes, and the sight of the distant water. From time to time McTeague played his six mournful airs upon his concertina.

After a while they began walking up and down the tracks, McTeague talking about his profession, Trina listening, very interested and absorbed, trying to understand.

"For pulling the roots of the upper molars we use the cow-horn forceps," continued the dentist, monotonously. "We get the inside beak over the palatal roots and the cow-horn beak over the buccal roots—that's the roots on the outside, you see. Then we close the forceps, and that breaks right through the alveolus—that's the part of the socket in the jaw, you understand."

At another moment he told her of his one unsatisfied desire. "Some day I'm going to have a big gilded tooth outside my window for a sign. Those big gold teeth are beautiful, beautiful—only they cost so much, I can't afford one just now."

"Oh, it's raining," suddenly exclaimed Trina, holding out her palm. They turned back and reached the station in a drizzle. The afternoon was closing in dark and rainy. The tide was coming back, talking and lapping for miles along the mud bank. Far off across the flats, at the edge of the town, an electric car went by, stringing out a long row of diamond sparks on the overhead wires.

"Say, Miss Trina," said McTeague, after a while, "what's the good of waiting any longer? Why can't us two get married?"

Trina still shook her head, saying "No" instinctively, in spite of herself.

"Why not?" persisted McTeague. "Don't you like me well enough?"

5. The popular name for Yerba Buena Island.

"Yes."

"Then why not?"

"Because."

"Ah, come on," he said, but Trina still shook her head.

"Ah, come on," urged McTeague. He could think of nothing else to say, repeating the same phrase over and over again to all her refusals.

"Ah, come on! Ah, come on!"

Suddenly he took her in his enormous arms, crushing down her struggle with his immense strength. Then Trina gave up, all in an instant, turning her head to his. They kissed each other, grossly, full in the mouth.

A roar and a jarring of the earth suddenly grew near and passed them in a reek of steam and hot air. It was the Overland, with its flaming headlight, on its way across the continent.[6]

The passage of the train startled them both. Trina struggled to free herself from McTeague. "Oh, please! please!" she pleaded, on the point of tears. McTeague released her, but in that moment a slight, a barely perceptible, revulsion of feeling had taken place in him. The instant that Trina gave up, the instant she allowed him to kiss her, he thought less of her. She was not so desirable, after all. But this reaction was so faint, so subtle, so intangible, that in another moment he had doubted its occurrence. Yet afterward it returned. Was there not something gone from Trina now? Was he not disappointed in her for doing that very thing for which he had longed? Was Trina the submissive, the compliant, the attainable just the same, just as delicate and adorable as Trina the inaccessible? Perhaps he dimly saw that this must be so, that it belonged to the changeless order of things—the man desiring the woman only for what she withholds; the woman worshipping the man for that which she yields up to him. With each concession gained the man's desire cools; with every surrender made the woman's adoration increases. But why should it be so?

Trina wrenched herself free and drew back from McTeague, her little chin quivering; her face, even to the lobes of her pale ears, flushed scarlet; her narrow blue eyes brimming. Suddenly she put her head between her hands and began to sob.

"Say, say, Miss Trina, listen—listen here, Miss Trina," cried McTeague, coming forward a step.

"Oh, don't!" she gasped, shrinking. "I must go home," she cried, springing to her feet. "It's late. I must. I must. Don't come with me, please. Oh, I'm so—so,"—she could not find any words. "Let me go alone," she went on. "You may—you come Sunday. Good-by."

"Good-by," said McTeague, his head in a whirl at this sudden,

6. The Overland Express left the Oakland Mole a short distance away and passed through the B Street Station on its way to Sacramento, Reno, and the East.

unaccountable change. "Can't I kiss you again?" But Trina was firm now. When it came to his pleading—a mere matter of words —she was strong enough.

"No, no, you must not!" she exclaimed, with energy. She was gone in another instant. The dentist, stunned, bewildered, gazed stupidly after her as she ran up the extension of B Street through the rain.

But suddenly a great joy took possession of him. He had won her. Trina was to be for him, after all. An enormous smile distended his thick lips; his eyes grew wide, and flashed; and he drew his breath quickly, striking his mallet-like fist upon his knee, and exclaiming under his breath:

"I got her, by God! I got her, by God!" At the same time he thought better of himself; his self-respect increased enormously. The man that could win Trina Sieppe was a man of extraordinary ability.

Trina burst in upon her mother while the latter was setting a mousetrap in the kitchen.

"Oh, mamma!"

"Eh, Trina? Ach, what has happun?"

Trina told her in a breath.

"Soh soon?" was Mrs. Sieppe's first comment. "Eh, well, what you cry for, then?"

"I don't know," wailed Trina, plucking at the end of her handkerchief.

"You loaf der younge doktor?"

"I don't know."

"Well, what for you kiss him?"

"I don't know."

"You don' know, you don' know? Where haf your sensus gone, Trina? You kiss der doktor. You cry, and you don' know. Is ut Marcus den?"

"No, it's not Cousin Mark."

"Den ut must be der doktor."

Trina made no answer.

"Eh?"

"I—I guess so."

"You loaf him?"

"I don't know."

Mrs. Sieppe set down the mousetrap with such violence that it sprung with a sharp snap.

VI

No, Trina did not know. "Do I love him? Do I love him?" A thousand times she put the question to herself during the next two or three days. At night she hardly slept, but lay broad awake for hours in her little, gayly painted bed, with its white netting, torturing herself with doubts and questions. At times she remembered the scene in the station with a veritable agony of shame, and at other times she was ashamed to recall it with a thrill of joy. Nothing could have been more sudden, more unexpected, than that surrender of herself. For over a year she had thought that Marcus would some day be her husband. They would be married, she supposed, some time in the future, she did not know exactly when; the matter did not take definite shape in her mind. She liked Cousin Mark very well. And then suddenly this cross-current had set in; this blond giant had appeared, this huge, stolid fellow, with his immense, crude strength. She had not loved him at first, that was certain. The day he had spoken to her in his "Parlors" she had only been terrified. If he had confined himself to merely speaking, as did Marcus, to pleading with her, to wooing her at a distance, forestalling her wishes, showing her little attentions, sending her boxes of candy, she could have easily withstood him. But he had only to take her in his arms, to crush down her struggle with his enormous strength, to subdue her, conquer her by sheer brute force, and she gave up in an instant.

But why—why had she done so? Why did she feel the desire, the necessity of being conquered by a superior strength? Why did it please her? Why had it suddenly thrilled her from head to foot with a quick, terrifying gust of passion, the like of which she had never known? Never at his best had Marcus made her feel like that, and yet she had always thought she cared for Cousin Mark more than for any one else.

When McTeague had all at once caught her in his huge arms, something had leaped to life in her—something that had hitherto lain dormant, something strong and overpowering. It frightened her now as she thought of it, this second self that had wakened within her, and that shouted and clamored for recognition. And yet, was it to be feared? Was it something to be ashamed of? Was it not, after all, natural, clean, spontaneous? Trina knew that she was a pure girl; knew that this sudden commotion within her carried with it no suggestion of vice.

Dimly, as figures seen in a waking dream, these ideas floated through Trina's mind. It was quite beyond her to realize them clearly; she could not know what they meant. Until that rainy day by the shore of the bay Trina had lived her life with as little self-consciousness as a tree. She was frank, straightforward, a healthy, natural human being, without sex as yet. She was almost like a boy. At once there had been a mysterious disturbance. The woman within her suddenly awoke.

Did she love McTeague? Difficult question. Did she choose him for better or for worse, deliberately, of her own free will, or was Trina herself allowed even a choice in the taking of that step that was to make or mar her life? The Woman is awakened, and, starting from her sleep, catches blindly at what first her newly opened eyes light upon. It is a spell, a witchery, ruled by chance alone, inexplicable—a fairy queen enamored of a clown with ass's ears.[1]

McTeague had awakened the Woman, and, whether she would or no, she was his now irrevocably; struggle against it as she would, she belonged to him, body and soul, for life or for death. She had not sought it, she had not desired it. The spell was laid upon her. Was it a blessing? Was it a curse? It was all one; she was his, indissolubly for evil or for good.

And he? The very act of submission that bound the woman to him forever had made her seem less desirable in his eyes. Their undoing had already begun. Yet neither of them was to blame. From the first they had not sought each other. Chance had brought them face to face, and mysterious instincts as ungovernable as the winds of heaven were at work knitting their lives together. Neither of them had asked that this thing should be—that their destinies, their very souls, should be the sport of chance. If they could have known, they would have shunned the fearful risk. But they were allowed no voice in the matter. Why should it all be?

It had been on a Wednesday that the scene in the B Street station had taken place. Throughout the rest of the week, at every hour of the day, Trina asked herself the same question: "Do I love him? Do I really love him? Is this what love is like?" As she recalled McTeague—recalled his huge, square-cut head, his salient jaw, his shock of yellow hair, his heavy, lumbering body, his slow wits—she found little to admire in him beyond his physical strength, and at such moments she shook her head decisively. "No, surely she did not love him." Sunday afternoon, however, McTeague called. Trina had prepared a little speech for him. She was to tell him that she did not know what had been the matter with her that Wednesday afternoon; that she had acted like a bad girl; that she did not love him well enough to marry him; that she had told him as much once before.

McTeague saw her alone in the little front parlor. The instant she appeared he came straight towards her. She saw what he was bent upon doing. "Wait a minute," she cried, putting out her hands. "Wait. You don't understand. I have got something to say to you." She might as well have talked to the wind. McTeague put

1. The allusion is to *A Midsummer Night's Dream*. Titania, while asleep, has been cast into a spell which requires that she fall in love with the first creature she sees upon awakening. She awakens to discover Bottom, who has himself been bewitched into the form of an ass.

aside her hands with a single gesture, and gripped her to him in a bearlike embrace that all but smothered her. Trina was but a reed before that giant strength. McTeague turned her face to his and kissed her again upon the mouth. Where was all Trina's resolve then? Where was her carefully prepared little speech? Where was all her hesitation and torturing doubts of the last few days? She clasped McTeague's huge red neck with both her slender arms; she raised her adorable little chin and kissed him in return, exclaiming: "Oh, I do love you! I do love you!" Never afterward were the two so happy as at that moment.

A little later in that same week, when Marcus and McTeague were taking lunch at the car conductors' coffee-joint, the former suddenly exclaimed:

"Say, Mac, now that you've got Trina, you ought to do more for her. By damn! you ought to, for a fact. Why don't you take her out somewhere—to the theatre, or somewhere? You ain't on to your job."

Naturally, McTeague had told Marcus of his success with Trina. Marcus had taken on a grand air.

"You've got her, have you? Well, I'm glad of it, old man. I am, for a fact. I know you'll be happy with her. I know how I would have been. I forgive you; yes, I forgive you, freely."

McTeague had not thought of taking Trina to the theatre.

"You think I ought to, Mark?" he inquired, hesitating. Marcus answered, with his mouth full of suet pudding:

"Why, of course. That's the proper caper."

"Well—well, that's so. The theatre—that's the word."

"Take her to the variety show at the Orpheum.[2] There's a good show there this week; you'll have to take Mrs. Sieppe, too, of course," he added. Marcus was not sure of himself as regarded certain proprieties, nor, for that matter, were any of the people of the little world of Polk Street. The shop girls, the plumbers' apprentices, the small tradespeople, and their like, whose social position was not clearly defined, could never be sure how far they could go and yet preserve their "respectability." When they wished to be "proper," they invariably overdid the thing. It was not as if they belonged to the "tough" element, who had no appearances to keep up. Polk Street rubbed elbows with the "avenue" one block above. There were certain limits which its dwellers could not overstep; but unfortunately for them, these limits were poorly defined. They could never be sure of themselves. At an unguarded moment they might be taken for "toughs," so they generally erred in the other

2. On O'Farrell near Powell, in downtown San Francisco, the Orpheum was long the principal vaudeville theatre of the city.

direction, and were absurdly formal. No people have a keener eye
for the amenities than those whose social position is not assured.

"Oh, sure, you'll have to take her mother," insisted Marcus. "It
wouldn't be the proper racket if you didn't."

McTeague undertook the affair. It was an ordeal. Never in his
life had he been so perturbed, so horribly anxious. He called upon
Trina the following Wednesday and made arrangements. Mrs.
Sieppe asked if little August might be included. It would console
him for the loss of his steamboat.

"Sure, sure," said McTeague. "August too—everybody," he
added, vaguely.

"We always have to leave so early," complained Trina, "in order
to catch the last boat. Just when it's becoming interesting."

At this McTeague, acting upon a suggestion of Marcus Schouler's, insisted they should stay at the flat over night. Marcus and the
dentist would give up their rooms to them and sleep at the dog hospital. There was a bed there in the sick ward that old Grannis
sometimes occupied when a bad case needed watching. All at once
McTeague had an idea, a veritable inspiration.

"And we'll—we'll—we'll have—what's the matter with having
something to eat afterward in my 'Parlors?' "

"Vairy goot," commented Mrs. Sieppe. "Bier, eh? And some
damales."

"Oh, I love *tamales!*" exclaimed Trina, clasping her hands.

McTeague returned to the city, rehearsing his instructions over
and over. The theatre party began to assume tremendous proportions. First of all, he was to get the seats, the third or fourth row
from the front, on the left-hand side, so as to be out of the hearing
of the drums in the orchestra; he must make arrangements about
the rooms with Marcus, must get in the beer, but not the tamales;
must buy for himself a white lawn tie[3]—so Marcus directed; must
look to it that Maria Macapa put his room in perfect order; and,
finally, must meet the Sieppes at the ferry slip at half-past seven the
following Monday night.

The real labor of the affair began with the buying of the tickets.
At the theatre McTeague got into wrong entrances; was sent from
one wicket to another; was bewildered, confused; misunderstood
directions; was at one moment suddenly convinced that he had not
enough money with him, and started to return home. Finally he
found himself at the box-office wicket.

"Is it here you buy your seats?"

"How many?"

"Is it here——"

3. A linen cravat.

"What night do you want 'em? Yes, sir, here's the place."

McTeague gravely delivered himself of the formula he had been reciting for the last dozen hours.

"I want four seats for Monday night in the fourth row from the front, and on the right-hand side."

"Right hand as you face the house or as you face the stage?" McTeague was dumfounded.

"I want to be on the right-hand side," he insisted, stolidly; adding, "in order to be away from the drums."

"Well, the drums are on the right of the orchestra as you face the stage," shouted the other impatiently; "you want to the left, then, as you face the house."

"I want to be on the right-hand side," persisted the dentist.

Without a word the seller threw out four tickets with a magnificent, supercilious gesture.

"There's four seats on the right-hand side, then, and you're right up against the drums."

"But I don't want to be near the drums," protested McTeague, beginning to perspire.

"Do you know what you want at all?" said the ticket seller with calmness, thrusting his head at McTeague. The dentist knew that he had hurt this young man's feelings.

"I want—I want," he stammered. The seller slammed down a plan of the house in front of him and began to explain excitedly. It was the one thing lacking to complete McTeague's confusion.

"There are your seats," finished the seller, shoving the tickets into McTeague's hands. "They are the fourth row from the front, and away from the drums. Now are you satisfied?"

"Are they on the right-hand side? I want on the right—no, I want on the left. I want—I don' know, I don' know."

The seller roared. McTeague moved slowly away, gazing stupidly at the blue slips of pasteboard. Two girls took his place at the wicket. In another moment McTeague came back, peering over the girls' shoulders and calling to the seller:

"Are these for Monday night?"

The other disdained reply. McTeague retreated again timidly, thrusting the tickets into his immense wallet. For a moment he stood thoughtful on the steps of the entrance. Then all at once he became enraged, he did not know exactly why; somehow he felt himself slighted. Once more he came back to the wicket.

"You can't make small of me," he shouted over the girls' shoulders; "you—you can't make small of me. I'll thump you in the head, you little—you little—you little—little—little pup." The ticket seller shrugged his shoulders wearily. "A dollar and a half," he said to the two girls.

McTeague glared at him and breathed loudly. Finally he decided to let the matter drop. He moved away, but on the steps was once more seized with a sense of injury and outraged dignity.

"You can't make small of me," he called back a last time, wagging his head and shaking his fist. "I will—I will—I will—yes, I will." He went off muttering.

At last Monday night came. McTeague met the Sieppes at the ferry, dressed in a black Prince Albert coat[4] and his best slate-blue trousers, and wearing the made-up lawn necktie that Marcus had selected for him. Trina was very pretty in the black dress that McTeague knew so well. She wore a pair of new gloves. Mrs. Sieppe had on lisle-thread mits,[5] and carried two bananas and an orange in a net reticule. "For Owgooste," she confided to him. Owgooste was in a Fauntleroy "costume" very much too small for him.[6] Already he had been crying.

"Woult you pelief, Doktor, dot bube has torn his stockun alreatty? Walk in der front, you; stop cryun. Where is dot berliceman?"

At the door of the theatre McTeague was suddenly seized with a panic terror. He had lost the tickets. He tore through his pockets, ransacked his wallet. They were nowhere to be found. All at once he remembered, and with a gasp of relief removed his hat and took them out from beneath the sweatband.

The party entered and took their places. It was absurdly early. The lights were all darkened, the ushers stood under the galleries in groups, the empty auditorium echoing with their noisy talk. Occasionally a waiter with his tray and clean white apron sauntered up and down the aisle. Directly in front of them was the great iron curtain of the stage, painted with all manner of advertisements. From behind this came a noise of hammering and of occasional loud voices.

While waiting they studied their programmes. First was an overture by the orchestra, after which came "The Gleasons, in their mirth-moving musical farce, entitled 'McMonnigal's Courtship.'" This was to be followed by "The Lamont Sisters, Winnie and Violet, serio-comiques and skirt dancers." And after this came a great array of other "artists" and "specialty performers," musical wonders, acrobats, lightning artists, ventriloquists, and last of all, "The feature of the evening, the crowning scientific achievement of the nineteenth century, the kinetoscope."[7] McTeague was excited,

---

4. A long double-breasted frock coat.
5. Long cotton gloves (usually spelled "mitts") which leave the fingers uncovered.
6. The notoriously prissy costume worn by Little Lord Fauntleroy in the popular novel of the same name published in 1886 by Frances Hodgson Burnett. Two notable characteristics of the costume were a lace collar and short velvet trousers.
7. A primitive form of the motion picture invented by Thomas A. Edison and William Dickson in 1891.

dazzled. In five years he had not been twice to the theatre. Now he beheld himself inviting his "girl" and her mother to accompany him. He began to feel that he was a man of the world. He ordered a cigar.

Meanwhile the house was filling up. A few side brackets were turned on. The ushers ran up and down the aisles, stubs of tickets between their thumb and finger, and from every part of the auditorium could be heard the sharp clap-clapping of the seats as the ushers flipped them down. A buzz of talk arose. In the gallery a street gamin whistled shrilly, and called to some friends on the other side of the house.

"Are they go-wun to begin pretty soon, ma?" whined Owgooste for the fifth or sixth time; adding, "Say, ma, can't I have some candy?" A cadaverous little boy had appeared in their aisle, chanting, "Candies, French mixed candies, popcorn, peanuts and candy." The orchestra entered, each man crawling out from an opening under the stage, hardly larger than the gate of a rabbit hutch. At every instant now the crowd increased; there were but few seats that were not taken. The waiters hurried up and down the aisles, their trays laden with beer glasses. A smell of cigar-smoke filled the air, and soon a faint blue haze rose from all corners of the house.

"Ma, when are they go-wun to begin?" cried Owgooste. As he spoke the iron advertisement curtain rose, disclosing the curtain proper underneath. This latter curtain was quite an affair. Upon it was painted a wonderful picture. A flight of marble steps led down to a stream of water; two white swans, their necks arched like the capital letter S, floated about. At the head of the marble steps were two vases filled with red and yellow flowers, while at the foot was moored a gondola. This gondola was full of red velvet rugs that hung over the side and trailed in the water. In the prow of the gondola a young man in vermilion tights held a mandolin in his left hand, and gave his right to a girl in white satin. A King Charles spaniel, dragging a leading-string in the shape of a huge pink sash, followed the girl. Seven scarlet roses were scattered upon the two lowest steps, and eight floated in the water.

"Ain't that pretty, Mac?" exclaimed Trina, turning to the dentist.

"Ma, ain't they go-wun to begin now-wow?" whined Owgooste. Suddenly the lights all over the house blazed up. "Ah!" said everybody all at once.

"Ain't ut crowdut?" murmured Mrs. Sieppe. Every seat was taken; many were even standing up.

"I always like it better when there is a crowd," said Trina. She was in great spirits that evening. Her round, pale face was positively pink.

The orchestra banged away at the overture, suddenly finishing with a great flourish of violins. A short pause followed. Then the orchestra played a quick-step strain, and the curtain rose on an interior furnished with two red chairs and a green sofa. A girl in a short blue dress and black stockings entered in a hurry and began to dust the two chairs. She was in a great temper, talking very fast, disclaiming against the "new lodger." It appeared that this latter never paid his rent; that he was given to late hours. Then she came down to the footlights and began to sing in a tremendous voice, hoarse and flat, almost like a man's. The chorus, of a feeble originality, ran:

"Oh, how happy I will be,
When my darling's face I'll see;
Oh, tell him for to meet me in the moonlight,
Down where the golden lilies bloom."

The orchestra played the tune of this chorus a second time, with certain variations, while the girl danced to it. She sidled to one side of the stage and kicked, then sidled to the other and kicked again. As she finished with the song, a man, evidently the lodger in question, came in. Instantly McTeague exploded in a roar of laughter. The man was intoxicated, his hat was knocked in, one end of his collar was unfastened and stuck up into his face, his watch-chain dangled from his pocket, and a yellow satin slipper was tied to a button-hole of his vest; his nose was vermilion, one eye was black and blue. After a short dialogue with the girl, a third actor appeared. He was dressed like a little boy, the girl's younger brother. He wore an immense turned-down collar, and was continually doing hand-springs and wonderful back somersaults. The "act" devolved upon these three people; the lodger making love to the girl in the short blue dress, the boy playing all manner of tricks upon him, giving him tremendous digs in the ribs or slaps upon the back that made him cough, pulling chairs from under him, running on all fours between his legs and upsetting him, knocking him over at inopportune moments. Every one of his falls was accentuated by a bang upon the bass drum. The whole humor of the "act" seemed to consist in the tripping up of the intoxicated lodger.

This horse-play delighted McTeague beyond measure. He roared and shouted every time the lodger went down, slapping his knee, wagging his head. Owgooste crowed shrilly, clapping his hands and continually asking, "What did he say, ma? What did he say?" Mrs. Sieppe laughed immoderately, her huge fat body shaking like a mountain of jelly. She exclaimed from time to time, "Ach, Gott, dot fool!" Even Trina was moved, laughing demurely, her lips closed, putting one hand with its new glove to her mouth.

The performance went on. Now it was the "musical marvels," two men extravagantly made up as negro minstrels, with immense shoes and plaid vests. They seemed to be able to wrestle a tune out of almost anything—glass bottles, cigar-box fiddles, strings of sleigh-bells, even graduated brass tubes, which they rubbed with resined fingers. McTeague was stupefied with admiration.

"That's what you call musicians," he announced gravely. "Home, Sweet Home," played upon a trombone. Think of that! Art could go no farther.

The acrobats left him breathless. They were dazzling young men with beautifully parted hair, continually making graceful gestures to the audience. In one of them the dentist fancied he saw a strong resemblance to the boy who had tormented the intoxicated lodger and who had turned such marvellous somersaults. Trina could not bear to watch their antics. She turned away her head with a little shudder. "It always makes me sick," she explained.

The beautiful young lady, "The Society Contralto," in evening dress, who sang the sentimental songs, and carried the sheets of music at which she never looked, pleased McTeague less. Trina, however, was captivated. She grew pensive over

> "You do not love me—no;
> Bid me good-by and go;"

and split her new gloves in her enthusiasm when it was finished.

"Don't you love sad music, Mac?" she murmured.

Then came the two comedians. They talked with fearful rapidity; their wit and repartee seemed inexhaustible.

"As I was going down the street yesterday—"

"Ah! as you were going down the street—all right."

"I saw a girl at a window——"

"You saw a girl at a window."

"And this girl she was a corker——"

"Ah! as you were going down the street yesterday you saw a girl at a window, and this girl she was a corker. All right, go on."

The other comedian went on. The joke was suddenly evolved. A certain phrase led to a song, which was sung with lightning rapidity, each performer making precisely the same gestures at precisely the same instant. They were irresistible. McTeague, though he caught but a third of the jokes, could have listened all night.

After the comedians had gone out, the iron advertisement curtain was let down.

"What comes now?" said McTeague, bewildered.

"It's the intermission of fifteen minutes now."

The musicians disappeared through the rabbit hutch, and the audience stirred and stretched itself. Most of the young men left their seats.

During this intermission McTeague and his party had "refreshments." Mrs. Sieppe and Trina had Queen Charlottes,[8] McTeague drank a glass of beer, Owgooste ate the orange and one of the bananas. He begged for a glass of lemonade, which was finally given him.

"Joost to geep um quiet," observed Mrs. Sieppe.

But almost immediately after drinking his lemonade Owgooste was seized with a sudden restlessness. He twisted and wriggled in his seat, swinging his legs violently, looking about him with eyes full of a vague distress. At length, just as the musicians were returning, he stood up and whispered energetically in his mother's ear. Mrs. Sieppe was exasperated at once.

"No, no," she cried, reseating him brusquely.[9]

The performance was resumed. A lightning artist appeared, drawing caricatures and portraits with incredible swiftness. He even went so far as to ask for subjects from the audience, and the names of prominent men were shouted to him from the gallery. He drew portraits of the President, of Grant, of Washington, of Napoleon Bonaparte, of Bismarck, of Garibaldi, of P. T. Barnum.

And so the evening passed. The hall grew very hot, and the smoke of innumerable cigars made the eyes smart. A thick blue mist hung low over the heads of the audience. The air was full of varied smells—the smell of stale cigars, of flat beer, of orange peel, of gas, of sachet powders, and of cheap perfumery.

One "artist" after another came upon the stage. McTeague's attention never wandered for a minute. Trina and her mother enjoyed themselves hugely. At every moment they made comments to one another, their eyes never leaving the stage.

"Ain't dot fool joost too funny?"

"That's a pretty song. Don't you like that kind of a song?"

"Wonderful! It's wonderful! Yes, yes, wonderful! That's the word."

Owgooste, however, lost interest. He stood up in his place, his back to the stage, chewing a piece of orange peel and watching a little girl in her father's lap across the aisle, his eyes fixed in a glassy, ox-like stare. But he was uneasy. He danced from one foot to the other, and at intervals appealed in hoarse whispers to his mother, who disdained an answer.

"Ma, say, ma-ah," he whined, abstractedly chewing his orange peel, staring at the little girl.

8. A pastry consisting of a hard crust and a custard or marmalade filling.

9. The two preceding paragraphs were replaced in the second impression of *McTeague* by:

The quarter of an hour intermission seemed interminable to McTeague. He continually consulted his watch, wondering when the musicians would come back, listening anxiously to the vague clamor of footsteps and voices that issued confusedly from behind the curtain and from the direction of the wings. Mrs. Sieppe pretended to recognize a friend two rows back of where she was sitting.

"Ach! sure dot's her," she murmured continually.

"Ma-ah, say, ma." At times his monotonous plaint reached his mother's consciousness. She suddenly realized what this was that was annoying her.

"Owgooste, will you sit down?" She caught him up all at once, and jammed him down into his place. "Be quiet, den; loog; listun at der yunge girls."

Three young women and a young man who played a zither occupied the stage. They were dressed in Tyrolese costume; they were yodlers, and sang in German about "mountain tops" and "bold hunters" and the like. The yodling chorus was a marvel of flute-like modulations. The girls were really pretty, and were not made up in the least. Their "turn" had a great success. Mrs. Sieppe was entranced. Instantly she remembered her girlhood and her native Swiss village.

"Ach, dot is heavunly; joost like der old country. Mein gran'mutter used to be one of der mos' famous yodlers. When I was leedle, I haf seen dem joost like dat."

"Ma-ah," began Owgooste fretfully, as soon as the yodlers had departed. He could not keep still an instant; he twisted from side to side, swinging his legs with incredible swiftness.[1]

"Ma-ah, I want to go ho-ome."

"Pehave!" exclaimed his mother, shaking him by the arm; "loog, der leedle girl is watchun you. Dis is der last dime I take you to der blay, you see."

"I don't ca-are; I'm sleepy." At length, to their great relief, he went to sleep, his head against his mother's arm.

The kinetoscope fairly took their breaths away.

"What will they do next?" observed Trina, in amazement. "Ain't that wonderful, Mac?"

McTeague was awe-struck.

"Look at that horse move his head," he cried excitedly, quite carried away. "Look at that cable-car coming—and the man going across the street. See, here comes a truck. Well, I never in all my life! What would Marcus say to this?"

"It's all a drick!" exclaimed Mrs. Sieppe, with sudden conviction. "I ain't no fool; dot's nothun but a drick."

"Well, of course, mamma," exclaimed Trina, "it's——"

But Mrs. Sieppe put her head in the air.

"I'm too old to be fooled," she persisted. "It's a drick." Nothing more could be got out of her than this.

The party stayed to the very end of the show, though the kinetoscope was the last number but one on the programme, and fully half the audience left immediately afterward. However, while the

---

1. The preceding paragraph was replaced in the second impression of *McTeague* by:
   "Ma'ah," began Owgooste fretfully, as soon as the yodlers had departed. He protested that he was sleepy, as though it was a matter for which the party were indiscriminately responsible.

unfortunate Irish comedian went through his "act" to the backs of
the departing people, Mrs. Sieppe woke Owgooste, very cross and
sleepy, and began getting her "things together." As soon as he was
awake Owgooste began fidgeting again.[2]

"Save der brogramme, Trina," whispered Mrs. Sieppe. "Take ut
home to popper. Where is der hat of Owgooste?[3] Haf you got mein
handkerchief, Trina?"

But at this moment a dreadful accident happened to Owgooste;
his distress reached its climax; his fortitude collapsed. What a
misery! It was a veritable catastrophe, deplorable, lamentable, a
thing beyond words! For a moment he gazed wildly about him, helpless and petrified with astonishment and terror. Then his grief
found utterance, and the closing strains of the orchestra were mingled with a prolonged wail of infinite sadness.

"Owgooste, what is ut?" cried his mother, eyeing him with dawn-
ing suspicion; then suddenly, "What haf you done? You haf ruin
your new Vauntleroy gostume!" Her face blazed; without more ado
she smacked him soundly. Then it was that Owgooste touched the
limit of his misery, his unhappiness, his horrible discomfort; his
utter wretchedness was complete. He filled the air with his doleful
outcries. The more he was smacked and shaken, the louder he wept.

"What—what is the matter?" inquired McTeague.

Trina's face was scarlet. "Nothing, nothing," she exclaimed hastily, looking away. "Come, we must be going. It's about over." The
end of the show and the breaking up of the audience tided over the
embarrassment of the moment.[4]

The party filed out at the tail end of the audience. Already the
lights were being extinguished and the ushers spreading druggeting
over the upholstered seats.

McTeague and the Sieppes took an uptown car that would bring
them near Polk Street. The car was crowded; McTeague and Ow-

2. The preceding sentence was replaced
in the second impression of *McTeague*
by:

    McTeague groped under his seat,
    reaching about for his hat.
3. The preceding sentence was replaced
in the second impression of *McTeague*
by:

    Where is der net redicule, eh?
4. The four preceding paragraphs were
replaced in the second impression of
McTeague by:

    But McTeague was in distress. He
    had lost his hat. What could have be-
    come of it? Again and again he thrust
    his hand blindly underneath the seat,
    feeling about upon the dusty floor. His
    face became scarlet with embarrass-
    ment and with the effort of bending
    his great body in so contracted a
    space; he bumped his head upon the
    backs of the seats in front of him.

    At length he recovered it from a re-
mote corner, in company with Mrs. Sieppe's reticule, sadly battered by a score of
feet. He clapped it upon his head with a
breath of relief. But when he turned about
to hand her reticule to Mrs. Sieppe he was
struck with bewilderment. Neither Mrs.
Sieppe, Trina, nor Owgooste was anywhere in sight. McTeague found himself
staring into the faces of some dozen people
whose progress he was blocking.

    "What—where are they gone?" mut-
tered McTeague.

    He gazed about him in great embarrass-
ment, rolling his eyes. But the moving audience had carried the Sieppes farther
down the aisle. At last McTeague discovered them and crushed his way to them
with bull-like force and directness. They,
meanwhile, sidled into an empty row of
seats to wait for him.

gooste were obliged to stand. The little boy fretted to be taken in his mother's lap, but Mrs. Sieppe emphatically refused.

On their way home they discussed the performance.

"I—I like best der yodlers."

"Ah, the soloist was the best—the lady who sang those sad songs."

"Wasn't—wasn't that magic lantern wonderful, where the figures moved? Wonderful—ah, wonderful! And wasn't that first act funny, where the fellow fell down all the time? And that musical act, and the fellow with the burnt-cork face who played 'Nearer, My God to Thee' on the beer bottles."

They got off at Polk Street and walked up a block to the flat. The street was dark and empty; opposite the flat, in the back of the deserted market, the ducks and geese were calling persistently.

As they were buying their *tamales* from the half-breed Mexican at the street corner, McTeague observed:

"Marcus ain't gone to bed yet. See, there's a light in his window. There!" he exclaimed at once, "I forgot the door-key. Well, Marcus can let us in."

Hardly had he rung the bell at the street door of the flat when the bolt was shot back. In the hall at the top of the long, narrow staircase there was the sound of a great scurrying. Maria Macapa stood there, her hand upon the rope that drew the bolt; Marcus was at her side; Old Grannis was in the background, looking over their shoulders; while little Miss Baker leant over the banisters, a strange man in a drab overcoat at her side. As McTeague's party stepped into the doorway a half-dozen voices cried;

"Yes, it's them."

"Is that you, Mac?"

"Is that you, Miss Sieppe?"

"Is your name Trina Sieppe?"

Then, shriller than all the rest, Maria Macapa screamed:

"Oh, Miss Sieppe, come up here quick. Your lottery ticket has won five thousand dollars!"

VII

"What nonsense!" answered Trina.

"Ach Gott! What *is* ut?" cried Mrs. Sieppe, misunderstanding, supposing a calamity.

"What—what—what," stammered the dentist, confused by the lights, the crowded stairway, the medley of voices. The party reached the landing. The others surrounded them. Marcus alone seemed to rise to the occasion.

"Le' me be the first to congratulate you," he cried, catching Trina's hand. Every one was talking at once.

"Miss Sieppe, Miss Sieppe, your ticket has won five thousand dollars," cried Maria. "Don't you remember the lottery ticket I sold you in Doctor McTeague's office?"

"Trina!" almost screamed her mother. "Five tausend thalers! five tausend thalers! If popper were only here!"

"What is it—what is it?" exclaimed McTeague, rolling his eyes.

"What are you going to do with it, Trina?" inquired Marcus.

"You're a rich woman, my dear," said Miss Baker, her little false curls quivering with excitement, "and I'm glad for your sake. Let me kiss you. To think I was in the room when you bought the ticket!"

"Oh, oh!" interrupted Trina, shaking her head, "there is a mistake. There must be. Why—why should I win five thousand dollars? It's nonsense!"

"No mistake, no mistake," screamed Maria. "Your number was 400,012. Here it is in the paper this evening. I remember it well, because I keep an account."

"But I know you're wrong," answered Trina, beginning to tremble in spite of herself. "Why should I win?"

"Eh? Why shouldn't you?" cried her mother.

In fact, why shouldn't she? The idea suddenly occurred to Trina. After all, it was not a question of effort or merit on her part. Why should she suppose a mistake? What if it were true, this wonderful fillip of fortune striking in there like some chance-driven bolt?

"Oh, do you think so?" she gasped.

The stranger in the drab overcoat came forward.

"It's the agent," cried two or three voices, simultaneously.

"I guess you're one of the lucky ones, Miss Sieppe," he said. "I suppose you have kept your ticket."

"Yes, yes; four three oughts twelve—I remember."

"That's right," admitted the other. "Present your ticket at the local branch office as soon as possible—the address is printed on the back of the ticket—and you'll receive a check on our bank for five thousand dollars. Your number will have to be verified on our official list, but there's hardly a chance of a mistake. I congratulate you."

All at once a great thrill of gladness surged up in Trina. She was to possess five thousand dollars. She was carried away with the joy of her good fortune, a natural, spontaneous joy—the gaiety of a child with a new and wonderful toy.

"Oh, I've won, I've won, I've won!" she cried, clapping her hands. "Mamma, think of it. I've won five thousand dollars, just by buying a ticket. Mac, what do you say to that? I've got five thousand dollars. August, do you hear what's happened to sister?"

"Kiss your mommer, Trina," suddenly commanded Mrs. Sieppe. "What efer will you do mit all dose money, eh, Trina?"

"Huh!" exclaimed Marcus. "Get married on it for one thing."
Thereat they all shouted with laughter. McTeague grinned, and
looked about sheepishly. "Talk about luck," muttered Marcus,
shaking his head at the dentist; then suddenly he added:

"Well, are we going to stay talking out here in the hall all night?
Can't we all come into your 'Parlors,' Mac?"

"Sure, sure," exclaimed McTeague, hastily unlocking his door.

"Efery botty gome," cried Mrs. Sieppe, genially. "Ain't ut so,
Doktor?"

"Everybody," repeated the dentist. "There's—there's some beer."

"We'll celebrate, by damn!" exclaimed Marcus. "It ain't every
day you win five thousand dollars. It's only Sundays and legal holidays." Again he set the company off into a gale of laughter. Anything was funny at a time like this. In some way every one of them
felt elated. The wheel of fortune had come spinning close to them.
They were near to this great sum of money. It was as though they
too had won.

"Here's right where I sat when I bought that ticket," cried Trina,
after they had come into the "Parlors," and Marcus had lit the gas.
"Right here in this chair." She sat down in one of the rigid chairs
under the steel engraving. "And, Marcus, you sat here——"

"And I was just getting out of the operating chair," interposed
Miss Baker.

"Yes, yes. That's so; and you," continued Trina, pointing to
Maria, "came up and said, 'Buy a ticket in the lottery; just a dollar.'
Oh, I remember it just as plain as though it was yesterday, and I
wasn't going to at first——"

"And don't you know I told Maria it was against the law?"

"Yes, I remember, and then I gave her a dollar and put the ticket
in my pocketbook. It's in my pocketbook now at home in the top
drawer of my bureau—oh, suppose it should be stolen now," she
suddenly exclaimed.

"It's worth big money now," asserted Marcus.

"Five thousand dollars. Who would have thought it? It's wonderful." Everybody started and turned. It was McTeague. He stood in
the middle of the floor, wagging his huge head. He seemed to have
just realized what had happened.

"Yes, sir, five thousand dollars!" exclaimed Marcus, with a
sudden unaccountable mirthlessness. "Five thousand dollars! Do
you get on to that? Cousin Trina and you will be rich people."

"At six per cent, that's twenty-five dollars a month," hazarded
the agent.

"Think of it. Think of it," muttered McTeague. He went aimlessly about the room, his eyes wide, his enormous hands dangling.

"A cousin of mine won forty dollars once," observed Miss Baker.

"But he spent every cent of it buying more tickets, and never won anything."

Then the reminiscences began. Maria told about the butcher on the next block who had won twenty dollars the last drawing. Mrs. Sieppe knew a gas-fitter in Oakland who had won several times; once a hundred dollars. Little Miss Baker announced that she had always believed that lotteries were wrong; but, just the same, five thousand was five thousand.

"It's all right when you win, ain't it, Miss Baker?" observed Marcus, with a certain sarcasm. What was the matter with Marcus? At moments he seemed singularly out of temper.

But the agent was full of stories. He told his experiences, the legends and myths that had grown up around the history of the lottery; he told of the poor newsboy with a dying mother to support who had drawn a prize of fifteen thousand; of the man who was driven to suicide through want, but who held (had he but known it) the number that two days after his death drew the capital prize of thirty thousand dollars; of the little milliner who for ten years had played the lottery without success, and who had one day declared that she would buy but one more ticket and then give up trying, and of how this last ticket had brought her a fortune upon which she could retire; of tickets that had been lost or destroyed, and whose numbers had won fabulous sums at the drawing; of criminals, driven to vice by poverty, and who had reformed after winning competencies; of gamblers who played the lottery as they would play a faro bank, turning in their winnings again as soon as made,[1] buying thousands of tickets all over the country; of superstitions as to terminal and initial numbers, and as to lucky days of purchase; of marvellous coincidences—three capital prizes drawn consecutively by the same town; a ticket bought by a millionaire and given to his bootblack, who won a thousand dollars upon it; the same number winning the same amount an indefinite number of times; and so on to infinity. Invariably it was the needy who won, the destitute and starving woke to wealth and plenty, the virtuous toiler suddenly found his reward in a ticket bought at a hazard; the lottery was a great charity, the friend of the people, a vast beneficent machine that recognized neither rank nor wealth nor station.

The company began to be very gay. Chairs and tables were brought in from the adjoining rooms, and Maria was sent out for more beer and tamales, and also commissioned to buy a bottle of wine and some cake for Miss Baker, who abhorred beer.

The "Dental Parlors" were in great confusion. Empty beer bottles stood on the movable rack where the instruments were kept; plates

1. Faro is a card game in which only two cards are dealt between the settling of bets.

and napkins were upon the seat of the operating chair and upon the stand of shelves in the corner, side by side with the concertina and the volumes of "Allen's Practical Dentist." The canary woke and chittered crossly, his feathers puffed out; the husks of tamales littered the floor; the stone pug dog sitting before the little stove stared at the unusual scene, his glass eyes starting from their sockets.

They drank and feasted in impromptu fashion. Marcus Schouler assumed the office of master of ceremonies; he was in a lather of excitement, rushing about here and there, opening beer bottles, serving the tamales, slapping McTeague upon the back, laughing and joking continually. He made McTeague sit at the head of the table, with Trina at his right and the agent at his left; he—when he sat down at all—occupied the foot, Maria Macapa at his left, while next to her was Mrs. Sieppe, opposite Miss Baker. Owgooste had been put to bed upon the bed-lounge.

"Where's Old Grannis?" suddenly exclaimed Marcus. Sure enough, where had the old Englishman gone? He had been there at first.

"I called him down with everybody else," cried Maria Macapa, "as soon as I saw in the paper that Miss Sieppe had won. We all came down to Mr. Schouler's room and waited for you to come home. I think he must have gone back to his room. I'll bet you'll find him sewing up his books."

"No, no," observed Miss Baker, "not at this hour."

Evidently the timid old gentleman had taken advantage of the confusion to slip unobtrusively away.

"I'll go bring him down," shouted Marcus; "he's got to join us." Miss Baker was in great agitation.

"I—I hardly think you'd better," she murmured; "he—he—I don't think he drinks beer."

"He takes his amusement in sewin' up books," cried Maria.

Marcus brought him down, nevertheless, having found him just preparing for bed.

"I—I must apologize," stammered Old Grannis, as he stood in the doorway. "I had not quite expected—I—find—find myself a little unprepared." He was without collar and cravat, owing to Marcus Schouler's precipitate haste. He was annoyed beyond words that Miss Baker saw him thus. Could anything be more embarrassing?

Old Grannis was introduced to Mrs. Sieppe and to Trina as Marcus's employer. They shook hands solemnly.

"I don't believe that he an' Miss Baker have ever been introduced," cried Maria Macapa, shrilly, "an' they've been livin' side by side for years."

The two old people were speechless, avoiding each other's gaze. It had come at last; they were to know each other, to talk together, to touch each other's hands.

Marcus brought Old Grannis around the table to little Miss Baker, dragging him by the coat sleeve, exclaiming: "Well, I thought you two people knew each other long ago. Miss Baker, this is Mr. Grannis; Mr. Grannis, this is Miss Baker." Neither spoke. Like two little children they faced each other, awkward, constrained, tongue-tied with embarrassment. Then Miss Baker put out her hand shyly. Old Grannis touched it for an instant and let it fall.

"Now you know each other," cried Marcus, "and it's about time." For the first time their eyes met; Old Grannis trembled a little, putting his hand uncertainly to his chin. Miss Baker flushed ever so slightly, but Maria Macapa passed suddenly between them, carrying a half empty beer bottle. The two old people fell back from one another, Miss Baker resuming her seat.

"Here's a place for you over here, Mr. Grannis," cried Marcus, making room for him at his side. Old Grannis slipped into the chair, withdrawing at once from the company's notice. He stared fixedly at his plate and did not speak again. Old Miss Baker began to talk volubly across the table to Mrs. Sieppe about hot-house flowers and medicated flannels.[2]

It was in the midst of this little impromptu supper that the engagement of Trina and the dentist was announced. In a pause in the chatter of conversation Mrs. Sieppe leaned forward and, speaking to the agent, said:

"Vell, you know also my daughter Trina get married bretty soon. She and der dentist, Doktor McTeague, eh, yes?"

There was a general exclamation.

"I thought so all along," cried Miss Baker, excitedly. "The first time I saw them together I said, 'What a pair!' "

"Delightful!" exclaimed the agent, "to be married and win a snug little fortune at the same time."

"So—So," murmured Old Grannis, nodding at his plate.

"Good luck to you," cried Maria.

"He's lucky enough already," growled Marcus under his breath, relapsing for a moment into one of those strange moods of sullenness which had marked him throughout the evening.

Trina flushed crimson, drawing shyly nearer her mother. McTeague grinned from ear to ear, looking around from one to another, exclaiming "Huh! Huh!"

But the agent rose to his feet, a newly filled beer glass in his hand. He was a man of the world, this agent. He knew life. He was suave and easy. A diamond was on his little finger.

2. Woolen underwear which has been treated with a medicinal substance.

"Ladies and gentlemen," he began. There was an instant silence. "This is indeed a happy occasion. I—I am glad to be here to-night; to be a witness to such good fortune; to partake in these—in this celebration. Why, I feel almost as glad as if I had held four three oughts twelve myself; as if the five thousand were mine instead of belonging to our charming hostess. The good wishes of my humble self go out to Miss Sieppe in this moment of her good fortune, and I think—in fact, I am sure I can speak for the great institution, the great company I represent. The company congratulates Miss Sieppe. We—they—ah— They wish her every happiness her new fortune can procure her. It has been my duty, my—ah—cheerful duty to call upon the winners of large prizes and to offer the felicitation of the company. I have, in my experience, called upon many such; but never have I seen fortune so happily bestowed as in this case. The company have dowered the prospective bride. I am sure I but echo the sentiments of this assembly when I wish all joy and happiness to this happy pair, happy in the possession of a snug little fortune, and happy—happy in—" he finished with a sudden inspiration— "in the possession of each other; I drink to the health, wealth, and happiness of the future bride and groom. Let us drink standing up." They drank with enthusiasm. Marcus was carried away with the excitement of the moment.

"Outa sight, outa sight," he vociferated, clapping his hands. "Very well said. To the health of the bride. McTeague, McTeague, speech, speech!"

In an instant the whole table was clamoring for the dentist to speak. McTeague was terrified; he gripped the table with both hands, looking wildly about him.

"Speech, speech!" shouted Marcus, running around the table and endeavoring to drag McTeague up.

"No—no—no," muttered the other. "No speech." The company rattled upon the table with their beer glasses, insisting upon a speech. McTeague settled obstinately into his chair, very red in the face, shaking his head energetically.

"Ah, go on!" he exclaimed; "no speech."

"Ah, get up and say somethun, anyhow," persisted Marcus; "you ought to do it. It's the proper caper."

McTeague heaved himself up; there was a burst of applause; he looked slowly about him, then suddenly sat down again, shaking his head hopelessly.

"Oh, go on, Mac," cried Trina.

"Get up, say somethun, anyhow," cried Marcus, tugging at his arm; "you *got* to."

Once more McTeague rose to his feet.

"Huh! he exclaimed, looking steadily at the table. Then he began:

"I don' know what to say—I—I—I ain't never made a speech before; I—I ain't never made a speech before. But I'm glad Trina's won the prize——"

"Yes, I'll bet you are," muttered Marcus.

"I—I—I'm glad Trina's won, and I—I want to—I want to—I want to—want to say that—you're—all—welcome, an' drink hearty, an' I'm much obliged to the agent. Trina and I are goin' to be married, an' I'm glad everybody's here to-night, an' you're—all—welcome, an' drink hearty, an' I hope you'll come again, an' you're always welcome—an'—I—an'—an'— That's—about—all—I—gotta say." He sat down, wiping his forehead, amidst tremendous applause.

Soon after that the company pushed back from the table and relaxed into couples and groups. The men, with the exception of Old Grannis, began to smoke, the smell of their tobacco mingling with the odors of ether, creosote, and stale bedding, which pervaded the "Parlors." Soon the windows had to be lowered from the top. Mrs. Sieppe and old Miss Baker sat together in the bay window exchanging confidences. Miss Baker had turned back the overskirt of her dress; a plate of cake was in her lap; from time to time she sipped her wine with the delicacy of a white cat. The two women were much interested in each other. Miss Baker told Mrs. Sieppe all about Old Grannis, not forgetting the fiction of the title and the unjust stepfather.

"He's quite a personage really," said Miss Baker.

Mrs. Sieppe led the conversation around to her children. "Ach, Trina is sudge a goote girl," she said; "always gay, yes, und sing from morgen to night. Und Owgooste, he is soh smart also, yes, eh? He has der genius for machines, always making somethun mit wheels und sbrings."

"Ah, if—if—I had children," murmured the little old maid a trifle wistfully, "one would have been a sailor; he would have begun as a midshipman on my brother's ship; in time he would have been an officer. The other would have been a landscape gardener."

"Oh, Mac!" exclaimed Trina, looking up into the dentist's face, "think of all this money coming to us just at this very moment. Isn't it wonderful? Don't it kind of scare you?"

"Wonderful, wonderful!" muttered McTeague, shaking his head. "Let's buy a lot of tickets," he added, struck with an idea.

"Now, that's how you can always tell a good cigar," observed the agent to Marcus as the two sat smoking at the end of the table. "The light end should be rolled to a point."

"Ah, the Chinese cigar-makers," cried Marcus, in a passion, brandishing his fist. "It's them as is ruining the cause of white labor. They are, they are for a *fact*. Ah, the rat-eaters! Ah, the white-livered curs!"

Over in the corner, by the stand of shelves, Old Grannis was listening to Maria Macapa. The Mexican woman had been violently stirred over Trina's sudden wealth; Maria's mind had gone back to her younger days. She leaned forward, her elbows on her knees, her chin in her hands, her eyes wide and fixed. Old Grannis listened to her attentively.

"There wa'n't a piece that was so much as scratched," Maria was saying. "Every piece was just like a mirror, smooth and bright; oh, bright as a little sun. Such a service as that was—platters and soup tureens and an immense big punch-bowl. Five thousand dollars, what does that amount to? Why, that punch-bowl alone was worth a fortune."

"What a wonderful story!" exclaimed Old Grannis, never for an instant doubting its truth. "And it's all lost now, you say?"

"Lost, lost," repeated Maria.

"Tut, tut! What a pity! What a pity!"

Suddenly the agent rose and broke out with;

"Well, I must be going, if I'm to get any car."

He shook hands with everybody, offered a parting cigar to Marcus, congratulated McTeague and Trina a last time, and bowed himself out.

"What an elegant gentleman," commented Miss Baker.

"Ah," said Marcus, nodding his head, "there's a man of the world for you. Right on to himself, by damn!"

The company broke up.

"Come along, Mac," cried Marcus; "we're to sleep with the dogs to-night, you know."

The two friends said "Good-night" all around and departed for the little dog hospital.

Old Grannis hurried to his room furtively, terrified lest he should again be brought face to face with Miss Baker. He bolted himself in and listened until he heard her foot in the hall and the soft closing of her door. She was there close beside him; as one might say, in the same room; for he, too, had made the discovery as to the similarity of the wall-paper. At long intervals he could hear a faint rustling as she moved about. What an evening that had been for him! He had met her, had spoken to her, had touched her hand; he was in a tremor of excitement. In a like manner the little old dressmaker listened and quivered. *He* was there in that same room which they shared in common, separated only by the thinnest board partition. He was thinking of her, she was almost sure of it. They were strangers no longer; they were acquaintances, friends. What an event that evening had been in their lives!

Late as it was, Miss Baker brewed a cup of tea and sat down in her rocking chair close to the partition; she rocked gently, sipping her tea, calming herself after the emotions of that wonderful evening.

Old Grannis heard the clinking of the tea things and smelt the faint odor of the tea. It seemed to him a signal, an invitation. He drew his chair close to his side of the partition, before his work-table. A pile of half-bound "Nations" was in the little binding apparatus; he threaded his huge upholsterer's needle with stout twine and set to work.

It was their *tête-à-tête*. Instinctively they felt each other's presence, felt each other's thought coming to them through the thin partition. It was charming; they were perfectly happy. There in the stillness that settled over the flat in the half hour after midnight the two old people "kept company," enjoying after their fashion their little romance that had come so late into the lives of each.

On the way to her room in the garret Maria Macapa paused under the single gas-jet that burned at the top of the well of the staircase; she assured herself that she was alone, and then drew from her pocket one of McTeague's "tapes" of non-cohesive gold. It was the most valuable steal she had ever yet made in the dentist's "Parlors." She told herself that it was worth at least a couple of dollars. Suddenly an idea occurred to her, and she went hastily to a window at the end of the hall, and, shading her face with both hands, looked down into the little alley just back of the flat. On some nights Zerkow, the red-headed Polish Jew, sat up late, taking account of the week's rag-picking. There was a dim light in his window now.

Maria went to her room, threw a shawl around her head, and descended into the little back yard of the flat by the back stairs. As she let herself out of the back gate into the alley, Alexander, Marcus's Irish setter, woke suddenly with a gruff bark. The collie who lived on the other side of the fence, in the back yard of the branch post-office, answered with a snarl. Then in an instant the endless feud between the two dogs was resumed. They dragged their respective kennels to the fence, and through the cracks raged at each other in a frenzy of hate; their teeth snapped and gleamed; the hackles on their backs rose and stiffened. Their hideous clamor could have been heard for blocks around. What a massacre should the two ever meet!

Meanwhile, Maria was knocking at Zerkow's miserable hovel.

"Who is it? Who is it?" cried the rag-picker from within, in his hoarse voice, that was half whisper, starting nervously, and sweeping a handful of silver into his drawer.

"It's me, Maria Macapa;" then in a lower voice, and as if speaking to herself, "had a flying squirrel an' let him go."

"Ah, Maria," cried Zerkow, obsequiously opening the door. "Come in, come in, my girl; you're always welcome, even as late as this. No junk, hey? But you're welcome for all that. You'll have a drink, won't you?" He led her into his back room and got down the whiskey bottle and the broken red tumbler.

After the two had drunk together Maria produced the gold "tape." Zerkow's eyes glittered on the instant. The sight of gold invariably sent a qualm all through him; try as he would, he could not repress it. His fingers trembled and clawed at his mouth; his breath grew short.

"Ah, ah, ah!" he exclaimed, "give it here, give it here; give it to me, Maria. That's a good girl, come give it to me."

They haggled as usual over the price, but to-night Maria was too excited over other matters to spend much time in bickering over a few cents.

"Look here, Zerkow," she said as soon as the transfer was made, "I got something to tell you. A little while ago I sold a lottery ticket to a girl at the flat; the drawing was in this evening's papers. How much do you suppose that girl has won?"

"I don't know. How much? How much?"

"Five thousand dollars."

It was as though a knife had been run through the Jew; a spasm of an almost physical pain twisted his face—his entire body. He raised his clenched fists into the air, his eyes shut, his teeth gnawing his lip.

"Five thousand dollars," he whispered; "five thousand dollars. For what? For nothing, for simply buying a ticket; and I have worked so hard for it, so hard, so hard. Five thousand dollars, five thousand dollars. Oh, why couldn't it have come to me?" he cried, his voice choking, the tears starting to his eyes; "why couldn't it have come to me? To come so close, so close, and yet to miss me—me who have worked for it, fought for it, starved for it, am dying for it every day. Think of it, Maria, five thousand dollars, all bright, heavy pieces——"

"Bright as a sunset," interrupted Maria, her chin propped on her hands. "Such a glory, and heavy. Yes, every piece was heavy, and it was all you could do to lift the punch-bowl. Why, that punch-bowl was worth a fortune alone——"

"And it rang when you hit it with your knuckles, didn't it?" prompted Zerkow, eagerly, his lips trembling, his fingers hooking themselves into claws.

"Sweeter'n any church bell," continued Maria.

"Go on, go on, go on," cried Zerkow, drawing his chair closer, and shutting his eyes in ecstasy.

"There were more than a hundred pieces, and every one of them gold——"

"Ah, every one of them gold."

"You should have seen the sight when the leather trunk was opened. There wa'n't a piece that was so much as scratched; every one was like a mirror, smooth and bright, polished so that it looked black——you know how I mean."

"Oh, I know, I know," cried Zerkow, moistening his lips.

Then he plied her with questions——questions that covered every detail of that service of plate. It was soft, wasn't it? You could bite into a plate and leave a dent? The handles of the knives, now, were they gold too? All the knife was made from one piece of gold, was it? And the forks the same? The interior of the trunk was quilted, of course? Did Maria ever polish the plates herself? When the company ate off this service, it must have made a fine noise— these gold knives and forks clinking together upon these gold plates.

"Now, let's have it all over again, Maria," pleaded Zerkow. "Begin now with 'There were more than a hundred pieces, and every one of them gold.' Go on, begin, begin, begin!"

The red-headed Pole was in a fever of excitement. Maria's recital had become a veritable mania with him. As he listened, with closed eyes and trembling lips, he fancied he could see that wonderful plate before him, there on the table, under his eyes, under his hand, ponderous, massive, gleaming. He tormented Maria into a second repetition of the story—into a third. The more his mind dwelt upon it, the sharper grew his desire. Then, with Maria's refusal to continue the tale, came the reaction. Zerkow awoke as from some ravishing dream. The plate was gone, was irretrievably lost. There was nothing in that miserable room but grimy rags and rust-corroded iron. What a torment! what agony! to be so near—so near, to see it in one's distorted fancy as plain as in a mirror. To know every individual piece as an old friend; to feel its weight; to be dazzled by its glitter; to call it one's own, own; to have it to oneself, hugged to the breast; and then to start, to wake, to come down to the horrible reality.

"And you, *you* had it once," gasped Zerkow, clawing at her arm; "you had it once, all your own. Think of it, and now it's gone."

"Gone for good and all."

"Perhaps it's buried near your old place somewhere."

"It's gone—gone—gone," chanted Maria in a monotone.

Zerkow dug his nails into his scalp, tearing at his red hair.

"Yes, yes, it's gone, it's gone—lost forever! Lost forever!"

Marcus and the dentist walked up the silent street and reached the little dog hospital. They had hardly spoken on the way. McTeague's brain was in a whirl; speech failed him. He was busy thinking of the great thing that had happened that night, and was trying to realize what its effect would be upon his life—his life and

Trina's. As soon as they had found themselves in the street, Marcus had relapsed at once to a sullen silence, which McTeague was too abstracted to notice.

They entered the tiny office of the hospital with its red carpet, its gas stove, and its colored prints of famous dogs hanging against the walls. In one corner stood the iron bed which they were to occupy.

"You go on an' get to bed, Mac," observed Marcus. "I'll take a look at the dogs before I turn in."

He went outside and passed along into the yard, that was bounded on three sides by pens where the dogs were kept. A bull terrier dying of gastritis recognized him and began to whimper feebly.

Marcus paid no attention to the dogs. For the first time that evening he was alone and could give vent to his thoughts. He took a couple of turns up and down the yard, then suddenly in a low voice exclaimed:

"You fool, you fool, Marcus Schouler! If you'd kept Trina you'd have had that money. You might have had it yourself. You've thrown away your chance in life—to give up the girl, yes—but *this*," he stamped his foot with rage—"to throw five thousand dollars out of the window—to stuff it into the pockets of someone else, when it might have been yours, when you might have had Trina *and* the money—and all for what? Because we were pals. Oh, 'pals' is all right—but five thousand dollars—to have played it right into his hands—God *damn* the luck!"

VIII

The next two months were delightful. Trina and McTeague saw each other regularly, three times a week. The dentist went over to B Street Sunday and Wednesday afternoons as usual; but on Fridays it was Trina who came to the city. She spent the morning between nine and twelve o'clock down town, for the most part in the cheap department stores, doing the weekly shopping for herself and the family. At noon she took an uptown car and met McTeague at the corner of Polk Street. The two lunched together at a small uptown hotel just around the corner on Sutter Street. They were given a little room to themselves. Nothing could have been more delicious. They had but to close the sliding door to shut themselves off from the whole world.

Trina would arrive breathless from her raids upon the bargain counters, her pale cheeks flushed, her hair blown about her face and into the corners of her lips, her mother's net reticule stuffed to bursting. Once in their tiny private room, she would drop into her chair with a little groan.

"Oh, *Mac*, I am so tired; I've just been all *over* town. Oh, it's good to sit down. Just think, I had to stand up in the car all the way, after being on my feet the whole blessed morning. Look here what I've bought. Just things and things. Look, there's some dotted veiling I got for myself; see now, do you think it looks pretty?"— she spread it over her face—"and I got a box of writing paper, and a roll of crépe paper to make a lamp shade for the front parlor; and —what do you suppose—I saw a pair of Nottingham lace curtains for *forty-nine cents*; isn't that cheap?[1] and some chenille portieres for two and a half. Now what have *you* been doing since I last saw you? Did Mr. Heise finally get up enough courage to have his tooth pulled yet?" Trina took off her hat and veil and rearranged her hair before the looking-glass.

"No, no—not yet. I went down to the sign painter's yesterday afternoon to see about that big gold tooth for a sign. It costs too much; I can't get it yet a while. There's two kinds, one German gilt and the other French gilt; but the German gilt is no good."[2]

McTeague sighed, and wagged his head. Even Trina and the five thousand dollars could not make him forget this one unsatisfied longing.

At other times they would talk at length over their plans, while Trina sipped her chocolate and McTeague devoured huge chunks of butterless bread. They were to be married at the end of May, and the dentist already had his eye on a couple of rooms, part of the suite of a bankrupt photographer. They were situated in the flat, just back of his "Parlors," and he believed the photographer would sublet them furnished.

McTeague and Trina had no apprehensions as to their finances. They could be sure, in fact, of a tidy little income. The dentist's practice was fairly good, and they could count upon the interest of Trina's five thousand dollars. To McTeague's mind this interest seemed wofully small. He had had uncertain ideas about that five thousand dollars; had imagined that they would spend it in some lavish fashion; would buy a house, perhaps, or would furnish their new rooms with overwhelming luxury—luxury that implied red velvet carpets and continued feasting. The old-time miner's idea of wealth easily gained and quickly spent persisted in his mind. But when Trina had begun to talk of investments and interests and per cents, he was troubled and not a little disappointed. The lump sum of five thousand dollars was one thing, a miserable little twenty or twenty-five a month was quite another; and then someone else had the money.

"But don't you see, Mac," explained Trina, "it's ours just the

---

1. Nottingham lace is machine-made and is thus much cheaper than handmade lace.

2. "French" gilt is prepared from gold leaf; "German" gilt (see p. 85) is merely gold paint.

same. We could get it back whenever we wanted it; and then it's the reasonable way to do. We mustn't let it turn our heads, Mac, dear, like that man that spent all he won in buying more tickets. How foolish we'd feel after we'd spent it all! We ought to go on just the same as before; as if we hadn't won. We must be sensible about it, mustn't we?"

"Well, well, I guess perhaps that's right," the dentist would answer, looking slowly about on the floor.

Just what should ultimately be done with the money was the subject of endless discussion in the Sieppe family. The savings bank would allow only three per cent., but Trina's parents believed that something better could be got.

"There's Uncle Oelbermann," Trina had suggested, remembering the rich relative who had the wholesale toy store in the Mission.

Mr. Sieppe struck his hand to his forehead. "Ah, an idea," he cried. In the end an agreement was made. The money was invested in Mr. Oelbermann's business. He gave Trina six per cent.

Invested in this fashion, Trina's winning would bring in twenty-five dollars a month. But, besides this, Trina had her own little trade. She made Noah's ark animals for Uncle Oelbermann's store. Trina's ancestors on both sides were German-Swiss, and some long-forgotten forefather of the sixteenth century, some worsted-leggined wood-carver of the Tyrol, had handed down the talent of the national industry, to reappear in this strangely distorted guise.

She made Noah's ark animals, whittling them out of a block of soft wood with a sharp jack-knife, the only instrument she used. Trina was very proud to explain her work to McTeague as he had already explained his own to her.

"You see, I take a block of straight-grained pine and cut out the shape, roughly at first, with the big blade; then I go over it a second time with the little blade, more carefully; then I put in the ears and tail with a drop of glue, and paint it with a 'non-poisonous' paint —Vandyke brown for the horses, foxes, and cows; slate gray for the elephants and camels; burnt umber for the chickens, zebras, and so on; then, last, a dot of Chinese white for the eyes, and there you are, all finished. They sell for nine cents a dozen. Only I can't make the manikins."

"The manikins?"

"The little figures, you know—Noah and his wife, and Shem, and all the others."

It was true. Trina could not whittle them fast enough and cheap enough to compete with the turning lathe, that could throw off whole tribes and peoples of manikins while she was fashioning one family. Everything else, however, she made—the ark itself, all windows and no door; the box in which the whole was packed; even down to pasting on the label, which read, "Made in France." She earned from three to four dollars a week.

The income from these three sources, McTeague's profession, the interest of the five thousand dollars, and Trina's whittling, made a respectable little sum taken altogether. Trina declared they could even lay by something, adding to the five thousand dollars little by little.

It soon became apparent that Trina would be an extraordinarily good housekeeper. Economy was her strong point. A good deal of peasant blood still ran undiluted in her veins, and she had all the instinct of a hardy and penurious mountain race—the instinct which saves without any thought, without idea of consequence— saving for the sake of saving, hoarding without knowing why. Even McTeague did not know how closely Trina held to her new-found wealth.

But they did not always pass their luncheon hour in this discussion of incomes and economies. As the dentist came to know his little woman better she grew to be more and more of a puzzle and a joy to him. She would suddenly interrupt a grave discourse upon the rents of rooms and the cost of light and fuel with a brusque outburst of affection that set him all a-tremble with delight. All at once she would set down her chocolate, and, leaning across the narrow table, would exclaim:

"Never mind all that! Oh, Mac, do you truly, really love me— love me *big*?"

McTeague would stammer something, gasping, and wagging his head, beside himself for the lack of words.

"Old bear," Trina would answer, grasping him by both huge ears and swaying his head from side to side. "Kiss me, then. Tell me, Mac, did you think any less of me that first time I let you kiss me there in the station? Oh, Mac, dear, what a funny nose you've got, all full of hairs inside; and, Mac, do you know you've got a bald spot—" she dragged his head down towards her—"right on the top of your head." Then she would seriously kiss the bald spot in question, declaring:

"That'll make the hair grow."

Trina took an infinite enjoyment in playing with McTeague's great square-cut head, rumpling his hair till it stood on end, putting her fingers in his eyes, or stretching his ears out straight, and watching the effect with her head on one side. It was like a little child playing with some gigantic, good-natured Saint Bernard.

One particular amusement they never wearied of. The two would lean across the table toward each other, McTeague folding his arms under his breast. Then Trina, resting on her elbows, would part his mustache—the great blond mustache of a viking—with her two hands, pushing it up from his lips, causing his face to assume the appearance of a Greek mask. She would curl it around either fore-finger, drawing it to a fine end. Then all at once McTeague would make a fearful snorting noise through his nose. Invariably—though she was expecting this, though it was part of the game—Trina would jump with a stifled shriek. McTeague would bellow with laughter till his eyes watered. Then they would recommence upon the instant, Trina protesting with a nervous tremulousness:

"Now—now—now, Mac, *don't*; you *scare* me so."

But these delicious *tête-à-têtes* with Trina were offset by a certain coolness that Marcus Schouler began to affect towards the dentist. At first McTeague was unaware of it; but by this time even his slow wits began to perceive that his best friend—his "pal"—was not the same to him as formerly. They continued to meet at lunch nearly every day but Friday at the car conductors' coffee-joint. But Marcus was sulky; there could be no doubt about that. He avoided talking to McTeague, read the paper continually, answering the dentist's timid efforts at conversation in gruff monosyllables. Sometimes, even, he turned sideways to the table and talked at great length to Heise the harness-maker, whose table was next to theirs. They took no more long walks together when Marcus went out to exercise the dogs. Nor did Marcus ever again recur to his generosity in renounc-ing Trina.

One Tuesday, as McTeague took his place at the table in the coffee-joint, he found Marcus already there.

"Hello, Mark," said the dentist, "you here already?"

"Hello," returned the other, indifferently, helping himself to tomato catsup. There was a silence. After a long while Marcus sud-denly looked up.

"Say, Mac," he exclaimed, "when you going to pay me that money you owe me?"

McTeague was astonished.

"Huh? What? I don't—do I owe you any money, Mark?"

"Well, you owe me four bits," returned Marcus, doggedly. "I paid for you and Trina that day at the picnic, and you never gave it back."

"Oh—oh!" answered McTeague, in distress. "That's so, that's so. I—you ought to have told me before. Here's your money, and I'm obliged to you."

"It ain't much," observed Marcus, sullenly. "But I need all I can get now-a-days."

"Are you—are you broke?" inquired McTeague.

"And I ain't saying anything about your sleeping at the hospital that night, either," muttered Marcus, as he pocketed the coin.

"Well—well—do you mean—should I have paid for that?"

"Well, you'd 'a' had to sleep *somewheres*, wouldn't you?" flashed out Marcus. "You'd 'a' had to pay half a dollar for a bed at the flat." "All right, all right," cried the dentist, hastily, feeling in his pockets. "I don't want you should be out anything on my account, old man. Here, will four bits du?"

"I don't *want* your damn money," shouted Marcus in a sudden rage, throwing back the coin. "I ain't no beggar."

McTeague was miserable. How had he offended his pal?

"Well, I want you should take it, Mark," he said, pushing it towards him.

"I tell you I won't touch your money," exclaimed the other through his clenched teeth, white with passion. "I've been played for a sucker long enough."

"What's the matter with you lately, Mark?" remonstrated McTeague. "You've got a grouch about something. Is there anything I've done?"

"Well, that's all right, that's all right," returned Marcus as he rose from the table. "That's all right. I've been played for a sucker long enough, that's all. I've been played for a sucker long enough." He went away with a parting malevolent glance.

At the corner of Polk Street, between the flat and the car conductors' coffee-joint, was Frenna's. It was a corner grocery; advertisements for cheap butter and eggs, painted in green marking-ink upon wrapping paper, stood about on the sidewalk outside. The doorway was decorated with a huge Milwaukee beer sign. Back of the store proper was a bar where white sand covered the floor. A few tables and chairs were scattered here and there. The walls were hung with gorgeously-colored tobacco advertisements and colored lithographs of trotting horses. On the wall behind the bar was a model of a full-rigged ship enclosed in a bottle.

It was at this place that the dentist used to leave his pitcher to be filled on Sunday afternoons. Since his engagement to Trina he had discontinued this habit. However, he still dropped into Frenna's one or two nights in the week. He spent a pleasant hour there, smoking his huge porcelain pipe and drinking his beer. He never joined any of the groups of piquet[3] players around the tables. In fact, he hardly spoke to anyone but the bartender and Marcus.

For Frenna's was one of Marcus Schouler's haunts; a great deal of his time was spent there. He involved himself in fearful political and social discussions with Heise the harness-maker, and with one or two old Germans, *habitués* of the place. These discussions Marcus carried on, as was his custom, at the top of his voice, gesticulating fiercely, banging the table with his fists, brandishing the plates and glasses, exciting himself with his own clamor.

3. A card game played by two to four players.

On a certain Saturday evening, a few days after the scene at the coffee-joint, the dentist bethought him to spend a quiet evening at Frenna's. He had not been there for some time, and, besides that, it occurred to him that the day was his birthday. He would permit himself an extra pipe and a few glasses of beer. When McTeague entered Frenna's back room by the street door, he found Marcus and Heise already installed at one of the tables. Two or three of the old Germans sat opposite them, gulping their beer from time to time. Heise was smoking a cigar, but Marcus had before him his fourth whiskey cocktail. At the moment of McTeague's entrance Marcus had the floor.

"It can't be proven," he was yelling. "I defy any sane politician whose eyes are not blinded by party prejudices, whose opinions are not warped by a personal bias, to substantiate such a statement. Look at your facts, look at your figures. I am a free American citizen, ain't I? I pay my taxes to support a good government, don't I? It's a contract between me and the government, ain't it? Well, then, by damn! if the authorities do not or *will* not afford me protection for life, liberty, and the pursuit of happiness, then my obligations are at an end; I withhold my taxes. I do—I do—I say I do. What?" He glared about him, seeking opposition.

"That's nonsense," observed Heise, quietly. "Try it once; you'll get jugged." But this observation of the harness-maker's roused Marcus to the last pitch of frenzy.

"Yes, ah, yes!" he shouted, rising to his feet, shaking his finger in the other's face. "Yes, I'd go to jail; but because I—I am crushed by a tyranny, does that make the tyranny right? Does might make right?"

"You must make less noise in here, Mister Schouler," said Frenna, from behind the bar.

"Well, it makes me mad," answered Marcus, subsiding into a growl and resuming his chair. "Hullo, Mac."

"Hullo, Mark."

But McTeague's presence made Marcus uneasy, rousing in him at once a sense of wrong. He twisted to and fro in his chair, shrugging first one shoulder and then another. Quarrelsome at all times, the heat of the previous discussion had awakened within him all his natural combativeness. Besides this, he was drinking his fourth cocktail.

McTeague began filling his big porcelain pipe. He lit it, blew a great cloud of smoke into the room, and settled himself comfortably in his chair. The smoke of his cheap tobacco drifted into the faces of the group at the adjoining table, and Marcus strangled and coughed. Instantly his eyes flamed.

"Say, for God's sake," he vociferated, "choke off on that pipe! If you've got to smoke rope like that, smoke it in a crowd of muckers; don't come here amongst gentlemen."

"Shut up, Schouler!" observed Heise in a low voice.

McTeague was stunned by the suddenness of the attack. He took his pipe from his mouth, and stared blankly at Marcus; his lips moved, but he said no word. Marcus turned his back on him, and the dentist resumed his pipe.

But Marcus was far from being appeased. McTeague could not hear the talk that followed between him and the harness-maker, but it seemed to him that Marcus was telling Heise of some injury, some grievance, and that the latter was trying to pacify him. All at once their talk grew louder. Heise laid a retaining hand upon his companion's coat sleeve, but Marcus swung himself around in his chair, and, fixing his eyes on McTeague, cried as if in answer to some protestation on the part of Heise:

"All I know is that I've been soldiered out of five thousand dollars."

McTeague gaped at him, bewildered. He removed his pipe from his mouth a second time, and stared at Marcus with eyes full of trouble and perplexity.

"If I had my rights," cried Marcus, bitterly, "I'd have part of that money. It's my due—it's only justice." The dentist still kept silence.

"If it hadn't been for me," Marcus continued, addressing himself directly to McTeague, "you wouldn't have had a cent of it—no, not a cent. Where's my share, I'd like to know? Where do I come in? No, I ain't in it any more. I've been played for a sucker, an' now that you've got all you can out of me, now that you've done me out of my girl and out of my money, you give me the go-by. Why, where would you have been *to-day* if it hadn't been for me?" Marcus shouted in a sudden exasperation, "You'd a been plugging teeth at two bits an hour. Ain't you got any gratitude? Ain't you got any sense of decency?"

"Ah, hold up, Schouler," grumbled Heise. "You don't want to get into a row."

"No, I don't, Heise," returned Marcus, with a plaintive, aggrieved air. "But it's too much sometimes when you think of it. He stole away my girl's affections, and now that he's rich and prosperous, and has got five thousand dollars that I might have had, he gives me the go-by; he's played me for a sucker. Look here," he cried, turning again to McTeague, "do I get any of that money?"

"It ain't mine to give," answered McTeague. "You're drunk, that's what you are."

"Do I get any of that money?" cried Marcus, persistently.

The dentist shook his head. "No, you don't get any of it."

"Now—*now*," clamored the other, turning to the harness-maker, as though this explained everything. "Look at that, look at that. Well, I've done with you from now on." Marcus had risen to his feet by this time and made as if to leave, but at every instant he came back, shouting his phrases into McTeague's face, moving off again as he spoke the last words, in order to give them better effect. "This settles it right here. I've done with you. Don't you ever dare speak to me again"—his voice was shaking with fury—"and don't you sit at my table in the restaurant again. I'm sorry I ever lowered myself to keep company with such dirt. Ah, one-horse dentist! Ah, ten-cent zinc-plugger—hoodlum—*mucker*! Get your damn smoke outa my face."

Then matters reached a sudden climax. In his agitation the dentist had been pulling hard on his pipe, and as Marcus for the last time thrust his face close to his own, McTeague, in opening his lips to reply, blew a stifling, acrid cloud directly in Marcus Schouler's eyes. Marcus knocked the pipe from his fingers with a sudden flash of his hand; it spun across the room and broke into a dozen fragments in a far corner.

McTeague rose to his feet, his eyes wide. But as yet he was not angry, only surprised, taken all aback by the suddenness of Marcus Schouler's outbreak as well as by its unreasonableness. Why had Marcus broken his pipe? What did it all mean, anyway? As he rose the dentist made a vague motion with his right hand. Did Marcus misinterpret it as a gesture of menace? He sprang back as though avoiding a blow. All at once there was a cry. Marcus had made a quick, peculiar motion, swinging his arm upward with a wide and sweeping gesture; his jack-knife lay open in his palm; it shot forward as he flung it, glinted sharply by McTeague's head, and struck quivering into the wall behind.

A sudden chill ran through the room; the others stood transfixed, as at the swift passage of some cold and deadly wind. Death had stooped there for an instant, had stooped and passed, leaving a trail of terror and confusion. Then the door leading to the street slammed; Marcus had disappeared.

Thereon a great babel of exclamation arose. The tension of that all but fatal instant snapped, and speech became once more possible.

"He would have knifed you."

"Narrow escape."

"What kind of a man do you call *that*?"

" 'Tain't his fault he ain't a murderer."

"I'd have him up for it."

"And they two have been the greatest kind of friends."

"He didn't touch you, did he?"

"No—no—no."

"What a—what a devil! What treachery! A regular greaser trick!"

"Look out he don't stab you in the back. If that's the kind of man he is, you never can tell."

Frenna drew the knife from the wall.

"Guess I'll keep this toad-stabber," he observed. "That fellow won't come round for it in a hurry; good-sized blade, too." The group examined it with intense interest.

"Big enough to let the life out of any man," observed Heise.

"What—what—what did he do it for?" stammered McTeague. "I got no quarrel with him."

He was puzzled and harassed by the strangeness of it all. Marcus would have killed him; had thrown his knife at him in the true, uncanny "greaser" style. It was inexplicable. McTeague sat down again, looking stupidly about on the floor. In a corner of the room his eye encountered his broken pipe, a dozen little fragments of painted porcelain and the stem of cherry wood and amber.

At that sight his tardy wrath, ever lagging behind the original affront, suddenly blazed up. Instantly his huge jaws clicked together.

"He can't make small of *me*," he exclaimed, suddenly. "I'll show Marcus Schouler—I'll show him—I'll——"

He got up and clapped on his hat.

"Now, Doctor," remonstrated Heise, standing between him and the door, "don't go make a fool of yourself."

"Let 'um alone," joined in Frenna, catching the dentist by the arm; "he's full, anyhow."

"He broke my pipe," answered McTeague.

It was this that had roused him. The thrown knife, the attempt on his life, was beyond his solution; but the breaking of his pipe he understood clearly enough.

"I'll show him," he exclaimed.

As though they had been little children, McTeague set Frenna and the harness-maker aside, and strode out at the door like a raging elephant. Heise stood rubbing his shoulder.

"Might as well try to stop a locomotive," he muttered. "The man's made of iron."

Meanwhile, McTeague went storming up the street toward the flat, wagging his head and grumbling to himself. Ah, Marcus would break his pipe, would he? Ah, he was a zinc-plugger, was he? He'd show Marcus Schouler. No one should make small of him. He tramped up the stairs to Marcus's room. The door was locked. The dentist put one enormous hand on the knob and pushed the door in, snapping the wood-work, tearing off the lock. Nobody—the room was dark and empty. Never mind, Marcus would have to come home some time that night. McTeague would go down and wait for him in his "Parlors." He was bound to hear him as he came up the stairs.

As McTeague reached his room he stumbled over, in the darkness, a big packing-box that stood in the hallway just outside his door. Puzzled, he stepped over it, and lighting the gas in his room, dragged it inside and examined it.

It was addressed to him. What could it mean? He was expecting nothing. Never since he had first furnished his room had packing-cases been left for him in this fashion. No mistake was possible. There were his name and address unmistakably. "Dr. McTeague, dentist,—Polk Street, San Francisco, Cal.," and the red Wells-Fargo tag.

Seized with the joyful curiosity of an overgrown boy, he pried off the boards with the corner of his fire-shovel. The case was stuffed full of excelsior. On the top lay an envelope addressed to him in Trina's handwriting. He opened it and read, "For my dear Mac's birthday, from Trina;" and below, in a kind of postscript, "The man will be round tomorrow to put it in place." McTeague tore away the excelsior. Suddenly he utter an exclamation.

It was the Tooth—the famous golden molar with its huge prongs —his sign, his ambition, the one unrealized dream of his life; and it was French gilt, too, not the cheap German gilt that was no good. Ah, what a dear little woman was this Trina, to keep so quiet, to remember his birthday!

"Ain't she—ain't she just a—just a *jewel*," exclaimed McTeague under his breath, "a *jewel*—yes, just a *jewel*; that's the word."

Very carefully he removed the rest of the excelsior, and lifting the ponderous Tooth from its box, set it upon the marble-top centre table. How immense it looked in that little room! The thing was tremendous, overpowering—the tooth of a gigantic fossil, golden and dazzling. Beside it everything seemed dwarfed. Even McTeague himself, big boned and enormous as he was, shrank and dwindled in the presence of the monster. As for an instant he bore it in his hands, it was like a puny Gulliver struggling with the molar of some vast Brobdingnag.[4]

The dentist circled about that golden wonder, gasping with delight and stupefaction, touching it gingerly with his hands as if it were something sacred. At every moment his thought returned to Trina. No, never was there such a little woman as his—the very thing he wanted—how had she remembered? And the money, where had that come from? No one knew better than he how expensive were these signs; not another dentist on Polk Street could

4. A giant-size citizen of Brobdingnag in Book II of Swift's *Gulliver's Travels.*

afford one. Where, then, had Trina found the money? It came out of her five thousand dollars, no doubt.

But what a wonderful, beautiful tooth it was, to be sure, bright as a mirror, shining there in its coat of French gilt, as if with a light of its own! No danger of that tooth turning black with the weather, as did the cheap German gilt impostures. What would that other dentist, that poser, that rider of bicycles, that courser of greyhounds, say when he should see this marvellous molar run out from McTeague's bay window like a flag of defiance? No doubt he would suffer veritable convulsions of envy; would be positively sick with jealousy. If McTeague could only see his face at the moment!

For a whole hour the dentist sat there in his little "Parlor," gazing ecstatically at his treasure, dazzled, supremely content. The whole room took on a different aspect because of it. The stone pug dog before the little stove reflected it in his protruding eyes; the canary woke and chittered feebly at this new gilt, so much brighter than the bars of its little prison. Lorenzo de' Medici, in the steel engraving, sitting in the heart of his court, seemed to ogle the thing out of the corner of one eye, while the brilliant colors of the unused rifle manufacturer's calendar seemed to fade and pale in the brilliance of this greater glory.

At length, long after midnight, the dentist started to go to bed, undressing himself with his eyes still fixed on the great tooth. All at once he heard Marcus Schouler's foot on the stairs; he started up with his fists clenched, but immediately dropped back upon the bed-lounge with a gesture of indifference.

He was in no truculent state of mind now. He could not reinstate himself in that mood of wrath wherein he had left the corner grocery. The tooth had changed all that. What was Marcus Schouler's hatred to him, who had Trina's affection? What did he care about a broken pipe now that he had the tooth? Let him go. As Frenna said, he was not worth it. He heard Marcus come out into the hall, shouting aggrievedly to anyone within sound of his voice:

"An' now he breaks into my room—into my room, by damn! How do I know how many things he's stolen? It's come to stealing from me, now, has it?" He went into his room, banging his splintered door.

McTeague looked upward at the ceiling, in the direction of the voice, muttering:

"Ah, go to bed, you."

He went to bed himself, turning out the gas, but leaving the window-curtains up so that he could see the tooth the last thing before he went to sleep and the first thing as he arose in the morning.

But he was restless during the night. Every now and then he was awakened by noises to which he had long since become accustomed. Now it was the cackling of the geese in the deserted market across the street; now it was the stoppage of the cable, the sudden silence coming almost like a shock; and now it was the infuriated barking of the dogs in the back yard—Alec, the Irish setter, and the collie that belonged to the branch post-office raging at each other through the fence, snarling their endless hatred into each other's faces. As often as he woke, McTeague turned and looked for the tooth, with a sudden suspicion that he had only that moment dreamed the whole business. But he always found it—Trina's gift, his birthday present from his little woman—a huge, vague bulk, looming there through the half darkness in the centre of the room, shining dimly out as if with some mysterious light of its own.

IX

Trina and McTeague were married on the first day of June, in the photographer's rooms that the dentist had rented. All through May the Sieppe household had been turned upside down. The little box of a house vibrated with excitement and confusion, for not only were the preparations for Trina's marriage to be made, but also the preliminaries were to be arranged for the hegira of the entire Sieppe family.

They were to move to the southern part of the State the day after Trina's marriage, Mr. Sieppe having bought a third interest in an upholstering business in the suburbs of Los Angeles. It was possible that Marcus Schouler would go with them.

Not Stanley penetrating for the first time into the Dark Continent, not Napoleon leading his army across the Alps, was more weighted with responsibility, more burdened with care, more overcome with the sense of the importance of his undertaking, than was Mr. Sieppe during this period of preparation. From dawn to dark, from dark to early dawn, he toiled and planned and fretted, organizing and reorganizing, projecting and devising. The trunks were lettered, A, B, and C, the packages and smaller bundles numbered. Each member of the family had his especial duty to perform, his particular bundles to oversee. Not a detail was forgotten—fares, prices, and tips were calculated to two places of decimals. Even the amount of food that it would be necessary to carry for the black greyhound was determined. Mrs. Sieppe was to look after the lunch, "der gomisariat." Mr. Sieppe would assume charge of the checks, the money, the tickets, and, of course, general supervision. The twins would be under the command of Owgooste, who, in turn, would report for orders to his father.

Day in and day out these minutiæ were rehearsed. The children were drilled in their parts with a military exactitude; obedience and punctuality became cardinal virtues. The vast importance of the undertaking was insisted upon with scrupulous iteration. It was a manœuvre, an army changing its base of operations, a veritable tribal migration.

On the other hand, Trina's little room was the centre around which revolved another and different order of things. The dressmaker came and went, congratulatory visitors invaded the little front parlor, the chatter of unfamiliar voices resounded from the front steps; bonnet-boxes and yards of dress-goods littered the beds and chairs; wrapping paper, tissue paper, and bits of string strewed the floor; a pair of white satin slippers stood on a corner of the toilet table; lengths of white veiling, like a snow-flurry, buried the little work-table; and a mislaid box of artificial orange blossoms was finally discovered behind a bureau.

The two systems of operation often clashed and tangled. Mrs. Sieppe was found by her harassed husband helping Trina with the waist of her gown when she should have been slicing cold chicken in the kitchen. Mr. Sieppe packed his frock coat, which he would have to wear at the wedding, at the very bottom of "Truck C." The minister, who called to offer his congratulations and to make arrangements, was mistaken for the expressman.

McTeague came and went furtively, dizzied and made uneasy by all this bustle. He got in the way; he trod upon and tore breadths of silk; he tried to help carry the packing-boxes, and broke the hall gas fixture; he came in upon Trina and the dressmaker at an ill timed moment, and retiring precipitately, overturned the piles of pictures stacked in the hall.

There was an incessant going and coming at every moment of the day, a great calling up and down stairs, a shouting from room to room, an opening and shutting of doors, and an intermittent sound of hammering from the laundry, where Mr. Sieppe in his shirt sleeves labored among the packing-boxes. The twins clattered about on the carpetless floors of the denuded rooms. Owgooste was smacked from hour to hour, and wept upon the front stairs; the dressmaker called over the banisters for a hot flatiron; expressmen tramped up and down the stairway. Mrs. Sieppe stopped in the preparation of the lunches to call "Hoop, Hoop" to the greyhound, throwing lumps of coal. The dog-wheel creaked, the front door bell rang, delivery wagons rumbled away, windows rattled—the little house was in a positive uproar.

Almost every day of the week now Trina was obliged to run over to town and meet McTeague. No more philandering over their lunch now-a-days. It was business now. They haunted the house-furnishing floors of the great department houses, inspecting and pricing ranges, hardware, china, and the like. They rented the photographer's rooms furnished, and fortunately only the kitchen and dining-room utensils had to be bought.

The money for this as well as for her trousseau came out of Trina's five thousand dollars. For it had been finally decided that two hundred dollars of this amount should be devoted to the establishment of the new household. Now that Trina had made her great winning, Mr. Sieppe no longer saw the necessity of dowering her further, especially when he considered the enormous expense to which he would be put by the voyage of his own family.

It had been a dreadful wrench for Trina to break in upon her precious five thousand. She clung to this sum with a tenacity that was surprising; it had become for her a thing miraculous, a god-from-the machine, suddenly descending upon the stage of her humble little life;[1] she regarded it as something almost sacred and inviolable. Never, never should a penny of it be spent. Before she could be induced to part with two hundred dollars of it, more than one scene had been enacted between her and her parents.

Did Trina pay for the golden tooth out of this two hundred? Later on, the dentist often asked her about it, but Trina invariably laughed in his face, declaring that it was her secret. McTeague never found out.

One day during this period McTeague told Trina about his affair with Marcus. Instantly she was aroused.

"He threw his knife at you! The coward! He wouldn't of dared stand up to you like a man. Oh, Mac, suppose he *had* hit you?"

"Came within an inch of my head," put in McTeague, proudly.

"Think of it!" she gasped; "and he wanted part of my money. Well, I do like his cheek; part of my five thousand! Why, it's *mine*, every single penny of it. Marcus hasn't the least bit of right to it. It's mine, mine—I mean, it's ours, Mac, dear."

The elder Sieppes, however, made excuses for Marcus. He had probably been drinking a good deal and didn't know what he was about. He had a dreadful temper, anyhow. Maybe he only wanted to scare McTeague.

The week before the marriage the two men were reconciled. Mrs. Sieppe brought them together in the front parlor of the B Street house.

"Now, you two fellers, don't be dot foolish. Schake hands und maig ut oop, soh."

Marcus muttered an apology. McTeague, miserably embarrassed, rolled his eyes about the room, murmuring, "That's all right—that's all right—that's all right."

1. An allusion to the convention of classic drama in which a god is introduced (brought on stage by a "ma-chine") to solve a seemingly insoluble dilemma.

However, when it was proposed that Marcus should be McTeague's best man, he flashed out again with renewed violence. Ah, no! ah, *no*! He'd make up with the dentist now that he was going away, but he'd be damned—yes, he would—before he'd be his best man. That *was* rubbing it in. Let him get Old Grannis. "I'm friends with um all right," vociferated Marcus, "but I'll not stand up with um. I'll not be *anybody's* best man, I won't."

The wedding was to be very quiet; Trina preferred it that way. McTeague would invite only Miss Baker and Heise the harness-maker. The Sieppes sent cards to Selina, who was counted on to furnish the music; to Marcus, of course; and to Uncle Oelbermann.

At last the great day, the first of June, arrived. The Sieppes had packed their last box and had strapped the last trunk. Trina's two trunks had already been sent to her new home—the remodelled photographer's rooms. The B Street house was deserted; the whole family came over to the city on the last day of May and stopped over night at one of the cheap downtown hotels. Trina would be married the following evening, and immediately after the wedding supper the Sieppes would leave for the South.

McTeague spent the day in a fever of agitation, frightened out of his wits each time that Old Grannis left his elbow.

Old Grannis was delighted beyond measure at the prospect of acting the part of best man in the ceremony. This wedding in which he was to figure filled his mind with vague ideas and half-formed thoughts. He found himself continually wondering what Miss Baker would think of it. During all that day he was in a reflective mood.

"Marriage is a—a noble institution, is it not, Doctor?" he observed to McTeague. "The—the foundation of society. It is not good that man should be alone. No, no," he added, pensively, "it is not good."

"Huh? Yes, yes," McTeague answered, his eyes in the air, hardly hearing him. "Do you think the rooms are all right? Let's go in and look at them again."

They went down the hall to where the new rooms were situated, and the dentist inspected them for the twentieth time.

The rooms were three in number—first, the sitting-room, which was also the dining-room; then the bedroom, and back of this the tiny kitchen.

The sitting-room was particularly charming. Clean matting covered the floor, and two or three bright-colored rugs were scattered here and there. The backs of the chairs were hung with knitted worsted tidies, very gay. The bay window should have been occupied by Trina's sewing machine, but this had been moved to the other side of the room to give place to a little black walnut table with spiral legs, before which the pair were to be married. In one corner stood the parlor melodeon,[2] a family possession of the Sieppes, but given now to Trina as one of her parents' wedding presents. Three pictures hung upon the walls. Two were companion pieces. One of these represented a little boy wearing huge spectacles and trying to smoke an enormous pipe. This was called "I'm Grandpa," the title being printed in large black letters; the companion picture was entitled "I'm Grandma," a little girl in cap and "specs," wearing mitts, and knitting. These pictures were hung on either side of the mantelpiece. The other picture was quite an affair, very large and striking. It was a colored lithograph of two little golden-haired girls in their nightgowns. They were kneeling down and saying their prayers; their eyes—very large and very blue—rolled upward. This picture had for name, "Faith," and was bordered with a red plush mat and a frame of imitation beaten brass.

A door hung with chenille portières—a bargain at two dollars and a half—admitted one to the bedroom. The bedroom could boast a carpet, three-ply ingrain, the design being bunches of red and green flowers in yellow baskets on a white ground. The wall-paper was admirable—hundreds and hundreds of tiny Japanese mandarins, all identically alike, helping hundreds of almond-eyed ladies into hundreds of impossible junks, while hundreds of bamboo palms overshadowed the pair, and hundreds of long-legged storks trailed contemptuously away from the scene. This room was prolific in pictures. Most of them were framed colored prints from Christmas editions of the London "Graphic" and "Illustrated News," the subject of each picture inevitably involving very alert fox terriers and very pretty moon-faced little girls.

Back of the bedroom was the kitchen, a creation of Trina's, a dream of a kitchen, with its range, its porcelain-lined sink, its copper boiler, and its overpowering array of flashing tinware. Everything was new; everything was complete.

Maria Macapa and a waiter from one of the restaurants in the street were to prepare the wedding supper here. Maria had already put in an appearance. The fire was crackling in the new stove, that smoked badly; a smell of cooking was in the air. She drove McTeague and Old Grannis from the room with great gestures of her bare arms.

This kitchen was the only one of the three rooms they had been obliged to furnish throughout. Most of the sitting-room and bedroom furniture went with the suite; a few pieces they had bought; the remainder Trina had brought over from the B Street house.

The presents had been set out on the extension table in the sitting-room. Besides the parlor melodeon, Trina's parents had given

2. A small and inexpensive organ.

her an ice-water set, and a carving knife and fork with elk-horn handles. Selina had painted a view of the Golden Gate upon a polished
slice of redwood that answered the purposes of a paper weight.
Marcus Schouler—after impressing upon Trina that his gift was to
her, and not to McTeague—had sent a chatelaine watch of German
silver;[3] Uncle Oelbermann's present, however, had been awaited
with a good deal of curiosity. What would *he* send? He was very
rich; in a sense Trina was his *protegé*. A couple of days before that
upon which the wedding was to take place, two boxes arrived with
his card. Trina and McTeague, assisted by Old Grannis, had
opened them. The first was a box of all sorts of toys.

"But what—what—I don't make it out," McTeague had
exclaimed. "Why should he send us toys? We have no need of
toys." Scarlet to her hair, Trina dropped into a chair and laughed
till she cried behind her handkerchief.

"We've no use of toys," muttered McTeague, looking at her in
perplexity. Old Grannis smiled discreetly, raising a tremulous hand
to his chin.

The other box was heavy, bound with withes at the edges, the
letters and stamps burnt in.

"I think—I really think it's champagne," said Old Grannis in a
whisper. So it was. A full case of Monopole. What a wonder! None
of them had seen the like before. Ah, this Uncle Oelbermann!
That's what it was to be rich. Not one of the other presents produced so deep an impression as this.

After Old Grannis and the dentist had gone through the rooms,
giving a last look around to see that everything was ready, they
returned to McTeague's "Parlors." At the door Old Grannis
excused himself.

At four o'clock McTeague began to dress, shaving himself first
before the hand-glass that was hung against the woodwork of the
bay window. While he shaved he sang with strange inappropri-
ateness:

> "No one to love, none to caress,
> Left all alone in this world's wilderness."

But as he stood before the mirror, intent upon his shaving, there
came a roll of wheels over the cobbles in front of the house. He
rushed to the window. Trina had arrived with her father and
mother. He saw her get out, and as she glanced upward at his
window, their eyes met.

Ah, there she was. There she was, his little woman, looking up at
him, her adorable little chin thrust upward with that familiar move-

3. A watch worn on an ornamental   and copper.
chain and made of an alloy of nickel

ment of innocence and confidence. The dentist saw again, as if for the first time, her small, pale face looking out from beneath her royal tiara of black hair; he saw again her long, narrow blue eyes; her lips, nose, and tiny ears, pale and bloodless, and suggestive of anæmia, as if all the vitality that should have lent them color had been sucked up into the strands and coils of that wonderful hair.

As their eyes met they waved their hands gayly to each other; then McTeague heard Trina and her mother come up the stairs and go into the bedroom of the photographer's suite, where Trina was to dress.

No, no; surely there could be no longer any hesitation. He knew that he loved her. What was the matter with him, that he should have doubted it for an instant? The great difficulty was that she was too good, too adorable, too sweet, too delicate for him, who was so huge, so clumsy, so brutal.

There was a knock at the door. It was old Grannis. He was dressed in his one black suit of broadcloth, much wrinkled; his hair was carefully brushed over his bald forehead.

"Miss Trina has come," he announced, "and the minister. You have an hour yet."

The dentist finished dressing. He wore a suit bought for the occasion—a ready made "Prince Albert" coat too short in the sleeves, striped "blue" trousers, and new patent leather shoes—veritable instruments of torture. Around his collar was a wonderful necktie that Trina had given him; it was of salmon-pink satin; in its centre Selina had painted a knot of blue forget-me-nots.

At length, after an interminable period of waiting, Mr. Sieppe appeared at the door.

"Are you reatty?" he asked in a sepulchral whisper. "Gome, den." It was like King Charles summoned to execution. Mr. Sieppe preceded them into the hall, moving at a funereal pace. He paused. Suddenly, in the direction of the sitting-room, came the strains of the parlor melodeon. Mr. Sieppe flung his arm into the air.

"Vowaarts!" he cried.

He left them at the door of the sitting-room, he himself going into the bedroom where Trina was waiting, entering by the hall door. He was in a tremendous state of nervous tension, fearful lest something should go wrong. He had employed the period of waiting in going through his part for the fiftieth time, repeating what he had to say in a low voice. He had even made chalk marks on the matting in the places where he was to take positions.

The dentist and Old Grannis entered the sitting-room; the minister stood behind the little table in the bay window, holding a book, one finger marking the place; he was rigid, erect, impassive. On either side of him, in a semi-circle, stood the invited guests. A little

pock-marked gentleman in glasses, no doubt the famous Uncle Oelbermann; Miss Baker, in her black grenadine, false curls, and coral
brooch; Marcus Schouler, his arms folded, his brows bent, grand
and gloomy; Heise the harness-maker, in yellow gloves, intently
studying the pattern of the matting; and Owgooste, in his Fauntleroy "costume," stupefied and a little frightened, rolling his eyes
from face to face. Selina sat at the parlor melodeon, fingering the
keys, her glance wandering to the chenille portières. She stopped
playing as McTeague and Old Grannis entered and took their
places. A profound silence ensued. Uncle Oelbermann's shirt front
could be heard creaking as he breathed. The most solemn expression pervaded every face.

All at once the portières were shaken violently. It was a signal.
Selina pulled open the stops and swung into the wedding march.

Trina entered. She was dressed in white silk, a crown of orange
blossoms was around her swarthy hair—dressed high for the first
time—her veil reached to the floor. Her face was pink, but otherwise she was calm. She looked quietly around the room as she
crossed it, until her glance rested on McTeague, smiling at him
then very prettily and with perfect self-possession.

She was on her father's arm. The twins, dressed exactly alike,
walked in front, each carrying an enormous bouquet of cut flowers
in a "lace-paper" holder. Mrs. Sieppe followed in the rear. She was
crying; her handkerchief was rolled into a wad. From time to time
she looked at the train of Trina's dress through her tears. Mr. Sieppe
marched his daughter to the exact middle of the floor, wheeled at
right angles, and brought her up to the minister. He stepped back
three paces, and stood planted upon one of his chalk marks, his face
glistening with perspiration.

Then Trina and the dentist were married. The guests stood in
constrained attitudes, looking furtively out of the corners of their
eyes. Mr. Sieppe never moved a muscle; Mrs. Sieppe cried into her
handkerchief all the time. At the melodeon Selina played "Call Me
Thine Own," very softly, the tremulo stop pulled out. She looked
over her shoulder from time to time. Between the pauses of the
music one could hear the low tones of the minister, the responses of
the participants, and the suppressed sounds of Mrs. Sieppe's weeping. Outside the noises of the street rose to the windows in muffled
undertones, a cable car rumbled past, a newsboy went by chanting
the evening papers; from somewhere in the building itself came a
persistent noise of sawing.

Trina and McTeague knelt. The dentist's knees thudded on the
floor and he presented to view the soles of his shoes, painfully new
and unworn, the leather still yellow, the brass nail heads still glittering. Trina sank at his side very gracefully, settling her dress and

train with a little gesture of her free hand. The company bowed their heads, Mr. Sieppe shutting his eyes tight. But Mrs. Sieppe took advantage of the moment to stop crying and make furtive gestures towards Owgooste, signing him to pull down his coat. But Owgooste gave no heed; his eyes were starting from their sockets, his chin had dropped upon his lace collar, and his head turned vaguely from side to side with a continued and maniacal motion.

All at once the ceremony was over before any one expected it. The guests kept their positions for a moment, eying one another, each fearing to make the first move, not quite certain as to whether or not everything were finished. But the couple faced the room, Trina throwing back her veil. She—perhaps McTeague as well—felt that there was a certain inadequateness about the ceremony. Was that all there was to it? Did just those few muttered phrases make them man and wife? It had been over in a few moments, but it had bound them for life. Had not something been left out? Was not the whole affair cursory, superficial? It was disappointing.

But Trina had no time to dwell upon this. Marcus Schouler, in the manner of a man of the world, who knew how to act in every situation, stepped forward and, even before Mr. or Mrs. Sieppe, took Trina's hand.

"Let me be the first to congratulate Mrs. McTeague," he said, feeling very noble and heroic. The strain of the previous moments was relaxed immediately, the guests crowded around the pair, shaking hands—a babel of talk arose.

"Owgooste, *will* you pull down your goat, den?"

"Well, my dear, now you're married and happy. When I first saw you two together, I said, 'What a pair!' We're to be neighbors now; you must come up and see me very often and we'll have tea together."

"Did you hear that sawing going on all the time? I declare it regularly got on my nerves."

Trina kissed her father and mother, crying a little herself as she saw the tears in Mrs. Sieppe's eyes.

Marcus came forward a second time, and, with an air of great gravity, kissed his cousin upon the forehead. Heise was introduced to Trina and Uncle Oelbermann to the dentist.

For upwards of half an hour the guests stood about in groups, filling the little sitting-room with a great chatter of talk. Then it was time to make ready for supper.

This was a tremendous task, in which nearly all the guests were obliged to assist. The sitting-room was transformed into a dining-room. The presents were removed from the extension table and the table drawn out to its full length. The cloth was laid, the chairs—rented from the dancing academy hard by—drawn up, the dishes set out, and the two bouquets of cut flowers taken from the twins under their shrill protests, and "arranged" in vases at either end of the table.

There was a great coming and going between the kitchen and the sitting room. Trina, who was allowed to do nothing, sat in the bay window and fretted, calling to her mother from time to time: "The napkins are in the right-hand drawer of the pantry."

"Yes, yes, I got um. Where do you geep der zoup blates?"

"The soup plates are here already."

"Say, Cousin Trina, is there a corkscrew? What is home without a corkscrew?"

"In the kitchen-table drawer, in the left-hand corner."

"Are these the forks you want to use, Mrs. McTeague?"

"No, no, there's some silver forks. Mamma knows where."

They were all very gay, laughing over their mistakes, getting in one another's way, rushing into the sitting-room, their hands full of plates or knives or glasses, and darting out again after more. Marcus and Mr. Sieppe took their coats off. Old Grannis and Miss Baker passed each other in the hall in a constrained silence, her grenadine brushing against the elbow of his wrinkled frock coat. Uncle Oelbermann superintended Heise opening the case of champagne with the gravity of a magistrate. Owgooste was assigned the task of filling the new salt and pepper canisters of red and blue glass.

In a wonderfully short time everything was ready. Marcus Schouler resumed his coat, wiping his forehead, and remarking:

"I tell you, I've been doing *chores* for *my* board."

"To der table!" commanded Mr. Sieppe.

The company sat down with a great chatter, Trina at the foot, the dentist at the head, the others arranged themselves in haphazard fashion. But it happened that Marcus Schouler crowded into the seat beside Selina, towards which Old Grannis was directing himself. There was but one other chair vacant, and that at the side of Miss Baker. Old Grannis hesitated, putting his hand to his chin. However, there was no escape. In great trepidation he sat down beside the retired dressmaker. Neither of them spoke. Old Grannis dared not move, but sat rigid, his eyes riveted on his empty soup plate.

All at once there was a report like a pistol. The men started in their places. Mrs. Sieppe uttered a muffled shriek. The waiter from the cheap restaurant, hired as Maria's assistant, rose from a bending posture, a champagne bottle frothing in his hand; he was grinning from ear to ear.

"Don't get scairt," he said, reassuringly, "it ain't loaded."

When all their glasses had been filled, Marcus proposed the health of the bride, "standing up." The guests rose and drank.

Hardly one of them had ever tasted champagne before. The moment's silence after the toast was broken by McTeague exclaiming with a long breath of satisfaction: "That's the best beer I ever drank."

There was a roar of laughter. Especially was Marcus tickled over the dentist's blunder; he went off in a very spasm of mirth, banging the table with his fist, laughing until his eyes watered. All through the meal he kept breaking out into cackling imitations of McTeague's words: "That's the best *beer* I ever drank. Oh, Lord, ain't that a break!"

What a wonderful supper that was! There was oyster soup; there were sea bass and barracuda; there was a gigantic roast goose stuffed with chestnuts; there were egg-plant and sweet potatoes—Miss Baker called them "yams." There was calf's head in oil, over which Mr. Sieppe went into ecstasies; there was lobster salad; there were rice pudding, and strawberry ice cream, and wine jelly, and stewed prunes, and cocoanuts, and mixed nuts, and raisins, and fruit, and tea, and coffee, and mineral waters, and lemonade.

For two hours the guests ate; their faces red, their elbows wide, the perspiration beading their foreheads. All around the table one saw the same incessant movement of jaws and heard the same uninterrupted sound of chewing. Three times Heise passed his plate for more roast goose. Mr. Sieppe devoured the calf's head with long breaths of contentment; McTeague ate for the sake of eating, without choice; everything within reach of his hands found its way into his enormous mouth.

There was but little conversation, and that only of the food; one exchanged opinions with one's neighbor as to the soup, the egg-plant, or the stewed prunes. Soon the room became very warm, a faint moisture appeared upon the windows, the air was heavy with the smell of cooked food. At every moment Trina or Mrs. Sieppe urged some one of the company to have his or her plate refilled. They were constantly employed in dishing potatoes or carving the goose or ladling gravy. The hired waiter circled around the room, his limp napkin over his arm, his hands full of plates and dishes. He was a great joker; he had names of his own for different articles of food, that sent gales of laughter around the table. When he spoke of a bunch of parsley as "scenery," Heise all but strangled himself over a mouthful of potato. Out in the kitchen Maria Macapa did the work of three, her face scarlet, her sleeves rolled up; every now and then she uttered shrill but unintelligible outcries, supposedly addressed to the waiter.

"Uncle Oelbermann," said Trina, "let me give you another helping of prunes."

The Sieppes paid great deference to Uncle Oelbermann, as

indeed did the whole company. Even Marcus Schouler lowered his voice when he addressed him. At the beginning of the meal he had nudged the harness-maker and had whispered behind his hand, nodding his head toward the wholesale toy dealer, "Got thirty thousand dollars in the bank; has, for a fact."

"Don't have much to say," observed Heise.

"No, no. That's his way; never opens his face."

As the evening wore on, the gas and two lamps were lit. The company were still eating. The men, gorged with food, had unbuttoned their vests. McTeague's cheeks were distended, his eyes wide, his huge, salient jaw moved with a machine-like regularity; at intervals he drew a series of short breaths through his nose. Mrs. Sieppe wiped her forehead with her napkin.

"Hey, dere, poy, gif me some more oaf dat—what you call— 'bubble-water.' "

That was how the waiter had spoken of the champagne— "bubble-water." The guests had shouted applause, "Outa sight." He was a heavy josher was that waiter.

Bottle after bottle was opened, the women stopping their ears as the corks were drawn. All of a sudden the dentist uttered an exclamation, clapping his hand to his nose, his face twisting sharply.

"Mac, what is it?" cried Trina in alarm.

"That champagne came to my nose," he cried, his eyes watering. "It stings like everything."

"Great *beer*, ain't ut?" shouted Marcus.

"Now, Mark," remonstrated Trina in a low voice. "Now, Mark, you just shut up; that isn't funny any more. I don't want you should make fun of Mac. He called it beer on purpose. I guess *he* knows."

Throughout the meal old Miss Baker had occupied herself largely with Owgooste and the twins, who had been given a table by themselves—the black walnut table before which the ceremony had taken place. The little dressmaker was continually turning about in her place, inquiring of the children if they wanted for anything; inquiries they rarely answered other than by stare, fixed, ox-like, expressionless.

Suddenly the little dressmaker turned to Old Grannis and exclaimed:

"I'm so very fond of little children."

"Yes, yes, they're very interesting. I'm very fond of them, too."

The next instant both of the old people were overwhelmed with confusion. What! They had spoken to each other after all these years of silence; they had for the first time addressed remarks to each other.

The old dressmaker was in a torment of embarrassment. How was it she had come to speak? She had neither planned nor wished it. Suddenly the words had escaped her, he had answered, and it was all over—over before they knew it.

Old Grannis's fingers trembled on the table ledge, his heart beat heavily, his breath fell short. He had actually talked to the little dressmaker. That possibility to which he had looked forward, it seemed to him for years—that companionship, that intimacy with his fellow-lodger, that delightful acquaintance which was only to ripen at some far distant time, he could not exactly say when— behold, it had suddenly come to a head, here in this over-crowded, over-heated room, in the midst of all this feeding, surrounded by odors of hot dishes, accompanied by the sounds of incessant mastication. How different he had imagined it would be! They were to be alone—he and Miss Baker—in the evening somewhere, withdrawn from the world, very quiet, very calm and peaceful. Their talk was to be of their lives, their lost illusions, not of other people's children.

The two old people did not speak again. They sat there side by side, nearer than they had ever been before, motionless, abstracted; their thoughts far away from that scene of feasting. They were thinking of each other and they were conscious of it. Timid, with the timidity of their second childhood, constrained and embarrassed by each other's presence, they were, nevertheless, in a little Elysium of their own creating. They walked hand in hand in a delicious garden where it was always autumn; together and alone they entered upon the long retarded romance of their commonplace and uneventful lives.

At last that great supper was over, everything had been eaten; the enormous roast goose had dwindled to a very skeleton. Mr. Sieppe had reduced the calf's head to a mere skull; a row of empty champagne bottles—"dead soldiers," as the facetious waiter had called them—lined the mantelpiece. Nothing of the stewed prunes remained but the juice, which was given to Owgooste and the twins. The platters were as clean as if they had been washed; crumbs of bread, potato parings, nutshells, and bits of cake littered the table; coffee and ice-cream stains and spots of congealed gravy marked the position of each plate. It was a devastation, a pillage; the table presented the appearance of an abandoned battlefield.

"Ouf," cried Mrs. Sieppe, pushing back, "I haf eatun und eatun, ach, Gott, how I haf eatun!"

"Ah, dot kaf's het," murmured her husband, passing his tongue over his lips.

The facetious waiter had disappeared. He and Maria Macapa foregathered in the kitchen. They drew up to the washboard of the sink, feasting off the remnants of the supper, slices of goose, the remains of the lobster salad, and half a bottle of champagne. They were obliged to drink the latter from teacups.

"Here's how," said the waiter gallantly, as he raised his teacup, bowing to Maria across the sink. "Hark," he added, "they're singing inside."

The company had left the table and had assembled about the melodeon, where Selina was seated. At first they attempted some of the popular songs of the day, but were obliged to give over as none of them knew any of the words beyond the first line of the chorus. Finally they pitched upon "Nearer, My God, to Thee," as the only song which they all knew. Selina sang the "alto," very much off the key; Marcus intoned the bass, scowling fiercely, his chin drawn into his collar. They sang in very slow time. The song became a dirge, a lamentable, prolonged wail of distress:

> "Nee-rah, my Gahd, to Thee,
> Nee-rah to Thee-ah."

At the end of the song, Uncle Oelbermann put on his hat without a word of warning. Instantly there was a hush. The guests rose.

"Not going so soon, Uncle Oelbermann?" protested Trina, politely. He only nodded. Marcus sprang forward to help him with his overcoat. Mr. Sieppe came up and the two men shook hands.

Then Uncle Oelbermann delivered himself of an oracular phrase. No doubt he had been meditating it during the supper. Addressing Mr. Sieppe, he said:

"You have not lost a daughter, but have gained a son."

These were the only words he had spoken the entire evening. He departed; the company was profoundly impressed.

About twenty minutes later, when Marcus Schouler was entertaining the guests by eating almonds, shells and all, Mr. Sieppe started to his feet, watch in hand.

"Haf-bast elevun," he shouted. "Attention! Der dime haf arrive, shtop eferyting. We depart."

This was a signal for tremendous confusion. Mr. Sieppe immediately threw off his previous air of relaxation, the calf's head was forgotten, he was once again the leader of vast enterprises.

"To me, to me," he cried. "Mommer, der tervins, Owgooste." He marshalled his tribe together, with tremendous commanding gestures. The sleeping twins were suddenly shaken into a dazed consciousness; Owgooste, whom the almond-eating of Marcus Schouler had petrified with admiration, was smacked to a realization of his surroundings.

Old Grannis, with a certain delicacy that was one of his characteristics, felt instinctively that the guests—the mere outsiders— should depart before the family began its leave-taking of Trina. He withdrew unobtrusively, after a hasty good-night to the bride and groom. The rest followed almost immediately.

"Well, Mr. Sieppe," exclaimed Marcus, "we won't see each other for some time." Marcus had given up his first intention of joining in the Sieppe migration. He spoke in a large way of certain affairs that would keep him in San Francisco till the fall. Of late he had entertained ambitions of a ranch life, he would breed cattle, he had a little money and was only looking for some one "to go in with." He dreamed of a cowboy's life and saw himself in an entrancing vision involving silver spurs and untamed bronchos. He told himself that Trina had cast him off, that his best friend had "played him for a sucker," that the "proper caper" was to withdraw from the world entirely.

"If you hear of anybody down there," he went on, speaking to Mr. Sieppe, "that wants to go in for ranching, why just let me know."

"Soh, soh," answered Mr. Sieppe abstractedly, peering about for Owgooste's cap.

Marcus bade the Sieppes farewell. He and Heise went out together. One heard them, as they descended the stairs, discussing the possibility of Frenna's place being still open.

Then Miss Baker departed after kissing Trina on both cheeks. Selina went with her. There was only the family left.

Trina watched them go, one by one, with an increasing feeling of uneasiness and vague apprehension. Soon they would all be gone.

"Well, Trina," exclaimed Mr. Sieppe, "goot-py; perhaps you gome visit us somedime."

Mrs. Sieppe began crying again.

"Ach, Trina, ven shall I efer see you again?"

Tears came to Trina's eyes in spite of herself. She put her arms around her mother.

"Oh, sometime, sometime," she cried. The twins and Owgooste clung to Trina's skirts, fretting and whimpering.

McTeague was miserable. He stood apart from the group, in a corner. None of them seemed to think of him; he was not one of them.

"Write to me very often, mamma, and tell me about everything —about August and the twins."

"It is dime," cried Mr. Sieppe, nervously. "Goot-py, Trina. Mommer, Owgooste, say goot-py, den we must go. Goot-py, Trina." He kissed her. Owgooste and the twins were lifted up. "Gome, gome," insisted Mr. Sieppe, moving toward the door.

"Goot-py, Trina," exclaimed Mrs. Sieppe, crying harder than ever. "Doktor—where is der doktor—Doktor, pe goot to her, eh? pe vairy goot, eh, won't you? Zum day, Dokter, you vill haf a daughter, den you know berhaps how I feel, yes."

They were standing at the door by this time. Mr. Sieppe, half way down the stairs, kept calling "Gome, gome, we miss der drain." Mrs. Sieppe released Trina and started down the hall, the twins and Owgooste following. Trina stood in the doorway, looking after them through her tears. They were going, going. When would she ever see them again? She was to be left alone with this man to whom she had just been married. A sudden vague terror seized her; she left McTeague and ran down the hall and caught her mother around the neck.

"I don't *want* you to go," she whispered in her mother's ear, sobbing. "Oh, mamma, I—I'm 'fraid."

"Ach, Trina, you preak my heart. Don't gry, poor leetle girl." She rocked Trina in her arms as though she were a child again. "Poor leetle scairt girl, don't gry—soh—soh—soh, dere's nuttun to pe 'fraid oaf. Dere, go to your hoasban'. Listen, popper's galling again; go den; goot-by."

She loosened Trina's arms and started down the stairs. Trina leaned over the banisters, straining her eyes after her mother.

"What is ut, Trina?"

"Oh, good-by, good-by."

"Gome, gome, we miss der drain."

"Mamma, oh, mamma!"

"What is ut, Trina?"

"Good-by."

"Goot-py, leetle daughter."

"Good-by, good-by, good-by."

The street door closed. The silence was profound.

For another moment Trina stood leaning over the banisters, looking down into the empty stairway. It was dark. There was nobody. They—her father, her mother, the children—had left her, left her alone. She faced about toward the rooms—faced her husband, faced her new home, the new life that was to begin now.

The hall was empty and deserted. The great flat around her seemed new and huge and strange; she felt horribly alone. Even Maria and the hired waiter were gone. On one of the floors above she heard a baby crying. She stood there an instant in the dark hall, in her wedding finery, looking about her, listening. From the open door of the sitting-room streamed a gold bar of light.

She went down the hall, by the open door of the sitting-room, going on toward the hall door of the bedroom.

As she softly passed the sitting-room she glanced hastily in. The lamps and the gas were burning brightly, the chairs were pushed back from the table just as the guests had left them, and the table itself, abandoned, deserted, presented to view the vague confusion of its dishes, its knives and forks, its empty platters and crumpled napkins. The dentist sat there leaning on his elbows, his back toward her; against the white blur of the table he looked colossal. Above his giant shoulders rose his thick, red neck and mane of yellow hair. The light shone pink through the gristle of his enormous ears.

Trina entered the bedroom, closing the door after her. At the sound, she heard McTeague start and rise.

"Is that you, Trina?"

She did not answer, but paused in the middle of the room, holding her breath, trembling.

The dentist crossed the outside room, parted the chenille portières, and came in. He came toward her quickly, making as if to take her in his arms. His eyes were alight.

"No, no," cried Trina, shrinking from him. Suddenly seized with the fear of him—the intuitive feminine fear of the male—her whole being quailed before him. She was terrified at his huge, square-cut head; his powerful, salient jaw; his huge, red hands; his enormous, resistless strength.

"No, no—I'm afraid," she cried, drawing back from him to the other side of the room.

"Afraid?" answered the dentist in perplexity. "What are you afraid of, Trina? I'm not going to hurt you. What are you afraid of?"

What, indeed, was Trina afraid of? She could not tell. But what did she know of McTeague, after all? Who was this man that had come into her life, who had taken her from her home and from her parents, and with whom she was now left alone here in this strange, vast flat?

"Oh, I'm afraid. I'm afraid," she cried.

McTeague came nearer, sat down beside her and put one arm around her.

"What are you afraid of, Trina?" he said, reassuringly. "I don't want to frighten you."

She looked at him wildly, her adorable little chin quivering, the tears brimming in her narrow blue eyes. Then her glance took on a certain intentness, and she peered curiously into his face, saying almost in a whisper:

"I'm afraid of *you.*"

But the dentist did not heed her. An immense joy seized upon him—the joy of possession. Trina was his very own now. She lay there in the hollow of his arm, helpless and very pretty.

Those instincts that in him were so close to the surface suddenly leaped to life, shouting and clamoring, not to be resisted. He loved her. Ah, did he not love her? The smell of her hair, of her neck, rose to him.

Suddenly he caught her in both his huge arms, crushing down

her struggle with his immense strength, kissing her full upon the mouth. Then her great love for McTeague suddenly flashed up in Trina's breast; she gave up to him as she had done before, yielding all at once to that strange desire of being conquered and subdued. She clung to him, her hands clasped behind his neck, whispering in his ear:

"Oh, you must be good to me—very, very good to me, dear—for you're all that I have in the world now."

x

That summer passed, then the winter. The wet season began in the last days of September and continued all through October, November, and December. At long intervals would come a week of perfect days, the sky without a cloud, the air motionless, but touched with a certain nimbleness, a faint effervescence that was exhilarating. Then, without warning, during a night when a south wind blew, a gray scroll of cloud would unroll and hang high over the city, and the rain would come pattering down again, at first in scattered showers, then in an uninterrupted drizzle.

All day long Trina sat in the bay window of the sitting-room that commanded a view of a small section of Polk Street. As often as she raised her head she could see the big market, a confectionery store, a bell-hanger's shop, and, farther on, above the roofs, the glass sky-lights and water tanks of the big public baths. In the nearer fore-ground ran the street itself; the cable cars trundled up and down, thumping heavily over the joints of the rails; market carts by the score came and went, driven at a great rate by preoccupied young men in their shirt sleeves, with pencils behind their ears, or by reck-less boys in blood-stained butcher's aprons. Upon the sidewalks the little world of Polk Street swarmed and jostled through its daily round of life. On fine days the great ladies from the avenue, one block above, invaded the street, appearing before the butcher stalls, intent upon their day's marketing. On rainy days their servants—the Chinese cooks or the second girls—took their places. These servants gave themselves great airs, carrying their big cotton umbrel-las as they had seen their mistresses carry their parasols, and hag-gling in supercilious fashion with the market men, their chins in the air.

The rain persisted. Everything in the range of Trina's vision, from the tarpaulins on the market-cart horses to the panes of glass in the roof of the public baths, looked glazed and varnished. The asphalt of the sidewalks shone like the surface of a patent leather boot; every hollow in the street held its little puddle, that winked like an eye each time a drop of rain struck into it.

Trina still continued to work for Uncle Oelbermann. In the mornings she busied herself about the kitchen, the bedroom, and the sitting-room; but in the afternoon, for two or three hours after lunch, she was occupied with the Noah's ark animals. She took her work to the bay window, spreading out a great square of canvas underneath her chair, to catch the chips and shavings, which she used afterwards for lighting fires. One after another she caught up the little blocks of straight-grained pine, the knife flashed between her fingers, the little figure grew rapidly under her touch, was finished and ready for painting in a wonderfully short time, and was tossed into the basket that stood at her elbow.

But very often during that rainy winter after her marriage Trina would pause in her work, her hands falling idly into her lap, her eyes—her narrow, pale blue eyes—growing wide and thoughtful as she gazed, unseeing, out into the rain-washed street.

She loved McTeague now with a blind, unreasoning love that admitted of no doubt or hesitancy. Indeed, it seemed to her that it was only *after* her marriage with the dentist that she had really begun to love him. With the absolute final surrender of herself, the irrevocable, ultimate submission, had come an affection the like of which she had never dreamed in the old B Street days. But Trina loved her husband, not because she fancied she saw in him any of those noble and generous qualities that inspire affection. The dentist might or might not possess them, it was all one with Trina. She loved him because she had given herself to him freely, unreservedly; had merged her individuality into his; she was his, she belonged to him forever and forever. Nothing that he could do (so she told herself), nothing that she herself could do, could change her in this respect. McTeague might cease to love her, might leave her, might even die; it would be all the same, *she was his.*

But it had not been so at first. During those long, rainy days of the fall, days when Trina was left alone for hours, at that time when the excitement and novelty of the honeymoon were dying down, when the new household was settling into its grooves, she passed through many an hour of misgiving, of doubt, and even of actual regret.

Never would she forget one Sunday afternoon in particular. She had been married but three weeks. After dinner she and little Miss Baker had gone for a bit of a walk to take advantage of an hour's sunshine and to look at some wonderful geraniums in a florist's window on Sutter Street. They had been caught in a shower, and on returning to the flat the little dressmaker had insisted on fetching Trina up to her tiny room and brewing her a cup of strong tea, "to take the chill off." The two women had chatted over their tea-cups the better part of the afternoon, then Trina had returned to her rooms. For nearly three hours McTeague had been out of her thoughts, and as she came through their little suite, singing softly to herself, she suddenly came upon him quite unexpectedly. Her husband was in the "Dental Parlors," lying back in his operating chair, fast asleep. The little stove was crammed with coke, the room was overheated, the air thick and foul with the odors of ether, of coke gas, of stale beer and cheap tobacco. The dentist sprawled his gigantic limbs over the worn velvet of the operating chair; his coat and vest and shoes were off, and his huge feet, in their thick gray socks, dangled over the edge of the foot-rest; his pipe, fallen from his half-open mouth, had spilled the ashes into his lap; while on the floor, at his side, stood the half-empty pitcher of steam beer. His head had rolled limply upon one shoulder, his face was red with sleep, and from his open mouth came a terrific sound of snoring.

For a moment Trina stood looking at him as he lay thus, prone, inert, half-dressed, and stupefied with the heat of the room, the steam beer, and the fumes of the cheap tobacco. Then her little chin quivered and a sob rose to her throat; she fled from the "Parlors," and locking herself in her bedroom, flung herself on the bed and burst into an agony of weeping. Ah, no, ah, no, she could not love him. It had all been a dreadful mistake, and now it was irrevocable; she was bound to this man for life. If it was as bad as this now, only three weeks after her marriage, how would it be in the years to come? Year after year, month after month, hour after hour, she was to see this same face, with its salient jaw, was to feel the touch of those enormous red hands, was to hear the heavy, elephantine tread of those huge feet—in thick gray socks. Year after year, day after day, there would be no change, and it would last all her life. Either it would be one long continued revulsion, or else—worse than all—she would come to be content with him, would come to be like him, would sink to the level of steam beer and cheap tobacco, and all her pretty ways, her clean, trim little habits, would be forgotten, since they would be thrown away upon her stupid, brutish husband. "Her husband!" *That*, was her husband in there —she could yet hear his snores—for life, for life. A great despair seized upon her. She buried her face in the pillow and thought of her mother with an infinite longing.

Aroused at length by the chittering of the canary, McTeague had awakened slowly. After a while he had taken down his concertina and played upon it the six very mournful airs that he knew.

Face downward upon the bed, Trina still wept. Throughout that little suite could be heard but two sounds, the lugubrious strains of the concertina and the noise of stifled weeping.

That her husband should be ignorant of her distress seemed to Trina an additional grievance. With perverse inconsistency she began to wish him to come to her, to comfort her. He ought to know that she was in trouble, that she was lonely and unhappy.

"Oh, Mac," she called in a trembling voice. But the concertina still continued to wail and lament. Then Trina wished she were dead, and on the instant jumped up and ran into the "Dental Parlors," and threw herself into her husband's arms, crying; "Oh, Mac, dear, love me, love me *big*! I'm *so* unhappy."

"What—what—what—" the dentist exclaimed, starting up bewildered, a little frightened.

"Nothing, nothing, only *love* me, love me always and always."

But this first crisis, this momentary revolt, as much a matter of high-strung feminine nerves as of anything else, passed, and in the end Trina's affection for her "old bear" grew in spite of herself. She began to love him more and more, not for what he was, but for what she had given up to him. Only once again did Trina undergo a reaction against her husband, and then it was but the matter of an instant, brought on, curiously enough, by the sight of a bit of egg on McTeague's heavy mustache one morning just after breakfast.

Then, too, the pair had learned to make concessions, little by little, and all unconsciously they adapted their modes of life to suit each other. Instead of sinking to McTeague's level as she had feared, Trina found that she could make McTeague rise to hers, and in this saw a solution of many a difficult and gloomy complication.

For one thing, the dentist began to dress a little better, Trina even succeeding in inducing him to wear a high silk hat and a frock coat of a Sunday. Next he relinquished his Sunday afternoon's nap and beer in favor of three or four hours spent in the park with her —the weather permitting. So that gradually Trina's misgivings ceased, or when they did assail her, she could at last meet them with a shrug of the shoulders, saying to herself meanwhile, "Well, it's done now and it can't be helped; one must make the best of it."

During the first months of their married life these nervous relapses of hers had alternated with brusque outbursts of affection when her only fear was that her husband's love did not equal her own. Without an instant's warning, she would clasp him about the neck, rubbing her cheek against his, murmuring;

"Dear old Mac, I love you so, I love you so. Oh, aren't we happy together, Mac, just us two and no one else? You love me as much as I love you, don't you, Mac? Oh, if you shouldn't—if you *shouldn't*."

But by the middle of the winter Trina's emotions, oscillating at first from one extreme to another, commenced to settle themselves to an equilibrium of calmness and placid quietude. Her household

duties began more and more to absorb her attention, for she was an
admirable housekeeper, keeping the little suite in marvellous good
order and regulating the schedule of expenditure with an economy
that often bordered on positive niggardliness. It was a passion with
her to save money. In the bottom of her trunk, in the bedroom, she
hid a brass match-safe that answered the purposes of a savings bank.
Each time she added a quarter or a half dollar to the little store she
laughed and sang with a veritable childish delight; whereas, if the
butcher or milkman compelled her to pay an overcharge she was
unhappy for the rest of the day. She did not save this money for
any ulterior purpose, she hoarded instinctively, without knowing
why, responding to the dentist's remonstrances with:

"Yes, yes, I know I'm a little miser, I know it."

Trina had always been an economical little body, but it was only
since her great winning in the lottery that she had become especially penurious. No doubt, in her fear lest their great good luck
should demoralize them and lead to habits of extravagance, she had
recoiled too far in the other direction. Never, never, never should a
penny of that miraculous fortune be spent; rather should it be added
to. It was a nest egg, a monstrous, roc-like[1] nest egg, not so large,
however, but that it could be made larger. Already by the end of
that winter Trina had begun to make up the deficit of two hundred
dollars that she had been forced to expend on the preparations for
her marriage.

McTeague, on his part, never asked himself now-a-days whether
he loved Trina the wife as much as he had loved Trina the young
girl. There had been a time when to kiss Trina, to take her in his
arms, had thrilled him from head to heel with a happiness that was
beyond words; even the smell of her wonderful odorous hair had
sent a sensation of faintness all through him. That time was long
past now. Those sudden outbursts of affection on the part of his
little woman, outbursts that only increased in vehemence the longer
they lived together, puzzled rather than pleased him. He had come
to submit to them good-naturedly, answering her passionate inquiries with a "Sure, sure, Trina, sure I love you. What—what's the
matter with you?"

There was no passion in the dentist's regard for his wife. He
dearly liked to have her near him, he took an enormous pleasure in
watching her as she moved about their rooms, very much at home,
gay and singing from morning till night; and it was his great delight
to call her into the "Dental Parlors" when a patient was in the
chair and, while he held the plugger, to have her rap in the gold fillings with the little box-wood mallet as he had taught her. But that
tempest of passion, that overpowering desire that had suddenly

[1]. The roc is a legendary bird of great size.

taken possession of him that day when he had given her ether, again when he had caught her in his arms in the B Street station, and again and again during the early days of their married life, rarely stirred him now. On the other hand, he was never assailed with doubts as to the wisdom of his marriage.

McTeague had relapsed to his wonted stolidity. He never questioned himself, never looked for motives, never went to the bottom of things. The year following upon the summer of his marriage was a time of great contentment for him; after the novelty of the honeymoon had passed he slipped easily into the new order of things without a question. Thus his life would be for years to come. Trina was there; he was married and settled. He accepted the situation. The little animal comforts which for him constituted the enjoyment of life were ministered to at every turn, or when they were interfered with—as in the case of his Sunday afternoon's nap and beer —some agreeable substitute was found. In her attempts to improve McTeague—to raise him from the stupid animal life to which he had been accustomed in his bachelor days—Trina was tactful enough to move so cautiously and with such slowness that the dentist was unconscious of any process of change. In the matter of the high silk hat, it seemed to him that the initiative had come from himself.

Gradually the dentist improved under the influence of his little wife. He no longer went abroad with frayed cuffs about his huge red wrists—or worse, without any cuffs at all. Trina kept his linen clean and mended, doing most of his washing herself, and insisting that he should change his flannels—thick red flannels they were, with enormous bone buttons—once a week, his linen shirts twice a week, and his collars and cuffs every second day. She broke him of the habit of eating with his knife, she caused him to substitute bottled beer in the place of steam beer, and she induced him to take off his hat to Miss Baker, to Heise's wife, and to the other women of his acquaintance. McTeague no longer spent an evening at Frenna's. Instead of this he brought a couple of bottles of beer up to the rooms and shared it with Trina. In his "Parlors" he was no longer gruff and indifferent to his female patients; he arrived at that stage where he could work and talk to them at the same time; he even accompanied them to the door, and held it open for them when the operation was finished, bowing them out with great nods of his huge square-cut head.

Besides all this, he began to observe the broader, larger interests of life, interests that affected him not as an individual, but as a member of a class, a profession, or a political party. He read the papers, he subscribed to a dental magazine; on Easter, Christmas, and New Year's he went to church with Trina. He commenced to have opinions, convictions—it was not fair to deprive tax-paying women of the privilege to vote; a university education should not be a prerequisite for admission to a dental college; the Catholic priests were to be restrained in their efforts to gain control of the public schools.

But most wonderful of all, McTeague began to have ambitions —very vague, very confused ideas of something better—ideas for the most part borrowed from Trina. Some day, perhaps, he and his wife would have a house of their own. What a dream! A little home all to themselves, with six rooms and a bath, with a grass plat[2] in front and calla-lilies. Then there would be children. He would have a son, whose name would be Daniel, who would go to High School, and perhaps turn out to be a prosperous plumber or house painter. Then this son Daniel would marry a wife, and they would all live together in that six-room-and-bath house; Daniel would have little children. McTeague would grow old among them all. The dentist saw himself as a venerable patriarch surrounded by children and grandchildren.

So the winter passed. It was a season of great happiness for the McTeagues; the new life jostled itself into its grooves. A routine began.

On week-days they rose at half-past six, being awakened by the boy who brought the bottled milk, and who had instructions to pound upon the bedroom door in passing. Trina made breakfast— coffee, bacon and eggs, and a roll of Vienna bread from the bakery. The breakfast was eaten in the kitchen, on the round deal table covered with the shiny oilcloth table-spread tacked on. After breakfast the dentist immediately betook himself to his "Parlors" to meet his early morning appointments—those made with the clerks and shop girls who stopped in for half an hour on their way to their work.

Trina, meanwhile, busied herself about the suite, clearing away the breakfast, sponging off the oilcloth table-spread, making the bed, pottering about with a broom or duster or cleaning rag. Towards ten o'clock she opened the windows to air the rooms, then put on her drab jacket,[3] her little round turban with its red wing, took the butcher's and grocer's books from the knife basket in the drawer of the kitchen table, and descended to the street, where she spent a delicious hour—now in the huge market across the way, now in the grocer's store with its fragrant aroma of coffee and spices, and now before the counters of the haberdasher's, intent on a bit of shopping, turning over ends of veiling, strips of elastic, or slivers of whalebone. On the street she rubbed elbows with the

2. A small plot of ground.   3. A jacket made from a brown cotton fabric.

great ladies of the avenue in their beautiful dresses, or at intervals she met an acquaintance or two—Miss Baker, or Heise's lame wife, or Mrs. Ryer. At times she passed the flat and looked up at the windows of her home, marked by the huge golden molar that projected, flashing, from the bay window of the "Parlors." She saw the open windows of the sitting-room, the Nottingham lace curtains stirring and billowing in the draft, and she caught sight of Maria Macapa's towelled head as the Mexican maid-of-all-work went to and fro in the suite, sweeping or carrying away the ashes. Occasionally in the windows of the "Parlors" she beheld McTeague's rounded back as he bent to his work. Sometimes, even, they saw each other and waved their hands gayly in recognition.

By eleven o'clock Trina returned to the flat, her brown net reticule—once her mother's—full of parcels. At once she set about getting lunch—sausages, perhaps, with mashed potatoes; or last evening's joint warmed over or made into a stew; chocolate, which Trina adored, and a side dish or two—a salted herring or a couple of artichokes or a salad. At half-past twelve the dentist came in from the "Parlors," bringing with him the smell of creosote and of ether. They sat down to lunch in the sitting-room. They told each other of their doings throughout the forenoon; Trina showed her purchases, McTeague recounted the progress of an operation. At one o'clock they separated, the dentist returning to the "Parlors," Trina settling to her work on the Noah's ark animals. At about three o'clock she put this work away, and for the rest of the afternoon was variously occupied—sometimes it was the mending, sometimes the wash, sometimes new curtains to be put up, or a bit of carpet to be tacked down, or a letter to be written, or a visit—generally to Miss Baker—to be returned. Towards five o'clock the old woman whom they had hired for that purpose came to cook supper, for even Trina was not equal to the task of preparing three meals a day.

This woman was French, and was known to the flat as Augustine, no one taking enough interest in her to inquire for her last name; all that was known of her was that she was a decayed French laundress, miserably poor, her trade long since ruined by Chinese competition. Augustine cooked well, but she was otherwise undesirable, and Trina lost patience with her at every moment. The old French woman's most marked characteristic was her timidity. Trina could scarcely address her a simple direction without Augustine quailing and shrinking; a reproof, however gentle, threw her into an agony of confusion; while Trina's anger promptly reduced her to a state of nervous collapse, wherein she lost all power of speech, while her head began to bob and nod with an incontrollable twitching of the muscles, much like the oscillations of the head of a toy donkey. Her timidity was exasperating, her very presence in the room unstrung the nerves, while her morbid eagerness to avoid offence only served to develop in her a clumsiness that was at times beyond belief. More than once Trina had decided that she could no longer put up with Augustine, but each time she had retained her as she reflected upon her admirably cooked cabbage soups and tapioca puddings, and—which in Trina's eyes was her chiefest recommendation—the pittance for which she was contented to work.

Augustine had a husband. He was a spirit-medium—a "professor." At times he held seances in the larger rooms of the flat, playing vigorously upon a mouth-organ and invoking a familiar whom he called "Edna," and whom he asserted was an Indian maiden.[4]

The evening was a period of relaxation for Trina and McTeague. They had supper at six, after which McTeague smoked his pipe and read the papers for half an hour, while Trina and Augustine cleared away the table and washed the dishes. Then, as often as not, they went out together. One of their amusements was to go "down town" after dark and promenade Market and Kearney Streets.[5] It was very gay; a great many others were promenading there also. All of the stores were brilliantly lighted and many of them still open. They walked about aimlessly, looking into the shop windows. Trina would take McTeague's arm, and he, very much embarrassed at that, would thrust both hands into his pockets and pretend not to notice. They stopped before the jewellers' and milliners' windows, finding a great delight in picking out things for each other, saying how they would choose this and that if they were rich. Trina did most of the talking, McTeague merely approving by a growl or a movement of the head or shoulders; she was interested in the displays of some of the cheaper stores, but he found an irresistible charm in an enormous golden molar with four prongs that hung at a corner of Kearney Street.[6] Sometimes they would look at Mars or at the moon through the street telescopes or sit for a time in the rotunda of a vast department store where a band played every evening.

Occasionally they met Heise the harness-maker and his wife, with whom they had become acquainted. Then the evening was concluded by a four-cornered party in the Luxembourg, a quite German restaurant under a theatre. Trina had a *tamale* and a glass of beer, Mrs. Heise (who was a decayed writing teacher) ate salads, with glasses of grenadine and currant syrups. Heise drank cocktails and

---

4. A satiric glance at the popularity of spiritualism during the period. At his seances, Augustine's husband regularly called forth the spirit Edna, who then answered questions about spirits who had recently entered the spirit world.

5. Market and Kearny was the princi-pal corner of downtown San Francisco. Here and elsewhere Norris uses the spelling "Kearney."

6. See Robert D. Lundy, "The Polk Street Background of *McTeague*," pp. 263–64 below.

whiskey straight, and urged the dentist to join him. But McTeague was obstinate, shaking his head. "I can't drink that stuff," he said. "It don't agree with me, somehow; I go kinda crazy after two glasses." So he gorged himself with beer and frankfurter sausages plastered with German mustard.

When the annual Mechanics' Fair opened,[7] McTeague and Trina often spent their evenings there, studying the exhibits carefully (since in Trina's estimation education meant knowing things and being able to talk about them). Wearying of this they would go up into the gallery, and, leaning over, look down into the huge amphitheatre full of light and color and movement.

There rose to them the vast shuffling noise of thousands of feet and a subdued roar of conversation like the sound of a great mill. Mingled with this was the purring of distant machinery, the splashing of a temporary fountain, and the rhythmic jangling of a brass band, while in the piano exhibit a hired performer was playing upon a concert grand with a great flourish. Nearer at hand they could catch ends of conversation and notes of laughter, the noise of moving dresses, and the rustle of stiffly starched skirts. Here and there school children elbowed their way through the crowd, crying shrilly, their hands full of advertisement pamphlets, fans, picture cards, and toy whips, while the air itself was full of the smell of fresh popcorn.

They even spent some time in the art gallery. Trina's cousin Selina, who gave lessons in hand painting at two bits an hour, generally had an exhibit on the walls, which they were interested to find. It usually was a bunch of yellow poppies painted on black velvet and framed in gilt. They stood before it some little time, hazarding their opinions, and then moved on slowly from one picture to another. Trina had McTeague buy a catalogue and made a duty of finding the title of every picture. This, too, she told McTeague, was a kind of education one ought to cultivate. Trina professed to be fond of art, having perhaps acquired a taste for painting and sculpture from her experience with the Noah's ark animals.

"Of course," she told the dentist, "I'm no critic, I only know what I like." She knew that she liked the "Ideal Heads," lovely girls with flowing straw-colored hair and immense, upturned eyes. These always had for title, "Reverie," or "An Idyll," or "Dreams of Love."

"I think those are lovely, don't you, Mac?" she said.

"Yes, yes," answered McTeague, nodding his head, bewildered, trying to understand. "Yes, yes, lovely, that's the word. Are you dead sure now, Trina, that all that's hand-painted just like the poppies?"

Thus the winter passed, a year went by, then two. The little life

7. Organized by the Mechanics' Institute in aid of its library, the Mechanics' Fair was a major social and cultural event.

of Polk Street, the life of small traders, drug clerks, grocers, stationers, plumbers, dentists, doctors, spirit-mediums, and the like, ran on
monotonously in its accustomed grooves. The first three years of
their married life wrought little change in the fortunes of the
McTeagues. In the third summer the branch post-office was moved
from the ground floor of the flat to a corner farther up the street in
order to be near the cable line that ran mail cars. Its place was
taken by a German saloon, called a "Wein Stube," in the face of
the protests of every female lodger. A few months later quite a little
flurry of excitement ran through the street on the occasion of "The
Polk Street Open Air Festival," organized to celebrate the introduction there of electric lights. The festival lasted three days and was
quite an affair. The street was garlanded with yellow and white
bunting; there were processions and "floats" and brass bands.
Marcus Schouler was in his element during the whole time of the
celebration. He was one of the marshals of the parade, and was to
be seen at every hour of the day, wearing a borrowed high hat and
cotton gloves, and galloping a broken-down cab-horse over the cobbles. He carried a baton covered with yellow and white calico, with
which he made furious passes and gestures. His voice was soon
reduced to a whisper by continued shouting, and he raged and fretted over trifles till he wore himself thin. McTeague was disgusted
with him. As often as Marcus passed the window of the flat the
dentist would mutter:

"Ah, you think you're smart, don't you?"

The result of the festival was the organizing of a body known as
the "Polk Street Improvement Club," of which Marcus was elected
secretary. McTeague and Trina often heard of him in this capacity
through Heise the harness-maker. Marcus had evidently come to
have political aspirations. It appeared that he was gaining a reputation as a maker of speeches, delivered with fiery emphasis, and occasionally reprinted in the "Progress," the organ of the club—"outraged constituencies," "opinions warped by personal bias," "eyes
blinded by party prejudice," etc.

Of her family, Trina heard every fortnight in letters from her
mother. The upholstery business which Mr. Sieppe had bought was
doing poorly, and Mrs. Sieppe bewailed the day she had ever left B
Street. Mr. Sieppe was losing money every month. Owgooste, who
was to have gone to school, had been forced to go to work in "the
store," picking waste.[8] Mrs. Sieppe was obliged to take a lodger or
two. Affairs were in a very bad way. Occasionally she spoke of
Marcus. Mr. Sieppe had not forgotten him despite his own troubles,
but still had an eye out for some one whom Marcus could "go in
with" on a ranch.

It was toward the end of this period of three years that Trina and

8. Removing excess yarn from upholstery.

McTeague had their first serious quarrel. Trina had talked so much about having a little house of their own at some future day, that McTeague had at length come to regard the affair as the end and object of all their labors. For a long time they had had their eyes upon one house in particular. It was situated on a cross street close by, between Polk Street and the great avenue one block above, and hardly a Sunday afternoon passed that Trina and McTeague did not go and look at it. They stood for fully half an hour upon the other side of the street, examining every detail of its exterior, hazarding guesses as to the arrangement of the rooms, commenting upon its immediate neighborhood—which was rather sordid. The house was a wooden two-story arrangement, built by a misguided contractor in a sort of hideous Queen Anne style, all scrolls and meaningless millwork, with a cheap imitation of stained glass in the light over the door. There was a microscopic front yard full of dusty calla-lilies. The front door boasted an electric bell. But for the McTeagues it was an ideal home. Their idea was to live in this little house, the dentist retaining merely his office in the flat. The two places were but around the corner from each other, so that McTeague could lunch with his wife, as usual, and could even keep his early morning appointments and return to breakfast if he so desired.

However, the house was occupied. A Hungarian family lived in it. The father kept a stationery and notion "bazaar" next to Heise's harness-shop on Polk Street, while the oldest son played a third violin in the orchestra of a theatre. The family rented the house unfurnished for thirty-five dollars, paying extra for the water.

But one Sunday as Trina and McTeague on their way home from their usual walk turned into the cross street on which the little house was situated, they became promptly aware of an unwonted bustle going on upon the sidewalk in front of it. A dray was back against the curb, an express wagon drove away loaded with furniture; bedsteads, looking-glasses, and washbowls littered the sidewalks. The Hungarian family were moving out.

"Oh, Mac, look!" gasped Trina.

"Sure, sure," muttered the dentist.

After that they spoke but little. For upwards of an hour the two stood upon the sidewalk opposite, watching intently all that went forward, absorbed, excited.

On the evening of the next day they returned and visited the house, finding a great delight in going from room to room and imagining themselves installed therein. Here would be the bedroom, here the dining-room, here a charming little parlor. As they came out upon the front steps once more they met the owner, an enormous, red-faced fellow, so fat that his walking seemed merely a certain movement of his feet by which he pushed his stomach along in front of him. Trina talked with him a few moments, but arrived at no understanding, and the two went away after giving him their address. At supper that night McTeague said:

"Huh—what do you think, Trina?"

Trina put her chin in the air, tilting back her heavy tiara of swarthy hair.

"I'm not so sure yet. Thirty-five dollars and the water extra. I don't think we can afford it, Mac."

"Ah, pshaw!" growled the dentist, "sure we can."

"It isn't only that," said Trina, "but it'll cost so much to make the change."

"Ah, you talk's though we were paupers. Ain't we got five thousand dollars?"

Trina flushed on the instant, even to the lobes of her tiny pale ears, and put her lips together.

"Now, Mac, you know I don't want you should talk like that. That money's never, never to be touched."

"And you've been savun up a good deal, besides," went on McTeague, exasperated at Trina's persistent economies. "How much money have you got in that little brass match-safe in the bottom of your trunk? Pretty near a hundred dollars, I guess—ah, sure." He shut his eyes and nodded his great head in a knowing way.

Trina had more than that in the brass match-safe in question, but her instinct of hoarding had led her to keep it a secret from her husband. Now she lied to him with prompt fluency.

"A hundred dollars! What are you talking of, Mac? I've not got fifty. I've not got *thirty*."

"Oh, let's take that little house," broke in McTeague. "We got the chance now, and it may never come again. Come on, Trina, shall we? Say, come on, shall we, huh?"

"We'd have to be awful saving if we did, Mac."

"Well, sure, *I* say let's take it."

"I don't know," said Trina, hesitating. "Wouldn't it be lovely to have a house all to ourselves? But let's not decide until to-morrow."

The next day the owner of the house called. Trina was out at her morning's marketing and the dentist, who had no one in the chair at the time, received him in the "Parlors." Before he was well aware of it, McTeague had concluded the bargain. The owner bewildered him with a world of phrases, made him believe that it would be a great saving to move into the little house, and finally offered it to him "water free."

"All right, all right," said McTeague, "I'll take it."

The other immediately produced a paper.

"Well, then, suppose you sign for the first month's rent, and we'll call it a bargain. That's business, you know," and McTeague, hesitating, signed.

"I'd like to have talked more with my wife about it first," he said, dubiously.

"Oh, that's all right," answered the owner, easily. "I guess if the head of the family wants a thing, that's enough."

McTeague could not wait until lunch time to tell the news to Trina. As soon as he heard her come in, he laid down the plaster-of-paris mould he was making and went out into the kitchen and found her chopping up onions.

"Well, Trina," he said, "we got that house. I've taken it."

"What do you mean?" she answered, quickly. The dentist told her.

"And you signed a paper for the first month's rent?"

"Sure, sure. That's business, you know."

"Well, why did you *do* it?" cried Trina. "You might have asked *me* something about it. Now, what have you done? I was talking with Mrs. Ryer about that house while I was out this morning, and she said the Hungarians moved out because it was absolutely unhealthy; there's water been standing in the basement for months. And she told me, too," Trina went on indignantly, "that she knew the owner, and she was sure we could get the house for thirty if we'd bargain for it. Now what have you gone and done? I hadn't made up my mind about taking the house at all. And now I *won't* take it, with the water in the basement and all."

"Well—well," stammered McTeague, helplessly, "we needn't go in if it's unhealthy."

"But you've signed a *paper*," cried Trina, exasperated. "You've got to pay that first month's rent, anyhow—to forfeit it. Oh, you are so stupid! There's thirty-five dollars just thrown away. I *shan't* go into that house; we won't move a *foot* out of here. I've changed my mind about it, and there's water in the basement besides."

"Well, I guess we can stand thirty-five dollars," mumbled the dentist, "if we've got to."

"Thirty-five dollars just thrown out of the window," cried Trina, her teeth clicking, every instinct of her parsimony aroused. "Oh, you are the thick-wittedest man that I ever knew. Do you think we're millionaires? Oh, to think of losing thirty-five dollars like that." Tears were in her eyes, tears of grief as well as of anger. Never had McTeague seen his little woman so aroused. Suddenly she rose to her feet and slammed the chopping-bowl down upon the table. "Well, *I* won't pay a nickel of it," she exclaimed.

"Huh? What, what?" stammered the dentist, taken all aback by her outburst.

"I say that you will find that money, that thirty-five dollars, yourself."

"Why—why——"

"It's your stupidity got us into this fix, and you'll be the one that'll suffer by it."

"I can't do it, I *won't* do it. We'll—we'll share and share alike. Why, you said—you told me you'd take the house if the water was free."

"I *never* did. I *never* did. How can you stand there and say such a thing?"

"You did tell me that," vociferated McTeague, beginning to get angry in his turn.

"Mac, I didn't, and you know it. And what's more, I won't pay a nickel. Mr. Heise pays his bill next week, it's forty-three dollars, and you can just pay the thirty-five out of that."

"Why, you got a whole hundred dollars saved up in your match-safe," shouted the dentist, throwing out an arm with an awkward gesture. "You pay half and I'll pay half, that's only fair."

"No, no, *no*," exclaimed Trina. "It's not a hundred dollars. You won't touch it; you won't touch my money, I tell you."

"Ah, how does it happen to be yours, I'd like to know?"

"It's mine! It's mine! It's mine!" cried Trina, her face scarlet, her teeth clicking like the snap of a closing purse.

"It ain't any more yours than it is mine."

"Every penny of it is mine."

"Ah, what a fine fix you'd get me into," growled the dentist. "I've signed the paper with the owner; that's business, you know, that's business, you know; and now you go back on me. Suppose we'd taken the house, we'd 'a' shared the rent, wouldn't we, just as we do here?"

Trina shrugged her shoulders with a great affectation of indifference and began chopping the onions again.

"You settle it with the owner," she said. "It's your affair; you've got the money." She pretended to assume a certain calmness as though the matter was something that no longer affected her. Her manner exasperated McTeague all the more.

"No, I won't; no, I won't; I won't either," he shouted. "I'll pay my half and he can come to you for the other half." Trina put a hand over her ear to shut out his clamor.

"Ah, don't try and be smart," cried McTeague. "Come, now, yes or no, will you pay your half?"

"You heard what I said."

"Will you pay it?'

"No."

"Miser!" shouted McTeague. "Miser! you're worse than old Zerkow. All right, all right, keep your money. I'll pay the whole thirty-five. I'd rather lose it than be such a miser as you."

"Haven't you got anything to do," returned Trina, "instead of staying here and abusing me?"

"Well, then, for the last time, will you help me out?" Trina cut the heads of a fresh bunch of onions and gave no answer.

"Huh? will you?"

"I'd like to have my kitchen to myself, please," she said in a mincing way, irritating to a last degree. The dentist stamped out of the room, banging the door behind him.

For nearly a week the breach between them remained unhealed. Trina only spoke to the dentist in monosyllables, while he, exasperated at her calmness and frigid reserve, sulked in his "Dental Parlors," muttering terrible things beneath his mustache, or finding solace in his concertina, playing his six lugubrious airs over and over again, or swearing frightful oaths at his canary. When Heise paid his bill, McTeague, in a fury, sent the amount to the owner of the little house.

There was no formal reconciliation between the dentist and his little woman. Their relations readjusted themselves inevitably. By the end of the week they were as amicable as ever, but it was long before they spoke of the little house again. Nor did they ever revisit it of a Sunday afternoon. A month or so later the Ryers told them that the owner himself had moved in. The McTeagues never occupied that little house.

But Trina suffered a reaction after the quarrel. She began to be sorry she had refused to help her husband, sorry she had brought matters to such an issue. One afternoon as she was at work on the Noah's ark animals, she surprised herself crying over the affair. She loved her "old bear" too much to do him an injustice, and perhaps, after all, she had been in the wrong. Then it occurred to her how pretty it would be to come up behind him unexpectedly, and slip the money, thirty-five dollars, into his hand, and pull his huge head down to her and kiss his bald spot as she used to do in the days before they were married.

Then she hesitated, pausing in her work, her knife dropping into her lap, a half-whittled figure between her fingers. If not thirty-five dollars, then at least fifteen or sixteen, her share of it. But a feeling of reluctance, a sudden revolt against this intended generosity, arose in her.

"No, no," she said to herself. "I'll give him ten dollars. I'll tell him it's all I can afford. It *is* all I can afford."

She hastened to finish the figure of the animal she was then at work upon, putting in the ears and tail with a drop of glue, and tossing it into the basket at her side. Then she rose and went into the bedroom and opened her trunk, taking the key from under a corner of the carpet where she kept it hid.

At the very bottom of her trunk, under her bridal dress, she kept her savings. It was all in change—half dollars and dollars for the most part, with here and there a gold piece. Long since the little brass match-box had overflowed. Trina kept the surplus in a chamois-skin sack she had made from an old chest protector.[9] Just now, yielding to an impulse which often seized her, she drew out the match-box and the chamois sack, and emptying the contents on the bed, counted them carefully. It came to one hundred and sixty-five dollars, all told. She counted it and recounted it and made little piles of it, and rubbed the gold pieces between the folds of her apron until they shone.

"Ah, yes, ten dollars is all I can afford to give Mac," said Trina, "and even then, think of it, ten dollars—it will be four or five months before I can save that again. But, dear old Mac, I know it would make him feel glad, and perhaps," she added, suddenly taken with an idea, "perhaps Mac will refuse to take it."

She took a ten-dollar piece from the heap and put the rest away. Then she paused:

"No, not the gold piece," she said to herself. It's too pretty. He can have the silver." She made the change and counted out ten silver dollars into her palm. But what a difference it made in the appearance and weight of the little chamois bag! The bag was shrunken and withered, long wrinkles appeared running downward from the draw-string. It was a lamentable sight. Trina looked longingly at the ten broad pieces in her hand. Then suddenly all her intuitive desire of saving, her instinct of hoarding, her love of money for the money's sake, rose strong within her.

"No, no, no," she said. "I can't do it. It may be mean, but I can't help it. It's stronger than I." She returned the money to the bag and locked it and the brass match-box in her trunk, turning the key with a long breath of satisfaction.

She was a little troubled, however, as she went back into the sitting-room and took up her work.

"I didn't use to be so stingy," she told herself. "Since I won in the lottery I've become a regular little miser. It's growing on me, but never mind, it's a good fault, and, anyhow, I can't help it."

XI

On that particular morning the McTeagues had risen a half hour earlier than usual and taken a hurried breakfast in the kitchen on

9. A woman's undergarment.

the deal table with its oilcloth cover. Trina was house-cleaning that week and had a presentiment of a hard day's work ahead of her, while McTeague remembered a seven o'clock appointment with a little German shoemaker.

At about eight o'clock, when the dentist had been in his office for over an hour, Trina descended upon the bedroom, a towel about her head and the roller-sweeper in her hand. She covered the bureau and sewing machine with sheets, and unhooked the chenille portières between the bedroom and the sitting-room. As she was tying the Nottingham lace curtains at the window into great knots, she saw old Miss Baker on the opposite sidewalk in the street below, and raising the sash called down to her.

"Oh, it's you, Mrs. McTeague," cried the retired dressmaker, facing about, her head in the air. Then a long conversation was begun, Trina, her arms folded under her breast, her elbows resting on the window ledge, willing to be idle for a moment; old Miss Baker, her market-basket on her arm, her hands wrapped in the ends of her worsted shawl against the cold of the early morning. They exchanged phrases, calling to each other from window to curb, their breath coming from their lips in faint puffs of vapor, their voices shrill, and raised to dominate the clamor of the waking street. The newsboys had made their appearance on the street, together with the day laborers. The cable cars had begun to fill up; all along the street could be seen the shopkeepers taking down their shutters; some were still breakfasting. Now and then a waiter from one of the cheap restaurants crossed from one sidewalk to another, balancing on one palm a tray covered with a napkin.

"Aren't you out pretty early this morning, Miss Baker?" called Trina.

"No, no," answered the other. "I'm always up at half-past six, but I don't always get out so soon. I wanted to get a nice head of cabbage and some lentils for a soup, and if you don't go to market early, the restaurants get all the best."

"And you've been to market already, Miss Baker?"

"Oh, my, yes; and I got a fish—a sole—see." She drew the sole in question from her basket.

"Oh, the lovely sole!" exclaimed Trina.

"I got this one at Spadella's; he always has good fish on Friday. How is the doctor, Mrs. McTeaguc?"

"Ah, Mac is always well, thank you, Miss Baker."

"You know, Mrs. Ryer told me," cried the little dressmaker, moving forward a step out of the way of a "glass-put-in" man, "that Doctor McTeague pulled a tooth of that Catholic priest, Father— oh, I forget his name—anyhow, he pulled his tooth with his fingers. Was that true, Mrs. McTeague?"

"Oh, of course. Mac does that almost all the time now, 'specially with front teeth. He's got a regular reputation for it. He says it's brought him more patients than even the sign I gave him," she added, pointing to the big golden molar projecting from the office window.

"With his fingers! Now, think of that," exclaimed Miss Baker, wagging her head. "Isn't he that strong! It's just wonderful. Cleaning house to-day?" she inquired, glancing at Trina's towelled head.

"Um hum," answered Trina. "Maria Macapa's coming in to help pretty soon."

At the mention of Maria's name the little old dressmaker suddenly uttered an exclamation.

"Well, if I'm not here talking to you and forgetting something I was just dying to tell you. Mrs. McTeague, what ever in the world do you suppose? Maria and old Zerkow, that red-headed Polish Jew, the rag-bottles-sacks man, you know, they're going to be married."

"No!" cried Trina, in blank amazement. "You don't mean it."

"Of course I do. Isn't it the funniest thing you ever heard of?"

"Oh, tell me all about it," said Trina, leaning eagerly from the window. Miss Baker crossed the street and stood just beneath her.

"Well, Maria came to me last night and wanted me to make her a new gown, said she wanted something gay, like what the girls at the candy store wear when they go out with their young men. I couldn't tell what had got into the girl, until finally she told me she wanted something to get married in, and that Zerkow had asked her to marry him, and that she was going to do it. Poor Maria! I guess it's the first and only offer she ever received, and it's just turned her head."

"But what *do* those two see in each other?" cried Trina. "Zerkow is a horror, he's an old man, and his hair is red and his voice is gone, and then he's a Jew, isn't he?"

"I know, I know; but it's Maria's only chance for a husband, and she don't mean to let it pass. You know she isn't quite right in her head, anyhow. I'm awfully sorry for poor Maria. But *I* can't see what Zerkow wants to marry her for. It's not possible that he's in love with Maria, it's out of the question. Maria hasn't a sou, either, and I'm just positive that Zerkow has lots of money."

"I'll bet I know why," exclaimed Trina, with sudden conviction; "yes, I know just why. See here, Miss Baker, you know how crazy old Zerkow is after money and gold and those sort of things."

"Yes, I know; but you know Maria hasn't——"

"Now, just listen. You've heard Maria tell about that wonderful service of gold dishes she says her folks used to own in Central America; she's crazy on that subject, don't you know. She's all right on everything else, but just start her on that service of gold plate and she'll talk you deaf. She can describe it just as though she saw it, and she can make you see it, too, almost. Now, you see, Maria and Zerkow have known each other pretty well. Maria goes to him every two weeks or so to sell him junk; they got acquainted that way, and I know Maria's been dropping in to see him pretty often this last year, and sometimes he comes here to see her. He's made Maria tell him the story of that plate over and over and over again, and Maria does it and is glad to, because he's the only one that believes it. Now he's going to marry her just so's he can hear that story every day, every hour. He's pretty near as crazy on the subject as Maria is. They're a pair for you, aren't they? Both crazy over a lot of gold dishes that never existed. Perhaps Maria'll marry him because it's her only chance to get a husband, but I'm sure it's more for the reason that she's got some one to talk to now who believes her story. Don't you think I'm right?"

"Yes, yes, I guess you're right," admitted Miss Baker.

"But it's a queer match anyway you put it," said Trina, musingly.

"Ah, you may well say that," returned the other, nodding her head. There was a silence. For a long moment the dentist's wife and the retired dressmaker, the one at the window, the other on the sidewalk, remained lost in thought, wondering over the strangeness of the affair.

But suddenly there was a diversion. Alexander, Marcus Schouler's Irish setter, whom his master had long since allowed the liberty of running untrammelled about the neighborhood, turned the corner briskly and came trotting along the sidewalk where Miss Baker stood. At the same moment the Scotch collie who had at one time belonged to the branch post-office issued from the side door of a house not fifty feet away. In an instant the two enemies had recognized each other. They halted abruptly, their fore feet planted rigidly. Trina uttered a little cry.

"Oh, look out, Miss Baker. Those two dogs hate each other just like humans. You best look out. They'll fight sure." Miss Baker sought safety in a nearby vestibule, whence she peered forth at the scene, very interested and curious. Maria Macapa's head thrust itself from one of the top-story windows of the flat, with a shrill cry. Even McTeague's huge form appeared above the half curtains of the "Parlor" windows, while over his shoulder could be seen the face of the "patient," a napkin tucked in his collar, the rubber dam depending from his mouth. All the flat knew of the feud between the dogs, but never before had the pair been brought face to face.

Meanwhile, the collie and the setter had drawn near to each other; five feet apart they paused as if by mutual consent. The collie turned sidewise to the setter; the setter instantly wheeled himself flank on to the collie. Their tails rose and stiffened, they raised their lips over their long white fangs, the napes of their necks bristled, and they showed each other the vicious whites of their eyes, while they drew in their breaths with prolonged and rasping snarls. Each dog seemed to be the personification of fury and unsatisfied hate. They began to circle about each other with infinite slowness, walking stiff-legged and upon the very points of their feet. Then they wheeled about and began to circle in the opposite direction. Twice they repeated this motion, their snarls growing louder. But still they did not come together, and the distance of five feet between them was maintained with an almost mathematical precision. It was magnificent, but it was not war. Then the setter, pausing in his walk, turned his head slowly from his enemy. The collie sniffed the air and pretended an interest in an old shoe lying in the gutter. Gradually and with all the dignity of monarchs they moved away from each other. Alexander stalked back to the corner of the street. The collie paced toward the side gate whence he had issued, affecting to remember something of great importance. They disappeared. Once out of sight of one another they began to bark furiously.

"Well, I *never!*" exclaimed Trina in great disgust. "The way those two dogs have been carrying on you'd 'a' thought they would 'a' just torn each other to pieces when they had the chance, and here I'm wasting the whole morning——" she closed her window with a bang.

"Sick 'im, sick 'im," called Maria Macapa, in a vain attempt to promote a fight.

Old Miss Baker came out of the vestibule, pursing her lips, quite put out at the fiasco. "And after all that fuss," she said to herself aggrievedly.

The little dressmaker bought an envelope of nasturtium seeds at the florist's, and returned to her tiny room in the flat. But as she slowly mounted the first flight of steps she suddenly came face to face with Old Grannis, who was coming down. It was between eight and nine, and he was on his way to his little dog hospital, no doubt. Instantly Miss Baker was seized with trepidation, her curious little false curls shook, a faint—a very faint—flush came into her withered cheeks, and her heart beat so violently under the worsted shawl that she felt obliged to shift the market-basket to her other arm and put out her free hand to steady herself against the rail.

On his part, Old Grannis was instantly overwhelmed with confusion. His awkwardness seemed to paralyze his limbs, his lips twitched and turned dry, his hand went tremblingly to his chin. But what added to Miss Baker's miserable embarrassment on this occasion was the fact that the old Englishman should meet her thus, carrying a sordid market-basket full of sordid fish and cabbage. It seemed as if a malicious fate persisted in bringing the two old people face to face at the most inopportune moments.

Just now, however, a veritable catastrophe occurred. The little old dressmaker changed her basket to her other arm at precisely the wrong moment, and Old Grannis, hastening to pass, removing his hat in a hurried salutation, struck it with his forearm, knocking it from her grasp, and sending it rolling and bumping down the stairs. The sole fell flat upon the first landing; the lentils scattered themselves over the entire flight; while the cabbage, leaping from step to step, thundered down the incline and brought up against the street floor with a shock that reverberated through the entire building.

The little retired dressmaker, horribly vexed, nervous and embarassed, was hard put to it to keep back the tears. Old Grannis stood for a moment with averted eyes, murmuring; "Oh, I'm so sorry, I'm so sorry, I—I really—I beg your pardon, really—really."

Marcus Schouler, coming down stairs from his room, saved the situation.

"Hello, people," he cried. "By damn! You've upset your basket —you have, for a fact. Here, let's pick um up." He and Old Grannis went up and down the flight, gathering up the fish, the lentils, and the sadly battered cabbage. Marcus was raging over the pusillanimity of Alexander, of which Maria had just told him.

"I'll cut him in two with the whip," he shouted. "I will, I will, I say I will, for a fact. He wouldn't fight, hey? I'll give um all the fight he wants, nasty, mangy cur. If he won't fight he won't eat. I'm going to get the butcher's bull pup and I'll put um both in a bag and shake um up. I will, for a fact, and I guess Alec will fight. Come along, Mister Grannis," and he took the old Englishman away.

Little Miss Baker hastened to her room and locked herself in. She was excited and upset during all the rest of the day, and listened eagerly for Old Grannis's return that evening. He went instantly to work binding up "The Breeder and Sportsman," and back numbers of the "Nation." She heard him softly draw his chair and the table on which he had placed his little binding apparatus close to the wall. At once she did the same, brewing herself a cup of tea. All through that evening the two old people "kept company" with each other, after their own peculiar fashion. "Setting out with each other" Miss Baker had begun to call it. That they had been presented, that they had even been forced to talk together, had made no change in their relative positions. Almost immediately they had fallen back into their old ways again, quite unable to master their timidity, to overcome the stifling embarrassment that seized upon them when in each other's presence. It was a sort of hypnotism, a thing stronger than themselves. But they were not altogether dissatisfied with the way things had come to be. It was their little romance, their last, and they were living through it with supreme enjoyment and calm contentment.

Marcus Schouler still occupied his old room on the floor above the McTeagues. They saw but little of him, however. At long intervals the dentist or his wife met him on the stairs of the flat. Sometimes he would stop and talk with Trina, inquiring after the Sieppes, asking her if Mr. Sieppe had yet heard of any one with whom he, Marcus, could "go in with on a ranch." McTeague, Marcus merely nodded to. Never had the quarrel between the two men been completely patched up. It did not seem possible to the dentist now that Marcus had ever been his "pal," that they had ever taken long walks together. He was sorry that he had treated Marcus gratis for an ulcerated tooth, while Marcus daily recalled the fact that he had given up his "girl" to his friend—the girl who had won a fortune—as the great mistake of his life. Only once since the wedding had he called upon Trina, at a time when he knew McTeague would be out. Trina had shown him through the rooms and had told him, innocently enough, how gay was their life there. Marcus had come away fairly sick with envy; his rancor against the dentist—and against himself, for that matter—knew no bounds. "And you might 'a' had it all yourself, Marcus Schouler," he muttered to himself on the stairs. "You mush-head, you damn fool!"

Meanwhile, Marcus was becoming involved in the politics of his ward. As secretary of the Polk Street Improvement Club—which soon developed into quite an affair and began to assume the proportions of a Republican political machine—he found he could make a little, a very little more than enough to live on. At once he had given up his position as Old Grannis's assistant in the dog hospital. Marcus felt that he needed a wider sphere. He had his eye upon a place connected with the city pound. When the great railroad strike occurred, he promptly got himself engaged as deputy-sheriff, and spent a memorable week in Sacramento, where he involved himself in more than one terrible melée with the strikers.[1] Marcus had that quickness of temper and passionate readiness to take offence which passes among his class for bravery. But whatever were his motives, his promptness to face danger could not for a moment be doubted. After the strike he returned to Polk Street, and throwing himself into the Improvement Club, heart, soul, and body, soon became one of its ruling spirits. In a certain local election, where a huge paving contract was at stake, the club made itself felt in the ward, and Marcus so managed his cards and pulled his wires that, at the end of the matter, he found himself some four hundred dollars to the good.

When McTeague came out of his "Parlors" at noon of the day upon which Trina had heard the news of Maria Macapa's intended

---

1. During the nationwide railway strike of June and July, 1895, rioting occurred in several California cities, including Sacramento.

marriage, he found Trina burning coffee on a shovel in the sitting-room. Try as she would, Trina could never quite eradicate from their rooms a certain faint and indefinable odor, particularly offensive to her. The smell of the photographer's chemicals persisted in spite of all Trina could do to combat it. She burnt pastilles and Chinese punk,[2] and even, as now, coffee on a shovel, all to no purpose. Indeed, the only drawback to their delightful home was the general unpleasant smell that pervaded it—a smell that arose partly from the photographer's chemicals, partly from the cooking in the little kitchen, and partly from the ether and creosote of the dentist's "Parlors."

As McTeague came in to lunch on this occasion, he found the table already laid, a red cloth figured with white flowers was spread, and as he took his seat his wife put down the shovel on a chair and brought in the stewed codfish and the pot of chocolate. As he tucked his napkin into his enormous collar, McTeague looked vaguely about the room, rolling his eyes.

During the three years of their married life the McTeagues had made but few additions to their furniture, Trina declaring that they could not afford it. The sitting-room could boast of but three new ornaments. Over the melodeon hung their marriage certificate in a black frame. It was balanced upon one side by Trina's wedding bouquet under a glass case, preserved by some fearful unknown process, and upon the other by the photograph of Trina and the dentist in their wedding finery. This latter picture was quite an affair, and had been taken immediately after the wedding, while McTeague's broadcloth was still new, and before Trina's silks and veil had lost their stiffness. It represented Trina, her veil thrown back, sitting very straight in a rep armchair, her elbows well in at her sides, holding her bouquet of cut flowers directly before her. The dentist stood at her side, one hand on her shoulder, the other thrust into the breast of his "Prince Albert," his chin in the air, his eyes to one side, his left foot forward in the attitude of a statue of a Secretary of State.

"Say, Trina," said McTeague, his mouth full of codfish, "Heise looked in on me this morning. He says 'What's the matter with a basket picnic over at Schuetzen Park next Tuesday?' You know the paper-hangers are going to be in the "Parlors" all that day, so I'll have a holiday. That's what made Heise think of it. Heise says he'll get the Ryers to go too. It's the anniversary of their wedding day. We'll ask Selina to go; she can meet us on the other side. Come on, let's go, huh, will you?"

Trina still had her mania for family picnics, which had been one

2. Norris is probably referring to "joss sticks," an incense burned in Chinese religious ceremonies.

of the Sieppes most cherished customs; but now there were other considerations.

"I don't know as we can afford it this month, Mac," she said, pouring the chocolate. "I got to pay the gas bill next week, and there's the papering of your office to be paid for some time."

"I know, I know," answered her husband. "But I got a new patient this week, had two molars and an upper incisor filled at the very first sitting, and he's going to bring his children round. He's a barber on the next block."

"Well, you pay half, then," said Trina. "It'll cost three or four dollars at the very least; and mind, the Heises pay their *own* fare both ways, Mac, and everybody gets their own lunch. Yes," she added, after a pause, "I'll write and have Selina join us. I haven't seen Selina in months. I guess I'll have to put up a lunch for her, though," admitted Trina, "the way we did last time, because she lives in a boarding-house now, and they make a fuss about putting up a lunch."

They could count on pleasant weather at this time of the year— it was May—and that particular Tuesday was all that could be desired. The party assembled at the ferry slip at nine o'clock, laden with baskets. The McTeagues came last of all; Ryer and his wife had already boarded the boat. They met the Heises in the waiting-room.

"Hello, Doctor," cried the harness-maker as the McTeagues came up. "This is what you'd call an old folks' picnic, all married people this time."

The party foregathered on the upper deck as the boat started, and sat down to listen to the band of Italian musicians who were playing outside this morning because of the fineness of the weather.

"Oh, we're going to have lots of fun," cried Trina. "If it's anything I do love it's a picnic. Do you remember our first picnic, Mac?"

"Sure, sure," replied the dentist; "we had a Gotha truffle."

"And August lost his steamboat," put in Trina, "and papa smacked him. I remember it just as well."

"Why, look there," said Mrs. Heise, nodding at a figure coming up the companion-way. "Ain't that Mr. Schouler?"

It was Marcus, sure enough. As he caught sight of the party he gaped at them a moment in blank astonishment, and then ran up, his eyes wide.

"Well, by damn!" he exclaimed, excitedly. "What's up? Where you all going, anyhow? Say, ain't ut queer we should all run up against each other like this?" He made great sweeping bows to the three women, and shook hands with "Cousin Trina," adding, as he turned to the men of the party, "Glad to see you, Mister Heise.

How do, Mister Ryer?" The dentist, who had formulated some sort of reserved greeting, he ignored completely. McTeague settled himself in his seat, growling inarticulately behind his mustache.

"Say, say, what's all up, anyhow?" cried Marcus again.

"It's a picnic," exclaimed the three women, all speaking at once; and Trina added, "We're going over to the same old Schuetzen Park again. But you're all fixed up yourself, Cousin Mark; you look as though you were going somewhere yourself."

In fact, Marcus was dressed with great care. He wore a new pair of slate-blue trousers, a black "cutaway,"[3] and a white lawn "tie" (for him the symbol of the height of elegance). He carried also his cane, a thin wand of ebony with a gold head, presented to him by the Improvement Club in "recognition of services."

"That's right, that's right," said Marcus, with a grin. "I'm takun a holiday myself to-day. I had a bit of business to do over at Oakland, an' I thought I'd go up to B Street afterward and see Selina. I haven't called on——"

But the party uttered an exclamation.

"Why, Selina is going with us."

"She's going to meet us at the Schuetzen Park station," explained Trina.

Marcus's business in Oakland was a fiction. He was crossing the bay that morning solely to see Selina. Marcus had "taken up with" Selina a little after Trina had married, and had been "rushing" her ever since, dazzled and attracted by her accomplishments, for which he pretended a great respect. At the prospect of missing Selina on this occasion, he was genuinely disappointed. His vexation at once assumed the form of exasperation against McTeague. It was all the dentist's fault. Ah, McTeague was coming between him and Selina now as he had come between him and Trina. Best look out, by damn! how he monkeyed with him now. Instantly his face flamed and he glanced over furiously at the dentist, who, catching his eye, began again to mutter behind his mustache.

"Well, say," began Mrs. Ryer, with some hesitation, looking to Ryer for approval, "why can't Marcus come along with us?"

"Why, of course," exclaimed Mrs. Heise, disregarding her husband's vigorous nudges. "I guess we got lunch enough to go round, all right; don't you say so, Mrs. McTeague?"

Thus appealed to, Trina could only concur.

"Why, of course, Cousin Mark," she said; "of course, come along with us if you want to."

"Why, you bet I will," cried Marcus, enthusiastic in an instant. "Say, this is outa sight; it is, for a fact; a picnic—ah, sure—and we'll meet Selina at the station."

3. Marcus is wearing a coat in which the skirts taper off from the front waist-line to the tails.

Just as the boat was passing Goat Island, the harness-maker proposed that the men of the party should go down to the bar on the lower deck and shake for the drinks. The idea had an immediate success.

"Have to see you on that," said Ryer.

"By damn, we'll have a drink! Yes, sir, we will, for a fact."

"Sure, sure, drinks, that's the word."

At the bar Heise and Ryer ordered cocktails, Marcus called for a "crème Yvette" in order to astonish the others. The dentist spoke for a glass of beer.

"Say, look here," suddenly exclaimed Heise as they took their glasses. "Look here, you fellahs," he had turned to Marcus and the dentist. "You two fellahs have had a grouch at each other for the last year or so; now what's the matter with your shaking hands and calling quits?"

McTeague was at once overcome with a great feeling of magnanimity. He put out his great hand.

"I got nothing against Marcus," he growled.

"Well, I don't care if I shake," admitted Marcus, a little shamefacedly, as their palms touched. "I guess that's all right."

"That's the idea," exclaimed Heise, delighted at his success. "Come on, boys, now let's drink." Their elbows crooked and they drank silently.

Their picnic that day was very jolly. Nothing had changed at Schuetzen Park since the day of that other memorable Sieppe picnic four years previous. After lunch the men took themselves off to the rifle range, while Selina, Trina, and the other two women put away the dishes. An hour later the men joined them in great spirits. Ryer had won the impromptu match which they had arranged, making quite a wonderful score, which included three clean bulls' eyes, while McTeague had not been able even to hit the target itself.

Their shooting match had awakened a spirit of rivalry in the men, and the rest of the afternoon was passed in athletic exercises between them. The women sat on the slope of the grass, their hats and gloves laid aside, watching the men as they strove together. Aroused by little feminine cries of wonder and the clapping of their ungloved palms, these latter began to show off at once. They took off their coats and vests, even their neckties and collars, and worked themselves into a lather of perspiration for the sake of making an impression on their wives. They ran hundred-yard sprints on the cinder path and executed clumsy feats on the rings and on the parallel bars. They even found a huge round stone on the beach and "put the shot" for a while. As long as it was a question of agility, Marcus was easily the best of the four; but the dentist's enormous strength, his crude, untutored brute force, was a matter of wonder for the entire party. McTeague cracked English walnuts —taken from the lunch baskets—in the hollow of his arm, and tossed the round stone a full five feet beyond their best mark. Heise believed himself to be particularly strong in the wrists, but the dentist, using but one hand, twisted a cane out of Heise's two with a wrench that all but sprained the harness-maker's arm. Then the dentist raised weights and chinned himself on the rings till they thought he would never tire.

His great success quite turned his head; he strutted back and forth in front of the women, his chest thrown out, and his great mouth perpetually expanded in a triumphant grin. As he felt his strength more and more, he began to abuse it; he domineered over the others, gripping suddenly at their arms till they squirmed with pain, and slapping Marcus on the back so that he gasped and gagged for breath. The childish vanity of the great fellow was as undisguised as that of a schoolboy. He began to tell of wonderful feats of strength he had accomplished when he was a young man. Why, at one time he had knocked down a half-grown heifer with a blow of his fist between the eyes, sure, and the heifer had just stiffened out and trembled all over and died without getting up.

McTeague told this story again, and yet again. All through the afternoon he could be overheard relating the wonder to any one who would listen, exaggerating the effect of his blow, inventing terrific details. Why, the heifer had just frothed at the mouth, and his eyes had rolled up—ah, sure, his eyes rolled up just like that—and the butcher had said his skull was all mashed in—just all mashed in, sure, that's the word—just as if from a sledge-hammer.

Notwithstanding his reconciliation with the dentist on the boat, Marcus's gorge rose within him at McTeague's boasting swagger. When McTeague had slapped him on the back, Marcus had retired to some little distance while he recovered his breath, and glared at the dentist fiercely as he strode up and down, glorying in the admiring glances of the women.

"Ah, one-horse dentist," he muttered between his teeth. "Ah, zinc-plugger, cow-killer, I'd like to show you once, you overgrown mucker, you—you—cow-killer!"

When he rejoined the group, he found them preparing for a wrestling bout.

"I tell you what," said Heise, "we'll have a tournament. Marcus and I will rastle, and Doc and Ryer, and then the winners will rastle each other."

The women clapped their hands excitedly. This would be exciting. Trina cried:

"Better let me hold your money, Mac, and your keys, so as you won't lose them out of your pockets." The men gave their valuables into the keeping of their wives and promptly set to work.

The dentist thrust Ryer down without even changing his grip; Marcus and the harness-maker struggled together for a few moments till Heise all at once slipped on a bit of turf and fell backwards. As they toppled over together, Marcus writhed himself from under his opponent, and, as they reached the ground, forced down first one shoulder and then the other.

"All right, all right," panted the harness-maker, good-naturedly, "I'm down. It's up to you and Doc now," he added, as he got to his feet.

The match between McTeague and Marcus promised to be interesting. The dentist, of course, had an enormous advantage in point of strength, but Marcus prided himself on his wrestling, and knew something about strangle-holds and half-Nelsons. The men drew back to allow them a free space as they faced each other, while Trina and the other women rose to their feet in their excitement.

"I bet Mac will throw him, all the same," said Trina.

"All ready!" cried Ryer.

The dentist and Marcus stepped forward, eying each other cautiously. They circled around the impromptu ring, Marcus watching eagerly for an opening. He ground his teeth, telling himself he would throw McTeague if it killed him. Ah, he'd show him now. Suddenly the two men caught at each other; Marcus went to his knees. The dentist threw his vast bulk on his adversary's shoulders and, thrusting a huge palm against his face, pushed him backwards and downwards. It was out of the question to resist that enormous strength. Marcus wrenched himself over and fell face downward on the ground.

McTeague rose on the instant with a great laugh of exultation.

"You're down!" he exclaimed.

Marcus leaped to his feet.

"Down nothing," he vociferated, with clenched fists. "Down nothing, by damn! You got to throw me so's my shoulders touch."

McTeague was stalking about, swelling with pride.

"Hoh, you're down. I threw you. Didn't I throw him, Trina? Hoh, you can't rastle *me*."

Marcus capered with rage.

"You didn't! you didn't! you didn't! and you can't! You got to give me another try."

The other men came crowding up. Everybody was talking at once.

"He's right."

"You didn't throw him."

"Both his shoulders at the same time."

Trina clapped and waved her hand at McTeague from where she stood on the little slope of lawn above the wrestlers. Marcus broke through the group, shaking all over with excitement and rage.

"I tell you that ain't the *way* to rastle. You've got to throw a man so's his shoulders touch. You got to give me another bout."

"That's straight," put in Heise, "both his shoulders down at the same time. Try it again. You and Schouler have another try."

McTeague was bewildered by so much simultaneous talk. He could not make out what it was all about. Could he have offended Marcus again?

"What? What? Huh? What is it?" he exclaimed in perplexity, looking from one to the other.

"Come on, you must rastle me again," shouted Marcus.

"Sure, sure," cried the dentist. "I'll rastle you again. I'll rastle everybody," he cried, suddenly struck with an idea. Trina looked on in some apprehension.

"Mark gets so mad," she said, half aloud.

"Yes," admitted Selina. "Mister Schouler's got an awful quick temper, but he ain't afraid of anything."

"All ready!" shouted Ryer.

This time Marcus was more careful. Twice, as McTeague rushed at him, he slipped cleverly away. But as the dentist came in a third time, with his head bowed, Marcus, raising himself to his full height, caught him with both arms around the neck. The dentist gripped at him and rent away the sleeve of his shirt. There was a great laugh.

"Keep your shirt on," cried Mrs. Ryer.

The two men were grappling at each other wildly. The party could hear them panting and grunting as they labored and struggled. Their boots tore up great clods of turf. Suddenly they came to the ground with a tremendous shock. But even as they were in the act of falling, Marcus, like a very eel, writhed in the dentist's clasp and fell upon his side. McTeague crashed down upon him like the collapse of a felled ox.

"Now, you gotta turn him on his back," shouted Heise to the dentist. "He ain't down if you don't."

With his huge salient chin digging into Marcus's shoulder, the dentist heaved and tugged. His face was flaming, his huge shock of yellow hair fell over his forehead, matted with sweat. Marcus began to yield despite his frantic efforts. One shoulder was down, now the other began to go; gradually, gradually it was forced over. The little audience held its breath in the suspense of the moment. Selina broke the silence, calling out shrilly:

"Ain't Doctor McTeague just that strong!"

Marcus heard it, and his fury came instantly to a head. Rage at his defeat at the hands of the dentist and before Selina's eyes, the hate he still bore his old-time "pal" and the impotent wrath of his own powerlessness were suddenly unleashed.

"God damn you! get off of me," he cried under his breath, spitting the words as a snake spits its venom. The little audience uttered a cry. With the oath Marcus had twisted his head and had bitten through the lobe of the dentist's ear. There was a sudden flash of bright-red blood.

Then followed a terrible scene. The brute that in McTeague lay so close to the surface leaped instantly to life, monstrous, not to be resisted. He sprang to his feet with a shrill and meaningless clamor, totally unlike the ordinary bass of his speaking tones. It was the hideous yelling of a hurt beast, the squealing of a wounded elephant. He framed no words; in the rush of high-pitched sound that issued from his wide-open mouth there was nothing articulate. It was something no longer human; it was rather an echo from the jungle.

Sluggish enough and slow to anger on ordinary occasions, McTeague when finally aroused became another man. His rage was a kind of obsession, an evil mania, the drunkenness of passion, the exalted and perverted fury of the Berserker,[4] blind and deaf, a thing insensate.

As he rose he caught Marcus's wrist in both his hands. He did not strike, he did not know what he was doing. His only idea was to batter the life out of the man before him, to crush and annihilate him upon the instant. Gripping his enemy in his enormous hands, hard and knotted, and covered with a stiff fell of yellow hair—the hands of the old-time car-boy—he swung him wide, as a hammer-thrower swings his hammer. Marcus's feet flipped from the ground, he spun through the air about McTeague as helpless as a bundle of clothes. All at once there was a sharp snap, almost like the report of a small pistol. Then Marcus rolled over and over upon the ground as McTeague released his grip; his arm, the one the dentist had seized, bending suddenly, as though a third joint had formed between wrist and elbow. The arm was broken.

But by this time every one was crying out at once. Heise and Ryer ran in between the two men. Selina turned her head away. Trina was wringing her hands and crying in an agony of dread:

"Oh, stop them, stop them! Don't let them fight. Oh, it's too awful."

"Here, here, Doc, quit. Don't make a fool of yourself," cried Heise, clinging to the dentist. "That's enough now. *Listen* to me, will you?"

"Oh, Mac, Mac," cried Trina, running to her husband. "Mac, dear, listen; it's me, it's Trina, look at me, you——"

---

4. A Norse term for a warrior driven into a frenzy by the excitement of battle.

"Get hold of his other arm, will you, Ryer?" panted Heise. "Quick!"

"Mac, Mac," cried Trina, her arms about his neck.

"For God's sake, hold up, Doc, will you?" shouted the harness-maker. "You don't want to kill him, do you?"

Mrs. Ryer and Heise's lame wife were filling the air with their outcries. Selina was giggling with hysteria. Marcus, terrified, but too brave to run, had picked up a jagged stone with his left hand and stood on the defensive. His swollen right arm, from which the shirt sleeve had been torn, dangled at his side, the back of the hand twisted where the palm should have been. The shirt itself was a mass of grass stains and was spotted with the dentist's blood.

But McTeague, in the centre of the group that struggled to hold him, was nigh to madness. The side of his face, his neck, and all the shoulder and breast of his shirt were covered with blood. He had ceased to cry out, but kept muttering between his gripped jaws, as he labored to tear himself free of the retaining hands:

"Ah, I'll kill him! Ah, I'll kill him! I'll kill him! Damn you, Heise," he exclaimed suddenly, trying to strike the harness-maker, "let go of me, will you!"

Little by little they pacified him, or rather (for he paid but little attention to what was said to him) his bestial fury lapsed by degrees. He turned away and let fall his arms, drawing long breaths, and looking stupidly about him, now searching helplessly upon the ground, now gazing vaguely into the circle of faces about him. His ear bled as though it would never stop.

"Say, Doctor," asked Heise, "what's the best thing to do?"

"Huh?" answered McTeague. "What—what do you mean? What is it?"

"What'll we do to stop this bleeding here?"

McTeague did not answer, but looked intently at the blood-stained bosom of his shirt.

"Mac," cried Trina, her face close to his, "tell us something—the best thing we can do to stop your ear bleeding."

"Collodium," said the dentist.

"But we can't get to that right away; we——"

"There's some ice in our lunch basket," broke in Heise. "We brought it for the beer; and take the napkins and make a bandage."

"Ice," muttered the dentist, "sure, ice, that's the word."

Mrs. Heise and the Ryers were looking after Marcus's broken arm. Selina sat on the slope of the grass, gasping and sobbing. Trina tore the napkins into strips, and, crushing some of the ice, made a bandage for her husband's head.

The party resolved itself into two groups; the Ryers and Mrs.

Heise bending over Marcus, while the harness-maker and Trina came and went about McTeague, sitting on the ground, his shirt, a mere blur of red and white, detaching itself violently from the background of pale-green grass. Between the two groups was the torn and trampled bit of turf, the wrestling ring; the picnic baskets, together with empty beer bottles, broken egg-shells, and discarded sardine tins, were scattered here and there. In the middle of the improvised wrestling ring the sleeve of Marcus's shirt fluttered occasionally in the sea breeze.

Nobody was paying any attention to Selina. All at once she began to giggle hysterically again, then cried out with a peal of laughter: "Oh, what a way for our picnic to end!"

XII

"Now, then, Maria," said Zerkow, his cracked, strained voice just rising above a whisper, hitching his chair closer to the table, "now, then, my girl, let's have it all over again. Tell us about the gold plate—the service. Begin with, 'There were over a hundred pieces and every one of them gold.'"

"I don' know what you're talking about, Zerkow," answered Maria. "There never was no gold plate, no gold service. I guess you must have dreamed it."

Maria and the red-headed Polish Jew had been married about a month after the McTeague's picnic which had ended in such lamentable fashion. Zerkow had taken Maria home to his wretched hovel in the alley back of the flat, and the flat had been obliged to get another maid of all work. Time passed, a month, six months, a whole year went by. At length Maria gave birth to a child, a wretched, sickly child, with not even strength enough nor wits enough to cry. At the time of its birth Maria was out of her mind, and continued in a state of dementia for nearly ten days. She recovered just in time to make the arrangements for the baby's burial. Neither Zerkow nor Maria was much affected by either the birth or the death of this little child. Zerkow had welcomed it with pronounced disfavor, since it had a mouth to be fed and wants to be provided for. Maria was out of her head so much of the time that she could scarcely remember how it looked when alive. The child was a mere incident in their lives, a thing that had come undesired and had gone unregretted. It had not even a name; a strange, hybrid little being, come and gone within a fortnight's time, yet combining in its puny little body the blood of the Hebrew, the Pole, and the Spaniard.

But the birth of this child had peculiar consequences. Maria came out of her dementia, and in a few days the household settled itself again to its sordid régime and Maria went about her duties as usual. Then one evening, about a week after the child's burial, Zerkow had asked Maria to tell him the story of the famous service of gold plate for the hundredth time.

Zerkow had come to believe in this story infallibly. He was immovably persuaded that at one time Maria or Maria's people had possessed these hundred golden dishes. In his perverted mind the hallucination had developed still further. Not only had that service of gold plate once existed, but it existed now, entire, intact; not a single burnished goldén piece of it was missing. It was somewhere, somebody had it, locked away in that leather trunk with its quilted lining and round brass locks. It was to be searched for and secured, to be fought for, to be gained at all hazards. Maria must know where it was; by dint of questioning, Zerkow would surely get the information from her. Some day, if only he was persistent, he would hit upon the right combination of questions, the right suggestion that would disentangle Maria's confused recollections. Maria would tell him where the thing was kept, was concealed, was buried, and he would go to that place and secure it, and all that wonderful gold would be his forever and forever. This service of plate had come to be Zerkow's mania.

On this particular evening, about a week after the child's burial, in the wretched back room of the junk shop, Zerkow had made Maria sit down to the table opposite him—the whiskey bottle and the red glass tumbler with its broken base between them—and had said:

"Now, then, Maria, tell us that story of the gold dishes again."

Maria stared at him, an expression of perplexity coming into her face.

"What gold dishes?" said she.

"The ones your people used to own in Central America. Come on, Maria, begin, begin." The Jew craned himself forward, his lean fingers clawing eagerly at his lips.

"What gold plate?" said Maria, frowning at him as she drank her whiskey. "What gold plate? I don' know what you're talking about, Zerkow."

Zerkow sat back in his chair, staring at her.

"Why, your people's gold dishes, what they used to eat off of. You've told me about it a hundred times."

"You're crazy, Zerkow," said Maria. "Push the bottle here, will you?"

"Come, now," insisted Zerkow, sweating with desire, "come, now, my girl, don't be a fool; let's have it, let's have it. Begin now,

'There were more'n a hundred pieces, and every one of 'em gold.' Oh, *you* know; come on, come on."

"I don't remember nothing of the kind," protested Maria, reaching for the bottle. Zerkow snatched it from her.

"You fool!" he wheezed, trying to raise his broken voice to a shout. "You fool! Don't you dare try an' cheat *me*, or I'll *do* for you. You know about the gold plate, and you know where it is." Suddenly he pitched his voice at the prolonged rasping shout with which he made his street cry. He rose to his feet, his long, prehensile fingers curled into fists. He was menacing, terrible in his rage. He leaned over Maria, his fists in her face.

"I believe you've got it!" he yelled. "I believe you've got it, an' are hiding it from me. Where is it, where is it? Is it here?" he rolled his eyes wildly about the room. "Hey? hey?" he went on, shaking Maria by the shoulders. "Where is it? Is it here? Tell me where it is. Tell me, or I'll do for you!"

"It ain't here," cried Maria, wrenching from him. "It ain't anywhere. What gold plate? What are you talking about? I don't remember nothing about no gold plate at all."

No, Maria did not remember. The trouble and turmoil of her mind consequent upon the birth of her child seemed to have readjusted her disordered ideas upon this point. Her mania had come to a crisis, which in subsiding had cleared her brain of its one illusion. She did not remember. Or it was possible that the gold plate she had once remembered had had some foundation in fact, that her recital of its splendors had been truth, sound and sane. It was possible that now her *forgetfulness* of it was some form of brain trouble, a relic of the dementia of childbirth. At all events Maria did not remember; the idea of the gold plate had passed entirely out of her mind, and it was now Zerkow who labored under its hallucination. It was now Zerkow, the raker of the city's muck heap, the searcher after gold, that saw that wonderful service in the eye of his perverted mind. It was he who could now describe it in a language almost eloquent. Maria had been content merely to remember it; but Zerkow's avarice goaded him to a belief that it was still in existence, hid somewhere, perhaps in that very house, stowed away there by Maria. For it stood to reason, didn't it, that Maria could not have described it with such wonderful accuracy and such careful detail unless she had seen it recently—the day before, perhaps, or that very day, or that very hour, that *very hour?*

"Look out for yourself," he whispered, hoarsely, to his wife. "Look out for yourself, my girl. I'll hunt for it, and hunt for it, and hunt for it, and some day I'll find it—*I* will, you'll see—I'll find it, I'll find it; and if I don't, I'll find a way that'll make you tell me

where it is. I'll make you speak—believe me, I will, I will, my girl
—trust me for that."

And at night Maria would sometimes wake to find Zerkow gone
from the bed, and would see him burrowing into some corner by
the light of his dark-lantern and would hear him mumbling to himself: "There were more'n a hundred pieces, and every one of 'em
gold—when the leather trunk was opened it fair dazzled your eyes
—why, just that punch-bowl was worth a fortune, I guess; solid,
solid, heavy, rich, pure gold, nothun but gold, gold, heaps and
heaps of it—what a glory! I'll find it yet, I'll find it. It's here somewheres, hid somewheres in this house."

At length his continued ill success began to exasperate him. One
day he took his whip from his junk wagon and thrashed Maria with
it, gasping the while, "Where is it, you beast? Where is it? Tell me
where it is; I'll make you speak."

"I don' know, I don' know," cried Maria, dodging his blows.
"I'd tell you, Zerkow, if I knew; but I don' know nothing about it.
How can I tell you if I don' know?"

Then one evening matters reached a crisis. Marcus Schouler was
in his room, the room in the flat just over McTeague's "Parlors"
which he had always occupied. It was between eleven and twelve
o'clock. The vast house was quiet; Polk Street outside was very still,
except for the occasional whirr and trundle of a passing cable car
and the persistent calling of ducks and geese in the deserted market
directly opposite. Marcus was in his shirt sleeves, perspiring and
swearing with exertion as he tried to get all his belongings into an
absurdly inadequate trunk. The room was in great confusion. It
looked as though Marcus was about to move. He stood in front of
his trunk, his precious silk hat in its hat-box in his hand. He was
raging at the perverseness of a pair of boots that refused to fit in his
trunk, no matter how he arranged them.

"I've tried you *so*, and I've tried you *so*," he exclaimed fiercely,
between his teeth, "and you won't go." He began to swear horribly,
grabbing at the boots with his free hand. "Pretty soon I won't take
you at all; I won't, for a fact."

He was interrupted by a rush of feet upon the back stairs and a
clamorous pounding upon his door. He opened it to let in Maria
Macapa, her hair dishevelled and her eyes starting with terror.

"Oh, *Mister* Schouler," she gasped, "lock the door quick. Don't
let him get me. He's got a knife, and he says sure he's going to do
for me, if I don't tell him where it is."

"Who has? What has? Where is what?" shouted Marcus,
flaming with excitement upon the instant. He opened the door and
peered down the dark hall, both fists clenched, ready to fight—he
did not know whom, and he did not know why.

"It's Zerkow," wailed Maria, pulling him back into the room and bolting the door, "and he's got a knife as long as *that*. Oh, my Lord, here he comes now! Ain't that him? Listen."

Zerkow was coming up the stairs, calling for Maria.

"Don't you let him get me, will you, Mister Schouler?" gasped Maria.

"I'll break him in two," shouted Marcus, livid with rage. "Think I'm afraid of his knife?"

"I know where you are," cried Zerkow, on the landing outside. "You're in Schouler's room. What are you doing in Schouler's room at this time of night? Come outa there; you oughta be ashamed. I'll do for you yet, my girl. Come outa there once, an' see if I don't."

"I'll do for you myself, you dirty Jew," shouted Marcus, unbolting the door and running out into the hall.

"I want my wife," exclaimed the Jew, backing down the stairs. "What's she mean by running away from me and going into your room?"

"Look out, he's got a knife!" cried Maria through the crack of the door.

"Ah, there you are. Come outa that, and come back home," exclaimed Zerkow.

"Get outa here yourself," cried Marcus, advancing on him angrily. "Get outa here."

"Maria's gota come too."

"Get outa here," vociferated Marcus, "an' put up that knife. I see it; you needn't try an' hide it behind your leg. Give it to me, anyhow," he shouted suddenly, and before Zerkow was aware, Marcus had wrenched it away. "Now, get outa here."

Zerkow backed away, peering and peeping over Marcus's shoulder.

"I want Maria."

"Get outa here. Get along out, or I'll *put* you out." The street door closed. The Jew was gone.

"Huh!" snorted Marcus, swelling with arrogance. "Huh! Think I'm afraid of his knife? I ain't afraid of *anybody*," he shouted pointedly, for McTeague and his wife, roused by the clamor, were peering over the banisters from the landing above. "Not of anybody," repeated Marcus.

Maria came out into the hall.

"Is he gone? Is he sure gone?"

"What was the trouble?" inquired Marcus, suddenly.

"I woke up about an hour ago," Maria explained, "and Zerkow wasn't in bed; maybe he hadn't come to bed at all. He was down on his knees by the sink, and he'd pried up some boards off the floor and was digging there. He had his dark-lantern. He was digging with that knife, I guess, and all the time he kept mumbling to himself, 'More'n a hundred pieces, an' every one of 'em gold; more'n a hundred pieces, an' every one of 'em gold.' Then, all of a sudden, he caught sight of me. I was sitting up in bed, and he jumped up and came at me with his knife, an' he says, 'Where is it? Where is it? I know you got it hid somewheres. Where is it? Tell me or I'll knife you.' I kind of fooled him and kept him off till I got my wrapper on, an' then I run out. I didn't dare stay."

"Well, what did you tell him about your gold dishes for in the first place?" cried Marcus.

"I never told him," protested Maria, with the greatest energy. "I never told him; I never heard of any gold dishes. I don' know where he got the idea; he must be crazy."

By this time Trina and McTeague, Old Grannis, and little Miss Baker—all the lodgers on the upper floors of the flat—had gathered about Maria. Trina and the dentist, who had gone to bed, were partially dressed, and Trina's enormous mane of black hair was hanging in two thick braids far down her back. But, late as it was, Old Grannis and the retired dressmaker had still been up and about when Maria had aroused them.

"Why, Maria," said Trina, "you always used to tell us about your gold dishes. You said your folks used to have them."

"Never, never, never!" exclaimed Maria, vehemently. "You folks must all be crazy. I never *heard* of any gold dishes."

"Well," spoke up Miss Baker, "you're a queer girl, Maria; that's all I can say." She left the group and returned to her room. Old Grannis watched her go from the corner of his eye, and in a few moments followed her, leaving the group as unnoticed as he had joined it. By degrees the flat quieted down again. Trina and McTeague returned to their rooms.

"I guess I'll go back now," said Maria. "He's all right now. I ain't afraid of him so long as he ain't got his knife."

"Well, say," Marcus called to her as she went down stairs, "if he gets funny again, you just yell out; *I'll* hear you. *I* won't let him hurt you."

Marcus went into his room again and resumed his wrangle with the refractory boots. His eye fell on Zerkow's knife, a long, keen-bladed hunting-knife, with a buckhorn handle. "I'll take you along with me," he exclaimed, suddenly. "I'll just need you where I'm going."

Meanwhile, óld Miss Baker was making tea to calm her nerves after the excitement of Maria's incursion. This evening she went so far as to make tea for two, laying an extra place on the other side of her little tea-table, setting out a cup and saucer and one of the

Gorham silver spoons. Close upon the other side of the partition Old Grannis bound uncut numbers of the "Nation."

"Do you know what I think, Mac?" said Trina, when the couple had returned to their rooms. "I think Marcus is going away."

"What? What?" muttered the dentist, very sleepy and stupid, "what you saying? What's that about Marcus?"

"I believe Marcus has been packing up, the last two or three days. I wonder if he's going away."

"Who's going away?" said McTeague, blinking at her.

"Oh, go to bed," said Trina, pushing him good-naturedly. "Mac, you're the stupidest man I ever knew."

But it was true. Marcus was going away. Trina received a letter the next morning from her mother. The carpet-cleaning and upholstery business in which Mr. Sieppe had involved himself was going from bad to worse. Mr. Sieppe had even been obliged to put a mortgage upon their house. Mrs. Sieppe didn't know what was to become of them all. Her husband had even begun to talk of emigrating to New Zealand. Meanwhile, she informed Trina that Mr. Sieppe had finally come across a man with whom Marcus could "go in with on a ranch," a cattle ranch in the southeastern portion of the State. Her ideas were vague upon the subject, but she knew that Marcus was wildly enthusiastic at the prospect, and was expected down before the end of the month. In the meantime, could Trina send them fifty dollars?

"Marcus *is* going away, after all, Mac," said Trina to her husband that day as he came out of his "Parlors" and sat down to the lunch of sausages, mashed potatoes, and chocolate in the sitting-room.

"Huh?" said the dentist, a little confused. "Who's going away? Schouler going away? Why's Schouler going away?"

Trina explained. "Oh!" growled McTeague, behind his thick mustache, "he can go far before *I'll* stop him."

"And, say, Mac," continued Trina, pouring the chocolate, "what do you think? Mamma wants me—wants us to send her fifty dollars. She says they're hard up."

"Well," said the dentist, after a moment, "well, I guess we can send it, can't we?"

"Oh, that's easy to say," complained Trina, her little chin in the air, her small pale lips pursed. "I wonder if mamma thinks we're millionaires?"

"Trina, you're getting to be regular stingy," muttered McTeague. "You're getting worse and worse every day."

"But fifty dollars is fifty dollars, Mac. Just think how long it takes you to earn fifty dollars. Fifty dollars! That's two months of our interest."

"Well," said McTeague, easily, his mouth full of mashed potato, "you got a lot saved up."

Upon every reference to that little hoard in the brass match-safe and chamois-skin bag at the bottom of her trunk, Trina bridled on the instant.

"Don't *talk* that way, Mac. 'A lot of money.' What do you call a lot of money? I don't believe I've got fifty dollars saved."

"Hoh!" exclaimed McTeague. "Hoh! I guess you got nearer a hundred *an'* fifty. That's what I guess *you* got."

"I've *not*, I've *not*," declared Trina, "and you know I've not. I wish mamma hadn't asked me for any money. Why can't she be a little more economical? *I* manage all right. No, no, I can't possibly afford to send her fifty."

"Oh, pshaw! What *will* you do, then?" grumbled her husband.

"I'll send her twenty-five this month, and tell her I'll send the rest as soon as I can afford it."

"Trina, you're a regular little miser," said McTeague.

"I don't care," answered Trina, beginning to laugh. "I guess I am, but I can't help it, and it's a good fault."

Trina put off sending this money for a couple of weeks, and her mother made no mention of it in her next letter. "Oh, I guess if she wants it so bad," said Trina, "she'll speak about it again." So she again postponed the sending of it. Day by day she put it off. When her mother asked her for it a second time, it seemed harder than ever for Trina to part with even half the sum requested. She answered her mother, telling her that they were very hard up themselves for that month, but that she would send down the amount in a few weeks.

"I'll tell you what we'll do, Mac," she said to her husband, "you send half and I'll send half; we'll send twenty-five dollars altogether. Twelve and a half apiece. That's an idea. How will that do?"

"Sure, sure," McTeague had answered, giving her the money. Trina sent McTeague's twelve dollars, but never sent the twelve that was to be her share. One day the dentist happened to ask her about it.

"You sent that twenty-five to your mother, didn't you?" said he.

"Oh, long ago," answered Trina, without thinking.

In fact, Trina never allowed herself to think very much of this affair. And, in fact, another matter soon came to engross her attention.

One Sunday evening Trina and her husband were in their sitting-room together. It was dark, but the lamp had not been lit. McTeague had brought up some bottles of beer from the "Wein Stube" on the ground floor, where the branch post-office used to be. But they had not opened the beer. It was a warm evening in summer. Trina was sitting on McTeague's lap in the bay window, and had looped back the Nottingham curtains so the two could look out into the darkened street and watch the moon coming up over the glass roof of the huge public baths. On occasions they sat like this for an hour or so, "philandering," Trina cuddling herself down upon McTeague's enormous body, rubbing her cheek against the grain of his unshaven chin, kissing the bald spot on the top of his head, or putting her fingers into his ears and eyes. At times, a brusque access of passion would seize upon her, and, with a nervous little sigh, she would clasp his thick red neck in both her small arms and whisper in his ear:

"Do you love me, Mac, dear? love me *big, big?* Sure, do you love me as much as you did when we were married?"

Puzzled, McTeague would answer; "Well, you know it, don't you, Trina?"

"But I want you to *say* so; say so always and always."

"Well, I do, of course I do."

"Say it, then."

"Well, then, I love you."

"But you don't say it of your own accord."

"Well, what—what—what—I don't understand," stammered the dentist, bewildered.

There was a knock on the door. Confused and embarrassed, as if they were not married, Trina scrambled off McTeague's lap, hastening to light the lamp, whispering, "Put on your coat, Mac, and smooth your hair," and making gestures for him to put the beer bottles out of sight. She opened the door and uttered an exclamation.

"Why, Cousin Mark!" she said. McTeague glared at him, struck speechless, confused beyond expression. Marcus Schouler, perfectly at his ease, stood in the doorway, smiling with great affability.

"Say," he remarked, "can I come in?"

Taken all aback, Trina could only answer:

"Why—I suppose so. Yes, of course—come in."

"Yes, yes, come in," exclaimed the dentist, suddenly, speaking without thought. "Have some beer?" he added, struck with an idea.

"No, thanks, Doctor," said Marcus, pleasantly.

McTeague and Trina were puzzled. What could it all mean? Did Marcus want to become reconciled to his enemy? "I know." Trina said to herself. "He's going away, and he wants to borrow some money. He won't get a penny, not a penny." She set her teeth together hard.

"Well," said Marcus, "how's business, Doctor?"

"Oh," said McTeague, uneasily, "oh, I don' know. I guess—I guess," he broke off in helpless embarrassment. They had all sat down by now. Marcus continued, holding his hat and his cane—the black wand of ebony with the gold top presented to him by the "Improvement Club."

"Ah!" said he, wagging his head and looking about the sitting-room, "you people have got the best fixed rooms in the whole flat. Yes, sir; you have, for a fact." He glanced from the lithograph framed in gilt and red plush—the two little girls at their prayers— to the "I'm Grandpa" and "I'm Grandma" pictures, noted the clean white matting and the gay worsted tidies over the chair backs, and appeared to contemplate in ecstasy the framed photograph of McTeague and Trina in their wedding finery.

"Well, you two are pretty happy together, ain't you?" said he, smiling good-humoredly.

"Oh, we don't complain," answered Trina.

"Plenty of money, lots to do, everything fine, hey?"

"We've got lots to do," returned Trina, thinking to head him off, "but we've not got lots of money."

But evidently Marcus wanted no money.

"Well, Cousin Trina," he said, rubbing his knee, "I'm going away."

"Yes, mamma wrote me; you're going on a ranch."

"I'm going in ranching with an English duck," corrected Marcus. "Mr. Sieppe has fixed things. We'll see if we can't raise some cattle. I know a lot about horses, and he's ranched some before—this English duck. And then I'm going to keep my eye open for a political chance down there. I got some introductions from the President of the Improvement Club. I'll work things somehow, oh, sure."

"How long you going to be gone?" asked Trina.

Marcus stared.

"Why, I ain't ever coming back," he vociferated. "I'm going to-morrow, and I'm going for good. I come to say good-by."

Marcus stayed for upwards of an hour that evening. He talked on easily and agreeably, addressing himself as much to McTeague as to Trina. At last he rose.

"Well, good-by, Doc."

"Good-by, Marcus," returned McTeague. The two shook hands.

"Guess we won't ever see each other again," continued Marcus. "But good luck to you, Doc. Hope some day you'll have the patients standing in line on the stairs."

"Huh! I guess so, I guess so," said the dentist.

"Good-by, Cousin Trina."

"Good-by, Marcus," answered Trina. "You be sure to remember me to mamma, and papa, and everybody. I'm going to make two great big sets of Noah's ark animals for the twins on their next birthday; August is too old for toys. But you tell the twins that I'll make them some great big animals. Good-by, success to you, Marcus."

"Good-by, good-by. Good luck to you both."

"Good-by, Cousin Mark."

"Good-by, Marcus."

He was gone.

XIII

One morning about a week after Marcus had left for the southern part of the State, McTeague found an oblong letter thrust through the letter-drop of the door of his "Parlors." The address was typewritten. He opened it. The letter had been sent from the City Hall and was stamped in one corner with the seal of the State of California, very official; the form and file numbers superscribed.

McTeague had been making fillings when this letter arrived. He was in his "Parlors," pottering over his movable rack underneath the bird cage in the bay window. He was making "blocks" to be used in large proximal cavities and "cylinders" for commencing fillings. He heard the postman's step in the hall and saw the envelopes begin to shuttle themselves through the slit of his letter-drop. Then came the fat oblong envelope, with its official seal, that dropped flat-wise to the floor with a sodden, dull impact.

The dentist put down the broach and scissors and gathered up his mail. There were four letters altogether. One was for Trina, in Selina's "elegant" handwriting; another was an advertisement of a new kind of operating chair for dentists; the third was a card from a milliner on the next block, announcing an opening; and the fourth, contained in the fat oblong envelope, was a printed form with blanks left for names and dates, and addressed to McTeague, from an office in the City Hall. McTeague read it through laboriously. "I don' know, I don' know," he muttered, looking stupidly at the rifle manufacturer's calendar. Then he heard Trina, from the kitchen, singing as she made a clattering noise with the breakfast dishes. "I guess I'll ask Trina about it," he muttered.

He went through the suite, by the sitting-room, where the sun was pouring in through the looped backed Nottingham curtains upon the clean white matting and the varnished surface of the melodeon, passed on through the bedroom, with its framed lithographs of round-cheeked English babies and alert fox terriers, and came out into the brick-paved kitchen. The kitchen was clean as a new whistle; the freshly blackened cook stove glowed like a negro's hide; the tins and porcelain-lined stewpans might have been of silver and of ivory. Trina was in the centre of the room, wiping off, with a damp sponge, the oilcloth table-cover, on which they had breakfasted.

Never had she looked so pretty. Early though it was, her enormous tiara of swarthy hair was neatly combed and coiled, not a pin was so much as loose. She wore a blue calico skirt with a white figure, and a belt of imitation alligator skin clasped around her small, firmly-corseted waist; her shirt waist was of pink linen, so new and crisp that it crackled with every movement, while around the collar, tied in a neat knot, was one of McTeague's lawn ties which she had appropriated. Her sleeves were carefully rolled up almost to her shoulders, and nothing could have been more delicious than the sight of her small round arms, white as milk, moving back and forth as she sponged the table-cover, a faint touch of pink coming and going at the elbows as they bent and straightened. She looked up quickly as her husband entered, her narrow eyes alight, her adorable little chin in the air; her lips rounded and opened with the last words of her song, so that one could catch a glint of gold in the fillings of her upper teeth.

The whole scene—the clean kitchen and its clean brick floor; the smell of coffee that lingered in the air; Trina herself, fresh as if from a bath, and singing at her work; the morning sun, striking obliquely through the white muslin half-curtain of the window and spanning the little kitchen with a bridge of golden mist—gave off, as it were, a note of gayety that was not to be resisted. Through the opened top of the window came the noises of Polk Street, already long awake. One heard the chanting of street cries, the shrill calling of children on their way to school, the merry rattle of a butcher's cart, the brisk noise of hammering, or the occasional prolonged roll of a cable car trundling heavily past, with a vibrant whirring of its jostled glass and the joyous clanging of its bells.

"What is it, Mac, dear?" said Trina.

McTeague shut the door behind him with his heel and handed her the letter. Trina read it through. Then suddenly her small hand gripped tightly upon the sponge, so that the water started from it and dripped in a little pattering deluge upon the bricks.

The letter—or rather printed notice—informed McTeague that he had never received a diploma from a dental college, and that in consequence he was forbidden to practise his profession any longer. A legal extract bearing upon the case was attached in small type.

"Why, what's all this?" said Trina, calmly, without thought as yet.

"I don' know, *I* don' know," answered her husband.

"You can't practise any longer," continued Trina,—" 'is herewith prohibited and enjoined from further continuing——' " She re-read the extract, her forehead lifting and puckering. She put the sponge carefully away in its wire rack over the sink, and drew up a chair to the table, spreading out the notice before her. "Sit down," she said to McTeague. "Draw up to the table here, Mac, and let's see what this is."

"I got it this morning," murmured the dentist. "It just now came. I was making some fillings—there, in the 'Parlors,' in the window—and the postman shoved it through the door. I thought it was a number of the 'American System of Dentistry' at first, and when I'd opened it and looked at it I thought I'd better——"

"Say, Mac," interrupted Trina, looking up from the notice, "*didn't* you ever go to a dental college?"

"Huh? What? What?" exclaimed McTeague.

"How did you learn to be a dentist? Did you go to a college?"

"I went along with a fellow who came to the mine once. My mother sent me. We used to go from one camp to another. I sharp-ened his excavators for him, and put up his notices in the towns—stuck them up in the post-offices and on the doors of the Odd Fel-lows' halls. He had a wagon."

"But didn't you never go to a college?"

"Huh? What? College? No, I never went, learned from the fellow."

Trina rolled down her sleeves. She was a little paler than usual. She fastened the buttons into the cuffs and said:

"But do you know you can't practise unless you're graduated from a college? You haven't the right to call yourself, 'doctor.'"

McTeague stared a moment; then:

"Why, I've been practising ten years. More—nearly twelve."

"But it's the law."

"What's the law?"

"That you can't practise, or call yourself doctor, unless you've got a diploma."

"What's that—a diploma?"

"I don't know exactly. It's a kind of paper that—that—oh, Mac, we're ruined." Trina's voice rose to a cry.

"What do you mean, Trina? Ain't I a dentist? Ain't I a doctor? Look at my sign, and the gold tooth you gave me. Why, I've been practising nearly twelve years."

Trina shut her lips tightly, cleared her throat, and pretended to resettle a hair-pin at the back of her head.

"I guess it isn't as bad as that," she said, very quietly. "Let's read this again. 'Herewith prohibited and enjoined from further continuing——'" She read to the end.

"Why, it isn't possible," she cried. "They can't mean—oh, Mac, I do believe—phsaw!" she exclaimed, her pale face flushing. "They don't know how good a dentist you are. What difference does a diploma make, if you're a first-class dentist? I guess that's all right. Mac, didn't you ever go to a dental college?"

"No," answered McTeague, doggedly. "What was the good? I learned how to operate; wa'n't that enough?"

"Hark," said Trina, suddenly. "Wasn't that the bell of your office?" They had both heard the jangling of the bell that McTeague had hung over the door of his "Parlors." The dentist looked at the kitchen clock.

"That's Vanovitch," said he. "He's a plumber round on Sutter Street. He's got an appointment with me to have a bicuspid pulled. I got to go back to work." He rose.

"But you can't" cried Trina, the back of her hand upon her lips, her eyes brimming. "Mac, don't you see? Can't you understand? You've got to stop. Oh, it's dreadful! Listen." She hurried around the table to him and caught his arm in both her hands.

"Huh?" growled McTeague, looking at her with a puzzled frown.

"They'll arrest you. You'll go to prison. You can't work—can't work any more. We're ruined."

Vanovitch was pounding on the door of the sitting-room.

"He'll be gone in a minute," exclaimed McTeague.

"Well, let him go. Tell him to go; tell him to come again."

"Why, he's got an *appointment* with me," exclaimed McTeague, his hand upon the door.

Trina caught him back. "But, Mac, you ain't a dentist any longer; you ain't a doctor. You haven't the right to work. You never went to a dental college."

"Well, suppose I never went to a college, ain't I a dentist just the same? Listen, he's pounding there again. No, I'm going, sure."

"Well, of course, go," said Trina, with sudden reaction. "It ain't possible they'll make you stop. If you're a good dentist, that's all that's wanted. Go on, Mac; hurry, before he goes."

McTeague went out, closing the door. Trina stood for a moment looking intently at the bricks at her feet. Then she returned to the table, and sat down again before the notice, and, resting her head in both her fists, read it yet another time. Suddenly the conviction seized upon her that it was all true. McTeague would be obliged to stop work, no matter how good a dentist he was. But why had the authorities at the City Hall waited this long before serving the notice? All at once Trina snapped her fingers, with a quick flash of intelligence.

"It's Marcus that's done it," she cried.

.   .   .   .

It was like a clap of thunder. McTeague was stunned, stupefied. He said nothing. Never in his life had he been so taciturn. At times he did not seem to hear Trina when she spoke to him, and often she had to shake him by the shoulder to arouse his attention. He would sit apart in his "Parlors," turning the notice about in his enormous clumsy fingers, reading it stupidly over and over again. He couldn't understand. What had a clerk at the City Hall to do with him? Why couldn't they let him alone?

"Oh, what's to become of us *now*?" wailed Trina. "What's to become of us now?" We're paupers, beggars—and all so sudden." And once, in a quick, inexplicable fury, totally unlike anything that McTeague had noticed in her before, she had started up, with fists and teeth shut tight, and had cried, "Oh, if you'd only *killed* Marcus Schouler that time he fought you!"

McTeague had continued his work, acting from sheer force of habit; his sluggish, deliberate nature, methodical, obstinate, refusing to adapt itself to the new conditions.

"Maybe Marcus was only trying to scare us," Trina had said. "How are they going to know whether you're practising or not?"

"I got a mould to make to-morrow," McTeague said, "and Vanovitch, that plumber round on Sutter Street, he's coming again at three."

"Well, you go right ahead," Trina told him, decisively; "you go right ahead and make the mould, and pull every tooth in Vanovitch's head if you want to. Who's going to know? Maybe they just sent that notice as a matter of form. Maybe Marcus got that paper and filled it in himself."

The two would lie awake all night long, staring up into the dark, talking, talking, talking.

"Haven't you got any right to practise if you've not been to a dental college, Mac? Didn't you ever go?" Trina would ask again and again.

"No, no," answered the dentist, "I never went. I learnt from the fellow I was apprenticed to. I don' know anything about a dental college. Ain't I got a right to do as I like?" he suddenly exclaimed.

"If you know your profession, isn't that enough?" cried Trina.

"Sure, sure," growled McTeague. "I ain't going to stop for them."

"You go right on," Trina said, "and I bet you won't hear another word about it.'

"Suppose I go round to the City Hall and see them," hazarded McTeague.

"No, no, don't you do it, Mac," exclaimed Trina. "Because, if Marcus has done this just to scare you, they won't know anything about it there at the City Hall; but they'll begin to ask you questions, and find out that you never *had* graduated from a dental college, and you'd be just as bad off as ever."

"Well, I ain't going to quit for just a piece of paper," declared the dentist. The phrase stuck to him. All day long he went about their rooms or continued at his work in the "Parlors," growling behind his thick mustache: "I ain't going to quit for just a piece of paper. No, I ain't going to quit for just a piece of paper. Sure not."

The days passed, a week went by, McTeague continued his work as usual. They heard no more from the City Hall, but the suspense of the situation was harrowing. Trina was actually sick with it. The terror of the thing was ever at their elbows, going to bed with them, sitting down with them at breakfast in the kitchen, keeping them company all through the day. Trina dared not think of what would be their fate if the income derived from McTeague's practice was suddenly taken from them. Then they would have to fall back on the interest of her lottery money and the pittance she derived from the manufacture of the Noah's ark animals, a little over thirty dollars a month. No, no, it was not to be thought of. It could not be that their means of livelihood was to be thus stricken from them.

A fortnight went by. "I guess we're all right, Mac," Trina allowed herself to say. "It looks as though we were all right. How *are* they going to tell whether you're practising or not?"

That day a second and much more peremptory notice was served upon McTeague by an official in person. Then suddenly Trina was seized with a panic terror, unreasoned, instinctive. If McTeague persisted they would both be sent to a prison, she was sure of it; a place where people were chained to the wall, in the dark, and fed on bread and water.

"Oh, Mac, you've got to quit," she wailed. "You can't go on. They can make you stop. Oh, why didn't you go to a dental college? Why didn't you find out that you had to have a college degree? And now we're paupers, beggars. We've got to leave here— leave this flat where I've been—where *we've* been so happy, and sell all the pretty things; sell the pictures and the melodeon, and—Oh, it's too dreadful!"

"Huh? Huh? What? What?" exclaimed the dentist, bewildered. "I ain't going to quit for just a piece of paper. Let them put me out. I'll show them. They—they can't make small of me."

"Oh, that's all very fine to talk that way, but you'll have to quit."

"Well, we ain't paupers," McTeague suddenly exclaimed, an idea entering his mind. "We've got our money yet. You've got your five thousand dollars and the money you've been saving up. People ain't paupers when they've got over five thousand dollars."

"What do you mean, Mac?" cried Trina, apprehensively.

"Well, we can live on *that* money until—until—until—" he broke off with an uncertain movement of his shoulders, looking about him stupidly.

"Until *when*?" cried Trina. "There ain't ever going to be any '*until*.' We've got the *interest* of that five thousand and we've got what Uncle Oelbermann gives me, a little over thirty dollars a month, and that's all we've got. You'll have to find something else to do."

"What will I find to do?"

What, indeed? McTeague was over thirty now, sluggish and slow-witted at best. What new trade could he learn at this age?

Little by little Trina made the dentist understand the calamity that had befallen them, and McTeague at last began cancelling his appointments. Trina gave it out that he was sick.

"Not a soul need know what's happened to us," she said to her husband.

But it was only by slow degrees that McTeague abandoned his profession. Every morning after breakfast he would go into his "Parlors" as usual and potter about his instruments, his dental engine, and his washstand in the corner behind his screen where he made his moulds. Now he would sharpen a "hoe" excavator, now he would busy himself for a whole hour making "mats" and "cylinders." Then he would look over his slate where he kept a record of his appointments.

One day Trina softly opened the door of the "Parlors" and came in from the sitting-room. She had not heard McTeague moving about for some time and had begun to wonder what he was doing. She came in, quietly shutting the door behind her.

McTeague had tidied the room with the greatest care. The volumes of the "Practical Dentist" and the "American System of Dentistry" were piled upon the marble-top centre-table in rectangular blocks. The few chairs were drawn up against the wall under the steel engraving of "Lorenzo de' Medici" with more than usual precision. The dental engine and the nickelled trimmings of the operating chair had been furbished till they shone, while on the movable rack in the bay window, McTeague had arranged his instruments with the greatest neatness and regularity. "Hoe" excavators, pluggers, forceps, pliers, corundum disks and burrs, even the boxwood mallet that Trina was never to use again, all were laid out and ready for immediate use.

McTeague himself sat in his operating chair, looking stupidly out of the windows, across the roofs opposite, with an unseeing gaze, his red hands lying idly in his lap. Trina came up to him. There was something in his eyes that made her put both arms around his neck and lay his huge head with its coarse blond hair upon her shoulder.

"I—I got everything fixed," he said. "I got everything fixed an' ready. See, everything ready an' waiting, an'—an'—an' nobody comes, an' nobody's ever going to come any more. Oh, Trina!" He put his arms about her and drew her down closer to him.

"Never mind, dear; never mind," cried Trina, through her tears.

"It'll all come right in the end, and we'll be poor together if we have to. You can sure find something else to do. We'll start in again."

"Look at the slate there," said McTeague, pulling away from her and reaching down the slate on which he kept a record of his appointments. "Look at them. There's Vanovitch at two on Wednesday, and Loughhead's wife Thursday morning, and Heise's little girl Thursday afternoon at one-thirty; Mrs. Watson on Friday, and Vanovitch again Saturday morning early—at seven. That's what I was to have had, and they ain't going to come. They ain't ever going to come any more."

Trina took the little slate from him and looked at it ruefully.

"Rub them out," she said, her voice trembling; "rub it all out;" and as she spoke her eyes brimmed again, and a great tear dropped on the slate. "That's it," she said; "that's the way to rub it out, by me crying on it." Then she passed her fingers over the tear-blurred writing and washed the slate clean. "All gone, all gone," she said.

"All gone," echoed the dentist. There was a silence. Then McTeague heaved himself up to his full six feet two, his face purpling, his enormous mallet-like fists raised over his head. His massive jaw protruded more than ever, while his teeth clicked and grated together; then he growled:

"If ever I meet Marcus Schouler—" he broke off abruptly, the white of his eyes growing suddenly pink.

"Oh, if ever you *do*," exclaimed Trina, catching her breath.

XIV

"Well, what do you think?" said Trina.

She and McTeague stood in a tiny room at the back of the flat and on its very top floor. The room was whitewashed. It contained a bed, three cane-seated chairs, and a wooden washstand with its washbowl and pitcher. From its single uncurtained window one looked down into the flat's dirty back yard and upon the roofs of the hovels that bordered the alley in the rear. There was a rag carpet on the floor. In place of a closet some dozen wooden pegs were affixed to the wall over the washstand. There was a smell of cheap soap and of ancient hair-oil in the air.

"That's a single bed," said Trina, "but the landlady says she'll put in a double one for us. You see——"

"I ain't going to live here," growled McTeague.

"Well, you've got to live somewhere," said Trina, impatiently. "We've looked Polk Street over, and this is the only thing we can afford."

"Afford, afford," muttered the dentist. "You with your five thousand dollars, and the two or three hundred you got saved up, talking about 'afford.' You make me sick."

"Now, Mac," exclaimed Trina, deliberately, sitting down in one of the cane-seated chairs; "now, Mac, let's have this thing——"

"Well, I don't figure on living in one room," growled the dentist, sullenly. "Let's live decently until we can get a fresh start. We've got the money."

"Who's got the money?"

"*We've* got it."

"We!"

"Well, it's all in the family. What's yours is mine, and what's mine is yours, ain't it?"

"No, it's not; no, it's not; no, it's not," cried Trina, vehemently. "It's all mine, mine. There's not a penny of it belongs to anybody else. I don't like to have to talk this way to you, but you just make me. We're not going to touch a penny of my five thousand nor a penny of that little money I managed to save—that seventy-five."

"That *two hundred,* you mean."

"That *seventy-five.* We're just going to live on the interest of that and on what I earn from Uncle Oelbermann—on just that thirty-one or two dollars."

"Huh! Think I'm going to do that, an' live in such a room as this?"

Trina folded her arms and looked him squarely in the face. "Well, what *are* you going to do, then?"

"Huh?"

"I say, what *are* you going to do? You can go on and find something to do and earn some more money, and *then* we'll talk."

"Well, I ain't going to live here."

"Oh, very well, suit yourself. *I'm* going to live here."

"You'll live where I *tell* you," the dentist suddenly cried, exasperated at the mincing tone she affected.

"Then *you'll* pay the rent," exclaimed Trina, quite as angry as he.

"Are you my boss, I'd like to know? Who's the boss, you or I?"

"Who's got the *money,* I'd like to know?" cried Trina, flushing to her pale lips. "Answer me that, McTeague, who's got the money?"

"You make me sick, you and your money. Why, you're a miser. I never saw anything like it. When I was practising, I never thought of my fees as my own; we lumped everything in together."

"Exactly; and *I'm* doing the working now. I'm working for Uncle Oelbermann, and you're not lumping in *anything* now. I'm doing it all. Do you know what I'm doing, McTeague? I'm supporting you."

"Ah, shut up; you make me sick."

"You got no *right* to talk to me that way. I won't let you. I—I won't have it." She caught her breath. Tears were in her eyes.

"Oh, live where you like, then," said McTeague, sullenly.

"Well, shall we take this room then?"

"All right, we'll take it. But why can't you take a little of your money an'—an'—sort of fix it up?"

"Not a penny, not a single penny."

"Oh, I don't care *what* you do." And for the rest of the day the dentist and his wife did not speak.

This was not the only quarrel they had during these days when they were occupied in moving from their suite and in looking for new quarters. Every hour the question of money came up. Trina had become more niggardly than ever since the loss of McTeague's practice. It was not mere economy with her now. It was a panic terror lest a fraction of a cent of her little savings should be touched; a passionate eagerness to continue to save in spite of all that had happened. Trina could have easily afforded better quarters than the single whitewashed room at the top of the flat, but she made McTeague believe that it was impossible.

"I can still save a little," she said to herself, after the room had been engaged; "perhaps almost as much as ever. I'll have three hundred dollars pretty soon, and Mac thinks it's only two hundred. It's almost two hundred and fifty; and I'll get a good deal out of the sale."

But this sale was a long agony. It lasted a week. Everything went —everything but the few big pieces that went with the suite, and that belonged to the photographer. The melodeon, the chairs, the black walnut table before which they were married, the extension table in the sitting-room, the kitchen table with its oilcloth cover, the framed lithographs from the English illustrated papers, the very carpets on the floors. But Trina's heart nearly broke when the kitchen utensils and furnishings began to go. Every pot, every stewpan, every knife and fork, was an old friend. How she had worked over them! How clean she had kept them! What a pleasure it had been to invade that little brick-paved kitchen every morning, and to wash up and put to rights after breakfast, turning on the hot water at the sink, raking down the ashes in the cook-stove, going and coming over the warm bricks, her head in the air, singing at her work, proud in the sense of her proprietorship and her independence! How happy had she been the day after her marriage when she had first entered that kitchen and knew that it was all her own! And how well she remembered her raids upon the bargain counters in the house-furnishing departments of the great down-town stores! And now it was all to go. Some one else would have it all, while she was relegated to cheap restaurants and meals cooked by hired servants. Night after night she sobbed herself to sleep at the thought of her past happiness and her present wretchedness. However, she was not alone in her unhappiness.

"Anyhow, I'm going to keep the steel engraving an' the stone pug dog," declared the dentist, his fist clenching. When it had come to the sale of his office effects McTeague had rebelled with the instinctive obstinacy of a boy, shutting his eyes and ears. Only little by little did Trina induce him to part with his office furniture. He fought over every article, over the little iron stove, the bed-lounge, the marble-topped centre table, the whatnot in the corner, the bound volumes of "Allen's Practical Dentist," the rifle manufacturer's calendar, and the prim, military chairs. A veritable scene took place between him and his wife before he could bring himself to part with the steel engraving of "Lorenzo de' Medici and His Court" and the stone pug dog with its goggle eyes.

"Why," he would cry, "I've had 'em ever since—ever since I *began*; long before I knew you, Trina. That steel engraving I bought in Sacramento one day when it was raining. I saw it in the window of a second-hand store, and a fellow *gave* me that stone pug dog. He was a druggist. It was in Sacramento too. We traded. I gave him a shaving-mug and a razor, and he gave me the pug dog."

There were, however, two of his belongings that even Trina could not induce him to part with.

"And your concertina, Mac," she prompted, as they were making out the list for the second-hand dealer. "The concertina, and—oh, yes, the canary and the bird cage."

"No."

"Mac, you *must* be reasonable. The concertina would bring quite a sum, and the bird cage is as good as new. I'll sell the canary to the bird-store man on Kearney Street."

"No."

"If you're going to make objections to every single thing, we might as well quit. Come, now, Mac, the concertina and the bird cage. We'll put them in Lot D."

"No."

"You'll have to come to it sooner or later. *I'm* giving up everything. I'm going to put them down, see."

"No."

And she could get no further than that. The dentist did not lose his temper, as in the case of the steel engraving or the stone pug dog; he simply opposed her entreaties and persuasions with a passive, inert obstinacy that nothing could move. In the end Trina was obliged to submit. McTeague kept his concertina and his canary, even going so far as to put them both away in the bedroom, attaching to them tags on which he had scrawled in immense round letters, "Not for Sale."

One evening during that same week the dentist and his wife were in the dismantled sitting-room. The room presented the appearance of a wreck. The Nottingham lace curtains were down. The extension table was heaped high with dishes, with tea and coffee pots, and with baskets of spoons and knives and forks. The melodeon was hauled out into the middle of the floor, and covered with a sheet marked "Lot A," the pictures were in a pile in a corner, the chenille portières were folded on top of the black walnut table. The room was desolate, lamentable. Trina was going over the inventory; McTeague, in his shirt sleeves, was smoking his pipe, looking stupidly out of the window. All at once there was a brisk rapping at the door.

"Come in," called Trina, apprehensively. Now-a-days at every unexpected visit she anticipated a fresh calamity. The door opened to let in a young man wearing a checked suit, a gay cravat, and a marvellously figured waistcoat. Trina and McTeague recognized him at once. It was the Other Dentist, the debonair fellow whose clients were the barbers and the young women of the candy stores and soda-water fountains, the poser, the wearer of waistcoats, who bet money on greyhound races.

"How'do?" said this one, bowing gracefully to the McTeagues as they stared at him distrustfully. "How'do? They tell me, Doctor, that you are going out of the profession."

McTeague muttered indistinctly behind his mustache and glowered at him.

"Well, say," continued the other, cheerily, "I'd like to talk business with you. That sign of yours, that big golden tooth that you got outside of your window, I don't suppose you'll have any further use for it. Maybe I'd buy it if we could agree on terms."

Trina shot a glance at her husband. McTeague began to glower again.

"What do you say?" said the Other Dentist.

"I guess not," growled McTeague.

"What do you say to ten dollars?"

"Ten dollars!" cried Trina, her chin in the air.

"Well, what figure *do* you put on it?"

Trina was about to answer when she was interrupted by McTeague.

"You go out of here."

"Hey? What?"

"You go out of here."

The other retreated toward the door.

"You can't make small of me. Go out of here."

McTeague came forward a step, his great red fist clenching. The young man fled. But half way down the stairs he paused long enough to call back:

"You don't want to trade anything for a diploma, do you?"
McTeague and his wife exchanged looks.
"How did he know?" exclaimed Trina, sharply. They had invented and spread the fiction that McTeague was merely retiring from business, without assigning any reason. But evidently every one knew the real cause. The humiliation was complete now. Old Miss Baker confirmed their suspicions on this point the next day. The little retired dressmaker came down and wept with Trina over her misfortune, and did what she could to encourage her. But she too knew that McTeague had been forbidden by the authorities from practising. Marcus had evidently left them no loophole of escape.

"It's just like cutting off your husband's hands, my dear," said Miss Baker. "And you two were so happy. When I first saw you together I said, 'What a pair!' "

Old Grannis also called during this period of the breaking up of the McTeague household.

"Dreadful, dreadful," murmured the old Englishman, his hand going tremulously to his chin. "It seems unjust; it does. But Mr. Schouler could not have set them on to do it. I can't quite believe it of him."

"Of Marcus!" cried Trina. "Hoh! Why, he threw his knife at Mac one time, and another time he bit him, actually bit him with his teeth, while they were wrestling just for fun. Marcus would do anything to injure Mac."

"Dear, dear," returned Old Grannis, genuinely pained. "I had always believed Schouler to be such a good fellow."

"That's because you're so good yourself, Mr. Grannis," responded Trina.

"I tell you what, Doc," declared Heise the harness-maker, shaking his finger impressively at the dentist, "you must fight it; you must appeal to the courts; you've been practising too long to be debarred now. The statute of limitations, you know."

"No, no," Trina had exclaimed, when the dentist had repeated this advice to her. "No, no, don't go near the law courts. *I* know them. The lawyers take all your money, and you lose your case. We're bad off as it is, without lawing about it."

Then at last came the sale. McTeague and Trina, whom Miss Baker had invited to her room for that day, sat there side by side, holding each other's hands, listening nervously to the turmoil that rose to them from the direction of their suite. From nine o'clock till dark the crowds came and went. All Polk Street seemed to have invaded the suite, lured on by the red flag that waved from the front windows. It was a *fête*, a veritable holiday, for the whole

neighborhood. People with no thought of buying presented themselves. Young women—the candy-store girls and florist's apprentices
—came to see the fun, walking arm in arm from room to room,
making jokes about the pretty lithographs and mimicking the picture of the two little girls saying their prayers.

"Look here," they would cry, "look here what she used for curtains—*Nottingham lace,* actually! Whoever thinks of buying Nottingham's lace now-a-days? Say, don't that *jar* you?"

"And a melodeon," another one would exclaim, lifting the sheet.
"A melodeon, when you can rent a piano for a dollar a week; and
say, I really believe they used to eat in the kitchen."

"Dollarn-half, dollarn-half, dollarn-half, give me two," intoned
the auctioneer from the second-hand store. By noon the crowd
became a jam. Wagons backed up to the curb outside and departed
heavily laden. In all directions people could be seen going away
from the house, carrying small articles of furniture—a clock, a water
pitcher, a towel rack. Every now and then old Miss Baker, who had
gone below to see how things were progressing, returned with
reports of the foray.

"Mrs. Heise bought the chenille portières. Mister Ryer made a
bid for your bed, but a man in a gray coat bid over him. It was
knocked down for three dollars and a half. The German shoemaker
on the next block bought the stone pug dog. I saw our postman
going away with a lot of the pictures. Zerkow has come, on my
word! the rags-bottles-sacks man; he's buying lots; he bought all
Doctor McTeague's gold tape and some of the instruments. Maria's
there too. That dentist on the corner took the dental engine, and
wanted to get the sign, the big gold tooth," and so on and so on.
Cruelest of all, however, at least to Trina, was when Miss Baker
herself began to buy, unable to resist a bargain. The last time she
came up she carried a bundle of the gay tidies that used to hang
over the chair backs.

"He offered them, three for a nickel," she explained to Trina,
"and I thought I'd spend just a quarter. You don't mind, now, do
you, Mrs. McTeague?"

"Why, no, of course not, Miss Baker," answered Trina, bravely.

"They'll look very pretty on some of my chairs," went on the
little old dressmaker, innocently. "See," she spread one of them on
a chair back for inspection. Trina's chin quivered.

"Oh, *very* pretty," she answered.

At length that dreadful day was over. The crowd dispersed. Even
the auctioneer went at last, and as he closed the door with a bang,
the reverberation that went through the suite gave evidence of its
emptiness.

"Come," said Trina to the dentist, "let's go down and look—take a last look."

They went out of Miss Baker's room and descended to the floor below. On the stairs, however, they were met by Old Grannis. In his hands he carried a little package. Was it possible that he too had taken advantage of their misfortunes to join in the raid upon the suite?

"I went in," he began, timidly, "for—for a few moments. This" —he indicated the little package he carried—"this was put up. It was of no value but to you. I—I ventured to bid it in. I thought perhaps"—his hand went to his chin, "that you wouldn't mind; that—in fact, I bought it for you—as a present. Will you take it?" He handed the package to Trina and hurried on. Trina tore off the wrappings.

It was the framed photograph of McTeague and his wife in their wedding finery, the one that had been taken immediately after the marriage. It represented Trina sitting very erect in a rep armchair, holding her wedding bouquet straight before her, McTeague standing at her side, his left foot forward, one hand upon her shoulder, and the other thrust into the breast of his "Prince Albert" coat, in the attitude of a statue of a Secretary of State.

"Oh, it *was* good of him, it *was* good of him," cried Trina, her eyes filling again. "I had forgotten to put it away. Of course it was not for sale."

They went on down the stairs, and arriving at the door of the sitting-room, opened it and looked in. It was late in the afternoon, and there was just light enough for the dentist and his wife to see the results of that day of sale. Nothing was left, not even the carpet. It was a pillage, a devastation, the barrenness of a field after the passage of a swarm of locusts. The room had been picked and stripped till only the bare walls and floor remained. Here where they had been married, where the wedding supper had taken place, where Trina had bade farewell to her father and mother, here where she had spent those first few hard months of her married life, where afterward she had grown to be happy and contented, where she had passed the long hours of the afternoon at her work of whittling, and where she and her husband had spent so many evenings looking out of the window before the lamp was lit—here in what had been her home, nothing was left but echoes and the emptiness of complete desolation. Only one thing remained. On the wall between the windows, in its oval glass frame, preserved by some unknown and fearful process, a melancholy relic of a vanished happiness, unsold, neglected, and forgotten, a thing that nobody wanted, hung Trina's wedding bouquet.

XV

Then the grind began. It would have been easier for the McTeagues to have faced their misfortunes had they befallen them immediately after their marriage, when their love for each other was fresh and fine, and when they could have found a certain happiness in helping each other and sharing each other's privations. Trina, no doubt, loved her husband more than ever, in the sense that she felt she belonged to him. But McTeague's affection for his wife was dwindling a little every day—*had* been dwindling for a long time, in fact. He had become used to her by now. She was part of the order of the things with which he found himself surrounded. He saw nothing extraordinary about her; it was no longer a pleasure for him to kiss her and take her in his arms; she was merely his wife. He did not dislike her; he did not love her. She was his wife, that was all. But he sadly missed and regretted all those little animal comforts which in the old prosperous life Trina had managed to find for him. He missed the cabbage soups and steaming chocolate that Trina had taught him to like; he missed his good tobacco that Trina had educated him to prefer; he missed the Sunday afternoon walks that she had caused him to substitute in place of his nap in the operating chair; and he missed the bottled beer that she had induced him to drink in place of the steam beer from Frenna's. In the end he grew morose and sulky, and sometimes neglected to answer his wife when she spoke to him. Besides this, Trina's avarice was a perpetual annoyance to him. Oftentimes when a considerable alleviation of this unhappiness could have been obtained at the expense of a nickel or a dime, Trina refused the money with a pettishness that was exasperating.

"No, no," she would exclaim. "To ride to the park Sunday afternoon, that means ten cents, and I can't afford it."

"Let's walk there, then."

"I've got to work."

"But you've worked morning and afternoon every day this week."

"I don't care, I've got to work."

There had been a time when Trina had hated the idea of McTeague drinking steam beer as common and vulgar.

"Say, let's have a bottle of beer to-night. We haven't had a drop of beer in three weeks."

"We can't afford it. It's fifteen cents a bottle."

"But I haven't had a swallow of beer in three weeks."

"Drink *steam* beer, then. You've got a nickel. I gave you a quarter day before yesterday."

"But I don't like steam beer now."

It was so with everything. Unfortunately, Trina had cultivated tastes in McTeague which now could not be gratified. He had come to be very proud of his silk hat and "Prince Albert" coat, and liked to wear them on Sundays. Trina had made him sell both. He preferred "Yale mixture" in his pipe; Trina had made him come down to "Mastiff," a five-cent tobacco with which he was once contented, but now abhorred. He liked to wear clean cuffs; Trina allowed him a fresh pair on Sundays only. At first these deprivations angered McTeague. Then, all of a sudden, he slipped back into the old habits (that had been his before he knew Trina) with an ease that was surprising. Sundays he dined at the car conductors' coffee-joint once more, and spent the afternoon lying full length upon the bed, crop-full, stupid, warm, smoking his huge pipe, drinking his steam beer, and playing his six mournful tunes upon his concertina, dozing off to sleep towards four o'clock.

The sale of their furniture had, after paying the rent and outstanding bills, netted about a hundred and thirty dollars. Trina believed that the auctioneer from the second-hand store had swindled and cheated them and had made a great outcry to no effect. But she had arranged the affair with the auctioneer herself, and offset her disappointment in the matter of the sale by deceiving her husband as to the real amount of the returns. It was easy to lie to McTeague, who took everything for granted; and since the occasion of her trickery with the money that was to have been sent to her mother, Trina had found falsehood easier than ever.

"Seventy dollars is all the auctioneer gave me," she told her husband; "and after paying the balance due on the rent, and the grocer's bill, there's only fifty left."

"Only fifty?" murmured McTeague, wagging his head, "only fifty? Think of that."

"Only fifty," declared Trina. Afterwards she said to herself with a certain admiration for her cleverness:

"Couldn't save sixty dollars much easier than that," and she had added the hundred and thirty to the little hoard in the chamois-skin bag and brass match-box in the bottom of her trunk.

In these first months of their misfortunes the routine of the McTeagues was as follows: They rose at seven and breakfasted in their room, Trina cooking the very meagre meal on an oil stove. Immediately after breakfast Trina sat down to her work of whittling the Noah's ark animals, and McTeague took himself off to walk down town. He had by the greatest good luck secured a position with a manufacturer of surgical instruments, where his manual dexterity in the making of excavators, pluggers, and other dental contrivances stood him in fairly good stead. He lunched at a sailor's boarding-house near the water front, and in the afternoon worked till six. He was home at six-thirty, and he and Trina had supper together in the "ladies' dining parlor," an adjunct of the car conductors' coffee-joint. Trina, meanwhile, had worked at her whittling all day long, with but half an hour's interval for lunch, which she herself prepared upon the oil stove. In the evening they were both so tired that they were in no mood for conversation, and went to bed early, worn out, harried, nervous, and cross.

Trina was not quite so scrupulously tidy now as in the old days. At one time while whittling the Noah's ark animals she had worn gloves. She never wore them now. She still took pride in neatly combing and coiling her wonderful black hair, but as the days passed she found it more and more comfortable to work in her blue flannel wrapper. Whittlings and chips accumulated under the window where she did her work, and she was at no great pains to clear the air of the room vitiated by the fumes of the oil stove and heavy with the smell of cooking. It was not gay, that life. The room itself was not gay. The huge double bed sprawled over nearly a fourth of the available space; the angles of Trina's trunk and the washstand projected into the room from the walls, and barked shins and scraped elbows. Streaks and spots of the "non-poisonous" paint that Trina used were upon the walls and woodwork. However, in one corner of the room, next the window, monstrous, distorted, brilliant, shining with a light of its own, stood the dentist's sign, the enormous golden tooth, the tooth of a Brobdingnag.

One afternoon in September, about four months after the McTeagues had left their suite, Trina was at her work by the window. She had whittled some half-dozen sets of animals, and was now busy painting them and making the arks. Little pots of "non-poisonous" paint stood at her elbow on the table, together with a box of labels that read, "Made in France." Her huge clasp-knife was stuck into the under side of the table. She was now occupied solely with the brushes and the glue pot. She turned the little figures in her fingers with a wonderful lightness and deftness, painting the chickens Naples yellow, the elephants blue gray, the horses Vandyke brown, adding a dot of Chinese white for the eyes and sticking in the ears and tail with a drop of glue. The animals once done, she put together and painted the arks, some dozen of them, all windows and no doors, each one opening only by a lid which was half the roof. She had all the work she could handle these days, for, from this time till a week before Christmas, Uncle Oelbermann could take as many "Noah's ark sets" as she could make.

Suddenly Trina paused in her work, looking expectantly toward the door. McTeague came in.

"Why, Mac," exclaimed Trina. "It's only three o'clock. What are you home so early for? Have they discharged you?"

"They've fired me," said McTeague, sitting down on the bed.

"Fired you! What for?"

"I don' know. Said the times were getting hard an' they had to let me go."

Trina let her paint-stained hands fall into her lap.

"*Oh!*" she cried. "If we don't have the *hardest* luck of any two people I ever heard of. What can you do now? Is there another place like that where they make surgical instruments?"

"Huh? No, I don' know. There's three more."

"Well, you must try them right away. Go down there right now."

"Huh? Right now? No, I'm tired. I'll go down in the morning."

"Mac," cried Trina, in alarm, "what are you thinking of? You talk as though we were millionaires. You must go down this minute. You're losing money every second you sit there." She goaded the huge fellow to his feet again, thrust his hat into his hands, and pushed him out of the door, he obeying the while, docile and obedient as a big cart horse. He was on the stairs when she came running after him.

"Mac, they paid you off, didn't they, when they discharged you?"

"Yes."

"They you must have some money. Give it to me."

The dentist heaved a shoulder uneasily.

"No, I don' want to."

"I've got to have that money. There's no more oil for the stove, and I must buy some more meal tickets to-night."

"Always after me about money," muttered the dentist; but he emptied his pockets for her, nevertheless.

"I—you've taken it all," he grumbled. "Better leave me something for car fare. It's going to rain."

"Pshaw! You can walk just as well as not. A big fellow like you 'fraid of a little walk; and it ain't going to rain."

Trina had lied again both as to the want of oil for the stove and the commutation ticket for the restaurant. But she knew by instinct that McTeague had money about him, and she did not intend to let it go out of the house. She listened intently until she was sure McTeague was gone. Then she hurriedly opened her trunk and hid the money in the chamois bag at the bottom.

The dentist presented himself at every one of the makers of surgical instruments that afternoon and was promptly turned away in each case. Then it came on to rain, a fine, cold drizzle, that chilled him and wet him to the bone. He had no umbrella, and Trina had not left him even five cents for car fare. He started to walk home through the rain. It was a long way to Polk Street, as the last manufactory he had visited was beyond even Folsom Street, and not far from the city front.[1]

[1.] McTeague is south of Market near the bay and is thus at the other end of the city from Polk and Sutter.

By the time McTeague reached Polk Street his teeth were chattering with the cold. He was wet from head to foot. As he was passing Heise's harness shop a sudden deluge of rain overtook him and he was obliged to dodge into the vestibule for shelter. He, who loved to be warm, to sleep and to be well fed, was icy cold, was exhausted and footsore from tramping the city. He could look forward to nothing better than a badly-cooked supper at the coffee-joint—hot meat on a cold plate, half done suet pudding, muddy coffee, and bad bread, and he was cold, miserably cold, and wet to the bone. All at once a sudden rage against Trina took possession of him. It was her fault. She knew it was going to rain, and she had not let him have a nickel for car fare—she who had five thousand dollars. She let him walk the streets in the cold and in the rain. "Miser," he growled behind his mustache. "Miser, nasty little old miser. You're worse than old Zerkow, always nagging about money, money, and you got five thousand dollars. You got more, an' you live in that stinking hole of a room, and you won't drink any decent beer. I ain't going to stand it much longer. She knew it was going to rain. She *knew* it. Didn't I *tell* her? And she drives me out of my own home in the rain, for me to get money for her; more money, and she takes it. She took that money from me that I earned. 'Twasn't hers; it was mine, I earned it—and not a nickel for car fare. She don't care if I get wet and get a cold and *die*. No, she don't, as long as she's warm and's got her money." He became more and more indignant at the picture he made of himself. "I ain't going to stand it much longer," he repeated.

"Why, hello, Doc. Is that you?" exclaimed Heise, opening the door of the harness shop behind him. "Come in out of the wet. Why, you're soaked through," he added as he and McTeague came back into the shop, that reeked of oiled leather. "Didn't you have any umbrella? Ought to have taken a car."

"I guess so—I guess so," murmured the dentist, confused. His teeth were chattering.

"*You're* going to catch your death-a-cold," exclaimed Heise. "Tell you what," he said, reaching for his hat, "come in next door to Frenna's and have something to warm you up. I'll get the old lady to mind the shop." He called Mrs. Heise down from the floor above and took McTeague into Joe Frenna's saloon, which was two doors above his harness shop.

"Whiskey and gum[2] twice, Joe," said he to the barkeeper as he and the dentist approached the bar.

"Huh? What?" said McTeague. "Whiskey? No, I can't drink whiskey. It kind of disagrees with me."

2. Whiskey and gum is whiskey in a mixer of hot water and sugar.

"Oh, the hell!" returned Heise, easily. "Take it as medicine. You'll get your death-a-cold if you stand round soaked like that. Two whiskey and gum, Joe."

McTeague emptied the pony glass at a single enormous gulp.

"That's the way," said Heise, approvingly. "Do you good." He drank his off slowly.

"I'd—I'd ask you to have a drink with me, Heise," said the dentist, who had an indistinct idea of the amenities of the barroom, "only," he added shamefacedly, "only—you see, I don't believe I got any change." His anger against Trina, heated by the whiskey he had drank, flamed up afresh. What a humiliating position for Trina to place him in, not to leave him the price of a drink with a friend, she who had five thousand dollars!

"Sha! That's all right, Doc," returned Heise, nibbling on a grain of coffee. "Want another? Hey? This my treat. Two more of the same, Joe."

McTeague hesitated. It was lamentably true that whiskey did not agree with him; he knew it well enough. However, by this time he felt very comfortably warm at the pit of his stomach. The blood was beginning to circulate in his chilled finger-tips and in his soggy, wet feet. He had had a hard day of it; in fact, the last week, the last month, the last three or four months, had been hard. He deserved a little consolation. Nor could Trina object to this. It wasn't costing a cent. He drank again with Heise.

"Get up here to the stove and warm yourself," urged Heise, drawing up a couple of chairs and cocking his feet upon the guard The two fell to talking while McTeague's draggled coat and trousers smoked.

"What a dirty turn that was that Marcus Schouler did you!" said Heise, wagging his head. "You ought to have fought that, Doc, sure. You'd been practising too long." They discussed this question some ten or fifteen minutes and then Heise rose.

"Well, this ain't earning any money. I got to get back to the shop." McTeague got up as well, and the pair started for the door. Just as they were going out Ryer met them.

"Hello, hello," he cried. "Lord, what a wet day! You two are going the wrong way. You're going to have a drink with me. Three whiskey punches, Joe."

"No, no," answered McTeague, shaking his head. "I'm going back home. I've had two glasses of whiskey already."

"Sha!" cried Heise, catching his arm. "A strapping big chap like you ain't afraid of a little whiskey."

"Well, I—I—I got to go right afterwards," protested McTeague.

About half an hour after the dentist had left to go down town,

Maria Macapa had come in to see Trina. Occasionally Maria dropped in on Trina in this fashion and spent an hour or so chatting with her while she worked. At first Trina had been inclined to resent these intrusions of the Mexican woman, but of late she had begun to tolerate them. Her days were long and cheerless at the best, and there was no one to talk to. Trina even fancied that old Miss Baker had come to be less cordial since their misfortune. Maria retailed to her all the gossip of the flat and the neighborhood, and, which was much more interesting, told her of her troubles with Zerkow.

Trina said to herself that Maria was common and vulgar, but one had to have some diversion, and Trina could talk and listen without interrupting her work. On this particular occasion Maria was much excited over Zerkow's demeanor of late.

"He's gettun worse an' worse," she informed Trina as she sat on the edge of the bed, her chin in her hand. "He says he knows I got the dishes and am hidun them from him. The other day I thought he'd gone off with his wagon, and I was doin' a bit of ir'ning, an' by an' by all of a sudden I saw him peeping at me through the crack of the door. I never let on that I saw him, and, honest, he stayed there over two hours, watchun everything I did. I could just feel his eyes on the back of my neck all the time. Last Sunday he took down part of the wall, 'cause he said he'd seen me making figures on it. Well, I was, but it was just the wash list. All the time he says he'll kill me if I don't tell?"

"Why, what do you stay with him for?" exclaimed Trina. "I'd be deathly 'fraid of a man like that; and he did take a knife to you once."

"Hoh! *he* won't kill me, never fear. If he'd kill me he'd never know where the dishes were; that's what *he* thinks."

"But I can't understand, Maria; you told him about those gold dishes yourself."

"Never, never! I never saw such a lot of crazy folks as you are."

"But you say he hits you sometimes."

"Ah!" said Maria, tossing her head scornfully, "I ain't afraid of him. He takes his horsewhip to me now and then, but I can always manage. I say, 'If you touch me with that, then I'll *never* tell you.' Just pretending, you know, and he drops it as though it was red hot. Say, Mrs. McTeague, have you got any tea? Let's make a cup of tea over the stove."

"No, no," cried Trina, with niggardly apprehension; "no, I haven't got a bit of tea." Trina's stinginess had increased to such an extent that it had gone beyond the mere hoarding of money. She grudged even the food that she and McTeague ate, and even brought away half loaves of bread, lumps of sugar, and fruit from the car conductors' coffee-joint. She hid these pilferings away on the shelf by the window, and often managed to make a very creditable lunch from them, enjoying the meal with the greater relish because it cost her nothing.

"No, Maria, I haven't got a bit of tea," she said, shaking her head decisively. "Hark, ain't that Mac?" she added, her chin in the air. "That's his step, sure."

"Well, I'm going to skip," said Maria. She left hurriedly, passing the dentist in the hall just outside the door.

"Well?" said Trina interrogatively as her husband entered. McTeague did not answer. He hung his hat on the hook behind the door and dropped heavily into a chair.

"Well," asked Trina, anxiously, "how did you make out, Mac?"

Still the dentist pretended not to hear, scowling fiercely at his muddy boots.

"Tell me, Mac, I want to know. Did you get a place? Did you get caught in the rain?"

"Did I? Did I?" cried the dentist, sharply, an alacrity in his manner and voice that Trina had never observed before.

"Look at me. Look at me," he went on, speaking with an unwonted rapidity, his wits sharp, his ideas succeeding each other quickly. "Look at me, drenched through, shivering cold. I've walked the city over. Caught in the rain! Yes, I guess I did get caught in the rain, and it ain't your fault I didn't catch my death-a-cold; wouldn't even let me have a nickel for car fare."

"But, Mac," protested Trina, "I didn't know it was going to rain."

The dentist put back his head and laughed scornfully. His face was very red, and his small eyes twinkled. "Hoh! no, you didn't know it was going to rain. Didn't I *tell* you it was?" he exclaimed, suddenly angry again. "Oh, you're a *daisy*, you are. Think I'm going to put up with your foolishness *all* the time? Who's the boss, you or I?"

"Why, Mac, I never saw you this way before. You talk like a different man."

"Well, I *am* a different man," retorted the dentist, savagely. "You can't make small of me *always*."

"Well, never mind that. You know I'm not trying to make small of you. But never mind that. Did you get place?"

"Give me my money," exclaimed McTeague, jumping up briskly. There was an activity, a positive nimbleness about the huge blond giant that had never been his before; also his stupidity, the sluggishness of his brain, seemed to be unusually stimulated.

"Give me my money, the money I gave you as I was going away."

"I can't," exclaimed Trina. "I paid the grocer's bill with it while you were gone."

"Don't believe you."

"Truly, truly, Mac. Do you think I'd lie to you? Do you think I'd lower myself to do that?"

"Well, the next time I earn any money I'll keep it myself."

"But tell me, Mac, *did* you get a place?"

McTeague turned his back on her.

"Tell me, Mac, please, did you?"

The dentist jumped up and thrust his face close to hers, his heavy jaw protruding, his little eyes twinkling meanly.

"No," he shouted. "No, no, *no*. Do you hear? *No*."

Trina cowered before him. Then suddenly she began to sob aloud, weeping partly at his strange brutality, partly at the disappointment of his failure to find employment.

McTeague cast a contemptuous glance about him, a glance that embraced the dingy, cheerless room, the rain streaming down the panes of the one window, and the figure of his weeping wife.

"Oh, ain't this all *fine?*" he exclaimed. "Ain't it lovely?"

"It's not my fault," sobbed Trina.

"It is too," vociferated McTeague. "It is too. We could live like Christians and decent people if you wanted to. You got more'n five thousand dollars, and you're so damned stingy that you'd rather live in a rat hole—and make me live there too—before you'd part with a nickel of it. I tell you I'm sick and tired of the whole business."

An allusion to her lottery money never failed to rouse Trina.

"And I'll tell you this much too," she cried, winking back the tears. "Now that you're out of a job, we can't afford even to live in your rat hole, as you call it. We've got to find a cheaper place than *this* even."

"What!" exclaimed the dentist, purple with rage. "What, get into a worse hole in the wall than this? Well, we'll *see* if we will. We'll just see about that. You're going to do just as I tell you after this, Trina McTeague," and once more he thrust his face close to hers.

"I know what's the matter," cried Trina, with a half sob; "I know, I can smell it on your breath. You've been drinking whiskey."

"Yes, I've been drinking whiskey," retorted her husband. "I've been drinking whiskey. Have you got anything to say about it? Ah, yes, you're *right*, I've been drinking whiskey. What have *you* got to say about my drinking whiskey? Let's hear it.'

"Oh! Oh! Oh!" sobbed Trina, covering her face with her hands. McTeague caught her wrists in one palm and pulled them down. Trina's pale face was streaming with tears; her long, narrow blue eyes were swimming; her adorable little chin upraised and quivering.

"Let's hear what you got to say," exclaimed McTeague.

"Nothing, nothing," said Trina, between her sobs.

"Then stop that noise. Stop it, do you hear me? Stop it." He
threw up his open hand threateningly. "*Stop!*" he exclaimed.
Trina looked at him fearfully, half blinded with weeping. Her
husband's thick mane of yellow hair was disordered and rumpled
upon his great square-cut head; his big red ears were redder than
ever; his face was purple; the thick eyebrows were knotted over the
small, twinkling eyes; the heavy yellow mustache, that smelt of alcohol, drooped over the massive, protruding chin, salient, like that of
the carnivora; the veins were swollen and throbbing on his thick red
neck; while over her head Trina saw his upraised palm, calloused,
enormous.

"Stop!" he exclaimed. And Trina, watching fearfully, saw the
palm suddenly contract into a fist, a fist that was hard as a wooden
mallet, the fist of the old-time car-boy. And then her ancient terror
of him, the intuitive fear of the male, leaped to life again. She was
afraid of him. Every nerve of her quailed and shrank from him. She
choked back her sobs, catching her breath.

"There," growled the dentist, releasing her, "that's more like.
Now," he went on, fixing her with his little eyes, "now listen to me.
I'm beat out. I've walked the city over—ten miles, I guess—an' I'm
going to bed, an' I don't want to be bothered. You understand? I
want to be let alone." Trina was silent.

"Do you *hear?*" he snarled.

"Yes, Mac."

The dentist took off his coat, his collar and necktie, unbuttoned
his vest, and slipped his heavy-soled boots from his big feet. Then
he stretched himself upon the bed and rolled over towards the wall.
In a few minutes the sound of his snoring filled the room.

Trina craned her neck and looked at her husband over the footboard of the bed. She saw his red, congested face; the huge mouth
wide open; his unclean shirt, with its frayed wristbands; and his
huge feet encased in thick woollen socks. Then her grief and the
sense of her unhappiness returned more poignant than ever. She
stretched her arms out in front of her on her work-table, and, burying her face in them, cried and sobbed as though her heart would
break.

The rain continued. The panes of the single window ran with
sheets of water; the eaves dripped incessantly. It grew darker. The
tiny, grimy room, full of the smells of cooking and of "non-poisonous" paint, took on an aspect of desolation and cheerlessness
lamentable beyond words. The canary in its little gilt prison chittered feebly from time to time. Sprawled at full length upon the
bed, the dentist snored and snored, stupefied, inert, his legs wide
apart, his hands lying palm upward at his sides.

At last Trina raised her head, with a long, trembling breath. She rose, and going over to the washstand, poured some water from the pitcher into the basin, and washed her face and swollen eyelids, and rearranged her hair. Suddenly, as she was about to return to her work, she was struck with an idea.

"I wonder," she said to herself, "I wonder where he got the money to buy his whiskey." She searched the pockets of his coat, which he had flung into a corner of the room, and even came up to him as he lay upon the bed and went through the pockets of his vest and trousers. She found nothing.

"I wonder," she murmured, "I wonder if he's got any money he don't tell me about. I'll have to look out for that."

XVI

A week passed, then a fortnight, then a month. It was a month of the greatest anxiety and unquietude for Trina. McTeague was out of a job, could find nothing to do; and Trina, who saw the impossibility of saving as much money as usual out of her earnings under the present conditions, was on the lookout for cheaper quarters. In spite of his outcries and sulky resistance Trina had induced her husband to consent to such a move, bewildering him with a torrent of phrases and marvellous columns of figures by which she proved conclusively that they were in a condition but one remove from downright destitution.

The dentist continued idle. Since his ill success with the manufacturers of surgical instruments he had made but two attempts to secure a job. Trina had gone to see Uncle Oelbermann and had obtained for McTeague a position in the shipping department of the wholesale toy store. However, it was a position that involved a certain amount of ciphering, and McTeague had been obliged to throw it up in two days.

Then for a time they had entertained a wild idea that a place on the police force could be secured for McTeague. He could pass the physical examination with flying colors, and Ryer, who had become the secretary of the Polk Street Improvement Club, promised the requisite political "pull." If McTeague had shown a certain energy in the matter the attempt might have been successful; but he was too stupid, or of late had become too listless to exert himself greatly, and the affair resulted only in a violent quarrel with Ryer.

McTeague had lost his ambition. He did not care to better his situation. All he wanted was a warm place to sleep and three good meals a day. At the first—at the very first—he had chafed at his idleness and had spent the days with his wife in their one narrow room, walking back and forth with the restlessness of a caged brute, or sitting motionless for hours, watching Trina at her work, feeling a dull glow of shame at the idea that she was supporting him. This feeling had worn off quickly, however. Trina's work was only hard when she chose to make it so, and as a rule she supported their misfortunes with a silent fortitude.

Then, wearied at his inaction and feeling the need of movement and exercise, McTeague would light his pipe and take a turn upon the great avenue one block above Polk Street. A gang of laborers were digging the foundations for a large brownstone house, and McTeague found interest and amusement in leaning over the barrier that surrounded the excavations and watching the progress of the work. He came to see it every afternoon; by and by he even got to know the foreman who superintended the job, and the two had long talks together. Then McTeague would return to Polk Street and find Heise in the back room of the harness shop, and occasionally the day ended with some half dozen drinks of whiskey at Joe Frenna's saloon.

It was curious to note the effect of the alcohol upon the dentist. It did not make him drunk, it made him vicious. So far from being stupefied, he became, after the fourth glass, active, alert, quick-witted, even talkative; a certain wickedness stirred in him then; he was intractable, mean; and when he had drunk a little more heavily than usual, he found a certain pleasure in annoying and exasperating Trina, even in abusing and hurting her.

It had begun on the evening of Thanksgiving Day, when Heise had taken McTeague out to dinner with him. The dentist on this occasion had drunk very freely. He and Heise had returned to Polk Street towards ten o'clock, and Heise at once suggested a couple of drinks at Frenna's.

"All right, all right," said McTeague. "Drinks, that's the word. I'll go home and get some money and meet you at Joe's."

Trina was awakened by her husband pinching her arm.

"Oh, Mac," she cried, jumping up in bed with a little scream, "how you hurt! Oh, that hurt me dreadfully."

"Give me a little money," answered the dentist, grinning, and pinching her again.

"I haven't a cent. There's not a—oh, Mac, will you stop? I won't have you pinch me that way."

"Hurry up," answered her husband, calmly, nipping the flesh of her shoulder between his thumb and finger. "Heise's waiting for me." Trina wrenched from him with a sharp intake of breath, frowning with pain, and caressing her shoulder. "Mac, you've no idea how that hurts. Mac, *stop!*"

"Give me some money, then."

In the end Trina had to comply. She gave him half a dollar from her dress pocket, protesting that it was the only piece of money she had.

"One more, just for luck," said McTeague, pinching her again; "and another."

"How can you—how *can* you hurt a woman so!" exclaimed Trina, beginning to cry with the pain.

"Ah, now, *cry*," retorted the dentist. "That's right, *cry*. I never saw such a little fool." He went out, slamming the door in disgust.

But McTeague never became a drunkard in the generally received sense of the term. He did not drink to excess more than two or three times in a month, and never upon any occasion did he become maudlin or staggering. Perhaps his nerves were naturally too dull to admit of any excitation; perhaps he did not really care for the whiskey, and only drank because Heise and the other men at Frenna's did. Trina could often reproach him with drinking too much; she never could say that he was drunk. The alcohol had its effect for all that. It roused the man, or rather the brute in the man, and now not only roused it, but goaded it to evil. McTeague's nature changed. It was not only the alcohol, it was idleness and a general throwing off of the good influence his wife had had over him in the days of their prosperity. McTeague disliked Trina. She was a perpetual irritation to him. She annoyed him because she was so small, so prettily made, so invariably correct and precise. Her avarice incessantly harassed him. Her industry was a constant reproach to him. She seemed to flaunt her work defiantly in his face. It was the red flag in the eyes of the bull. One time when he had just come back from Frenna's and had been sitting in the chair near her, silently watching her at her work, he exclaimed all of a sudden:

"Stop working. Stop it, I tell you. Put 'em away. Put 'em all away, or I'll pinch you."

"But why—why?" Trina protested.

The dentist cuffed her ears. "I won't have you work." He took her knife and her paint-pots away, and made her sit idly in the window the rest of the afternoon.

It was, however, only when his wits had been stirred with alcohol that the dentist was brutal to his wife. At other times, say three weeks of every month, she was merely an incumbrance to him. They often quarrelled about Trina's money, her savings. The dentist was bent upon having at least a part of them. What he would do with the money once he had it, he did not precisely know. He would spend it in royal fashion, no doubt, feasting continually, buying himself wonderful clothes. The miner's idea of money quickly gained and lavishly squandered, persisted in his mind. As for Trina, the more her husband stormed, the tighter she drew the strings of the little chamois-skin bag that she hid at the bottom of her trunk underneath her bridal dress. Her five thousand dollars invested in Uncle Oelbermann's business was a glittering, splendid dream which came to her almost every hour of the day as a solace and a compensation for all her unhappiness.

At times, when she knew that McTeague was far from home, she would lock her door, open her trunk, and pile all her little hoard on her table. By now it was four hundred and seven dollars and fifty cents. Trina would play with this money by the hour, piling it, and repiling it, or gathering it all into one heap, and drawing back to the farthest corner of the room to note the effect, her head on one side. She polished the gold pieces with a mixture of soap and ashes until they shone, wiping them carefully on her apron. Or, again, she would draw the heap lovingly toward her and bury her face in it, delighted at the smell of it and the feel of the smooth, cool metal on her cheeks. She even put the smaller gold pieces in her mouth, and jingled them there. She loved her money with an intensity that she could hardly express. She would plunge her small fingers into the pile with little murmurs of affection, her long, narrow eyes half closed and shining, her breath coming in long sighs.

"Ah, the dear money, the dear money," she would whisper. "I love you so! All mine, every penny of it. No one shall ever, ever get you. How I've worked for you! How I've slaved and saved for you! And I'm going to get more; I'm going to get more, more, more; a little every day."

She was still looking for cheaper quarters. Whenever she could spare a moment from her work, she would put on her hat and range up and down the entire neighborhood from Sutter to Sacramento Streets, going into all the alleys and by-streets, her head in the air, looking for the "Rooms-to-let" sign. But she was in despair. All the cheaper tenements were occupied. She could find no room more reasonable than the one she and the dentist now occupied.

As time went on, McTeague's idleness became habitual. He drank no more whiskey than at first, but his dislike for Trina increased with every day of their poverty, with every day of Trina's persistent stinginess. At times—fortunately rare—he was more than ever brutal to her. He would box her ears or hit her a great blow with the back of a hairbrush, even with his closed fist. His old-time affection for his "little woman," unable to stand the test of privation, had lapsed by degrees, and what little of it was left was changed, distorted, and made monstrous by the alcohol.

The people about the house and the clerks at the provision stores often remarked that Trina's finger-tips were swollen and the nails purple as though they had been shut in a door. Indeed, this was the explanation she gave. The fact of the matter was that

McTeague, when he had been drinking, used to bite them, crunching and grinding them with his immense teeth, always ingenious enough to remember which were the sorest. Sometimes he extorted money from her by this means, but as often as not he did it for his own satisfaction.

And in some strange, inexplicable way this brutality made Trina all the more affectionate; aroused in her a morbid, unwholesome love of submission, a strange, unnatural pleasure in yielding, in surrendering herself to the will of an irresistible, virile power.

Trina's emotions had narrowed with the narrowing of her daily life. They reduced themselves at last to but two, her passion for her money and her perverted love for her husband when he was brutal. She was a strange woman during these days.

Trina had come to be on very intimate terms with Maria Macapa, and in the end the dentist's wife and the maid of all work became great friends. Maria was constantly in and out of Trina's room, and, whenever she could, Trina threw a shawl over her head and returned Maria's calls. Trina could reach Zerkow's dirty house without going into the street. The back yard of the flat had a gate that opened into a little inclosure where Zerkow kept his decrepit horse and ramshackle wagon, and from thence Trina could enter directly into Maria's kitchen. Trina made long visits to Maria during the morning in her dressing-gown and curl papers, and the two talked at great length over a cup of tea served on the edge of the sink or a corner of the laundry table. The talk was all of their husbands and of what to do when they came home in aggressive moods.

"You never ought to fight um," advised Maria. "It only makes um worse. Just hump your back, and it's soonest over."

They told each other of their husbands' brutalities, taking a strange sort of pride in recounting some particularly savage blow, each trying to make out that her own husband was the most cruel. They critically compared each other's bruises, each one glad when she could exhibit the worst. They exaggerated, they invented details, and, as if proud of their beatings, as if glorying in their husbands' mishandling, lied to each other, magnifying their own maltreatment. They had long and excited arguments as to which were the most effective means of punishment, the rope's ends and cart whips such as Zerkow used, or the fists and backs of hair-brushes affected by McTeague. Maria contended that the lash of the whip hurt the most; Trina, that the butt did the most injury.[1]

Maria showed Trina the holes in the walls and the loosened boards in the flooring where Zerkow had been searching for the

1. An expanded version of the subject matter of this paragraph served as the material of Norris's short story "Fantaisie Printaniere," San Francisco Wave, XVI (November 6, 1897), 7; reprinted in Frank Norris of the "Wave" (San Francisco, 1931).

gold plate. Of late he had been digging in the back yard and had ransacked the hay in his horse-shed for the concealed leather chest he imagined he would find. But he was becoming impatient, evidently.

"The way he goes on," Maria told Trina, "is somethun dreadful. He's gettun regularly sick with it—got a fever every night—don't sleep, and when he does, talks to himself. Says 'More'n a hundred pieces, an' every one of 'em gold. More'n a hundred pieces, an' every one of 'em gold.' Then he'll whale me with his whip, and shout, 'You know where it is. Tell me, tell me, you swine, or I'll do for you.' An' then he'll get down on his knees and whimper, and beg me to tell um where I've hid it. He's just gone plum crazy. Sometimes he has regular fits, he gets so mad, and rolls on the floor and scratches himself."

One morning in November, about ten o'clock, Trina pasted a "Made in France" label on the bottom of a Noah's ark, and leaned back in her chair with a long sigh of relief. She had just finished a large Christmas order for Uncle Oelbermann, and there was nothing else she could do that morning. The bed had not yet been made, nor had the breakfast things been washed. Trina hesitated for a moment, then put her chin in the air indifferently.

"Bah!" she said, "let them go till this afternoon. I don't care *when* the room is put to rights, and I know Mac don't." She determined that instead of making the bed or washing the dishes she would go and call on Miss Baker on the floor below. The little dressmaker might ask her to stay to lunch, and that would be something saved, as the dentist had announced his intention that morning of taking a long walk out to the Presidio to be gone all day.

But Trina rapped on Miss Baker's door in vain that morning. She was out. Perhaps she was gone to the florist's to buy some geranium seeds. However, Old Grannis's door stood a little ajar, and on hearing Trina at Miss Baker's room, the old Englishman came out into the hall.

"She's gone out," he said, uncertainly, and in a half whisper, "went out about half an hour ago. I—I think she went to the drug store to get some wafers for the goldfish."

"Don't you go to your dog hospital any more, Mister Grannis?" said Trina, leaning against the balustrade in the hall, willing to talk a moment.

Old Grannis stood in the doorway of his room, in his carpet slippers and faded corduroy jacket that he wore when at home.

"Why—why," he said, hesitating, tapping his chin thoughtfully. "You see I'm thinking of giving up the little hospital."

"Giving it up?"

"You see, the people at the book store where I buy my pamphlets have found out—I told them of my contrivance for binding books, and one of the members of the firm came up to look at it. He offered me quite a sum if I would sell him the right of it—the—the patent of 'it—quite a sum. In fact—in fact—yes, quite a sum, quite." He rubbed his chin tremulously and looked about him on the floor.,

"Why, isn't that fine?" said Trina, good-naturedly. "I'm very glad, Mister Grannis. Is it a good price?"

"Quite a sum—quite. In fact, I never dreamed of having so much money."

"Now, see here, Mister Grannis," said Trina, decisively, "I want to give you a good piece of advice. Here are you and Miss Baker ——" The old Englishman started nervously—"You and Miss Baker, that have been in love with each other for——"

"Oh, Mrs. McTeague, that subject—if you would please—Miss Baker is such an estimable lady."

"Fiddlesticks!" said Trina. "You're in love with each other, and the whole flat knows it; and you two have been living here side by side year in and year out, and you've never said a word to each other. It's all nonsense. Now, I want you should go right in and speak to her just as soon as she comes home, and say you've come into money and you want her to marry you."

"Impossible—impossible!" exclaimed the old Englishman, alarmed and perturbed. "It's quite out of the question. I wouldn't presume."

"Well, do you love her, or not?"

"Really, Mrs McTeague, I—I—you must excuse me. It's a matter so personal—so—I—Oh, yes, I love her. Oh, yes, indeed," he exclaimed, suddenly.

"Well, then, she loves you. She told me so."

"Oh!"

"She did. She said those very words."   .

Miss Baker had said nothing of the kind—would have died sooner than have made such a confession; but Trina had drawn her own conclusions, like every other lodger of the flat, and thought the time was come for decided action.

"Now you do just as I tell you, and when she comes home, go right in and see her, and have it over with. Now don't say another word. I'm going; but you do just as I tell you."

Trina turned about and went down-stairs. She had decided, since Miss Baker was not at home, that she would run over and see Maria; possibly she could have lunch there. At any rate, Maria would offer her a cup of tea.

Old Grannis stood for a long time as Trina had left him, his hands trembling, the blood coming and going in his withered cheeks.

"She said, she—she—she told her—she said that—that——" he could get no farther.

Then he faced about and entered his room, closing the door behind him. For a long time he sat in his armchair, drawn close to the wall in front of the table on which stood his piles of pamphlets and his little binding apparatus.

"I wonder," said Trina, as she crossed the yard back of Zerkow's house, "I wonder what rent Zerkow and Maria pay for this place. I'll bet it's cheaper than where Mac and I are."

Trina found Maria sitting in front of the kitchen stove, her chin upon her breast. Trina went up to her. She was dead. And as Trina touched her shoulder, her head rolled sideways and showed a fearful gash in her throat under her ear. All the front of her dress was soaked through and through.

Trina backed sharply away from the body, drawing her hands up to her very shoulders, her eyes staring and wide, an expression of unutterable horror twisting her face.

"Oh-h-h!" she exclaimed in a long breath, her voice hardly rising above a whisper. "Oh-h, isn't that horrible!" Suddenly she turned and fled through the front part of the house to the street door, that opened upon the little alley. She looked wildly about her. Directly across the way a butcher's boy was getting into his two-wheeled cart drawn up in front of the opposite house, while near by a peddler of wild game was coming down the street, a brace of ducks in his hand.

"Oh, say—say," gasped Trina, trying to get her voice, "say, come over here quick."

The butcher's boy paused, one foot on the wheel, and stared. Trina beckoned frantically.

"Come over here, come over here quick."

The young fellow swung himself into his seat.

"What's the matter with that woman?" he said, half aloud.

"There's a murder been done," cried Trina, swaying in the doorway.

The young fellow drove away, his head over his shoulder, staring at Trina with eyes that were fixed and absolutely devoid of expression.

"What's the matter with that woman?" he said again to himself as he turned the corner.

Trina wondered why she didn't scream, how she could keep from it—how, at such a moment as this, she could remember that it was improper to make a disturbance and create a scene in the street.

The peddler of wild game was looking at her suspiciously. It would not do to tell him. He would go away like the butcher's boy.

"Now, wait a minute," Trina said to herself, speaking aloud. She put her hands to her head. "Now, wait a minute. It won't do for me to lose my wits now. What must I do?" She looked about her. There was the same familiar aspect of Polk Street. She could see it at the end of the alley. The big market opposite the flat, the delivery carts rattling up and down, the great ladies from the avenue at their morning shopping, the cable cars trundling past, loaded with passengers. She saw a little boy in a flat leather cap whistling and calling for an unseen dog, slapping his small knee from time to time. Two men came out of Frenna's saloon, laughing heartily. Heise the harness-maker stood in the vestibule of his shop, a bundle of whittlings in his apron of greasy ticking. And all this was going on, people were laughing and living, buying and selling, walking about out there on the sunny sidewalks, while behind her in there —in there—in there——

Heise started back from the sudden apparition of a white-lipped woman in a blue dressing-gown that seemed to rise up before him from his very doorstep.

"Well, Mrs. McTeague, you did scare me, for——"

"Oh, come over here quick." Trina put her hand to her neck, swallowing something that seemed to be choking her. "Maria's killed—Zerkow's wife—I found her."

"Get out!" exclaimed Heise, "you're joking."

"Come over here—over into the house—I found her—she's dead."

Heise dashed across the street on the run, with Trina at his heels, a trial of spilled whittlings marking his course. The two ran down the alley. The wild-game peddler, a woman who had been washing down the steps in a neighboring house, and a man in a broad-brimmed hat stood at Zerkow's doorway, looking in from time to time, and talking together. They seemed puzzled.

"Anything wrong in here?" asked the wild-game peddler as Heise and Trina came up. Two more men stopped on the corner of the alley and Polk Street and looked at the group. A woman with a towel round her head raised a window opposite Zerkow's house and called to the woman who had been washing the steps, "What is it, Mrs. Flint?"

Heise was already inside the house. He turned to Trina, panting from his run.

"Where did you say—where was it—where?"

"In there," said Trina, "farther in—the next room." They burst into the kitchen.

"*Lord!*" ejaculated Heise, stopping a yard or so from the body, and bending down to peer into the gray face with its brown lips.

"By God! he's killed her."

"Who?"

"Zerkow, by God! he's killed her. Cut her throat. He always said he would."

"Zerkow?"

"He's killed her. Her throat's cut. Good Lord, how she did bleed! By God! he's done for her in *good* shape this time."

"Oh, I told her—I *told* her," cried Trina.

"He's done for her *sure* this time."

"She said she could always manage—Oh-h! It's horrible."

"He's done for her sure this trip. Cut her throat. *Lord*, how she has *bled!* Did you ever *see* so much—that's murder—that's cold-blooded murder. He's killed her. Say, we must get a policeman. Come on."

They turned back through the house. Half a dozen people—the wild-game peddler, the man with the broad-brimmed hat, the wash-woman, and three other men—were in the front room of the junk shop, a bank of excited faces surged at the door. Beyond this, out-side, the crowd was packed solid from one end of the alley to the other. Out in Polk Street the cable cars were nearly blocked and were bunting a way slowly through the throng with clanging bells. Every window had its group. And as Trina and the harness-maker tried to force the way from the door of the junk shop the throng suddenly parted right and left before the passage of two blue-coated policemen who clove a passage through the press, working their elbows energetically. They were accompanied by a third man in citizen's clothes.

Heise and Trina went back into the kitchen with the two police-men, the third man in citizen's clothes cleared the intruders from the front room of the junk shop and kept the crowd back, his arm across the open door.

"Whew!" whistled one of the officers as they came out into the kitchen, "cutting scrape? By George! *somebody's* been using his knife all right." He turned to the other officer. "Better get the wagon. There's a box on the second corner south. Now, then," he continued, turning to Trina and the harness-maker and taking out his note-book and pencil, "I want your names and addresses."

It was a day of tremendous excitement for the entire street. Long after the patrol wagon had driven away, the crowd remained. In fact, until seven o'clock that evening groups collected about the door of the junk shop, where a policeman stood guard, asking all manner of questions, advancing all manner of opinions.

"Do you think they'll get him?" asked Ryer of the policeman. A dozen necks craned forward eagerly.

"Hoh, we'll get him all right, easy enough," answered the other, with a grand air.

"What? What's that? What did he say?" asked the people on the outskirts of the group. Those in front passed the answer back.

"He says they'll get him all right, easy enough."

The group looked at the policeman admiringly.

"He's skipped to San José."

Where the rumor started, and how, no one knew. But every one seemed persuaded that Zerkow had gone to San José.

"But what did he kill her for? Was he drunk?"

"No, he was crazy, I tell you—crazy in the head. Thought she was hiding some money from him."

Frenna did a big business all day long. The murder was the one subject of conversation. Little parties were made up in his saloon—parties of twos and threes—to go over and have a look at the outside of the junk shop. Heise was the most important man in the length and breadth of Polk Street; almost invariably he accompanied these parties, telling again and again of the part he had played in the affair.

"It was about eleven o'clock. I was standing in front of the shop, when Mrs. McTeague—you know, the dentist's wife—came running across the street," and so on and so on.

The next day came a fresh sensation. Polk Street read of it in the morning papers. Towards midnight on the day of the murder Zerkow's body had been found floating in the bay near Black Point. No one knew whether he had drowned himself or fallen from one of the wharves. Clutched in both his hands was a sack full of old and rusty pans, tin dishes—fully a hundred of them—tin cans, and iron knives and forks, collected from some dump heap.

"And all this," exclaimed Trina, "on account of a set of gold dishes that never existed."

XVII

One day, about a fortnight after the coroner's inquest had been held, and when the excitement of the terrible affair was calming down and Polk Street beginning to resume its monotonous routine, Old Grannis sat in his clean, well-kept little room, in his cushioned armchair, his hands lying idly upon his knees. It was evening; not quite time to light the lamps. Old Grannis had drawn his chair close to the wall—so close, in fact, that he could hear Miss Baker's grenadine brushing against the other side of the thin partition, at his very elbow, while she rocked gently back and forth, a cup of tea in her hands.

Old Grannis's occupation was gone. That morning the book-selling firm where he had bought his pamphlets had taken his little binding apparatus from him to use as a model. The transaction had been concluded. Old Grannis had received his check. It was large enough, to be sure, but when all was over, he returned to his room and sat there sad and unoccupied, looking at the pattern in the carpet and counting the heads of the tacks in the zinc guard that was fastened to the wall behind his little stove. By and by he heard Miss Baker moving about. It was five o'clock, the time when she was accustomed to make her cup of tea and "keep company" with him on her side of the partition. Old Grannis drew up his chair to the wall near where he knew she was sitting. The minutes passed; side by side, and separated by only a couple of inches of board, the two old people sat there together, while the afternoon grew darker.

But for Old Grannis all was different that evening. There was nothing for him to do. His hands lay idly in his lap. His table, with its pile of pamphlets, was in a far corner of the room, and, from time to time, stirred with an uncertain trouble, he turned his head and looked at it sadly, reflecting that he would never use it again. The absence of his accustomed work seemed to leave something out of his life. It did not appear to him that he could be the same to Miss Baker now; their little habits were disarranged, their customs broken up. He could no longer fancy himself so near to her. They would drift apart now, and she would no longer make herself a cup of tea and "keep company" with him when she knew that he would never again sit before his table binding uncut pamphlets. He had sold his happiness for money; he had bartered all his tardy romance for some miserable bank-notes. He had not foreseen that it would be like this. A vast regret welled up within him. What was that on the back of his hand? He wiped it dry with his ancient silk handkerchief.

Old Grannis leant his face in his hands. Not only did an inexplicable regret stir within him, but a certain great tenderness came upon him. The tears that swam in his faded blue eyes were not altogether those of unhappiness. No, this long-delayed affection that had come upon him in his later years filled him with a joy for which tears seemed to be the natural expression. For thirty years his eyes had not been wet, but to-night he felt as if he were young again. He had never loved before, and there was still a part of him that was only twenty years of age. He could not tell whether he was profoundly sad or deeply happy; but he was not ashamed of the tears that brought the smart to his eyes and the ache to his throat.

He did not hear the timid rapping on his door, and it was not until the door itself opened that he looked up quickly and saw the little retired dressmaker standing on the threshold, carrying a cup of tea on a tiny Japanese tray. She held it toward him.

"I was making some tea," she said, "and I thought you would like to have a cup."

Never after could the little dressmaker understand how she had brought herself to do this thing. One moment she had been sitting quietly on her side of the partition, stirring her cup of tea with one of her Gorham spoons. She was quiet, she was peaceful. The evening was closing down tranquilly. Her room was the picture of calmness and order. The geraniums blooming in the starch boxes in the window, the aged goldfish occasionally turning his iridescent flank to catch a sudden glow of the setting sun. The next moment she had been all trepidation. It seemed to her the most natural thing in the world to make a steaming cup of tea and carry it in to Old Grannis next door. It seemed to her that he was wanting her, that she ought to go to him. With the brusque resolve and intrepidity that sometimes seizes upon very timid people—the courage of the coward greater than all others—she had presented herself at the old Englishman's half-open door, and, when he had not heeded her knock, had pushed it open, and at last, after all these years, stood upon the threshold of his room. She had found courage enough to explain her intrusion.

"I was making some tea, and I thought you would like to have a cup."

Old Grannis dropped his hands upon either arm of his chair, and, leaning forward a little, looked at her blankly. He did not speak.

The retired dressmaker's courage had carried her thus far; now it deserted her as abruptly as it had come. Her cheeks became scarlet; her funny little false curls trembled with her agitation. What she had done seemed to her indecorous beyond expression. It was an enormity. Fancy, she had gone into his room, *into his room*— Mister Grannis's room. She had done this—she who could not pass him on the stairs without a qualm. What to do she did not know. She stood, a fixture, on the threshold of his room, without even resolution enough to beat a retreat. Helplessly, and with a little quaver in her voice, she repeated obstinately:

"I was making some tea, and I thought you would like to have a cup of tea." Her agitation betrayed itself in the repetition of the word. She felt that she could not hold the tray out another instant. Already she was trembling so that half the tea was spilled.

Old Grannis still kept silence, still bending forward, with wide eyes, his hands gripping the arms of his chair.

Then with the tea-tray still held straight before her, the little dressmaker exclaimed tearfully:

"Oh, I didn't mean—I didn't mean—I didn't know it would seem like this. I only meant to be kind and bring you some tea; and now it seems *so* improper. I—I—I'm *so* ashamed! I don't know what you will think of me. I—" she caught her breath—"improper—" she managed to exclaim, "unlady-like—you can never think well of me—I'll go. I'll go." She turned about.

"Stop," cried Old Grannis, finding his voice at last. Miss Baker paused, looking at him over her shoulder, her eyes very wide open, blinking through her tears, for all the world like a frightened child.

"Stop," exclaimed the old Englishman, rising to his feet. "I didn't know it was you at first. I hadn't dreamed—I couldn't believe you would be so good, so kind to me. Oh," he cried, with a sudden sharp breath, "oh, you *are* kind. I—I—you have—have made me very happy."

"No, no," exclaimed Miss Baker, ready to sob. "It was unlady-like. You will—you must think ill of me." She stood in the hall. The tears were running down her cheeks, and she had no free hand to dry them.

"Let me—I'll take the tray from you," cried Old Grannis, coming forward. A tremulous joy came upon him. Never in his life had he been so happy. At last it had come—come when he had least expected it. That which he had longed for and hoped for through so many years, behold, it was come tonight. He felt his awkwardness leaving him. He was almost certain that the little dressmaker loved him, and the thought gave him boldness. He came toward her and took the tray from her hands, and, turning back into the room with it, made as if to set it upon his table. But the piles of his pamphlets were in the way. Both of his hands were occupied with the tray; he could not make a place for it on the table. He stood for a moment uncertain, his embarrassment returning.

"Oh, won't you—won't you please—" He turned his head, looking appealingly at the little old dressmaker.

"Wait, I'll help you," she said. She came into the room, up to the table, and moved the pamphlets to one side.

"Thanks, thanks," murmured Old Grannis, setting down the tray.

"Now—now—now I will go back," she exclaimed, hurriedly.

"No—no," returned the old Englishman. "Don't go, don't go. I've been so lonely to-night—and last night too—all this year—all my life," he suddenly cried.

"I—I—I've forgotten the sugar."

"But I never take sugar in my tea."

"But it's rather cold, and I've spilled it—almost all of it."

"I'll drink it from the saucer." Old Grannis had drawn up his armchair for her.

"Oh, I shouldn't. This is—this is *so*— You must think ill of me." Suddenly she sat down, and resting her elbows on the table, hid her face in her hands.

"Think *ill* of you?" cried Old Grannis, "think *ill* of you? Why, you don't know—you have no idea—all these years—living so close to you, I—I—" he paused suddenly. It seemed to him as if the beating of his heart was choking him.

"I thought you were binding your books tonight," said Miss Baker, suddenly, "and you looked tired. I thought you looked tired when I last saw you, and a cup of tea, you know, it—that—that does you so much good when you're tired. But you weren't binding books."

"No, no," returned Old Grannis, drawing up a chair and sitting down. "No, I—the fact is, I've sold my apparatus; a firm of book-sellers has bought the rights of it."

"And aren't you going to bind books any more?" exclaimed the little dressmaker, a shade of disappointment in her manner. "I thought you always did about four o'clock. I used to hear you when I was making tea."

It hardly seemed possible to Miss Baker that she was actually talking to Old Grannis, that the two were really chatting together, face to face, and without the dreadful embarrassment that used to overwhelm them both when they met on the stairs. She had often dreamed of this, but had always put it off to some far-distant day. It was to come gradually, little by little, instead of, as now, abruptly and with no preparation. That she should permit herself the indiscretion of actually intruding herself into his room had never so much as occurred to her. Yet here she was, *in his room*, and they were talking together, and little by little her embarrassment was wearing away.

"Yes, yes, I always heard you when you were making tea," returned the old Englishman; "I heard the tea things. Then I used to draw my chair and my work-table close to the wall on my side, and sit there and work while you drank your tea just on the other side; and I used to feel very near to you then. I used to pass the whole evening that way."

"And, yes—yes—I did too," she answered. "I used to make tea just at that time and sit there for a whole hour."

"And didn't you sit close to the partition on your side? Sometimes I was sure of it. I could even fancy that I could hear your dress brushing against the wall-paper close beside me. Didn't you sit close to the partition?"

"I—I don't know where I sat."

Old Grannis shyly put out his hand and took hers as it lay upon her lap.

"Didn't you sit close to the partition on your side?" he insisted.

"No—I don't know—perhaps—sometimes. Oh, yes," she exclaimed, with a little gasp, "Oh, yes, I often did."

Then Old Grannis put his arm about her, and kissed her faded cheek, that flushed to pink upon the instant.

After that they spoke but little. The day lapsed slowly into twilight, and the two old people sat there in the grey evening, quietly, quietly, their hands in each other's hands, "keeping company," but now with nothing to separate them. It had come at last. After all these years they were together; they understood each other. They stood at length in a little Elysium of their own creating. They walked hand in hand in a delicious garden where it was always autumn. Far from the world and together they entered upon the long retarded romance of their commonplace and uneventful lives.

XVIII

That same night McTeague was awakened by a shrill scream, and woke to find Trina's arms around his neck. She was trembling so that the bed-springs creaked.

"Huh?" cried the dentist, sitting up in bed, raising his clinched fists. "Huh? What? What? What is it? What is it?"

"Oh, Mac," gasped his wife, "I had such an awful dream. I dreamed about Maria. I thought she was chasing me, and I couldn't run, and her throat was—Oh, she was all covered with blood. Oh-h, I am so frightened!"

Trina had borne up very well for the first day or so after the affair, and had given her testimony to the coroner with far greater calmness than Heise. It was only a week later that the horror of the thing came upon her again. She was so nervous that she hardly dared to be alone in the daytime, and almost every night woke with a cry of terror, trembling with the recollection of some dreadful nightmare. The dentist was irritated beyond all expression by her nervousness, and especially was he exasperated when her cries woke him suddenly in the middle of the night. He would sit up in bed, rolling his eyes wildly, throwing out his huge fists—at what, he did not know—exclaiming, "What—what—" bewildered and hopelessly confused. Then when he realized that it was only Trina, his anger kindled abruptly.

"Oh, you and your dreams! You go to sleep, or I'll give you a dressing down." Sometimes he would hit her a great thwack with his open palm, or catch her hand and bite the tops of her fingers.

Trina would lie awake for hours afterward, crying softly to herself.
Then, by and by, "Mac," she would say timidly.

"Huh?"

"Mac, do you love me?"

"Huh? What? Go to sleep."

"Don't you love me any more, Mac?"

"Oh, go to sleep. Don't bother me."

"Well, do you *love* me, Mac?"

"*I* guess so."

"Oh, Mac, I've only you now, and if *you* don't love me, what is
going to become of me?"

"Shut up, an' let me go to sleep."

"Well, just tell me that you love me."

The dentist would turn abruptly away from her, burying his big
blond head in the pillow, and covering up his ears with the blankets. Then Trina would sob herself to sleep.

The dentist had long since given up looking for a job. Between
breakfast and supper time Trina saw but little of him. Once the
morning meal over, McTeague bestirred himself, put on his cap—
he had given up wearing even a hat since his wife had made him
sell his silk hat—and went out. He had fallen into the habit of
taking long and solitary walks beyond the suburbs of the city. Sometimes it was to the Cliff House, occasionally to the Park (where he
would sit on the sun-warmed benches, smoking his pipe and reading
ragged ends of old newspapers), but more often it was to the Presidio Reservation. McTague would walk out to the end of the Union
Street car line, entering the Reservation at the terminus, then he
would work down to the shore of the bay, follow the shore line to
the Old Fort at the Golden Gate, and, turning the Point here,
come out suddenly upon the full sweep of the Pacific. Then he
would follow the beach down to a certain point of rocks that he
knew. Here he would turn inland, climbing the bluffs to a rolling
grassy down sown with blue iris and a yellow flower that he did not
know the name of. On the far side of this down was a broad, well-
kept road. McTeague would keep to this road until he reached the
city again by the way of the Sacramento Street car line.[1] The dentist loved these walks. He liked to be alone. He liked the solitude of
the tremendous, tumbling ocean; the fresh, windy downs; he liked
to feel the gusty Trades flogging his face, and he would remain for
hours watching the roll and plunge of the breakers with the silent,
unreasoned enjoyment of a child. All at once he developed a passion for fishing. He would sit all day nearly motionless upon a point

1. McTeague would have walked ap-
proximately ten miles on this circuit.
The Park is Lincoln Park, the Old Fort
is Fort Winfield Scott, and the Point is
Fort Point, at the foot of the present
Golden Gate Bridge.

of rocks, his fish-line between his fingers, happy if he caught three perch in twelve hours. At noon he would retire to a bit of level turf around an angle of the shore and cook his fish, eating them without salt or knife or fork. He thrust a pointed stick down the mouth of the perch, and turned it slowly over the blaze. When the grease stopped dripping, he knew that it was done, and would devour it slowly and with tremendous relish, picking the bones clean, eating even the head. He remembered how often he used to do this sort of thing when he was a boy in the mountains of Placer County, before he became a car-boy at the mine. The dentist enjoyed himself hugely during these days. The instincts of the old-time miner were returning. In the stress of his misfortune McTeague was lapsing back to his early estate.

One evening as he reached home after such a tramp, he was surprised to find Trina standing in front of what had been Zerkow's house, looking at it thoughtfully, her finger on her lips.

"What you doing here?" growled the dentist as he came up. There was a "Rooms-to-let" sign on the street door of the house.

"Now we've found a place to move to," exclaimed Trina.

"What?" cried McTeague. "There, in that dirty house, where you found Maria?"

"I can't afford that room in the flat any more, now that you can't get any work to do."

"But there's where Zerkow killed Maria—the very house—an' you wake up an' squeal in the night just thinking of it."

"I know. I know it will be bad at first, but I'll get used to it, an' it's just half again as cheap as where we are now. I was looking at a room; we can have it dirt cheap. It's a back room over the kitchen. A German family are going to take the front part of the house and sublet the rest. I'm going to take it. It'll be money in my pocket."

"But it won't be any in mine," vociferated the dentist, angrily. "I'll have to live in that dirty rat hole just so's you can save money. I ain't any the better off for it."

"Find work to do, and then we'll talk," declared Trina. "I'm going to save up some money against a rainy day; and if I can save more by living here I'm going to do it, even if it is the house Maria was killed in. I don't care."

"All right," said McTeague, and did not make any further protest. His wife looked at him surprised. She could not understand this sudden acquiescence. Perhaps McTeague was so much away from home of late that he had ceased to care where or how he lived. But this sudden change troubled her a little for all that.

The next day the McTeagues moved for a second time. It did not take them long. They were obliged to buy the bed from the landlady, a circumstance which nearly broke Trina's heart; and this bed, a couple of chairs, Trina's trunk, an ornament or two, the oil stove, and some plates and kitchen ware were all that they could call their own now; and this back room in that wretched house with its grisly memories, the one window looking out into a grimy maze of back yards and broken sheds, was what they now knew as their home.

The McTeagues now began to sink rapidly lower and lower. They became accustomed to their surroundings. Worst of all, Trina lost her pretty ways and her good looks. The combined effects of hard work, avarice, poor food, and her husband's brutalities told on her swiftly. Her charming little figure grew coarse, stunted, and dumpy. She who had once been of a cat-like neatness, now slovened all day about the room in a dirty flannel wrapper, her slippers clap-clapping after her as she walked. At last she even neglected her hair, the wonderful swarthy tiara, the coiffure of a queen, that shaded her little pale forehead. In the morning she braided it before it was half combed, and piled and coiled it about her head in haphazard fashion. It came down half a dozen times a day; by evening it was an unkempt, tangled mass, a veritable rat's nest.

Ah, no, it was not very gay, that life of hers, when one had to rustle for two, cook and work and wash, to say nothing of paying the rent. What odds was it if she was slatternly, dirty, coarse? Was there time to make herself look otherwise, and who was there to be pleased when she was all prinked out? Surely not a great brute of a husband who bit you like a dog, and kicked and pounded you as though you were made of iron. Ah, no, better let things go, and take it as easy as you could. Hump your back, and it was soonest over.

The one room grew abominably dirty, reeking with the odors of cooking and of "non-poisonous" paint. The bed was not made until late in the afternoon, sometimes not at all. Dirty, unwashed crockery, greasy knives, sodden fragments of yesterday's meals cluttered the table, while in one corner was the heap of evil-smelling, dirty linen. Cockroaches appeared in the crevices of the woodwork, the wall-paper bulged from the damp walls and began to peel. Trina had long ago ceased to dust or to wipe the furniture with a bit of rag. The grime grew thick upon the window panes and in the corners of the room. All the filth of the alley invaded their quarters like a rising muddy tide.

Between the windows, however, the faded photograph of the couple in their wedding finery looked down upon the wretchedness, Trina still holding her set bouquet straight before her, McTeague standing at her side, his left foot forward, in the attitude of a Secretary of State; while near by hung the canary, the one thing the dentist clung to obstinately, piping and chittering all day in its little gilt prison.

And the tooth, the gigantic golden molar of French gilt, enormous and ungainly, sprawled its branching prongs in one corner of the room, by the footboard of the bed. The McTeagues had come to use it as a sort of substitute for a table. After breakfast and supper Trina piled the plates and greasy dishes upon it to have them out of the way.

One afternoon the Other Dentist, McTeague's old-time rival, the wearer of marvellous waistcoats, was surprised out of all countenance to receive a visit from McTeague. The Other Dentist was in his operating room at the time, at work upon a plaster-of-paris mould. To his call of "Come right in. Don't you see the sign, 'Enter without knocking'?" McTeague came in. He noted at once how airy and cheerful was the room. A little fire coughed and tittered on the hearth, a brindled greyhound sat on his haunches watching it intently, a great mirror over the mantle offered to view an array of actresses' pictures thrust between the glass and the frame, and a big bunch of freshly-cut violets stood in a glass bowl on the polished cherry-wood table. The Other Dentist came forward briskly, exclaiming cheerfully:

"Oh, Doctor—Mister McTeague, how do? how do?"

The fellow was actually wearing a velvet smoking jacket. A cigarette was between his lips; his patent leather boots reflected the firelight. McTeague wore a black surah negligé shirt[2] without a cravat; huge buckled brogans, hob-nailed, gross, encased his feet; the hems of his trousers were spotted with mud; his coat was frayed at the sleeves and a button was gone. In three days he had not shaved; his shock of heavy blond hair escaped from beneath the visor of his woolen cap and hung low over his forehead. He stood with awkward, shifting feet and uncertain eyes before this dapper young fellow who reeked of the barber shop, and whom he had once ordered from his rooms.

"What can I do for you this morning, Mister McTeague? Something wrong with the teeth, eh?"

"No, no." McTeague, floundering in the difficulties of his speech, forgot the carefully rehearsed words with which he had intended to begin this interview.

"I want to sell you my sign," he said, stupidly. "That big tooth of French guilt—*you* know—that you made an offer for once."

"Oh, I don't want that now," said the other loftily. "I prefer a little quiet signboard, nothing pretentious—just the name, and "Dentist" after it. These big signs are vulgar. No, I don't want it."

2. An open-necked shirt made of soft cloth.

McTeague remained, looking about on the floor, horribly embarrassed, not knowing whether to go or to stay.

"But I don't know," said the Other Dentist, reflectively. "If it will help you out any—I guess you're pretty hard up—I'll—well, I tell you what—I'll give you five dollars for it."

"All right, all right."

On the following Thursday morning McTeague woke to hear the eaves dripping and the prolonged rattle of the rain upon the roof.

"Raining," he growled, in deep disgust, sitting up in bed, and winking at the blurred window.

"It's been raining all night," said Trina. She was already up and dressed, and was cooking breakfast on the oil stove.

McTeague dressed himself, grumbling, "Well, I'll go, *anyhow*. The fish will bite all the better for the rain."

"Look here, Mac," said Trina, slicing a bit of bacon as thinly as she could. "Look here, why don't you bring some of your fish home sometime?"

"Huh!" snorted the dentist, "so's we could have 'em for breakfast. Might save you a nickel, mightn't it?"

"Well, and if it did! Or you might fish for the market. The fisherman across the street would buy 'em of you."

"Shut up!" exclaimed the dentist, and Trina obediently subsided.

"Look here," continued her husband, fumbling in his trousers pocket and bringing out a dollar, "I'm sick and tired of coffee and bacon and mashed potatoes. Go over to the market and get some kind of meat for breakfast. Get a steak, or chops, or something."

"Why, Mac, that's a whole dollar, and he only gave you five for your sign. We can't afford it. Sure, Mac. Let me put that money away against a rainy day. You're just as well off without meat for breakfast."

"You do as I tell you. Get some steak, or chops, or something."

"Please, Mac, dear."

"Go on, now. I'll bite your fingers again pretty soon."

"But——"

The dentist took a step towards her, snatching at her hand.

"All right, I'll go," cried Trina, wincing and shrinking. "I'll go."

She did not get the chops at the big market, however. Instead, she hurried to a cheaper butcher shop on a side street two blocks away, and bought fifteen cents' worth of chops from a side of mutton some two or three days old. She was gone some little time.

"Give me the change," exclaimed the dentist as soon as she returned. Trina handed him a quarter; and when McTeague was about to protest, broke in upon him with a rapid stream of talk that confused him upon the instant. But for that matter, it was never difficult for Trina to deceive the dentist. He never went to the bottom of things. He would have believed her if she had told him the chops had cost a dollar.

"There's sixty cents saved, anyhow," thought Trina, as she clutched the money in her pocket to keep it from rattling.

Trina cooked the chops, and they breakfasted in silence.

"Now," said McTeague as he rose, wiping the coffee from his thick mustache with the hollow of his palm, "now I'm going fishing, rain or no rain. I'm going to be gone all day."

He stood for a moment at the door, his fish-line in his hand, swinging the heavy sinker back and forth. He looked at Trina as she cleared away the breakfast things.

"So long," said he, nodding his huge square-cut head. This amiability in the matter of leave taking was unusual. Trina put the dishes down and came up to him, her little chin, once so adorable, in the air:

"Kiss me good-by, Mac," she said, putting her arms around his neck. "You *do* love me a little yet, don't you, Mac? We'll be happy again some day. This is hard times now, but we'll pull out. You'll find something to do pretty soon."

"*I* guess so," growled McTeague, allowing her to kiss him.

The canary was stirring nimbly in its cage, and just now broke out into a shrill trilling, its little throat bulging and quivering. The dentist stared at it. "Say," he remarked slowly, "I think I'll take that bird of mine along."

"Sell it?" inquired Trina.

"Yes, yes, sell it."

"Well, you *are* coming to your senses at last," answered Trina, approvingly. "But don't you let the bird-store man cheat you. That's a good songster; and with the cage, you ought to make him give you five dollars. You stick out for that at first, anyhow."

McTeague unhooked the cage and carefully wrapped it in an old newspaper, remarking, "He might get cold. Well, so long," he repeated, "so long."

"Good-by, Mac."

When he was gone, Trina took the sixty cents she had stolen from him out of her pocket and recounted it. "It's sixty cents, all right," she said proudly. "But I *do* believe that dime is too smooth." She looked at it critically. The clock on the power-house of the Sutter Street cable struck eight. "Eight o'clock already," she exclaimed. "I must get to work." She cleared the breakfast things from the table, and drawing up her chair and her workbox began painting the sets of Noah's ark animals she had whittled the day before. She worked steadily all the morning. At noon she lunched, warming over the coffee left from breakfast, and frying a couple of sausages. By one she was bending over her table again. Her fingers—

some of them lacerated by McTeague's teeth—flew, and the little pile of cheap toys in the basket at her elbow grew steadily.

"Where *do* all the toys go to?" she mummured. "The thousands and thousands of these Noah's arks that I have made—horses and chickens and elephants—and always there never seems to be enough. It's a good thing for me that children break their things, and that they all have to have birthdays and Christmases." She dipped her brush into a pot of Vandyke brown and painted one of the whittled toy horses in two strokes. Then a touch of ivory black with a small flat brush created the tail and mane, and dots of Chinese white made the eyes. The turpentine in the paint dried it almost immediately, and she tossed the completed little horse into the basket.

At six o'clock the dentist had not returned. Trina waited until seven, and then put her work away, and ate her supper alone.

"I wonder what's keeping Mac," she exclaimed as the clock from the power-house on Sutter Street struck half-past seven. "I *know* he's drinking somewhere," she cried, apprehensively. "He had the money from his sign with him."

At eight o'clock she threw a shawl over her head and went over to the harness shop. If anybody would know where McTeague was it would be Heise. But the harness-maker had seen nothing of him since the day before.

"He was in here yesterday afternoon, and we had a drink or two at Frenna's. Maybe he's been in there to-day."

"Oh, won't you go in and see?" said Trina. "Mac always came home to his supper—he never likes to miss his meals—and I'm getting frightened about him."

Heise went into the barroom next door, and returned with no definite news. Frenna had not seen the dentist since he had come in with the harness-maker the previous afternoon. Trina even humbled herself to ask of the Ryers—with whom they had quarrelled—if they knew anything of the dentist's whereabouts, but received a contemptuous negative.

"Maybe he's come in while I've been out," said Trina to herself. She went down Polk Street again, going towards the flat. The rain had stopped, but the sidewalks were still glistening. The cable cars trundled by, loaded with theatregoers. The barbers were just closing their shops. The candy store on the corner was brilliantly lighted and was filling up, while the green and yellow lamps from the drug store directly opposite threw kaleidoscopic reflections deep down into the shining surface of the asphalt. A band of Salvationists began to play and pray in front of Frenna's saloon. Trina hurried on down the gay street, with its evening's brilliancy and small activities, her shawl over her head, one hand lifting her faded skirt from off the wet pavements. She turned into the alley, entered Zerkow's old home by the ever-open door, and ran up-stairs to the room. Nobody.

"Why, isn't this *funny*," she exclaimed, half aloud, standing on the threshold, her little milk-white forehead curdling to a frown, one sore finger on her lips. Then a great fear seized upon her. Inevitably she associated the house with a scene of violent death.

"No, no," she said to the darkness, "Mac is all right. He can take care of himself." But for all that she had a clear-cut vision of her husband's body, bloated with sea-water, his blond hair streaming like kelp, rolling inertly in shifting waters.

"He couldn't have fallen off the rocks," she declared firmly. "There—*there* he is now." She heaved a great sigh of relief as a heavy tread sounded in the hallway below. She ran to the banisters, looking over, and calling, "Oh, Mac! Is that you, Mac?" It was the German whose family occupied the lower floor. The power-house clock struck nine.

"My God, where *is* Mac?" cried Trina, stamping her foot.

She put the shawl over her head again, and went out and stood on the corner of the alley and Polk Street, watching and waiting, craning her neck to see down the street. Once, even, she went out upon the sidewalk in front of the flat and sat down for a moment upon the horse-block there. She could not help remembering the day when she had been driven up to that horse-block in a hack. Her mother and father and Owgooste and the twins were with her. It was her wedding day. Her wedding dress was in a huge tin trunk on the driver's seat. She had never been happier before in all her life. She remembered how she got out of the hack and stood for a moment upon the horse-block, looking up at McTeague's windows. She had caught a glimpse of him at his shaving, the lather still on his cheek, and they had waved their hands at each other. Instinctively Trina looked up at the flat behind her; looked up at the bay window where her husband's "Dental Parlors" had been. It was all dark; the windows had the blind, sightless appearance imparted by vacant, untenanted rooms. A rusty iron rod projected mournfully from one of the window ledges.

"There's where our sign hung once," said Trina. She turned her head and looked down Polk Street towards where the Other Dentist had his rooms, and there, overhanging the street from his window, newly furbished and brightened, hung the huge tooth, her birthday present to her husband, flashing and glowing in the white glare of the electric lights like a beacon of defiance and triumph.

"Ah, no; ah, no," whispered Trina, choking back a sob. "Life isn't so gay. But I wouldn't mind, no I wouldn't mind anything, if only Mac was home all right." She got up from the horse-block and stood again on the corner of the alley, watching and listening.

It grew later. The hours passed. Trina kept at her post. The noise of approaching footfalls grew less and less frequent. Little by little Polk Street dropped back into solitude. Eleven o'clock struck from the power-house clock; lights were extinguished; at one o'clock the cable stopped, leaving an abrupt and numbing silence in the air. All at once it seemed very still. The only noises were the occasional footfalls of a policeman and the persistent calling of ducks and geese in the closed market across the way. The street was asleep.

When it is night and dark, and one is awake and alone, one's thoughts take the color of the surroundings; become gloomy, sombre, and very dismal. All at once an idea came to Trina, a dark, terrible idea; worse, even, than the idea of McTeague's death.

"Oh, no," she cried. "Oh, no. It isn't true. But suppose—suppose."

She left her post and hurried back to the house.

"No, no," she was saying under her breath, "it isn't possible. Maybe he's even come home already by another way. But suppose—suppose—suppose."

She ran up the stairs, opened the door of the room, and paused, out of breath. The room was dark and empty. With cold, trembling fingers she lighted the lamp, and, turning about, looked at her trunk. The lock was burst.

"No, no, no," cried Trina, "it's not true; it's not true." She dropped on her knees before the trunk, and tossed back the lid, and plunged her hands down into the corner underneath her wedding dress, where she always kept the savings. The brass match-safe and the chamois-skin bag were there. They were empty.

Trina flung herself full length upon the floor, burying her face in her arms, rolling her head from side to side. Her voice rose to a wail.

"No, no, no, it's not true; it's not true; it's not true. Oh, he couldn't have done it. Oh, how could he have done it? All my money, all my little savings—and deserted me. He's gone, my money's gone, my dear money—my dear, dear gold pieces that I've worked so hard for. Oh, to have deserted me—gone for good—gone and never coming back—gone with my gold pieces. Gone—gone—gone. I'll never see them again, and I've worked so hard, so so hard for him—for them. No, no, *no*, it's not true. It *is* true. What will become of me now? Oh, if you'll only come back you can have all the money—half of it. Oh, give me back my money. Give me back my money, and I'll forgive you. You can leave me then if you want to. Oh, my money. Mac, Mac, you've gone for good. You don't love me any more, and now I'm a beggar. My money's gone, my husband's gone, gone, gone, gone!"

Her grief was terrible. She dug her nails into her scalp, and clutching the heavy coils of her thick black hair tore it again and again. She struck her forehead with her clenched fists. Her little body shook from head to foot with the violence of her sobbing. She ground her small teeth together and beat her head upon the floor with all her strenght.

Her hair was uncoiled and hanging a tangled, dishevelled mass far below her waist; her dress was torn; a spot of blood was upon her forehead; her eyes were swollen; her cheeks flamed vermilion from the fever that raged in her veins. Old Miss Baker found her thus towards five o'clock the next morning.

What had happened between one o'clock and dawn of that fearful night Trina never remembered. She could only recall herself, as in a picture, kneeling before her broken and rifled trunk, and then —weeks later, so it seemed to her—she woke to find herself in her own bed with an iced bandage about her forehead and the little old dressmaker at her side, stroking her hot, dry palm.

The facts of the matter were that the German woman who lived below had been awakened some hours after midnight by the sounds of Trina's weeping. She had come up-stairs and into the room to find Trina stretched face downward upon the floor, half conscious and sobbing, in the throes of an hysteria for which there was no relief. The woman, terrified, had called her husband, and between them they had got Trina upon the bed. Then the German woman happened to remember that Trina had friends in the big flat near by, and had sent her husband to fetch the retired dressmaker, while she herself remained behind to undress Trina and put her to bed. Miss Baker had come over at once, and began to cry herself at the sight of the dentist's poor little wife. She did not stop to ask what the trouble was, and indeed it would have been useless to attempt to get any coherent explanation from Trina at that time. Miss Baker had sent the German woman's husband to get some ice at one of the "all-night" restaurants of the street; had kept cold, wet towels on Trina's head; had combed and recombed her wonderful thick hair; and had sat down by the side of the bed, holding her hot hand, with its poor maimed fingers, waiting patiently until Trina should be able to speak.

Towards morning Trina awoke—or perhaps it was a mere regaining of consciousness—looked a moment at Miss Baker, then about the room until her eyes fell upon her trunk with its broken lock. Then she turned over upon the pillow and began to sob again. She refused to answer any of the little dressmaker's questions, shaking her head violently, her face hidden in the pillow.

By breakfast time her fever had increased to such a point that Miss Baker took matters into her own hands and had the German woman call a doctor. He arrived some twenty minutes later. He was a big, kindly fellow who lived over the drug store on the corner. He had a deep voice and a tremendous striding gait less suggestive of a physician than of a sergeant of a cavalry troop.

By the time of his arrival little Miss Baker had divined intuitively the entire trouble. She heard the doctor's swinging tramp in the entry below, and heard the German woman saying:

"Righd oop der stairs, at der back of der halle. Der room mit der door oppen."

Miss Baker met the doctor at the landing, she told him in a whisper of the trouble.

"Her husband's deserted her, I'm afraid, doctor, and took all of her money—a good deal of it. It's about killed the poor child. She was out of her head a good deal of the night, and now she's got a raging fever."

The doctor and Miss Baker returned to the room and entered, closing the door. The big doctor stood for a moment looking down at Trina rolling her head from side to side upon the pillow, her face scarlet, her enormous mane of hair spread out on either side of her. The little dressmaker remained at his elbow, looking from him to Trina.

"Poor little woman!" said the doctor; "poor little woman!"

Miss Baker pointed to the trunk, whispering:

"See, there's where she kept her savings. See, he broke the lock."

"Well, Mrs. McTeague," said the doctor, sitting down by the bed, and taking Trina's wrist, "a little fever, eh?"

Trina opened her eyes and looked at him, and then at Miss Baker. She did not seem in the least surprised at the unfamiliar faces. She appeared to consider it all as a matter of course.

"Yes," she said, with a long, tremulous breath, "I have a fever, and my head—my head aches and aches."

The doctor prescribed rest and mild opiates. Then his eye fell upon the fingers of Trina's right hand. He looked at them sharply. A deep red glow, unmistakable to a physician's eyes, was upon some of them, extending from the finger tips up to the second knuckle.

"Hello," he exclaimed, "what's the matter here?" In fact something was very wrong indeed. For days Trina had noticed it. The fingers of her right hand had swollen as never before, aching and discolored. Cruelly lacerated by McTeague's brutality as they were, she had nevertheless gone on about her work on the Noah's ark animals, constantly in contact with the "non-poisonous" paint. She told as much to the doctor in answer to his questions. He shook his head with an exclamation.

"Why, this is blood-poisoning, you know," he told her; "the worst kind. You'll have to have those fingers amputated, beyond a doubt, or lose the entire hand—or even worse."

"And my work!" exclaimed Trina.

XIX

One can hold a scrubbing-brush with two good fingers and the stumps of two others even if both joints of the thumb are gone, but it takes considerable practice to get used to it.

Trina became a scrub-woman. She had taken council of Selina, and through her had obtained the position of care-taker in a little memorial kindergarten over on Pacific Street.[1] Like Polk Street, it was an accommodation street, but running through a much poorer and more sordid quarter. Trina had a little room over the kindergarten schoolroom. It was not an unpleasant room. It looked out upon a sunny little court floored with boards and used as the children's playground. Two great cherry trees grew here, the leaves almost brushing against the window of Trina's room and filtering the sunlight so that it fell in round golden spots upon the floor of the room. "Like gold pieces," Trina said to herself.

Trina's work consisted in taking care of the kindergarten rooms, scrubbing the floors, washing the windows, dusting and airing, and carrying out the ashes. Besides this she earned some five dollars a month by washing down the front steps of some big flats on Washington Street, and by cleaning out vacant houses after the tenants had left. She saw no one. Nobody knew her. She went about her work from dawn to dark, and often entire days passed when she did not hear the sound of her own voice. She was alone, a solitary, abandoned woman, lost in the lowest eddies of the great city's tide —the tide that always ebbs.

When Trina had been discharged from the hospital after the operation on her fingers, she found herself alone in the world, alone with her five thousand dollars. The interest of this would support her, and yet allow her to save a little.

But for a time Trina had thought of giving up the fight altogether and of joining her family in the southern part of the State. But even while she hesitated about this she received a long letter from her mother, an answer to one she herself had written just before the amputation of her right-hand fingers—the last letter she would ever be able to write. Mrs. Sieppe's letter was one long lamentation; she had her own misfortunes to bewail as well as those of her daughter. The carpet-cleaning and upholstery business had failed. Mr. Sieppe and Owgooste had left for New Zealand with a colonization company, whither Mrs. Sieppe and the twins were to follow them as soon as the colony established itself. So far from helping Trina in her ill fortune, it was she, her mother, who might

---

1. It was a San Francisco custom for well-to-do families to found kindergartens, and Norris's family had founded the Lester Norris Memorial Kindergarten on Pacific Street. See also Norris's reference to the "grand ladies of the Kindergarten Board" on p. 208.

some day in the near future be obliged to turn to Trina for aid. So
Trina had given up the idea of any help from her family. For that
matter she needed none. She still had her five thousand, and Uncle
Oelbermann paid her the interest with a machine-like regularity.
Now that McTeague had left her, there was one less mouth to feed;
and with this saving, together with the little she could earn as
scrub-woman, Trina could almost manage to make good the amount
she lost by being obliged to cease work upon the Noah's ark animals.

Little by little her sorrow over the loss of her precious savings
overcame the grief of McTeague's desertion of her. Her avarice had
grown to be her one dominant passion; her love of money for the
money's sake brooded in her heart, driving out by degrees every
other natural affection. She grew thin and meagre; her flesh clove
tight to her small skeleton; her small pale mouth and little uplifted
chin grew to have a certain feline eagerness of expression; her long,
narrow eyes glistened continually, as if they caught and held the
glint of metal. One day as she sat in her room, the empty brass
match-box and the limp chamois bag in her hands, she suddenly
exclaimed:

"I could have forgiven him if he had only gone away and left me
my money. I could have—yes, I could have forgiven him even
this"—she looked at the stumps of her fingers. "But now," her teeth
closed tight and her eyes flashed, "now—I'll—never—forgive—him
—as—long—as—I—live."

The empty bag and the hollow, light match-box troubled her.
Day after day she took them from her trunk and wept over them as
other women weep over a dead baby's shoe. Her four hundred dollars were gone, were gone, were gone. She would never see them
again. She could plainly see her husband spending her savings by
handfuls; squandering her beautiful gold pieces that she had been at
such pains to polish with soap and ashes. The thought filled her
with an unspeakable anguish. She would wake at night from a
dream of McTeague revelling down her money, and ask of the darkness, "How much did he spend to-day? How many of the gold
pieces are left? Has he broken either of the two twenty-dollar pieces
yet? What did he spend it for?"

The instant she was out of the hospital Trina had begun to save
again, but now it was with an eagerness that amounted at times to
a veritable frenzy. She even denied herself lights and fuel in order
to put by a quarter or so, grudging every penny she was obliged to
spend. She did her own washing and cooking. Finally she sold her
wedding dress, that had hitherto lain in the bottom of her trunk.

The day she moved from Zerkow's old house, she came suddenly
upon the dentist's concertina under a heap of old clothes in the

closet. Within twenty minutes she had sold it to the dealer in second-hand furniture, returning to her room with seven dollars in her pocket, happy for the first time since McTeague had left her.

But for all that the match-box and the bag refused to fill up; after three weeks of the most rigid economy they contained but eighteen dollars and some small change. What was that compared with four hundred? Trina told herself that she must have her money in hand. She longed to see again the heap of it upon her work-table, where she could plunge her hands into it, her face into it, feeling the cool, smooth metal upon her cheeks. At such moments she would see in her imagination her wonderful five thousand dollars piled in columns, shining and gleaming somewhere at the bottom of Uncle Oelbermann's vault. She would look at the paper that Uncle Oelbermann had given her, and tell herself that it represented five thousand dollars. But in the end this ceased to satisfy her, she must have the money itself. She must have her four hundred dollars back again, there in her trunk, in her bag and her match-box, where she could touch it and see it whenever she desired.

At length she could stand it no longer, and one day presented herself before Uncle Oelbermann as he sat in his office in the wholesale toy store, and told him she wanted to have four hundred dollars of her money.

"But this is very irregular, you know, Mrs. McTeague," said the great man. "Not business-like at all."

But his niece's misfortunes and the sight of her poor maimed hand appealed to him. He opened his check-book. "You understand, of course," he said, "that this will reduce the amount of your interest by just so much."

"I know, I know. I've thought of that," said Trina.

"Four hundred, did you say?" remarked Uncle Oelbermann, taking the cap from his fountain pen.

"Yes, four hundred," exclaimed Trina, quickly, her eyes glistening.

Trina cashed the check and returned home with the money—all in twenty-dollar pieces as she had desired—in an ecstasy of delight. For half of that night she sat up playing with her money, counting it and recounting it, polishing the duller pieces until they shone. Altogether there were twenty twenty-dollar gold pieces.

"Oh-h, you beauties!" murmured Trina, running her palms over them, fairly quivering with pleasure. "You beauties! *Is* there anything prettier than a twenty-dollar gold piece? You dear, dear money! Oh, don't I *love* you! Mine, mine, mine—all of you mine."

She laid them out in a row on the ledge of the table, or arranged them in patterns—triangles, circles, and squares—or built them all up into a pyramid which she afterward overthrew for the sake of hearing the delicious clink of the pieces tumbling against each other. Then at last she put them away in the brass match-box and chamois bag, delighted beyond words that they were once more full and heavy.

Then, a few days after, the thought of the money still remaining in Uncle Oelbermann's keeping returned to her. It was hers, all hers —all that four thousand six hundred. She could have as much of it or as little of it as she chose. She only had to ask. For a week Trina resisted, knowing very well that taking from her capital was proportionately reducing her monthly income. Then at last she yielded.

"Just to make it an even five hundred, anyhow," she told herself. That day she drew a hundred dollars more, in twenty-dollar gold pieces as before. From that time Trina began to draw steadily upon her capital, a little at a time. It was a passion with her, a mania, a veritable mental disease; a temptation such as drunkards only know.

It would come upon her all of a sudden. While she was about her work, scrubbing the floor of some vacant house; or in her room, in the morning, as she made her coffee on the oil stove, or when she woke in the night, a brusque access of cupidity would seize upon her. Her cheeks flushed, her eyes glistened, her breath came short. At times she would leave her work just as it was, put on her old bonnet of black straw, throw her shawl about her, and go straight to Uncle Oelbermann's store and draw against her money. Now it would be a hundred dollars, now sixty; now she would content herself with only twenty; and once, after a fortnight's abstinence, she permitted herself a positive debauch of five hundred. Little by little she drew her capital from Uncle Oelbermann, and little by little her original interest of twenty-five dollars a month dwindled.

One day she presented herself again in the office of the wholesale toy store.

"Will you let me have a check for two hundred dollars, Uncle Oelbermann?" she said.

The great man laid down his fountain pen and leaned back in his swivel chair with great deliberation.

"I don't understand, Mrs. McTeague," he said. "Every week you come here and draw out a little of your money. I've told you that it is not at all regular or business-like for me to let you have it this way. And more than this, it's a great inconvenience to me to give you these checks at unstated times. If you wish to draw out the whole amount let's have some understanding. Draw it in monthly installments of, say, five hundred dollars, or else," he added, abruptly, "draw it all at once, now, today. I would even prefer it that way. Otherwise it's—it's annoying. Come, shall I draw you a check for thirty-seven hundred, and have it over and done with?"

"No, no," cried Trina, with instinctive apprehension, refusing, she did not know why. "No, I'll leave it with you. I won't draw out any more."

She took her departure, but paused on the pavement outside the store, and stood for a moment lost in thought, her eyes beginning to glisten and her breath coming short. Slowly she turned about and reentered the store; but she came back into the office, and stood trembling at the corner of Uncle Oelbermann's desk. He looked up sharply. Twice Trina tried to get her voice, and when it did come to her, she could hardly recognize it. Between breaths she said:

"Yes, all right—I'll—you can give me—will you give me a check for thirty-seven hundred? Give me *all* of my money."

A few hours later she entered her little room over the kindergarten, bolted the door with shaking fingers, and emptied a heavy canvas sack upon the middle of her bed. Then she opened her trunk, and taking thence the brass match-box and the chamois-skin bag added their contents to the pile. Next she laid herself upon the bed and gathered the gleaming heaps of gold pieces to her with both arms, burying her face in them with long sighs of unspeakable delight.

It was a little past noon, and the day was fine and warm. The leaves of the huge cherry trees threw off a certain pungent aroma that entered through the open window, together with long thin shafts of golden sunlight. Below, in the kindergarten, the children were singing gayly and marching to the jangling of the piano. Trina heard nothing, saw nothing. She lay on her bed, her eyes closed, her face buried in a pile of gold that she encircled with both her arms.

Trina even told herself at last that she was happy once more. McTeague became a memory—a memory that faded a little every day—dim and indistinct in the golden splendor of five thousand dollars.

"And yet," Trina would say, "I did love Mac, loved him dearly, only a little while ago. Even when he hurt me, it only made me love him more. How is it I've changed so sudden? How *could* I forget him so soon? It must be because he stole my money. That is it. I couldn't forgive anyone that—no, not even my *mother*. And I never—never—will forgive him."

What had become of her husband Trina did not know. She never saw any of the old Polk Street people. There was no way she could have news of him, even if she had cared to have it. She had her money, that was the main thing. Her passion for it excluded every other sentiment. There it was in the bottom of her trunk, in the canvas sack, the chamois-skin bag, and the little brass match-safe. Not a day passed that Trina did not have it out where she could see and touch it. One evening she had even spread all the gold pieces between the sheets, and had then gone to bed, stripping herself, and had slept all night upon the money, taking a strange and ecstatic pleasure in the touch of the smooth flat pieces the length of her entire body.

One night, some three months after she had come to live at the kindergarten, Trina was awakened by a sharp tap on the pane of the window. She sat up quickly in bed, her heart beating thickly, her eyes rolling wildly in the direction of her trunk. The tap was repeated. Trina rose and went fearfully to the window. The little court below was bright with moonlight, and standing just on the edge of the shadow thrown by one of the cherry trees was McTeague. A bunch of half-ripe cherries was in his hand. He was eating them and throwing the pits at the window. As he caught sight of her, he made an eager sign for her to raise the sash. Reluctant and wondering, Trina obeyed, and the dentist came quickly forward. He was wearing a pair of blue overalls; a navy-blue flannel shirt without a cravat; an old coat, faded, rain-washed, and ripped at the seams; and his woollen cap.

"Say, Trina," he exclaimed, his heavy bass voice pitched just above a whisper, "let me in, will you, huh? Say, will you? I'm regularly starving, and I haven't slept in a Christian bed for two weeks."

At sight at him standing there in the moonlight, Trina could only think of him as the man who had beaten and bitten her, had deserted her and stolen her money, had made her suffer as she had never suffered before in all her life. Now that he had spent the money that he had stolen from her, he was whining to come back —so that he might steal more, no doubt. Once in her room he could not help but smell out her five thousand dollars. Her indignation rose.

"No," she whispered back at him. "No, I will not let you in."

"But listen here, Trina, I tell you I am starving, regularly——"

"Hoh!" interrupted Trina scornfully. "A man can't starve with four hundred dollars, I guess."

"Well—well—I—well—" faltered the dentist. "Never mind now. Give me something to eat, an' let me in an' sleep. I've been sleeping in the Plaza[2] for the last ten nights, and say, I—Damn it, Trina, I ain't had anything to eat since——"

"Where's the four hundred dollars you robbed me of when you deserted me?" returned Trina, coldly.

"Well, I've spent it," growled the dentist. "But you *can't* see me starve, Trina, no matter what's happened. Give me a little money, then."

"I'll see you starve before you get any more of *my* money."

2. The popular name for Portsmouth Square. The square was in the oldest section of city and was close to the Chinese quarter and the red-light district.

The dentist stepped back a pace and stared up at her, wonder-stricken. His face was lean and pinched. Never had the jaw bone looked so enormous, nor the square-cut head so huge. The moonlight made deep black shadows in the shrunken cheeks.

"Huh?" asked the dentist, puzzled. "What did you say?"

"I won't give you any money—never again—not a cent."

"But do you know that I'm hungry?"

"Well, I've been hungry myself. Besides, I *don't* believe you."

"Trina, I ain't had a thing to eat since yesterday morning; that's God's truth. Even if I did get off with your money, you *can't* see me starve, can you? You can't see me walk the streets all night because I ain't got a place to sleep. Will you let me in? Say, will you? Huh?

"No."

"Well, will you give me some money then—just a little? Give me a dollar. Give me half a dol—— Say, give me a *dime*, an' I can get a cup of coffee."

"No."

The dentist paused and looked at her with curious intentness, bewildered, nonplussed.

"Say, you—you must be crazy, Trina. I—I—wouldn't let a *dog* go hungry."

"Not even if he'd bitten you, perhaps."

The dentist stared again.

There was another pause. McTeague looked up at her in silence, a mean and vicious twinkle coming into his small eyes. He uttered a low exclamation, and then checked himself.

"Well, look here, for the last time. I'm starving. I've got nowhere to sleep. Will you give me some money, or something to eat? Will you let me in?"

"No—no—no."

Trina could fancy she almost saw the brassy glint in her husband's eyes. He raised one enormous lean fist. Then he growled:

"If I had hold of you for a minute, by God, I'd make you dance. An' I will yet, I will yet. Don't you be afraid of that."

He turned about, the moonlight showing like a layer of snow upon his massive shoulders. Trina watched him as he passed under the shadow of the cherry trees and crossed the little court. She heard his great feet grinding on the board flooring. He disappeared.

Miser though she was, Trina was only human, and the echo of the dentist's heavy feet had not died away before she began to be sorry for what she had done. She stood by the open window in her nightgown, her finger upon her lips.

"He did looked pinched," she said half aloud. "Maybe he *was* hungry. I ought to have given him something. I wish I had, I *wish* I had. Oh," she cried, suddenly, with a frightened gesture of both hands, "what have I come to be that I would see Mac—my husband—that I would see him starve rather than give him money? No, no. It's too dreadful. I *will* give him some. I'll send it to him to-morrow. Where?—well, he'll come back." She leaned from the window and called as loudly as she dared, "Mac, oh, Mac." There was no answer.

When McTeague had told Trina he had been without food for nearly two days he was speaking the truth. The week before he had spent the last of the four hundred dollars in the bar of a sailor's lodging-house near the water front, and since that time had lived a veritable hand-to-mouth existence.

He had spent her money here and there about the city in royal fashion, absolutely reckless of the morrow, feasting and drinking for the most part with companions he picked up heaven knows where, acquaintances of twenty-four hours, whose names he forgot in two days. Then suddenly he found himself at the end of his money. He no longer had any friends. Hunger rode him and rowelled him. He was no longer well fed, comfortable. There was no longer a warm place for him to sleep. He went back to Polk Street in the evening, walking on the dark side of the street, lurking in the shadows, ashamed to have any of his old-time friends see him. He entered Zerkow's old house and knocked at the door of the room Trina and he had occupied. It was empty.

Next day he went to Uncle Oelbermann's store and asked news of Trina. Trina had not told Uncle Oelbermann of McTeague's brutalities, giving him other reasons to explain the loss of her fingers; neither had she told him of her husband's robbery. So when the dentist had asked where Trina could be found, Uncle Oelbermann, believing that McTeague was seeking a reconciliation, had told him without hesitation, and, he added:

"She was in here only yesterday and drew out the balance of her money. She's been drawing against her money for the last month or so. She's got it all now, I guess."

"Ah, she's got it all."

The dentist went away from his bootless visit to his wife shaking with rage, hating her with all the strength of a crude and primitive nature. He clenched his fists till his knuckles whitened, his teeth ground furiously upon one another.

"Ah, if I had hold of you once, I'd make you dance. She had five thousand dollars in that room, while I stood there, not twenty feet away, and told her I was starving, and she wouldn't give me a dime to get a cup of coffee with; not a dime to get a cup of coffee. Oh, if I once get my hands on you!" His wrath strangled him. He clutched at the darkness in front of him, his breath fairly whistling between his teeth.

That night he walked the streets until the morning, wondering what now he was to do to fight the wolf away. The morning of the next day towards ten o'clock he was on Kearney Street, still walking, still tramping the streets, since there was nothing else for him to do. By and by he paused on a corner near a music store, finding a momentary amusement in watching two or three men loading a piano upon a dray. Already half its weight was supported by the dray's backboard. One of the men, a big mulatto, almost hidden under the mass of glistening rosewood, was guiding its course, while the other two heaved and tugged in the rear. Something in the street frightened the horses and they shied abruptly. The end of the piano was twitched sharply from the backboard. There was a cry, the mulatto staggered and fell with the falling piano, and its weight dropped squarely upon his thigh, which broke with a resounding crack.

An hour later McTeague had found his job. The music store engaged him as handler at six dollars a week. McTeague's enormous strength, useless all his life, stood him in good stead at last.

He slept in a tiny back room opening from the storeroom of the music store. He was in some sense a watchman as well as handler, and went the rounds of the store twice every night. His room was a box of a place that reeked with odors of stale tobacco smoke. The former occupant had papered the walls with newspapers and had pasted up figures cut out from the posters of some Kiralfy ballet, very gaudy.[3] By the one window, chittering all day in its little gilt prison, hung the canary bird, a tiny atom of life that McTeague still clung to with a strange obstinacy.

McTeague drank a good deal of whiskey in these days, but the only effect it had upon him was to increase the viciousness and bad temper that had developed in him since the beginning of his misfortunes. He terrorized his fellow-handlers, powerful men though they were. For a gruff word, for an awkward movement in lading the pianos, for a surly look or a muttered oath, the dentist's elbow would crook and his hand contract to a mallet-like fist. As often as not the blow followed, colossal in its force, swift as the leap of the piston from its cylinder.

His hatred of Trina increased from day to day. He'd make her dance yet. Wait only till he got his hands upon her. She'd let him starve, would she? She'd turn him out of doors while she hid her five thousand dollars in the bottom of her trunk. Aha, he would see

---

3. During the 1880s and 1890s Arnold Kiralfy formed a number of "ballet" troupes which featured pretty girls in tights and which were a staple of music hall entertainment.

about that some day. She couldn't make small of him. Ah, no. She'd dance all right—all right. McTeague was not an imaginative man by nature, but he would lie awake nights, his clumsy wits galloping and frisking under the lash of the alcohol, and fancy himself thrashing his wife, till a sudden frenzy of rage would overcome him, and he would shake all over, rolling upon the bed and biting the mattress.

On a certain day, about a week after Christmas of that year, McTeague was on one of the top floors of the music store, where the second-hand instruments were kept, helping to move about and rearrange some old pianos. As he passed by one of the counters he paused abruptly, his eye caught by an object that was strangely familiar.

"Say," he inquired, addressing the clerk in charge, "say, where'd this come from?"

"Why, let's see. We got that from a second-hand store up on Polk Street, I guess. It's a fairly good machine; a little tinkering with the stops and a bit of shellac, and we'll make it about's good as new. Good tone. See." And the clerk drew a long, sonorous wail from the depths of McTeague's old concertina.

"Well, it's mine," growled the dentist.

The other laughed. "It's yours for eleven dollars."

"It's mine," persisted McTeague. "I want it."

"Go 'long with you, Mac. What do you mean?"

"I mean that it's mine, that's what I mean, You got no right to it. It was *stolen* from me, that's what I mean," he added, a sullen anger flaming up in his little eyes.

The clerk raised a shoulder and put the concertina on an upper shelf.

"You talk to the boss about that; t'ain't none of *my* affair. If you want to buy it, it's eleven dollars."

The dentist had been paid off the day before and had four dollars in his wallet at the moment. He gave the money to the clerk.

"Here, there's part of the money. You—you put that concertina aside for me, an' I'll give you the rest in a week or so—I'll give it to you tomorrow," he exclaimed, struck with a sudden idea.

McTeague had sadly missed his concertina. Sunday afternoons when there was no work to be done, he was accustomed to lie flat on his back on his springless bed in the little room in the rear of the music store, his coat and shoes off, reading the paper, drinking steam beer from a pitcher, and smoking his pipe. But he could no longer play his six lugubrious airs upon his concertina, and it was a deprivation. He often wondered where it was gone. It had been lost, no doubt, in the general wreck of his fortunes. Once, even, the dentist had taken a concertina from the lot kept by the music store. It was a Sunday and no one was about. But he found he could not play upon it. The stops were arranged upon a system he did not understand.

Now his own concertina was come back to him. He would buy it back. He had given the clerk four dollars. He knew where he would get the remaining seven.

The clerk had told him the concertina had been sold on Polk Street to the second-hand store there. Trina had sold it. McTeague knew it. Trina had sold his concertina—had stolen it and sold it—his concertina, his beloved concertina, that he had had all his life. Why, barring the canary, there was not one of all his belongings that McTeague had cherished more dearly. His steel engraving of "Lorenzo de' Medici and his Court" might be lost, his stone pug dog might go, but his concertina!

"And she sold it—stole it from me and sold it. Just because I happened to forget to take it along with me. Well, we'll just see about that. You'll give me the money to buy it back, or——"

His rage loomed big within him. His hatred of Trina came back upon him like a returning surge. He saw her small, prim mouth, her narrow blue eyes, her black mane of hair, and uptilted chin, and hated her the more because of them. Aha, he'd show her; he'd make her dance. He'd get that seven dollars from her, or he'd know the reason why. He went through his work that day, heaving and hauling at the ponderous pianos, handling them with the ease of a lifting crane, impatient for the coming of evening, when he could be left to his own devices. As often as he had a moment to spare he went down the street to the nearest saloon and drank a pony of whiskey. Now and then as he fought and struggled with the vast masses of ebony, rosewood, and mahogany on the upper floor of the music store, raging and chafing at their inertness and unwillingness, while the whiskey pirouetted in his brain, he would mutter to himself:

"An' I got to do this. I got to work like a dray horse while she sits at home by her stove and counts her money—and sells my concertina."

Six o'clock came. Instead of supper, McTeague drank some more whiskey, five ponies in rapid succession. After supper he was obliged to go out with the dray to deliver a concert grand at the Odd Fellows' Hall, where a piano "recital" was to take place.

"Ain't you coming back with us?" asked one of the handlers as he climbed upon the driver's seat after the piano had been put in place.

"No, no," returned the dentist; "I got something else to do."

The brilliant lights of a saloon near the City Hall caught his eye. He decided he would have another drink of whiskey. It was about eight o'clock.

The following day was to be a *fête* day at the kindergarten, the Christmas and New Year festivals combined. All that afternoon the little two-story building on Pacific Street had been filled with a number of grand ladies of the Kindergarten Board, who were hanging up ropes of evergreen and sprays of holly, and arranging a great Christmas tree that stood in the centre of the ring in the schoolroom. The whole place was pervaded with a pungent, piney odor. Trina had been very busy since the early morning, coming and going at everybody's call, now running down the street after another tack-hammer or a fresh supply of cranberries, now tying together the ropes of evergreen and passing them up to one of the grand ladies as she carefully balanced herself on a step-ladder. By evening everything was in place. As the last grand lady left the school, she gave Trina an extra dollar for her work, and said:

"Now, if you'll just tidy up here, Mrs. McTeague, I think that will be all. Sweep up the pine needles here—you see they are all over the floor—and look through all the rooms, and tidy up generally. Good night—and a Happy New Year," she cried pleasantly as she went out.

Trina put the dollar away in her trunk before she did anything else and cooked herself a bit of supper. Then she came down-stairs again.

The kindergarten was not large. On the lower floor were but two rooms, the main schoolroom and another room, a cloakroom, very small, where the children hung their hats and coats. This cloakroom opened off the back of the main schoolroom. Trina cast a critical glance into both of these rooms. There had been a great deal of going and coming in them during the day, and she decided that the first thing to do would be to scrub the floors. She went up again to her room overhead and heated some water over her oil stove; then, re-descending, set to work vigorously.

By nine o'clock she had almost finished with the schoolroom. She was down on her hands and knees in the midst of a steaming muck of soapy water. On her feet were a pair of man's shoes fastened with buckles; a dirty cotton gown, damp with the water, clung about her shapeless, stunted figure. From time to time she sat back on her heels to ease the strain of her position, and with one smoking hand, white and parboiled with the hot water, brushed her hair, already streaked with gray, out of her weazened, pale face and the corners of her mouth.

It was very quiet. A gas-jet without a globe lit up the place with a crude, raw light. The cat who lived on the premises, preferring to be dirty rather than to be wet, had got into the coal scuttle, and over its rim watched her sleepily with a long, complacent purr.

All at once he stopped purring, leaving an abrupt silence in the air like the sudden shutting off of a stream of water, while his eyes grew wide, two lambent disks of yellow in the heap of black fur.

"Who is there?" cried Trina, sitting back on her heels. In the stillness that succeeded, the water dripped from her hands with the steady tick of a clock. Then a brutal fist swung open the street door of the schoolroom and McTeague came in. He was drunk; not with that drunkenness which is stupid, maudlin, wavering on its feet, but with that which is alert, unnaturally intelligent, vicious, perfectly steady, deadly wicked. Trina only had to look once at him, and in an instant, with some strange sixth sense, born of the occasion, knew what she had to expect.

She jumped up and ran from him into the little cloakroom. She locked and bolted the door after her, and leaned her weight against it, panting and trembling, every nerve shrinking and quivering with the fear of him.

McTeague put his hand on the knob of the door outside and opened it, tearing off the lock and bolt guard, and sending her staggering across the room.

"Mac," she cried to him, as he came in, speaking with horrid rapidity, cringing and holding out her hands, "Mac, listen. Wait a minute—look here—listen here. It wasn't my fault. I'll give you some money. You can come back. I'll do *anything* you want. Won't you just *listen* to me? Oh, don't! I'll scream. I can't help it, you know. The people will hear."

McTeague came towards her slowly, his immense feet dragging and grinding on the floor; his enormous fists, hard as wooden mallets, swinging at his sides. Trina backed from him to the corner of the room, cowering before him, holding her elbow crooked in front of her face, watching him with fearful intentness, ready to dodge.

"I want that money," he said, pausing in front of her.

"What money?" cried Trina.

"I want that money. You got it—that five thousand dollars. I want every nickel of it! You understand?"

"I haven't it. It isn't here. Uncle Oelbermann's got it."

"That's a lie. He told me that you came and got it. You've had it long enough; now *I* want it. Do you hear?"

"Mac, I can't give you that money. I—I *won't* give it to you," Trina cried, with sudden resolution.

"Yes, you will. You'll give me every nickel of it."

"No, *no*."

"You ain't going to make small of me this time. Give me that money."

"No."

"For the last time, will you give me that money?'

"No."

"You won't, huh? You won't give me it? For the last time."

"No, *no.*"

Usually the dentist was slow in his movements, but now the alcohol had awakened in him an ape-like agility. He kept his small dull eyes upon her, and all at once sent his fist into the middle of her face with the suddenness of a relaxed spring.

Beside herself with terror, Trina turned and fought him back; fought for her miserable life with the exasperation and strength of a harassed cat; and with such energy and such wild, unnatural force, that even McTeague for the moment drew back from her. But her resistance was the one thing to drive him to the top of his fury. He came back at her again, his eyes drawn to two fine twinkling points, and his enormous fists, clenched till the knuckles whitened, raised in the air.

Then it became abominable.

In the schoolroom outside, behind the coal scuttle, the cat listened to the sounds of stamping and struggling and the muffled noise of blows, wildly terrified, his eyes bulging like brass knobs. At last the sounds stopped on a sudden; he heard nothing more. Then McTeague came out, closing the door. The cat followed him with distended eyes as he crossed the room and disappeared through the street door.

The dentist paused for a moment on the sidewalk, looking carefully up and down the street. It was deserted and quiet. He turned sharply to the right and went down a narrow passage that led into the little court yard behind the school. A candle was burning in Trina's room. He went up by the outside stairway and entered.

The trunk stood locked in one corner of the room. The dentist took the lid-lifter from the little oil stove, put it underneath the lock-clasp and wrenched it open. Groping beneath a pile of dresses he found the chamois-skin bag, the little brass match-box, and, at the very bottom, carefully thrust into one corner, the canvas sack crammed to the mouth with twenty-dollar gold pieces. He emptied the chamois-skin bag and the match-box into the pockets of his trousers. But the canvas sack was too bulky to hide about his clothes.

"I guess I'll just naturally have to carry *you,*" he muttered. He blew out the candle, closed the door, and gained the street again.

The dentist crossed the city, going back to the music store. It was a little after eleven o'clock. The night was moonless, filled with a gray blur of faint light that seemed to come from all quarters of the horizon at once. From time to time there were sudden explosions of a southeast wind at the street corners. McTeague went on, slanting his head against the gusts, to keep his cap from blowing off, carrying the sack close to his side. Once he looked critically at the sky.

"I bet it'll rain to-morrow," he muttered, "if this wind works round to the south."

Once in his little den behind the music store, he washed his hands and forearms, and put on his working clothes, blue overalls and a jumper, over cheap trousers and vest. Then he got together his small belongings—an old campaign hat, a pair of boots, a tin of tobacco, and a pinchbeck bracelet[4] which he had found one Sunday in the Park, and which he believed to be valuable. He stripped his blanket from his bed and rolled up in it all these objects, together with the canvas sack, fastening the roll with a half hitch such as miners use, the instincts of the old-time car-boy coming back to him in his present confusion of mind. He changed his pipe and his knife—a huge jacknife with a yellowed bone handle—to the pockets of his overalls.

Then at last he stood with his hand on the door, holding up the lamp before blowing it out, looking about to make sure he was ready to go. The wavering light woke his canary. It stirred and began to chitter feebly, very sleepy and cross at being awakened. McTeague started, staring at it, and reflecting. He believed that it would be a long time before anyone came into that room again. The canary would be days without food; it was likely it would starve, would die there, hour by hour, in its little gilt prison. McTeague resolved to take it with him. He took down the cage, touching it gently with his enormous hands, and tied a couple of sacks about it to shelter the little bird from the sharp night wind.

Then he went out, locking all the doors behind him, and turned toward the ferry slips. The boats had ceased running hours ago, but he told himself that by waiting till four o'clock he could get across the bay on the tug that took over the morning papers.

. . . .

Trina lay unconscious, just as she had fallen under the last of McTeague's blows, her body twitching with an occasional hiccough that stirred the pool of blood in which she lay face downward. Towards morning she died with a rapid series of hiccoughs that sounded like a piece of clockwork running down.

The thing had been done in the cloakroom where the kindergarten children hung their hats and coats. There was no other entrance except by going through the main schoolroom. McTeague going out

4. A bracelet in which an alloy of copper and zinc (invented by Christo- pher Pinchbeck) is used as an imitation gold.

had shut the door of the cloakroom, but had left the street door open; so when the children arrived in the morning, they entered as usual.

About half-past eight, two or three five-year-olds, one a little colored girl, came into the schoolroom of the kindergarten with a great chatter of voices, going across to the cloakroom to hang up their hats and coats as they had been taught.

Half way across the room one of them stopped and put her small nose in the air, crying, "Um-o-o, what a funnee smell!" The others began to sniff the air as well, and one, the daughter of a butcher, exclaimed, " 'Tsmells like my pa's shop," adding in the next breath, "Look, what's the matter with the kittee?"

In fact, the cat was acting strangely. He lay quite flat on the floor, his nose pressed close to the crevice under the door of the little cloakroom, winding his tail slowly back and forth, excited, very eager. At times he would draw back and make a strange little clacking noise down in his throat.

"Ain't he funnee?" said the little girl again. The cat slunk swiftly away as the children came up. Then the tallest of the little girls swung the door of the little cloakroom wide open and they all ran in.

xx

The day was very hot, and the silence of high noon lay close and thick between the steep slopes of the cañons like an invisible, muffling fluid. At intervals the drone of an insect bored the air and trailed slowly to silence again. Everywhere were pungent, aromatic smells. The vast, moveless heat seemed to distil countless odors from the brush—odors of warm sap, of pine needles, and of tarweed, and above all the medicinal odor of witch hazel. As far as one could look, uncounted multitudes of trees and manzanita bushes were quietly and motionlessly growing, growing, growing. A tremendous, immeasurable Life pushed steadily heavenward without a sound, without a motion. At turns of the road, on the higher points, cañons disclosed themselves far away, gigantic grooves in the landscape, deep blue in the distance, opening one into another, ocean-deep, silent, huge, and suggestive of colossal primeval forces held in reserve. At their bottoms they were solid, massive; on their crests they broke delicately into fine serrated edges where the pines and redwoods outlined their million of tops against the high white horizon. Here and there the mountains lifted themselves out of the narrow river beds in groups like giant lions rearing their heads after drinking. The entire region was untamed. In some places east of the Mississippi nature is cosey, intimate, small, and homelike, like a good-natured housewife. In Placer County, California, she is a vast, unconquered brute of the Pliocene epoch, savage, sullen, and magnificently indifferent to man.

But there were men in these mountains, like lice on mammoths' hides, fighting them stubbornly, now with hydraulic "monitors," now with drill and dynamite, boring into the vitals of them, or tearing away great yellow gravelly scars in the flanks of them, sucking their blood, extracting gold.[1]

Here and there at long distances upon the cañon sides rose the headgear of a mine, surrounded with its few unpainted houses, and topped by its never-failing feather of black smoke. On near approach one heard the prolonged thunder of the stamp-mill, the crusher, the insatiable monster, gnashing the rocks to powder with its long iron teeth, vomiting them out again in a thin stream of wet gray mud. Its enormous maw, fed night and day with the car-boy's loads, gorged itself with gravel, and spat out the gold, grinding the rocks between its jaws, glutted, as it were, with the very entrails of the earth, and growling over its endless meal, like some savage animal, some legendary dragon, some fabulous beast, symbol of inordinate and monstrous gluttony.

McTeague had left the Overland train at Colfax, and the same afternoon had ridden some eight miles across the mountains in the stage that connects Colfax with Iowa Hill. Iowa Hill was a small one-street town, the headquarters of the mines of the district.[2] Originally it had been built upon the summit of a mountain, but the sides of this mountain have long since been "hydraulicked" away, so that the town now clings to a mere back bone, and the rear windows of the houses on both sides of the street look down over sheer precipices, into vast pits hundreds of feet deep.

The dentist stayed over night at the Hill, and the next morning started off on foot farther into the mountains. He still wore his blue overalls and jumper; his woollen cap was pulled down over his eyes; on his feet were hob-nailed boots he had bought at the store in Colfax; his blanket roll was over his back; in his left hand swung the bird cage wrapped in sacks.

Just outside the town he paused, as if suddenly remembering something.

1. In this passage and in the chapters that follow Norris describes the three forms of gold mining common in California in the late nineteenth century: hydraulic mining, in which a high-pressure stream of water (from a "monitor" or nozzle) works gold-bearing rock and gravel loose from hillsides; vein mining, in which a mine shaft is sunk to a vein of gold-bearing rock which is blasted free; and placer mining, in which gold-bearing sand from surface veins near streams is mined by hand. Placer mining had characterized most of the early gold mining in the state; by the 1890s most mining was hydraulic or deep vein and required a stamp mill to pound the rock or gravel into sand.

2. McTeague is in the heart of the gold-mining area of Placer County. First settled in the early 1850s, Iowa Hill in the 1890s was still an important mining town.

"There ought to be a trail just off the road here," he muttered. "There used to be a trail—a short cut." The next instant, without moving from his position, he saw where it opened just before him. His instinct had halted him at the exact spot. The trail zigzagged down the abrupt descent of the cañon, debouching into a gravelly river bed. "Indian River," muttered the dentist. "I remember—I remember. I ought to hear the Morning Star's stamps from here." He cocked his head. A low, sustained roar, like a distant cataract, came to his ears from across the river. "That's right," he said, contentedly. He crossed the river and regained the road beyond. The slope rose under his feet; a little farther on he passed the Morning Star mine, smoking and thundering. McTeague pushed steadily on. The road rose with the rise of the mountain, turned at a sharp angle where a great live-oak grew, and held level for nearly a quarter of a mile. Twice again the dentist left the road and took to the trail that cut through deserted hydraulic pits. He knew exactly where to look for these trails; not once did his instinct deceive him. He recognized familiar points at once. Here was Cold Cañon, where invariably, winter and summer, a chilly wind was blowing; here was where the road to Spencer's branched off; here was Bussy's old place, where at one time there were so many dogs; here was Delmue's cabin, where unlicensed whiskey used to be sold; here was the plank bridge with its one rotten board; and here the flat overgrown with manzanita, where he once had shot three quail.

At noon, after he had been tramping for some two hours, he halted at a point where the road dipped suddenly. A little to the right of him, and flanking the road, an enormous yellow gravel-pit like an emptied lake gaped to heaven. Farther on, in the distance, a cañon zigzagged toward the horizon, rugged with pine-clad mountain crests. Nearer at hand, and directly in the line of the road, was an irregular cluster of unpainted cabins. A dull, prolonged roar vibrated in the air. McTeague nodded his head as if satisfied. "That's the place," he muttered.

He reshouldered his blanket roll and descended the road. At last he halted again. He stood before a low one-story building, differing from the others in that it was painted. A verandah, shut in with mosquito netting, surrounded it. McTeague dropped his blanket roll on a lumber pile outside, and came up and knocked at the open door. Some one called to him to come in.

McTeague entered, rolling his eyes about him, noting the changes that had been made since he had last seen this place. A partition had been knocked down, making one big room out of the two former small ones. A counter and railing stood inside the door. There was a telephone on the wall. In one corner he also observed a stack of surveyor's instruments; a big drawing-board straddled on spindle legs across one end of the room, a mechanical drawing of some kind, no doubt the plan of the mine, unrolled upon it; a chromo representing a couple of peasants in a ploughed field (Millet's "Angelus") was nailed unframed upon the wall,³ and hanging from the same wire nail that secured one of its corners in place was a bullion bag and a cartridge belt with a loaded revolver in the pouch.

The dentist approached the counter and leaned his elbows upon it. Three men were in the room—a tall, lean young man, with a thick head of hair surprisingly gray, who was playing with a half-grown great Dane puppy; another fellow about as young, but with a jaw almost as salient as McTeague's, stood at the letter-press taking a copy of a letter; a third man, a little older than the other two, was pottering over a transit.⁴ This latter was massively built, and wore overalls and low boots streaked and stained and spotted in every direction with gray mud. The dentist looked slowly from one to the other; then at length, "Is the foreman about?" he asked.

The man in the muddy overalls came forward.

"What you want?"

He spoke with a strong German accent.

The old invariable formula came back to McTeague on the instant.

"What's the show for a job?"

At once the German foreman became preoccupied, looking aimlessly out of the window. There was a silence.

"You hev been miner alretty?"

"Yes, yes."

"Know how to hendle pick'n shov'le?"

"Yes, I know."

The other seemed unsatisfied. "Are you a 'cousin Jack'?"⁵

The dentist grinned. This prejudice against Cornishmen he remembered too.

"No. American."

"How long sence you mine?"

"Oh, year or two."

"Show your hends." McTeague exhibited his hard, calloused palms.

3. A chromo (or chromolithograph) was a cheaply produced print, usually of a sentimental subject, as in this instance of Jean Francois Millet's painting of peasants saying their evening prayers in the fields.

4. Of the three figures, the first is Norris himself (Norris was prematurely gray, and he had visited the Big Dipper in the fall of 1897 in order to complete *McTeague*), and the second is Seymour Waterhouse, Norris's college friend and the owner of the Big Dipper. A transit is part of a surveyor's kit.

5. A common term for a Cornishman. Cornish miners were often unwelcome to American mine operators because of their reputation for independence and impermanence.

"When ken you go to work? I want a chuck-tender on der night-shift."[6]

"I can tend a chuck. I'll go on to-night."

"What's your name?"

The dentist started. He had forgotten to be prepared for this.

"Huh? What?"

"What's the name?"

McTeague's eyes was caught by a railroad calender hanging over the desk. There was no time to think.

"Burlington," he said, loudly.

The German took a card from a file and wrote it down.

"Give dis card to der boarding-boss, down at der boarding-haus, den gome find me bei der mill at sex o'clock, und I set you to work."

Straight as a homing pigeon, and following a blind and unreasoned instinct, McTeague had returned to the Big Dipper mine. Within a week's time it seemed to him as though he had never been away. He picked up his life again exactly where he had left it the day when his mother had sent him away with the travelling dentist, the charlatan who had set up his tent by the bunk house. The house McTeague had once lived in was still there, occupied by one of the shift bosses and his family. The dentist passed it on his way to and from the mine.

He himself slept in the bunk house with some thirty others of his shift. At half-past five in the evening the cook at the boarding-house sounded a prolonged alarm upon a crowbar bent in the form of a triangle, that hung upon the porch of the boarding-house. McTeague rose and dressed, and with his shift had supper. Their lunch-pails were distributed to them. Then he made his way to the tunnel mouth, climbed into a car in the waiting ore train, and was hauled into the mine.

Once inside, the hot evening air turned to a cool dampness, and the forest odors gave place to the smell of stale dynamite smoke, suggestive of burning rubber. A cloud of steam came from McTeague's mouth; underneath, the water swashed and rippled around the car-wheels, while the light from the miner's candlesticks threw wavering blurs of pale yellow over the gray rotting quartz of the roof and walls. Occasionally McTeague bent down his head to avoid the lagging of the roof or the projections of an overhanging shute. From car to car all along the line the miners called to one another as the train trundled along, joshing and laughing.

A mile from the entrance the train reached the breast where McTeague's gang worked. The men clambered from the cars and

6. As a deep vein mine, the Big Dipper used drilling to prepare the quartz rock of the vein for blasting. Mc- Teague's job was to replace the drills in the gripping device (the chuck) of the drilling machine. See also p. 217 below.

took up the labor where the day shift had left it, burrowing their way steadily through a primeval river bed.

The candlesticks thrust into the crevices of the gravel strata lit up faintly the half dozen moving figures befouled with sweat and with wet gray mould. The picks struck into the loose gravel with a yielding shock. The long-handled shovels clinked amidst the pile of bowlders and scraped dully in the heaps of rotten quartz. The Burly drill[7] boring for blasts broke out from time to time in an irregular chug-chug, chug-chug, while the engine that pumped the water from the mine coughed and strangled at short intervals.

McTeague tended the chuck. In a way he was the assistant of the man who worked the Burly. It was his duty to replace the drills in the Burly, putting in longer ones as the hole got deeper and deeper. From time to time he rapped the drill with a pole-pick when it stuck fast or fitchered.[8]

Once it even occurred to him that there was a resemblance between his present work and the profession he had been forced to abandon. In the Burly drill he saw a queer counterpart of his old-time dental engine; and what were the drills and chucks but enormous hoe excavators, hard bits, and burrs? It was the same work he had so often performed in his "Parlors," only magnified, made monstrous, distorted, and grotesqued, the caricature of dentistry.

He passed his nights thus in the midst of the play of crude and simple forces—the powerful attacks of the Burly drills; the great exertions of bared, bent backs overlaid with muscle; the brusque, resistless expansion of dynamite; and the silent, vast, Titanic force, mysterious and slow, that cracked the timbers supporting the roof of the tunnel, and that gradually flattened the lagging till it was thin as paper.

The life pleased the dentist beyond words. The still, colossal mountains took him back again like a returning prodigal, and vaguely, without knowing why, he yielded to their influence—their immensity, their enormous power, crude and blind, reflecting themselves in his own nature, huge, strong, brutal in its simplicity. And this, though he only saw the mountains at night. They appeared far different then than in the daytime. At twelve o'clock he came out of the mine and lunched on the contents of his dinner-pail, sitting upon the embankment of the track, eating with both hands, and looking around him with a steady ox-like gaze. The mountains rose sheer from every side, heaving their gigantic crests far up into the night, the black peaks crowding together, and looking now less like beasts than like a company of cowled giants. In the daytime they were silent; but at night they seemed to stir and rouse themselves. Occasionally the stamp-mill stopped, its thunder ceasing abruptly.

7. More accurately, the Burleigh drill.   8. To "fitcher" is to move very slowly.

Then one could hear the noises that the mountains made in their living. From the cañon, from the crowding crests, from the whole immense landscape, there rose a steady and prolonged sound, coming from all sides at once. It was that incessant and muffled roar which disengages itself from all vast bodies, from oceans, from cities, from forests, from sleeping armies, and which is like the breathing of an infinitely great monster, alive, palpitating.

McTeague returned to his work. At six in the morning his shift was taken off, and he went out of the mine and back to the bunk house. All day long he slept, flung at length upon the strong-smelling blankets—slept the dreamless sleep of exhaustion, crushed and overpowered with the work, flat and prone upon his belly, till again in the evening the cook sounded the alarm upon the crowbar bent into a triangle.

Every alternate week the shifts were changed. The second week McTeague's shift worked in the daytime and slept at night. Wednesday night of this second week the dentist woke suddenly. He sat up in his bed in the bunk house, looking about him from side to side; an alarm clock hanging on the wall, over a lantern, marked half-past three.

"What was it?" muttered the dentist. "I wonder what it was." The rest of the shift were sleeping soundly, filling the room with the rasping sound of snoring. Everything was in its accustomed place; nothing stirred. But for all that McTeague got up and lit his miner's candlestick and went carefully about the room, throwing the light into the dark corners, peering under all the beds, including his own. Then he went to the door and stepped outside. The night was warm and still; the moon, very low, and canted on her side like a galleon foundering. The camp was very quiet; nobody was in sight. "I wonder what it was," muttered the dentist. "There was something—why did I wake up? Huh?" He made a circuit about the bunk house, unusually alert, his small eyes twinkling rapidly, seeing everything. All was quiet. An old dog who invariably slept on the steps of the bunk house had not even wakened. McTeague went back to bed, but did not sleep.

"There was *something*," he muttered, looking in a puzzled way at his canary in the cage that hung from the wall at his bedside; "something. What was it? There is something *now*. There it is again—the same thing." He sat up in bed with eyes and ears strained. "What is it? I don' know what it is. I don' hear anything, an' I don' see anything. I feel something—right now; feel it now. I wonder—I don' know—I don' know."

Once more he got up, and this time dressed himself. He made a complete tour of the camp, looking and listening, for what he did not know. He even went to the outskirts of the camp and for nearly half an hour watched the road that led into the camp from the direction of Iowa Hill. He saw nothing; not even a rabbit stirred. He went to bed.

But from this time on there was a change. The dentist grew restless, uneasy. Suspicion of something, he could not say what, annoyed him incessantly. He went wide around sharp corners. At every moment he looked sharply over his shoulder. He even went to bed with his clothes and cap on, and at every hour during the night would get up and prowl about the bunk house, one ear turned down the wind, his eyes gimleting the darkness. From time to time he would murmur:

"There's something. What is it? I wonder what it is."

What strange sixth sense stirred in McTeague at this time? What animal cunning, what brute instinct clamored for recognition and obedience? What lower faculty was it that roused his suspicion, that drove him out into the night a score of times between dark and dawn, his head in the air, his eyes and ears keenly alert?

One night as he stood on the steps of the bunk house, peering into the shadows of the camp, he uttered an exclamation as of a man suddenly enlightened. He turned back into the house, drew from under his bed the blanket roll in which he kept his money hid, and took the canary down from the wall. He strode to the door and disappeared into the night. When the sheriff of Placer County and the two deputies from San Francisco reached the Big Dipper mine, McTeague had been gone two days.

XXI

"Well," said one of the deputies, as he backed the horse into the shafts of the buggy in which the pursuers had driven over from the Hill, "we've about as good as got him. It isn't hard to follow a man who carries a bird cage with him wherever he goes."

McTeague crossed the mountains on foot the Friday and Saturday of that week, going over through Emigrant Gap, following the line of the Overland railroad. He reached Reno Monday night.[1] By degrees a vague plan of action outlined itself in the dentist's mind.

"Mexico," he muttered to himself. "Mexico, that's the place. They'll watch the coast and they'll watch the Eastern trains, but they won't think of Mexico."

The sense of pursuit which had harassed him during the last week of his stay at the Big Dipper mine had worn off, and he believed himself to be very cunning.

"I'm pretty far ahead now, I guess," he said. At Reno he boarded

---

1. As described in the next several pages, McTeague's journey from Colfax to Keeler is about 350 miles.

a south-bound freight on the line of the Carson and Colorado railroad, paying for a passage in the caboose. "Freights don' run on schedule time," he muttered, "and a conductor on a passenger train makes it his business to study faces. I'll stay with this train as far as it goes."

The freight worked slowly southward, through western Nevada, the country becoming hourly more and more desolate and abandoned. After leaving Walker Lake the sage-brush country began, and the freight rolled heavily over tracks that threw off visible layers of heat. At times it stopped whole half days on sidings or by water tanks, and the engineer and fireman came back to the caboose and played poker with the conductor and train crew. The dentist sat apart, behind the stove, smoking pipe after pipe of cheap tobacco. Sometimes he joined in the poker games. He had learned poker when a boy at the mine, and after a few deals his knowledge returned to him; but for the most part he was taciturn and unsociable, and rarely spoke to the others unless spoken to first. The crew recognized the type, and the impression gained ground among them that he had "done for" a livery-stable keeper at Truckee and was trying to get down into Arizona.

McTeague heard two brakemen discussing him one night as they stood outside by the halted train. "The livery-stable keeper called him a bastard; that's what Picachos told me," one of them remarked, "and started to draw his gun; an' this fellar did for him with a hayfork. He's a horse doctor, this chap is, and the livery-stable keeper had got the law on him so's he couldn't practise any more, an' he was sore about it."

Near a place called Queen's the train reëntered California, and McTeague observed with relief that the line of track which had hitherto held westward curved sharply to the south again. The train was unmolested; occasionally the crew fought with a gang of tramps who attempted to ride the brake beams, and once in the northern part of Inyo County, while they were halted at a water tank, an immense Indian buck, blanketed to the ground, approached McTeague as he stood on the roadbed stretching his legs, and without a word presented to him a filthy, crumped letter. The letter was to the effect that the buck Big Jim was a good Indian and deserving of charity; the signature was illegible. The dentist stared at the letter, returned it to the buck, and regained the train just as it started. Neither had spoken; the buck did not move from his position, and fully five minutes afterward, when the slow-moving freight was miles away, the dentist looked back and saw him still standing motionless between the rails, a forlorn and solitary point of red, lost in the immensity of the surrounding white blur of the desert.

At length the mountains began again, rising up on either side of the track; vast, naked hills of white sand and red rock, spotted with blue shadows. Here and there a patch of green was spread like a gay table-cloth over the sand. All at once Mount Whitney leaped over the horizon. Independence was reached and passed; the freight, nearly emptied by now, and much shortened, rolled along the shores of Owen Lake. At a place called Keeler it stopped definitely. It was the terminus of the road.

The town of Keeler was a one-street town, not unlike Iowa Hill —the post-office, the bar and hotel, the Odd Fellows' Hall, and the livery stable being the principal buildings.

"Where to now?" muttered McTeague to himself as he sat on the edge of the bed in his room in the hotel. He hung the canary in the window, filled its little bathtub, and watched it take its bath with enormous satisfaction. "Where to now?" he muttered again. "This is as far as the railroad goes, an' it won' do for me to stay in a town yet a while; no, it won' do. I got to clear out. Where to? That's the word, where to? I'll go down to supper now"—He went on whispering his thoughts aloud, so that they would take more concrete shape in his mind—"I'll go down to supper now, an' then I'll hang aroun' the bar this evening till I get the lay of this land. Maybe this is fruit country, though it looks more like a cattle country. Maybe it's a mining country. If it's a mining country," he continued, puckering his heavy eyebrows, "if it's a mining country, an' the mines are far enough off the roads, maybe I'd better get to the mines an' lay quiet for a month before I try to get any farther south."

He washed the cinders and dust of a week's railroading from his face and hair, put on a fresh pair of boots, and went down to supper. The dining-room was of the invariable type of the smaller interior towns of California. There was but one table, covered with oilcloth; rows of benches answered for chairs; a railroad map, a chromo with a gilt frame protected by mosquito netting, hung on the walls, together with a yellowed photograph of the proprietor in Masonic regalia. Two waitresses whom the guests—all men—called by their first names, came and went with large trays.

Through the windows outside McTeague observed a great number of saddle horses tied to trees and fences. Each one of these horses had a riata[2] on the pommel of the saddle. He sat down to the table, eating his thick hot soup, watching his neighbors covertly, listening to everything that was said. It did not take him long to gather that the country to the east and south of Keeler was a cattle country.

2. A lariat.

Not far off, across a range of hills, was the Panamint Valley, where the big cattle ranges were. Every now and then this name was tossed to and fro across the table in the flow of conversation— "Over in the Panamint." "Just going down for a rodeo in the Panamint." "Panamint brands." "Has a range down in the Panamint." Then by and by the remark, "Hoh, yes, Gold Gulch,[3] they're down to good pay there. That's on the other side the Panamint Range. Peters came in yesterday and told me."

McTeague turned to the speaker.

"Is that a gravel mine?" he asked.

"No, no, quartz."

"I'm a miner; that's why I asked."

"Well I've mined some too. I had a hole in the ground meself, but she was silver; and when the skunks at Washington lowered the price of silver, where was I? Fitchered, b'God!"[4]

"I was looking for a job."

"Well, it's mostly cattle down here in the Panamint, but since the strike over at Gold Gulch some of the boys have gone prospecting. There's gold in them damn Panamint Mountains. If you can find a good long 'contact' of country rocks you ain't far from it. There's a couple of fellars from Redlands has located four claims around Gold Gulch. They got a vein eighteen inches wide, an' Peters says you can trace it for more'n a thousand feet. Were you thinking of prospecting over there?"

"Well, well, I don' know, I don' know."

"Well, I'm going over to the other side of the range day after t'morrow after some ponies of mine, an' I'm going to have a look around. You say you've been a miner?"

"Yes, yes."

"If you're going over that way, you might come along and see if we can't find a contact, or copper sulphurets, or something.[5] Even if we don't find color we may find silver-bearing galena." Then, after a pause, "Let's see, I didn't catch your name."

"Huh? My name's Carter," answered McTeague, promptly. Why he should change his name again the dentist could not say. "Carter" came to his mind at once, and he answered without reflecting that he had registered as "Burlington" when he had arrived at the hotel.

"Well, my name's Cribbens," answered the other. The two shook hands solemnly.

---

3. A fictitious place.

4. A reference to the "Crime of 73," when Congress demonetized silver and thus lowered its price. Cribbens is "fitchered" in the sense of being "caught" or "trapped."

5. Here and elsewhere Cribbens is full of the "lingo" of placer mining. A "contact" is the junction of two different kinds of rock and often indicates the presence of gold ore; "country" rock is rock containing mineral deposits; "color" is a particle of gold visible to the eye.

"You're about finished?" continued Cribbens, pushing back. "Le's go out in the bar an' have a drink on it."

"Sure, sure," said the dentist.

The two sat up late that night in a corner of the barroom discussing the probability of finding gold in the Panamint hills. It soon became evident that they held differing theories. McTeague clung to the old prospector's idea that there was no way of telling where gold was until you actually saw it. Cribbens had evidently read a good many books upon the subject, and had already prospected in something of a scientific manner.

"Shucks!" he exclaimed. "Gi' me a long distinct contact between sedimentary and igneous rocks, an' I'll sink a shaft without ever *seeing* 'color.' "

The dentist put his huge chin in the air. "Gold is where you find it," he returned, doggedly.

"Well, it's my idea as how pardners ought to work along different lines," said Cribbens. He tucked the corners of his mustache into his mouth and sucked the tobacco juice from them. For a moment he was thoughtful, then he blew out his mustache abruptly, and exclaimed:

"Say, Carter, le's make a go of this. You got a little cash I suppose—fifty dollars or so?"

"Huh? Yes—I—I——"

"Well, *I* got about fifty. We'll go pardners on the proposition, an' we'll dally 'round the range yonder an' see what we can see. What do you say?"

"Sure, sure," answered the dentist.

"Well, it's a go then, hey?"

"That's the word."

"Well, le's have a drink on it."

They drank with profound gravity.

They fitted out the next day at the general merchandise store of Keeler—picks, shovels, prospectors' hammers, a couple of cradles,[6] pans, bacon, flour, coffee, and the like, and they bought a burro on which to pack their kit.

"Say, by jingo, you ain't got a horse," suddenly exclaimed Cribbens as they came out of the store. "You can't get around this country without a pony of some kind.'

Cribbens already owned and rode a buckskin cayuse that had to be knocked in the head and stunned before it could be saddled. "I got an extry saddle an' a headstall[7] at the hotel that you can use," he said, "but you'll have to get a horse."

In the end the dentist bought a mule at the livery stable for forty

___

6. A device used to wash out sand and gravel from ore.

7. A bridle.

dollars. It turned out to be good bargain, however, for the mule was a good traveller and seemed actually to fatten on sage-brush and potato parings. When the actual transaction took place, McTeague had been obliged to get the money to pay for the mule out of the canvas sack. Cribbens was with him at the time, and as the dentist unrolled his blankets and disclosed the sack, whistled in amazement.

"An' me asking you if you had fifty dollars!" he exclaimed. "You carry your mine right around with you, don't you?"

"Huh, I guess so," muttered the dentist. "I—I just sold a claim I had up in El Dorado County," he added.

At five o'clock on a magnificent May morning[8] the "pardners" jogged out of Keeler, driving the burro before them. Cribbens rode his cayuse, McTeague following in his rear on the mule.

"Say," remarked Cribbens, "why in thunder don't you leave that fool canary behind at the hotel? It's going to be in your way all the time, an' it will sure die. Better break its neck an' chuck it."

"No, no," insisted the dentist. "I've had it too long. I'll take it with me."

"Well, that's the craziest idea I ever heard of," remarked Cribbens, "to take a canary along prospecting. Why not kid gloves, and be done with it?"

They travelled leisurely to the southeast during the day, following a well-beaten cattle road, and that evening camped on a spur of some hills at the head of the Panamint Valley where there was a spring. The next day they crossed the Panamint itself.

"That's a smart looking valley," observed the dentist.

"Now you're talking straight talk," returned Cribbens, sucking his mustache. The valley was beautiful, wide, level, and very green. Everywhere were herds of cattle, scarcely less wild than deer. Once or twice cowboys passed them on the road, big-boned fellows, picturesque in their broad hats, hairy trousers, jingling spurs, and revolver belts, surprisingly like the pictures McTeague remembered to have seen. Everyone of them knew Cribbens, and almost invariably joshed him on his venture.

"Say, Crib, ye'd best take a wagon train with ye to bring your dust back."

Cribbens resented their humor, and after they had passed, chewed fiercely on his mustache.

"I'd like to make a strike, b'God! if it was only to get the laugh on them joshers."

By noon they were climbing the eastern slope of the Panamint Range. Long since they had abandoned the road; vegetation ceased;

---

8. Norris has forgotten that McTeague murders Trina in late December (p. 203) and that McTeague has been no more than a month at the Big Dipper and on the road.

not a tree was in sight. They followed faint cattle trails that led from one water hole to another. By degrees these water holes grew dryer and dryer, and at three o'clock Cribbens halted and filled their canteens.

"There ain't any *too* much water on the other side," he observed grimly.

"It's pretty hot," muttered the dentist, wiping his streaming forehead with the back of his hand.

"Huh!" snorted the other more grimly than ever. The motionless air was like the mouth of a furnace. Cribbens's pony lathered and panted. McTeague's mule began to droop his long ears. Only the little burro plodded resolutely on, picking the trail where McTeague could see but trackless sand and stunted sage. Towards evening Cribbens, who was in the lead, drew rein on the summit of the hills.

Behind them was the beautiful green Panamint Valley, but before and below them for miles and miles, as far as the eye could reach, a flat, white desert, empty even of sage-brush, unrolled toward the horizon. In the immediate foreground a broken system of arroyos, and little cañons tumbled down to meet it. To the north faint blue hills shouldered themselves above the horizon.

"Well," observed Cribbens, "we're on the top of the Panamint Range now. It's along this eastern slope, right below us here, that we're going to prospect. Gold Gulch"—he pointed with the butt of his quirt—"is about eighteen or nineteen miles along here to the north of us. Those hills way over yonder to the northeast are the Telescope hills."

"What do you call the desert out yonder?" McTeague's eyes wandered over the illimitable stretch of alkali that stretched out forever and forever to the east, to the north, and to the south.

"That," said Cribbens, "that's Death Valley."

There was a long pause. The horses panted irregularly, the sweat dripping from their heaving bellies. Cribbens and the dentist sat motionless in their saddles, looking out over that abominable desolation, silent, troubled.

"God!" ejaculated Cribbens at length, under his breath, with a shake of his head. Then he seemed to rouse himself. "Well," he remarked, "first thing we got to do now is to find water."

This was a long and difficult task. They descended into one little cañon after another, followed the course of numberless arroyos, and even dug where there seemed indications of moisture, all to no purpose. But at length McTeague's mule put his nose in the air and blew once or twice through his nostrils.

"Smells it, the son of a gun!" exclaimed Cribbens. The dentist let the animal have his head, and in a few minutes he had brought

them to the bed of a tiny cañon where a thin stream of brackish
water filtered over a ledge of rocks.

"We'll camp here," observed Cribbens, "but we can't turn the
horses loose. We'll have to picket 'em with the lariats. I saw some
loco-weed back here a piece, and if they get to eating that, they'll
sure go plum crazy. The burro won't eat it, but I wouldn't trust the
others."

A new life began for McTeague. After breakfast the "pardners"
separated, going in opposite directions along the slope of the range,
examining rocks, picking and chipping at ledges and bowlders, looking for signs, prospecting. McTeague went up into the little cañons
where the streams had cut through the bed rock, searching for
veins of quartz, breaking out this quartz when he had found it, pul-
verizing and panning it. Cribbens hunted for "contacts," closely
examining country rocks and out-crops, continually on the lookout
for spots where sedimentary and igneous rock came together.

One day, after a week of prospecting, they met unexpectedly on
the slope of an arroyo. It was late in the afternoon. "Hello, pardner," exclaimed Cribbens as he came down to where McTeague was
bending over his pan. "What luck?"

The dentist emptied his pan and straightened up. "Nothing,
nothing. You struck anything?"

"Not a trace. Guess we might as well be moving towards camp."
They returned together, Cribbens telling the dentist of a group of
antelope he had seen.

"We might lay off to-morrow, an' see if we can plug a couple of
them fellers. Antelope steak would go pretty well after beans an'
bacon an' coffee week in an' week out."

McTeague was answering, when Cribbens interrupted him with
an exclamation of profound disgust. "I thought we were the first to
prospect along in here, an' now look at that. Don't it make you
sick?"

He pointed out evidences of an abandoned prospector's camp just
before them—charred ashes, empty tin cans, one or two gold-min-
er's pans, and a broken pick. "Don't that make you sick?" muttered
Cribbens, sucking his mustache furiously. "To think of us mushheads going over ground that's been covered already! Say, pardner,
we'll dig out of here to-morrow. I've been thinking, anyhow, we'd
better move to the south; that water of ours is pretty low."

"Yes, yes, I guess so," assented the dentist. "There ain't any gold
here."

"Yes, there is," protested Cribbens doggedly; "there's gold all
through these hills, if we could only strike it. I tell you what, pardner, I got a place in mind where I'll bet no one ain't prospected—
least not very many. There don't very many care to try an' get to it.

It's over on the other side of Death Valley. It's called Gold Mountain, an' there's only one mine been located there, an' it's paying
like a nitrate bed.⁹ There ain't many people in that country,
because it's all hell to get into. First place, you got to cross Death
Valley and strike the Armagosa Range fur off to the south. Well,
no one ain't stuck on crossing the Valley, not if they can help it.
But we could work down the Panamint some hundred or so miles,
maybe two hundred, an' fetch around by the Armagosa River, way
to the south'erd. We could prospect on the way. But I guess the
Armagosa'd be dried up at this season. Anyhow," he concluded,
"we'll move camp to the south to-morrow. We got to get new feed
an' water for the horses. We'll sce if we can knock over a couple of
antelope to-morrow, and then we'll scoot."

"I ain't got a gun," said the dentist; "not even a revolver. I—"

"Wait a second," said Cribbens, pausing in his scramble down
the side of one of the smaller gulches. "Here's some slate here; I
ain't seen no slate around here yet. Let's see where it goes to."

McTeague followed him along the side of the gulch. Cribbens
went on ahead, muttering to himself from time to time:

"Runs right along here, even enough, and here's water too.
Didn't know this stream was here; pretty near dry, though. Here's
the slate again. See where it runs, pardner?"

"Look at it up there ahead," said McTeague. "It runs right up
over the back of this hill."

"That's right," assented Cribbens. "Hi!" he shouted suddenly,
"*here's a 'contact,'* and here it is again, and there, and yonder. Oh,
look at it, will you? That's grano-diorite on slate. Couldn't want it
any more distinct than that. *God!* if we could only find the quartz
between the two now."

"Well, there it is," exclaimed McTeague. "Look on ahead there;
ain't that quartz?"

"You're shouting right out loud," vociferated Cribbens, looking
where McTeague was pointing. His face went suddenly pale. He
turned to the dentist, his eyes wide.

"By God, pardner," he exclaimed, breathlessly, "By God—" he
broke off abruptly.

"That's what you been looking for, ain't it?" asked the dentist.

"*Looking* for! *Looking* for!" Cribbens checked himself. "That's
slate all right, and that's grano-diorite, *I* know"—he bent down and
examined the rock—"and here's the quartz between 'em; there
can't be no mistake about that. Gi' me that hammer," he cried,
excitedly. "Come on, git to work. Jab into the quartz with your
pick; git out some chunks of it." Cribbens went down on his hands

9. Mines rich in sodium nitrate had a
ready market for this byproduct as a   fertilizer.

and knees, attacking the quartz vein furiously. The dentist followed his example, swinging his pick with enormous force, splintering the rocks at every stroke. Cribbens was talking to himself in his excitement.

"Got you *this* time, you son of a gun! By God! I guess we got you *this* time, at last. Looks like it, anyhow. *Get* a move on, pardner. There ain't anybody 'round, is there? How?" Without looking, he drew his revolver and threw it to the dentist. "Take the gun an' look around, pardner. If you see any son of a gun *anywhere, plug* him. This yere's *our* claim. I guess we got it *this* time, pardner. Come on." He gathered up the chunks of quartz he had broken out, and put them in his hat and started towards their camp. The two went along with great strides, hurrying as fast as they could over the uneven ground.

"I don' know," exclaimed Cribbens, breathlessly, "I don' want to say too much. Maybe we're fooled. Lord, that damn camp's a long ways off. Oh, I ain't goin' to fool along this way. Come on, pardner." He broke into a run. McTeague followed at a lumbering gallop. Over the scorched, parched ground, stumbling and tripping over sage-brush and sharp-pointed rocks, under the palpitating heat of the desert sun, they ran and scrambled, carrying the quartz lumps in their hats.

"See any *'color'* in it, pardner?" gasped Cribbens. "I can't, can you? 'Twouldn't be visible nohow, I guess. Hurry up. Lord, we ain't ever going to get to that camp."

Finally they arrived. Cribbens dumped the quartz fragments into a pan.

"You pestle her, pardner, an' I'll fix the scales." McTeague ground the lumps to fine dust in the iron mortar while Cribbens set up the tiny scales and got out the "spoons" from their outfit.

"That's fine enough," Cribbens exclaimed, impatiently. "Now we'll spoon her. Gi' me the water."

Cribbens scooped up a spoonful of the fine white powder and began to spoon it carefully. The two were on their hands and knees upon the ground, their heads close together, still panting with excitement and the exertion of their run.

"Can't do it," exalaimed Cribbens, sitting back on his heels, "hand shakes so. *You* take it, pardner. Careful, now."

McTeague took the horn spoon and began rocking it gently in his huge fingers, sluicing the water over the edge a little at a time, each movement washing away a little more of the powdered quartz. The two watched it with the intensest eagerness.

"Don't see it yet; don't see it yet," whispered Cribbens, chewing his mustache. "*Leetle* faster, pardner. That's the ticket. Careful, steady, now; lettle more, leetle more. Don't see color yet, do you?"

The quartz sediment dwindled by degrees as McTeague spooned it steadily. Then at last a thin streak of a foreign substance began to show just along the edge. It was yellow.

Neither spoke. Cribbens dug his nails into the sand, and ground his mustache between his teeth. The yellow streak broadened as the quartz sediment washed away. Cribbens whispered:

"We got it, pardner. That's gold."

McTeague washed the last of the white quartz dust away, and let the water trickle after it. A pinch of gold, fine as flour, was left in the bottom of the spoon.

"There you are," he said. The two looked at each other. Then Cribbens rose into the air with a great leap and a yell that could have been heard for half a mile.

"Yee-e-ow! We *got* it, we struck it. Pardner, we got it. Out of sight. We're millionaires." He snatched up his revolver and fired it with inconceivable rapidity. "*Put* it there, old man," he shouted, gripping McTeague's palm.

"That's gold, all right," muttered McTeague, studying the contents of the spoon.

"You bet your great-grandma's Cochin-China Chessy cat[1] it's gold," shouted Cribbens. "Here, now, we got a lot to do. We got to stake her out an' put up the location notice. We'll take our full acreage, you bet. You—we haven't weighed this yet. Where's the scales?" He weighed the pinch of gold with shaking hands. "Two grains," he cried. "That'll run five dollars to the ton. Rich, it's rich; it's the richest kind of pay, pardner. We're millionaires. Why don't you say something? Why don't you get excited? Why don't you run around an' *do* something?"

"Huh!" said McTeague, rolling his eyes. "Huh! *I* know, I know, we've struck it pretty rich."

"Come on," exclaimed Cribbens, jumping up again. "We'll stake her out an' put up the location notice.[2] Lord, suppose anyone should have come on her while we've been away." He reloaded his revolver deliberately. "We'll drop *him* all right, if there's anyone fooling round there; I'll tell you those right now. Bring the rifle, pardner, an' if you see anyone, *plug* him, an' ask him what he wants afterward."

They hurried back to where they had made their discovery.

"To think," exclaimed Cribbens, as he drove the first stake, "to think those other mushheads had their camp within gunshot of her and never located her. Guess they didn't know the meaning of a 'contact.' Oh, I knew I was solid on 'contacts.'"

1. That is, a grinning cat (the allusion is to the Cheshire Cat in *Alice in Wonderland*) from Southeast Asia.
2. Mining law required that the boundaries of a claim be marked by visible stakes and that a notice stating the details of the claim be posted on the claim.

They staked out their claim, and Cribbens put up the notice of location. It was dark before they were through. Cribbens broke off some more chunks of quartz in the vein.

"I'll spoon this too, just for the fun of it, when I get home," he explained, as they tramped back to the camp.

"Well," said the dentist, "we got the laugh on those cowboys."

"Have we?" shouted Cribbens. "Have we? Just wait and see the rush for this place when we tell 'em about it down in Keeler. Say, what'll we call her?"

"I don' know, I don' know."

"We might call her the 'Last Chance.' 'Twas our last chance, wasn't it? We'd 'a' gone antelope shooting to-morrow, and the next day we'd 'a'—say, what you stopping for?" he added, interrupting himself. "What's up?"

The dentist had paused abruptly on the crest of a cañon. Cribbens, looking back, saw him standing motionless in his tracks.

"What's up?" asked Cribbens a second time.

McTeague slowly turned his head and looked over one shoulder, then over the other. Suddenly he wheeled sharply about, cocking the Winchester and tossing it to his shoulder.

Cribbens ran back to his side, whipping out his revolver.

"What is it?" he cried. "See anybody?" He peered on ahead through the gathering twilight.

"No, no."

"Hear anything?"

"No, didn't hear anything."

"What is it then? What's up?"

"I don' know, I don' know," muttered the dentist, lowering the rifle. "There was something."

"What?"

"Something—didn't you notice?"

"Notice what?"

"I don' know. Something—something or other."

"Who? What? Notice what? What did you see?"

The dentist let down the hammer of the rifle.

"I guess it wasn't anything," he said rather foolishly.

"What d'you think you saw—anybody on the claim?"

"I didn't see anything. I didn't hear anything either. I had an idea, that's all; came all of a sudden, like that. Something, I don' know what."

"I guess you just imagined something. There ain't anybody within twenty miles of us, I guess."

"Yes, I guess so, just imagined it, that's the word."

Half an hour later they had the fire going. McTeague was frying strips of bacon over the coals, and Cribbens was still chattering and exclaiming over their great strike. All at once McTeague put down the frying-pan.

"What's that?" he growled.

"Hey? What's what?" exclaimed Cribbens, getting up.

"Didn't you notice something?"

"Where?"

"Off there." The dentist made a vague gesture toward the eastern horizon. "Didn't you hear something—I mean see something—I mean——"

"What's the matter with you, pardner?"

"Nothing. I guess I just imagined it."

But it was not imagination. Until midnight the partners lay broad awake, rolled in their blankets under the open sky, talking and discussing and making plans. At last Cribbens rolled over on his side and slept. The dentist could not sleep.

What! It was warning him again, that strange sixth sense, that obscure brute instinct. It was aroused again and clamoring to be obeyed. Here, in these desolate barren hills, twenty miles from the nearest human being, it stirred and woke and rowelled him to be moving on. It had goaded him to flight from the Big Dipper mine, and he had obeyed. But now it was different; now he had suddenly become rich; he had lighted on a treasure—a treasure far more valuable than the Big Dipper mine itself. How was he to leave that? He could not move on now. He turned about in his blankets. No, he would not move on. Perhaps it was his fancy, after all. He saw nothing, heard nothing. The emptiness of primeval desolation stretched from him leagues and leagues upon either hand. The gigantic silence of the night lay close over everything, like a muffling Titanic palm. Of what was he suspicious? In that treeless waste an object could be seen at half a day's journey distant. In the vast silence the click of a pebble was as audible as a pistol-shot. And yet there was nothing, nothing.

The dentist settled himself in his blankets and tried to sleep. In five minutes he was sitting up, staring into the blue-gray shimmer of the moonlight, straining his ears, watching and listening intently. Nothing was in sight. The browned and broken flanks of the Panamint hills lay quiet and familiar under the moon. The burro moved its head with a clinking of its bell; and McTeague's mule, dozing on three legs, changed its weight to another foot, with a long breath. Everything fell silent again.

"What is it?" muttered the dentist. "If I could only see something, hear something."

He threw off the blankets, and, rising, climbed to the summit of the nearest hill and looked back in the direction in which he and Cribbens had travelled a fortnight before. For half an hour he waited, watching and listening in vain. But as he returned to camp, and prepared to roll his blankets about him, the strange impulse rose in him again abruptly, never so strong, never so insistent. It seemed as though he were bitted and ridden; as if some unseen hand were turning him toward the east; some unseen heel spurring him to precipitate and instant flight.

Flight from what? "No," he muttered under his breath. "Go now and leave the claim, and leave a fortune! What a fool I'd be, when I can't see anything or hear anything. To leave a fortune! No, I won't. No, by God!" He drew Cribbens's Winchester toward him and slipped a cartridge into the magazine.

"No," he growled. "Whatever happens, I'm going to stay. If anybody comes—" He depressed the lever of the rifle, and sent the cartridge clashing into the breech.

"I ain't going to sleep," he muttered under his mustache. "I can't sleep; I'll watch." He rose a second time, clambered to the nearest hilltop and sat down, drawing the blanket around him, and laying the Winchester across his knees. The hours passed. The dentist sat on the hilltop a motionless, crouching figure, inky black against the pale blur of the sky. By and by the edge of the eastern horizon began to grow blacker and more distinct in outline. The dawn was coming. Once more McTeague felt the mysterious intuition of approaching danger; an unseen hand seemed reining his head eastward; a spur was in his flanks that seemed to urge him to hurry, hurry, hurry. The influence grew stronger with every moment. The dentist set his great jaws together and held his ground.

"No," he growled between his set teeth. "No, I'll stay." He made a long circuit around the camp, even going as far as the first stake of the new claim, his Winchester cocked, his ears pricked, his eyes alert. There was nothing; yet as plainly as though it were shouted at the very nape of his neck he felt an enemy. It was not fear. McTeague was not afraid.

"If I could only *see* something—somebody," he muttered, as he held the cocked rifle ready, "I—I'd show him."

He returned to camp. Cribbens was snoring. The burro had come down to the stream for its morning drink. The mule was awake and browsing. McTeague stood irresolutely by the cold ashes of the camp-fire, looking from side to side with all the suspicion and wariness of a tracked stag. Stronger and stronger grew the strange impulse. It seemed to him that on the next instant he *must* perforce wheel sharply eastward and rush away headlong in a clumsy, lumbering gallop. He fought against it with all the ferocious obstinacy of his simple brute nature.

"Go, and leave the mine? Go and leave a million dollars? No, *no*, I won't go. No, I'll stay. Ah," he exclaimed, under his breath, with a shake of his huge head, like an exasperated and harassed brute, "ah, show yourself, will you?" He brought the rifle to his shoulder and covered point after point along the range of hills to the west. "Come on, show yourself. Come on a little, all of you. I ain't afraid of you; but don't skulk this way. You ain't going to drive me away from my mine. I'm going to *stay*."

An hour passed. Then two. The stars winked out, and the dawn whitened. The air became warmer. The whole east, clean of clouds, flamed opalescent from horizon to zenith, crimson at the base, where the earth blackened against it; at the top fading from pink to pale yellow, to green, to light blue, to the turquoise iridescence of the desert sky. The long, thin shadows of the early hours drew backward like receding serpents, then suddenly the sun looked over the shoulder of the world, and it was day.

At that moment McTeague was already eight miles away from the camp, going steadily eastward. He was descending the lowest spurs of the Panamint hills, following an old and faint cattle trail. Before him he drove his mule, laden with blankets, provisions for six days, Cribbens's rifle, and a canteen full of water. Securely bound to the pommel of the saddle was the canvas sack with its precious five thousand dollars, all in twenty-dollar gold pieces. But strange enough in that horrid waste of sand and sage was the object that McTeague himself persistently carried—the canary in its cage, about which he had carefully wrapped a couple of old flour-bags.

At about five o'clock that morning McTeague had crossed several trails which seemed to be converging, and, guessing that they led to a water hole, had followed one of them and had brought up at a sort of small sun-dried sink which nevertheless contained a little water at the bottom. He had watered the mule here, refilled the canteen, and drank deep himself. He had also dampened the old flour-sacks around the bird cage to protect the little canary as far as possible from the heat that he knew would increase now with every hour. He had made ready to go forward again, but had paused irresolute again, hesitating for the last time.

"I'm a fool," he growled, scowling back at the range behind him. "I'm a fool. What's the matter with me? I'm just walking right away from a million dollars. I know it's there. No, by God!" he exclaimed, savagely, "I ain't going to do it. I'm going back. I can't leave a mine like that." He had wheeled the mule about, and had started to return on his tracks, grinding his teeth fiercely, inclining his head forward as though butting against a wind that would beat him back. "Go on, go on," he cried, sometimes addressing the

mule, sometimes himself. "Go on, go back, go back. I *will* go back."
It was as though he were climbing a hill that grew steeper with
every stride. The strange impelling instinct fought his advance yard
by yard. By degrees the dentist's steps grew slower; he stopped,
went forward again cautiously, almost feeling his way, like someone
approaching a pit in the darkness. He stopped again, hesitating,
gnashing his teeth, clinching his fists with blind fury. Suddenly he
turned the mule about, and once more set his face to the eastward.
"I can't," he cried aloud to the desert; "I can't, I can't. It's
stronger than I am. I *can't* go back. Hurry now, hurry, hurry,
hurry."

He hastened on furtively, his head and shoulders bent. At times
one could almost say he crouched as he pushed forward with long
strides; now and then he even looked over his shoulder. Sweat rolled
from him, he lost his hat, and the matted mane of thick yellow hair
swept over his forehead and shaded his small, twinkling eyes. At
times, with a vague, nearly automatic gesture, he reached his hand
forward, the fingers prehensile, and directed towards the horizon, as
if he would clutch it and draw it nearer; and at intervals he muttered, "Hurry, hurry, hurry on, hurry on." For now at last
McTeague was afraid.

His plans were uncertain. He remembered what Cribbens had
said about the Armagosa Mountains in the country on the other
side of Death Valley. It was all hell to get into that country, Cribbens had said, and not many men went there, because of the terrible valley of alkali that barred the way, a horrible vast sink of white
sand and salt below even the sea level, the dry bed, no doubt, of
some prehistoric lake. But McTeague resolved to make a circuit of
the valley, keeping to the south, until he should strike the Armagosa River. He would make a circuit of the valley and come up on
the other side. He would get into that country around Gold Mountain in the Armagosa hills, barred off from the world by the leagues
of the red-hot alkali of Death Valley. "They" would hardly reach
him there. He would stay at Gold Mountain two or three months,
and then work his way down into Mexico.

McTeague tramped steadily forward, still descending the lower
irregularities of the Panamint Range. By nine o'clock the slope flattened out abruptly; the hills were behind him; before him, to the
east, all was level. He had reached the region where even the sand
and sage-brush begin to dwindle, giving place to white, powdered
alkali. The trails were numerous, but old and faint; and they had
been made by cattle, not by men. They led in all directions but one
—north, south, and west; but not one, however faint, struck out
towards the valley.

"If I keep along the edge of the hills where these trails are," muttered the dentist, "I ought to find water up in the arroyos from time to time."

At once he uttered an exclamation. The mule had begun to squeal and lash out with alternate hoofs, his eyes rolling, his ears flattened. He ran a few steps, halted, and squealed again. Then, suddenly wheeling at right angles, set off on a jog trot to the north, squealing and kicking from time to time. McTeague ran after him shouting and swearing, but for a long time the mule would not allow himself to be caught. He seemed more bewildered than frightened.

"He's eatun some of that loco-weed that Cribbens spoke about," panted McTeague. "Whoa, there; steady, you." At length the mule stopped of his own accord, and seemed to come to his senses again. McTeague came up and took the bridle rein, speaking to him and rubbing his nose.

"There, there, what's the matter with you?" The mule was docile again. McTeague washed his mouth and set forward once more.

The day was magnificent. From horizon to horizon was one vast span of blue, whitening as it dipped earthward. Miles upon miles to the east and southeast the desert unrolled itself, white, naked, inhospitable, palpitating and shimmering under the sun, unbroken by so much as a rock or cactus stump. In the distance it assumed all manner of faint colors, pink, purple, and pale orange. To the west rose the Panamint Range, sparsely sprinkled with gray sage-brush; here the earths and sands were yellow, ochre, and rich, deep red, the hollows and cañons picked out with intense blue shadows. It seemed strange that such barrenness could exhibit this radiance of color, but nothing could have been more beautiful than the deep red of the higher bluffs and ridges, seamed with purple shadows, standing sharply out against the pale-blue whiteness of the horizon.

By nine o'clock the sun stood high in the sky. The heat was intense; the atmosphere was thick and heavy with it. McTeague gasped for breath and wiped the beads of perspiration from his forehead, his cheeks, and his neck. Every inch and pore of his skin was tingling and pricking under the merciless lash of the sun's rays.

"If it gets much hotter," he muttered, with a long breath, "If it gets much hotter, I—I don' know—" he wagged his head and wiped the sweat from his eyelids, where it was running like tears.

The sun rose higher; hour by hour, as the dentist tramped steadily on, the heat increased. The baked dry sand crackled into innumerable tiny flakes under his feet. The twigs of the sage-brush snapped like brittle pipestems as he pushed through them. It grew hotter. At eleven the earth was like the surface of a furnace; the air, as McTeague breathed it in, was hot to his lips and the roof of his mouth. The sun was a disk of molten brass swimming in the burnt-out blue of the sky. McTeague stripped off his woollen shirt, and even unbuttoned his flannel undershirt, tying a handkerchief loosely about his neck.

"Lord!" he exclaimed. "I never knew it *could* get as hot as this." The heat grew steadily fiercer; all distant objects were visibly shimmering and palpitating under it. At noon a mirage appeared on the hills to the northwest. McTeague halted the mule, and drank from the tepid water in the canteen, dampening the sack around the canary's cage. As soon as he ceased his tramp and the noise of his crunching, grinding footsteps died away, the silence, vast, illimitable, enfolded him like an immeasurable tide. From all that gigantic landscape, that colossal reach of baking sand, there arose not a single sound. Not a twig rattled, not an insect hummed, not a bird or beast invaded that huge solitude with call or cry. Everything as far as the eye could reach, to north, to south, to east, and west, lay inert, absolutely quiet and moveless under the remorseless scourge of the noon sun. The very shadows shrank away, hiding under sage-bushes, retreating to the farthest nooks and crevices in the cañons of the hills. All the world was one gigantic blinding glare, silent, motionless. "If it gets much hotter," murmured the dentist again, moving his head from side to side, "If it gets much hotter, I don' know what I'll do."

Steadily the heat increased. At three o'clock it was even more terrible than it had been at noon.

"Ain't it *ever* going to let up?" groaned the dentist, rolling his eyes at the sky of hot blue brass. Then, as he spoke, the stillness was abruptly stabbed through and through by a shrill sound that seemed to come from all sides at once. It ceased; then, as McTeague took another forward step, began again with the suddenness of a blow, shriller, nearer at hand, a hideous, prolonged note that brought both man and mule to an instant halt.

"I know what *that* is," exclaimed the dentist. His eyes searched the ground swiftly until he saw what he expected he should see— the round thick coil, the slowly waving clover-shaped head and erect whirling tail with its vibrant rattles.

For fully thirty seconds the man and snake remained looking into each other's eyes. Then the snake uncoiled and swiftly wound from sight amidst the sage-brush. McTeague drew breath again, and his eyes once more beheld the illimitable leagues of quivering sand and alkali.

"Good Lord! What a country!" he exclaimed. But his voice was trembling as he urged forward the mule once more.

Fiercer and fiercer grew the heat as the afternoon advanced. At four McTeague stopped again. He was dripping at every pore, but there was no relief in perspiration. The very touch of his clothes upon his body was unendurable. The mule's ears were drooping and his tongue lolled from his mouth. The cattle trails seemed to be drawing together toward a common point; perhaps a water hole was near by.

"I'll have to lay up, sure," muttered the dentist. "I ain't made to travel in such heat as this."

He drove the mule up into one of the larger cañons and halted in the shadow of a pile of red rock. After a long search he found water, a few quarts, warm and brackish, at the bottom of a hollow of sun-cracked mud; it was little more than enough to water the mule and refill his canteen. Here he camped, casing the mule of the saddle, and turning him loose to find what nourishment he might. A few hours later the sun set in a cloudless glory of red and gold, and the heat became by degrees less intolerable. McTeague cooked his supper, chiefly coffee and bacon, and watched the twilight come on, revelling in the delicious coolness of the evening. As he spread his blankets on the ground he resolved that hereafter he would travel only at night, laying up in the daytime in the shade of the cañons. He was exhausted with his terrible day's march. Never in his life had sleep seemed so sweet to him.

But suddenly he was broad awake, his jaded senses all alert.

"What was that?" he muttered. "I thought I heard something— saw something."

He rose to his feet, reaching for the Winchester. Desolation lay still around him. There was not a sound but his own breathing; on the face of the desert not a grain of sand was in motion. McTeague looked furtively and quickly from side to side, his teeth set, his eyes rolling. Once more the rowel was in his flanks, once more an unseen hand reined him toward the east. After all the miles of that dreadful day's flight he was no better off than when he started. If anything, he was worse, for never had that mysterious instinct in him been more insistent than now; never had the impulse toward precipitate flight been stronger; never had the spur bit deeper. Every nerve of his body cried aloud for rest; yet every instinct seemed aroused and alive, goading him to hurry on, to hurry on.

"What *is* it, then? What *is* it?" he cried, between his teeth. "Can't I ever get rid of you? Ain't I *ever* going to shake you off? Don' keep it up this way. Show yourselves. Let's have it out right away. Come on. I ain't afraid if you'll only come on; but don't skulk this way." Suddenly he cried aloud in a frenzy of exasperation, "Damn you, come on, will you? Come on and have it out." His rifle was at his shoulder, he was covering bush after bush, rock after rock, aiming at every denser shadow. All at once, and quite involuntarily, his forefinger crooked, and the rifle spoke and flamed. The cañons roared back the echo, tossing it out far over the desert in a rippling, widening wave of sound.

McTeague lowered the rifle hastily, with an exclamation of dismay.

"You fool," he said to himself, "you fool. You've done it now. They could hear that miles away. You've done it now."

He stood listening intently, the rifle smoking in his hands. The last echo died away. The smoke vanished, the vast silence closed upon the passing echoes of the rifle as the ocean closes upon a ship's wake. Nothing moved; yet McTeague bestirred himself sharply, rolling up his blankets, resaddling the mule, getting his outfit together again. From time to time he muttered.

"Hurry now; hurry on. You fool, you've done it now. They could hear that miles away. Hurry now. They ain't far off now."

As he depressed the lever of the rifle to reload it, he found that the magazine was empty. He clapped his hands to his sides, feeling rapidly first in one pocket, then in another. He had forgotten to take extra cartridges with him. McTeague swore under his breath as he flung the rifle away. Henceforth he must travel unarmed.

A little more water had gathered in the mud hole near which he had camped. He watered the mule for the last time and wet the sacks around the canary's cage. Then once more he set forward.

But there was a change in the direction of McTeague's flight. Hitherto he had held to the south, keeping upon the very edge of the hills; now he turned sharply at right angles. The slope fell away beneath his hurrying feet; the sage-brush dwindled, and at length ceased; the sand gave place to a fine powder, white as snow; and an hour after he had fired the rifle his mule's hoofs were crisping and cracking the sun-baked flakes of alkali on the surface of Death Valley.

Tracked and harried, as he felt himself to be, from one camping place to another, McTeague had suddenly resolved to make one last effort to rid himself of the enemy that seemed to hang upon his heels. He would strike straight out into that horrible wilderness where even the beasts were afraid. He would cross Death Valley at once and put its arid wastes between him and his pursuer.

"You don't dare follow me now," he muttered, as he hurried on. "Let's see you come out *here* after me."

He hurried on swiftly, urging the mule to a rapid racking walk. Towards four o'clock the sky in front of him began to flush pink and golden. McTeague halted and breakfasted, pushing on again immediately afterward. The dawn flamed and glowed like a brazier, and the sun rose a vast red-hot coal floating in fire. An hour passed, then another, and another. It was about nine o'clock. Once more the dentist paused, and stood panting and blowing, his arms dangling, his eyes screwed up and blinking as he looked about him.

Far behind him the Panamint hills were already but blue hummocks on the horizon. Before him and upon either side, to the north and to the east and to the south, stretched primordial desolation. League upon league the infinite reaches of dazzling white alkali laid themselves out like an immeasurable scroll unrolled from horizon to horizon; not a bush, not a twig relieved that horrible monotony. Even the sand of the desert would have been a welcome sight; a single clump of sage-brush would have fascinated the eye; but this was worse than the desert. It was abominable, this hideous sink of alkali, this bed of some primeval lake lying so far below the level of the ocean. The great mountains of Placer County had been merely indifferent to man; but this awful sink of alkali was openly and unreservedly iniquitous and malignant.

McTeague had told himself that the heat upon the lower slopes of the Panamint had been dreadful; here in Death Valley it became a thing of terror. There was no longer any shadow but his own. He was scorched and parched from head to heel. It seemed to him that the smart of his tortured body could not have been keener if he had been flayed.

"If it gets much hotter," he muttered, wringing the sweat from his thick fell of hair and mustache, "If it gets much hotter, I don' know what I'll do." He was thirsty, and drank a little from his canteen. "I ain't got any too much water," he murmured, shaking the canteen. "I got to get out of this place in a hurry, sure."

By eleven o'clock the heat had increased to such an extent that McTeague could feel the burning of the ground come pringling and stinging through the soles of his boots. Every step he took threw up clouds of impalpable alkali dust, salty and choking, so that he strangled and coughed and sneezed with it.

"Lord! what a country!" exclaimed the dentist.

An hour later, the mule stopped and lay down, his jaws wide open, his ears dangling. McTeague washed his mouth with a handful of water and for a second time since sunrise wetted the floursacks around the bird cage. The air was quivering and palpitating like that in the stoke-hold of a steamship. The sun, small and contracted, swam molten overhead.

"I can't stand it," said McTeague at length. "I'll have to stop and make some kinda shade."

The mule was crouched upon the ground, panting rapidly, with half-closed eyes. The dentist removed the saddle, and unrolling his blanket, propped it up as best he could between him and the sun.

As he stooped down to crawl beneath it, his palm touched the ground. He snatched it away with a cry of pain. The surface alkali was oven-hot; he was obliged to scoop out a trench in it before he dared to lie down.

By degrees the dentist began to doze. He had had little or no sleep the night before, and the hurry of his flight under the blazing sun had exhausted him. But his rest was broken; between waking and sleeping, all manner of troublous images galloped through his brain. He thought he was back in the Panamint hills again with Cribbens. They had just discovered the mine and were returning toward camp. McTeague saw himself as another man, striding along over the sand and sage-brush. At once he saw himself stop and wheel sharply about, peering back suspiciously. There was something behind him; something was following him. He looked, as it were, over the shoulder of this other McTeague, and saw down there, in the half light of the cañon, something dark crawling upon the ground, an indistinct gray figure, man or brute, he did not know. Then he saw another, and another; then another. A score of black, crawling objects were following him, crawling from bush to bush, converging upon him. "*They*" were after him, were closing in upon him, were within touch of his hand, were at his feet—*were at his throat.*

McTeague jumped up with a shout, oversetting the blanket. There was nothing in sight. For miles around, the alkali was empty, solitary, quivering and shimmering under the pelting fire of the afternoon's sun.

But once more the spur bit into his body, goading him on. There was to be no rest, no going back, no pause, no stop. Hurry, hurry, hurry on. The brute that in him slept so close to the surface was alive and alert, and tugging to be gone. There was no resisting that instinct. The brute felt an enemy, scented the trackers, clamored and struggled and fought, and would not be gainsaid.

"I *can't* go on," groaned McTeague, his eyes sweeping the horizon behind him, "I'm beat out. I'm dog tired. I ain't slept any for two nights." But for all that he roused himself again, saddled the mule, scarcely less exhausted than himself, and pushed on once more over the scorching alkali and under the blazing sun.

From that time on the fear never left him, the spur never ceased to bite, the instinct that goaded him to flight never was dumb; hurry or halt, it was all the same. On he went, straight on, chasing the receding horizon; flagellated with heat; tortured with thirst; crouching over; looking furtively behind, and at times reaching his hand forward, the fingers prehensile, grasping, as it were, toward the horizon, that always fled before him.

The sun set upon the third day of McTeague's flight, night came on, the stars burned slowly into the cool dark purple of the sky. The gigantic sink of white alkali glowed like snow. McTeague, now far into the desert, held steadily on, swinging forward with great strides. His enormous strength held him doggedly to his work. Sullenly, with his huge jaws gripping stolidly together, he pushed on. At midnight he stopped.

"Now," he growled, with a certain desperate defiance, as though he expected to be heard, "Now, I'm going to lay up and get some sleep. You can come or not."

He cleared away the hot surface alkali, spread out his blanket, and slept until the next day's heat aroused him. His water was so low that he dared not make coffee now, and so breakfasted without it. Until ten o'clock he tramped forward, then camped again in the shade of one of the rare rock ledges, and "lay up" during the heat of the day. By five o'clock he was once more on the march.

He travelled on for the greater part of that night, stopping only once towards three in the morning to water the mule from the canteen. Again the red-hot day burned up over the horizon. Even at six o'clock it was hot.

"It's going to be worse than ever to-day," he groaned. "I wish I could find another rock to camp by. Ain't I *ever* going to get out of this place?"

There was no change in the character of the desert. Always the same measureless leagues of white-hot alkali stretched away toward the horizon on every hand. Here and there the flat, dazzling surface of the desert broke and raised into long low mounds, from the summit of which McTeague could look for miles and miles over its horrible desolation. No shade was in sight. Not a rock, not a stone broke the monotony of the ground. Again and again he ascended the low unevennesses, looking and searching for a camping place, shading his eyes from the glitter of sand and sky.

He tramped forward a little farther, then paused at length in a hollow between two breaks, resolving to make camp there.

Suddenly there was a shout.

"Hands up. By damn, I got the drop on you!"

McTeague looked up.

It was Marcus.

XXII

Within a month after his departure from San Francisco, Marcus had "gone in on a cattle ranch" in the Panamint Valley with an Englishman, an acquaintance of Mr. Sieppe's. His headquarters were at a place called Modoc,[1] at the lower extremity of the valley, about fifty miles by trail to the south of Keeler.

His life was the life of a cowboy. He realized his former vision of himself, booted, sombreroed, and revolvered, passing his days in the saddle and the better part of his nights around the poker tables in Modoc's one saloon. To his intense satisfaction he even involved himself in a gun fight that arose over a disputed brand, with the result that two fingers of his left hand were shot away.

News from the outside world filtered slowly into the Panamint Valley, and the telegraph had never been built beyond Keeler. At intervals one of the local papers of Independence, the nearest large town, found its way into the cattle camps on the ranges, and occasionally one of the Sunday editions of a Sacramento journal, weeks old, was passed from hand to hand. Marcus ceased to hear from the Sieppes. As for San Francisco, it was as far from him as was London or Vienna.

One day, a fortnight after McTeague's flight from San Francisco, Marcus rode into Modoc, to find a group of men gathered about a notice affixed to the outside of the Wells-Fargo office. It was an offer of reward for the arrest and apprehension of a murderer. The crime had been committed in San Francisco, but the man wanted had been traced as far as the western portion of Inyo County, and was believed at that time to be in hiding in either the Pinto or Panamint hills, in the vicinity of Keeler.

Marcus reached Keeler on the afternoon of that same day. Half a mile from the town his pony fell and died from exhaustion. Marcus did not stop even to remove the saddle. He arrived in the barroom of the hotel in Keeler just after the posse had been made up. The sheriff, who had come down from Independence that morning, at first refused his offer of assistance. He had enough men already—too many, in fact. The country travelled through would be hard, and it would be difficult to find water for so many men and horses.

"But none of you fellers have ever seen um," vociferated Marcus, quivering· with excitement and wrath. "I know um well. I could pick um out in a million. I can identify um, and you fellers can't. And I knew—I knew—good God! I knew that girl—his wife—in Frisco. She's a cousin of mine, she is—she was—I thought once of — This thing's a personal matter of mine—an' that money he got away with, that five thousand, belongs to me by rights. Oh, never mind, I'm going along. Do you hear?" he shouted, his fists raised, "I'm going along, I tell you. There ain't a man of you big enough to stop me. Let's see you try and stop me going. Let's see you once, any two of you." He filled the barroom with his clamor.

"Lord love you, come along, then," said the sheriff.

1. A fictitious place.

The posse rode out of Keeler that same night. The keeper of the general merchandise store, from whom Marcus had borrowed a second pony, had informed them that Cribbens and his partner, whose description tallied exactly with that given in the notice of reward, had outfitted at his place with a view to prospecting in the Panamint hills. The posse trailed them at once to their first camp at the head of the valley. It was an easy matter. It was only necessary to inquire of the cowboys and range riders of the valley if they had seen and noted the passage of two men, one of whom carried a bird cage.

Beyond this first camp the trail was lost, and a week was wasted in a bootless search around the mine at Gold Gulch, whither it seemed probable the partners had gone. Then a travelling peddler, who included Gold Gulch in his route, brought in the news of a wonderful strike of gold-bearing quartz some ten miles to the south on the western slope of the range. Two men from Keeler had made a strike, the peddler had said, and added the curious detail that one of the men had a canary bird in a cage with him.

The posse made Cribbens's camp three days after the unaccountable disappearance of his partner. Their man was gone, but the narrow hoof prints of a mule, mixed with those of huge hob-nailed boots, could be plainly followed in the sand. Here they picked up the trail and held to it steadily till the point was reached where, instead of tending southward it swerved abruptly to the east. The men could hardly believe their eyes.

"It ain't reason," exclaimed the sheriff. "What in thunder is he up to? This beats me. Cutting out into Death Valley at this time of year."

"He's heading for Gold Mountain over in the Armagosa, sure."

The men decided that this conjecture was true. It was the only inhabited locality in that direction. A discussion began as to the further movements of the posse.

"I don't figure on going into that alkali sink with no eight men and horses," declared the sheriff. "One man can't carry enough water to take him and his mount across, let alone *eight*. No, sir. Four couldn't do it. No, *three* couldn't. We've got to make a circuit round the valley and come up on the other side and head him off at Gold Mountain. That's what we got to do, and ride like hell to do it, too."

But Marcus protested with all the strength of his lungs against abandoning the trail now that they had found it. He argued that they were but a day and a half behind their man now. There was no possibility of their missing the trail—as distinct in the white alkali as in snow. They could make a dash into the valley, secure their man, and return long before their water failed them. He, for one, would not give up the pursuit, now that they were so close. In the haste of the departure from Keeler the sheriff had neglected to swear him in. He was under no orders. He would do as he pleased. "Go on, then, you darn fool," answered the sheriff. "We'll cut on round the valley, for all that. It's a gamble he'll be at Gold Mountain before you're half way across. But if you catch him, here"—he tossed Marcus a pair of handcuffs—"put 'em on him and bring him back to Keeler."

Two days after he had left the posse, and when he was already far out in the desert, Marcus's horse gave out.[2] In the fury of his impatience he had spurred mercilessly forward on the trail, and on the morning of the third day found that his horse was unable to move. The joints of his legs seemed locked rigidly. He would go his own length, stumbling and interfering, then collapse helplessly upon the ground with a pitiful groan. He was used up.

Marcus believed himself to be close upon McTeague now. The ashes at his last camp had still been smoldering. Marcus took what supplies of food and water he could carry, and hurried on. But McTeague was farther ahead than he had guessed, and by evening of his third day upon the desert Marcus, raging with thirst, had drunk his last mouthful of water and had flung away the empty canteen.

"If he ain't got water with um," he said to himself as he pushed on, "If he ain't got water with um, by damn! I'll be in a bad way. I will, for a fact."

. . . .

At Marcus's shout McTeague looked up and around him. For the instant he saw no one. The white glare of alkali was still unbroken. Then his swiftly rolling eyes lighted upon a head and shoulder that protruded above the low crest of the break directly in front of him. A man was there, lying at full length upon the ground, covering him with a revolver. For a few seconds McTeague looked at the man stupidly, bewildered, confused, as yet without definite thought. Then he noticed that the man was singularly like Marcus Schouler. It *was* Marcus Schouler. How in the world did Marcus Schouler come to be in that desert? What did he mean by pointing a pistol at him that way? He'd best look out or the pistol would go off. Then his thoughts readjusted themselves with a swiftness born of a vivid sense of danger. Here was the enemy at last, the tracker he had felt upon his footsteps. Now at length he had "come on" and shown himself, after all those days of skulking. McTeague was glad of it. He'd show him now. They two would have it out right then

2. Since Death Valley is only fifteen miles wide at its widest point, it seems unlikely that it would take Marcus several days to reach McTeague.

and there. His rifle! He had thrown it away long since. He was helpless. Marcus had ordered him to put up his hands. If he did not,
Marcus would kill him. He had the drop on him. McTeague stared,
scowling fiercely at the levelled pistol. He did not move.

"Hands up!" shouted Marcus a second time. "I'll give you three
to do it in. One, two——"

Instinctively McTeague put his hands above his head.

Marcus rose and came towards him over the break.

"Keep 'em up," he cried. "If you move 'em once I'll kill you,
sure."

He came up to McTeague and searched him, going through his
pockets; but McTeague had no revolver; not even a hunting knife.

"What did you do with that money, with that five thousand dollars?"

"It's on the mule," answered McTeague, sullenly.

Marcus grunted, and cast a glance at the mule, who was standing
some distance away, snorting nervously, and from time to time flattening his long ears.

"Is that it there on the horn of the saddle, there in that canvas
sack?" Marcus demanded.

"Yes, that's it."

A gleam of satisfaction came into Marcus's eyes, and under his
breath he muttered:

"Got it at last."

He was singularly puzzled to know what next to do. He had got
McTeague. There he stood at length, with his big hands over his
head, scowling at him sullenly. Marcus had caught his enemy, had
run down the man for whom every officer in the State had been
looking. What should he do with him now? He couldn't keep him
standing there forever with his hands over his head.

"Got any water?" he demanded.

"There's a canteen of water on the mule."

Marcus moved toward the mule and made as if to reach the
bridle-rein. The mule squealed, threw up his head, and galloped
to a little distance, rolling his eyes and flattening his ears.

Marcus swore wrathfully.

"He acted that way once before," explained McTeague, his hands
still in the air. "He ate some loco-weed back in the hills before I
started."

For a moment Marcus hesitated. While he was catching the
mule McTeague might get away. But where to, in heaven's name?
A rat could not hide on the surface of that glistening alkali, and
besides, all McTeague's store of provisions and his priceless supply
of water were on the mule. Marcus ran after the mule, revolver in

hand, shouting and cursing. But the mule would not be caught. He acted as if possessed, squealing, lashing out, and galloping in wide circles, his head high in the air.

"Come on," shouted Marcus, furious, turning back to McTeague. "Come on, help me catch him. We got to catch him. All the water we got is on the saddle."

McTeague came up.

"He's eatun some loco-weed," he repeated. "He went kinda crazy once before."

"If he should take it into his head to bolt and keep on running——"

Marcus did not finish. A sudden great fear seemed to widen around and inclose the two men. Once their water gone, the end would not be long.

"We can catch him all right," said the dentist. "I caught him once before."

"Oh, I guess we can catch him," answered Marcus, reassuringly.

Already the sense of enmity between the two had weakened in the face of a common peril. Marcus let down the hammer of his revolver and slid it back into the holster.

The mule was trotting on ahead, snorting and throwing up great clouds of alkali dust. At every step the canvas sack jingled, and McTeague's bird cage, still wrapped in the flour-bags, bumped against the saddle-pads. By and by the mule stopped, blowing out his nostrils excitedly.

"He's clean crazy," fumed Marcus, panting and swearing.

"We ought to come up on him quiet," observed McTeague.

"I'll try and sneak up," said Marcus; "two of us would scare him again. You stay here."

Marcus went forward a step at a time. He was almost within arm's length of the bridle when the mule shied from him abruptly and galloped away.

Marcus danced with rage, shaking his fists, and swearing horribly. Some hundred yards away the mule paused and began blowing and snuffing in the alkali as though in search of feed. Then, for no reason, he shied again, and started off on a jog trot toward the east.

"We've got to follow him," exclaimed Marcus as McTeague came up. "There's no water within seventy miles of here."

Then began an interminable pursuit. Mile after mile, under the terrible heat of the desert sun, the two men followed the mule, racked with a thirst that grew fiercer every hour. A dozen times they could almost touch the canteen of water, and as often the distraught animal shied away and fled before them. At length Marcus cried:

"It's no use, we can't catch him, and we're killing ourselves with thirst. We got to take our chances." He drew his revolver from its holster, cocked it, and crept forward.

"Steady, now," said McTeague; "it won' do to shoot through the canteen." Within twenty yards Marcus paused, made a rest of his left forearm and fired.

"You *got* him," cried McTeague. "No, he's up again. Shoot him again. He's going to bolt." Marcus ran on, firing as he ran. The mule, one foreleg trailing, scrambled along, squealing and snorting. Marcus fired his last shot. The mule pitched forward upon his head, then, rolling sideways, fell upon the canteen, bursting it open and spilling its entire contents into the sand.

Marcus and McTeague ran up, and Marcus snatched the battered canteen from under the reeking, bloody hide. There was no water left. Marcus flung the canteen from him and stood up, facing McTeague. There was a pause.

"We're dead men," said Marcus.

McTeague looked from him out over the desert. Chaotic desolation stretched from them on either hand, flaming and glaring with the afternoon heat. There was the brazen sky and the leagues upon leagues of alkali, leper white. There was nothing more. They were in the heart of Death Valley.

"Not a drop of water," muttered McTeague; "not a drop of water."

"We can drink the mule's blood," said Marcus. "It's been done before. But—but—" he looked down at the quivering, gory body— "but I ain't thirsty enough for that yet."

"Where's the nearest water?"

"Well, it's about a hundred miles or more back of us in the Panamint hills," returned Marcus, doggedly. "We'd be crazy long before we reached it. I tell you, we're done for, by damn, we're *done* for. We ain't ever going to get outa here."

"Done for?" murmured the other, looking about stupidly. "Done for, that's the word. Done for? Yes, I guess we're done for."

"What are we going to do *now*?" exclaimed Marcus, sharply, after a while.

"Well, let's—let's be moving along—somewhere."

"*Where*, I'd like to know? What's the good of moving on?"

"What's the good of stopping here?"

There was a silence.

"Lord, it's hot," said the dentist, finally, wiping his forehead with the back of his hand. Marcus ground his teeth.

"Done for," he muttered; "done for."

"I never *was* so thirsty," continued McTeague. "I'm that dry I can hear my tongue rubbing against the roof of my mouth."

"Well, we can't stop here," said Marcus, finally; "we got to go somewhere. We'll try and get back, but it ain't no manner of use. Anything we want to take along with us from the mule? We can——"

Suddenly he paused. In an instant the eyes of the two doomed men had met as the same thought simultaneously rose in their minds. The canvas sack with its five thousand dollars was still tied to the horn of the saddle.

Marcus had emptied his revolver at the mule, and though he still wore his cartridge belt, he was for the moment as unarmed as McTeague.

"I guess," began McTeague coming forward a step, "I guess, even if we are done for, I'll take——some of my truck along."

"Hold on," exclaimed Marcus, with rising aggressiveness. "Let's talk about that. I ain't so sure about who that——who that money belongs to."

"Well, I *am*, you see," growled the dentist.

The old enmity between the two men, their ancient hate, was flaming up again.

"Don't try an' load that gun either," cried McTeague, fixing Marcus with his little eyes.

"Then don't lay your finger on that sack," shouted the other. "You're my prisoner, do you understand? You'll do as I say." Marcus had drawn the handcuffs from his pocket, and stood ready with his revolver held as a club. "You soldiered me out of that money once, and played me for a sucker, an' it's *my* turn now. Don't you lay your finger on that sack."

Marcus barred McTeague's way, white with passion. McTeague did not answer. His eyes drew to two fine, twinkling points, and his enormous hands knotted themselves into fists, hard as wooden mallets. He moved a step nearer to Marcus, then another.

Suddenly the men grappled, and in another instant were rolling and struggling upon the hot white ground. McTeague thrust Marcus backward until he tripped and fell over the body of the dead mule. The little bird cage broke from the saddle with the violence of their fall, and rolled out upon the ground, the flour-bags slipping from it. McTeague tore the revolver from Marcus's grip and struck out with it blindly. Clouds of alkali dust, fine and pungent, enveloped the two fighting men, all but strangling them.

McTeague did not know how he killed his enemy, but all at once Marcus grew still beneath his blows. Then there was a sudden last return of energy. McTeague's right wrist was caught, something clicked upon it, then the struggling body fell limp and motionless with a long breath.

As McTeague rose to his feet, he felt a pull at his right wrist; something held it fast. Looking down, he saw that Marcus in that last struggle had found strength to handcuff their wrists together. Marcus was dead now; McTeague was locked to the body. All about him, vast, interminable, stretched the measureless leagues of Death Valley.

McTeague remained stupidly looking around him, now at the distant horizon, now at the ground, now at the half-dead canary chittering feebly in its little gilt prison.

THE END

Backgrounds and Sources

The Sources and Composition of McTeague

The San Francisco Background

FRANK NORRIS

An Opening for Novelists: Great Opportunities for Fiction Writers in San Francisco†

There are certain cities in the world which are adaptable to the uses of the writer of fiction, and there are others which are not. Things can happen in some cities and the tale of them will be interesting; the same story laid in another city would be ridiculous. It is hard to say, why this is so, but a moment's review of the world's centers with this thought in mind will prove the truth of the statement beyond any shadow of doubt. Paris, London and Rome are "good material." Berlin, Vienna and Hamburg are not. Stories of New Orleans or of Constantinople could easily be made interesting, but no romancer has yet had the hardihood to attempt to write of Chicago or Buffalo. Imagine a novel of Chicago.[1] The fact is very curious and the choice very arbitrary. There seems to be no rule applicable. A city need not necessarily be old, nor a seaport, nor "cosmopolitan," nor picturesque, nor beautifully built, nor large nor small. Any one who has the instinct for fiction can tell on the instant whether or not it is suitable as a background for a novel, a short story or a drama.

But consider San Francisco. It is not necessary to hesitate a moment. "Things can happen" in San Francisco. Kearny street, Montgomery street, Nob Hill, Telegraph Hill, of course Chinatown, Lone Mountain, the Poodle Dog, the Palace Hotel and the What Cheer House, the Barbary Coast, the Crow's Nest, the Mission, the Bay, the Bohemian Club, the Presidio, Spanish town, Fisherman's wharf.

There is an indefinable air about all these places that is suggestive of stories at once. You fancy the names would look well on a book's page. The people who frequent them could walk right into a novel or short story and be at home.

† From the San Francisco *Wave*, XVI (May 22, 1897), 7; text as reprinted in *The Literary Criticism of Frank Norris*, edited by Donald Pizer. Copyright 1964 by Donald Pizer. (Austin, Tex.: University of Texas Press, 1964; reprinted, New York: Russell & Russell, 1976).

1. Norris was apparently unaware of H. B. Fuller's *The Cliff-Dwellers* (1893) and *With the Procession* (1895), both set in Chicago, and of Hamlin Garland's *Rose of Dutcher's Coolly* (1895), partially set in Chicago. Nor, of course, did he anticipate his own *The Pit* (1903).

It occurs to me that there is perhaps one feature of the city that conduces to this effect, that is its isolation. Perhaps no great city of the world is so isolated as we are. Did you ever think of that? There is no great city to the north of us, to the south none nearer than Mexico, to the west is the waste of the Pacific, to the east the waste of the deserts. Here we are set down as a pin point in a vast circle of solitude. Isolation produces individuality, originality. The place has grown up independently. Other cities grow by accretion from without. San Francisco must grow by expansion from within; and so we have time and opportunity to develop certain unhampered types and characters and habits unbiased by outside influence, types that are admirably adapted to fictitious treatment.

It is a significant fact that the little that has been done in the way of gripping hold upon and impressing this life of ours between the covers of works of fiction has been done in the way of short stories. London had her Dickens, New Orleans her Cable, New York her Davis, Boston her Howells, Paris her Zola, but San Francisco still waits for her novelist. She will wait long, we believe. The conditions of our life are suited finely to the short story, but not as yet to the novel. We are growing and living, as it were, in spots, here a little and there a little, scattered bits of life and movement, quite independent of each other—short stories that are happening every day. But we are not settled enough yet for the novelist, who demands large, co-ordinated, broad and simple lines upon which to work, something far more unified than we can yet give him.[2] But the short stories. There's the chance. Who shall be our Kipling? Where is the man that shall get at the heart of us, the blood and bones and fiber of us, that shall go a-gunning for stories up and down our streets and into our houses and parlors and lodging houses and saloons and dives and along our wharves and into our theaters; yes, and into the secretest chambers of our homes as well as our hearts?

Les Jeunes.[3] Yes, there are Les Jeunes, and the *Lark* was delightful—delightful fooling, but there's a graver note and a more virile to be sounded. Les Jeunes can do better than the *Lark*. Give us stories now, give us men, strong, brutal men, with red-hot blood in 'em, with unleashed passions rampant in 'em, blood and bones and viscera in 'em, and women, too, that move and have their being, people that love and hate something better now than Vivettes and Perilles and Goups.[4] They are here, these living men and women.

2. A somewhat anomalous remark considering that Norris had completed *Vandover and the Brute* and had almost finished *McTeague*. Indeed, he had subtitled *Vandover*, "A Study of Life and Manners in an American City at the End of the Nineteenth Century," and that city was San Francisco.

3. A group of San Francisco Bohemians, led by Gelett Burgess; the group were the principal contributors to the San Francisco little magazine *The Lark*.

4. Vivette and Perilla (not *Perille*) were imaginary characters of refinement and sensitivity to whom many of the essays in the *Lark* were either dedicated or addressed. Goops (not *goups*) were boneless figures drawn by Burgess for cartoons in the *Lark*.

Think of the short stories that are happening every hour of the time. Get hold of them, some of you younger writers, grip fast upon the life of them. It's the Life that we want, the vigorous, real thing, not the curious weaving of words and the polish of literary finish. Damn the "style" of a story, so long as we get the swing and rush and trample of the things that live. While you are rounding a phrase a sailor has been shanghaied down there along the water front; while you are sustaining a metaphor, another See Yup has been hatcheted yonder in Gambler's alley; a man has time to be stabbed while you are composing a villanelle; the crisis of a life has come and gone while you have been niggling with your couplet. "Murder and sudden death," say you? Yes, but it's the life that lives; it's reality, it's the thing that counts. We don't want literature, we want life. We don't want fine writing, we want short stories. Kipling saw it here and Stevenson as they passed through—read the unwritten tales of us as they ran.[5]

The tales are here. The public is here. A hundred clashing presses are hungry for you, future young story-writer of San Francisco, whoever you may be. Strike but the right note, and strike it with all your might, strike it with iron instead of velvet, and the clang of it shall go the round of the nations.

Aqui le tour, who shall be our Kipling?

From the *San Francisco Examiner*†

TWENTY-NINE FATAL WOUNDS

SARAH COLLINS SLAUGHTERED BY HER HUSBAND
BECAUSE SHE WOULD NOT GIVE HIM MONEY

*He Followed Her to Her Work at a Kindergarten
and Fulfilled His Oft-Made Threat*

ARRESTED WHILE AT PRAYER

*The Murderer Found by the Police While Kneeling in a Church
—The Victim Lives Long Enough to Tell Her
Slayer's Name—Her Life of Poverty and Toil for Her
Children's Sake—Collins Tried to Kill Her
Once Before and Served a Term in Prison for It.*

A brute named Pat Collins stabbed his wife to death in the Felix

---

5. Norris refers to passages on San Francisco in Kipling's *American Notes* (1891) and Stevenson's *The Wrecker* (1892). Loudon Dodd in *The Wrecker* (always one of Norris's favorite novels) thought San Francisco the most interesting city in America.

† From the *San Francisco Examiner,* October 10, 1893, p. 12.

Adler Free Kindergarten yesterday morning.

She was the janitress of the school, and he followed her there when she went to her work in the early morning. Two minutes after Collins entered the school he ran out again and escaped, and immediately she dragged herself down the stairs bleeding and dying and with the knife he buried to the hilt in the last gash. He had stabbed her more than thirty times.

She died in the Receiving Hospital half an hour later.

He killed her because she would not give him money and would not live with him. He had told her he would do it, and once before he attempted to kill her. He served a short term in jail for this attempt.

She knew he would carry out his threats, for she told the neighbors that some day he would surely take her life.

They were married nine years ago. He was an iron-worker, but soon gave up his trade, and has been a common laborer ever since. He abused his wife almost from the start, and his treatment of her became worse as the years went by. Whenever he got drunk he beat her, and if she did not give him money he knocked her down. They had a couple of children, both boys, and the mother had to support these as well as herself and her worthless husband.

Just about a year ago Collins got into a tantrum and tried to kill his wife with a razor. He did cut her rather severely, but she recovered. Collins was arrested for assault to murder, but when the case went to the Superior Court he got off with a conviction of simple assault. He was sent to the House of Correction for six months and the wretched wife had peace for that period.

She lived with her children in the rear of "Flannery's," a saloon and tenement house at 18 Tehama street, in two wretched rooms.

To her neighbors she was a marvel. They could talk of nothing else yesterday but her patience and her industry. She was janitress of the Occidental Kindergarten as well as the other.

The Felix Adler School is a charity kindergarten in the upper story of an old barn at the corner of Folsom and Second Streets. The Occidental is another school of the same sort on Second and Howard.

She could not earn enough to live on by keeping these poor schools clean, so she took in washing. The wondering neighbors told of her life in these two rooms. Every morning she went to her work in the kindergarten. She had to finish that in time to dress the two boys and sent them off to school. Then she began on the washing. That was her life every day.

"And many's the time I've seen her so dead tired at dark that she couldn't stand," said Mrs. Flannery, who tends the bar at 18 Tehama street. "All she did was to work and pray God that she'd be well enough to work the next day."

Things are very squalid down in that part of town. Mrs. Collins slept and cooked and worked all in the same room.

There is but a single cover on the bed, and that was ragged and threadbare. There was the look and odor of abject poverty everywhere. It was more like a picture of wretchedness in London than a room in rich San Francisco.

Like Kipling's Badalia Herodsfoot,[1] who died in much the same way, Sarah Collins took up with no other man while her own was in jail or otherwise away.

All she asked was for him to keep away and give her a chance to support her children.

Collins served out his time and wanted to come back to his wife, but she kept him away till last Friday. Then he came to see her. He had been out in the country picking grapes or tramping. Of course he wanted money, and she would not give him any.

He sat in her room with a knife in his hand, and alternately coaxed and threatened. He told her he would kill her, and though she heard him say it often, she thought that the time was near when he would carry out his threat. She left him talking to the children, and appealed to some men in the neighborhood for help.

It is not customary to interfere between husband and wife in that part of Tehama street, and they advised her to apply to the police for protection. She went to the Southern Police Station and was told to swear out a warrant for her husband's arrest; but when she returned Collins was gone, so she did not bother about a warrant.

She went to her work as usual yesterday morning. A little before 8 o'clock a man ran up the steps that lead to the kindergarten. A track-cleaner, John Kelly, saw him go in. "He had hardly got inside," Kelly says, "when I heard a woman scream. She only screamed two or three times and then the man ran out and started up to Harrison street. Then he turned around and ran down Second toward Bryant street.

Accusing Her Husband

Then the woman appeared, dragging herself, or sliding from step to step. I ran to her and asked her what was wrong.

"Oh, my God! my man cut me," she said. Then she asked me to take her to the hospital. I took the knife from the wound in her neck. She asked me for it. "It's what he stabbed me with," she said.

"Who?" I asked.

1. Kipling's story "The Record of Badalia Herodsfoot" (1890) is set in a London slum.

"My husband Collins."

The dying woman was taken in a partol wagon to the Receiving Hospital. She asked for a priest, but before one came she was dead.

She was taken to the Morgue, and the doctors there made an autopsy. There were knife wounds all over her—gashes in her breast, in her throat, on her head and her face. The doctors found over thirty cuts before the ghastly count was concluded, and stated that any one of twenty-nine of them would have caused death.

The weapon the murderer used was an ordinary rough horn-handled pocket-knife with a freshly sharpened blade about two inches long. She must have fought him hard while he was cutting her for the palms of both her hands were gashed, showing that she caught the knife and tried to wrest it from him. There were finger-marks on her face—he had held her with one hand while he stabbed with the others, and the prints of his nails are plain on the dead woman's cheek.

The little hatroom of the kindergarten showed what a struggle there had been. The walls were splashed with blood and the floors were covered with it. Some of the hooks for the children's hats and coats were broken. The red stain extended out into the hall and down the steps to the street, but the teachers of the kindergarten had the dreadful traces cleaned away before the children got there.

Mrs. Collins' two little boys went to school as usual when their mother did not return. The youngest, five years old, attended the Occidental Kindergarten, the other, ten years old, went to the Tehama-street school. Both were taken in charge by the Youths' Directory, and do not know even now of their mother's terrible death.

Arrested While at Prayer

Collins was arrested about 10 o'clock last night in the sanctuary of St. Ignatius' Church, where he was found on his knees engaged in prayer. Patrolmen Flynn and Foley got their clew as to the where-abouts of the man from a lot of young fellows who were sitting in a McAllister-street saloon about 9:30 o'clock when Collins entered the place. He called for a drink and invited the crowd to join him. Then he proposed a game of cards, which they refused to join. Collins then left the saloon, saying:

"I'm going to the church and take the pledge."

As he went out of the door one of the men said "I believe that is Collins," and he ran over to the New City Hall station and notified the police.

When the policemen came upon Collins in the sanctuary one of them advanced, and laying his hand on the shoulder of the kneeling man asked him if his name was Collins.

"Yes," was the reply. "What's that to you?"

"Then I arrest you for the murder of your wife."

Collins offered no resistance, and was brought to the Old City Hall, where he was searched and afterward stripped of his outer clothing. He had on a clean shirt, but his underclothing was found to be covered with blood, and blood stains were found on his pantaloons. Collins refused to answer any questions except to say that he had not seen his wife since Friday. To all other questions he made the one reply: "That is my business."

He was apparently sober and seemed to realize his position. He denied ever having had a knife of any sort, and refused to say a word about the killing of his wife or about the blood on his underclothing.

From the *San Francisco Examiner*†

HE WAS BORN FOR THE ROPE

PATRICK COLLINS, THE SAVAGE OF CIVILIZATION, WHO STABBED
AND HACKED HIS WIFE TO DEATH

*What the Murderous, Human Beast Looks Like,
and His Motives for the Horrible Crime*

A DEEPLY INJURED HUSBAND

*The Wife's Refusal to Give Him Money for Drink Was More than
He Could Stand—The Man a Mixture of Moral Idiocy,
Egotism and Shallow Cunning—The Hapless Orphaned
Children in Different Asylums—The Father Is
Formally Charged with Murder*

If a good many of Patrick Collins' ancestors did not die on the scaffold then either they escaped their desert or there is nothing in heredity. Collins fell upon his wife the other morning with his knife and stabbed and slashed until his lust for murder was glutted. Seeing him, you can understand that murder is as natural to such a man when his temper is up as hot speech is to the anger of the civilized.

He came out of his cell yesterday when the turnkey unlocked the

† From the *San Francisco Examiner*, October 14, 1893, p. 8.

door and commanded him. Standing under a gas jet in the corridor of the Old City Prison he eyes his visitor loweringly. Hitherto he had been surly and insolent to all questioners, but yesterday he was civil enough.

"Sit down, Collins, I want to talk to you," said the visitor, motioning to a bench.

"What's your business with me?" he asked, not truculently, but with doubt and caution.

When told that it was the *Examiner* that wished him to speak, he answered:

"No, I haven't got anything to say just now. When the time comes I'll talk."

Collins' Portrait

Collins is a young man in his early thirties, healthy and muscular. The hang of his arms, his blue shirt and the hitch that he gave his waistband with the backs of his hands all suggested the sailor. The face is not degraded, but brutish. That is to say, he is not a man who has sunk, but one who was made an animal by nature to start with. The face is broad, the brown eyes are set wide apart, the nose is flattened at the bridge and as broad as a negro's. The jaw is heavy and cruel. Fancy a first cousin of John L. Sullivan's in Collins dress and situation and you have the man. He is not devoid of intelligence, but it is of a low kind, with foolish cunning as its highest manifestations. Collins has been in jail before. Something over a year ago he flew at his wife with a razor. She escaped death, and he went to the House of Correction for six months. This experience, and perhaps others of a like kind, has led him into the belief that he knows enough of the law not to be caught napping. If he were a sailor his cunning would make him that wise man of the forecastle whose wisdom is forever getting him into trouble—a "sea lawyer." He would know exactly what rations were due him, and by testing the bread in his hand could tell to an ounce's fraction if it were under weight. He could relate to his mates his conversations with the officers, in which he would figure as admirably shrewd and impudent. A Collins is never annoyed by the want of a good opinion of himself. A grotesque egotism is at the bottom of the concentrated selfishness which marks the character of all such brutes and pushes them into their crimes. Self excludes the capacity to feel for others.

He Is a Type

Normal people take it for granted that when a man does a deed so horrible as that of Collins he must, when his rage has passed, have at least a faint perception of its enormity. Nothing of the sort troubles the vanity of the human species to which Collins belongs. He is not a rarity by any means. His counterparts are numerous enough. He killed his wife because she had inflamed him with a sense of injury which he considered, and doubtless still considers, thoroughly well grounded. To his moral sense murder is what a curse, or perhaps a blow, would be with men of a more highly organized type.

Collins as he appears to Collins is a radically different person from Collins as he appears to others.

Realize his wrongs as he realized them before he avenged them. His wife had left him and was earning what appeared to him a comfortable living by taking in washing and acting as janitress for two kindergartens that were supported and visited by high-toned ladies who roll in gold. She had a roof over her head—two tidy rooms in the rear of 18 Tehama street, where she and the kids enjoyed everything they wanted. Long since he had ceased to feel that he was in any degree bound to be the bread-winner. His wife's industry had accustomed him to the view that she was a money-maker who needed no help from him. True, he had lost employment at his trade through his irregular habits and had been forced to do odd jobs along the water front, an occupation that did not yield half as much as he required for himself, not to speak of the family. True, also, that he drank whenever he could get drink, and when in liquor was liable to be rough with the old woman, but then every good fellow, every man who is a man, has his little weaknesses.

A Husband's Wrongs

Because she had exasperated him into giving her a little bit of a slash with a razor, she had testified against him and made him do time and then refused to live with him afterwards. To be sure she had given him a meal once in a way and let him have a little money out of her plenty.

Observe his claims upon this woman. She was his wife; he had begotten her children; he had been kind to her when they were first married, before she got to be an old story; but in spite of all she was down on him for his small faults. No man ought to submit to having his own wife shut the door in his face.

Reflect on how the ill-used Collins must have felt on that unfortunate Monday morning. He had been drunk overnight on water front whisky, and every man knows what that means in the way of misery next day. His last cent was gone. There was nowhere that he could take that burning thirst, those tormenting nerves and nausea for relief. It was infamous that not one barkeeper of his acquaintance on the front would trust him for a drink. He hated them all, hated everybody he knew, for not a friend remained who would lend him a dime. There is an immense capacity for hatred in a Collins. The memory of a dozen benefactions bestowed is lost in the rancor inspired by one refused. That morning he could gladly have murdered all the barkeepers, all the friends; but he encountered none of them, and then they were strangers after all—not like his wife, bound to him by the most sacred of ties. What did the woman mean by treating him as if he was dirt under her feet? By the lord, he'd see whether she'd give him money or not. If she had none she could get it from some of those fine friends of hers at the school. He would bring her to her senses or know the reason why.

The Husband Asserts Himself

The wife grew frightened when he shouldered his way into her poor little room. He gave not even a glance at the two wide-eyed, shrinking children who knew him as their father, but had seldom seen him. The woman in her life of hard and patient drudgery, her decency and her determination to rear the young ones respectably, had about her always the dread of what she felt was sure to come, and which did come. But she had escaped her fate before and might again this time. She refused his demand for money; she refused his demand for breakfast. To yield would be but to entail further visits, and the children needed all the money she could earn and all the food.

Collins glowered, swung around, and marched out in silence.

Given Collins and the hell's fire of anger that burned in his dull little brain and savage's breast can be understood. Action with him was as inevitable as a roused animal's biting onrush. Rope or no rope the thing had to be done.

As she swept the schoolroom he entered. The broom fell from her hand and a scream was strangled in her throat.

Without a word he plunged the knife into her body. He seized her and dug the blade into her time and again with limitless relief to his own breast. Thirty-five plunges, slashes, and rips—every one of them good and hearty and satisfying. Then he flung her down, leaving the knife sticking in her side.

She was not dead. Crawling out to the steps she sat in the sunshine bleeding.

A man came up, horrified, and plucked the knife from her flesh. "My husband did it," she said, and fainted.

Virtue in the Ascendant

The husband, his brute vindictiveness comfortably abated, gave his thought to his own safety. Confident that his cunning would suffice to outwit the conceited police, he spent the day seeking a change of clothing, and washed the blood from his hands in a saloon.

As night fell Collins experienced a doubt as to the entire propriety of his conduct. Perhaps he had gone a trifle too far. If he hadn't been drinking, if his temper hadn't been heated from his suffering from last night's spree, he might have been content to give her a beating. In view of the way the law regards killing there was no denying he was in some peril. But the resources of one so clever as himself would doubtless get him out of the scrape. As for the drink, however, he would give that a rest for a while, since he needed all his bright wits for his own service.

So Collins, braced by that agreeable sense of virtue which one resolved upon reform over experiences, made his way to St. Ignatius' Church and with manly frankness told the priest that he had made up his mind to do the right thing and wanted to swear off.

Happily, the priest recognized the murderer from the description in the evening papers and sent for the police.

Collins made no resistance. He was too clever for that. To the officers, to the Chief of Police, to the reporters, he had but one self-confident, sneering, swaggering answer: "That's my business."

Collins trusts Collins. Collins is no fool and will show the detectives and lawyers that he is a match for them. Let them prove it, if they can. He has no regrets, except so far as the punishment inflicted on his wife may cause him trouble. For one thing, he doesn't like to be in jail. As he lies on his mattress, if a face peers at him through the wicket, Collins looks up with a shrewd eye and scowling brow. You have seen a chained bulldog bare his teeth and growl softly when a kind word was tossed to him. That is Collins.

ROBERT D. LUNDY

[The Polk Street Background of *McTeague*]†

There was no dentist on the street at the spot where Norris placed McTeague's "parlors." The idea of McTeague's profession probably originated in Norris's fascination with a large gilded tooth that hung before the offices of Dr. L. A. Teague at the corner of Geary and Kearney downtown. In the novel, McTeague, who real-

† From Robert D. Lundy, "The Making of *McTeague* and *The Octopus*" (Ph. D. diss., University of California, 1956), pp. 145–53. Reprinted by permission of the author.

Some of the details in Lundy's account of the San Francisco background of *McTeague* have been corrected by Jesse S. Crisler in his "A Critical and Textual Study of Frank Norris's *McTeague*" (Ph. D. diss., University of South Carolina, 1973).

References to *McTeague* in the notes are changed to correspond with pages in this Norton Critical Edition.

ized his heart's desire when Trina presented him with a similar sign, "found an irresistible charm in an enormous golden molar with four prongs that hung at a corner of Kearney Street."[1] Amused by the gaudy vulgarity of the sign, Norris's eye may have been caught by news stories in 1894 about its owner, Dr. Teague, a former president of both the San Francisco and California dental societies, who became involved in a heated fight about the organization of a dental congress held at the mid-winter fair.[2] What better way to insure the authenticity of the name for his own dentist? And what a fine private joke, to baptize him with the name of one of San Francisco's most prominent practitioners and to endow him with this man's garish taste.

Several decades after the novel appeared, Norris's contemporaries were certain that McTeague's office was modeled upon an actual one on Polk Street, and his brother published pictures to prove it.[3] This dental parlor is indeed over the branch post office where Norris placed McTeague's. But this is a case of life imitating art, for the street directory shows that it was not until some years after Norris had written that a dentist moved into this location.[4] The mistake of Norris's friends is easily understood when the general reliability of his reproduction of the street is known.

Having introduced one fictional element, the dentist's offices, into the street, Norris meticulously drew the rest of its profile from life, observing the most trivial details, from the actual locations of shops to the real names of their owners. It is possible through a street directory of the period to reconstruct the street's actual countenance. Let us begin at the outer edge of McTeague's daily movements on the street and work inward to his office and note how Norris duplicated actuality.

The dentist often ate his dinner at the car conductors' "coffee-joint," a block below his office. In actuality, this was Glavinovich and Brown's of 1210½ Polk Street, a "coffee saloon," a block from Branch Post Office A of 1309 Polk Street, above which Norris placed McTeague's office and home. On the southwest corner of Polk and Bush, the cross street between the coffee joint and the "parlors," was Burmeister's "groceries and liquors," which, as Frenna's in the novel, was the setting of several major scenes; "At the corner of Polk Street, between the flat and the car conductors' coffee-joint, was Frenna's. It was a corner grocery. . . . Back of the store proper was a bar where white sand covered the floor."[5]

Across the street from McTeague's office was the big market, S.

1. *McTeague*, p. 111.
2. *San Francisco Chronicle*, February 22, 1894, p. 10; June 10, 1894, p. 24. A portrait of Teague appears June 12, 1894, p. 24.
3. Charles G. Norris, *Frank Norris,* *An Intimate Sketch* (New York, 1914), p. 8.
4. *Crocker-Langley San Francisco Directory, 1897* (San Francisco, 1897).
5. *McTeague*, p. 79.

Sactina's at 1318, a confectionary store (Huber's) at 1308, and a bell-hanger's shop (Frizzi's) at 1324, which Trina saw from her flat: "All day long Trina sat in the bay window of the sitting room that commanded a view of a small section of Polk Street. As often as she raised her head she could see the big market, a confectionary store, a bell-hanger's shop, and, farther on, above the roofs, the glass skylights and water tanks of the big public baths."[6] Opposite McTeague's office was a well-known dancing academy, "Lunt's Dancing School," of 1310 Polk Street.[7]

The way in which Norris's observation of the street contributed to the novel's life is glimpsed in a passing reference to this school. When extra chairs are needed for the wedding dinner, they are "rented from the dancing academy hard by."[8] The specific reference enhances verisimilitude and nourishes the illusion that we are participating in a real world. Norris had made himself so thoroughly at home in his setting that such details flowed easily from his pen.

It is not fanciful, given his relentless use of the actual street, to speculate that observation of it suggested at least one crucial turn in the plot. Norris would have seen workers carving and painting toys at two companies, O. Vrachliotti's at 1206 Polk and Fannie Guttman's at 1330 Polk. Their activity may have been instrumental in suggesting the change of Trina's occupation from teaching to toymaking. Because her fingers are lacerated by McTeague's brutality, Trina's carving and painting ultimately lead to the amputation of her fingers when she suffers from blood poisoning induced by the "non-poisonous" paint she used. It is not unlikely that this development was suggested by the deformity of a salesgirl at G. F. Roberts's candy store at 1301 Polk—"the candy store on the corner"[9] —who had one thumb missing and was notorious for dispensing wares more appealing to young men than candy.[1] It was just such odd details as a missing thumb that intrigued Norris; the girl's fame and the several allusions in the novel to the candy store and the candy store girls make it certain that he had observed her.[2] Casting about for some way to employ this detail, he may have conceived one of the most gratuitous and most effective bits of horror in the story.

The street also furnished several of the characters' names. Frenna's, the name of the saloon, came from a barber, Joseph Frenna,

6. Ibid., p. 103.
7. Amelia Ransome Neville, *The Fantastic City, Memories of the Social and Romantic Life of Old San Francisco* (Boston, 1932), p. 251, notes that Norris was taught to dance at "Lunt's dancing-school, which was almost a social institution."
8. *McTeague*, p. 94.
9. Ibid., p. 192.

1. Mr. L. W. Neustadter, a contemporary of Norris's, supplied this bit of local color in a letter.
2. *McTeague*, p. 121: Maria ". . . wanted something gay, like what the girls at the candy store wear when they go out with their young men." P. 158: "Young women—the candy-store girls and florist's apprentices—came . . ."

who had a shop at 1207 Polk. His name having been used for the bartender, the real Frenna appears anonymously in the novel as "the barber on the next block,"[3] one of the dentist's patients. Heise, the harness maker, a friend of McTeague's who has as large a role as any minor character, owed his name to a Walter L. Heise, who lived close by Polk Street at 905 Sutter and owned the California Wagon and Carriage Shop. Norris was either friendly with these men or blithely indifferent to the legal penalties he could face for using their names.

Two other names came from the neighborhood. "Loughhead's wife," a patient of McTeague who is casually mentioned,[4] was a name taken from Loughhead Hall at 1605 Polk. A Gerstle who lived at 1517 Van Ness, just one street above McTeague's rooms, loaned his name to the owner of the Wein Stube. (This name is not mentioned in the novel, but appears in "Fantaisie Printaniere," a short story, which almost certainly was an episode originally written as part of the novel.)

Norris became a connoisseur of Polk Street. Throughout the three years during which he worked on *McTeague*, he eagerly scanned the street. The slightest change in its make-up or in its daily activities was of interest to him, and because of the minuteness of his chronicle it is possible to date his progress on it. Although exactly how much of the novel was finished by the end of 1895 is uncertain, *terminus ad quem* of chapter nine can be determined. The rest, almost two-thirds, was written during 1897.

The basis for this dating is a passage in chapter ten which could not have been written until after December 1896. Many references in later chapters to the events introduced in this passage verify that it was not introduced in revision. It reads:

> The first three years of their married life wrought little change in the fortunes of the McTeagues. In the third summer the branch post-office was moved from the ground floor of the flat to a corner farther up the street in order to be near the cable line that ran mail cars. Its place was taken by a German saloon, called a "Wein Stube," in the face of the protests of every female lodger. A few months later quite a little flurry of excitement ran through the street on the occasion of "The Polk Street Open Air Festival," organized to celebrate the introduction there of electric lights. The festival lasted three days and was quite an affair. The street was garlanded with yellow and white bunting; there were processions and "floats" and brass bands. Marcus Schouler was in his element during the whole time of the celebration. He was one of the marshals of the parade, and was to be seen at every hour of the day, wearing a borrowed high hat and cotton gloves, and galloping a broken-down cab-horse over the cobbles. He carried a

3. Ibid., p. 127. 4. Ibid., p. 152.

baton covered with yellow and white calico, with which he made furious passes and gestures. . . .

The result of the festival was the organizing of a body known as the "Polk Street Improvement Club," of which Marcus was elected secretary.[5] The post office actually moved at some time between April 1896 and May 1897 and its place was taken by Kollig's liquor store.[6] Norris's description of the festival owed its existence to the "Polk Street Fiesta," organized by the Polk Street Improvement Association, which was held on the last three days of 1896 to celebrate the street's acquisition of electric lights.[7] The "Mardi Gras Fete," as one newspaper described it, had all the customary trimmings, colors of yellow and cardinal (a slight discrepancy), street dancing, and a parade, with a Grand Marshal, and a King of the Fiesta, J. P. Frenna, "the well-known barber," who is pictured in one account, complete with top hat and gloves, mounted on an imposing horse.[8]

Norris did not use these happenings or the real names from any fetish of realism. He did believe that they were more telling than anything he could event; but he did not believe that the novelist's task consisted in passively recording the scene he observed. The novelist had to establish a coherent image of life by weaving "facts" into a system of cross-references. Norris's imaginative use of his "data" is evidenced in what he made of the Wein Stube's location and Marcus Schouler's position in the Improvement Club. Marcus's position is not casually mentioned and then dropped, but becomes part of the texture of the life Norris describes. The work becomes a full-time job for Marcus. He carries a cane "presented to him by the Improvement Club in 'recognition of services.'" He obtains introductions from the president of the club when he leaves San Francisco for southern California.[9]

The new liquor store also becomes a part of the environment and is referred to several times. Marcus comes to bid the McTeagues farewell on an evening when they "had brought up some bottles of beer from the 'Wein Stube' on the ground floor, where the branch post-office used to be."[1] Among the comforts which McTeague misses in his poverty is "the bottled beer that she had induced him to drink in place of the steam beer from Frenna's."[2] This is one of many instances of the particularity which helps to give the action the stamp of reality. Norris imagines his characters in their setting and relates them fully to it. It is his imaginative comprehension of his materials that imparts to them the glow of life.

5. Ibid., p. 113.
6. *Crocker-Langley San Francisco Directory, 1897* (San Francisco, 1897).
7. Although this fete marks the introduction of electric lights, the street has been described since the beginning of the novel as blazing with light. Cf. p. 5.
8. *San Francisco Call,* January 1, 1897, p. 8.
9. *McTeague,* pp. 125, 128, 144.
1. Ibid., p. 142.
2. Ibid., p. 160.

He did not reproduce his observations verbatim but skillfully manipulated them. There is rarely a one-to-one observation. They come from his mind working on his notes. For example, there had undoubtedly once been a photographer who occupied the rooms into which Norris shows McTeague and Trina moving after their marriage.[3] This fact by itself has little part in the novel's substance. But Norris links it with the McTeagues' lives—some fifty pages after the former resident has been identified—and shows Trina "burning coffee on a shovel in the sitting-room. Try as she would, Trina could never quite eradicate from their rooms a certain faint and indefinable odor, particularly offensive to her. The smell of the photographer's chemicals persisted in spite of all Trina could do to combat it."[4] A trivial detail, a random observation, has been transformed into part of the novel's life.

French Naturalism and Émile Zola

LARS ÅHNEBRINK

Naturalism in France[†]

Naturalism[1] is a term somewhat loosely applied to the literary movement that may be said to have taken its inception from Flaubert's Madame Bovary (1857) and developed in the works of the brothers Goncourt, Zola, Daudet, Maupassant, and others. Zola became the champion of the new literary tendencies. After 1870 this movement took on the dignity of a naturalistic school of letters which greatly influenced French literature in the seventies and eighties. When in 1877 Zola achieved his success with L'Assommoir, naturalism was gaining rapid headway and the ten years between the publication of this novel about the lower classes and La Terre (1887) marked the climax of the movement in France. As early as 1884, however, a reaction set in, for in that year J.-K. Huysmans, Zola's friend and at first a faithful disciple of naturalism, published his famous A Rebours, in which he abjured his allegiance to the

3. Ibid., p. 86.
4. Ibid., p. 126.
† From Lars Åhnebrink, The Beginnings of Naturalism in American Fiction (1950), New York: Russell & Russell, 1961. Reprinted by permission.
1. Essential for this chapter were, besides Zola's critical writings, P. Martino, Le Naturalisme français (1870–1895)

(Paris, 1930) and Poul Levin, Den Naturalistiske Roman (Copenhagen and Christiana, 1907). See also Johan Mortensen, Från Röda Rummet till sekelskiftet (Stockholm, 1918), pp. 5–47, Vernon Louis Parrington, Main Currents in American Thought (New York, 1930), III, 323–34, and Hans Röhl, Der Naturalismus (Leipzig, 1927).

school. In 1887 there appeared the well-known *Manifeste des Cinq*, in which five of Zola's former disciples repudiated naturalism, or, more correctly, the Zolaism and bestiality of *La Terre*.

French naturalism, which exerted a certain influence on the literatures of other countries, developed out of the realism of the reign of Louis-Philippe and of the second Empire. It was a logical outgrowth of nineteenth century thought in the realm of letters. Great discoveries in the natural sciences affected the intellectual outlook of the century—the leading idea was evolution—and offered new visions and new prospects to mankind. The mid-century discoveries seemed revolutionary. Traditional thinking about man and the universe was challenged. The scientific tendencies of the period were characterized by a repudiation of previously accepted propositions and by a reliance on observation, experience, and facts; the century may be described as analytic, intellectual, and interrogative, in search of truth and exactness. Science put its imprint on it and became a sort of fetish which people worshiped for it seemed to offer a solution of the riddles of the universe. Nothing occult or transcendental existed; spiritual and organic phenomena were equally deduced from matter; natural laws were omnipotent and controlled everything; matter was the entire reality. Science invaded many fields of learning and rapid changes were effectuated through its impact on philosophy, religion, politics, belles-lettres, etc. In the field of religion, for instance, it threatened the supremacy of orthodoxy. The metaphysical school of philosophy was partly superseded by positivism, and realism received a new tenor, a new substance of ideas, which eventually led to naturalism. The basic philosophy of literary naturalism was deterministic and positivistic and consequently the naturalists focused their interests on the external reality. Darwin's interpretation of the mechanism of the universe, the positivism of Comte, and Marx's socialism were adopted by the naturalistic school. Mill, Spencer, Buckle, Huzley, Haeckel, and other scholars substantially influenced the new generation. The new scientific, philosophical, and social ideas were merged in the naturalistic novel and gave to it its specific character.

The scientific method of the natural sciences was applied to fields where emotion, speculation, and imagination predominated. For instance, Renan, an intimate friend of Berthelot, the chemist, used it in writing of religion. Claude Bernard's *Introduction à l'étude de la médecine expérimentale* (1865) did much to establish medicine as an exact science and he successfully advocated an experimental method. Upon this book Zola founded *Le Roman expérimental*, which demanded a literature governed by science and in which he used the same method as the scientist. By substituting for the word "doctor" the word "novelist," he could make his meaning clear and give to the work of art the rigidity of a scientific truth. He formulated the theory of naturalism and illustrated it in his gigantic study of degeneracy, Les Rougon-Macquart. To him literature, like medicine, was no longer an art; it was a science. By applying the method of the scientist to literature, he hoped to raise the novel to the level of science, since to him and to others of his time the voice of science was ultimate truth. He based his ideas on the theories of Taine, who became the philosopher and theorist of naturalism. His theories about the causes of human actions and particularly his doctrines of race, milieu, and moment challenged traditional conceptions of man; these ideas were, of course, mainly derived from Darwin. Taine reduced psychology to physiology and the study of character to the study of temperament, and he applied his positivistic formula to literary criticism. He taught moreover that the physical milieu constantly affected the individual, who was subjected to the rigidity of determinism.[2] Zola reduced Taine's doctrines to the study of heredity and milieu, the two basic factors which, to him, fundamentally transformed and reshaped human destinies.

Zola and other naturalists introduced into the novel a pseudo scientific terminology. Many naturalistic novels were saturated with scientific terms and technical detail; the brothers Goncourt spoke of "la méthode anatomique," and the novel was nothing but "une analyse," "une étude," "un cas pathologique." In Les Rougon-Macquart Zola's intentions were purely scientific, for he stated explicitly in the preface to La Fortune des Rougon (1871) that he wanted to "expliquer" the development of a family through the "analyse" based upon "des documents" and that "l'hérédité" had its laws as "la pesanteur." The method of clinical dissection was successfully used in Madame Bovary by Flaubert, who, a doctor's son, said: "Je me suis moi-même franchement disséqué au vif en des moments peu drôles."[3] Scientific methods and beliefs became of great importance to the contents and the technique of the naturalistic novel. It became "un roman documentaire," based solidly on physical reality and crammed with facts and data actually seen and experienced. The naturalistic writer was to seek the truth in the spirit of a scientist, for Zola and his followers did not admit of anything occult; reality, hard and brutal as it was, had to be described with exact minuteness of detail. The naturalist was to collect "human documents" and make a series of preliminary studies, sketches, etc., before he set about doing the real work.[4] This

2. Martino, op. cit., p. 21.

3. Quoted by Sten Linder in Ernst Ahlgren i hennes romaner (Stockholm, 1930), p. 166. Cf. also Flaubert, Correspondance (Paris, 1920), III, 168. [Author.] "I have openly dissected myself at moments that are not very amusing." [Editor's translation.]

4. In Les Romanciers naturalistes in OEuvres complètes (50 vols., Paris, 1927–9), XLII, 307–9, Zola described in detail Daudet's method of novel writing.

involved careful preparation and endless toil; Zola was a great
worker and his slogan was: "Travaillez, tout est là!" Imagination
and plot were reduced to a minimum.
The result was both beneficial and detrimental to the novel. On
the one hand it increased the sense of fidelity to reality and
observed facts. Successful handling of the documents Zola exhibited, for instance, in *L'Assommoir* and *Germinal*. On the other
hand he often went to extremes and created such distortions of reality as *La Faute de l'abbé Mouret* and *Le Ventre de Paris*. The naturalist had learnt from Taine that the milieu was of primary importance in the life of the individual and as a result much of the space
was given to the description of setting. Furthermore, the French
writers had a predilection for a certain kind of setting. Usually their
stories took place in great industrial cities, preferably in the slums,
which were exposed without mercy. Sometimes the descriptions
expanded into accurate surveys of an epoch and became veritable
documents of historical value. The naturalists liked to paint the
ugly details of modern civilization. With scientific zeal they chose
exact localities and used exact names, etc., for, according to Zola,
the naturalistic novel was to be "la reproduction exacte de la vie."
The study of the milieu was to be carried out methodically and
objectively so that the novelist might reproduce it accurately.

Because of their scientific pretensions the naturalists felt free to
choose for their study or analysis any subject however brutal or
revolting. They excused their audacity and frankness and their lack
of restraint and taste by resorting to the mystic word "science." As
early as 1865 Taine had given the naturalistic writer certain fundamental doctrines:

Du roman à la critique et de la critique au roman, la distance au-
jourd'hui n'est pas grande. Si le roman s'emploie à montrer ce
que nous sommes, la critique s'emploie à montrer ce que nous
avons été. L'un et l'autre sont maintenant une grande enquête
sur l'homme, sur toutes les variétés, toutes les situations, toutes
les floraisons, toutes les dégénérescences de la nature humaine.
Par leur sérieux, par leur méthode, par leur exactitude rigoureuse,
par leurs avenirs et leurs espérances, tous deux se rapprochent de
la science.[5]

In following this advice the novelists enlarged the scope and field of
their work to embrace what seemed to them the entire man and the

5. Martino, *op. cit.*, p. 23. [*Author.*]
"From the novel to criticism and from
criticism to the novel is not a great distance today. If the novel seeks to demonstrate that which we are, criticism
seeks to demonstrate that which we have
been. Both are now investigating man in
all the varieties, all the circumstances,
all the flowerings, all the degeneracies of
human nature. Through their seriousness,
through their methodology, through their
rigorous accuracy, through their concern
for the future and their hope, both ap-
proximate science." [*Editor's translation.*]

entire reality—that is, the entire natural and physical reality. The naturalists took up subjects earlier shunned or prohibited, such as prostitution, free love, social misery of many sorts, and burning questions of the day; they held the convenient belief that "La morale n'avait plus rien à faire avec la littérature, pas plus qu'avec la science"[6] and that "Le vice et la vertu sont des produits comme le vitriol et le sucre."[7] The lower classes, the masses became heroes and heroines of grim tales, and the new subject matter was treated of with a sincerity and brutality uncommon before.

While the novels of the brothers Goncourt may be labeled analytical monographs, describing single topics, the novels of Zola and Daudet portrayed society at large. Zola, for instance, chose large subjects; he wanted to present a vast tableau of French society during the second Empire and pictured the political world, the financial world, the world of pleasure, and groups such as laborers, peasants, soldiers, etc. This was exactly what Taine had suggested: "une grande enquête sur l'homme, sur toutes les variétés." Balzac's *La Comédie humaine* was of course Zola's immediate model. Occasionally he was inebriated by his descriptions and everything took on a gigantic, exaggerated form: ". . . il anime un des détails, pour en faire une sorte de symbole, et du coup tous les autres enflent, deviennent énormes; pendant une page, ou deux, l'auteur, obéissant à un emballement lyrique, oublie son dessein, si souvent répété, de n'écrire que des 'procès-verbaux.' "[8] The mine in *Germinal*, for instance, became a living monster that devoured the miners.

Whereas in Flaubert, the brothers Goncourt, and some of their followers, the aim was fundamentally esthetic, in a naturalist like Zola the purpose was predominantly social and humanitarian. Flaubert and Maupassant were strictly objective, whereas Zola's objectivity was tinged with indignation. In this he deviated from strict naturalism, which claimed to be an objective study of life without any *Tendenz*. The naturalist was to be "as cold as a vivisectionist at a lecture," abstain from comment, never show his own personality, and never turn to the reader for sympathy. A classic illustration of this attitude was the description of the death scene in *Madame Bovary*, which Flaubert carried out with the detachment of a physician, for he believed that "le grand art est scientific et impersonnel." The naturalistic novel should not satirize nor preach, but only describe human life objectively; the naturalist should draw

6. *Ibid.* [*Author.*] "Morality no longer had anything to do with literature, and neither had it anything to do with science." [*Editor's translation.*]
7. Preface to Taine's *Histoire de la littérature anglaise* (Paris, 1863). [*Author.*] "Vice and virtue are products just as vitriol and sugar." [*Editor's translation.*]

8. Martino, *op. cit.*, pp. 77–8 [*Author.*] ". . . he animates a detail to make it into a symbol; in the process, all the other details swell up and become huge; in the course of one or two pages the author, yielding to a lyric impulse, forgets his oft-repeated plan to write only a record of the evidence." [*Editor's translation.*]

no conclusions because the conclusions were implicit in the material. Despite its so-called objectivity naturalism was critical of society. Zola, especially, had a reformer's zeal. He believed that society was responsible for all the misfortunes that befell the French people; he criticized violently "ce régime politique détesté," and associated the doctrine of naturalism with the Republican idea. He was a moralist and depicted repulsive scenes in order to arouse disgust for vice. He wanted to know why there were drunkards and harlots. He aimed his most violent attacks at the French bourgeoisie, devoting whole books to the criticism of this class of society, but, in general, his criticism was leveled at society at large. He saw flagrant class-distinctions, fathomless corruption, intellectual ambiguity, and moral rottenness, all of which he wanted to disclose and hold up for opprobrium. At heart, he was an optimistic Utopian, whose temperament clashed with the naturalistic formula, while naturalists like Flaubert[9] and Maupassant were misanthropists and pessimists who saw little hope for mankind.

Zola believed that, just as the animals were transformed by the surroundings to which they adapted themselves, the individual man was refashioned by the environment in which he lived. The individual could not be separated from the milieu that surrounded and molded him; it bound and enclosed him and he was unable to extricate himself. "Nous estimons," wrote Zola, "que l'homme ne peut être séparé de son milieu, qu'il est complété par son vêtement, par sa maison, par sa ville, et sa province; et, dès lors, nous ne noterons pas un seul phénomène de son cerveau ou de son cœur, sans en chercher les causes ou le contre-coup dans le milieu."[1] In order to demonstrate their hypotheses, Zola and his disciples selected men and women on whom the influence of the environment easily put its imprint: weak and passive characters, who were afflicted by an hereditary taint and who submissively responded to, and were affected by, their milieu.

In the preface to *La Fortune des Rougon* Zola wrote:

Je veux expliquer comment une famille, un petit groupe d'êtres, se comporte dans une société, en s'épanouissant pour donner naissance à dix, à vingt individus, qui paraissent, au premier coup d'œil, profondément dissemblables, mais que l'analyse montre intimement liés les uns aux autres. L'hérédité a ses lois, comme la pesanteur.

Je tâcherai de trouver et de suivre, en résolvant la double ques-

---

9. I refer, of course, only to the author of *Madame Bovary*.

1. *Le Roman expérimental* in *Œuvres*, XLI, 186 [Author]. "We believe that man cannot be separated from his milieu, that he is inseparable from his clothes, his house, his city, and his province; and therefore we do not observe a single phenomenon of his mind or heart without searching for its causes or effects in the milieu." [*Editor's translation.*]

tion des tempéraments et des milieux, le fil qui conduit mathématiquement d'un homme à un autre homme.[2]

These ideas concerning the influence of heredity and milieu, mainly derived from Taine, Claude Bernard, and Prosper Lucas, were basic pillars of Zola's naturalistic creed, and it was upon them that he built *Les Rougon-Macquart*. The fallacy of his arguments has been exposed by more than one critic, but to him, in the early seventies, they seemed true and unassailable. Man was a product generated by the struggle for life and was transformed by his surroundings. Thus, coal-miners grew crook-backed, heavy-built, anemic, brutal, wishing only to eat, to drink, and to sleep. The influence of heredity was of equal importance to the naturalistic writer and Zola founded *Les Rougon-Macquart* on "une mère affectée d'une tare nerveuse et un père alcoolique,"[3] and his novels show, like most naturalistic works, a process of dissolution and degeneration.

The naturalists extended the study of character to embrace the entire physical man with all his physical impulses and instincts and, in their emphasis on instincts and hidden, unconscious urges and the role these phenomena play in human life, they contributed to a deeper understanding of man. Too often, however, the novelists went to extremes. By stressing the Darwinian concept of man and his affinity with organic nature and the influence of heredity and environment on the individual, they identified him with the brute controlled by instincts, particularly sex.

The characters preferred by the French naturalists belonged to the lower classes. The heroes and heroines were workers, harlots, drunkards, servant-maids, forlorn creatures, and mass-individuals. They were generally portrayed as indolent and dull, devoid of free will and purpose, sensual, and often abnormal, the products of a certain milieu and a certain kind of work; but they were seldom pictured as evil. Usually they were depicted with shocking and sensual detail as creatures dominated by their instincts. Besides types with strong physiques the naturalists preferred characters of excitable and neurotic temperaments, and often these traits were merged into one character. The novelists' portraiture of character became superficial; they painted types instead of individuals, and since psychology was reduced to physiology, they were apt to view merely the animality and the primitiveness of man. Man was devoid of a soul and of higher ethical motives; he was a helpless creature determined by

2. "I want to make clear how a family, a small group of human beings, acts in society, expanding to give birth to ten, to twenty individuals, who appear, at first glance, profoundly dissimilar but whom analysis reveals to be intimately bound to each other. Heredity has its laws, like gravity.

"I will try to discover and to pursue, in resolving the twofold problem of temperament and milieu, the thread which leads mathematically from one man to another man." [*Editor's translation.*]
3. "A mother with a nervous disease, and an alcoholic father." [*Editor's translation.*]

heredity and environment. Consequently the characters were not ethically responsible for their actions, they were pawns driven by outer forces or inner urges; moral checks were always lacking. The principle of free will was denied and man was the victim of forces beyond his control. The universe was controlled by the mechanistic laws of causation and the struggle for life was tragic in its hopelessness. The individual did not have confidence in religion or social government; everywhere vice, malice, wickedness, "les tares héréditaires, la misère" stared him in the face. The outcome of life was usually hopeless sorrow, sometimes stolid resignation; often there was no other end than annihilation.

The frank portrayal of sex was particularly characteristic of French naturalism. Love was generally depicted as a physical craving like hunger and thirst, irresistible, a natural force that blindly struck its victim. This was in conformity with the naturalists' belief in the importance of the instincts and desires of man and their denial of free will and the capacity of the individual to control natural urges. Love was no longer ethically or intellectually conditioned, but was reduced to sexual desire. The ideal concept of love was swept away before the naturalistic one.

The naturalistic conception of nature denounced the traditional, romantic, and symbolic view that conceived of nature as a living, incarnate entity. Nature should be studied and reproduced objectively and truthfully. The novelist chose phenomena which had an everyday, close-to-the soil, and often repulsive effect on the reader; sounds became noises and odors bad smells. Climatic changes and the processes of nature were faithfully chronicled: heavy rains, supreme heat, growth, fructification, etc. The evolutionary doctrine placed man in a new and intimate affinity with the vegetative and the animal kingdom and in conformity with this concept the naturalist was apt to paint phenomena which directed one's attention toward the earth. Parallels between man, plant, and animal are often met with in naturalistic fiction. Take for instance the simultaneous births of a child and a calf in the opening chapter of *La Terre*, which illustrates the essence and quality of Zola's naturalism.

In spite of the fact that the naturalistic formula was both doctrinaise and extreme, and although the naturalistic school in France soon weakened, in the eighties naturalism as a literary movement, pregnant with the spirit and ideas of its age, and possessing an almost volcanic force, began to be felt in the literatures of other European countries, where it was adopted and transformed in conformity with tradition and prevailing taste. It opened up new paths to the delineation of man and nature and helped to break down prejudices and conventions.

*   *   *

ERNEST MARCHAND

[Norris and Zola†]

The many and close resemblances between the work of Zola and that of his American disciple are not alone the result of "influence" as it is commonly understood by critics, but depend ultimately on certain correspondences in the fundamental emotions and mental characters of the two men. Both have the wide-embracing imaginations of epic poets. Both have a romantic Hugoesque love for big effects, striking contrasts, dramatic (even melodramatic) situations. "Never forget," Zola cautioned himself, "that a drama must take the public by the throat."[1] Nothing could be more romantic than the Provençal boyhood of Zola. He devoured the works of De Musset, Hugo, Lamartine, De Vigny; he was a haunter of graveyards and mountain caves. His first writing was verse, a chivalric romance inspired by the reading of Michelet's *History of the Crusades*. As a youth in Paris, Norris eagerly garnered from the stalls along the quais of the Seine a cuirassier's helmet, a skeleton hand with the manacle still clanking upon it, and a quantity of blackletter books. He, too, wrote his poem of medieval lore and adventure. When each of the two writers had emerged from this early phase and adopted the doctrines of naturalism, he came to lay a great emphasis on the animal nature of man, if not to celebrate it. In *Thérèse Raquin*, Zola set himself a problem: "Given a strong man and an unsatisfied woman, to seek in them the beast, to see nothing but the beast. . . ."[2] Norris, with whom Zola's *La Bête Humaine* was a favorite, shows the triumph of the brute in Vandover. Both men have a genius for handling men in large masses; they love crowds. Witness the scene at the racecourse in *Nana*, the battles in *La Débâcle*; the scene at the opera which opens *The Pit*,[3] the rabbit drive, the plowing, and the mass meeting at Bonneville in *The Octopus*, the dance at the house of Henrietta Vance in *Vandover*. Like his master, Norris loves to set his people down at Gargantuan feasts which turn into veritable gastronomic debauches during which the faces of the sweating eaters grow scarlet and their veins become distended with their mighty labors. Such are the dinners in *Nana and L'Assommoir*, the wedding supper in *McTeague*, the dinner of the plow-hands, and the feasting at the conclusion of the

† From *Frank Norris: A Study*. Copyright © 1942 by the Board of Trustees of the Leland Stanford Junior University. Copyright renewed 1970 by Ernest Marchand. Reprinted by permission of Stanford University Press. Pp. 90–96.

For Norris's comments on the work of Zola, see "Norris's Definition of Naturalism," pp. 308–16 below.

1. Matthew Josephson, *Zola and His Time* (New York: The Macaulay Company, 1928), p. 150.
2. *Ibid.*, p. 117.
3. With the necessary changes for characters, this opera scene is repeated almost verbatim from chapter fourteen of *Vandover and the Brute*, which Norris was never able to get published. He never wasted literary material.

rabbit drive in *The Octopus*. Both men intoxicate themselves with swelling paeans to the fecund earth, employing a bold metaphorical language derived from ideas of sex and procreation. Matthew Josephson well says of *La Terre* that it is "a rude poem to the earth and its eternal act of life.[4] This hymning of earth is not a mere literary device, but a genuine feeling in Zola himself:

Ah! good earth, take me [he chants], thou who art our common mother. O unique source of life, eternal and immortal, in which circulates the soul of the world, like a sap arising now in the stones and now in the trees, our great motionless brothers! . . . . Yes, I desire to lose myself in thee; I feel thee down there under my limbs pressing and arousing me; it is thou alone who shalt be as a pristine force in my works, the end and the means at once of all things! . . . .

Norris speaks thus of the land at the moment when the battery of plows is about to attack it:

One could not take a dozen steps upon the ranches without the brusque sensation that underfoot the land was alive; roused at last from its sleep, palpitating with the desire of reproduction. Deep down there in the recesses of the soil, the great heart throbbed once more, thrilling with passion, vibrating with desire, offering itself to the caress of the plow, insistent, eager, imperious. Dimly one felt the deep-seated trouble of the earth, the uneasy agitation of its members, the hidden tumult of its womb, demanding to be made fruitful, to reproduce, to disengage the eternal renascent germ of Life that stirred and struggled in its loins.[5]

Both writers are capable of alternating delicate fantasies and elevated sentiment with their horrendous pictures of squalor and corruption; after the grim brutalities of *La Terre*, the purity of maiden love in *Le Rêve*;[6] after the harsh and somber *McTeague* and *Vandover*, the *Youth's Companion* "wholesomeness" of *Blix*. And did not Norris write the tender idyl of lost youth and late-recovered love set in an autumnal garden with its tumbled statue of Cupid?[7] and the delicately and reverently imagined *Miracle Joyeux*, in which a youthful Christ smiles upon the innocence of childhood?

Both Zola and Norris sense the world almost as much through their noses as through their eyes and ears. They are extraordinarily responsive to smells—mainly bad smells their enemies averred, though falsely. An interminable catalogue of odors might be com-

4. Josephson, *op. cit.*, p. 305.

5. *The Octopus* (Doubleday, Doran & Company, Inc., 1929), p. 127.

6. The name of Vanamee's love, Angéle, suggests that of the girl of similar purity in *Le Rêve*—Angélique. Franklin Walker (p. 250) assigns the origin of the seed ranch, with its bewildering profusion of blossoms, to a similar place observed by Norris during his stay in San Benito County, California. He may equally owe the idea to the garden of Paradou in Zola's *La Faute de l'Abbé Mouret*, to the description of whose intoxicating luxuriance of color and perfume nearly two hundred pages are devoted.

7. See "A Statue in an Old Garden," *Collected Writings*, p. 291.

piled from the work of Norris. He notes the smell of hot steam and smoke in the cab of a locomotive, of damp leather and upholstery in a carriage on a rainy night, the "acrid odor of ink" that rose from the branch post office beneath McTeague's "parlors." And in the great plowing scene of *The Octopus* a whole battery of smells discharge themselves upon the sense with smashing impact (p. 130): "the ammoniacal smell of the horses, the bitter reek of perspiration of beasts and men, the aroma of warm leather, the scent of dead stubble . . . . the heavy, enervating odour of the upturned, living earth."

Both men have the temperament of the moralist and the reformer and color their pessimism with hope. "To tell the truth and still to hope,"[8] Zola enjoined upon himself. But at first neither was sympathetic with agitators or radicals; rather the contrary. Lantier, in *L'Assommoir*, who on occasion inveighs against titles and privileges and cries for the "glorification of the proletariat," is a charlatan. Marcus Schouler of *McTeague* (though the role of social malcontent is brief and incidental with him) is equally a fraud, an ignorant ranter without even a personal grievance. Norris makes him ridiculous: " 'It's the capitalists that's ruining the cause of labor,' shouted Marcus, banging the table with his fist till the beer glasses danced; 'white-livered drones, traitors . . . . eatun the bread of widows and orphuns. . . .' " After *L'Assommoir*, Zola threw himself upon the works of the socialist writers with the furious energy which he brought to all he did. He was not constituted by nature, any more than his disciple Norris, to be a thinker on such subjects; but he at least confronted directly the theories of Marx, Proudhon, and Lassalle, and was ready to call himself a socialist. It is unlikely that Norris ever read a political or economic treatise in his life; but it is clear from *The Octopus* and from his later critical writing that his awakening sympathy for the underdog was beginning to push him, somewhat uncertainly, in the direction of socialism. Whether he would ever have arrived there or not cannot well be determined. But there is no doubt that toward the end of his life he had begun to take the role of social prophet very seriously. In his defense of the unsentimental rigors of naturalism he declared that if fiction "wears the camel's-hair and feeds upon the locusts, it is to cry aloud unto the people, 'Prepare ye the way of the Lord; make straight his path.' "[9]

Finally, both Zola and Norris were endowed with that kind of moral courage which dares opprobrium and even personal danger in defense of what it conceives to be justice. In Norris this trait is illustrated by an incident which occurred a few months before his death in 1902. The superintendent of the California state home for the feeble-minded at Glen Ellen, Dr. William Lawlor, was accused

8. Josephson, *op. cit.*, p. 370.   *Novelist*, p. 220.
9. Norris, *The Responsibilities of the*

by his political enemies of brutality toward the inmates of the institution. He was helpless to present his own case; for the press, controlled by the opposition, would print no word favorable to him. The public, systematically misinformed, clamored against the doctor. Norris was indignant, investigated the charges, satisfied himself they were false, and wrote a fiery denunciation which every newspaper in San Francisco cynically refused to print.[1] At length during a dramatic meeting of the board of directors, marked by hot words, a certain Colonel Harrington (appropriately from Kentucky) drew a pistol upon Dr. Lawlor. But before he could fire Norris seized his arm. Dr. Lawlor was eventually dismissed from his post, though officially exonerated. L'Affaire Dreyfus, at the center of which Zola placed himself, shook France from Paris to the borders during two years. The Lawlor episode agitated San Francisco for a few weeks. But for Norris it was his Dreyfus affair—in miniature.

Such comparisons of literary men are apt, however, to bear unjustly on the disciple. It should not be supposed, whatever he owed Zola, that Norris cannot stand firmly on his own feet as a writer. The words of a French critic, who is little likely to overestimate the worth of Zola's followers in other lands, are here of special interest. M. Marius Biencourt writes:

Le disciple a contracté envers le maître une dette considérable, mais son œuvre n'en laisse pas moins une forte impression de nouveauté et d'originalité. Il est resté américain dans ses défauts et dans ses qualités. . . .
Norris dont la devise était: faire de la vie et non de la littérature, a su créer vivant et faire passer dans son œuvre la vigueur et l'énergie de son tempérament épique.[2]

ÉMILE ZOLA

[The Wedding Party]†

Thereupon the wedding-party, much diverted, drew up to table with a great scraping of chairs. Gervaise was between Lorilleux and M. Madinier, and Coupeau between Madame Fauconnier and Madame Lorilleux. The other guests seated themselves where they

1. It was published, however, in the weekly *Argonaut*, San Francisco, August 11, 1902.
2. Marius Biencourt, *Une Influence du Naturalisme Français en Amérique: Frank Norris* (Paris: Marcel Giard, 1933), p. 230. [*Author*.]
"The disciple is much indebted to the master, but his work nevertheless leaves a strong impression of novelty and of originality. He remains American in his defects and in his strengths. . . . Norris, whose motto was life, not literature, knew how to create vividly and to transmit in his work the vigor and energy of his epic temperament." [*Editor's translation*.]
† From *The Drunkard (L'Assommoir)*, trans. Arthur Symons (London: Elek Books, 1958), pp. 84–90. Reprinted by permission of Elek Books Limited.
For the parallel scene in *McTeague*, see pp. 95–99 above. In Zola's novel, the wedding couple are Gervaise and Coupeau.

pleased, because there were always grumblings and jealousies when the places were arranged beforehand. Boche slipped into the seat by Madame Lerat. Bibi-la-Grillade had for neighbours Mademoiselle Remanjou and Madame Gaudron. As for Madame Boche and old Madame Coupeau, right at the end, they looked after the children, and promised to cut up their meat, and give them something to drink; above all, not much wine.

"Doesn't anyone say grace?" asked Boche, whilst the ladies were arranging their skirts under the table, for fear of staining them.

But Madame Lorilleux did not approve of such jokes. The vermicelli soup, almost cold, was eaten very quickly, with lips hissing in the spoons. Two waiters were in attendance, dressed in little greasy jackets and aprons of dubious whiteness. Through the four windows, opening on the acacias of the court, the air entered freely, a calm evening after storm, still with a lingering heat. The reflection of the dripping trees cast a greenish light over the smoky room, making the shadows of the leaves flicker over the table-cloth, smelling faintly of mouldiness. There were two fly-spotted mirrors, one at each end, seeming to lengthen out the table indefinitely, with its dingy plate turning yellow, the grease of the sink clotted black in the scratches of the knives. Every time that a waiter came up from the kitchen, a door at the end banged, letting through a strong smell of burning fat.

"Now don't speak all at once," said Boche, in the midst of a general silence, as they bent over their plates.

The first glass of wine was being drunk, and two force-meat pies were being served by the waiters, when Mes-Bottes entered.

"Well! you are a nice lot, you people!" he cried. "Here have I been kicking my heels on the road these three hours, till a gendarme actually came and asked for my papers. Is that the dirty way you serve your friends? You might at least have sent a cab for me. No, joking apart, it's a bit thick. Why it rained so hard my pockets were filled with water; there's still some small fry for the fishing in them."

The company went into fits of laughter. Mes-Bottes was quite screwed; he had already had his two bottles, merely as a sort of counter-blast to the dose of Adam's ale which the storm had soused him with.

"Now, daddy-long-legs!" said Coupeau, "go and sit down at the end by Madame Gaudron. You see, we waited for you!"

Oh, that was all the same to him, he would soon catch them up; and he called three times for soup, helpings of vermicelli, in which he cut up huge chunks of bread. When they attacked the pies, he became the wonderment of the whole table. How he did guzzle! The astonished waiters took turns in passing him the bread, little neat bits which he swallowed at one mouthful. At last he lost his temper, and demanded a whole length of bread to himself. The landlord looked in anxiously for a moment at the door, and the company, who were expecting his advent, went into fresh fits of laughter. And that fetched him, the poor old boss! And wasn't he a stunner, Mes-Bottes! One day he had eaten twelve hard-boiled eggs and drunk twelve glasses of wine, while it was striking twelve! There were not many like that! And Mademoiselle Remanjou, quite moved by his prowess, watched his jaws going, whilst M. Madinier, casting about for a word to express his astonishment, which amounted almost to respect, declared that such a capacity was extraordinary.

There was a silence. A waiter had just placed on the table a ragout of rabbit in a huge dish as deep as a salad-bowl. Thereupon Coupeau played off a famous bit of spoof.

"I say waiter, you've brought us a nice sort of rabbit. I should call it a gutter-rabbit. Why, it still mews."

And, indeed, a faint mew, perfectly imitated, seemed to issue from the plate. It was Coupeau who did it in his throat, without moving his lips; a show accomplishment which never failed of success, so that he never ordered a meal without including a rabbit. After that he purred. The women hid their faces in their handkerchiefs; they could not stop laughing.

Madame Fauconnier asked for the head; she only cared for the head. Mademoiselle Remanjou adored the fat. And when Boche said that he preferred the little onions when they were well done, Madame Lerat pursed up her lips and muttered:

"I can quite understand that."

She was as thin as a lath, lived a hard-working, cloistral existence, and had scarcely seen a man since her husband died, but she had a perfect mania for indecent allusions, so very obscure that only she herself could understand them. Boche bent over and asked her in a whisper to explain her meaning, but she only repeated:

"Oh, yes, the little onions. I fancy that will just do."

But the conversation became serious. Everyone talked shop. M. Madinier bragged about his cardboard making; there were genuine artists employed in it; and he referred to the fancy boxes, of which he knew the models, perfect wonders. Meanwhile Lorilleux sneered; he was very proud of working in gold, he seemed to see the glitter of it on his fingers, from head to foot. "Well," said he, "goldsmiths once upon a time used to wear swords," and he referred at random to Bernard Palissy.[1] Coupeau told of a weathercock that one of his fellow workmen had made; it was composed of a column, then of a sheaf, then of a basket of fruit, then of a flag, all copied to the life, and made merely out of bits of galvanized cut out and soldered together. Madame Lerat explained to Bibi-la-Grillade how the stalk

1. A celebrated sixteenth-century potter who rose to wealth and position.

of a rose was turned, making the handle of her knife revolve between her bony fingers. Meanwhile voices grew louder, and spoke all at once. In the midst of the noise Madame Fauconnier was heard complaining of one of her work-girls, a bit of trash, who had caught fire to a pair of her sheets only last night.

"You may say as you like," cried Lorilleux, bringing down his fist on the table, "gold is gold."

And, in the silence caused by this truism, nothing was heard but the thin voice of Mademoiselle Remanjou continuing:

"Then I pull up their skirts, I stitch inside, I stick a pin into the head to keep on the bonnet, and it is finished. They are sold at sixpence."

She was explaining her dolls to Mes-Bottes, whose jaws worked on slowly and steadily, like millstones. He paid no attention, but wagged his head, and kept an eye on the waiters, so that they should not change the plates before they were well scraped out. They had had a *fricandeau au jus* and French beans. Now the roast was brought in, two meagre fowls laid out on cress, faded and frizzled by the heat. Outside, the sun was fading behind the high branches of the acacias. In the room, the greenish reflection grew darker in the steam that rose from the table, stained with wine and sauce, and encumbered with all the dishes. And along the wall, the dirty plates and empty bottles, placed there by the waiters, seemed the sweepings of the feast. It was very hot. The men took off their coats, and went on eating in their shirt-sleeves.

"Madame Boche, please don't let the children stuff so much," said Gervaise, who had spoken little, keeping an eye on Claude and Étienne from a distance.

She got up, and went round behind their chairs to speak to them for a moment. The children, you may be sure, would eat all day long without refusing anything; and she gave them herself some fowl, a bit of the white. But old Madame Coupeau declared that they might have an indigestion if they would, for once. Madame Boche, in a low voice, accused Boche of pinching Madame Lerat's knee. He was a sly dog; he was easily worked up. She saw his hand go out of sight. If he did it again she had a good mind to fling a decanter at his head; she had indeed.

In the midst of the general silence M. Madinier talked politics.

"Their law of the 31st of May is an abomination. Now you are obliged to have been a householder for two years. Three thousand citizens are struck off the lists. They say that Bonaparte is really at heart much put out about it, for he loves the people, he has shown it."[2]

2. The law of May 31, 1850 (the wedding feast of Gervaise and Coupeau occurs in the summer of 1850), restricted suffrage. The period between the riots of June 1848 and the establishment of Napoleon III as emperor of France in 1852 saw a gradual repression of public liberties.

For his part he was a Republican, but he admired the prince on account of his uncle, a man the like of whom would never be seen again. Bibi-la-Grillade grew wroth. He had worked at the Élysée; he had seen Bonaparte as well as he saw Mes-Bottes there opposite to him. Well, as for the president, the bounder looked for all the world like a nark! It was reported that he was going on a tour Lyons way: it would be a good riddance if he were to break his neck in a ditch. And as the discussion grew heated, Coupeau had to interfere.

"Well, you are simpletons to quarrel over politics! There's a nice business, politics! What have we to do with politics, I should like to know? They can have what they like, a king, an emperor, or nothing, but will that hinder me from earning my five francs, from eating and sleeping, eh? It's too ridiculous!"

Lorilleux shook his head. He was born the same day as the Comte de Chambord, the 29th of September, 1820. This coincidence impressed him deeply; and he had vague dreams, in which there was a certain connection between the return of the king and his own luck. He did not say exactly what he hoped for, but he gave out that it would be something uncommonly pleasant. So, whenever he hoped for anything that was not likely to be realized, he put it off till later, "when the king comes back".

"Besides," he went on, "I saw the Comte de Chambord one day. . . ."

Every face turned in his direction.

"Certainly. A big good-natured looking man in a greatcoat. I was at Péquignot's, a friend of mine who sells furniture, Grande-Rue de la Chapelle. The Comte de Chambord had left his umbrella there the day before. Well, he came in, he said, 'Would you kindly give me my umbrella?' just like that, quite simply. Fact! it was he himself, Péquignot gave me his word."

None of the guests threw any doubt on the story. By this time they had come to the dessert. The waiters cleared the table with a great clatter of dishes. And Madame Lorilleux, who till then had behaved in the most genteel and ladylike manner, screamed out "Damn your butter fingers!" as one of the waiters, in removing a dish, dropped something wet on the back of her neck. Her silk dress must surely be stained. M. Madinier had to look up and down her back, but he swore there was nothing to be seen. Meanwhile some *œufs à la neige* were laid out in a salad bowl in the middle of the table, with two plates of cheese on one side and two plates of fruit on the other. The *œufs à la neige*, the over-done white crumbling into the yellow cream, caused quite a sensation; they were something unexpected, quite stylish. Mes-Bottes continued to eat. He had asked for another roll of bread. He finished up both sorts of cheese; then, finding some cream left, he had the salad bowl passed to him, and proceeded to ladle out huge pieces, as if it were soup.

"The gentleman is really very remarkable," said M. Madinier, once more lost in admiration.

Then the men rose to fill their pipes. They stopped for a moment behind Mes-Bottes, slapping him on the shoulder, and asking him if he felt better now. Bibi-la-Grillade lifted him, chair and all; but God damn it, the fellow was twice as heavy as he was before. Coupeau declared jokingly that he was only just getting under way; that he would go on eating bread at that rate all night. The terrified waiters disappeared. Boche who had gone downstairs just before, came up declaring that the landlord was sitting pallid inside the bar, while his wife, all in a flurry, had sent out to see if the bakers were still open; the very cat went about looking the picture of misery. It was really absurd; it was worth the price of the dinner; it was impossible to have a proper feed without that great guzzler Mes-Bottes. And the men, as they smoked their pipes, looked at him enviously; for a man must be solidly built to be able to eat all that.

"I shouldn't like to have to look after your keep," said Madame Gaudron. "No, indeed!"

"I say, mother, none of that," replied Mes-Bottes, with a side-glance at the big belly of his neighbour. "You've swallowed more than I have."

Everyone applauded, and cried "Bravo!" It was a good hit. The light had now quite gone, and three gas-burners flickered in the room, giving a wavering light in the midst of the smoke of pipes. The waiters, after having served the coffee and cognac, had cleared away the last piles of dirty plates. Below, under the three acacias, the dancing had begun, a cornet and two violins playing loudly, the women's laughter sounding shrill in the warm night.

Composition and Revision:
Harvard and San Francisco

CHARLES KAPLAN

Fact into Fiction in *McTeague*†

Frank Norris came to Harvard in the autumn of 1894 as a special student, seeking to learn under Lewis E. Gates what he had failed

† From *Harvard Library Bulletin*, VIII (Autumn 1954), 381–85. Reprinted by permission of the author.

References to *McTeague* in the notes are changed to correspond with pages in this Norton Critical Edition.

to find at Berkeley in four disappointing years.[1] Taking up residence in 47 Grays Hall, he enrolled in English 22, Gates's creative writing course, and turned his attention to the business of becoming a writer. The results of his one year of study, although not immediately apparent, were important, for at Harvard he wrote nineteen chapters of a work which, when it was published four years later, became a major event in the history of the American novel. In gratitude to the man who, Norris declared, taught him more about writing than anyone else, he dedicated *McTeague* to 'L. E. Gates of Harvard University.'

Like his avowed master, Zola, Norris always drew heavily from the life around him in creating accurate and lifelike pictures in the realistic manner. *McTeague* recognizably depicted San Francisco and the inhabitants of its middle-class lower depths at the turn of the century, Norris incorporating into his novel actual locales and specific features of the San Francisco milieu—even to the 'huge gilded tooth, a molar with enormous prongs, something gorgeous and attractive,' which he transferred from 'Dental Parlors' on Polk Street to the office of his title character.[2]

Since McTeague was to be a dentist, it was necessary for Norris to become familiar with the technical details of dentistry. Willard E. Martin, Jr., listing the volumes Norris drew from the Harvard College Library during his year of residence, has indicated Thomas Fillebrown's *A Text-book of Operative Dentistry* as the probable source for these technical details.[3] However, Professor Martin did not consider the nature and extent of Norris' use of this source. The following quotations are intended to show that Norris leaned very heavily on Fillebrown, ranging widely through the 275-page textbook, and even going so far as to incorporate technical matter almost verbatim.[4]

Most of the details of dentistry, aside from scattered references to McTeague's tools—his hoe-excavators, hard bits, burrs, and so forth—are given in the second chapter, which shows the dentist at work.

1. Lewis E. Gates, A.B. *s.c.l.* Harvard 1884, had been instructor in forensics and English since graduation. He became Assistant Professor of English in 1896, and of Comparative Literature in 1901, but ill health forced his resignation the following year, and he remained quietly in retirement until his death in 1924.

2. Ernest Peixotto, 'Romanticist under the Skin,' *Saturday Review of Literature,* IX (27 May 1933), 614.

3. 'Willard E. Martin, Jr., 'Frank Norris' Reading at Harvard College,' *American Literature,* VII (May 1935), 203–204.

4. Thomas Fillebrown (1836–1908), nationally recognized as a leader in his profession at the turn of the century, was one of six to receive the D.M.D. degree at the first commencement of the Harvard Dental School, 1869. Fillebrown was Professor of Operative Dentistry at Harvard 1883–97 and in addition of Oral Surgery 1897–1904. His textbook, undertaken at the invitation of the National Association of Dental Faculties, was long standard in the field, and Norris could not have turned to a more authoritative source. The copy used by Norris was transferred in 1914 from the Harvard College Library to the Library of the Harvard Dental School, where it is still available for consultation.

One of the minor characters, a resident in the rooming house, comes to him for treatment:

> . . . In examining Miss Baker's teeth at the preliminary sitting he had found a cavity in one of the incisors. Miss Baker had decided to have it filled with gold. McTeague remembered now that it was what is called a "proximate case," where there is not sufficient room to fill with large pieces of gold. He told himself that he should have to use "mats" in the filling. He made some dozen of these "mats" from his tape of non-cohesive gold, cutting it transversely into small pieces that could be inserted edgewise between the teeth and consolidated by packing. After he had made his "mats" he continued with the other kind of gold fillings, such as he would have occasion to use during the week; "blocks" to be used in large proximal cavities, made by folding the tape on itself a number of times and then shaping it with the soldering pliers; "cylinders" for commencing fillings, which he formed by rolling the tape around a needle called a "broach," cutting it afterwards into different lengths. . . .
> After he had finished his fillings, he made a hook broach from a bit of piano wire . . .[5]

This lump of technical information is to be compared with Fillebrown's enumeration of the types of gold fillings:

> . . . If it is desirable for any reason to use small portions of the tape, it is cut transversely in small pieces, which are called mats. These, when of non-cohesive gold, are of considerable use in very small cavities. . . . The mat is of most service in proximate cases where there may not be sufficient room to introduce larger and thicker pieces of gold. These can be inserted edgewise between the teeth, and afterward be carried into place and consolidated according to the method of packing employed . . .
> . . . The compact block is formed by folding a tape on itself a number of times, which is done by seizing it in the pliers and making turns of any desired size . . . These blocks are useful in commencing large proximate cavities . . .
> . . . This form [the compact cylinder] is made by rolling a tape of non-cohesive gold on a fine brooch . . .
> . . . When the brooch is removed, they are cut into definite lengths . . .
> They are employed in the commencement of fillings . . .[6]
> Fine hook broaches are also made of fine piano-wire . . .[7]

When Trina, McTeague's future wife, is first brought to his office to have a broken tooth repaired, the dentist offers the following diagnosis:

5. *McTeague*, pp. 10–11.
6. Thomas Fillebrown, *A Text-Book of Operative Dentistry* (Philadelphia, 1889), pp. 70–71.
7. Fillebrown, *Text-Book*, p. 34.

"Well," answered McTeague . . . "the roots of the broken tooth are still in the gum; they'll have to come out, and I guess I'll have to pull that other bicuspid. . . ." The tooth was loose, discolored, and evidently dead. "It's a curious case," McTeague went on. "I don't know as I ever had a tooth like that before. It's what's called necrosis. It don't often happen. It'll have to come out sure."

. . . McTeague reasoned with her, tried in vain to make her understand that there was no vascular connection between the root and the gum. . . .[8]

This passage is a reconstruction from Fillebrown's definition and discussion of necrosis:

Necrosis, as applied to a tooth, means death of the entire organ, both pulp and pericementum. It rarely occurs.
. It is caused by dead pulp, violence, long use of mercury, calcular deposit, exhausting diseases, or impaired nutrition.
Signs.—Tooth much discolored, loose, with little or no vascular connection.
Treatment.—Removal.[9]

McTeague decides to attempt his most difficult operation, in response to Trina's wishes, and proceeds as follows:

It was the first bicuspid that was missing, and though part of the root of the second (the loose one) would remain after its extraction, he was sure it would not be strong enough to sustain a crown. . . . He turned over in his mind the technicalities of the case. No, evidently the root was not strong enough to sustain a crown; besides that, it was placed a little irregularly in the arch. But, fortunately, there were cavities in the two teeth on either side of the gap—one in the first molar and one in the palatine surface of the cuspid; might he not drill a socket in the remaining root and sockets in the molar and cuspid, and, partly by bridging, partly by crowning, fill in the gap? . . .
. . . He extracted the loose tooth with his bayonet forceps and prepared the roots of the broken one as if for filling, fitting into them a flattened piece of platinum wire to serve as a dowel. . . .[1]
By degrees the operation progressed. One day . . . [he] put in the temporary gutta-percha fillings . . .[2]

The source for this account is found in Fillebrown's case history of a similar unusual operation:

. . . In the mouth of a student at the Philadelphia Dental College, where the first right superior bicuspid was missing, and there remained a portion of the root of the second bicuspid not strong enough to sustain a crown, and likewise irregular as to pos-

8. *McTeague,* pp. 14–15.
9. Fillebrown, *Text-Book,* p. 110.

1. *McTeague,* p. 15.
2. *McTeague,* p. 17.

ition in the arch . . . the following operation was performed: There was a cavity on the disto-palatine surface of the cuspid and a mesial and crown cavity in the first molar. The above mentioned root was treated and prepared as for filling. . . . A piece of slightly flattened platinum wire was fitted into the root for a dowel. . . . The fillings can be temporarily made of oxychloride of zinc or gutta percha . . .[3]

In filling another cavity, McTeague decides to use an anaesthetic so that he will not hurt Trina:

> . . . He had a notion that the nitrous oxide gas was dangerous, so on this occasion, as on all others, used ether.
> He put the sponge a half dozen times to Trina's face, more nervous than he had ever been before, watching the symptoms closely. Her breathing became short and irregular; there was a slight twitching of the muscles. When her thumbs turned inward toward the palms, he took the sponge away. She passed off very quickly, and with a long sigh, sank back into the chair.[4]

When Trina awakens, the crude but childlike dentist frightens her by blurting out a proposal of marriage:

> . . . "No, no," she cried, terrified. Then, as she exclaimed, "Oh, I am sick," was suddenly taken with a fit of vomiting. It was the not unusual after effect of the ether . . . He poured some bromide of potassium into a graduated glass and held it to her lips.[5]

In using the following data from his textbook source, Norris seems either to have made a mistake or to have deliberately but unaccountably reversed the sense of the original:

> *Nitrous Oxide.*—Relaxation of the muscles is not constant nor common in anæsthesia produced by nitrous oxide gas. Contraction instead of relaxation is likely to follow, and a spasmodic twitching of the muscles takes place, an interrupted, jerky inspiration, and a turning inward of the thumbs toward the palm of the hand. . . .[6]
> Nausea and vomiting are sometimes persistent and distressing [as the aftereffects of ether]. Bromide of potassium in doses of fifteen to thirty grains, repeated if necessary, is a good remedy.[7]

Because Norris in other instances was known to have personally consulted and interviewed people in order to get the jargon of their special professions and crafts, it has been assumed that a similar practice obtained in the writing of *McTeague*. Marius Biencourt, for example, says that 'pour les termes d'odontologie, il consulta sans doute le dentiste dont le cabinet, situé dans Polk Street, est

3. Fillebrown, *Text-Book*, pp. 253–254.
4. *McTeague*, p. 17.
5. *McTeague*, p. 20.
6. Fillebrown, *Text-Book*, pp. 143–144.
7. Fillebrown, *Text-Book*, p. 148.

décrit dans *McTeague.*[8] Although Norris did draw many of his details from real life, 'les termes d'odontologie' were not among them, being rather the fruit of the simplest kind of research in the Harvard College Library.

FRANK NORRIS

[Harvard Themes from *McTeague*]†

23

JANUARY 7, 1895

The other teachers at the kindergarten often noticed that Bessie's fingertips were swollen and the nails purple as thought they had been shut in a door. This was in fact the explanation she offered. But she lied to them. McTeague her husband used to bite her fingertips when he came home after drinking whiskey, crunching them between his strong large teeth, always ingenious enough to remember which were the sorest. If she resisted he brought her down with a blow of his immense bony fist between the eyes.

Often these brutalities inflamed his sensual passions and he threw her, bleeding and stupid from his fists across the bed and then it was abominable, bestial, unspeakable.

[Abbott] Reader's comment: "Morbid and repulsive in subject matter. Your manner is strong and effective but ask yourself why you present us with this subject. To force upon our unwilling attention a repulsive, painful and debasing image has in itself something akin to the brutal."

[Hart] For the first time Norris introduces McTeague into his themes. Like Vandover, who appeared only three days earlier in Theme 21, he is a figure from the larger fiction that Norris was writing outside of class assignments. In the novel that was starting

---

8. Marius Biencourt, *Une influence du naturalisme français en Amérique: Frank Norris* (Paris, 1933), p. 133. "For his dental terminology, he no doubt consulted the dentist whose office, located in Polk Street, is described in *McTeague.*" [*Editor's translation.*]
   † From *A Novelist in the Making: A Collection of Student Themes, and the Novels "Blix" and "Vandover and the Brute,"* by *Frank Norris,* James D. Hart, ed. (Cambridge, Mass.: The Belknap Press of Harvard University Press), pp.

78–89. Copyright 1970 by the President and Fellows of Harvard College. Reprinted by permission of the publishers and Frank C. Preston, Jr.
   The numbered passages are from Norris's themes for Professor Lewis E. Gates's class in writing, Harvard, 1894–95. The "reader's comment" on each theme is by Herbert V. Abbott, then a graduate assistant at Harvard and later a professor of English at Smith College. The numbering and the closing comments are by James D. Hart.

to take on final form there now began to loom the story of the tragic marriage of McTeague and the kindergarten teacher Bessie, who was the friend of the loose Ida whom Vandover had seduced. Throughout January and February McTeague figures as the central subject of Norris' themes, with different aspects of his sordid story displayed in Themes 23 through 28, until finally on March 8 his story has become an integral work that can be told in resumé form as Theme 32. The story of Vandover is picked up again only after that of McTeague has been clearly shaped as a separate work.

Theme 23 is reworked in Ch. XVI of *McTeague* so that Bessie changes her name to Trina and her occupation from kindergarten teacher to a beaten housewife who soon becomes a scrubwoman in a kindergarten. In this fallen state it is she who is conceived as pathologically sexual, for whereas the theme states that "these brutalities inflamed his sensual passions," the book attributes the perverse sexuality to her, in that brutality arouses "in her a morbid, unwholesome love of submission, a strange, unnatural pleasure in yielding, in surrendering herself to the will of an irresistible, virile power." In the concluding sentence Norris, for the first time, employs his tripling of adjectives for a trip-hammer effect on the reader. Curiously, it is so effective that it leads Abbott to employ the same device in his comment.

24

JANUARY 8, 1895

Bessie told all sorts of different stories to the other kindergarten teachers to account for the state of her fingertips after McTeague had been chewing them. The last was that it was a form of gout. Yes *wasn't* it funny to have gout in your fingers, but that's what the doctor had said it was. She didn't dare eat any more spiced food. No she didn't suffer much with them.

At last they began to look so bad that she pretended her hands were cold and wore her gloves all the time.

[Abbott] Reader's comment: "An ineffective postscript."

[Hart] In Theme 23 Norris had excerpted from his novel a passage not only long enough to satisfy the daily requirement but also complete in itself, concluding with a shocking denouement. In Theme 24, presented a day later, he continues the subject in a less horrifyingly direct style and in a form that makes little sense by itself. Abbott's criticism is wholly justified. Although the text could have served as a continuation of the theme that preceded it, Norris never used it in *McTeague*.

25

JANUARY 11, 1895

That week McTeague had his first attack of tremens. It came on him quite suddenly on a Thursday evening just after supper as he was shaking up the fire in the kitchen stove. All day he had been burning up with fever; while a certain nervous trembling beginning just between his shoulders had spread to his arms and legs and even at last to his fingers and toes. All at once toward seven o'clock he began to feel cold; cold even inside his body as though his bones had turned to ice. He went out into the kitchen and crouched over the stove. Instead of trembling now, he was shivering. The fire was low and he picked up the poker to arouse it. The poker moved in his hand and grew cold. He looked at it and saw that it was a snake, a thick, black, wet snake, writhing slowly in his fist, its head and neck bent up sharply towards him, its tongue flickering in and out of its mouth. He flung it from him and saw it shrink into a coil as it struck the floor. Then he sprang back stretching out his hands and screaming until the effort brought the blood specks to his eyes. It was not because he knew the coiled horror upon the floor was a snake that he was afraid, a real snake would not have frightened him. It was because he knew that it was *not* a snake that he was afraid, horribly, frantically, unspeakably afraid.

[*Abbott*] Reader's comment: "A melodramatic subject not relieved by any felicity of treatment."

[*Hart*] The subject of drunkenness, not so important as other vices in the completed *McTeague*, obviously looms large as Norris begins to shape the novel, just as it is a major subject of *Vandover and the Brute* and is also the subject of isolated compositions, like that of January 3. Neither this whole theme nor the typical concluding sentence affected Abbott the way the comparable Theme 23 had done; his displeasure may have kept Norris from using this material in the finished novel.

26

FEBRUARY 15, 1895

On Sundays about two o'clock he took dinner at the car-conductor's coffee joint, next to the harness shop on Polk St. He had a gray soup, thick and oily, heavy meat, underdone and very hot on a cold plate, two kinds of greasy vegetables and a sort of suet pudding full of strong butter and sugar.

On his way back to his room he would stop at the corner grocery to get a pitcher of steam beer. Once in his room, he took off his coat and shoes, unbuttoned his vest and having crammed the little stove full of coke, sat at the window in his shirt sleeves and stocking feet, reading his paper, drinking his beer and smoking his huge porcelain pipe, while his food digested, crop-full, stupid and warm. Sometimes even, overcome by the heat of the room, the tobacco smoke and the effects of his heavy meal he dropped off to sleep.

Later on in the afternoon when he awoke he finished his beer very flat and stale by this time and played very mournful airs on his concertina. He always looked forward to these Sunday afternoons as a period of relaxation and enjoyment.

[*Abbott*] Reader's comment': "Good wording."

[*Hart*] Although Norris rewrote this theme before using it as the opening page of *McTeague*, his protagonist's character and tone are already set four years before the novel's publication. In the final text an office setting, appointment board, operating chair, and seven volumes of *Allen's Practical Dentist* are added to fit McTeague into the profession that is basic to the plot. Norris may actually have conceived McTeague as a dentist at this time and simply not made that clear in the theme; certainly by the March 8 theme his profession is fixed. McTeague already has his concertina but lacks his canary, even though both of these properties belonged to the comparable mate in Stevenson's *The Wrecker*, which Norris greatly admired. This theme was written for the newly conceived novel, yet its atmosphere and a few of its words are still to be found on the third page of Ch. X of *Vandover and the Brute*, and there is an echo of them in the final sentence of Ch. XVII.

28

FEBRUARY 19, 1895

Towards morning Trina died with a rapid series of hiccoughs, that stirred the great pool of blood in which she lay and which sounded like a piece of clock-work running down.

McTeague had killed her in the little room just off the kindergarten school-room where the children hung their hats and coats. McTeague going out had shut the door of this room but had left the street door open so the children, coming in the morning entered as usual.

About nine o'clock a half dozen babies one a little nigger-girl, came into the school-room with a great chatter going across to the

door of the little room to hang up their hats and coats as they had been taught. As they came near the door one of them put her little nose in the air crying "O what a funnee smell" another a butcher's little girl exclaimed "It smells like my pa's shop." The tallest of them swung the door of the little room wide open and they all ran in.

[*Abbott*] Reader's comment: "Not a toothsome subject."

[*Hart*] Six weeks after writing Themes 23 and 24 Norris has changed McTeague's wife from Bessie to Trina, and by now he probably has much of the finished novel *McTeague* well in mind. The themes between January 11 and February 15 are missing, perhaps because they developed the plot and several scenes in ways so close to the final version that Norris extracted them from his stack of work for use in a last revision. Indeed, Theme 28 is remarkably close to the final text in Ch. XIX of *McTeague,* except for its addition of a cat that sniffs at the closed cloakroom door. However, this theme, like most of the others, is both a first and final draft for the class, and it opens with another version of the first paragraph that has been crossed out. The reader's comment is so oddly inappropriate that one wonders if he could have been playing on the subject of McTeague's dentistry and his great gold tooth, perhaps introduced in an earlier, now lost theme.

29

FEBRUARY 20, 1895

McTeague's brother-in-law, Marcus, held advanced and radical ideas, having imperfectly grasped a few half-truths of Political Economy and of theories of population, picked up at some of the ward clubs. He was a clerk at the ribbon counter in one of the Polk street stores. He developed these ideas on all occasions to McTeague, vociferating at the top of his voice, shaking his fists, exciting himself with his own noise.

"The evil is *there,*" he would shout. "Self-control, that's the great secret, the masses must learn self-control. It stands to reason, look at the figures. Decrease the number of wage-earners and you increase wages, aint that true? ain't it? ain't it?"

McTeague understood never a word but would answer stupidly, "Yes, thats it, self-control, yes, yes."

Or it would be a question of strikes.

"It's the scabs that's ruining the cause of labor," Marcus would yell, banging the table with his fist until the beer glasses danced,

"White-livered cowards, traitors with their livers, white as snow, eating the bread of widows and orphans. There's where the evil is. It's them the real oppressors of the working man."

Stupefied by his clamor McTeague would answer wagging his head: "Yes that's it. I think it is their livers."

[*Abbott*] Reader's comment: "Connotative."

[*Hart*] At this time Norris thinks of Marcus as Trina's brother rather than as her cousin and a suitor for her hand, so the theme of rivalry with McTeague has not been conceived. Moreover, Norris has not yet cast Marcus as a veterinarian's assistant but rather as a clerk at a ribbon counter, a job far too dainty for this lusty, brawling man. The final revision of this theme appears in Ch. I of *McTeague*.

30

FEBRUARY 28, 1895

. . . air opened McTeague and Trina went very often in the evening. They even spent some time in the Art Gallery. A friend of Trina's had an exhibit there, a bunch of yellow poppies painted on black velvet which they were interested to find. They stood before it some little time hazarding their opinions and then moved on from one picture to another. Trina professed to be fond of painting and said she would have taken it up herself only the oil or turpentine or something was unhealthy for her. "Of course," she said, "I'm no critic. I only know what I like." She was much taken with the ideal "heads" pictures of young girls with an abundance of hair and large eyes with the titles of "Reverie" or "Pastoral" or "Faith." They bought a catalogue and Trina made it a duty to find the title of every picture. McTeague wondered helplessly at some of the huge landscapes, asking her if she was sure that "they were all hand-painted."

[*Abbott*] Reader's comment: "Suggests."

[*Hart*] As with Theme 8, the opening has been cut off, probably to remove Norris' autograph on the rear of the page. The first few words, including the partially preserved "Fair," can be reconstructed from Ch. X of *McTeague*, which is a revision of this text. The final version does not include Trina's comment that painting is unhealthy for her, although it is an aptly ironic foreshadowing of her blood poisoning by the so-called nonpoisonous paints with which

she decorates toys. Some of this text is also applied to Trina's alter ego, Bessie Laguna, when she visits the same Art Gallery with Ellis in *Vandover and the Brute* (Ch. VII).

32

MARCH 8, 1895

McTeague who is a third class dentist on an uptown business street marries Trina a kindergarten teacher. Their misfortunes begin after a few years. McTeague, having no diploma, is forbidden to practice and begins to drink heavily. For a long time Trina supports the two, until she finally loses her place and in a short while the household falls into great poverty and misery. McTeague goes from bad to worse and finally ends by killing his wife. He manages to escape and goes back to the mines where the first part of his life has been spent. The facts concerning him come to light here and he is obliged to run for it. His way is across an arm of an Arizona desert, here he is ridden down by a deputy sheriff. The two are sixty miles from the nearest human being and McTeague determines to fight, he kills the sheriff and is about to go on when he discovers that even in the fight the sheriff has managed to hand-cuff their wrists together. He is chained to the body sixty miles from help.

[*Abbott*] Reader's comment: "Gruesome."

[*Hart*] The plot summary for *McTeague* presented here seems complete, if sketchy, but it differs in a number of ways from the final work. First, the initial sentence plunges the protagonist into marriage, suggesting that Norris had not planned to treat McTeague's life as a single man or his courtship which cover about a third of the finished text. That sentence also identifies Trina as a kindergarten teacher and thus of a higher class than she appears in the final work. The second sentence suggests that there is to be little emphasis on the happy days of their marriage, such as are briefly shown in Theme 30, and a good deal of stress on the concluding sequence of McTeague's escape to the Sierra Nevada and the desert, to which more than half of this outline is devoted, whereas only the last three of the novel's twenty-three chapters treat this denouement. The composition also differs from the novel in larger ways, for it does not introduce the subjects of greed or of animosity and rivalry with Marcus, who is McTeague's captor in the final work. Nevertheless, the theme is important in showing how clearly Norris did have a full novel in mind and in general how close it already was to the work neither completed nor published for four more years.

DONALD PIZER

[The Genesis of *McTeague*†]

* * *

The initial inspiration for *McTeague* was probably a San Francisco murder in late 1893, when Norris was in his senior year at Berkeley and was deeply immersed in Zola's novels. A laborer named Collins, separated from his wife, stabbed her to death in the cloakroom of a kindergarten, for which she was the charwoman, when she refused him money.[1] Norris was no doubt intrigued by two aspects of the crime. First, the unusual setting for the murder, a kindergarten, was closely related to his mother's philanthropic activities. It was the custom for wealthy San Francisco society women to endow kindergartens, and Mrs. Norris had founded and continued to support the Lester Norris Memorial Kindergarten.[2] In *McTeague* Norris shifted the scene of the murder from Second and Folsom, where it had occurred, to Pacific Street, the location of the Lester Norris Kindergarten. He also introduced a number of "grand ladies of the Kindergarten Board" who are decorating the kindergarten for a children's festival (p. 208). His playfulness, however—which led him to describe himself in a scene at the Big Dipper Mine and to have Trina's dental appointments coincide with the meeting time of English 22[3]—did not extend to a portrayal of Mrs. Norris herself.

Besides the piquancy of the setting, Norris was attracted by the similarity of the murder to themes and incidents he was encountering in Zola. The newspaper accounts of Collins stressed that he was a drunken brute; "whenever he got drunk he beat [his wife] and if she did not give him money he knocked her down."[4] Indeed, "brute" was the key word in the reports of Collins, an interpretation encouraged by the viciousness of the crime ("Twenty-Nine Fatal Wounds" ran one headline),[5] by Collins's dull-witted, inept attempts to conceal it, and by his lack of remorse. "Collins has the face of a brute," the *Examiner* noted, while the *Chronicle* stated

† From *The Novels of Frank Norris* by Donald Pizer, copyright © 1966 by Indiana University Press. Reprinted by permission of the publishers, Indiana University Press, and Haskell House Publishers, Ltd. Pp. 52–63.
References to *McTeague* in the text and notes have been changed to correspond with pages in this Norton Critical Edition.
1. The murder was fully reported in the San Francisco newspapers on October 10, 1893, and for several days thereafter. This source was first noted by Charles Kaplan in his "Frank Norris and the Craft of Fiction" (Ph. D. diss.,

Northwestern University, 1952). For two of the newspaper reports, see pp. 255–63 above.
2. Eleanor Davenport, in a letter to Franklin Walker, October 5, 1930 (Franklin Walker Collection, Bancroft Library, University of California, Berkeley).
3. Trina's appointments are at 2:00 P.M., Tuesday, Thursday, and Saturday; English 22 met at 1:30 P.M. on those days.
4. *San Francisco Examiner*, October 10, 1893, p. 12. See p. 256 above.
5. Ibid.

that "Collins continues to bear himself with a stolid, brutish indifference that marks him as a type of all that is low in humanity.[6] In short, here was a vicious crime in a low-class setting involving drunkenness, poverty, and brutality—a combination characteristic of such Zola novels as *L'Assommoir, La Bête humaine, Thérèse Raquin,* and *Germinal.* "Terrible things must happen to the characters of the naturalistic tale," Norris wrote in June, 1896, referring to Zola's work at a time when *McTeague* was still incomplete. "They must be twisted from the ordinary, wrenched out from the quiet, uneventful round of every-day life, and flung into the throes of a vast and terrible drama that works itself out in unleased passions, in blood, and in sudden death."[7]

When Norris began writing *McTeague* at Harvard, he stressed those sensational elements common to both the Collins murder and Zola's novels. His Harvard themes on *McTeague,* eight in all, from January 7 to March 8, 1895, are primarily on McTeague's drunkenness, his brutal mistreatment of Trina, and his murder of her in the kindergarten. Norris's last theme, on March 8, is a plot summary:

McTeague who is a third class dentist on an uptown business street marries Trina a kindergarden teacher. Their misfortunes begin after a few years. McTeague, having no diploma, is forbidden to practice and begins to drink heavily. For a long time Trina supports the two, until she finally loses her place and in a short while the household falls into great poverty and misery. McTeague goes from bad to worse and finally ends by killing his wife. He manages to escape and goes back to the mines where the first part of his life has been spent. The facts concerning him come to light here and he is obliged to run for it. His way is across an arm of an Arizona desert, here he is ridden down by a deputy sheriff. The two are sixty miles from the nearest human being and McTeague determines to fight, he kills the sheriff and is about to go on when he discovers that even in the fight the sheriff has managed to hand-cuff their wrists together. He is chained to the body sixty miles from help.[8]

Some details of the finished novel, such as McTeague's lack of a diploma and the fight in the desert, are in this early summary. One detail now present—that Trina is a kindergarten teacher—was to be changed. Absent entirely from the summary are several major segments or themes in the novel: the lengthy account of the courtship and early married life of Trina and McTeague, the theme of Trina's avarice, and the two subplots.

Norris apparently continued to work on *McTeague* during the

6. *San Francisco Examiner,* October 11, 1893, p. 4, and *San Francisco Chronicle,* October 12, 1893, p. 4. Collins was eventually found guilty of murder and was executed.
7. Norris, "Zola as a Romantic Writer," *Wave,* XV (June 27, 1896), 3. See p. 309 below.
8. Frank Norris Collection, Bancroft Library, University of California, Berkeley. See p. 295 above.

spring of 1895, despite the fact that none of his extant themes after March 8 deal with the novel. On March 19 he drew out from the Harvard Library a book on dentistry from which he derived the technical dental details used in the novel.[9] Moreover, his letter to Lewis E. Gates, as well as his dedication to him, suggests that by the time he left Harvard he had carried McTeague beyond isolated scenes and a cursory plot summary.

How much of the novel he wrote at Harvard, however, is difficult to say. In his later accounts of McTeague's composition he said that though it was begun at Harvard, it was written in the fall of 1897, when he spent several months at the Placer County mine of his friend Seymour Waterhouse.[1] It is also uncertain whether he worked on McTeague between the late spring of 1895, after leaving Cambridge, and the fall of 1897. During this time he published three excerpts from McTeague in the Wave, but two of these appeared when he was rewriting the novel (October and November, 1897) and the third is a description of McTeague's dental parlor which comes early in the work.[2] In any case, the extant pages of the manuscript of McTeague suggest that the novel was either completely revised or freshly composed in late 1897. This manuscript is primarily a clean copy, with some minor revisions, and served as printer's copy. It was undoubtedly the copy which Norris made just before or after he completed his stay in the Sierras, which he then submitted to Doubleday and McClure early in 1898, soon after he joined the firm.[3] The novel was "held up by Doubleday's hesitancy because of the realistic contents," one of the company's editors later recalled,[4] but it was finally published in February, 1899. There were some protests from readers and reviewers about the scene in the theatre in which "Owgooste" Sieppi suffers a physiological calamity not uncommon among young children, and the scene was revised in later issues. It does not appear in its original form in the Complete Edition republication of McTeague, but it was restored in a private press edition in 1941 and in most editions since then.

In the interval between early March, 1895, and October, 1897, McTeague continued to grow and take shape in Norris's mind, whether he worked extensively on it during this time or not. It

9. Willard E. Martin, Jr., "Frank Norris's Reading at Harvard College," American Literature, VII (May 1935), 203–204 and Charles Kaplan, "Fact Into Fiction in McTeague," Harvard Library Bulletin, VIII (Autumn, 1954), 381–85.

1. See, for example, Norris to Charles F. Lummis, April 9, 1900; published by Donald Pizer, "Ten Letters by Frank Norris," Book Club of California Quarterly News-Letter, XXVII (Summer, 1962), 56.

2. Norris, "Suggestions IV. The Dental Parlors," XVI (March 13, 1897), 7; "Judy's Service of Gold Plate," XVI (Oct. 16, 1897), 6; and "Fantaisie Printaniere," XVI (Nov. 6, 1897), 7.

3. About seventy manuscript pages have been recovered (from what was a manuscript of over 300 pages) and are now in the Frank Norris Collection.

4. John S. Phillips, in a letter to Franklin Walker, April 18, 1932 (Franklin Walker Collection).

emerged finally, in his revision of late 1897, as rather a different work from what is suggested by his 1895 plot summary. The major influences on the novel during this intervening period need to be traced, since they will help explain much in the finished work. The Zola novels which had the greatest effect on the development of *McTeague* were *L'Assommoir* and *La Bête humaine*.[5] To the pivotal event of the Collins murder, Norris added much of the spirit and detail of *L'Assommoir*, including its love triangle, its plot movement of gradual decline after initial prosperity, and its detailed rendering of a middle- and lower-class milieu. It is possible to find traces of *L'Assommoir* throughout *McTeague*, from characterization (Lantier and Marcus, the initial suitors, are both intemperate radicals) to scene (a wedding feast) to plot (a crucial stroke of fate). But McTeague differs from the drunken Coupeau of *L'Assommoir* in two important ways—he commits a murder, and he himself is a brute of a man, huge, strong, dumb. In the characterization of McTeague, Norris appears to have been influenced primarily by the contemporary accounts of Collins and by Zola's portrait of an unrepentant vicious murderer in *La Bête humaine*. In that work Jacques Lantier, the victim of an inherited homicidal mania, stabs his mistress to death. What is particularly significant in the characterization of Lantier is that his mania is portrayed as an uncontrollable atavistic urge to kill any woman who arouses his sexual desire. The alcoholism and insanity of Lantier's forefathers have made him a "human beast," a man who exhibits psychological vestiges of the prehistoric savage. Moreover, though Lantier is neither stupid nor physically brutish, he does have a striking atavistic facial characteristic—a very prominent jaw.

Zola had dramatized the effects of inherited degeneracy throughout the Rougon-Macquart series, and his earlier *Thérèse Raquin* contains a brutish murderer. But in *La Bête humaine* he portrayed for the first time the instinctive homicidal criminal. In this portrait he was directly and acknowledgedly influenced by the late nineteenth-century school of criminal anthropology, and, more particularly, by Cesare Lombroso, the founder and leader of the school.[6] Lombroso's central and most widely disseminated belief was that the criminal is characterized by atavism resulting from degeneration

5. Zola's influence on Norris is one of the most thoroughly investigated fields in Norris criticism. The two standard studies are Marius Biencourt, *Une Influence du naturalisme français en Amérique: Frank Norris* (Paris, 1933) and Lars Ahnebrink, *The Beginnings of Naturalism in American Fiction* (Cambridge, Mass., 1950).

6. The fullest study of Lombroso's influence on Zola's conception of Jacques is by Martin Kanes, *Zola's "La Bête humaine": A Study in Literary Creation* (Berkeley and Los Angeles, 1962), pp. 35–36, 60–61. Lombroso himself critically examined Zola's dramatizations of his theories in "Illustrative Studies in Criminal Anthropology. I. 'La Bête Humaine' and Criminal Anthropology," *Monist*, I (Jan. 1891), 177–85.

of the nervous system, with alcohol one of the chief causes of that degeneration.[7] He held that criminals were members of a biological subspecies which was at an earlier stage of evolution than normal man, and he popularized the term "born criminal" to describe the lawbreaker who inherited his criminal tendencies either from criminal parents or from parents who had undergone a degenerative process. According to Lombroso, the born criminal exhibited physical and mental stigmata of his atavism. There were numerous stigmata, and they differed somewhat depending on the class of criminal (murderers, burglars, rapists, etc.), but among the most common were prognathism, square-headedness, and moral and physical insensitivity. ("Ne pas oublier les signes du criminel-né," Zola reminded himself in his notes for *La Bête*.)[8] Such characteristics, Lombroso believed, were the "outward and visible signs of a mysterious and complicated process of degeneration, which in the case of the criminal evokes evil impulses that are largely of atavistic origin."[9]

Lombroso's theories were popular in the late nineteenth century for several reasons. They not only confirmed superstitions about criminal physiognomy and about the effects of alcohol, but they also embodied an optimistic Darwinism, in which the criminal was a reversion to an earlier epoch rather than a product of evolutionary progress. Moreover, they supported the traditional belief in the "sins of the fathers," but did so by exact physical measurements and descriptions and by elaborate statistical proof. Zola was attracted to Lombroso's ideas because the entire Rougon-Macquart edifice was built on the foundation of hereditary alcoholic degeneracy; Norris because the idea of criminal atavism was a sensational endorsement of his ideas about the importance of man's animal past.

It is doubtful that Norris was aware of Lombroso's theories at first hand when he began writing *McTeague* in early 1895, despite the widespread knowledge of criminal anthropology at that time among both criminologists and laymen. Rather, the early influences in the novel appear to have been the Collins murder, *L'Assommoir*, and the characterization of Lantier in *La Bête humaine*. But by the time Norris completed *McTeague* in the fall of 1897, he had acquired and exhibited an acquaintance with Lombroso's ideas,

7. Lombroso's major work, *L'Uomo delinquente* (Milan, 1876; 5th rev. ed., 1896) was translated as *L'Homme criminel* (Paris, 1887). An English version, adapted by Gina Lombroso-Ferrero, did not appear until the publication of *Criminal Man, According to the Classification of Cesare Lombroso* (New York and London, 1911). Lombroso's ideas, however, were well known in England and America by the late 1880s. Havelock Ellis's *The Criminal* (London, 1892) and Arthur MacDonald's *Criminology* (New York, 1893) were heavily Lombrosian,

and Lombroso's translated articles appeared in such journals as the *Forum, Century,* and *Contemporary Review.* See also Arthur E. Fink, *Causes of Crime: Biological Theories in the United States, 1800–1915* (Philadelphia, 1938), pp. 99–150.

8. Kanes, Zola's "La Bête humaine," p. 61. "Don't forget the manifestations of the born criminal." [*Editor's translation.*]

9. Lombroso-Ferrero, *Criminal Man,* p. 24.

though he had apparently still not read Lombroso at first hand. The most obvious source for this increase in knowledge is Max Nordau's *Degeneration*, which was published in March, 1895, and which by June had become the most discussed book of the year.[1] Nordau's study was dedicated to Lombroso and was an attempt to use the idea of the stigmata of degeneracy in an attack on the major artists and art movements of the day. Nordau not only mentioned Lombroso throughout his work, but also defined degeneracy in Lombrosian terms. "The degenerate organism," he wrote, "has not the power to mount to the height of evolution already attained by the species, but stops on the way."[2] Norris's story "A Case for Lombroso," which appeared in the *Wave* on September 11, 1897, reveals that he associated Lombroso with Nordau. He subtitled his clipping of the story, "A Subject for Max Nordau,"[3] and its theme is related to Nordau's depiction of egomania and morbidity among degenerate artists.

Norris may also have learned of Lombroso's ideas from his friend Dr. Lawlor, who from mid-1895 to mid-1898 was prison doctor at San Quentin.[4] Norris wrote two articles on San Quentin for the *Wave*, and in one of them, "New Year's at San Quentin" (January 9, 1897), he both accepted the idea of inherited homicidal mania and mentioned Dr. Lawlor by name.[5] Dr. Lawlor, as a prison doctor, would probably have known of Lombroso's theories, particularly at San Quentin, where the prison chaplin, August Drähms, was a confirmed Lombrosian, whose book *The Criminal* (1900) contained a commendatory preface by the master.[6]

That Norris during 1896-1897 was responding to the complex of ideas involving degeneracy and inherited criminality is revealed by a number of articles and stories which he wrote for the *Wave* during this period. One of his earliest *Wave* sketches, "Man Proposes— No. 2" (May 30, 1896), is about a coal heaver whose mother had "drunk herself into an asylum." He is a huge brute of a man, dull-witted and slow, with "his lower jaw immense, probably like the jaws of the carnivora."[7] (There is much in this sketch which is also in *McTeague*, but it is impossible to tell whether it draws upon the novel or vice versa.) In "A Reversion to Type" (August 14, 1897), a seemingly docile department store floorwalker suddenly reverts to the criminality of his father. "Little Dramas of the Curbstone" (June 26, 1897) combines the themes of alcoholic atavism and criminal reversion. The "dramas" are accounts of parental degeneracy which has resulted in children who are idiots, cripples, and

1. See Grant C. Knight, *The Critical Period in American Literature* (Chapel Hill, N.C., 1951), pp. 70–76.

2. Max Nordau, *Degeneration* (New York, 1895), p. 556.

3. Frank Norris Collection.

4. See the *Biennial Report of the State Board of Prison Directors of the State of California* for the years 1895–1898.

5. The second article was "A Lag's Release," XVI (Mar. 27, 1897), 4.

6. See also Kenneth Lamott, *Chronicles of San Quentin: The Biography of a Prison* (New York, 1961), p. 129.

7. *Wave*, XV, 7.

criminals. Of one of the children, "a creature far below the brute," a medical student says, "Heredity . . ., father a degenerate, exhausted race, drank himself into a sanitarium." Norris concluded the sketch with the comment that "the chief actors [the fathers] in these three Little Dramas of the Curbstone had been somehow left out of the programme."[8]

These stories and sketches reveal Norris's preoccupation with the theme of atavism and reversion (the two terms were used interchangeably in his day), and particularly with the role of heredity in causing either an obvious physical or mental devolution or a return to an earlier family condition. Norris had dealt with the theme of reversion as early as 1891 in his story "The Son of a Sheik." It is a theme found frequently in Kipling, and indeed it appeared in much post-Darwinian literature once some of the implications of evolution were realized. ("Evolution ever climbing after some ideal good," Tennyson wrote, "and Reversion ever dragging evolution in the mud.") But in Norris's *Wave* pieces of 1896–1897, the theme appears in the context of alcoholism and criminality, which relates it significantly to Lombroso and *McTeague* rather than to Kipling.

Thus Norris's initial impulse to develop McTeague in terms of a brutish criminality caused by alcoholism was no doubt sharpened during the composition of the novel by the popularity of Nordau's and Lombroso's theories of degeneracy.[9] The result of this variety of influences impinging on the conception of McTeague is that though he is not a literal portrait of a Lombrosian born criminal, he does have sufficient characteristics of that type to indicate that Norris was loosely drawing upon contemporary ideas involving degeneracy and atavistic criminality. McTeague lacks many of the explicit stigmata listed by Lombroso, such as epilepsy and tattooing. McTeague's characteristics are rather those which indicate Norris's imaginative response to the dramatic possibilities inherent in the idea of alcoholic degeneracy resulting in atavistic criminality, particularly those characteristics which immediately suggest atavism, such as physical size and strength and mental slowness. So McTeague's father has died of acute alcoholism, and McTeague himself is huge, strong, stupid, and crude. Moreover, he has the protruding jaw,[1] square head, and alcoholic intolerance of the Lombrosian criminal.

8. *Wave*, XVI, 9.
9. Eugene S. Talbot, in *Degeneracy: Its Causes, Signs and Results* (London and New York, 1899), p. vii, noted that the topic of degeneracy received its "popular apotheosis under Lombroso and Nordau."
1. Many of Norris's characters have prominent jaws and yet are not criminals. Norris used prognathism as a crude symbol of the primitive strength which breaks down all barriers in its drive toward a goal or possession. He distinguished between criminal and noncriminal primitivism in terms of ends, not means. A prognathous Ward Bennett, for example, uses his strength beneficially, according to Norris, when he drives his men across the ice to safety in *A Man's Woman*, even though he commits inhuman acts in achieving that goal.

McTeague is dull and slow except when roused to anger or desire, at which time the beast within him—"the brute that in McTeague lay so close to the surface" (p. 133)[2]—prompts him to seize or destroy with uncontrollable violence. Early in the novel he is a potential criminal when he kisses the anesthetized Trina and when he breaks Marcus's arm while wrestling. Later, under the influence of alcohol, which stimulates the release of a vicious brutality in him, he tortures and then murders Trina. After the murder, McTeague displays one of the outstanding characteristics of the atavistic criminal—lack of remorse for his crime. On his return to the Placer County mining area, he feels an instinctive kinship with the primeval landscape. Finally, in fleeing his pursuers, his persistence in traveling with his canary causes him to be easily followed, yet he possesses an animalistic sixth sense which warns him of approaching danger.

Responsive to the dramatic possibilities of the atavistic criminal and encouraged by Zola's many animal-like characters, Norris exaggerated McTeague into a gross brute of a man, just as he had exaggerated Vandover's sensuality into lycanthropic hallucinations. Not that the struggle between flesh and spirit does not occur within McTeague. As he views the anesthetized Trina,

> Suddenly the animal in the man stirred and woke; the evil instincts that in him were so close to the surface leaped to life, shouting and clamouring.
> . . . Within him, a certain second self, another better McTeague rose with the brute; both were strong, with the huge crude strength of the man himself. . . . It was the old battle, old as the world, wide as the world—the sudden panther leap of the animal, lips drawn, fangs aflash, hideous, monstrous, not to be resisted, and the simultaneous arousing of the other man, the better self that cries. "Down, down," without knowing why; that grips the monster; that fights to strangle it, to thrust it down and back (p. 18).

In this first encounter with the "monster," however, McTeague succumbs immediately, as he crudely kisses Trina. Norris then asks the reason for this fall, and quickly answers his question:

> Why could he not always love her purely, cleanly? What was this perverse, vicious thing that lived within him, knitted to his flesh?
> Below the fine fabric of all that was good in him ran the foul stream of hereditary evil, like a sewer. The vices and sins of his father and of his father's father, to the third and fourth and five hundredth generation, tainted him. The evil of an entire race flowed in his veins. Why should it be? He did not desire it. Was he to blame? (p. 19)

2. Norris also indicated on pp. 18, 102, and 240 (in almost the exact words) the unusual volatility of McTeague's animal nature.

No wonder that Norris asks "Was he to blame?," for the implication is that, given McTeague's hereditary disposition toward atavism, the victory of the brute is beyond his control, though that victory—as all such victories—is to be deplored.

This notorious passage, blatant as it is, involves a more complex idea of McTeague's atavism than appears at first glance. For Norris's analysis of McTeague's "evil instincts" combines the limited theme of criminal atavism ("the vices and sins of his father") with the more generic theme of racial atavism—that is, the theme of man's animal sensuality going back to the "five hundredth generation." Norris further develops this larger theme—or rather suggests more firmly its earlier presence—when he writes in the next paragraph that the pull of sexual desire had at last faced McTeague "as sooner or later it faces every child of man." His use of the term "race" in the passage also implies a dual atavistic theme. The term embodies both the common meaning of "mankind as a whole" and the more specialized sense of "family heritage." Norris had used it in this second sense in "Little Dramas of the Curbstone" and "A Case for Lombroso."[3] The passage is confusing because it rather muddily combines these two sources of McTeague's "foul stream of hereditary evil." But it is out of this complexity, here fuzzy but elsewhere clearer, that the main theme of the novel emerges. McTeague's fall is the product of both his special circumstance as an atavistic criminal and his general sensual fallibility as a man. Both flaws stress man's atavistic nature, that he is frequently controlled by unanalyzable instincts which derive from his family and racial past.

Norris, therefore, seems to have begun *McTeague* as a story of alcoholic degeneracy, closely related to this theme in Zola. He then saw the possibility of heightening his portrait of McTeague by introducing some of Lombroso's ideas on criminal atavism. But as he filled out and rewrote the novel, he probably realized that the theme of atavism involved more than an explanation of the criminal, that it also embodied other central human characteristics which absorbed him, that most of all it was related to the source and nature of man's sexual desires. Under the impact of this larger conception of atavism, Norris expanded and developed the novel in directions either absent or barely implied in his original plan. He now gave more attention to the courtship and marriage of Trina and McTeague than to Trina's murder or McTeague's capture; he introduced two additional love subplots; and he made Trina's avarice a parallel atavistic theme to McTeague's criminality. And it is this expansion of the atavistic theme, until it transcends Norris's source of it in the Collins murder and in Zola and Lombroso, which almost succeeds in turning the novel into that mythical creature of literature, a naturalistic tragedy.

3. Norris, "Little Dramas of the Curbstone," *Wave*, XVI (June 26, 1897), 9, and "A Case for Lombroso," *Wave*, XVI (Sept. 11, 1897), 6.

Norris's Theory of Fiction

Introduction

DONALD PIZER
["Life, Not Literature"]†

Most discussions of Norris's ideas, or lack of them, owe much to Franklin Walker's biography of Norris. In that work Walker stressed Norris's "boyish enthusiasm" and his code of "feeling" raised above "thought." Walker implied by this emphasis that Norris was not a systematic thinker and that it would be futile to search for a coherent intellectual position in his fiction or criticism. But Walker's characterization of Norris is misleading for two reasons. A writer under thirty does not have to appear solemn to think seriously. And the rejection of "thought" for "feeling" is itself capable of expansion into an elaborate intellectual position. Because Norris advised others to feel does not mean that his advice was not reasoned. Indeed, in the history of man much thought has been devoted to the creation of anti-intellectual philosophies.

At the heart of the unified and coherent system of ideas underlying Norris's criticism is a primitivistic anti-intellectualism.[1] One method of describing this system is to adopt as convenient counterwords the key terms in Norris's cry that life is better than literature. Superficially, he affirmed by this statement that firsthand experience ("life") is better than secondhand experience ("literature"). But when the terms are placed in the context of Norris's critical essays, one realizes that they are Norris's inadequate symbols for two rich and opposing clusters of ideas and values. I therefore use "life" and "literature" both with a recognition of their deficiencies as generally viable critical terminology and with an appreciation of their usefulness and appropriateness when analyzing Norris's critical ideas.

To Norris, "life" included the emotions and the instincts. It incorporated both the world of nature (the outdoors and the country) and the kind of life which Norris believed "natural" (the life

† From *The Literary Criticism of Frank Norris* (Austin: University of Texas Press, 1964), pp. xiii–xvi. Reprinted by permission of the University of Texas Press.
1. It should be clear that I use "prim- itivism" in its cultural rather than chronological sense. Norris's primitivism establishes certain key values in nature; he does not claim that these values flourished more in the past than in the present.

305

of passion and violence, and the life of the low and fallen) because such life was closest to the primitive in man and furthest from the cultivated. "Literature," on the other hand, included thought, culture, overeducation, refinement, and excessive spirituality. "Life" was dominated by connotations of masculinity, naturalness, and strength; "literature" by suggestions of effeminacy, artificiality, and weakness. "Life" was the source of good art—from it sprang art which moved and led men—whereas from "literature" came imitative and affected art, written entirely for money or for the approval of a cult, or because the artist was unfortunate and unknowing enough to overrefine his temperament and to neglect the crude, raw, often violent world of action and affairs—the world of men and of nature.

From this primitivistic center Norris's critical system branches out in several important directions. Norris believed that the greatest attribute of the writer is sincerity, because the sincere writer rejects the artificialities of literary schools, vogues, and style, and turns rather to the true sources of power and worth—his own "heart" and his immersion in the rough and tumble of active life. By being faithful to his own vision of life, and by dealing with the full compass of life, including the sordid, the sincere writer avoids the two great interdependent flaws of "literature"—rejection of "life" and imitation of others. The correct formula for sincerity is individual knowledge of "life" and then individual use of one's vision of "life" as the material of fiction. Norris's faith in the intuitive or instinctive is thus the common foundation both for his mystique of sincerity and his call for "life, not literature."

Norris's primitivism and anti-intellectualism also contain the seeds for two other aspects of his critical system—his belief in the critical judgment of the "People" and his demand for the practical and useful, in both life and fiction.[2] Norris's minimizing of thought implied his confidence in the instinctive judgment shared by all men, regardless of position or education. He insisted that though the sincere writer who failed to conform to popular imitative vogues might not be immediately successful, the People in the long run would confirm his worth. Moreover, since Norris made action rather than the mind the center of experience, he valued the demonstrably useful in men's affairs above the independent cultivation or stimulation of the mind. He believed that the best fiction does not merely describe or amuse. Rather, it serves the practical moral purpose of revealing both the primary truths of human experience and the full extent of human injustice and deprivation, so

2. My understanding of the social implications of Norris's anti-intellectualism has been aided by two excellent articles: Merle Curti, "Intellectuals and Other People" (*American Historical Review*, LX [January, 1955], 259–282), and Walter E. Houghton, "Victorian Anti-Intellectualism" (*Journal of the History of Ideas*, XIII [June, 1952], 291–313).

that man might learn and mend his ways. The predominantly middle-class direction which Norris gave to his primitivistic values is revealed both by his faith in the majority and by his moral pragmatism.

Norris's ideas on the relationship of the American writer to the American scene also derive from his basic core of values. The American writer, confronted by a huge new reading public easily influenced by fiction, should above all recognize his responsibility to be sincere, to deal with life as it is, and to reveal the underlying realities of life as he finds it. But because American life is still heterogeneous, the American novelist must be a regionalist—not the describer of surface eccentricities, however, but the perceiver of fundamental regional characteristics.

Finally, naturalism—as defined by Norris—is the literary mode capable of encompassing the entire complex of ideas contained in the rejection of "literature" for "life." To Norris, naturalism was the only modern literature concerned with "life"—with the attempt to deal honestly with the richness and diversity of contemporary life, including the violent and low, and to describe the great forces underlying all experience. It was the method which penetrated beneath the commonplace outer surfaces of "civilization" and got at the heart of "life"—man at his most instinctive, emotional, and fundamental. It was the method to be used by the sincere American writer attempting to "prove something" both about man and about his region. In short, Norris defined naturalism primarily as a mode capable of expressing the values clustered around his idea of "life."

But now one comes to a vital paradox in Norris's critical thought. For Norris combined with his primitivistic ideas an equally confirmed faith in what he called "the mechanics of fiction"—that is, a belief that the form and technique of fiction have certain rules, "tricks," and procedures which can not only be described and codified, but which can also be taught, and which must be acquired through arduous discipline and application. In other words, as far as the form of the novel is concerned, Norris attacked the instinctive, the emotional, the natural. He believed that fictional form is an intellectual problem in selection and organization for the achievement of plausibility, effect, and theme, and that there are few substitutes for a considered and painstaking intellectual solution. It is upon this fundamental duality, then, that Norris's critical system rests—"life, not literature" as far as theme and content are concerned, but "literature, not life" as far as form is concerned. Of the two, he gave the first priority, as can be seen in his story "Dying Fires" and in his essays on New York as a literary center. Without "life" as a foundation, no amount of technical training would benefit a writer. The best novelist, however, was primitivistic in content and theme, sophisticated in form.

The duality in Norris's critical system anticipates and clarifies a major development in the American novel. A strong current of primitivistic anti-intellectualism had always existed in nineteenth-century American fiction, from Leatherstocking baiting Obed Bat in *The Prairie* to Huck Finn deciding to obey his heart rather than his conscience. This faith in the life of action, instinct, and emotion continues as a central force in the modern American novel, as in the work of Faulkner, Hemingway, and Steinbeck. There is little doubt that it is one of our distinctive national faiths.[3] The importance of Norris's criticism is that he is our earliest critic to found a complete aesthetic of the novel upon this faith. Moreover, Norris wrote at a time when there was an increasing sense of the artistic qualities and capacities of the novel. He thus combines with his primitivism a demand that the novel be cultivated as an art form, and thereby represents a major bridge between the ungainly novels of a Cooper or Twain and the virtuoso techniques of a Hemingway or Faulkner. Much of our best modern fiction therefore answers Norris's key demands, since it often combines an intense thematic primitivism with a striking facility in the manipulation of point of view, time, scene, and symbol. In short, the sophisticated primitivism which Norris required is a primary characteristic of twentieth-century American fiction. One finds this quality both among the established novelists and among the more promising post-war writers, such as Mailer, Bellow, and Styron. Whatever the crudities, the lapses, the journalistic short cuts of Norris's criticism, then, that criticism is important not only for the obvious reasons that it tells us much about Norris's own practice of fiction and that it clarifies the literary issues and temper of his age. His criticism is also significant because it increases our understanding of some of the most basic and seemingly most enduring characteristics of American fiction.

Norris's Definition of Naturalism

FRANK NORRIS

Zola as a Romantic Writer†

It is curious to notice how persistently M. Zola is misunderstood. How strangely he is misinterpreted even by those who conscien-

3. For discussions of the literary expression of this faith, see Philip Rahv, "The Cult of Experience in American Writing," *Image and Idea* (Norfolk, Connecticut: New Directions, 1949), pp. 6–21, and Lionel Trilling, "Reality in America," *The Liberal Imagination* (New York: The Viking Press, 1950), pp. 3–21.

† From the San Francisco *Wave*, XV (June 27, 1896), 3; text as reprinted in Pizer, ed., *The Literary Criticism of Frank Norris*, pp. 71–72.

tiously admire the novels of the "man of the iron pen." For most people Naturalism has a vague meaning. It is a sort of inner circle of realism—a kind of diametric opposite of romanticism, a theory of fiction wherein things are represented "as they really are," inexorably, with the truthfulness of a camera. This idea can be shown to be far from right, that Naturalism, as understood by Zola, is but a form of romanticism after all.

Observe the methods employed by the novelists who profess and call themselves "realists"—Mr. Howells, for instance. Howells's characters live across the street from us, they are "on our block." We know all about them, about their affairs, and the story of their lives. One can go even further. We ourselves are Mr. Howells's characters, so long as we are well behaved and ordinary and bourgeois, so long as we are not adventurous or not rich or not unconventional. If we are otherwise, if things commence to happen to us, if we kill a man or two, or get mixed up in a tragic affair, or do something on a large scale, such as the amassing of enormous wealth or power or fame, Mr. Howells cuts our acquaintance at once. He will none of us if we are out of the usual.

This is the real Realism. It is the smaller details of every-day life, things that are likely to happen between lunch and supper, small passions, restricted emotions, dramas of the reception-room, tragedies of an afternoon call, crises involving cups of tea. Every one will admit there is no romance here. The novel is interesting—which is after all the main point—but it is the commonplace tale of commonplace people made into a novel of far more than commonplace charm. Mr. Howells is not uninteresting; he is simply not romantic. But that Zola should be quoted as a realist, and as a realist of realists, is a strange perversion.

Reflect a moment upon his choice of subject and character and episode. The Rougon-Macquart live in a world of their own; they are not of our lives any more than are the Don Juans, the Jean Valjeans, the Gil Blases, the Marmions, or the Ivanhoes. We, the bourgeois, the commonplace, the ordinary, have no part nor lot in the *Rougon-Macquart*, in *Lourdes*, or in *Rome*; it is not our world, not because our social position is different, but because we are *ordinary*. To be noted of M. Zola we must leave the rank and the file, either run to the forefront of the marching world, or fall by the roadway; we must separate ourselves; we must become individual, unique. The naturalist takes no note of common people, common in so far as their interests, their lives, and the things that occur in them are common, are ordinary. Terrible things must happen to the characters of the naturalistic tale. They must be twisted from the ordinary, wrenched out from the quiet, uneventful round of every-day life, and flung into the throes of a vast and terrible drama that works itself out in unleashed passions, in blood, and in sudden death. The world of M. Zola is a world of big things; the enormous, the formidable, the terrible, is what counts; no teacup tragedies here. Here Nana holds her monstrous orgies, and dies horribly, her face distorted to a frightful mask; Etienne Lantier, carried away by the strike of coal miners of *Le Voreux*, (the strike that is almost war), is involved in the vast and fearful catastrophe that comes as a climax of the great drama; Claude Lantier, disappointed, disillusioned, acknowledging the futility of his art after a life of effort, hangs himself to his huge easel; Jacques Lantier, haunted by an hereditary insanity, all his natural desires hideously distorted, cuts the throat of the girl he loves, and is ground to pieces under the wheels of his own locomotive; Jean Macquart, soldier and tiller of the fields, is drawn into the war of 1870, passes through the terrible scenes of Sedan and the Siege of Paris only to bayonet to death his truest friend and sworn brother-at-arms in the streets of the burning capital.[1]

Everything is extraordinary, imaginative, grotesque even, with a vague note of terror quivering throughout like the vibration of an ominous and low-pitched diapason. It is all romantic, at times unmistakably so, as in *Le Rêve* or *Rome*, closely resembling the work of the greatest of all modern romanticists, Hugo. We have the same huge dramas, the same enormous scenic effects, the same love of the extraordinary, the vast, the monstrous, and the tragic.

Naturalism is a form of romanticism, not an inner circle of realism. Where is the realism in the *Rougon-Macquart*? Are such things likely to happen between lunch and supper? That Zola's work is not purely romantic as was Hugo's, lies chiefly in the choice of Milieu. These great, terrible dramas no longer happen among the personnel of a feudal and Renaissance nobility, those who are in the fore-front of the marching world, but among the lower—almost the lowest—classes; those who have been thrust or wrenched from the ranks, who are falling by the roadway. This is not romanticism—this drama of the people, working itself out in blood and ordure. It is not realism. It is a school by itself, unique, somber, powerful beyond words. It is naturalism.

FRANK NORRIS

Frank Norris' Weekly Letter†

It is not more than a week ago since the present writer, in going through the daily batch of volunteer manuscripts submitted to a

1. The novels referred to are, in order, *Nana, Germinal, L'Oeuvre, La Bête Humaine*, and *La Débâcle*.
† From the *Chicago American*, August

3, 1901, p. 5; text as reprinted in Pizer, ed., *The Literary Criticism of Frank Norris*, pp. 73–75.

certain firm of New York publishers, came across a letter pinned to the typewritten draft of a novel. The letter was, in a way, a note and commentary upon the novel, and its writer declared with some vehemence, and more than once, that the events in the novel were true—were taken from real life—actually occurred, etc., etc. The inference was plain as paint. The author believed his story to be better by just so much, because the things in it were taken from actual life, were based on fact—must, therefore, be true to life. Now, here is the point. Is an event that is taken from actual life, true to life? Let us consider now. Suppose one had overlooked this author's letter, and had written to him to say that one of the faults of his story lay in the fact that it was not true to life. What a chance! How that author would have countered! How he would have forever demolished the critic, or the reader, with the one phrase, "But, sir, it actually happened." Therefore, it must be true.

Well, I say no. Let us talk about this Truth in Fiction, and with a certain provincial magistrate ask—in the name of American literature—"What is Truth?" A thing has actually happened; that is the proposition. Given to prove that it is not necessarily true when told as fiction—not necessarily true even when told with the most scrupulous adherence to fact, even when narrated with the meticulous science of the phonograph or pictured with the incontestable precision of the photograph.,

Perhaps we will get a good grip of the problem at the outset if we make a difference, a wide difference, between Accuracy and Truth. A story can be accurate and yet lamentably—even wickedly—untrue. As, for instance, let us suppose that you have never seen a sheep, and that it devolves upon me to give you an idea of the animal—describe it, in fact. I go out into the fields and select a sheep. In size, build, habits, weight, wool-producing qualities and the like it is precisely like other sheep—but it is black. To you, then I bring this sheep. I call your attention to the characteristics. I falsify nothing, conceal nothing. I present the creature fairly in every detail, in every particular. I am, in a word, accurate. But what is the result? To your notion all sheep are black, which is an untruth.

So that Accuracy is not necessarily Truth, and the novelist who relies upon the accurate presentation of a crisis in life, hoping by this means to create the impression of Truth, is leaning upon a broken reed.

For further—Life itself is not necessarily True—not necessarily True to life. I admit that this is much easier to assert than to prove, and the sound of it is that of a flippant paradox. Let us try an illustration or two. How many times—how almost invariably, especially with us stoical Anglo-Saxons—do men or women confronted suddenly with great tragedy or great joy fail to "rise to the occasion." How seldom is it that their actions or words at the moment are adequate, are interpretive of their emotions, give an expression of themselves. Mr. Davis tells of a condemned murderer who received the news of his pardon with the words:

"That's good. That's good."

Death-bed scenes are notoriously tame; heroic rescuers are most frequently silent at their works; the soldier receiving a mortal wound, when not struck unconscious, shouts "Gee!" and sits down suddenly with straddled legs. Wellington, at Waterloo, never cried "Up guards and at 'em!" Louis Napoleon's tame eagle refused to fly at the fortress of Ham; and Newton, when his little dog, by overturning a lamp, had irreparably destroyed fifty years of work, could only exclaim, "Ah, Flo, Flo, thou little knowest the ruin thou hast wrought!" Suppose Newton had acted and spoken in proportion to the poignancy of his grief, what a noble, heroic strain of tragedy would have been given to the world. But if we all gave true expression to our feelings under stress there would be no need nor place for fiction.

And here comes the dividing line. Here stands the crux. Is it too much to say that fiction can be truer than Life itself? I take it that we can say this and yet be well within conservatism. For fiction must not be judged by standards of real life, but both life and fiction referred to a third standard. The expression "true to life" is false, is inadequate, for life itself is not always true.

To what, then, should the truth of a novel be referred—to what standard? By what touchstone may we recognize the true metal?

Difficult question. Standards vary for different works of fiction. We must not refer Tolstoy to the same standard as Victor Hugo— the one a realist, the other a romanticist. We can conceive of no standard which would be large enough to include both, unless it would be one so vague, so broad, so formless as to be without value. Take the grand scene in *Hernani*. How would Tolstoy have done it? He would have brought it home as close to the reader as possible. Hugo has elevated it as far as he could in the opposite direction. Tolstoy would have confined himself to probabilities only. Hugo is confined by nothing save the limitations of his own imagination. The realist would have been accurate—only in this case he would not have chosen a black sheep. The romanticist aims at the broad truth of the thing—puts into his people's mouths the words they would have spoken if only they could have given expression to his thoughts.

Then the conclusion. Is it permissible to say that Accuracy is realism and Truth romanticism? I am not so sure, but I feel that we come close to a solution here. The divisions seem natural and intended. It is not difficult to be accurate, but it is monstrously difficult to be True; at best the romanticists can only aim at it, while on the other hand, mere accuracy as an easily obtainable result is for that reason less worthy.

Does Truth after all "lie in the middle"? And what school, then, is midway between the Realists and Romanticists, taking the best from each? Is it not the school of Naturalism, which strives hard for accuracy and truth? The nigger is out of the fence at last, but must it not be admitted that the author of *La Débâcle* (not the author of *La Terre* and *Fécondité*)[1] is up to the present stage of literary development the most adequate, the most satisfactory, the most just of them all?

FRANK NORRIS

A Plea for Romantic Fiction[†]

Let us at the start make a distinction. Observe that one speaks of Romanticism and not of sentimentalism. One claims that the latter is as distinct from the former as is that other form of art which is called Realism. Romance has been often put upon and overburdened by being forced to bear the onus of abuse that by right should fall to sentiment; but the two should be kept very distinct, for a very high and illustrious place will be claimed for Romance, while sentiment will be handed down the scullery stairs.

Many people today are composing mere sentimentalism, and calling it and causing it to be called Romance, so with those who are too busy to think much upon these subjects, but who none the less love honest literature, Romance has fallen into disrepute. Consider now the cut-and-thrust stories. They are labelled Romances, and it is very easy to get the impression that Romance must be an affair of cloaks and daggers, or moonlight and golden hair. But this is not so at all. The true Romance is a more serious business than this. It is not merely a conjurer's trick box, full of flimsy quackeries, tinsel and clap traps, meant only to amuse, and relying upon deception to do even that. Is it not something better than this? Can we not see in it an instrument, keen, finely tempered, flawless—an instrument with which we may go straight through the clothes and tissues and wrappings of flesh down deep into the red, living heart of things?

Is all this too subtle, too merely speculative and intrinsic, too *précieuse* and nice and "literary"? Devoutly one hopes the contrary.

1. This choice of Zola novels is not entirely clear, but perhaps it can be explained by the contemporary reputation of the three works and by the fact that Norris was writing for a newspaper supplement. *La Débâcle* was well received in America, whereas *La Terre* was attacked for its gross sexuality and *Fécondité* was almost universally criticized for its excessive polemicism.

† From the *Boston Evening Transcript*, December 18, 1901, p. 14; text as reprinted in Pizer, ed., *The Literary Criticism of Frank Norris*, pp. 75–78.

So much is made of so-called Romanticism in present day fiction, that the subject seems worthy of discussion, and a protest against the misuse of a really noble and honest formula of literature appears to be timely—misuse, that is, in the sense of limited use. Let us suppose for the moment that a Romance can be made out of the cut-and-thrust business. Good Heavens, are there no other things that are romantic, even in this—falsely, falsely called—humdrum world of today? Why should it be that so soon as the novelist addresses himself—seriously—to the consideration of contemporary life he must abandon Romance and take up that harsh, loveless, colorless, blunt tool called Realism?

Now, let us understand at once what is meant by Romance and what by Realism. Romance—I take it—is the kind of fiction that takes cognizance of variations from the type of normal life. Realism is the kind of fiction that confines itself to the type of normal life. According to this definition, then, Romance may even treat of the sordid, the unlovely—as for instance, the novels of M. Zola. (Zola has been dubbed a Realist, but he is, on the contrary, the very head of Romanticists.) Also, Realism, used as it sometimes is as a term of reproach, need not be in the remotest sense or degree offensive, but on the other hand respectable as a church and proper as a deacon—as, for instance, the novels of Mr. Howells.

The reason why one claims so much for Romance, and quarrels so pointedly with Realism, is that Realism stultifies itself. It notes only the surface of things. For it Beauty is not even skin-deep, but only a geometrical plane, without dimensions of depth, a mere outside. Realism is very excellent so far as it goes, but it goes no farther than the Realist himself can actually see, or actually hear. Realism is minute, it is the drama of a broken teacup, the tragedy of a walk down the block, the excitement of an afternoon call, the adventure of an invitation to dinner. It is the visit to my neighbor's house, a formal visit, from which I may draw no conclusions. I see my neighbor and his friends—very, oh, such very! probable people—and that is all. Realism bows upon the doormat and goes away and says to me, as we link arms on the sidewalk: "That is life." And I say it is not. It is not, as you would very well see if you took Romance with you to call upon your neighbor.

Lately you have been taking Romance a weary journey across the water—ages and the flood of years—and haling her into the fubsy, musty, worm-eaten, moth-riddled, rust-corroded "Grandes Salles" of the Middle Ages and the Renaissance, and she has found the drama of a bygone age for you there. But would you take her across the street to your neighbor's front parlor (with the bisque fisher boy on the mantel and the photograph of Niagara Falls on glass hanging in the front window); would you introduce her there? Not you. Would you take a walk with her on Fifth avenue, or Beacon street, or Michigan avenue? No indeed. Would you choose her for a companion of a morning spent in Wall Street, or an afternoon in the Waldorf-Astoria? You just guess you would not.

She would be out of place, you say, inappropriate. She might be awkward in my neighbor's front parlor, and knock over the little bisque fisher boy. Well, she might. If she did, you might find underneath the base of the statuette, hidden away, tucked away—what? God knows. But something which would be a complete revelation of my neighbor's secretest life.

So you think Romance would stop in the front parlor and discuss medicated flannels and mineral waters with the ladies? Not for more than five minutes. She would be off upstairs with you, prying, peeping, peering into the closets of the bedrooms, into the nursery, into the sitting-room; yes, and into that little iron box screwed to the lower shelf of the closet in the library; and into those compartments and pigeon-holes of the *secrétaire* in the study. She would find a heartache (may-be) between the pillows of the mistress's bed, and a memory carefully secreted in the master's deedbox. She would come upon a great hope amid the books and papers of the study table of the young man's room, and—perhaps—who knows—an affair, or, great heavens, an intrigue, in the scented ribbons and gloves and hairpins of the young lady's bureau. And she would pick here a little and there a little, making up a bag of hopes and fears, and a package of joys and sorrows—great ones, mind you—and then come down to the front door, and stepping out into the street, hand you the bags and package, and say to you—"That is Life!"

Romance does very well in the castles of the Middle Ages and the Renaissance chateaux, and she has the entrée there and is very well received. That is all well and good. But let us protest against limiting her to such places and such times. You will find her, I grant you, in the chatelaine's chamber and the dungeon of the man-at-arms; but, if you choose to look for her, you will find her equally at home in the brownstone house on the corner and in the office building downtown. And this very day, in this very hour, she is sitting among the rags and wretchedness, the dirt and despair of the tenements of the East Side of New York.

"What?" I hear you say, "look for Romance—the lady of the silken robes and golden crown, our beautiful, chaste maiden of soft voice and gentle eyes—look for her among the vicious ruffians, male and female, of Allen Street and Mulberry Bend?" I tell you she is there, and to your shame be it said you will not know her in those surroundings. You, the aristocrats, who demand the fine linen and the purple in your fiction; you, the sensitive, the delicate, who will associate with your Romance only so long as she wears a silken gown. You will not follow her to the slums, for you believe that

Romance should only amuse and entertain you, singing you sweet songs and touching the harp of silver strings with rosy-tipped fingers. If haply she should call to you from the squalor of a dive, or the awful degradation of a disorderly house, crying: "Look! listen! This, too, is life. These, too, are my children, look at them, know them and, knowing, help!" Should she call thus, you would stop your ears; you would avert your eyes, and you would answer, "Come from there, Romance. Your place is not there!" And you would make of her a harlequin, a tumbler, a sword dancer, when, as a matter of fact, she should be by right divine a teacher sent from God.

She will not always wear a robe of silk, the gold crown, the jeweled shoon, will not always sweep the silver harp. An iron note is hers if so she choose, and coarse garments, and stained hands; and, meeting her thus, it is for you to know her as she passes—know her for the same young queen of the blue mantle and lilies. She can teach you, if you will be humble to learn. Teach you by showing. God help you, if at last you take from Romance her mission of teaching, if you do not believe that she has a purpose, a nobler purpose and a mightier than mere amusement, mere entertainment. Let Realism do the entertaining with its meticulous presentation of teacups, rag carpets, wall paper and haircloth sofas, stopping with these, going no deeper than it sees, choosing the ordinary, the untroubled, the commonplace.

But to Romance belongs the wide world for range, and the unplumbed depths of the human heart, and the mystery of sex, and the problems of life, and the black, unsearched penetralia of the soul of man. You, the indolent, must not always be amused. What matter the silken clothes, what matter the prince's houses? Romance, too, is a teacher, and if—throwing aside the purple—she wears the camel's hair and feeds upon the locusts, it is to cry aloud unto the people, "Prepare ye the way of the Lord; make straight his path."

The Mechanics of Fiction

FRANK NORRIS

Fiction Is Selection†

To the man who has ever so modestly assumed the pose of a writer of fiction is given a certain experience which is usually trying,

† From San Francisco *Wave*, XVI (September 11, 1897), 3; text as reprinted in Pizer, ed., *The Literary Criticism of Frank Norris*, pp. 50–53.

sometimes amusing, but that on rare occasions is profitable and entertaining to the last degree. People who wish him well give him "ideas" for stories, come to him with the remark "here's something you ought to make into a story," or "there's a character you ought to put in a book. More often than otherwise they clinch their recital with the remark; "This really happened, you know," as though it were any better for actually having happened. Take, for instance, a ca e like this: A very good friend of the writer's, a capital chap, but without the sense for fiction, tells him a yarn of a romantic elopement. As usual, he says, "this is something that actually happened, you know." Here is what actually happened: A young fellow is in love with a girl—parents on both sides opposed to the match—relentless. Young couple decide to elope—secret appointment at the gate at the bottom of the garden—carriage and horses there—start for the flight—pursuit—girl's brother on a horse (black for preference) pistol shots exchanged—black horse of pursuing brother killed—down he goes with a hideous sliding chatter—next town is reached and marriage performed—subsequent reconciliation, etc., etc., etc. "Now isn't that a story for you?" he exclaims. "That actually happened at ————" and he names the town and backs up his story with all manner of detail. "There's a story you ought to write," says he, in conclusion. No, indeed, not if the story were paid for at the rate of twenty-five dollars per hundred words. The thing may have happened. There can be no doubt that such stories have happened. But the truth of a story in this sense of the word has nothing to do with its availability, from the point of view of good fiction. In a written tale it would not seem real. It would seem like a rehash of some tawdry yellow-covered romance of fifty or a hundred years ago. Fiction is what seems real, not what is real.

But for all this, the story writer must go to real life for his story. You can never think out, or invent or imagine a tale that will be half so good as the things that have "really happened." The complications of real life are infinitely better, stronger and more original than anything you can make up. The only difference is in the matter of selection of details. The story writer's position in regards to the life of the world is like that of a maker of mosaics in front of a vast pile of tiny many-colored blocks. He doesn't make the blocks nor color them—the story writer does not invent nor imagine the parts of his story. Writer and mosaicist alike select and combine. The maker of a mosaic has a design in his brain, or, better still, infinitely better, sees in the pile of little colored blocks in front of him a certain little group or tiny heap that, by merest accident, has tumbled into a design of its own. The design is rough, very crude, the blocks do not fit together, and here and there a green or blue or red block jars in the color scheme. But, for all that, there is a suggestion of design there, much more original than any design he could work out. Well, he takes this group of blocks in hand, picks out and throws away the red and blue and the green that jar and fight, trims off the edges of the blocks and makes them fit compactly together; perhaps a gap or two is left. The whole vast heap is at his command. Deftly he goes over it, picking out here and there the blocks that he needs, a circular one here, a triangular one there, now one of a bright vermillion, now one of a sombre grey. Little by little, he pieces together that crude and rough design, gets everything to fit, everything to harmonize; possibly he combines the first design with another; possibly these two designs suggest a third still better; so he proceeds. At last the final design is complete. A little polishing, a very little, for in roughness there is strength and in sharp contrast, vividness; and there you are, a rounded whole, a definite, compact and complete thing, taken out of and isolated from a formless heap and jumble of shape and colors.

There may be—in fact, there is—in the heap a hundred and one other combinations of forms and shapes already arranged, "actually existing," made to hand, as it were, but the designer over-passes them because these combinations have been used by other designers before him, used so often that there is no longer any originality or freshness in them.

Some one objects at this point: "What about imagination? What about fancy? What about invention?" There is no such thing as imagination. What we elect to call imagination is mere combination of things not heretofore combined. The designer, before his heap of mosaic blocks, can only pick and choose. If he is daring enough, thoughtful enough, careful enough to combine two colors that have never before been combined, or two shapes never before fitted together, we call it "imagination." It is only observation, after all. The designer does not make his little blocks, does not color them. They are already made and colored for him. The fiction writer of the wildest and most untrammelled fancy cannot get away from real life. Imagination! There is no such thing; you can't imagine anything that you have not already seen and observed.

Like the skilled mosaic maker, any one with an eye accustomed to looking for short stories can run his glance over the heap of things we have elected to call life and here and there see combinations of form and color that are original, telling and worth working up. Such a one would not have given the elopement combination half a thought. The design may be in the heap, almost perfect as it lies; the story may have really happened; both are worthless for all that. Sometimes, however, the design does not exist at all except in your brain; you must go to your heap nevertheless. Here, for instance, is an "idea" for another kind of story. It has never happened, but it was told me by a man who has the fiction-sense rather keenly developed. Observe the difference between it and the other one of the elopement, but bear in mind that this last story is yet in its crude original state—needs, in fact, no end of handling and piecing and rearranging. It's a mere handful of blocks, so far. A Jew—sweats old clothes in a sordid basement—a wretched benighted man, squatting all day cross-legged in that sordid basement—has a wife no less sordid than himself. The Jew has no emotions, no fancies, no illusions. There is no poetry in the man. He sweats old clothes. Has not seen the country in fifteen or twenty years. However, in front of his shop stands a poplar tree—tall, very beautiful. Jew has a sort of blind, unreasoned attachment for the tree—looks at it in the evening after he is done with sweating old clothes—has watched its leaves come and go with the seasons—loves the tree, but doesn't know why—hardly knows that he does love the tree. All the starved poetry of the sordid man's life is centered about the tree. One day the tree is suddenly cut down—consternation—something gone out of the Jew's life—don't know exactly what—becomes morose and gloomy—goes from bad to worse—develops latent melancholia—insanity perhaps—quarrels with the sordid wife. All his peace of mind and little happiness gone—goes from worse to worst of all—one day kills the sordid wife without knowing why—is adjudged insane and strait-jacketed in a sanitarium—would it all have happened if the tree had been left standing?

FRANK NORRIS

The Mechanics of Fiction†

We approach a delicate subject. And if the manner of approach is too serious it will be very like the 40,000 men of the King of France who marched terribly and with banners to the top of the hill with the meagre achievement of simply getting there. Of all the arts, as one has previously observed, that of novel writing is the least mechanical. Perhaps after all rightly so; still it is hard to escape some formality, some forms. There must always be chapter divisions, also a beginning and an end, which implies a middle, continuity, which implies movement, which in turn implies a greater speed or less, an accelerated, retarded or broken action; and before the scoffer is well aware he is admitting a multitude of set forms. No one who sets a thing in motion but keeps an eye and a hand upon its speed. No one who constructs but keeps watch upon the build-

† From the *Boston Evening Transcript*, December 4, 1901, p. 22; text as reprinted in Pizer, ed., *The Literary Criticism of Frank Norris*, pp. 58–61.

ing, strengthening here, lightening there, here at the foundations cautious and conservative, there at the cornice fantastic and daring. In all human occupations, trades, arts or business, science, morals or religion, there exists way at the bottom a homogeneity and a certain family likeness, so that, quite possibly after all the discussion of the importance of the mechanics of fiction may be something more than mere speculative sophistry.

A novel addresses itself primarily to a reader, and it has been so indisputably established that the reader's time and effort of attention must be economized that the fact need not be mentioned in this place—it would not economize the reader's time nor effort of attention.

Remains then the means to be considered, or in other words: How best to tell your story.

It depends naturally upon the nature of the story. The formula which would apply to one would not be appropriate for another. That is very true, but at the same time it is hard to get away from that thing in any novel which, let us call, the pivotal event. All good novels have one. It is the peg upon which the fabric of the thing hangs, the nucleus around which the shifting drifts and currents must—suddenly—coagulate, the sudden releasing of the brake to permit for one instant the entire machinery to labor, full steam, ahead. Up to that point the action must lead; from it, it must decline.

But—and here one holds at least one mechanical problem—the approach, the leading up to this pivotal event must be infinitely slower than the decline. For the reader's interest in the story centres around it and once it is disposed of attention is apt to dwindle very rapidly—and thus back we go again to the economy proposition.

It is the slow approach, however, that tells. The unskilled, impatient of the tedium of meticulous elaboration, will rush at it in a furious gallop of short chapters and hurried episodes, so that he may come the sooner to the purple prose declamation and drama that he is sure he can handle with such tremendous effect.

Not so the masters. Watch them during the first third—say—of their novels. Nothing happens, or at least so you fancy. People come and go, plans are described, localities, neighborhoods; an incident crops up just for a second, for which you can see no reason, a note sounded that is puzzling inappropriate. The novel continues. There seems to be no progress; again that perplexing note, but a little less perplexing. By now we are well into the story. There are no more new people but the old ones come back again and again, and yet again; you remember them now after they are off the stage, you are more intimate with the two main characters. Then comes a series of petty incidents in which these two are prominent. The action still lags, but little by little you are getting more and more acquainted with these principal actors. Then perhaps comes the first acceleration of movement. The approach begins—ever so little—to rise, and that same note which seemed at first so out of tune sounds again and this time drops into place in the progression, beautifully harmonious, correlating the whole gamut. By now all the people are "on," by now all the groundwork is prepared. You know the localities so well that you could find your way about among them in the dark; hero and heroine are intimate acquaintances.

Now the action begins to increase in speed. The complication suddenly tightens, all along the line there runs a sudden alert. An episode far back there in the first chapter, an episode with its appropriate group of characters, is brought forward and coming suddenly to the front collides with the main line of development and sends it off upon an entirely unlooked for tangent. Another episode of the second chapter—let us suppose—all at once makes common cause with a more recent incident and the two produce a wholly unlooked for counter influence which swerves the main theme in still another direction and all this time the action is speeding faster and faster, the complication tightening and straining to the breaking point and then at last a "motif" that has been in preparation ever since the first paragraph of the first chapter of the novel suddenly comes to a head, and in a twinkling the complication is solved with all the violence of an explosion and the catastrophe, the climax, the pivotal event fairly leaps from the pages with a rush of action that leaves you stunned, breathless and overwhelmed with the sheer power of its presentation. And there is a master-work of fiction.

Reading as the uninitiated do without an eye to the mechanics, without a consciousness of the wires and wheels and cogs and springs of the affair, it seems inexplicable that these great scenes of fiction—short as they are—some of them less than a thousand words in length—should produce so tremendous an effect by such few words, such simple language; and that sorely overtaxed word, "genius," is made to do duty as the explanation. But the genius is rare that in one thousand simple words, taken by themselves, could achieve the effect—for instance—of the fight aboard *The Flying Scud* in Stevenson's *Wrecker*. Taken by itself, the scene is hardly important except from the point of view of style and felicity of expression. It is the context of the story that makes it so tremendous, and because Osbourne and Stevenson prepared for that very scene from the novel's initial chapter.

And it seems as if here in a phrase one could resume the whole system of fiction-mechanics—preparation of effect.

The unskilled will invariably attempt to atone for lack of such painstaking preparation for their "Grande Scenes" by hysteria, and by exclamation in presenting the catastrophe. They declaim, they shout, stamp, shake their fists and flood the page with sonorous adjectives, call upon heaven and upon God. They summon to their aid every broken down device to rouse the flaccid interest of the reader and conclusively, irretrievably and ignominiously fail. It is too late for heroic effort then, and the reader, uninterested in the character, unfamiliar with the locale, unattracted by any charm of "atmosphere," lays down the book unperturbed and forgets it before dinner.

Where is the fault? Is it not in defective machinery? The analogies are multitudinous. The liner with hastily constructed boilers will flounder when she comes to essay the storm, and no stoking, however vigorous, no oiling, however eager, if delayed till then, will avail to aid her to ride through successfully. It is not the time to strengthen a wall when the hurricane threatens, prop and stay will not brace it then. Then the thing that tells is the plodding, slow, patient, brick-by-brick work, that only half shows down there at the foot half-hidden in the grass, obscure, unnoted. No genius is necessary for this sort of work, only great patience and a willingness to plod, for the time being.

No one is expected to strike off the whole novel in one continued fine frenzy of inspiration. As well expect the stone mason to plant his wall in a single day. Nor is it possible to lay down any rule of thumb, any hard and fast schedule in the matter of novel writing. But no work is so ephemeral, so delicate, so—in a word—artistic that it cannot be improved by systematizing.

There is at least one indisputably good manner in which the unskilled may order his work—besides the one of preparation already mentioned. He may consider each chapter a unit, distinct, separate, having a definite beginning, rise, height and end, the action continuous, containing no break in time, the locality unchanged throughout—no shifting of the scene to another environment. Each chapter thus treated is a little work in itself, and the great story of the whole novel is told thus as it were in a series of pictures, the author supplying information as to what has intervened between the end of one chapter and the beginning of the next by suggestion or by actual résumé. As often as not the reader himself can fill up the gap by context.

This may be over-artificial, and it is conceivable that there are times when it is necessary to throw artificiality to the winds. But it is the method that many of the greatest fiction writers have employed, and even a defective system is—at any rate in fiction—better than none.

Criticism

Early Criticism

FRANK NORRIS

[To the Editor of *Book News*] †

New York, March 23, 1899

My chief object in writing "McTeague" was to produce an interesting story—nothing more. It has always seemed to me that this should be the final test in any work of fiction independent of style, "school," or theory of art. If I had any secondary motive in its production it was in the nature of a protest against and a revolt from the "decadent," artificial and morbid "prose fancies" of latter-day fiction. I believe that the future of American fiction lies in the direction of a return to the primitive elemental life, and an abandonment of "elegant prose" and "fine writing."

FRANK NORRIS

WILLIAM DEAN HOWELLS

A Case in Point‡

The question of expansion in American fiction lately agitated by a lady novelist of Chicago with more vehemence than power, and more courage than coherence, seems to me again palpitant in the case of a new book by a young writer, which I feel obliged at once to recognise as altogether a remarkable book. Whether we shall abandon the old-fashioned American ideal of a novel as something which may be read by all ages and sexes, for the European notion of it as something fit only for age and experience, and for men rather than women; whether we shall keep to the bounds of the provincial proprieties, or shall include within the imperial territory of our fiction the passions and the motives of the savage world

† From "Aims and Autographs of Authors," *Book News*, XVII (May 1899), 486; republished by Mukhtar Ali Isani, "Frank Norris on the Purpose of Mc-Teague," *American Notes and Queries*, X (April 1972), 118.
‡ From *Literature*, N.S. I (March 24, 1899), 241–42.

which underlies as well as environs civilisation, are points which this book sums up and puts concretely; and it is for the reader, not for the author, to make answer. There is no denying the force with which he makes the demand, and there is no denying the hypocrisies which the old-fashioned ideal of the novel involved. But society, as we have it, is a tissue of hypocrisies, beginning with the clothes in which we hide our nakedness, and we have to ask ourselves how far we shall part with them at his demand. The hypocrisies are the proprieties, the decencies, the morals; they are by no means altogether bad; they are, perhaps, the beginning of civilisation; but whether they should be the end of it is another affair. That is what we are to consider in entering upon a career of imperial expansion in a region where the Monroe Doctrine was never valid. From the very first Europe invaded and controlled in our literary world. The time may have come at last when we are to invade and control Europe in literature. I do not say that it has come, but if it has we may have to employ European means and methods.

It ought not to be strange that the impulse in this direction should have come from California, where, as I am always affirming rather than proving, a continental American fiction began. I felt, or fancied I felt, the impulse in Mr. Frank Norris' "Moran of the Lady Letty," and now in his "McTeague" I am so sure of it that I am tempted to claim the prophetic instinct of it. In the earlier book there were, at least, indications that forecast to any weather-wise eye a change from the romantic to the realistic temperature, and in the later we have it suddenly, and with the overwhelming effect of a blizzard. It is saying both too much and too little to say that Mr. Norris has built his book on Zolaesque lines, yet Zola is the master of whom he reminds you in a certain epical conception of life. He reminds you of Zola also in the lingering love of the romantic, which indulges itself at the end in an anti-climax worthy of Dickens. He ignores as simply and sublimely as Zola any sort of nature or character beyond or above those of Polk Street in San Francisco, but within the ascertained limits he convinces you, two-thirds of the time, of his absolute truth to them. He does not, of course, go to Zola's lengths, breadths, and depths; but he goes far enough to difference his work from the old-fashioned American novel.

Polite readers of the sort who do not like to meet in fiction people of the sort they never meet in society will not have a good time in "McTeague," for there is really not a society person in the book. They might, indeed, console themselves a little with an elderly pair of lovers on whom Mr. Norris wreaks all the sentimentality he denies himself in the rest of the story; and as readers of that sort do not mind murders as much as vulgarity, they may like to find three of them, not much varying in atrocity. Another sort of readers will not mind the hero's being a massive blond animal, not necessarily bad, though brutal, who has just wit enough to pick up a practical knowledge of dentistry and to follow it as a trade; or the heroine's being a little, pretty, delicate daughter of German-Swiss emigrants, perfectly common in her experience and ideals, but devotedly industrious, patient, and loyal. In the chemistry of their marriage McTeague becomes a prepotent ruffian, with always a base of bestial innocence; and Trina becomes a pitiless miser without altogether losing her housewifely virtues or ceasing to feel a woman's rapture in giving up everything but her money to the man who maltreats her more and more, and, finally, murders her.

This is rendering in coarse outline the shape of a story realised with a fulness which the outline imparts no sense of. It abounds in touches of character at once fine and free, in little miracles of observation, in vivid insight, in simple and subtle expression. Its strong movement carries with it a multiplicity of detail which never clogs it; the subordinate persons are never shabbed or faked; in the equality of their treatment their dramatic inferiority is lost; their number is great enough to give the feeling of a world revolving round the central figures without distracting the interest from these. Among the minor persons, Maria Macapa, the Mexican chorewoman, whose fable of a treasure of gold turns the head of the Polish Jew Zerkow, is done with rare imaginative force. But all these lesser people are well done; and there are passages throughout the book that live strongly in the memory, as only masterly work can live. The one folly is the insistence on the love-making of those silly elders, which is apparently introduced as an offset to the misery of the other love-making; the anti-climax is McTeague's abandonment in the alkali desert, handcuffed to the dead body of his enemy.

Mr. Norris has, in fact, learned his lesson well, but he has not learned it all. His true picture of life is not true, because it leaves beauty out. Life is squalid and cruel and vile and hateful, but it is noble and tender and pure and lovely, too. By and by he will put these traits in, and then his powerful scene will be a reflection of reality; by and by he will achieve something of the impartial fidelity of the photograph. In the mean time he has done a picture of life which has form, which has texture, which has color, which has what great original power and ardent study of Zola can give, but which lacks the spiritual light and air, the consecration which the larger art of Tolstoy gives. It is a little inhuman, and it is distinctly not for the walls of living-rooms, where the ladies of the family sit and the children go in and out. This may not be a penalty, but it is the inevitable consequence of expansion in fiction.

ERNEST MARCHAND

[1899 Reviews of *McTeague*]†

The reviews of *McTeague* make melancholy reading today. The violence of the revolt against the genteel tradition, especially among the generation that began to be heard about the time of the World War of 1914–1918, is sometimes decried; but the browser among these old reviews will feel that it was amply justified. The keen-nosed watchdogs of literature sensed immediately that here was something new and disturbing in native writing, and promptly set up their growl. *McTeague* came just at the moment when the critics were congratulating themselves that the invading foreign heresy of naturalistic realism, after a twenty-year struggle, had been stamped out—"swept out of sight," as one reviewer wrote, "five or six years ago by the sudden on-rush of works of ideality and romance, which arose like a fresh, sweet wind to clear the literary atmosphere.[1] With mingled prudery, priggishness, and Pecksniffery, Norris was admonished and chided and his novel deplored. A veritable chorus arose: "we trust that Mr. Norris's next plot will fall in more pleasant places"; "to be hoped that Mr. Norris will find subjects better worthy of his power"; "to be hoped he may henceforth use [his ability] in the writing of books that will be not less true but a good deal more agreeable." The author was accused of "searching out the degraded side of humanity." It was deemed "a misfortune that he should have devoted so much skill and virility to the description of a life so essentially without spiritual significance, and so repulsive in its habit and quality." His manner was "hard and cold." His book was "a monotony of brutality from beginning to end"; it was "about the most unpleasant American story that anybody has ever ventured to write"; it had "no moral, esthetical or artistic reason for being," and no one would "be the better for reading it."[2]

From the reviewer in *The Outlook* we learn why Kipling could concern himself with the lives of "coarse and even vulgar" men and yet become popular with a tender-minded generation intensely intolerant of ugliness, squalor, or brutality—in its books. Kipling, the writer explains, "has always exhibited such men at some point as possessing deep human feeling, a sense of duty, courage, fellow-

† *Frank Norris: A Study.* Copyright © 1942 by the Board of Trustees of the Leland Stanford Junior University. Copyright renewed 1970 by Ernest Marchand. Reprinted by permission of Stanford University Press. Pp. 201–208.
1. Nancy Huston Banks, "Two Recent Revivals in Realism," *The Bookman,* June 1899, p. 356.
2. So *Public Opinion* .(March 16, 1899), *The Outlook* (March 18, 1899), *The Review of Reviews* (June 1899), Nancy Huston Banks (*Bookman,* June 1899), and *The Independent* (April 6, 1899).

ship, or humor. In Mr. Norris's story there is not a trace of these higher qualities with the single exception of the two lovers."

Being themselves of a severe intellectual and verbal chastity, the critics were considerably embarrassed in their efforts to warn against Norris' "coarseness." They could deal only in cautious allusion. Thus the writer last quoted: "In two instances at least, . . . he descends to descriptions of incidents which have no place in print; to comment upon or even suggest them is vulgar to the last degree." It is likely that the chief cause of these fastidious shrinkings was the incident of little Owgoost's unfortunate urinary incontinence at the theater.[3]

Yet *McTeague* wrung from its adverse critics on all hands admissions, however grudging, of its original force and of its author's high talents. *The Literary World* (April 1, 1899), of Boston, was typical. To avoid compromising itself it was obliged to voice strongly its editorial[4] dissent from the opinion of its New York correspondent, John D. Barry, whose favorable review it had recently printed. It accused Norris of "grossness for the sake of grossness," declared the spirit of his work to be "false to the highest standards," prayed that the book might fall into the hands only of those of "vigorous mind . . . . and strong stomach," and concluded that though he had reason to be proud of his novel "the world will not be proud of it in that distant tomorrow which irrevocably sets the true value on books of today." But with all this it could not deny that he was a powerful writer, that his characters were drawn "with rare skill," and that the deterioration of McTeague's character was pictured with a "relentless truth" which would not afford the reader the "consolation of saying that in real life it could not have happened so." Neither the public, however, nor the official guardians of literature were prepared to accept excellence, no matter how commanding, on the terms offered by such a novel as *McTeague*. For from the preceding survey of the reviews may be inductively drawn the rules governing the writing of fiction, as that art was understood by the defenders of the genteel tradition: (1) fiction must deal with pleasant subjects; (2) the chief characters must be good people, respectable, such as one might safely introduce to his wife and family; (3) the chief figures may be poor if they go to church, are industrious, and are respectful to their betters; (4) since even the most happily circumstanced heroes or heroines are likely to meet bad, coarse, or vulgar people, let the latter be always redeemed by some conspicuous virtue; (5) lest there be any mistake about where

3. This entirely innocuous passage was removed by the publisher after the first copies had been sent out, and has not subsequently been restored till the appearance, in December 1941, of the limited edition issued by the Colt Press, San Francisco. The curious may also find the omitted passage in Walker's *Frank Norris*, pp. 221-22.

4. The editors were the Reverend Edward Abbott (brother of Lyman Abbott) and Madeline Vaughan Abbott.

the author stands on the subjects of beauty, goodness, and truth (always remembering that there are certain "untellable truths"), let him roll his eyes heavenward from time to time, or wipe away a tear of compassion and thus avoid the imputation of being hard and cold; (6) shun unhappy endings.

Several honorable exceptions, however, may be found to the general thin-lipped disapproval which greeted *McTeague*. Charles F. Lummis in *The Land of Sunshine* (July 1899) of Los Angeles, of which he was editor, thought it a "hideous story" but was not to be daunted by a hideous story when it was well done. And in *McTeague* he found "a fine and a powerful piece of work, an honor to its smith and a matter of pride to those of us who love literature . . . . and respect honest craft."

One of the earliest and one of the most intelligent of the reviews was that by John D. Barry, whose "New York Letter" to *The Literary World* (March 18, 1899) put the editors of that journal to the necessity of a rebuttal. *McTeague* "seems to me," he began boldly, "worthy to rank among the few great novels produced in this country." He declared himself astonished by the "profound insight into character . . . . shrewd humor . . . . brilliant massing of significant detail, and . . . . dramatic force" of Norris' novel, which he already knew at this early date was composed before *Moran of the Lady Letty*. Aware of the irrelevant objections provoked by the theme of the work, he replied: "for those who do not go to fiction merely to be amused and diverted, and who believe that fiction may profitably be made an expression of life, *McTeague* will be a revelation." An "authoritative reviewer" had recently disparaged the novel by calling it "a study of people who were on the verge of the criminal class." But even supposing the statement were true, why, Barry asked, should it be considered a reproach to the author? "People on the verge of the criminal classes, as well as the criminal classes themselves, offer excellent material for serious study in fiction."

The Old Grannis-Miss Baker love affair has always been a *locus criticus* in all discussion of *McTeague*. A majority of the reviewers, in their dogged search for something sweet in this lump of corruption, seized on it desperately as the only palatable episode in the novel. A minority saw it as an artistic defect. Thus Barry thought it had "a little of the unreality of romance."

He was one of the very first to link the name of Norris with that of Crane, an association that has been maintained in criticism ever since. The handling of the theme of *McTeague* suggested to him Crane's manner, but without a hint of imitation and with none of Crane's "striving for effect." If the novel had a fault it was that occasionally the author explained his characters "in a way that suggests superiority," whereas when he found it necessary to speak at all, he should have used language "wholly in harmony with theirs."

But it was again Howells who proved Norris' most influential champion. He had been sniffing the air and had ventured to predict that a shift in the wind was imminent. A period of expansion in American fiction, he believed, was drawing near, a time when it would lay aside the puerilities of romance and become a closer reflection of American actualities; when it would quit the provincialisms that had long confined it and become continental in scope. And the impulse which would set the new currents in motion would come from the foreign realists whose spokesman Howells had long been. *McTeague* seemed to him "A Case in Point" for all he had been prophesying, and with these words he entitled his review (*Literature*, March 24, 1899) of the novel. *McTeague*, he believed, posed an important question:

> Whether we shall abandon the old-fashioned American ideal of a novel as something which may be read by all ages and sexes, for the European notion of it as something fit only for age and experience, and for men rather than women; whether we shall keep to the bonds of the provincial proprieties, or shall include within the imperial territory of our fiction the passions and the motives of the savage world which underlies as well as environs civilization, are points which this book sums up and puts concretely . . .

Professing to have seen already in *Moran* signs of the coming change "from the romantic to the realistic temperament," he found that change fully accomplished in *McTeague*, "suddenly, and with the overwhelming effect of a blizzard." After drawing parallels with Zola and offering a close résumé of the narrative, he praised its "vivid insight," its "simply and subtle expression," the skill which could manage a mass of detail without encumbering the action, the creative power which showed no relaxation in the drawing of minor figures; "the subordinate persons are never shabbed or faked; in the equality of their treatment their dramatic inferiority is lost." He demurred only, as we have seen, at what he considered the anticlimax of the conclusion and at "those silly elders," Old Grannis and Miss Baker. In one of its larger aspects, however, he found *McTeague* wanting, and here he resorts to the argument and the language of the romantic and "idealistic" school of critics who had been belaboring Norris' novel in the reviews. "Mr. Norris," he wrote, "has . . . . learned his lesson well, but he has not learned it all. His true picture of life is not true, because it leaves beauty out. Life is squalid and cruel and vile and hateful, but it is noble and tender and pure and lovely too." By this assertion it might be thought that he would have welcomed the old lovers, for did not their romance form an oasis of the "noble, pure, and lovely," in the dreary waste of Polk Street? The idyl appeared to him, however, too obvious an effort at contrast, patched on, not organic to the whole.

But does Howells' dictum about life (which was everybody's dictum and surely nothing profound) carry with it any imperative to the artist? Why must the artist put everything into every picture? May he not, must he not (whether he wills or no) select? And if so, may he not, if he likes, use only the darkest pigments, and for objects only of the harshest outlines? The question answers itself; and as a criticism of *McTeague* Howells' complaint that beauty has been left out falls to the ground. *McTeague* has a beauty of its own, of another sort than Howells had in mind—the beauty of an imaginative creation executed with a high artistry.

Howells is a little like the veteran propagandist of revolution who, when the revolution comes, finds himself an exile. It is as if when he saw in action the forces he had invoked, he felt himself already assailed by regrets and a sense of loss. For all his tolerance and liberality of mind, the taboos of the genteel tradition "rode and rowelled" him, as Norris might have said, and he could never forget that vast audience of pious matrons and pure maidens to whom for a quarter of a century he had been addressing his own mild fictions. At the close of his review he wrote:

> It is a little inhuman, and it is distinctly not for the walls of living-rooms, where the ladies of the family sit and the children go in and out. This may not be a penalty, but it is the inevitable consequence of expansion in fiction.

Recent Criticism

MAXWELL GEISMAR

Frank Norris: And the Brute†

* * *

The early scene in the novel when Trina lay motionless in the dentist's chair, "unconscious and helpless and very pretty," while McTeague nervously stared at her, struck the chord indeed for a new set of feelings. "He was alone with her, and she was absolutely without defense." There was also a second self in Trina, despite her strict little world of lower middle class conventions, that responded

† From Maxwell Geismar, *Rebels and Ancestors: The American Novel, 1890–1915* (Boston: Houghton Mifflin, 1953), pp. 14–21. Copyright 1953 by Maxwell Geismar. Reprinted by permission of the publisher, Houghton Mifflin Company, Boston.

to McTeague's force. She is terrified of him physically, seized with fright at "his huge, square-cut head; his powerful, salient jaw; his huge red hands; his enormous, resistless strength." But when he had all at once caught her in his arms, something leaped to life in her, Norris said, and she felt the desire, the necessity of being conquered, of making an absolute final surrender of herself, while she thrilled from head to foot "with a quick, terrifying gust of passion."

So opened one of the famous love affairs in American literature at the turn of the century. It marked the advent of a new literature of realism (more concretely, unequivocally than Crane's work) and perhaps even, with these undertones of power and conquest, a new epoch of violence in human relations. It was a far cry from the innocent romances of William Dean Howells, who sponsored Norris's early work and represented the last reluctant surrender of a nineteenth century tradition to the new age. It was the reverse of the pure spirit and smiling side of life, and also, plunging deep into the pure animal drives as it did, of that popular notion of love—popular in print at least—in which a touch of the hand after three hundred pages was a consummation of passion and pledge of matrimony. The sexuality which in Norris's own work had been banished in effect from the primal emotions of *Moran of the Lady Letty*, and distilled off into the gay comradeship of *Blix*, had with a vengeance been restored to a proper position in human affairs.,

Restored: or imposed. There were still curious undertones in the story of *McTeague*. If the dentist first kissed the unconscious Trina "grossly, full on the mouth," later on he was subject to "a barely perceptible revulsion of feeling." The struggle between McTeague's brute self and his better self took on something of the character of an alcoholic conflict in Zola's work, from which, to be sure, Norris had derived his early notions of the scientific spirit in literature, but, as here, only to make a peculiar fusion of American moralism and European naturalism. "The foul stream of hereditary evil," so he said about his hero, "the evil of an entire race flowed in his veins." And one has the impression that the novelist who was so instrumental in establishing the role of sexuality in the main stream of modern fiction viewed it in part as a biological disease which must be recorded and diagnosed, but not necessarily condoned. At the moment of Trina's surrender to the dentist, he felt a lessening of her attraction. . . . The whole view of lower class figures in the novel (McTeague's friend Marcus, old Mr. Grannis, Miss Baker) was somewhat patronizing too; or literary and derivative when Norris dealt with the lower depths in the story of Maria and the Polish junk dealer Zerkow.

Nevertheless, *McTeague* still deserves its reputation as a pioneer work, and Norris's imagination transcended the limitations of his social background and early training. Very often careless and hasty, as well as sheltered and naïve in his late twenties, he could throw off passages like the description of Trina's hair. "All the vitality that should have given color to her face seemed to have been absorbed by this marvellous hair." There was the moment when McTeague himself—"this poor crude dentist of Polk Street, stupid, ignorant, vulgar, with his sham education and plebeian tastes, whose only relaxations were to eat, to drink steam beer, and to play upon his concertina"—when this hero, convincing as a human being if not as a brute, and still holding his mallet in one hand and a pellet of sponge gold in the other, proposed to Trina. And she, after smiling at him very prettily behind the rubber dam which she was wearing, was suddenly taken by a fit of vomiting, induced by ether and excitement. The notion of an obscure and touching, completely humdrum little love affair in these dingy, depressing Dental Parlors which were heavy with the smell of creosote and stale bedding—a romance which opens with a broken tooth and is played out against a background of bridges, crowns, plaster of Paris, nitric acid, molds and fillings—was a brilliant one, and had an underlying freshness and vitality of execution.

As so often when an artist first discovers and explores a completely new medium, one has the sense of a new insight about life. The "little world of Polk Street" charmed the first years of the McTeagues' married life; the theatre parties or kinetoscopes, the weddings and feasts, and picnics at Schuetzen Park where the husbands and beaus demonstrated their virility, and Trina affirmed her respectability by laughing demurely, her lips closed, putting one hand to her mouth. This lower middle class section of merchants and tradesmen was a fresh theme in our literature which Theodore Dreiser, for example, was to carry forward in *Sister Carrie*. The study of character took on power when Trina was caught between her physical dependence on McTeague and her growing fear of poverty after he had lost his license to practice dentistry and began a slow and painful decline in his empty office.

With her blind instinct to protect the money she had won in the lottery (and which helps to destroy her life), her "mincing tone" and airs of superiority in the quarrels which were a recurrent feature in the McTeagues' domestic scheme—and almost their only point of contact with each other; her underlying panic when her husband disintegrates before her eyes until even those few outbursts of affection which he had tolerated—"Oh, Mac, do you truly, really love me—love me big?"—are no longer possible, Trina becomes indeed the central figure in the novel. McTeague himself alternates between indifference and sullen rages ("You can't make small of me always") which turn into physical violence and torture during his drinking bouts. "And in some inexplicable way this brutality made Trina all the more affectionate; aroused in her a morbid, unwholesome love of submission. . . ." Her emotions had narrowed with the narrowing of her daily life. "They reduced themselves at last to but two, her passion for her money, and her perverted love for her husband when he was brutal. She was a strange woman during these days." Moreover, when even this form of human relationship deteriorates, she turns her thwarted sexual feeling into a physical love for money itself—her little hoard of savings in the chamois-skin bag. "She loved her money with an intensity that she could hardly express. She would plunger her small fingers into the pile with little murmurs of affection, her long, narrow eyes half closed and shining, her breath coming in long sighs."

McTeague was in this respect a study of greed; of a 'passion' in the manner of the nineteenth century French and English authors, that feeds upon and consumes the normal range of human emotions. The subordinate tale of Zerkow who beats and tortures Maria, "and all this . . . on account of a set of gold dishes that never existed," or had existed only in Maria's wandering fancy, prepares us for the denouement, just as the famous golden molar which hung outside of McTeague's dental parlors—and which represented the height of his aspirations—was another omen of danger. The novel was in fact structured upon images of gold, and one notices again, in Norris's case, that these early realists and naturalists were consciously using the technics of a literary symbolism. In a story of mutual disintegration, too, the McTeagues move from cheaper to cheaper rooms, while both husband and wife, gnawing and preying upon each other in their economic desperation, are driven to the extremes of their idiosyncracies. When Trina finds herself deserted and helpless—"a solitary abandoned woman, lost in the lowest eddies of the great city's tide"—a tide that always ebbs —she withdraws her remaining capital from Uncle Oelbermann's business in a final burst of desperation. She is in the last phase of a vice which has traded her true security (and the investment which might still support her dwindling existence) for a compulsion to take physical possession of her money.

"Not a day passed that Trina did not have it where she could see and touch it." At night, stripping herself, she slept upon the gold pieces, "taking a strange and ecstatic pleasure in the touch of the smooth flat pieces the length of her entire body." This was her dominant and only desire which had replaced the lost satisfaction of a husband, a home or children. The novel becomes the study of a mania, of "a temptation such as drunkards only know," and in such phrases as a "brusque access of cupidity," repeating a variation of the earlier description of Trina's love for her husband, Norris made clear the conscious parallelism of her greed with an inverted or re-versionary sexuality. McTeague himself discovers that his hatred of Trina comes back upon him "like a returning surge." Almost as though she were young and beautiful and tempting again, he remembers "her small, prim mouth, her narrow blue eyes, her black mane of hair" in his fantasies of whipping her, of "making her dance" in order to get at her money. He would lie awake at night, indeed, "and fancy himself thrashing his wife, till a sudden frenzy of rage would overcome him, and he would shake all over, rolling and biting the mattress." The impulse to murder her became con-crete when, at the end of his resources, quite desperate, he returned to beg for a night's shelter, and having been refused by Trina, he turns to go, outside her window, "the moonlight showing like a layer of snow upon his massive shoulders."

This was a clinching scene in the novel. And notice the artistry which invoked the pure and indifferent light of the heavens, or the immaculate, frozen innocence of nature (the sinful "whiteness" of Melville's diatribes, or the Chicago blizzard in Richard Wright's parable of a tormented Negro boy) to support the drama of inverted emotions. *McTeague* was also a study in pathology, in modern terminology—of a double pathology, in fact, or of the masochistic and sadistic impulses that are entwined around the chronicle; and perhaps this was even a more daring theme, in the literature at the turn of the century, than the outward story which became so famous as the little world of Polk Street.

To what degree was the concept of animality at the base of the central relationship consciously opposed to the prevailing idea of romance in nineteenth century American fiction? On McTeague's part at least, this love affair, opening with the fantasy of rape, was based on the notion of masculine virility that impales a woman rather than satisfies her, and that avoids all the true centrality of sexual feeling for a purely physical sensation of conquest. And per-haps this was an appropriate reaction—in part—to an extreme phase of repression and negation of sexuality in our native letters at the time of Norris's work. The unnaturally pure spirit, tutored in suppression and sublimation, imbued with terror and fear of normal instincts, is apt to release itself in a similar frustration and rage, and almost purely destructive impulses. "The very act of submission that bound the woman to him forever had made her seem less desir-able in his eyes," so Norris described his hero's reaction. "Their undoing had already begun." And if the first part of this proposi-tion were really true, the second might be.

We must ask, too, whether the young Norris, like Ellen Glasgow and even Jack London, attributed to the lower classes of the Victorian social hierarchy an animality which was not quite suitable or proper to the more privileged and wealthier members of the community. McTeague was intended to be a new version of the Darwinian man; we are constantly reminded of the brute in him that lay so close to the surface, "monstrous, not to be resisted," or the "demonic nature" which slumbered under his slow, heavy, clumsy placidity and could be roused to a bestial frenzy. But what is interesting, after all, is the slight degree to which this 'bestiality' was concentrated in the sensual areas of the novel, and how much it seemed to flourish in the realm of morbid and recessive passions. *McTeague* is not so much a study in sexual emotion as in sexual pathology, and the diffused libido we have noticed elsewhere in Norris's work—everywhere indeed but in its proper context—was only partly the product of and reaction to the social taboos which still prevailed in the fiction of the period.

* * *

CHARLES C. WALCUTT

Frank Norris and the Search for Form†

Writing for the San Francisco *Wave* in 1896, when he was still at work on *McTeague*, Norris averred that

> The naturalist takes no note of common people, common in so far as their interests, their lives, and the things that occur in them are common. are ordinary. Terrible things must happen to the characters of the naturalistic tale. They must be twisted from the ordinary, wrenched from the quiet, uneventful round of everyday life and flung into the throes of a vast and terrible drama that works itself out in unleashed passions, in blood, and in sudden death.

This pronouncement identifies at once the literary quality of Zola and the attraction which Norris found in his work. It was the surging vitality of Zola's style, the power of his conceptions, the superabundance of life in his work that Norris emulated. He did not care for theories except insofar as they released forces within him. The scientific outlook, the patient documentation, the use of physical and sociological monstrosities become with Norris, as they were in the work of Zola, the instruments of a new vigor as much as they are the causes of it. As in *Vandover*, these naturalistic qualities free

† From Charles C. Walcutt, *American Literary Naturalism, A Divided Stream* (Minneapolis: University of Minnesota Press, 1956), pp. 125, 128–32. Copyright © 1956 by The University of Minnesota. Reprinted by permission of the University of Minnesota Press and the author.

McTeague from the lifeless vapidness of contemporary romance and create the effect of newness—of new people seen with new closeness doing new and real things.

* * *

It will be obvious by this time that *McTeague* deals with the sordid side of life. McTeague is a brute, a primitive man unnaturally placed in a civilized environment. His life with Trina is degraded and ugly, and his lack of mentality makes his connection with his environment more intimate than it could be if he had those qualities of will or "soul" which, in different kinds of stories, cause characters to stand out as self-sufficient and autonomous in spite of whatever physical conditions may oppress them. Since it is in this respect that most American naturalistic novels fail to achieve inner consistency, the preponderance of sordid milieu over individual will may profitably be emphasized. McTeague probably thinks and chooses, but the novel concerns itself with the objects and actions that exist outside of his mind; in the crises, the actions of the leading characters are fully treated, while the accompanying cerebration is assumed to be a part or function of the action rather than its cause. The causes are physical, instinctive, and dependent upon external circumstance. In this respect the resemblance between *McTeague* and Zola's *L'Assommoir* is striking.

The lower spiritual plane upon which *McTeague* moves accounts for a difference in ethical tone from that which obtains in *Vandover* and suggests that it comes considerably closer to fulfilling the theoretical criteria of naturalism. The hero of *Vandover* starts from a social and moral plane as high as that of the average gentle reader, who consequently identifies himself with Vandover and in some degree judges and condemns him for the kind of moral lapses that he would condemn in himself. But where McTeague's rudimentary moral gropings appear beside his gigantic and instinctive activities, the reader feels no impulse to identify himself with their possessor; and if McTeague does make a reasoned choice (which he scarcely does in the whole book) the reader hardly thinks of judging it. Rather he observes—with curiosity, fascination, wonder, and pity. The terror proper to tragedy is absent. There is interest but no purgation.

Furthermore, the tone of *McTeague* is frequently facetious. Norris treats his characters as if they were exhibits in a side show, ridiculous monsters, or conversation pieces. He seems to delight in exhibiting their follies, to be grimacing at the reader over their shoulders, to be saying that these freaks from the grubby levels of society are at least as funny as they are pathetic. McTeague is absurd except when powerful emotion makes him terrifying. Trina is repulsive. Marcus Schouler, who is symbolically represented by yapping dogs, is vain, combative, petty. And as if this were not enough, Norris has introduced minor freaks. There is a crazy servant, Marie, who says, "I had a flying squirrel but I let him go," and who tells a burlesque miser about chests full of gold plate till she has him wild with avarice. And there is a pathetic old couple, Miss Baker and Old Grannis, who commune through the wall of the rooming house where they live, never daring to speak to each other. The assemblage of big and little monsters creates a sense of sociological extremes—of people or creatures who have to be seen in the new dimension of Darwinian thought rather than in the established frames of social conformity and orientation. For all the humor, there is a grotesque and nightmarish quality here that recalls similar effects in the work of Stephen Crane. This is the jungle at our back door, full of creatures who do not answer to the social norms.

That the philosophy is broadly deterministic is obvious from the character of the story. How explicitly so is another matter, for the forms of naturalism may be assumed without the writer's caring much about its theoretical basis. Let us see how Norris goes about working either internal or external determining forces into his action. With reference to the former, he gives careful attention to McTeague's heredity. His father died of acute alcoholism, and the evil is said to have been transmitted to the son: "Below the fine fabric of all that was good in him ran the foul stream of hereditary evil, like a sewer. The vices and sins of his father and of his father's father, to the third and fourth and fifth hundredth generation, tainted him." His physique and his intellectual slowness are also obviously products of his heredity which show why he does not act like the "ideal" social creature who thinks and chooses with perfect moral freedom. We are told of the forces which produce McTeague's "will," though his individuality is not impaired thereby. Trina's greed, further, is derived from her Swiss ancestry. Equal care is devoted to the external forces which operate upon the hereditary endowment of McTeague to bring about a change of state. But these external forces—Trina's greed, and Marcus's jealousy, especially—do not represent broad social or economic pressures and so do not in their operation demonstrate any sociological truths. In other words, the story of *McTeague* is put in motion by circumstance, by external forces which do not join perfectly together to form a chain of cause and effect. Norris points to the unalterable destiny that was created when McTeague and Trina met: "Their undoing had already begun. Yet neither of them was to blame. From the first they had not sought each other. Chance had brought them face to face and mysterious instincts as ungovernable as the winds of heaven were at work knitting their lives together."

In this story, however, we are not to witness the interaction of heredity and environment according to scientific rules, but to observe the web of circumstances which brings about the destruction of the leading characters. The structure of the novel, therefore, depends neither upon a "cycle of degeneration" in which internal forces direct the movement, nor upon a cycle of change induced by external pressures operating in their regular courses. The structure consists, rather, of very much the sort of plot that might be found in any novel of adventure or intrigue—except that it is not conceived in terms of free will. Its interlocking of cause and effect in such incidents as the winning of the lottery, the loss of McTeague's practice through Marcus's jealousy, and the finding by McTeague of his concertina which Trina has sold, is as statistically improbable as the melodrama of the conclusion. Yet the fact that the action is slow, so that there is ample time for detailed presentation of what appears to be a *complete* picture of the lives of McTeague and Trina, makes the incidents seem inevitable as they occur. In this ͡ ͡ of inevitability lies much of the aesthetic effect of the story. In ͡͡. ͡f the comic overtones the reader is touched by the pathos of McTeague's situation, by his dumb and helpless struggling against a sequence of events for which he is not personally responsible, and by the pathetic sense of isolation which attaches to a character who moves in a course which he cannot change.

The plot is one extra-naturalistic element in *McTeague* that accounts for its interest. Instead of illustrating natural laws, the structure of the novel draws the reader's attention to the people who move through it. The result is that one knows McTeague and Trina as individuals who do think and desire and struggle: instead of robbing them of their personalities, the deterministic forces direct us to feel the pathos of their inability to cope with the pressures which overcome them. It is a feeling for the desperation of human, or subhuman, impotence that the book communicates. The humanity of the characters is minimized somewhat by Norris's facetious tone, but nevertheless it comes through, sometimes forcefully, almost in spite of the author.

Because the writer's concern is always with his characters, we get only an inkling of his attitude toward nature. It is malignant toward McTeague, but he is not a representative American. Norris expresses no teleology; yet he does not deny one. He exhibits religious feeling which seems not to be related in his inchoate materialism. So shadowy are the philosophical assumptions, indeed, that he can endow McTeague with a sharp power of intuition through which, in the long final section devoted to his flight into the mountains and across the desert, he is constantly aware of his pursuers and knows when he must thrust on further into the hinterland. The suggestion is that this power of instinctive perception belongs to the atavistic animal nature which is strong in him. It is also a preview of the natural dynamism which derives from the romantic roots of naturalism and of which we shall see much more in *The Octopus* and *The Pit*.

McTeague is an advance toward pure naturalism beyond *Vandover* in that its characters are more convincingly dominated by a sordid milieu. The difficulty in *Vandover* was that Norris could produce no effective milieu in San Francisco. In *McTeague* he found one but lightened its burden by leaning heavily upon heredity and circumstance to control his action. The carefully wrought plot represents a literary advance; it does not draw away from "pure" naturalism so much as it distinctly and consciously subordinates it to the literary intention which was always uppermost with Norris. If it ends in outlandish melodrama rather than a controlled demonstration of inevitable consequences, it is merely because Norris shifted from the theory to the romantic extremes of naturalism.

RICHARD CHASE

McTeague†

Norris's first novel was mostly written in 1892 but it was not finished and published until 1899 (it was thus preceded by another important early document in American naturalism, Stephen Crane's *Maggie*, which was published earlier but made little impression). McTeague, the hero of the book, is an illiterate dentist in San Francisco, an innocent animal-like man who falls victim to the corrupt ways of city life. In telling the story Norris sticks close to the heredity-environment-degeneration theme. Marcus Schouler, McTeague's supposed friend, informs the authorities that McTeague is practicing dentistry without a license. This activates the fatal forces of environment and heredity and starts the hero off on his undeviating path to disaster.

McTeague is Norris's best book, having all the hallmarks of young genius and forming in its crude way a genuine art work. Like many American novels, *The Octopus* is all "picture," and the few "scenes" we are given are perfunctory, with the exception of one or

† From Richard Chase, *The American Novel and Its Tradition* (Garden City, N.Y.: Doubleday, 1957), 188–92. Copyright © 1957 by Richard Chase. Reprinted by permission of Doubleday & Company, Inc.

two that stick in the mind, like the ranch festival and accompanying jack-rabbit hunt, though even here everything is done with the wide brush. But *McTeague* has several closely observed and adequately dramatized scenes—even though others are so far overdramatized as to exceed the bounds of calculated distortion and to become self-parodies. But we do not easily forget McTeague in his Dental Parlors, the fight at the beach between McTeague and Marcus Schouler, the wedding of McTeague and Trina, the evening at the vaudeville, McTeague's weird and brutal murder of Trina, nor, melodramatic as it is, the final death struggle between McTeague and Marcus. Norris had an eye for social behavior when he chose to use it—although his overt comments on human manners are likely to be banal ("no people have a keener eye for amenities than those whose social position is not assured"). He often gets off passages of quiet and effective factual observation:

Then Trina and the dentist were married. The guests stood in constrained attitudes, looking furtively out of the corners of their eyes. Mr. Sieppe never moved a muscle; Mrs. Sieppe cried into her handkerchief all the time. At the melodeon Selina played "Call Me Thine Own," very softly, the tremulo stop pulled out. She looked over her shoulder from time to time. Between the pauses of the music one could hear the low tones of the minister, the responses of the participants, and the suppressed sounds of Mrs. Sieppe's weeping. Outside the noises of the street rose to the windows in muffled undertones, a cable car rumbled past, a newsboy went by chanting the evening papers; from somewhere in the building itself came a persistent noise of sawing.

Trina and McTeague knelt. The dentist's knees thudded on the floor and he presented to view the soles of his shoes, painfully new and unworn, the leather still yellow, the brass nail heads still glittering. Trina sank at his side very gracefully, setting her dress and train with a little gesture of her hand.

Having come to know McTeague and Trina in the circumstances of their ordinary lives, we are able to feel for them as their story unfolds. Thus they have an existence apart from the puppets they become as the pressure of their Fate, in the latter parts of the book, hurries them on to their annihilation.

These scenes are more successful in telling us about the characters than are Norris's theoretical devices. One of these latter is the trick of giving everyone a sort of Darwinian double existence, so that on the surface people are domesticated and conventionalized, whereas underneath they are carnivorous beasts. In the naturalistic novel the beast shows through the human exterior as in the older fiction the devil did; the modern Mephistopheles is a werewolf or, more likely, an apeman. There is a rampant animal imagery in *McTeague*, and often it occurs where people are being metaphorically hustled up and down the evolutionary ladder, between the animal and the human levels. There is a memorable moment in the book when, before she is married to McTeague, Trina reclines prettily in the dentist's chair. She is under ether, and McTeague's emotions are described thus:

> Suddenly the animal in the man stirred and woke; the evil instincts that in him were so close to the surface leaped to life, shouting and clamoring.
>
> It was a crisis—a crisis that had arisen all in an instant; a crisis for which he was totally unprepared. Blindly, and without knowing why, McTeague fought against it, moved by an unreasoned instinct of resistance. Within him, a certain second self, another better McTeague rose with the brute; both were strong, with the huge crude strength if the man himself. The two were at grapples. There in that cheap and shabby "Dental Parlor" a dreaded struggle began. It was the old battle, old as the world, wide as the world—the sudden panther leap of the animal, lips drawn, fangs aflash, hideous, monstrous, not to be resisted, and the simultaneous arousing of the other man, the better self that cries, "Down, down," without knowing why; that grips the monster; that fights to strangle it, to thrust it down and back.

To quote from the several passages of this sort is really unfair, because they tend to be rather trashy expressions of what, taking the book as a whole, is a satisfactory poetic metaphor. But it is certainly not much of a device of characterization. Nor are the pseudo-Homeric epithets Norris attaches to his people, repeating over and over again that Trina's hair is "moist" and "regal," that her ear lobes are "anemic" (though she herself does not seem to be), or that McTeague has "the hands of the old car boy" (the boy, that is, who pushes cars in mine tunnels, as McTeague had done before learning dentistry). There is little attempt to characterize lesser figures like Zerkow, the junk man, and Maria Macapa, the demented Mexican woman whom Zerkow marries in the hope of finding a solid gold table service she crazily remembers as having been once in her family's possession. Zerkow and Maria are only slightly less absurd than the pathetic Dickensian comic lovers, Miss Baker and Old Grannis.

Over against the scenic realism and the characterization of the main figures, however, there is a powerful tendency towards abstraction. In *McTeague* the circuit of life between the real and the ideal often ceases to operate and the two fly wildly asunder. One reason for the abstractness that makes so notable a part of the book is that McTeague himself is semilegendary; we should have to change our feeling about him if his name were Joe McTeague, say, instead of apparently just plain McTeague. He is of the confraternity of the blond beast, the "Nietzschean" or "Darwinian" Adam, so much admired by Norris and Jack London. In this respect McTeague is the spiritual father of mass-media heroes like Edgar Rice Burroughs's Tarzan. Also we feel blowing through the novel the cold ideology of the era of Herbert Spencer, as when Norris poetically exclaims of McTeague and Trina that "chance had brought them fact to face, and mysterious instincts as ungovernable as the winds of heaven were at work knitting their lives together."

And we come to see that Norris is moved most deeply (this is more obvious in The Octopus than in McTeague) not by people and their daily tragedies and adventures but by abstractions, by Forces, Environments, Accidents, and Influences.

Like almost every other interesting American naturalistic novel one might name, from the works of Norris himself to those of Faulkner, McTeague succeeds because the author is able to write instinctively out of his natural genius and with his considerable grasp of ordinary novelistic procedures. When he obtrudes his pet ideas and prejudices, his writing begins to be meretricious. The effects are forced, and the language sounds faked. The strong parts of McTeague are the dramatic scenes and the central fable of degeneration, melodramatic as this is. There is also a kind of crude but effective poetry that lends its somber color to the whole.

* * *

WILLIAM B. DILLINGHAM

The Old Folks of McTeague†

In McTeague Frank Norris portrays with sordid and stark detail the deterioration of a dentist and his miserly wife. The atmosphere reeks of steam beer and dirty back rooms with greasy walls. Most of the characters are dominated by primitive passions; greed and murder are rampant. Surrounded by this grossness and violence are the timid old veterinarian, Mr. Grannis, and the spinster dressmaker, Miss Baker. Unlike the other characters, these old people are delicately sensitive, and the story of their successful love affair at first seems out of place in the novel. Consequently, critics have accused Norris of inconsistency and have smiled at this apparent indulgence in sentimentality. For example, Ernest Marchand praises McTeague as "the first important naturalistic novel in American

† From *Nineteenth-Century Fiction,* XVI (September 1961), 169–73. Reprinted by permission of the author. References to *McTeague* in the text are changed to correspond with page numbers in this Norton Critical Edition.

fiction," but he feels that Norris's "pattern" of naturalism is "somewhat broken by the sentimental love story of old Grannis and Miss Baker. . . ."[1] Grant C. Knight writes that "the story of Old Grannis and Miss Baker is pure Dickens," and since he can see no other functional value in the affair, concludes that it is probably "intended to be comic relief."[2] Clarence Gohdes agrees that the old people are "Dickensian" and finds that they contribute "in a small way" to the novel by offering "humorous relief and romance."[3] Richard Chase dismisses the old lovers as "absurd,"[4] and their story is a "romantic flaw" in the novel according to the *Literary History of the United States.*[5] Charles C. Walcutt perhaps has come closest to seeing some useful purpose in this subplot in his brief suggestion that Old Grannis and Miss Baker help to create contrast or "a sense of sociological extremes."[6]

The contrast created by the old couple in *McTeague* is not, as Marchand has asserted, outside the pattern of thought otherwise represented in the theme of the story; nor is it simply comic relief, as others have suggested. Rather than a "romantic flaw," the subplot intensifies and broadens Norris's theme and is an integral part of the novel's structure.

In the theme of *McTeague,* Norris has attempted to illustrate the primary motivating forces in our lives: chance and instinct. The characters of the story act from instincts which are brought to the surface and intensified by chance occurrences. McTeague and Trina first meet when she comes to him for treatment after accidentally breaking her tooth: "Chance had brought them face to face. . . . Neither of them had asked that this thing should be—that their destinies, their very souls, should be the sport of chance" (p. 51). After they meet, they are drawn together by sexual instincts over which they have no control. When Trina wins $5,000.00 in the lottery her instinctive greed is stimulated and she begins saving without purpose: "A good deal of peasant blood still ran undiluted in her veins, and she had all the instincts of a hardy and penurious mountain race—the instinct which saves without any thought, without idea of consequence—saving for the sake of saving, hoarding without knowing why" (p. 77). Her hoarding gradually becomes unbearable to McTeague and finally results in her complete deterioration and the awakening in him of animal instincts inherited from

1. Marchand, *Frank Norris, A Study* (Stanford, Calif., 1942), p. 65.

2. Knight, *The Critical Period in American Literature* (Chapel Hill, N.C., 1952), pp. 163, 167.

3. Gohdes, "The Later Nineteenth Century," *The Literature of the American People,* ed. Arthur Hobson Quinn (New York, 1951), p. 752.

4. Chase, *The American Novel and its Tradition* (Garden City, N..Y, 1957), p. 191.

5. Robert E. Spiller *et al.* (eds.), *Literary History of the United States* (New York, 1955), p. 1029.

6. Walcutt, *American Literary Naturalism, A Divided Stream* (Minneapolis, 1956), p. 129.

his father, a miner who at times became "an irresponsible animal, a beast, a brute . . ." (p. 2).

At the same time that these "mysterious instincts as ungovernable as the winds of heaven" are knitting together the lives of McTeague and Trina and then pulling them apart toward destruction others are at work in the lives of Mr. Grannis and Miss Baker. They are as much the puppets of chance and instinct as are McTeague and Trina. That they are gentle instead of primitive, that their affair ends in happiness rather than misery, does not indicate that Norris has lapsed into romanticism. Rather, he is showing that the same forces which destroy his main characters also can create happiness. Like McTeague and Trina, Mr. Grannis and Miss Baker have no free will but are thrown together as a result of chance and uncontrollable instincts conquering their natural timidity.

In spite of their respect for each other, Old Grannis and Miss Baker are never formally acquainted until the residents in the flat celebrate Trina's winnings in the lottery. Until then they are not able to overcome their shyness enough to speak, even though "the emotion of one of these chance meetings remained with them during all the rest of the day" (p. 9). They "keep company" in their separate rooms, however, each feeling instinctively the presence of the other. While Miss Baker brews tea in her room, Old Grannis in his flat binds back issues of the *Nation* and the *Breeder and Sportsman*, and they somehow feel comfort in knowing each other's movements and habits.

Only by chance, not through their own volition, are the old people brought together and formally introduced. In the structure and theme of *McTeague*, the most important single occurrence is Trina's winning the $5,000.00. At this point the deterioration of Trina and McTeague begins. The entire series of misfortunes in their lives can be traced directly to this one result of chance. It brings out the greed in Trina, which in turn provokes the beastly nature of McTeague. It produces envy in Marcus Schouler, who causes McTeague to lose his dental practice. But at the same time it brings Mr. Grannis and Miss Baker together.

Grannis and Miss Baker next meet at McTeague's wedding banquet, where they impulsively exchange their first words. When the old dressmaker speaks to Mr. Grannis, it is as if she is controlled by some force outside herself. She is "in a torment of embarrassment. How was it she had come to speak? She had neither planned nor wished it. Suddenly the words had escaped her, he had answered, and it was all over—over before they knew it" (pp. 97–98). Thus at the time McTeague and Trina marry and thereby take a major step toward their mutual wretchedness, the aged lovers again advance in the other direction, toward a happy life together. The movement of the two plots is again brought into contrast as Mr. Grannis encounters the dressmaker on the steps outside their rooms. "It seemed," Norris writes, "as if a malicious fate persisted in bringing the two old people face to face at the most inopportune moments" (p. 123). When Mr. Grannis accidentally upsets Miss Baker's shopping basket, their chagrin and embarrassment are so keen that their relationship becomes seriously strained. It is Marcus Schouler who saves the situation by quickly picking up Miss Baker's cabbage and fish and taking the veterinarian away with him. Marcus serves as a link between the story of the old people and the main plot. He first forces Mr. Grannis and Miss Baker into the meeting at the celebration and then prevents a rift between them when they collide on the stairs. Marcus also introduces McTeague and Trina, and only a few pages after the incident on the stairs, he helps draw McTeague and Trina apart. He informs the authorities that McTeague has no license, and the dentist is forced to give up his practice. Marcus Schouler, then, is the unconscious agent of what Norris half-humorously calls "a malicious fate," bringing both couples together, then at the same time helping to save one relationship while aiding in the destruction of the other.

The subject ends in chapter xvii as the old people declare their mutual love. Old Grannis has sold his binding apparatus and like Trina has come unexpectedly into considerable wealth. As he sits alone in his room, no longer able to follow his habit of binding pamphlets, Miss Baker feels the same force that compelled her to speak to him at the wedding, and she bursts into his room to offer him a cup of tea. It was an action thoroughly out of keeping with her usual timidity, the result of instinct, not will. Her own action surprises Miss Baker; "That she should permit herself the indiscretion of actually intruding herself into his room had never so much as occurred to her" (p. 184). Yet she was there, and as their embarrassment fades, they confess their love. Immediately after, in chapter xviii, McTeague leaves Trina after mistreating her brutally and stealing her savings. Thus Norris has juxtaposed the final development in the happy relationship of the old folks and the completely broken marriage of McTeague and Trina and has made it clear that the same inexplicable forces are behind both affairs.

The story of Old Grannis and Miss Baker, therefore, serves as an effective contrast and balance to the main plot. Beginning at the celebration party, Norris weaves the growing happiness of the old lovers with the movement of McTeague and Trina toward unhappiness and destruction. Every important step in the progress of the

old pair's romance marks a stage in the deterioration of McTeague
and Trina. But rather than reflecting "romanticism" in one plot
and "naturalism" in the other, Norris has simply shown two results
of the same elemental forces in life. The destinies, the "very souls,"
of all the characters of *McTeague* are the "sport of chance."

DONALD PIZER

Late Nineteenth-Century American Naturalism†

Most literary critics and historians who attempt definitions are
aware of the dangers and advantages inherent in this enterprise. But
few, I believe, recognize that many literary genres and modes have
their barriers of established terms and ideas to overcome or out-
flank. The writer who seeks to define tragedy usually finds that his
definition takes shape around such traditional guideposts as the
tragic hero, the tragic flaw, recognition and catharsis, and so on.
American naturalism, as a concept, has two such channelled
approaches to its definition. The first is that since naturalism comes
after realism, and since it seems to take literature in the same direction as realism, it is primarily an "extension" or continuation of
realism—only a little different. The second almost inevitable
approach involves this difference. The major distinction between
realism and naturalism, most critics agree, is the particular philosophical orientation of the naturalists. A traditional and widely
accepted concept of American naturalism, therefore, is that it is
essentially realism infused with a pessimistic determinism. Richard
Chase argues that American naturalism is realism with a "necessi-
tarian ideology," and George J. Becker (defining all naturalism,
including American) considers it as "no more than an emphatic
and explicit philosophical position taken by some realists," the position being a "pessimistic materialistic determinism."[1] The common
belief is that the naturalists were like the realists in their fidelity to

† From *Realism and Naturalism in
Nineteenth-Century American Literature.*
Copyright 1966 by Donald Pizer. (Car-
bondale, Ill.: Southern Illinois University
Press, 1966; reprinted, New York: Russell & Russell, 1976). Reprinted by permission of Russell & Russell. References
to *McTeague* in the text are changed to
correspond with the Norton Critical Edition.

1. Richard Chase, *The American
Novel and Its Tradition* (Garden City,
N.Y., 1957), p. 186 n; George J. Becker,

"Modern Realism as a Literary Movement," in *Documents of Modern Literary Realism*, ed. George J. Becker
(Princeton, 1963), p. 35. See also the definitions by Lars Åhnebrink, *The Beginnings of Naturalism in American Fiction*
(Cambridge, Mass., 1950), pp. vi–vii;
Malcolm Cowley, "A Natural History
of American Naturalism," *Documents*,
pp. 429–30; and Philip Rahv, "Notes on
the Decline of Naturalism," *Documents*,
pp. 583–84.

the details of contemporary life, but that they depicted everyday life with a greater sense of the role of such causal forces as heredity and environment in determining behavior and belief.

This traditional approach to naturalism through realism and through philosophical determinism is historically justifiable and has served a useful purpose, but it has also handicapped thinking both about the movement as a whole and about individual works within the movement. It has resulted in much condescension toward those writers who are supposed to be naturalists yet whose fictional sensationalism (an aspect of romanticism) and moral ambiguity (a quality inconsistent with the absolutes of determinism) appear to make their work flawed specimens of the mode.

I would like, therefore, to propose a modified definition of late nineteenth-century American naturalism.[2] For the time being, let this be a working definition, to be amplified and made more concrete by the illustrations from which it has been drawn. I suggest that the naturalistic novel usually contains two tensions or contradictions, and that the two in conjunction comprise both an interpretation of experience and a particular aesthetic recreation of experience. In other words, the two constitute the theme and form of the naturalistic novel. The first tension is that between the subject matter of the naturalistic novel and the concept of man which emerges from this subject matter. The naturalist populates his novel primarily from the lower middle class or the lower class. His characters are the poor, the uneducated, the unsophisticated. His fictional world is that of the commonplace and unheroic in which life would seem to be chiefly the dull round of daily existence, as we ourselves usually conceive of our lives. But the naturalist discovers in this world those qualities of man usually associated with the heroic or adventurous, such as acts of violence and passion which involve sexual adventure or bodily strength and which culminate in desperate moments and violent death. A naturalistic novel is thus an extension of realism only in the sense that both modes often deal with the local and contemporary. The naturalist, however, discovers in this material the extraordinary and excessive in human nature.

The second tension involves the theme of the naturalistic novel. The naturalist often describes his characters as though they are conditioned and controlled by environment, heredity, instinct, or

2. The discussion of naturalism in the next two paragraphs resembles in several ways that by Charles C. Walcutt in his *American Literary Naturalism, A Divided Stream* (Minneapolis, 1956), pp. 3–29. In general, I accept Walcutt's analysis of naturalism's philosophical and literary ambivalences. I believe, however, that his discussion of the naturalists' divided view of nature and of their maintenance of the idea of free will by implicitly encouraging their readers to social action are ways of describing these ambivalances historically and socially—by source and effect—rather than as they function within the naturalistic novel itself.

chance. But he also suggests a compensating humanistic value in his characters or their fates which affirms the significance of the individual and of his life. The tension here is that between the naturalist's desire to represent in fiction the new, discomforting truths which he has found in the ideas and life of his late nineteenth-century world, and also his desire to find some meaning in experience which reasserts the validity of the human enterprise. The naturalist appears to say that although the individual may be a cipher in a world made amoral by man's lack of responsibility for his fate, the imagination refuses to accept this formula as the total meaning of life and so seeks a new basis for man's sense of his own dignity and importance.

The naturalistic novel is therefore not so superficial or reductive as it implicitly appears to be in its conventional definition. It involves a belief that life on its lowest levels is not so simple as it seems to be from higher levels. It suggests that even the least significant human being can feel and strive powerfully and can suffer the extraordinary consequences of his emotions, and that no range of human experience is free of the moral complexities and ambiguities which Milton set his fallen angels to debating.[3] Naturalism reflects an affirmative ethical conception of life, for it asserts the value of all life by endowing the lowest character with emotion and defeat and with moral ambiguity, no matter how poor or ignoble he may seem. The naturalistic novel derives much of its aesthetic effect from these contrasts. It involves us in the experience of a life both commonplace and extraordinary, both familiar and strange, both simple and complex. It pleases us with its sensationalism without affronting our sense of probability. It discovers the "romance of the commonplace," as Frank Norris put it. Thus, the melodramatic sensationalism and moral "confusion" which are often attacked in the naturalistic novel should really be incorporated into a normative definition of the mode and be recognized as its essential constituents.

* * *

II

A good deal of *McTeague* is devoted to depicting the routine, ordered world of Polk Street, the lower middle class service street in San Francisco on which McTeague practices and lives. The life of Polk Street enters the novel in two ways—through set pieces describing street activities or the daily lives of the central characters in relation to the life of the street, and through constant incidental

3. Erich Auerbach's *Mimesis: The Representation of Reality in Western Literature* (Princeton, 1953) deals with the representation of these ideas in imaginative literature from antiquity to our own day.

allusion to its activities and inhabitants. Norris dramatically establishes Polk Street as above all a life of the repetitious and constant. The street exists as a source of the ordered and the routine in McTeague's life, as a world where the harness shop, the grocery, and the car conductors' coffee joint are always available in their set roles, where the children go to school at the same time each day, followed by the shop clerks coming to work, and so on. McTeague is settled and content in this life, and we recognize that his inner needs and outer world are in harmony.

A central theme in Norris's work is that beneath the surface of our placid, everyday lives there is turbulence, that the romance of the extraordinary is not limited to the distant in time and place but can be found "in the brownstone house on the corner and in the office building downtown."[4] Norris therefore used the incident which had stimulated him to write the novel, a vicious murder in a San Francisco kindergarten, as a controlling paradox in *McTeague* as in scene after scene he introduces the sensational into the commonplace activities and setting of Polk Street. So we have such incidents as McTeague grossly kissing the anesthetized Trina in his dental parlor, or the nearly murderous fight between Marcus and McTeague at the picnic. Some of the best moments in the novel powerfully unite these two streams of the commonplace and the extraordinary. In one such moment the frightened and incoherent Trina, having just found Maria's corpse with its cut throat and its blood-soaked clothes, rushes out into the everyday routine of Polk Street and has difficulty convincing the butcher's boy that something is wrong or even convincing herself that it is not improper "to make a disturbance and create a scene in the street" (p. 177).

Norris believed that the source of this violence beneath the surface placidity of life is the presence in all men of animal qualities which have played a major role in man's evolutionary development but which are now frequently atavistic and destructive.[5] Norris's theme is that man's racial atavism (particularly his brute sexual desires) and man's individual family heritage (alcoholic degeneracy in McTeague's case) can combine as a force toward reversion, toward a return to the emotions and instincts of man's animal past. McTeague is in one sense a "special case" of reversion, since his atavistic brutality is in part caused by his degenerate parents. He is also, however, any man caught up in the net of sex, and in this second aspect of man's inherited animal nature Norris introduces a

4. Frank Norris, "A Plea for Romantic Fiction," *The Literary Criticism of Frank Norris*, ed. Donald Pizer (Austin, Texas, 1964), p. 77. See p. 315 above.
5. I discuss this aspect of Norris's thought at some length in my "Evolutionary Ethical Dualism in Frank Norris' *Vandover and the Brute* and *McTeague*," *PMLA*, LXXVI (December, 1961), 552–60.

tragic element into McTeague's fall, an element which contributes to the novel's thematic tension.

In describing the courtship of Trina and McTeague, Norris is at pains to stress their overt sexual innocence yet intuitive sexuality. The woman in Trina "was not yet awakened; she was yet, as one might say, without sex" (p. 14). For McTeague, Trina is his "first experience. With her the feminine element suddenly entered his little world. It was not only her that he saw and felt, it was the woman, the whole sex, an entire new humanity . . ." (p. 16). Despite their innocence and lack of experience, both react intuitively and atavistically—McTeague desiring to seize and possess her, she instinctively withdrawing yet desiring to be conquered.

The most important sexual encounter between McTeague and Trina occurs at the B Street Station where McTeague for a second time proposes. When Trina hesitates, he seizes her "in his enormous arms, crushing down her struggle with his immense strength. Then Trina gave up, all in an instant, turning her head to his. They kissed each other, grossly, full in the mouth" (p. 48). Within the literary conventions of the day, this kiss symbolizes Trina's sexual submission. At this moment the strands in the web of sexual determinism begin to pull taut, for "the instant she allowed him to kiss her, he thought less of her. She was not so desirable, after all" (p. 48). McTeague senses this diminution along with a dim awareness "that this must be so, that it belonged to the changeless order of things—the man desiring the woman only for what she withholds; the woman worshipping the man for that which she yields up to him. With each concession gained the man's desire cools; with every surrender made the woman's adoration increases" (p. 48). Norris is concerned in this second meeting not with a special flaw in McTeague or Trina but with a sexual determinism affecting all men. The possessive sexual desire of the man aroused by the first woman he experiences sensually, the instinctive desire of the woman for sexual submission responding to the first man who assaults her —these are the atavistic animal forces which bring Trina and McTeague together.

A major theme in *McTeague* is therefore that of the sexual tragedy of man and woman. Caught up by drives and instincts beyond their control or comprehension, they mate by chance. In *McTeague* sex is that which comes to all men and women, disrupting their lives and placing them in relationships which the sanctity of marriage cannot prevent from ending in chaos and destruction. Norris does not tell the old tale of the fallen fornicator, as he does in *Vandover and the Brute*, but rather reaches out toward the unexplored ground of the human dilemma of sexual attraction.

The tension between this deterministic aspect of *McTeague* and its humanistic element does not lie in McTeague as a fully developed tragic figure. Rather, it is contained in the theme that man can seldom escape the violence inherent in his own nature, that man's attempt to achieve an ordered world is constantly thwarted by man himself. Norris devotes much attention to the element of order in the details of McTeague's life not only because of his belief in the romance of the commonplace but because the destruction of that order is the source of the tragic quality in McTeague's fall and of our own compassionate involvement with him despite his grotesqueness. Norris carefully documents McTeague's life as a dentist and as an inhabitant of Polk Street because the habitual tasks and minor successes of this life represent the order and stability which McTeague requires. In the course of the novel we begin to feel compassion for him as he becomes a victim of Trina's avarice and as we recognize that his emerging brutality is at least partly the result of the destruction of his world. When McTeague learns that he can no longer practice dentistry, his reaction is that of man whose life is emptied of all meaning. In a scene of considerable power Trina comes upon him sitting in his dental chair, "looking stupidly out of the window, across the roofs opposite, with an unseeing gaze, his red hands lying idly in his lap" (p. 151). We are never completely one with McTeague; his brute strength and dull mind put us off. But because he is trapped in the universal net of sex, and because we recognize the poignancy of the loss of his world, we respond to him ultimately as a human being in distress, as a figure of some significance despite his limitations—as a man, in short, whose fall contains elements of the tragic.

For *McTeague* is in part a tragic novel. True, McTeague neither bears full responsibility for his fate nor is he in any sense noble or profound. He is rather like Gervaise in *L'Assommoir*: they are both poor creatures who want above all a place to rest and be content, yet who are brought low by their needs and desires. There is a sense of common humanity in McTeague's fall, and that quality is perhaps the modern residue of the tragic theme, since we are no longer certain of man's transcendent nobility or of the reality of major responsibility for our fates. The theme of *McTeague* is not that drunkenness leads to a tragic fall, but that tragedy is inherent in the human situation given man's animal past and the possibility that he will be dominated by that past in particular circumstances. Norris does not deny the strength of man's past or present animality, but neither does he deny the poignancy of the fall of even such a gross symbol of this animality as McTeague. It is out of this tension that much of the meaning and power of the novel arises.

WILLIAM B. DILLINGHAM

[Norris's Prose Style and the Gold Symbolism in McTeague]†

I

Style

Norris's style has vigor and freshness at times, but just as often it is excessive and too little controlled. It appears to best advantage when read in short stretches. His long series of adjectives can strike the ear forcefully, like the sound of a giant drum (or, as Norris himself would perhaps have described the effect he aimed at, like "a giant heartbeat"). In *The Pit* he saw the power of the wheat as "stupefying . . . coeval with the earthquake and glacier, merciless, all-powerful, a primal basic throe of creation itself, unassailable, inviolate, and untamed".[1] He called upon his vocabulary of super-adjectives with great frequency and often with surprisingly effective results. In *The Octopus*, for example, he portrayed the saga of the earth's reproduction by creating a metaphor of two colossal lovers in sexual embrace. Pounding adjectives suggest the violence and passion of the sex act:

It was the long stroking caress, vigorous, male, powerful, for which the Earth seemed panting. The heroic embrace of a multitude of iron hands, gripping deep into the brown, warm flesh of the land that quivered responsive and passionate under this rude advance, so robust as to be almost an assault, so violent as to be veritably brutal. There, under the sun and under the speckless sheen of the sky, the wooing of the Titan began, the vast primal passion, the two world-forces, the elemental Male and Female, locked in a colossal embrace, at grapples in the throes of an infinite desire, at once terrible and divine, knowing no law, untamed, savage, natural, sublime. (I, 125–26)

Some months after this agricultural act of conception, the wheat breaks through the soil and starts its growth that will culminate in the feeding of the earth's population. In the same style Norris described this "great, majestic, silent ocean of the wheat":

Indifferent, gigantic, resistless, it moved in its appointed grooves. Men. Lilliputians, gnats in the sunshine, buzzed impudently in

---

† From William B. Dillingham, *Frank Norris: Instinct and Art.* Riverside Studies in Literature (Boston: Houghton Mifflin Co., 1969), pp. 104–109; 115–119. Used by permission of the publisher. References to *McTeague* in text and notes are changed to correspond with page numbers in this Norton Critical Edition.

1. *The Collected Edition of Frank Norris* (Garden City, N.Y., 1928), IX, 371. [*Author.*] Except for *McTeague*, further references in the text are to this collected edition. [*Editor.*]

their tiny battles, were born, lived through their little day, died, and were forgotten; while the Wheat, wrapped in Nirvanic calm, grew steadily under the night, along with the stars and with God. (II, 161)

Norris's love affair with purple prose was of long duration. He was incurably similar to his character Condy Rivers, of whom Blix says, "There *is* that about you, Condy, you like to be too showy; you don't know when to stop" (III, 96). Carried away on the wings of titanic force, he did not realize that perhaps his reader might tire of so many male characters with "salient" chins or so many "prolonged" sounds, from rain falling on leaves to purring cats.

Once Norris discovered a word or phrase that caught his fancy, he never let it go. He had the same appetite for catch-phrases that Thomas Wolfe had. When Wolfe was in college he read a striking sentence in a cheap detective magazine: "His arm was hairy—hairy beyond all description." He was so taken with this sentence that he repeated it aloud over and over for several days.[2] To Norris a character with a salient jaw was always more interesting than one with an ordinary chin (if he had thought of it, he might also have given them Roman noses). Time and again the reader of *McTeague* is told that the junk man Zerkow had "claw-like" fingers and that Maria Macapa, the cleaning woman, before telling her strange story always put her chin in the air and shut her eyes "as though . . . she knew a long story about that if she had a mind to talk."[3] Norris used exactly the same phrase ("a vertiable god from the machine," III, 173, 304) to describe both a letter offering Condy Rivers a job in *Blix* and Ross Wilbur as he reappears in society in *Moran*. Characters in *The Octopus* are repeatedly described in exactly the same words. Vanamee's dead lover Angèle, Norris wrote many times, had gold hair "making three-cornered her round, white forehead" and lips of "Egyptian fulness."[4] Vanamee is described more than once as resembling "a half-inspired shepherd prophet of Hebraic legends." The nose of Harran Derrick is "hawk-like and prominent, such as one sees in the later portraits of the Duke of Wellington," and his hair has "a tendency to curl in a forward direction, just in front of the ears" (I, 6). Some pages later Norris stated that Magnus Derrick, Harran's father, has "a prominent hawk-like nose . . . thin, with a high bridge, such as one sees in the later portraits of the Duke of Wellington. His hair . . . had a tendency to curl in a forward direction just in front of his ears" (I, 59). Seldom did Norris describe any large scene without the word "vast" or any deep human feeling without the word "unreasoned." His boundless love

2. For this story I am indebted to Floyd C. Watkins; apparently it has not been printed before.

3. See, for example, *McTeague*, pp. 12, 26.

4. See, for example, *Collected Edition*, I, 33–34, 36, 146.

for metaphors of battle or some great force or movement involved him in similarly obnoxious repetitions. Every antagonistic force in *A Man's Woman*, from polar ice in the first of the book to the typhoid fever that kills the explorer Ferriss, is described as an "Enemy." "Brute" is a catch-all term for any kind of evil in man's nature. The repetition of such favorite words and expressions reveals Norris's sense of fiction gone awry.

Norris once wrote to Isaac F. Marcosson, who had reviewed *McTeague* favorably, that he believed in telling a story and letting his style "go to the devil."[5] His hasty composition and failure to revise carried his style if not to the devil at least sometimes down to the level of the not-too-bright college freshman who dangles his modifiers and mixes his metaphors. Describing Ross Wilbur's view of the sea in *Moran*, he wrote: "Standing on one of the latter projections and looking out to the west, the Pacific appeared as empty of life as the land" (III, 239). In *The Octopus* he wrote: ". . . while perched high upon the seat, under a yellow cotton wagon umbrella, Presley recognized Hooven . . ." (I, 3). The only problem here is that, as it turns out, it is not Presley but Hooven who is perched under the umbrella. The famous scene in *The Octopus* where a locomotive slaughters sheep that wander onto the tracks illustrates how Norris's enthusiasm could run amuck. It is difficult to imagine how the blood of the sheep ("winking in the starlight") "seeped down into the clinkers between the ties with a prolonged sucking murmur" (I, 47). His metaphors for the locomotive are also puzzling. It is at the same time the two-legged, one-eyed giant, Cyclops; a great horse with "iron hoofs"; a whale; and an octopus. Presley hears the train "filling the night with the terrific clamour of its iron hoofs . . . bellowing, ringing with the accents of menace and defiance; and abruptly Presley saw again, in his imagination, the galloping monster . . . with its single eye, Cyclopean . . . the leviathan, with tentacles of steel . . ." (I, 46, 48).

Norris's immaturity as a stylist is also illustrated in his fondness for clichés. His reading of Kipling and Richard Harding Davis furnished him with a storehouse of ready expressions for exciting situations. After Moran kicks the joss sticks of the Chinese coolies into the sea, they exclaim "with bated breaths" (III, 238). Later, in what should be the most exciting scene in the entire novel, inept dialogue makes Moran's attack on Wilbur humorous. Seeing the maddened daughter of the Vikings rush upon him, her dirk ready for the kill, Wilbur cries: "It's I. It's Wilbur—your mate, can't you see?" (III, 287). Norris's best work is seldom marred by the unskillful dialogue characteristic of *Moran*, *Blix*, and *A Man's Woman*,

5. Letter of March 14, 1899; *The Letters of Frank Norris*, ed. Franklin Walker (San Francisco, 1956), pp. 30–31.

but, even in the more serious novels, he simply could not resist the temptation to add such amateurish expressions as "It was true" after giving the thought or opinion of one of his characters. Not content with writing simply that Presley spoke to a waiter in Spanish, he had to add, "a language with which Presley was familiar" (I, 18). Effective as Norris's style is at times, it is often no better than that of countless dime novels long since forgotten.

More important to him than perfect prose was the creation of sharp and vivid pictures, images that remain in the mind long after one has forgotten how graceless the style is. He felt strongly, like Conrad, that art makes its primary appeal not through the intellect but through the senses, especially the visual sense.[6] Indeed, he once described the novel as a group of well-formed pictures: "The great story of the whole novel is told thus as it were in a series of pictures, the author supplying information as to what has intervened between the end of one chapter and the beginning of the next by suggestion or by actual résumé."[7]

Norris was at his best with the visual image. In *McTeague* the animal-like dentist stands in the middle of Death Valley, handcuffed to a dead man: "Chaotic desolation stretched from them on either hand, flaming and glaring with the afternoon heat. There was the brazen sky and the leagues upon leagues of alkali, leper white. There was nothing more" [p. 247]. Grettir, in "Grettir at Drangey," his hair and shoulders red with his enemy's blood, fights in vain as his burning shack falls down around him. On Sunday morning after a wild debauch, Vandover goes to church with the pure and innocent Turner Ravis, listens to the minister preaching repentance, holds on to the back of the pew in front of him until his fingernails turn white, and tries not to succumb to nausea and exhaustion. Such impressive tableaux are even to be found occasionally in his potboilers. Flawed as *Moran* is, it leaves idelible impressions: for example, the image of the wild Chinese beachcombers and their fantastic boat painted with two large eyes, one on either side of the bow. Norris can almost be forgiven for the sentimentality of *Blix* because of scenes such as that in which Blix and Condy sit alone in the bay window of her darkened apartment and watch in silence as evening gradually covers everything. The quantity and richness of such images account in large measure for the effectiveness of *The Octopus*, which projects just such a series of pictures as Norris described as the essence of fiction: Presley sitting in the midst of the great West, ideas for his epic poem running madly

6. Ernest Marchand, in *Frank Norris: A Study* (Palo Alto, 1942), points out this similarity between Norris and Conrad. As Marchand further explains, however, "Conrad's 'unremitting never-discouraged care for the shape and ring of sentences' was ever outside Norris's intention" (p. 174).

7. "The Mechanics of Fiction," *Boston Evening Transcript*, December 4, 1901, p. 22.

through his brain; a speeding locomotive slaughtering sheep; Hilma Tree with her bare feet in the waters of the cool spring that flows beneath the trestle; Vanamee, alone in the night, seeking his dead lover amidst the perfume of thousands of flowers within the seed ranch; Annixter chomping dried prunes and rereading *David Copperfield*; the great barn dance; the rabbit chase; Presley, almost insane with indignation, shouting incoherently to the ranchers at their mass meeting; the fight at the irrigation ditch. Whatever its faults, *The Octopus* is eminently successful in leaving a succession of lasting pictures in the reader's memory.

* * *

III

Symbolism

Literary symbolism derives from nature (Melville's white whale or Twain's great river) or from man's world (Hawthorne's scarlet letter). To review the great works of literature is to become impressed with the preponderance of natural symbolism. For some reason symbols from man's world succeed less often in conveying the richness and the profundity of meaning which are characteristic of great art. Few modern readers would be willing to accept fully Emerson's idea that "every natural fact is a symbol of some spiritual fact. Every appearance in nature corresponds to some state of the mind, and that state of the mind can only be described by presenting that natural appearance as its picture."[8] Nevertheless, the associational process which Emerson was describing does exist; certain images from nature do have great and universal emotional appeal. "Who looks upon a river in a meditative hour and is not reminded of the flux of all things? Throw a stone into the stream, and the circles that propagate themselves are the beautiful type of all influence."[9] Whether such associations are, as Emerson thought, the result of some mystical union of God and nature and man or whether they are the workings of our collective unconscious, as C. J. Jung believed, nature remains the richest source of symbols for the creative writer.

As a rule the American literary naturalists made only modest attempts to use symbols. In *Sister Carrie* Dreiser used a rocking chair to suggest the cyclic process of the characters' lives, the endless ebb and flow which actually arrives nowhere. This symbol is, however, rather obvious, superficial, and minor—somewhat like the windtower in Crane's "The Open Boat." It suggests the one meaning its author wanted it to convey and there its life ends. Symbol-

8. Ralph Waldo Emerson, *Nature,* in *Complete Works* (Boston, 1903), I, 26.   9. Ibid., p. 27.

ism in the writings of American naturalists is usually of this order: it comes from man's world and serves a minor purpose in the work. When Crane and Dreiser turned to nature, they generally found little to suggest the mystical energy Emerson saw. Indeed, they felt a poignant separation from nature. When Crane used the "high, cold star" to symbolize nature's indifference, he succeeded only in *stating* his meaning, not in making it come alive through symbolism. The natural setting in *The Red Badge of Courage* seems shallow and mechanical because that was precisely how Crane conceived of nature. He saw in it no great and enduring mysteries, no mystical connection with man, not even any terrifying evil. How, then, could he have created from nature a symbol with the complexity of Twain's river or Melville's whale?

Among the naturalists Norris had the best chance to become a great symbolist. He felt as none of the others did the wild and terrible force of nature. To be sure, he did not see in nature what Emerson saw, the transcendental God, the Oversoul, but he did sense the existence of a vast primeval force, with which man has both struggled and lived from the beginning. Nature could not, then, be as remote and cold for Norris as it was for Crane. To Norris nature was simply more meaningful than to Crane and Dreiser. In his three best novels, *McTeague*, *The Octopus*, and *The Pit*, he attempted with unique ambition for an American literary naturalist the creation of major natural symbols.

In *McTeague* he wanted to objectify the deepest instincts in his characters with the most precious of nature's metals, gold. It was a splendid concept. Gold is an apt materialization of the deepest yearnings of man. On the one hand, its rarity and untarnishable purity make it the symbol of fulfillment. In the Bible the New Jerusalem is of "pure gold," and "the street of the city was pure gold." Yeats used gold to symbolize perfection in art and spirit. The "artifice of eternity," which he writes of in "Sailing to Byzantium," is ". . . such a form as Grecian goldsmiths make / Of hammered gold. . . ." But if gold suggests beauty and spirit, it is also associated with all the materialistic cravings of man, and if it represents fulfillment, it can also imply the ultimate emptiness of success. Gold is thus a symbol from nature which relates easily but profoundly to man's existence; yet the full complexity of its symbolic value has seldom been exploited. It has generally been employed superficially by second-rate authors.

Norris saw the symbolic possibilities of gold, and he came remarkably close to realizing them. He was not thinking of a one-to-one equivalence of gold and greed. There is nothing greedy about McTeague's desire to have a big gilded tooth in front of his dental office. Rather, the gold tooth is the symbol of his "dream" of perfect contentment—perhaps not unlike other men's dream of a heaven with streets paved with gold. In *McTeague* Norris was thinking in terms of a complex of emotional meanings for gold that run all the way from McTeague's dream of the good life to the diseased desire of Zerkow. He thus hit upon the forerunner of the wheat as symbol of man's inner life. The characters in *McTeague* are driven to their destruction by different desires and motivations, but in each case gold is their immediate aim. They arrange themselves according to a scale and illustrate in varying degrees the meaning of gold to man. Those with the purest form of the obsession desire gold in its purest form, not possessions or what gold can buy, but the primal metal itself. Trina and Zerkow want to caress the metal, to make it a part of themselves. Zerkow attempts to "marry" gold when he takes Maria Macapa for his wife. He thinks she can bring him the gold dinner set. Trina sleeps with gold pieces in a symbolic sexual union. What, then, does gold *mean* to them? The most advanced degree of human obsession, as Norris realized, brings on a craving for the symbol itself rather than what lies behind it. To use Melville's example again, Ahab speaks of his desire to destroy evil, all evil in the world, and at one time he may have felt this desire. But as his bitterness grows, he more and more centers his hatred on Moby Dick, the symbol of evil for him. Ultimately, he wants only to destroy the symbol. Thus an obsession grows in two basic stages, expansion and then contraction. In the first stage, one recognizes the symbol as symbol and seeks what lies behind it. In the second stage, the desire contracts, and in the mind the symbol *becomes* what it earlier stood for. This is precisely the pattern Norris depicts in Trina.

Most of the major characters remain in a less advanced stage of obsession. Maria Macapa steals gold from McTeague's dental parlor, but only to buy smart dresses and to attract the attention of Zerkow. Marcus Schouler thinks of gold as money, which in turn will provide both pleasure and power. For these characters life is a conscious search for gold as symbol. But the harder they search for it, the more it escapes them. At the bottom of the scale of obsession is McTeague. Ironically the only one of the chief characters who has not sought frantically for gold, he finds it. During his prospecting, he discovers a mine of the primal metal, which he abandons when he senses that he is about to be arrested for Trina's murder and takes flight. Nevertheless, like the others, he is to a large extent destroyed by gold simply because his animalistic nature must have its comforts, which gold provides. His better side, his nobler self, is like his canary, which he carries with him even to Death Valley. It sleeps when he murders Trina. As he regresses toward the brute, the canary becomes weaker. By the time McTeague kills Marcus Schouler in the desert, the canary is almost dead, "chittering feebly in its little gilt prison." The bird's gilt cage objectifies the part gold has played in McTeague's life, imprisoning his less brutish side: life at the gold mine shaped his early life and helped to mold his animal-like body; Trina's love for gold alienates him from her; and finally, it is because of the gold that he kills Trina and has to escape to Death Valley.

Gold thus serves a dual function. It is the symbol of all those things which the major characters seek. Their desires range from the pure obsessions of Zerkow and Trina to McTeague's craving for simple, basic comforts. To each, gold has a different meaning. But in another way, it is the same to all of them. No matter how *they* think of gold, it suggests to the reader the deterministic force that destroys them all. They are all like McTeague's canary, imprisoned in the gilt cage of their deepest instinctive drives.

What, then, is wrong with the symbolism in *McTeague?* Norris's sense of fiction discovered one of those few symbols which, like the bottomless well, allow the diver to go to any depth he wishes. But his symbolism often ran away with him: it lacks subtlety and delicacy of treatment.[1] To illustrate, McTeague wants a huge gold tooth to advertise his "dental parlors," and after much discussion of the relative advantages of French and German gilt, he finally gets his tooth. He has the canary in the gilt cage. Maria Macapa continually babbles about the hundred-piece gold service and steals gold foil from McTeague. Zerkow is crazy for gold. Trina has gold fillings in her teeth and counts gold pieces until they are smooth, sometimes sleeping with them, wallowing in them like a pig in its mud. McTeague grew up at a gold mine; he goes back to it, and later he discovers gold near places called Gold Gulch and Gold Mountain. Even the sun streaming into Trina's room looks like gold coins. "The wonder is," wrote Vernon Louis Parrington, that Norris "didn't give Trina gold hair instead of black."[2] The real tribute to Norris's rough-hewn genius is that despite its obtrusiveness, the gold symbolism in *McTeague* is still richly meaningful.

JOSEPH H. GARDNER

Dickens, Romance, and *McTeague:* A Study in Mutual Interpretation†

In one of his more celebrated critical comments Frank Norris observed that "naturalism," far from being the "inner circle of realism" many of his contemporaries thought it, is actually a form of

1. By my count, "gold" (or "gilt") is mentioned 140 times.
2. Vernon Louis Parrington, *Main Currents in American Thought* (New York, 1930), III, 331.
† From *Essays in Literature,* I

(Spring 1974), 69–82. Reprinted by permission of Western Illinois University and the author.
   References to *McTeague* in the text have been changed to correspond with pages in this Norton Critical Edition.

"romance."[1] The twentieth-century commentator is apt to throw up his hands in despair over such statements, recognizing that terms like "naturalism," "realism," and "romance" have been used in so many ways to refer to so many things as to be nearly incapable of analysis and definition. However, we are also forced to admit that although notions concerning them might have to be inchoate and contradictory, such categories were nonetheless realities in the minds of a great many late nineteenth-century novelists and critics and that the belief in their existence exerted a considerable influence on critical opinion and novelistic techniques. Among others, one significant side effect of nineteenth-century belief in "naturalism," "realism," and "romance" as consistent, identifiable and definable literary modes was a markedly on-again-off-again pattern in both critical response to Dickens and novelistic use of Dickensian techniques and themes.

From the forties to the mid-seventies, when "romance" was in the ascendency, Dickens was the darling of American critics, who saw him as the great exemplar of all a novelist should be. Hence the growth of that peculiar paradox which haunted the period, the notion that the way to write The Great American Novel was to imitate Dickens.[2] Recalling the period of his youth and early manhood, Henry James asserted that Dickens had been "the great actuality of the current imagination."[3] Looking back to the same era Mark Twain observed that "there were a great many people in America at that time who were ambitiously and undisguisedly imitating Dickens."[4]

But when "romance" became a term of opprobrium and "realism" the beau ideal of critics and novelists, Dickens's fortunes suffered a slump so drastic that it inspired Sir Edmund Gosse to imitate Silas Wegg of *Our Mutual Friend* by "dropping into poetry" to pen a "Motto for the American Critic":

> Ho! the old school! Thackeray! Dickens!
> Throw them out to feed the chickens!
> Ho! the new school! James and [Howells]!
> Lay the flattery on with trowels![5]

1. *The Literary Criticism of Frank Norris*, ed. Donald Pizer (Austin: Univ. of Texas Press, 1964), p. 71.
2. Perhaps the most dramatic treatment of this notion can be found in a lecture by E. P. Whipple delivered before the Boston Mercantile Library Association in December, 1844, entitled "Novels and Novelists: Charles Dickens." The lecture was one of Whipple's greatest successes. It became a stand-by on his speaking tours, was published in the *North American Review*, October, 1849, and subsequently resuméed and pirated by newspapers and journals all over the country. Reprinted in a volume of *Lectures on Subjects Connected with Literature and Life* the following spring, it was largely responsible for that volume's having gone through six editions by 1866.
3. Henry James, *Autobiography*, ed. F. W. Dupee (New York: Criterion, 1956), p. 70.
4. Samuel Langhorne Clemens, *Mark Twain in Eruption*, ed. Bernard DeVoto (New York: Harper, 1940), p. 267.
5. Quoted in Leonard Lutwack, "William Dean Howells and 'The Editor's Study,'" *American Literature*, 24 (1952), 197.

The occasion for Gosse's excursion into doggerel was, of course, Howells's celebrated essay on James, published in *The Century*, November, 1882, in which he had maintained that "the art of fiction has become a finer art in our day than it was with Dickens and Thackeray. . . . These great men are of the past—they and their methods and interests."[6] Thus, although he had begun his own career as a novelist by writing what he himself had admitted were "bald parodies of *Bleak House*,"[7] Howells was to become increasingly dogmatic in his insistence that the "finer art" of "realism" demanded a systematic exclusion of Dickensian elements from the American novel. Significantly, his first edict, issued after he had elevated the easy chair in the "Editor's Study" of *Harper's Magazine* into the papal throne of American criticism, praised the Tennessee local colorist Mary Noailles Murfree for her "realistic" techniques but pronounced her occasional lapses into easy Dickensianisms anathema.[8] His major concern in *Criticism and Fiction* is to teach American novelists that they must see life "as it is" and not as it had been depicted in books, but he also realized that, because of his immense popularity with the uncritical reader, Dickens above all other writers stood in the way of a direct approach to experience. As he explained years later, young American authors frequently felt that "it was not permitted them, on pain of public rejection, to write anything but Dickens."[9] Hence one aim of *Criticism and Fiction* is, by repeated diatribes and elephantine ironies, to show them —and the public—why they should not imitate Dickens. Thus part of the significance of Norris's assertion that "naturalism" was not "the inner circle of realism" but rather represented a rebirth of "romance," is that it reflects a critical attitude in the nineties that could allow for the inclusion of Dickensian elements in American fiction by program as well as by actual performance—as, ironically, often happened in Howells's own novels. In other words, the return to "romance" brought with it a return to the paradox of earlier years that only Dickens could point the way to The Great American Novel, and the search for "The American Boz," abandoned in the eighties, became an agreeable pastime once more in the nineties.

A good example of the new attitude is an article entitled precisely "The Chance for an American Dickens," published by James L. Ford in *Munsey's Magazine*.[1] Noting that the vogue for "analytical realism" has run its course, Ford asserts that the times demand a return to story-telling, to narrative drive and dramatic, even melodramatic, power, to moral allegory rather than psychological analysis. The leaders of the "realistic school," Ford admits, sneer at Dickens as "a master of bathos, a caricaturist, a man whose pen had the

6. 25 (Nov. 1882), 28.
7. *My Literary Passions* (New York: Harper, 1895), pp. 86–87.
8. 72 (Jan. 1886), 323.
9. "Editor's Easy Chair," *Harper's Magazine*, 105 (July 1902), 311.
1. 23 (April 1900), 281–85.

newspaper taint," but, he claims, the writer who is to produce The Great American Novel must study the "magic art" of *Bleak House* and master it. The "realists" may be able to depict "certain corners" of America and "certain phases" of its social life; Dickens's greatness was his ability to present all of society from Chesney Wold to Tom-All-Alones's. Indeed, it is this class consciousness that is one of the most interesting facets of Ford's argument, for it indicates a radical shift in American critical definitions of "reality." Howells and his cohorts had moved the position of the "real" on a philosophical plane from the moral, essentially teleological, idealism that they tended to see as the basis of "romance" to the empirical materialism that formed the underpinnings of "realism." Ford moves it on a social and economic plane: the "real" is no longer upper middle-class. "I cannot," he insists, "conceive of a really great New York story springing from the brain of a man who does not know what a bung starter is." Predictably, Ford associates the depiction of lower-class life with sensation, lurid incident, and melodrama. Hence Dickens, whose skill in delineating the lower reaches of society and whose penchant for melodrama had formed part of his consistent mass appeal for American readers, becomes once again the exemplar for American novelists.[2]

Ford prescribes that the American Dickens must set his Great American Novel in New York City. Not all the young novelists of the nineties for whom he spoke would have agreed. One of them in particular vigorously maintained that there were suitable cities on the West Coast as well. Equally disillusioned with the limited range of "realism" and eager to portray life with a capital "L" by returning to a mode of "romance," Frank Norris had, three years prior to Ford's essay, pointed out that "London had her Dickens . . . but San Francisco still waits for her novelist."[3] And given the massive admixtures of Dickensian elements in *McTeague*, we must, I think, see the novel as programmatic in more ways than are generally recognized. Although Norris was wont, on occasion, to sign his letters "the Boy Zola," *McTeague* may well represent, among other things, his attempt to claim the title, if not of the American Dickens, at least of the Polk Street Boz. Unfortunately the most obvious of these Dickensian admixtures are among the least successful parts of

2. In a sense Ford is merely importing the main thrust of the "experimental school" of European "naturalism," the tendency, which Erich Auerbach traces back to the brothers Goncourt, to introduce the fourth estate into literature and present it "seriously" as the material for tragedy rather than relegating it to low comedy and farce. There is even in Ford's emphasis on the lurid and sensational a hint of what Auerbach calls in the Goncourts and their followers "the aesthetic attraction of the ugly and pathological" (*Mimesis,* trans. Willard Trask [Garden City, N.Y.: Doubleday, 1957], pp. 437–40, 445, 449–52). But the important thing to note here is that Ford bases his argument not on the example of the Goncourts or Zola but solely upon that of Dickens.

3. *Literary Criticism of Frank Norris,* p. 29.

the novel. The scattered references to Dickens's influence in earlier studies have focussed almost exclusively on its melodramatic conclusion and the sub-plot involving Old Grannis and Miss Baker. V. L. Parrington adds Norris's "patent effort" to achieve dramatic unity through the use of gold as symbol, labelling it "an exaggeration that is almost Dickens-like with its warping singleness."[4] One wonders, incidently, why the other sub-plot Zcrkow and Maria Macapa has not also been called Dickensian, especially since in many ways it seems more so than the Grannis-Baker action. But what Donald Pizer says of the old folks could be said of all these facile parallels: "They fail not because they are Dickensian but because they are weakly Dickensian."[5] The problem, primarily, is one of freshness and appropriateness. Melodrama, exaggerated symbolism, and especially grotesques and eccentrics, had been stocks in trade ever since Cornelius Matthews had attempted to claim the title of American Boz with *The Career of Puffer Hopkins* nearly sixty years earlier, and by the nineties they had long since become an anachronistic short-hand for second-rate novelists. As such they seem peculiarly out of place in the work of a writer whose other programmatic aims included the exploration of what he called "the unplumbed depths of the human heart, and the mystery of sex, and the problems of life, and the black, unsearched penetralia of the soul of man."[6] This does not mean that Dickens had nothing to offer Norris, but in order to find the real value for himself Norris had to probe deeper into the elements of Dickens's "romantic" mode than his commentators have previously acknowledged.

Indeed, Norris's case is particularly interesting in that it raises an important question of scholarly and critical technique. Since we tend to credit only what we can footnote, we restrict ourselves to "source studies" that can safely discuss Dickens's "influence" on Norris only in terms of "melodrama" and "eccentrics," and in so doing insulate ourselves from the kinds of critical insight that can come from "mutual interpretation." I borrow the term from Mark Spilka, whose *Dickens and Kafka* well illustrates both the merits and the liabilities of the approach. Spilka writes:

> A comparison that stops with parallels is, I believe, sterile; but a comparison which leads to mutual readings of specific texts, and to the illumination of related worlds, is critically rewarding. A fund of insights becomes available which might escape direct approach; and, through mutual reinforcement, a common vision emerges which supports the continuity of art and culture.[7]

4. *The Beginnings of Critical Realism in America: 1860–1920* (New York: Harbinger, 1958), p. 331.
5. *The Novels of Frank Norris* (Bloomington: Univ. of Indiana Press, 1966), p. 74.
6. *Literary Criticism of Frank Norris,* p. 78.
7. Mark Spilka, *Dickens and Kafka* (Bloomington: Univ. of Indiana Press, 1963), p. 23.

Moreover, "mutual interpretation" can be a double-edged sword. In this case, for example, if Dickens provides a way of seeing Norris, Norris, in turn, becomes an index of the man he called "Master": by seeing what is in this larger sense Dickensian in Norris, we may also learn something about Dickens.

From the perspective of mutual interpretation such things as Norris's curious shift in attitude and tone in depicting lower-class people is much more revealing than his use of melodrama and grotesques. Originally attracted to Polk Street for somewhat olympian —if not downright snobbish—reasons, Norris thought the poor people suitable subjects for fiction because they were simpler, somehow more pure in their conditioned responses, than the more complex members of his own social class. Thus a certain amount of aristocratic scorn vitiates the presentation of McTeague and his world in the early chapters. However, as Norris lives with and comes to know the dentist, his wife, and their associates, his objectivity is threatened from the other direction, the tone and attitude shifting to a sympathy, understanding, and even tenderness that is decidedly Dickensian. McTeague, "crop-full, stupid and warm," comes to demonstrate complexities that surprise his very creator. Norris may occasionally give way to an upper-class sneer at the dentist's taste in pictures, but the picnic and the theatre scene, even down to Owguste's celebrated mishap, for example, are treated with an empathetic understanding recalling such scenes in Dickens as the Nubles's trip to Astley's and Kit's determination to show little Jacob "what oysters meant" in *The Old Curiosity Shop*; Norris, like Dickens, realizes that there is something touching in the amusements of the poor.

But Norris's shift in tone indicates more than an awareness of the pathos of lower-class life. To be touched by the poor is in itself a kind of bourgeois condescension. His perhaps unexpected discovery of human complexity beneath the dentist's animalistic surface, his awareness as the novel progresses of the inadequacies in his original "naturalistic" formula of McTeague as draft-horse, "immensely strong, stupid, docile, obedient," living only by habit and seeking only animal comforts, bears significance not only for the history of Dickens's fortunes in America but also for the whole course of modern fiction. For it demonstrates that Norris had both instinctively fixed upon the fundamental technique that aligns Dickens with Shakespeare in literary greatness and, perhaps by accident but nonetheless effectively, exploited it as a way out of the *cul-de-sac* of "scientific" fiction that traps him in such woeful novels as *A Man's Woman*. The technique is so central to Dickens's art and so crucial to Norris's success in *McTeague* that the reader will, I hope, bear with me if I take some time to explain.

Cyril Connolly's famous aphorism maintains that inside every fat man there is a thin man struggling to be free; inside every so-called "flat" character of Dickens is a living human being either struggling to find his way out or, more often, happily acquiescing in his own eccentricities. Almost all Dickens's types, stock characters, eccentrics, grotesques, call them what you will, nurture underneath the dazzling array of peculiarities that forms their two-dimensional surface a spark of life and vitality that is all their own, and not, as the mainstream of Dickens criticism would have it, simply a conjured imputation from the author.[8] They may be ninety per cent mechanical, but they are also ten per cent human; this is, I think, what Spilka means when he observes that Dickens's characters, like Kafka's, "attempt to show the human spirit, alive and responsive, in the cage of its own making."[9] It is precisely the reader's shock at discovering individual humanity underneath the machinery that is the source of their power. Indeed, Dickens's most habitual practice is to play the one off against the other. Thus his characters haunt our imagination because they afford us a glimpse of life where we would least expect to find it.

The technique is not peculiar to Dickens. Ralph Baldwin observes that Chaucer brings the stock types of *The General Prologue* to life by catching the reader off-guard with a "quick glimpse of the interior man," an "unexpected percipient thrust which throws the character in momentary bold-relief."[1] Shakespeare is the great master of the technique. Like Chaucer's, like Dickens's, his characters are almost all stock types; they come to life when we discover a human spirit stirring under their typicality. Without it they are cardboard. Parolles, the hanger-on of *All's Well That Ends Well*, is an instructive case. Parolles is clearly a stock type; as befits a hanger-on he is the Imposter or *Poseur*. In E. M. Forster's terms he is a "flat" character in that we always recognize him when he re-enters and can always predict more or less what he is going to say and do. Above all we know that the plot is going to lead through one stratagem or another to his exposure. Yet when the stratagem is complete, when Parolles has been exposed (Act IV, Sc. iii), and we are prepared to see him disappear, he astounds us with a remarkable statement: "Who cannot be crushed with a plot?" (l. 360) Suddenly we are confronted not with a mechanical figure but with a

8. This tradition, which grows in part out of George Henry Lewes's pioneer study of Dickens's methods, is best stated by E. M. Forster, who attributes the paradoxical liveliness of Dickens's "flat" characters to a "conjuring trick" by which Dickens's own vitality is projected onto his otherwise dead creations who, vicariously, "borrow his life and appear to lead one of their own" (*As-pects of the Novel* [London: Edward Arnold, 1949], pp. 68–69). Unsatisfactory as it is, the theory is still very much alive.
9. Spilka, p. 69.
1. "The Unity of the Canterbury Tales," in *Chaucer Criticism*, ed. Richard J. Schoeck and Jerome Taylor (Notre Dame, Ind.: Univ. of Notre Dame Press, 1960), I, 25.

living human spirit. Having thus thrown us off balance, Parolles capitalizes on our amazement by bouncing back into his role, carrying all his new-found humanity with him and demonstrating beyond question that his cage is of his own creation. As he himself says, "Simply the thing I am/ Shall make me live" (ll. 369–70). Thus humanity flourishes where we least expect it, and Parolles redeems an otherwise rather left-handed play.

Dickens's importance is that he applied the same technique to the stock characters of prose fiction so consistently and so skillfully that in both the nineteenth and twentieth centuries the paradoxically flat, mechanical, yet vital character has been seen as his most distinctive creation. (Hence any such character in any novel written after 1836 can properly be called Dickensian.) To take but one example, Pecksniff is a stock type, like Parolles belonging to the tradition of the *Poseur* or Hypocrite. And like Parolles, he is flat; we always recognize him and can normally predict what he is going to say and do, although we never fail to enjoy it. Our interest is maintained by seeing Pecksniff act out himself as hypocrite and by the suspense of not knowing how or when he will receive his inevitable comeuppance. But as we watch him we begin, under Dickens's guidance, to see that Pecksniff is human as well as Hypocrite. In the drinking scene of chapter nine, for example, when punch and the charms of Mrs. Todger arouse his amorous propensities, we see him behaving not merely as a hypocrite but also as a very human spirit. The high comedy of the scene depends, no less, on our awareness of the juxtaposition of the mechanical and the human. Hence our deep disappointment when he is finally locked in his room, never to emerge and shock us again—until the next chapter.

When Pecksniff is finally unmasked by Old Martin, he does not point out that anyone can be crushed by a plot, but he does observe an equivalent: "'I have been struck this day,' said Mr. Pecksniff, 'with a walking stick (which I have every reason to believe has knobs upon it).'"[2] And like Parolles, he asserts and preserves his humanity by audaciously bouncing back into the stock role he has chosen for himself, demonstrating that a cage protects as well as imprisons. The *thing* he is makes him *live*. Our dissatisfaction with the ending (in which Pecksniff becomes a begging, whining alcoholic) stems not from his having abandoned his role, but from his having rejected his humanity.

The importance of this analysis of Dickens's fundamental technique to a discussion of *McTeague* should be fairly clear. Norris was

2. *The Works of Charles Dickens*, Gadshill Edition, ed. Andrew Lang [and B. W. Matz] (London: Chapman & Hall, 1897–1908), VII, 474. For ease of reference, all future citations to this edition will be included in the text, by volume (of the edition), chapter (of the individual novel) and page.

committed, at least in part, to a "scientific" theory that fostered an essentially mechanistic view of human existence and tended to reduce all men to certain rigidly fixed types. Yet types ruled by external and internal forces are recalcitrant, if not impossible, materials for fiction. Malcolm Cowley gets at part of the problem faced by American "naturalists" when he attacks their tendency always to explain the complex in terms of the simple: "To say that man is a beast of prey or a collection of chemical compounds omits most of man's special nature; it is a metaphor, not a scientific statement."[3] One may argue, of course, that to speak in terms of "special natures" is also to employ metaphor; nevertheless it is a metaphor embodying a set of assumptions absolutely essential to the production of literature. Norris's shift from a "naturalistic" to a Dickensian treatment of his lower-class characters is a shift from explaining human phenomena in terms of the simple to an honest attempt to grapple with the complex.

The shift redeems the novel from the "scientism" that makes *A Man's Woman* with its purely mechanical characters such a dreary affair and provides it with a great deal of its impact. What comes to fascinate us in *McTeague* is a sense of humanity struggling to survive under machinery that threatens to crush it. Norris's elaborate attempts to place the dentist in a world of force and rigid types only prepare us for the Dickensian shock of discovering life where we least expect it. "What is important," says Spilka of the Dickensian nature of Gregor Samsa, the gigantic insect of Kafka's *Metamorphosis*, "is the rich and careful portrayal of a way of life, an existence which continues under the most adverse conditions. For the principle at stake is Gregor's humanity, not his vileness."[4] The same may be said of McTeague; the principle at stake is Norris's discovery that the dentist is a human being and not a draft-horse. Paradoxically his draft-horse qualities become part of his humanity. Like Gregor's shell and, say, Wemmick's castle (*Great Expectations*) or Sairey Gamp's imaginary friend (*Martin Chuzzlewit*), they are the mechanical means by which the dentist strives to reach an accommodation with a hostile universe dominated by destructive forces. That McTeague is ultimately defeated does not deny his humanity; rather it merely pushes his story toward the realm of tragedy, that final affirmation of man's special nature. Hence, among other things, Norris's insistence—over the strong objections of his friends—on taking the canary into Death Valley. Like Miss Flite's finches (*Bleak House*), from whom it perhaps descends, the

3. " 'Not Men': A Natural History of American Naturalism," *Kenyon Review*, 9 (1947), 432.
4. Spilka, p. 77. A similar point is made by Edward Sackville-West in a comparison of Dickens, Kafka, and Dostoyevsky ("Books in General," *The New Statesman*, 11 Dec. 1948, p. 527).

canary is a symbol of life, alive and responsive, chittering—albeit feebly—in a cage constructed of vast, vague, social and psychological forces.

In his discovery of the ten per cent human lurking under the ninety per cent mechanical in McTeague, Norris uncovers a "romantic" element in the Dickensian mode capable of leading him out, in an effective and meaningful way, from what he thought were the stultifications of "realism." By juxtaposing the two positions, Norris, like Dickens, achieves his peculiar modernity. The twentieth-century reader may chafe at such sentimental Dickensianisms as Old Grannis and Miss Baker, but he will certainly credit a portrayal of life struggling to maintain and even assert itself in the face of a universe governed by impersonal, hostile force.

Norris penetrates beneath the surface of melodrama, overdrawn symbolism and eccentric characters again when, consciously or intuitively, he discovers in Dickens a reiterated pattern and theme useful to his purposes of re-opening the American novel to the concerns and techniques of "romance." Early commentators on *McTeague* describe it as a study of economic force and personal greed. More recently critics have read it as primarily concerned with sexuality. Actually the novel is about both, the two being combined in a manner that Norris more than likely absorbed from Dickens. Once again, to understand the pattern in Norris we must look closely in Dickens himself.

Throughout his career Dickens associated distorted attitudes toward money with grotesque or perverse sexuality. The most powerful presentation of the association is, of course, in *The Old Curiosity Shop*, where all the novel's sources of horror, from Old Trent gambling away his money to the satanic mills of the Black Country chapters, converge upon and are summed up by the single image of Quilp sprawled obscenely in Little Nell's bed. But it is elsewhere as well: in *Nicholas Nickleby, Martin Chuzzlewit, Little Dorrit, Our Mutual Friend*. In *David Copperfield*, the Dickens novel Norris seems most to have admired, Uriah Heep's ugliness is most effectively conveyed not through his greed but through his designs on Agnes. Indeed, the one functions as a euphemism for the other. The ultimate horror of the novel resides in the repeated references to his smacking his bloodless lips at the mention of Agnes and in David's mental vision of his repulsive form sharing a marriage bed with her ethereal purity. It is this nightmare, and not the monetary misfortunes of Old Wickfield to which it is allied, that haunts the book. At least four-fifths of the imagery surrounding Heep is either animalistic, slimy or phallic; often it is all three. In one paragraph alone he is associated with an eel, corkscrew and a snake (XV, xxxv, 97). When he announces, "Oh . . . with what a pure affection do I love the ground my Agnes walks on," David's reaction is itself almost pathological in its violence, vertigo, and sense of archetypal horror:

> I believe I had a delirious idea of seizing the red-hot poker out of the fire, and running him through with it. It went from me with a shock, like a ball fired from a rifle; but the image of Agnes, outraged by so much as a thought of this red-headed animal's, remained in my mind (when I looked at him, sitting all awry as if his mean soul gripped his body), and made me giddy. He seemed to swell and grow before my eyes; the room seemed full of the echoes of his voice; and the strange feeling (to which perhaps, no one is quite a stranger) that all this had occurred before, at some indefinite time, and that I knew what he was going to say next, took possession of me (XIV, xxv, 455).

The morbid extremes of David's reaction stem not only from the image of Agnes outraged by a red-headed animal but also from the very notion of sex itself; in David's world normal, "healthy" sexuality is virtually non-existent. Male-female relationships are shown only in two lights. In the one they are horrible and destructive. Betsy Trotwood's love for her husband becomes distorted by his cruelty and rapaciousness into a hatred of the institution of marriage itself: when she is not sending the maid out to chase donkeys, she is giving her lectures on the necessity of abjuring men. Annie Strong's normal desires, frustrated by her marriage to a man old enough to be her grandfather, bring disaster to all involved. Steerforth preys upon Emily's womanly aspirations, and two whole families are brought to ruin. Moreover, when these three plot lines are catalogued together, we notice that in all three, sex acts as a disruptive force primarily through the agency of its association with money. In the other half of the novel male-female relationships are shown to be so completely antiseptic that Freudian commentators have frequently described them as abortive sublimations of Dickens's own oedipal fantasies.[5] The only possible exceptions to this either/or pattern in *David Copperfield* are the Micawbers' fertile union and the somewhat alarming horse-play that goes on in the harem which Tommy Traddles assembles from his wife's flock of nubile sisters—and one hardly knows what to make of that except to hazard that Traddles's license is totally innocent because he is repeatedly shown to be (like Micawber) a financial incompetent.

Dickens's asexual male-female relationships are so notorious to modern criticism that they hardly require mention were it not for the importance one example has in the working out of the sex-greed

---

5. Long before he had worked out his theories of the oedipal relationship, Freud himself had been disturbed by Dickens's "colorless" (i.e., asexual) heroines (Ernest Jones, *The Life and Work of Sigmund Freud,* I [New York: Basic Books, 1953], 174).

association in *Copperfield*. No physical consummation crowns the Indian summer union of Barkis and Peggotty. Peggotty's attraction to the carrier is motivated only by her desire for economic stability, for a place to go after the Murdstones drive her out, and Barsis's desires do not extend beyond apple-pastries. David himself insists upon the post-climacteric "innocence" of their marriage (XIV, x, 175). Precisely because Barkis is without sex, his avarice is as innocent as his marriage. He is possessed by miserly greed, his love for the box containing his wealth exceeding even his love for sweetmeats. He is attached to it as if to a sexual fetish. He carries it with him everywhere he goes in his cart; when he retires he keeps it under his marriage bed. In his illness he banishes Peggotty from the bed and takes the box into it, finally dying with the box clasped in his arms as if it, and not Peggotty, were the wife of his bosom. Yet one immediately feels a strain when speaking of Barkis in terms of greed and sexual distortion; no one, certainly, would ever classify him with Quilp, Ralph Nickleby or Uriah Heep. But the only thing that seems to separate them is the simple fact that Barkis is impotent.

It is this pattern linking impotence with innocence as polar to sexuality and greed, quite distinctive to Dickens, that Norris, intuitively perhaps, absorbed. That the pattern is distinctly Dickensian can be seen by comparing his depiction of the union of sex and avarice with that of stage melodrama, in which the villain demands the rent while leering at the heroine. Dickens may have inherited the association from the melodrama, but he deepened it and made it his own; his villains demand the heroine and leer at the rent. Closer to the stage tradition are such novels as Thackeray's *The Newcomes* in which Barnes's villainy is exposed when it is discovered that he has seduced a mill-worker's daughter and abandoned his illegitimate children to starve. But unlike Dickens, Thackeray makes no attempt to link Barnes's greed with his sexuality. The two are presented merely as separate compartments of his multiform evil.[6]

Explaining the reasons why—or even the process by which—Norris was attracted to this recurrent theme in Dickens may be more properly the province of clinical psychology than literary history, but whatever the explanation, the greed-sex association is the controlling theme of *McTeague*. Norris may have set out to write a "naturalistic" study of heredity and environment; what he actually produced is a Dickensian exploration of the relationship between

6. Dickens's use of sex-greed association reflects not only his own insight into abnormal psychology but also certain unconscious attitudes inherent in the climate of his age. In his study of *My Secret Life*, Steven Marcus comments at length on the way in which the memoirist unconsciously associates money and sex, pointing out that the episode in which he fills a prostitute's vagina with coins hardly needs or deserves comment (*The Other Victorians* [New York: Basic Books, 1966], pp. 155–60).

attitudes toward sex and attitudes toward money. When we first meet Trina she is neither miserly nor even frugal. She gives Maria Macapa a dollar for the lottery ticket simply to avoid embarrassment, an action that would be unthinkable to her later in the novel when she refuses to give her husband even a nickel for carfare on a rainy day. The problem, then, becomes to define what has happened to her in the interim.

Trina can afford to be free with her dollars in chapter two precisely because she is yet a sexual neuter. Norris, in his fondness for tautology, makes the point three times over. McTeague is disturbed by Trina's feminine presence in his parlors, but she is "perfectly at ease; doubtless the woman in her was yet not awakened; she was yet . . . without sex. She was almost like a boy" [p. 14]. But if her womanhood is unawakened, it is shown to be there dormant; McTeague might well be troubled by her sexual allure.

As Trina and McTeague are forced into the grotesque physical intimacy imposed upon them by the processes of dental repairs, McTeague grows more and more troubled by the stirrings of that Old Adam which the nineteenth century preferred to call John Thomas. The dentist is plunged into confusion, for he can neither understand nor accept the forces that grip him. Norris focuses almost entirely on McTeague in these passages, but the aura of sensuality he describes as filling the parlors is so intense that Trina cannot escape it either. The first crisis comes when McTeague succumbs to his "lower nature" and kisses Trina "grossly, full on the mouth" as she lies helplessly etherized in his operating chair. Trina awakes—in more ways than one—to express a coyness that triumphs even over the sordid accoutrements of oral hygiene. " 'I never felt a thing' [she said], then she smiled at him very prettily beneath the rubber dam." At this point McTeague blurts out his first offer of marriage.

Trina's reaction is worth noting. She is immediately filled with terror, terror that Norris labels "the intuitive feminine fear of the male." The point of view suddenly shifts to her, and McTeague looms before us a monster, as her eyes focus on his huge hands and immense shoulders. McTeague stalks closer and closer. Trina vomits. Trina's nausea is more psychosomatic than physiological. Like David Copperfield's vertigo (in which Heep also swells to gigantic proportions) it is a violent reaction to the very notion of sexuality, in this case both McTeague's, as he towers over Trina, and her own as it is jolted into life and recoils from the dentist's suffocating bulk.

That Trina fears her own sexuality as much, if not more, than she fears McTeague's brute masculinity is shown repeatedly in the chapters describing their courtship. The long and curiously convincing analysis of her response to her engagement [pp. 49–51] illustrates the turmoil into which her awakened womanhood has thrown her. Well aware that McTeague's only appeal is sexual, she is incapable of accepting her own response. On the one hand McTeague's embrace and her yielding to it had "suddenly thrilled her from head to foot with a quick terrifying gust of passion, the like of which she had never known," while on the other she clings, baffled, to her knowledge that she is a "pure girl," that this "sudden commotion within her carried with it no suggestion of vice." Somehow the two will never come into balance; her only recourse is the fatalistic acceptance of her engagement, whether blessing or curse, as a *fait accompli*. But even fatalism proves inadequate. Her fear of herself, continually growing more and more exacerbated, begins to hint of the psychic distortion that will eventually destroy her. She comes to require stronger and stronger assertions of masculine force from McTeague, her demands to be overpowered by his brute strength representing, in Freudian terms, the need of the superego (her concept of herself as a "pure girl") to be violently crushed before the libido (her "gust of passion") can express itself openly. Only then can she and McTeague, who understands nothing of her turmoil, find release.

The crisis in Trina's development—or more properly, degeneration—comes with the wedding itself. In the atmosphere of crude sensuality established by the wedding dinner, Trina is suddenly left alone with her husband. Despite her mother's reassurances, she is again overcome by terror. Norris's writing rises to his very best as he presents Trina's fear in a way that can best be described as highly Dickensian, objectifying it in a powerful visual image of the dentist's enormous back, framed by a door-sill as if for illustration. It is here that Norris begins to plant the seeds of the money-sex association that is to control the rest of the novel. Seen from Trina's point of view, the light streams from the door like "a gold bar" [p. 101].

Trina's wedding night fears are primarily of McTeague, but that they are also of herself is indicated by Norris's reference to her "strange desire of being conquered and subdued" [p 103], her inability to accept the consummation of her marriage unless it is turned into symbolic rape. In the weeks following the wedding, even though she finds delight and fulfillment in having yielded, she is still unable to accept her sexuality. In one revelatory scene she steals to the door of the parlors to find McTeague spending Sunday in his old fashion:

> The little stove was crammed with coke, the room was over-heated, the air thick and foul with the odors of ether, of coke gas, of stale beer and cheap tobacco. The dentist sprawled his gi-

gantic limbs over the worn velvet of the operating chair; his coat
and vest and shoes were off, and his huge feet, in their thick grey
socks, dangled over the foot-rest; his pipe, fallen from his half-
opened mouth, had spilled the ashes into his lap; while on the
floor, at his side, stood the half-empty pitcher of steam-beer. His
head had rolled limply upon one shoulder, his face was red with
sleep, and from his open mouth came a terrific sound of snoring.
[p. 105]

She responds with horror and revulsion. What repulses her is not so
much McTeague, although the picture is certainly unattractive
enough, but McTeague as he here symbolizes her own sexuality. As
the object of her sexual desires, he becomes the projection of them;
that she is drawn to this obscene giant can, to her mind, only mean
that the drives that compel her are themselves obscene. In this
somewhat clinical climate the Dickensian pattern asserts itself.
Trina for a while oscillates between revulsion and sudden bursts of
passionate affection, but gradually settles into what Norris calls "an
equilibrium of calmness and placid quietude." The balm soothing
her ruffled psyche is none other than money, for we are told in the
same paragraph that she begins to regulate "the expenditure with
an economy that often bordered on positive niggardliness" [p.
107].

McTeague in the meanwhile has followed a different course of
development. Immediately following the wedding he is blissfully
happy in the consummation of his desires, but once his somewhat
limited needs are fulfilled, he slips into indifferent satiety. Moreover, he is both baffled and repulsed by the response he has released
in his wife. Whereas earlier he had been delighted by her sudden
bursts of passion and had roared with pleasure to have her perch on
his lap and tousle his hair, he is now only made uncomfortable by
such antics. Eventually he loses his interest in her altogether, his
previous love turning to bitter hatred.

Hence Trina's peculiar dilemma. The dentist has both awakened
in her drives that she is incapable of accepting and ceased to satisfy
those drives when they become most insistent. Her responses are
two, both of them following the Dickensian mold. First, she chan-
nels her sexual frustrations into a fetishistic attachment to her
money, whereby greed becomes an expression of sexuality; second,
she experiences a masochistic enjoyment of McTeague's sadism,
whereby his acts of hatred are inverted to the caresses of love and
her physical pain assuages the guilt she feels both for her sexuality
and for the avarice that has come to symbolize it.

As Trina's sex life degenerates, her greed grows, each stage of the
one marking out a step in the other. The farther apart the
McTeagues move, the closer she clutches her treasure trove, which,

with appropriate Dickensian symbolism, she keeps hidden beneath her wedding dress. After justifying her miserliness on the same fatalistic grounds on which she had earlier rationalized her sexuality, she comes to decide that avarice is "a good fault" [p. 119]. The stratagem is transparent; avarice is a "good" fault as sexuality is a "bad" one. The petting session that Schouler interrupts when he comes to say good-bye, having already reported McTeague to the licensing authorities, is the last physical expression of affection that passes between them. Correspondingly, Trina's niggardliness begins to show signs of pathology as she mimics the antics of Dickens's Noddy Boffin (*Our Mutual Friend*), but with the difference that Trina is in earnest. The earlier scene in which she had been repulsed by the sight of the dentist sprawled in his operating chair is repeated when McTeague, filled with whiskey, passes out on the bed, "stupefied, inert, his legs wide apart" [p. 169]. But far from feeling revulsion, Trina merely begins to search his pockets for coins. Norris sums up her regression in a sentence. Her emotions, he says, "reduced themselves at last to but two, her passion for her money and her perverted love for her husband when he was brutal" [p. 174]. She comes to reproduce on the clinical plane the comic antics of such Dickens characters as old Mrs. Smallweed (*Bleak House*), who cackles about coins and per cents until her husband knocks her out of her chair. After McTeague has deserted her, taking her savings along with him, she weeps over the bag in which she had kept the money "as other women weep over a dead baby's shoe" [p. 198]. In other words her money has become the symbol of her ultimate fulfillment as a woman. The nadir is soon reached; having retrieved all her lottery winnings from Oelbermann, she makes them the specific means of sexual release; "One evening she had even spread all the gold pieces between the sheets, and had then gone to bed, stripping herself, and had slept all night upon the money, taking a strange and ecstatic pleasure in the touch of the smooth flat pieces the length of her entire body" [pp. 201–2].

The two sub-plots reinforce the Dickensian pattern of the central action. Maria Macapa's sexual frustrations (she envies the soda-fountain girls and feebly attempts to imitate their dress because "they had their young men") express themselves in demented fantasies of golden tableware. In the trauma of childbirth the fulfillment of her womanhood purges her of her autism, even though the child, a reincarnation of Caddy Jellyby's ink-stained baby (*Bleak House*), dies. Zerkow, who is more than reminiscent of Dickens's Silas Wegg (*Our Mutural Friend*) is from the beginning a fetishist, the object of whose desires is gold, which he revealingly calls "the pure virgin metal." He marries Maria simply to hear her describe the gold dishes, as fetishists of a different sort have been known to marry overweight women simple to get near their corsets. Miss Baker and Old Grannis represent the other, the Barkis and Peggotty side of the coin. Although they are irresistibly drawn to each other, they are clearly past the age of sexual activity. Thus they run no risk of being destroyed by money. Like Trina, Grannis comes into a small fortune quite by chance. But far from having sold his happiness for "some miserable banknotes" as he originally thinks he has, he has precisely found it. Miss Baker, sensing his desolation, is emboldened to enter his room; the two declare their love; they "walked hand in hand in a delicious garden where it was always autumn" [p. 135]. Even the sentimental rhetoric is reminiscent of Barkis "drifting out with the tide," blissfully, but innocently (impotently) embracing his beloved box.

While the sub-plots of *McTeague* are either lurid or saccharine, the psychological penetration displayed in the depiction of Trina contributes toward making the novel the minor classic that it is. Above all, the affirmation of essential humanity struggling for existence in a world of dehumanizing force, in the story of McTeague, and the description of the human damage wrought by confusing money with the vital processes of life, in the story of Trina, demonstrate that as the nineteenth century became the twentieth, Dickens had lost none of his value as a presence in American fiction.

Selected Bibliography

FRANK NORRIS

NOVELS
Moran of the Lady Letty (1898)
McTeague (1899)
Blix (1899)
A Man's Woman (1900)
The Octopus (1901)
The Pit (1903)
Vandover and the Brute (1914)
SHORT STORIES AND SKETCHES
A Deal in Wheat and Other Stories (1903)
The Third Circle (1909)
Collected Writings Hitherto Unpublished in Book Form (Vol. 10 of *The Complete Edition of Frank Norris*, 1928)
Frank Norris of "The Wave" (1931)
POETRY
Yvernelle (1892)
LITERARY CRITICISM
The Responsibilities of the Novelist (1903)
The Literary Criticism of Frank Norris, ed. Donald Pizer (1964)
LETTERS
The Letters of Frank Norris, ed. Franklin Walker (1956)
COLLECTED EDITION
The Complete Edition of Frank Norris, 10 vols. (1928)

GENERAL BIBLIOGRAPHY, BIOGRAPHY, AND CRITICISM

BOOKS
Crisler, Jesse S., and McElrath, Joseph R. *Frank Norris: A Reference Guide.* 1974.
Dillingham, William B. *Frank Norris: Instinct and Art.* 1969.
French, Warren, *Frank Norris.* 1962.
Hart, James D., ed. *A Novelist in the Making . . . . Frank Norris.* 1970.
Lohf, Kenneth A., and Sheehy, Eugene P. *Frank Norris: A Bibliography.* 1959.
Lundy, Robert D. "The Making of *McTeague* and *The Octopus*" (Ph.D. diss., University of California). 1956.
Marchand, Ernest. *Frank Norris: A Study.* 1942.
Pizer, Donald. *The Novels of Frank Norris.* 1966.
Walker, Franklin D. *Frank Norris: A Biography.* 1932.
ARTICLES AND PARTS OF BOOKS
Ahnebrink, Lars. *The Beginnings of Naturalism in American Fiction.* 1950.
Geismar, Maxwell, *Rebels and Ancestors: The American Novel, 1890–1915.* 1953.
Howells, W. D. "Frank Norris," *North American Review*, CLXXV (December 1902), 769–78.
Johnson, George W. "Frank Norris and Romance," *American Literature*, XXXIII (March 1961), 52–63.
Knight, Grant C. *The Critical Period in American Literature.* 1951.
Lynn, Kenneth S. *The Dream of Success.* 1955.
Pizer, Donald. *Realism and Naturalism in Nineteenth-Century American Literature.* 1966.
Taylor, Walter F. *The Economic Novel in America.* 1942.
Walcutt, Charles C. *American Literary Naturalism, A Divided Stream.* 1956.
Ziff, Larzer. *The American 1890s.* 1966.

McTEAGUE

Essays republished in this volume are not included here.

Collins, Carvel. Introduction, *McTeague* (Rinehart Edition). 1950.

Cooperman, Stanley. "Frank Norris and the Werewolf of Guilt," *Modern Language Quarterly*, XX (September 1959), 252–58.

Crisler, Jesse S. "A Critical and Textual Study of Frank Norris's *McTeague*" (Ph.D. diss., University of South Carolina). 1973.

Dreiser, Theodore. Introduction, *McTeague* (Vol. 8 of *The Complete Edition of Frank Norris*). 1928.

Goldman, Suzy B. "*McTeague* and the Imagistic Network," *Western American Literature*, VII (Summer 1972), 83–99.

Hill, John S. "Trina Sieppe: First Lady of American Literary Naturalism," *University of Kansas City Review*, XXIX (Autumn 1962), 77–80.

Johnson, George W. "The Frontier Behind Frank Norris' *McTeague*," *Huntington Library Quarterly*, XXVI (November 1962), 91–104.

Pizer, Donald. "Evolutionary Ethical Dualism in Frank Norris's *Vandover and the Brute* and *McTeague*," *PMLA*, LXXVI (December 1961), 552–60.

Stronks, James B. "Frank Norris's *McTeague*: A Possible Source in H. C. Bunner," *Nineteenth-Century Fiction*, XXV (March, 1971), 474–78.

Taylor, Gordon O. *The Passages of Thought: Psychological Representation in the American Novel, 1870–1900.* 1969.

Watson, Charles S. "A Source for the Ending of *McTeague*," *American Literary Realism*, V (Spring 1972), 173–74.

NORTON CRITICAL EDITIONS

Juno and the Paycock, The Quare Fellow, Krapp's Last Tape, Translations) edited by John P. Harrington
MORE *Utopia* translated and edited by Robert M. Adams
NEWMAN *Apologia Pro Vita Sua* edited by David J. DeLaura
NORRIS *McTeague* edited by Donald Pizer
Restoration and Eighteenth-Century Comedy (The Country Wife, The Man of Mode, The Way of the World, The Conscious Lovers, The School for Scandal) edited by Scott McMillan
RICH *Adrienne Rich's Poetry* selected and edited by Barbara Charlesworth Gelpi and Albert Gelpi
ROUSSEAU *Rousseau's Political Writings* edited by Alan Ritter and Julia Conway Bondanella, translated by Julia Conway Bondanella
ST. PAUL *The Writings of St. Paul* edited by Wayne A. Meeks
SHAKESPEARE *Hamlet*, Second Edition, edited by Cyrus Hoy
SHAKESPEARE *Henry IV, Part I*, Second Edition, edited by James J. Sanderson
SHAW *Bernard Shaw's Plays* (Major Barbara, Heartbreak House, Saint Joan, Too True to be Good) edited by Warren Sylvester Smith
SHELLEY *Shelley's Poetry and Prose* edited by Donald H. Reiman and Sharon B. Powers
SMOLLETT *Humphry Clinker* edited by James Thorson
SOPHOCLES *Oedipus Tyrannus* translated and edited by Luci Berkowitz and Theodore F. Brunner
SPENSER *Edmund Spenser's Poetry*, Second Edition, selected and edited by Hugh Maclean
STENDHAL *Red and Black* translated and edited by Robert M. Adams
STERNE *Tristram Shandy* edited by Howard Anderson
SWIFT *Gulliver's Travels*, Second Edition, edited by Robert A. Greenberg
SWIFT *The Writings of Jonathan Swift* edited by Robert A. Greenberg and William B. Piper
TENNYSON *In Memoriam* edited by Robert Ross
TENNYSON *Tennyson's Poetry* selected and edited by Robert W. Hill, Jr.
THOREAU *Walden and Civil Disobedience* edited by Owen Thomas
TOLSTOY *Anna Karenina* (the Maude translation) edited by George Gibian
TOLSTOY *Tolstoy's Short Fiction* edited and with revised translations by Michael R. Katz
TOLSTOY *War and Peace* (the Maude translation) edited by George Gibian
TOOMER *Cane* edited by Darwin T. Turner
TURGENEV *Fathers and Sons*, Second Edition, edited with a thoroughly revised translation by Ralph E. Matlaw
VOLTAIRE *Candide* translated and edited by Robert M. Adams
WATSON *The Double Helix: A Personal Account of the Discovery of the Structure of DNA* edited by Gunther S. Stent
WHARTON *The House of Mirth* edited by Elizabeth Ammons
WHITMAN *Leaves of Grass* edited by Sculley Bradley and Harold W. Blodgett
WILDE *The Picture of Dorian Gray* edited by Donald L. Lawler
WOLLSTONECRAFT *A Vindication of the Rights of Woman*, Second Edition, edited by Carol H. Poston
WORDSWORTH *The Prelude: 1799, 1805, 1850* edited by Jonathan Wordsworth, M. H. Abrams, and Stephen Gill